ROXANA

Daniel Defoe

edited by Melissa Mowry

D1153723

broadview editions

Library and Archives Canada Cataloguing in Publication

Defoe, Daniel, 1661?-1731
    Roxana / Daniel Defoe ; edited by Melissa Mowry.

(Broadview editions)
Includes bibliographical references.
ISBN 978-1-55111-807-9

    I. Mowry, Melissa M., 1963- II. Title.

PR3404.R6 2009   823'.5   C2009-900201-9

Broadview Editions

The Broadview Editions series represents the ever-changing canon of literature in English by bringing together texts long regarded as classics with valuable lesser-known works.

Advisory editor for this volume: Betsy Struthers

Broadview Press is an independent, international publishing house, incorporated in 1985. Broadview believes in shared ownership, both with its employees and with the general public; since the year 2000 Broadview shares have traded publicly on the Toronto Venture Exchange under the symbol BDP.

We welcome comments and suggestions regarding any aspect of our publications—please feel free to contact us at the addresses below or at broadview@broadviewpress.com.

North America
Post Office Box 1243, Peterborough, Ontario, Canada K9J 7H5
2215 Kenmore Avenue, Buffalo, NY, USA 14207
Tel: (705) 743-8990; Fax: (705) 743-8353;
email: customerservice@broadviewpress.com

UK, Ireland, and continental Europe
NBN International, Estover Road, Plymouth UK PL6 7PY
Tel: 44 (0) 1752 202300   Fax: 44 (0) 1752 202330
email: enquiries@nbninternational.com

Australia and New Zealand
UNIREPS, University of New South Wales
Sydney, NSW, 2052 Australia
Tel: 61 2 9385 0150; Fax: 61 2 9385 0155
email: info.press@unsw.edu.au

www.broadviewpress.com

FSC

Mixed Sources
Product group from well-managed
forests, controlled sources and
recycled wood or fibre

Cert no. SW-COC-003438
www.fsc.org
© 1996 Forest Stewardship Council

This book is printed on paper containing 100% post-consumer waste.

Typesetting and assembly: True to Type Inc., Claremont, Canada.

PRINTED IN CANADA

ROXANA

broadview editions
series editor: L.W. Conolly

The Famous ROXANA.

Contents

Acknowledgements • 7
Introduction • 9
Daniel Defoe: A Brief Chronology • 29
Defoe's Times: A Brief Chronology • 33
A Note on the Text • 37

Roxana • 39

Appendix A: Roxana's Shifting Identity and the Tradition of
Whore Biography • 327
    1. From *The Lawyer's Clarke Trappan'd by the Crafty
       Whore of Canterbury* (1663) • 327
    2. From *The London Jilt* (1683) • 329
    3. From *The Whores Rhetorick* (1683) • 334

Appendix B: Women's Work • 341
    1. *A True Copie of the Petition of the Gentlewomen, and
       Tradesmens-Wives* (1641) • 341
    2. Mary Collier, *The Woman's Labour: An Epistle to
       Mr. Stephen Duck* (1739) • 346

Appendix C: Court Culture • 355
    1. *Poor-Whores Petition* (1668) • 355
    2. *The Gracious* ANSWER ... *To the Poor-Whores Petition*
       (1668) • 357
    3. John Dunton, *The Night-Walker* (1696) • 361

Appendix D: City Culture • 369
    1. *The Character of a Town-Miss* (1680) • 369
    2. *Auction of Whores* (1691) • 372

Appendix E: The Great Debate on the Poor • 377
    1. From Matthew Hale, *A Discourse Touching Provision
       for the Poor* (1683) • 377
    2. From Thomas Firman, *Some Proposals for the
       imployment of the Poor* (1681) • 384
    3. From Daniel Defoe, *The Poor Man's Plea* (1698) • 386
    4. From Daniel Defoe, *Every-Body's Business is No-
       Body's Business* (1725) • 388
    5. From Bernard Mandeville, *Modest Defense of the
       Publick Stews* (1724) • 389
    6. From Daniel Defoe, *Some Considerations Upon Street-
       Walkers* (1726) • 391

Appendix F: Women and Marriage • 395
1. From Mary Astell, *Some Considerations on Marriage*
   (1700/1706) • 395
2. From Daniel Defoe, *Conjugal Lewdness* (1727) • 397

Appendix G: Alternate Endings of *Roxana* • 399
1. Daniel Defoe, *The fortunate mistress* (1740) • 399
2. Daniel Defoe, *The history of Mademoiselle de Beleau*
   (1775) • 402

Appendix H: Defoe, *Roxana*, and Posterity • 405
1. From Charles Gildon, *The Life and Strange Surprizing
   Adventures of Mr. Daniel Defoe* (1719) • 405
2. From *The History of Mademoiselle de Beleau; or, The New
   Roxana* (1775) • 405
3. John Howlett, *The Insufficiency of the Causes to which the
   Increase of the Poor's Rates Have Been Commonly Ascribed*
   (1788) • 407
4. George Chalmers, *The Life of Daniel Defoe* (1790) • 407
5. Thomas Ruggles, *The History of the Poor* (1797) • 407
6. *The Penny Magazine of the Society for the Diffusion of
   Useful Knowledge* (1833) • 408

Select Bibliography • 413

Acknowledgements

I wish to thank St. John's University for a generous summer grant that allowed me to begin work on this project. In particular, I wish to thank the English Department for providing me with graduate assistants at crucial points in the process. As always, the library staff at St. John's met my requests for sometimes arcane and remote materials with both good cheer and good speed. Thanks too to numerous colleagues who have offered important insights and stimulating conversations during the process of editing this volume. I wish to thank Frances Dolan for encouraging me to pursue an edition of *Roxana* with Broadview. This book is for my children Helen and Alex in the hope that they too will come to know the pleasures of reading and inquiry.

Introduction

In 1724, Daniel Defoe published the last of his novels—*The For-tunate Mistress or, a History of the Life and Vast Variety of Fortunes of Mademoiselle de Beleau, afterwards called the Countess of Wintelsheim in Germany Being the Person known by the Name of the Lady Roxana in the time of Charles II*—and thereby ended his five-year experiment in long fiction. Like most of his fictions, and, indeed, those of many other writers at the time, *Roxana* carried no signature. Only a pamphlet, *The Great Law of Subordination consider'd; Or, The Insolence and Unsufferable Behaviour of Servants in England duly enquir'd into* (1724), announced "*The Fortunate Mistress*" as another work by the same author "Just Publish'd" and linked Defoe with the novel.[1] No subsequent edition of the novel carried Defoe's name until 1775.[2]

It remains a mystery why *Roxana* signaled the end of Defoe's career as a novelist. There is almost no information about how the novel was received upon its publication. We do know that, unlike *Robinson Crusoe* or *Moll Flanders*, only one edition of *Roxana* appeared during Defoe's lifetime and that subsequent editions, the first of which did not appear until 1735, four years after Defoe's death, altered the novel's ending.[3] Editors and pub-lishers of the multiple posthumous editions seemed uncomfort-able with *Roxana*'s troubling conclusion and ominous announce-ment that, following her daughter's apparent murder, she "was brought so low again, that [her] Repentance seem'd to be only the Consequence of [her] Misery, as [her] Misery was of [her] Crime" (326). They often added happy endings to the novel, making Defoe's fiction palatable to sentimental eighteenth- and nineteenth-century readers (see Appendix G). It is possible that Defoe's contemporaries similarly found Roxana's story disturb-

---

1 Janet E. Aikens, "*Roxana*: the Unfortunate Mistress of Conversation," *SEL* 25 (1985): 533.

2 Robert J. Griffin, "The Text in Motion: Eighteenth-Century *Roxanas*," *ELH* 72.2 (2005): 390.

3 John Mullen speculates that the single printing during Defoe's lifetime may have resulted from the fact that two of the four booksellers listed on *Roxana*'s 1724 title page also sold Defoe's earlier fictions; thus they would have been well-acquainted with their author's potential for com-mercial success and might have ventured a large print run. "Note on the Text," *Roxana*, ed. John Mullen (Oxford: Oxford UP, 1996), 333.

ing and rejected the novel's moral lessons. It may also be that *Roxana*'s ending reveals its author at a creative loss and that Defoe wrote no more novels because he had exhausted the genre's possibilities.[1] Unfortunately, he left no record of his creative decision-making process. About the only thing we can say for certain is that after *Roxana*'s publication, Defoe continued to enjoy a prolific writing career for the remaining seven years of his life.

Daniel Defoe was born in 1660, a watershed moment in England's history. During the eleven years preceding his birth, England had governed without a monarch. But in 1660 Parliament declared the nation's bold political experiment over, restored the monarchy, and invited the Stuarts to return to govern. Arguably, Parliament had been forced to reinstate the monarchy less because the nation had rejected parliamentary rule and more because two decades of war and economic upheaval had left England in dire economic straits. The rolls of charitable hospitals, such as London's Bridewell, are clogged with entries of people taken begging in the streets. The great hope was the Charles II would bring stability and economic prosperity back to England.

In many ways, Defoe's family was fortunate. They appear to have weathered the tumultuous years of mid-century well, and by the time Defoe was born, his father was making a prosperous living as a merchant. James Foe had come to London in the 1640s from Northamptonshire and served an apprenticeship to a tallow-chandler. He later became a merchant who rose to serve as warden in the Butcher's Company. As a member of one of London's guilds, James Foe was a fully enfranchised citizen who enjoyed what was referred to as the "freedom of the City" and could vote in municipal elections.

The political privileges associated with James Foe's business and guild membership, however, proved short-lived. Many of the religious and political conflicts, particularly those about the limits of Crown and ecclesiastical authority, that had driven England to civil war nearly twenty years earlier proved durable despite the monarchy's return and continued to structure the life of the nation. The Anglican Church hierarchy moved quickly to exclude those who refused to embrace English Protestantism in its pre-civil war form. Though in practice they belonged to a wide variety

---

1 Leopold Damrosch Jr., *God's Plot and Man's Stories: Studies in the Fictional Imagination from Milton to Fielding* (Chicago: U of Chicago P, 1985), 211-12.

of sects including Presbyterians, Quakers, and Baptists, among others, those who refused to take sacraments in the Anglican Church became known as Dissenters. In 1661, Parliament enacted the Act of Conformity, the first in a series of four acts passed during the next four years that would become known as the Clarendon Code. By this Act, James Foe was excluded from holding municipal office in the City. One year later, in 1662, the Foes joined the Dissenters and followed their pastor Samuel Annesley when he was expelled from his church by the Act of Uniformity, the second piece of legislation in the Clarendon Code. In thus following their consciences, the Foes made a number of sacrifices, including "their son's chance for a university education and civil or military career."[1] Instead of attending Oxford or Cambridge, Defoe was enrolled in Charles Morton's Dissenting academy in Newington Green, a suburb of west London where he spent the years between 1674 and 1680. Initially, Defoe may have intended to pursue a career in the ministry.[2] Though by 1681 he apparently had decided against this career path, the intersection of politics and conscience that structured the lives of Dissenters in Restoration London dominated his work and thought for the remainder of his life.

Defoe did not immediately turn to writing as a profession, however. Instead, he followed his father's path and became a merchant, setting up business around 1683 as a wholesale hosier. The following year, age 24, he married Mary Tuffley, daughter of a wealthy cooper. Shortly thereafter, he made a decision that jeopardized both his business and his life: he became engrossed in a dangerous political intrigue.

In 1685 Charles II died without a legitimate heir, leaving the English throne to his Catholic brother James II. James's designation as Charles's heir-apparent had been fiercely opposed for fifteen years by ministers and citizens alike who feared that a Catholic monarch would reinstate Catholicism as the state religion. During the preceding years, many of the King's ministers had tried to persuade Charles to designate his illegitimate but Protestant son, James Scott, Duke of Monmouth, heir to the throne in hopes of averting a religious crisis. Charles refused, but not before Monmouth's sense of entitlement to the throne had become so over-inflated that he embroiled himself in a failed plot

---

1   Paula R. Backscheider, *Daniel Defoe: His Life* (Baltimore: Johns Hopkins UP, 1989), 7.
2   Backscheider, 15.

to murder his father and uncle in 1683. The plot's discovery forced Monmouth to flee the country. Charles II's death reawakened Monmouth's political ambitions. The Dissenting community to which Defoe belonged was no less virulently anti-Catholic than its Anglican counterpart, and when news came that Monmouth planned to overthrow his Catholic uncle, now James II, Defoe cast his lot with the rebels. The plan failed miserably, and those who could escape fled the battlefield at Sedgemoor, July 6, 1685. Monmouth and many of his supporters were tried, convicted, and executed for treason. To save his life, Defoe was forced into hiding until at least March 1686 when James II issued a general pardon, though Defoe himself did not receive a personal pardon until May 1687.

Only after he had failed miserably at political and military rebellion, did Defoe embark on a career as a writer. In 1688 he channeled his political energies into his writing and published his first extant piece of writing: *A Letter to a Dissenter from his Friend at the Hague* in support of the accession of William III and Mary II to the English throne and the return of Protestant rule following James II's abdication.

The long career that serves as the prelude to *Roxana* began unevenly. During the 1690s, Defoe wrote sporadically, producing titles like *Reflections on the Late Great Revolution* (1689), *An Answer to the Lte K. James's Last Declaration* (1693), *An Essay on Projects* (1697), *An Arguement Shewing that a Standing Army, with Consent of Parliament, Is Not Inconsistent with a Free Government* (1698), *Some Reflections on a Pamphlet Lately Publish'd Entitl'd An Argument Shewing That a Standing Army Is Inconsistent with a Free Government* (1698), and *The Poor Man's Plea* (1698). He contributed occasionally to the *Athenian Mercury* published by John Dunton, another member of Annesley's congregation and Annesley's son-in-law, and began to write political satire. In 1702, however, Defoe's satirical sensibility missed its mark, and he was arrested for his pamphlet *The Shortest Way with Dissenters*. He was sentenced to stand in the pillory three times where he was subjected to ridicule and abuse at the hands of onlookers. However ignominious the punishment, Defoe's fate brought him to the attention of one of the most powerful men of the early eighteenth century—Robert Harley, Secretary of State for the North and close advisor to Queen Anne (1702-14). Through Harley's intercession, Defoe was released from prison, after which he served both as Harley's spy and journalist for the remainder of Anne's reign. Over the course of the following eleven years, he established himself as one of the most prolific writers of his day, writing not only pamphlets but also periodicals.

By the time Defoe put his hand to *Roxana*, he was among the most seasoned and successful writers of a generation that included satirists such as Jonathan Swift (1667-1745), Delariviere Manley (1670-1724), and Bernard Mandeville (1670-1733); essayists such as Joseph Addison (1673-1719) and Richard Steele (1672-1729); novelist Penelope Aubin (1679?-1731?); poet Alexander Pope (1688-1744), who famously excoriated Defoe in *The Dunciad* (1728) as a Grub-Street hack writing only for money; and novelist and essayist Eliza Haywood (1693-1756).

Roxana has been described as Defoe's "darkest novel" as it tells the tale of a young Huguenot émigré who rises to extraordinary wealth and notoriety as a courtesan, only to find that she cannot sever her ties with the past and live a virtuous life.[1] the novel ends ominously with the apparent murder of Roxana's daughter and her own fortunes devastated by the "Blast of Heaven" (326). If Defoe left no clear indication why he stopped writing novels after *Roxana*, his decision to focus on the life of a courtesan in the "time of Charles II" has been equally mystifying. On the one hand, *Roxana* continues his long-standing concern with social order and the devastating effects of its absence. Several of the pamphlets he published between 1724 and his death in 1731 are explicitly concerned with the corrosive effects of the sexual permissiveness believed to typify women from the lower social orders. But there is little in those commentaries that reflects the deep concern with courtesan culture and the libertine ethos so abundantly evident in *Roxana*. In many ways the morality it reflects is more typical of Defoe's earlier works, such as the pamphlet *The Poor Man's Plea* (1698) in which he reflected:

> In the Time of King *Charles* the Second, Lewdness and all manner of Debauchery arriv'd at its Meridian: The Encouragement it had from the Practice and Allowance of the Court, is an invincible Demonstration how far the Influence of our Governors extends in the Practice of the People. (5)

For Defoe, Charles II's court epitomized immorality and decadence, a flagrant disregard for social order, and, most importantly, an utter ignorance of the aristocracy's ancestral obligation

---

1   David Blewett, *Defoe's Art of Fiction:* Robinson Crusoe, Moll Flanders, Colonel Jack *and* Roxana (Toronto: U of Toronto P, 1979), 116.

to serve as a moral model for the lower orders of society. Because he was the heir to his father's throne and his life was therefore in jeopardy in England, Charles II spent most of the Interregnum (1649-60) in exile, mostly in France and the Netherlands, along with other supporters of the royalist cause. There the expatriate English cavaliers developed a reputation and taste for decadent and profligate living, a taste that the new King and his courtiers continued to pursue upon their return to power. Extramarital liaisons became a hallmark of the Caroline court beginning with the King's long-running affair (1660-70) with Barbara Villiers, Countess of Castlemaine, which he apparently initiated within two or three weeks of his arrival in England.[1] Two of Charles's mistresses, Barbara Villiers (d. 1709) and Louise de Kéroualle (d. 1734), remained socially prominent until their deaths. Notwithstanding the Interregnum, no one in Restoration England would have been surprised by the fact that Charles II had mistresses. What made the King's behavior so shocking and scandalous was his unapologetic lack of discretion. Not only did he carry on his liaisons openly, often with more than one mistress at a time, he frequently ensconced his mistresses in private apartments within the royal household. He was, moreover, politically generous with his mistresses and equally open-handed with the large number of illegitimate children they bore him. Women of genteel birth like Barbara Villiers, for instance, found themselves elevated to aristocratic status as the Countess of Castlemaine, and then included among the nobility when she was created Duchess of Cleveland. Likewise, Nell Gwyn, born a commoner, rose from orange girl to actress to royal mistress with extraordinary speed. Indeed, Alison Conway has suggested that Gwyn's status as Charles II's only Protestant mistress may have served as a model for Roxana.[2]

---

1   Charles II acknowledged Villiers's daughter Ann, who was born 25 February 1661, as his own, placing her conception sometime in May 1660.
2   Alison Conway, "Defoe's Protestant Whore," *Eighteenth-Century Studies* 35.2 (2002): 215-33. Indeed, there may be more to Conway's argument than she realizes. Defoe's description of Roxana's Pall Mall house with its "private Door into the King's Garden" echoes strikingly John Evelyn's description of a "'very familiar' discourse between the king and Nell, 'she looking out of her garden on a tarrace at the top of the wall, and [the king] standing on the greene walke under it' (Evelyn, 3.573)." Conway is quoting John Evelyn's diary here. S.M. Wynne, "Gwyn, Eleanor (1651?–1687)," *Oxford Dictionary of National Biography*, Oxford University Press, 2004 http://www.oxforddnb.com/view/article/11816, accessed 31 January 2007.

Additionally, their children enjoyed royal patronage that often translated into political privileges as adults, since their aristocratic status entitled them to a seat in the House of Lords. For a nation grudgingly returned from what was arguably Europe's first great experiment in democracy, however limited, the flaunting of social privilege and elite power did not sit well. The self-indulgence of Charles II's court and the King's disregard for the sober morality of his Dissenting subjects looked too much like his father's embrace of absolute royal authority and disdain for those he governed. Although Charles II gave his political enemies little room to maneuver, he was certainly vulnerable to popular observations that the King spent too much time indulging venal desire when he should have been attending to matters of state.

While there are ample indications in the text of *Roxana*, from the inclusion of famed Whig financier and director of the Bank of England Sir Robert Clayton (1629-1707) as Roxana's financial advisor to Roxana's suggestion that Charles II's son, the Duke Monmouth (1649-85), was among those nobles who witnessed her Turkish dance, most critics also recognize that Defoe's choice of place and setting was likely allegorical and probably reflects contemporary distaste for the similar excesses of George I's court (1714-27). In fact, Rodney Baine has argued that the novel's claim to be set in the time of Charles II belonged to Defoe's booksellers rather than the author himself.[1] According to the novel's own chronology, Roxana's tenure as courtesan and royal mistress corresponds much more closely to the reign of George I who was also a notorious libertine. The primary piece of evidence to support a Georgian setting for the novel stems from Roxana's observation that she arrived with her parents in England in 1683, when she was "about ten Years old" (46), placing her birth around 1673. Thus, Roxana could not have been both the child of twelve the novel claims she was when Charles II died in 1685 *and* the courtesan of forty who is said to have entertained Charles II's illegitimate son the "D— of M—th" (199), who was executed that same year. In 1718, four years after George I's accession, Defoe wrote in *Mist's Journal* "we are now running headlong, not into the same vile debauch'd Taste of King Charles the Second's Reign, but into as much worse as Thought can conceive."[2] Defoe and his publishers might well have been drawn to using the Car-

---

1 Rodney M. Baine, "*Roxana's* Georgian Setting," *Studies in English Literature: 1500-1900* 15.3 (1975): 459-71.
2 5 April 1719, cited in Blewett, 122.

oline court as a ruse for their more contemporary social criticism in order to protect themselves from libel charges.

Together with *Robinson Crusoe* (1719), *Moll Flanders* (1722), and *Journal of the Plague Year* (1722), *Roxana* belongs to a cluster of consecutively published works set in the 1600s. With the exception of *Journal of the Plague Year*, *Roxana* is the only work from this series whose story Defoe claims personally to have witnessed.[1] In the preface, he identifies himself as the "Writer" and claims that he "was particularly acquainted with this Lady's First Husband, the Brewer, and with his Father; and also with his Bad Circumstances; and knows that first Part of the Story to be the Truth" (44).

The first portion of the novel is critical to setting the stage for Roxana's subsequent moral conflicts. Unlike Moll Flanders, Defoe's earlier heroine, there is little definitive evidence to suggest that Roxana is based on a real person, although he clearly intended part of Roxana's story to evoke the seventeenth-century criminal Mary Carleton who similarly masqueraded as a European aristocrat and to whom Roxana compares herself when she proclaims that she "might as well have been the *German Princess*" (277). Critics have also proposed a number of literary sources for her character.[2] Whatever the model or models, it is also entirely likely that Defoe knew women who came from similar backgrounds. He, himself, would have been a young man of twenty-three when Roxana's parents emigrated from France in anticipation of Louis XIV's revocation of the Edict of Nantes in 1685. Coming from a prosperous merchant family and embarking on his own business ventures, Defoe probably associated with a good many sons like Roxana's future husband, as he suggests in the novel's preface.

Like Defoe's own family, Roxana's parents are affluent enough to afford an education for their child, though her education is both the first harbinger of her future corruption as well as the first hint we have of possible generic sources for the novel as it

---

1 In both *Robinson Crusoe* and *Moll Flanders*, Defoe claims only an editorial function.
2 John Mullan has suggested that Defoe's source for Roxana's pseudonym is the "semi-scandalous" *Memoirs of the Life of Count de Grammont* (1714) (see John Mullan, *Roxana, the Fortunate Mistress* by Daniel Defoe [New York: Oxford UP, 1996] 349), while Blewett (123) argues that there were likely multiple sources for Roxana's pseudonym in the Restoration theatre.

points to Defoe's knowledge of seventeenth-century whore biographies (see Appendix A). By the time Roxana had become school-age, education for girls was no longer a novelty, though it continued to be viewed with great suspicion. Indeed, Roxana's claims that along with learning to speak English, she "danc'd *as some say*, naturally, lov'd it extremely, and sung well also" (46) echoes a satire on prostitution published the year of her arrival in England, in which the title character was "sent to School to write and learn *French*, as also to Dance" and whose education similarly serves as the prelude to her own descent into whoring.[1]

If Roxana's education foreshadows what Defoe understood as her moral and sexual decadence and alludes to her author's awareness of the conventions of seventeenth-century whore biography, her life story also augments and updates the earlier genre. For unlike her seventeenth-century predecessors who were portrayed predominantly as coming from artisanal or working-poor backgrounds, Roxana grows up in a successful mercantile family. For a brief time she is able to defer her fate because her family's affluence gives her a dowry that makes marriage possible. She thus sustains her family's social status by marrying the son and heir-apparent of a wealthy London brewer. But her marriage also sets the stage for the novel's moral conflicts; it amplifies her "fall," making readers aware that she descends far further than the "common women" of seventeenth-century pornography. By her own admission, Roxana discovers that the vanity her education had fostered led her to marry a "fool" at the tender age of sixteen. Notwithstanding his attractiveness and athleticism, her husband has little to recommend him. When he inherits his father's business, he quickly drives it into the ground, squandering all his family's money. Thus destitute, he makes the cowardly and fateful decision to abandon his wife and five small children (all of whom are under the age of six). Receiving no relief either from her family or her husband's family, Roxana feels at a loss as to how to help herself or her children and faces what is arguably the most difficult decision of her life.

> If I had but one Child, or two Children, I would have done my Endeavour to have work'd for them with my Needle, and

---

1 *The London Jilt: or, the Politick Whore. Shewing all the Artifices and Strategems which the Ladies of Pleasure make use of for the Intreaguing and Decoying of Men; Interwoven with several Pleasant Stories of the Misses' Ingenious Performances* (1683).

should only have come to them to get them to help me to some Work, that I might get our Bread by my Labour; but to think of one single Woman not bred to Work, and at a Loss where to get Employment, to get the Bread of five Children, that was not possible, some of my Children being young too, and none of them big enough to help one another. (55)

To modern readers, Roxana's helplessness often seems like the self-indulgent statement of a woman who simply does not want to earn an honest living. Her accounts of the work available to women and the economic status they endured, however, are quite accurate. Many women in the late seventeenth century were employed in what were called "slop shops who put out material to be made into garments for sailors." Women were also heavily involved in making stock items for shops including stays, bodices, caps, gloves, etc.[1] But Roxana correctly surmises that such employment often set women on a downward spiral of poverty.

Paid work was something done for the most part by poor women and most women were poor but they got poorer as they struggled to raise their families, an inevitable feature of the poverty cycle, made worse by the fact that husbands had the unfortunate habit of deserting, falling sick, failing in their business, or being sent to the debtor's prison.[2]

Compounding the fact that women were often meagerly compensated for their labors as seamstresses were the series of economic recessions that hit the aggregate textile industries in the 1690s. That Roxana manages to feed herself and her children for a few months is more indicative of her resolve and her resourcefulness than anything else.

In short order, however, Roxana imagines that she faces an excruciating choice between keeping what's left of her family intact and thereby starving to death or sending her children off to be supported by her husband's family.

I was at first, sadly afflicted at the Thoughts of parting with my Children, and especially at that terrible thing, their being taken into the Parish-keeping; and then a hundred terrible

1   Peter Earle, "The Female Labour Market in London in the Late Seventeenth and Early Eighteenth Centuries," *Economic History Review* 42.3 (1989): 340.
2   Earle, 338.

things came into my Thoughts; *viz.* of Parish-Children being Starv'd at Nurse; of their being ruin'd, let grow crook'd, lam'd, and the like, for want of being taken care of; and this sunk my very Heart within me. (58-59)

Traditionally, critics have taken a dim view of Roxana's decision, regarding it as evidence of her "failure of maternal feeling."[1] As Toni Bowers points out, Roxana's is not an idle concern: a good many children met with abuse at the hands of wet-nurses and foster parents.[2] More recent critics, however, have observed that, unlike Moll Flanders, who seems to forget her children almost as soon as she has them, Roxana not only remembers her children with the Brewer, she makes it her singular aim to seek them out upon her return to England and "provide" for them: "After my coming to England, I was greatly desirous to hear how things stood with [my children]" (206). Laura Rosenthal points out that although Roxana's concern for her children appears late in the novel, it emerges at the earliest possible moment after her decision to become a "Woman of Business," which puts her in a position to provide for her children's welfare.[3]

Roxana's grudging decision to relinquish her children sets the stage for the novel's critical turn as their absence signals her sexual availability to her landlord. As Defoe repeatedly reminds his readers, illicit sex is inextricable from economics. Roxana admits that she is "no more able to maintain myself and My Maid *Amy* in [the house], than [she] was [her] five Children" (64). Roxana's landlord comes "oftener to see" her, professing to be "griev'd for [her] sake" (64). He restores Roxana's furniture and plate and orders Roxana to "put up a Bill for Letting Rooms, reserving one for himself, to come as he saw Occasion" (71). The novel makes no mention of the possibility that with a means to support herself and her children now available, Roxana might choose to reunite her family.

Prior to this arrangement, Roxana's maid Amy has already suggested that the landlord will want to "ask ... a Favour by and by" (66). Initially, Roxana is indignant and proclaims that she'd rather "starve first" (66). At last, she acquiesces.

---

1 Mullan xii.
2 Toni Bowers, *The Politics of Motherhood: British Writing and Culture, 1680–1760* (Cambridge: Cambridge UP, 1996), 106.
3 Laura J. Rosenthal, *Infamous Commerce: Prostitution in Eighteenth-Century British Literature and Culture* (Ithaca: Cornell UP, 2006), 90.

Amy put us to-Bed ... this may be farther Testimony what a hardness of Crime I was now arriv'd to, which was owing to the Conviction that was from the beginning, upon me, that I was a Whore, not a Wife; nor cou'd I ever frame my Mouth to call him Husband, when I was speaking of him. (81-82)

Having crossed a critical line, Roxana represents her decline as inevitable. Echoing Milton's God in *Paradise Lost*, Roxana condemns herself: "I sinn'd with open Eyes, and thereby had a double Guilt upon me" (80).[1] The guilt never leaves Roxana and alludes to another generic influence on Defoe's novel. In Roxana's repeated self-reproaches—"*Why am I a whore now?*" (217)—Marilyn Westfall reads traces of the Puritan Jeremiad sermon, popular during the late seventeenth century, which "censures and condemns acts against conscience."[2]

Roxana does not act against her conscience easily. Indeed, she refuses to succumb to her landlord's proposition without first ensuring her economic welfare. Initially, she objects to the landlord's proposal that they should live as man and wife, noting that "he was above the World, and I infinitely below it" (79). But her suitor is not to be deterred and he protests,

I have taken such Measures as shall make an Equality still; and with that, he shew'd me a Contract in Writing, wherein he engag'd himself to me; to cohabit constantly with me; to provide for me in all Respects as a Wife; and repeating in the Preamble, a long Account of the Nature and Reason of our living together, and an Obligation in the Penalty of 7000£ never to abandon me; and at last, shew'd me a Bond for 500£ to be paid to me, or my Assigns, within three Months after his Death. (79)

Because his wife abandoned him for an adulterous relationship and has thus abdicated any claims she might have made upon his estate, the Jeweller is free to make such arrangements, particularly since the award he makes Roxana is in money rather than

---

1 Roxana echoes God's observation to Christ about the difference between Satan's sin and Adam and Eve's sin in Book III of *Paradise Lost*: "The first sort by their own suggestion fell,/ Self-tempted, self-deprav'd: Man falls deceiv'd/ By the other first" (ll. 129-31).

2 Marilyn Westfall, "A Sermon by the Queen of Whores," *SEL: Studies in English Literature* 41.3 (2001): 485.

property. The prospect of a secure future entices Roxana to take the plunge, and she remains cognizant of her reasoning upon the Jeweller's fateful murder: "I had the Satisfaction not to be left in Distress, or in danger of Poverty ... [but] as I did not know how his Relations, or his Wife's Friends, might act on that Occasion, I order'd [Amy] to convey away all the Plate, Linnen, and other things of Value" at the house (90). It is never clear whether Roxana's preemptive actions are necessary since the Jeweller's wife makes no reappearance. Nonetheless, the contract she made with the Jeweller is honored, and Roxana never looks back on poverty again.

★★★

The sizable fortune Roxana inherits from the Jeweller draws her to the attention of the most wealthy and powerful aristocrats at the French court. Her subsequent liaison with a German Prince stationed on diplomatic duty at Versailles completes her transformation from a merchant-class woman of "Virtue and Honour" to a courtesan who moves with great ease in aristocratic circles. For the next eleven years, Roxana serves as the Prince's mistress.

Upon his wife's death, the Prince is stricken with remorse and terminates his liaison with Roxana. At this point, Defoe begins his heroine's transformation from a woman who seeks solace, protection, and economic support from men to a woman who is fiercely protective of her own independence and sees her sexual partners almost exclusively as a means of economic advancement. Roxana's adulterous relationships first with the Jeweller and then with the Prince have left her enormously wealthy, and her mind turns from acquiring the economic means of survival to accumulating further wealth. In the process she turns down a marriage proposal, bears another illegitimate child, takes on the Whig financier Robert Clayton as her financial advisor, and becomes mistress to a king. The reasons for Roxana's pursuit of money beyond her needs prove elusive, even to Defoe's heroine herself. Ultimately, they seem to revolve around her desire to live her life as a sovereign subject. Roxana's drive for economic independence proves to be among the most durable values in her life. It is the ground upon which she rejects the Dutch Merchant's first marriage proposal. Expounding upon the pitfalls of marriage, Roxana exclaims, "That the very Nature of the Marriage-Contract was, in short, nothing but giving up Liberty, Estate, Authority, and every-thing, to the

Man, and the Woman was indeed, a meer Woman ever after, that is to say, a Slave" (169).

As with many of Roxana's observations about the economic choices she has available, her assessment of the constraints imposed upon married women are correct. With some notable exceptions, marriage continued to be governed by common law, a complex combination of precedent, statute, and traditional practice. According to common law jurisprudence, marriage transformed a woman from a *femme sole* into a *femme covert*. According to this principle, husband and wife acquired a single identity at law and that identity was the husband's. In general, married women were barred from making business contracts on their own, and unless a marriage settlement stipulated that a woman's property and wealth be held in trust for her and her heirs, all her property became that of her husband. For a woman of Roxana's fortune, this was no small matter. Not only was a great deal of money and property at stake, but so too was Roxana's ability to provide for her children by the Brewer.

By 1724, Roxana's complaints about the pitfalls of marriage were familiar enough to women and men alike and had been articulated by writers such as Mary Astell, whose comments in her essay *Some Considerations on Marriage* (1706; see Appendix F) bear an uncanny resemblance to Roxana's observations. Writing nearly a quarter century before Defoe, Astell opined,

> The Domestic Sovereign is without Dispute Elected, and the Stipulations and Contract are mutual, is it not then partial in Men to the last degree, to contend for, and practise that Arbitrary Dominion in their Families, which they abhor and exclaim against in the State? For if Arbitrary Power is evil in it self, and an improper Method of Governing Rational and Free Agents, it ought not to be Practis'd any where; Nor is it less, but rather more mischievous in Families than in Kingdoms, by how much 100000 Tyrants are worse than one. What tho' a Husband can't deprive a Wife of Life without being responsible to the Law, he may however do what is much more grievous to a generous Mind, render Life miserable, for which she has no Redress, scarce Pity which is afforded to every other Complainant. It being thought a Wife's Duty to suffer every thing without Complaint. If all Men are born free, how is it that all Women are born Slaves? as they must be if the being subjected to the inconstant, uncertain, unknown, arbitrary Will of Men, be the perfect Condition of Slavery? and if the

Essence of Freedom consists, as our Masters say it does, in having a standing Rule to live by? And why is Slavery so much condemn'd and strove against in one Case, and so highly applauded, and held so necessary and so sacred in another? (Preface)

Defoe allows Roxana to repeat the argument again and again. And she admonishes Sir Robert Clayton, when he encourages her to marry a wealthy English merchant:

I told him, I knew no State of Matrimony, but what was, at best, a State of Inferiority, if not of Bondage: that I had no Notion of it; that I liv'd a Life of absolute Liberty now; was free as I was born, and having plentiful Fortune, I did not understand what Coherence the Words *Honour* and *Obey* had with the Liberty of a *Free Woman*; that I knew no Reason the Men had to engross the whole Liberty of the Race, and make the Women, notwithstanding any disparity of fortune, be subject to the Laws of Marriage, of their own making; that it was my Misfortune to be a Woman, but I was resolv'd it shou'd not be made worse by the Sex; and seeing Liberty seem'd to be the Men's Property, I wou'd be a Man-Woman; for as I was born free, I wou'd die also. (190)

The frequency with which Roxana repeats the argument is matched only by the frequency with which she reproaches herself for sustaining her liberty at the expense of her soul.

★★★

Amy's role in Roxana's fall has captivated critics for decades. Amy is, on the one hand, a loyal friend whom Roxana describes as "faithful to [her] as the Skin to [her] Back" (64). As Amy, herself puts the matter: "If I will starve for your sake, I will be a Whore, or any thing, for your sake; why I would die for you, if I were put to it" (67). As Terry Castle suggests, "Amy is the secret sharer in Roxana's life: she acts out her mistress's fantasies, she accepts the functions Roxana projects, both consciously and unconsciously onto her."[1] Not only is Amy the agent of Roxana's

---

1 Terry J. Castle, "'Amy, Who Knew My Disease': A Psychosexual Pattern in Defoe's Roxana," *ELH* 46.1 (1979): 84.

descent into prostitution, she also intermittently manages Roxana's financial affairs. In fact, it is Amy who actually makes the arrangements for Roxana's three surviving children from the Brewer to be educated and clothed in a manner befitting their origins in life. And, as Christopher Gabbard has pointed out, it is Amy who "has been keeping her mistress' books."[1] Indeed, when Amy leaves Roxana, apparently for good, Roxana finds herself at both a psychological and financial loss.

> I was, for want of *Amy*, destitute; I had lost my Right-Hand; she was my Steward, gather'd in my Rents, *I mean my Interest-Money*, and kept my Accompts, and, *in a word*, did all my Business. (317)

However, discomfited at Amy's departure Roxana seems, her emotional state reminds readers that the mistress has been uneasy with the intimacy between herself and her servant. Almost as soon as their partnership is formed, Roxana takes pains to remind Amy that she is not Roxana's social equal and certainly not her superior either socially or morally. As Roxana comes to recognize that she is on an inexorable course to becoming her landlord's lover, she laments that she "shou'd have repell'd this *Amy*, however faithful and honest to me in other things, as a Viper, and Engine of the Devil" (76). Shortly after Roxana consummates her relationship with the Jeweller, Amy makes the mistake of acting surprised that Roxana is not yet pregnant. She then goes on to boast that she would have been pregnant twice in the same time. The boast piques Roxana's pride, and she calls Amy's bluff by forcing the younger woman into bed with her own lover, after which she makes one of the novel's most remarkable and startling comments to her readers:

> Had I look'd upon myself as a Wife, you cannot suppose I would have been willing to have let my Husband lye with my Maid, much less, before my Face, for I stood-by all the while; but as I thought myself a Whore, I cannot say but that it was something design'd in my Thoughts, that my Maid should be a Whore too, and should not reproach me with it. (83)

---

1 D. Christopher Gabbard, "The Dutch Wives' Good Husbandry: Defoe's *Roxana* and Financial Literacy," *Eighteenth-Century Studies* 37.2 (2004): 238.

It turns out that what bothers Roxana most about her conscious decision to degrade herself is that in so doing she has traded social places with her own servant, elevating Amy to a morally superior position.

The apotheosis of this psychology comes towards the end of the novel when Roxana has reunited with the Dutch merchant and has begun to entertain thoughts of marriage. Ironically, Roxana has dispatched Amy to Europe to search out the merchant. In addition to reporting what Roxana already knows, that the merchant had taken up residence in London, Amy also reveals that her former lover, the German Prince, had been searching similarly for Roxana with the intention of sending his gentleman to marry her by proxy. The news erases all thoughts Roxana has of becoming an "honest wife" as visions of ascending to the rank of royalty begin to dance before her eyes:

> The Thoughts of being surrounded with Domesticks; honour'd with Titles; be call'd HER HIGHNESS; and live in all the Splendor of a Court; and *which was till more*, in the Arms of a Man of such Rank and who I knew lov'd and valued me; all this *in a word*, dazzl'd my Eyes; turn'd my Head; and I was as truly craz'd and distracted for about a Fortnight, as most of the People in *Bedlam*, tho' perhaps, not quite so far gone. (244)

Amy serves Roxana faithfully through the remainder of the novel, arranging her housing, seeing that all her worldly possessions are cared for, retrieving information, and most importantly seeing to it that her surviving children from her marriage to the Brewer are provided for. But it is in this context that Amy fatally oversteps her bounds. In the process of tending to Roxana's daughters, she learns that Roxana's daughter and namesake, Susan, suspects the truth that Roxana is her mother. That knowledge sends Amy and Roxana alike into a panic. They fear that Susan will expose the past, for, between the time that Roxana abandons her profligate past and the time that Susan begins to pursue the truth about her mother, Roxana and the Dutch merchant have rediscovered one another and married. That exposure, Defoe implies, would invalidate the contract Roxana and her husband agreed to wherein Roxana retains control and management of the couple's finances and thus retains the means to conceal the source of her ill-gotten gains. Roxana's solution is to avoid discovery by fleeing in the hope that Susan will simply become exhausted and give up looking for her. Amy has a darker solution.

Amy understands, too well perhaps, that a rising social tide lifts all boats, and this gives her a direct, vested interest in sustaining Roxana's prosperity, since Roxana is the means whereby Amy sustains her own wealth. Likewise, any threat to Roxana's wealth is also a threat to Amy's wealth. Amy has no maternal affection to temper her. In her eyes Susan must either go away voluntarily or be made to go away forcibly. Initially, Amy threatens the girl, but Susan is undaunted and continues to pursue Roxana. Amy tracks Susan down and menaces her, confessing to Roxana that had there not been witnesses, she would have thrown Susan out of the water taxi in which they were riding and drowned her. Roxana describes this as the last straw.

> I was so provok'd at her, that all my Rage turn'd against Amy, and I fell thorowly out with her: I had now kept Amy almost thirty Year, and found her, on all Occassions, the faithfulest Creature to me, that ever Woman had; *I say*, faithful to me; for however wicked she was, still she was true to me; and even this Rage of hers was all upon my Account, and for fear any Mischief shou'd befall me.... Upon these Words it was that I bade her get out of my Sight, and out of my House. (312-13)

Shortly after Roxana and Amy have their falling out, Susan disappears; Roxana assumes the worst, that Amy has carried out her threat.

Defoe never confirms for his readers that Susan is, in fact, murdered, but it almost doesn't matter. What matters is that Roxana is so tortured by the *possibility* that Susan has been killed that she is as tormented as if she had done the deed herself:

> As for the poor Girl herself, she was ever before my Eyes; I saw her by-Night, and by-Day; ... Sometimes I thought I saw her with her Throat cut; sometimes with her Head cut, and her Brains knock'd-out; other-times hang'd up upon a Beam; another time drown'd in the Great Pond at Camberwell. (323)

In the end, Roxana transforms her assumption that Susan has been murder'd into the *a priori* cause of her own misfortunes:

> After some few Years of flourishing and outwardly happy Circumstances, I fell into a dreadful Course of Calamities.... The

Blast of Heaven seem'd to follow the Injury done the poor girl, by us both; and I was brought so low again, that my Repentance seem'd to be only the Consequence of my Misery, as my Misery was of my Crime. (326)

Some years ago, G.A. Starr wrote of Roxana, "Defoe regards his heroine as a damned soul."[1] Yet she is not a character without redeeming qualities. For all her self-condemnations, Roxana is a bright, witty, and resourceful character, capable of profound emotional attachment, which she demonstrates repeatedly in her responses to the surviving children of her first marriage. How we judge her depends not only on the internal logic of Defoe's novel, but also on our ability to understand the generic traditions that underwrite Roxana's story as well as the material constraints late seventeenth- and early eighteenth-century women faced.

---

1 G.A. Starr, *Defoe and Casuistry* (Princeton: Princeton UP, 1971), 165.

Daniel Defoe: A Brief Chronology[1]

1660   Born Daniel Foe, probably in the east London parish of St. Giles Cripplegate, the son of a prosperous merchant and citizen.

1662   The Foes follow their pastor Dr. Samuel Annesley, who had been expelled from St. Giles Anglican Church as a result of the Act of Uniformity, to form a Dissenting Presbyterian congregation or conventicle.

1674-79   Attends Rev. Charles Morton's Dissenting Academy in Newington Green, perhaps to prepare for a career as a Presbyterian ministry. Morton's school was responsible for educating leading non-Anglican intellectuals, including, later in the eighteenth century, Mary Wollstonecraft.

1681-82   Begins to write, but remains unpublished.

c. 1683   Embarks on the first of several business ventures, setting up as a wholesale hosier in Cornhill, near the Royal Exchange.

1684   Marries Mary Tuffley, daughter of a wealthy cooper. Together they produce eight children in the space of fourteen years (1687-1701).

1685   Joins the Duke of Monmouth's rebellion against King James II. Between July and the end of the year Defoe is probably in hiding, but he resurfaces in London in January of the following year.

1686   James II issues a general pardon to Monmouth's rebels.

1687   Defoe is personally pardoned for his participation in the rebellion.

1688   Defoe's first extant publication appears, *A Letter to a Dissenter from his Friend at the Hague*, in which Defoe celebrates the "Glorious Revolution" of 1688 and the arrival of William and Mary as Protestant monarchs.

1691   Contributes occasionally to John Dunton's *Athenian Mercury* (1691-97). Dunton is Samuel Annesley's son-in-law and fellow member of the Dissenting Pres-

---

1 Adapted and modified from "Daniel Defoe: A Brief Chronology," *Moll Flanders by Daniel Defoe*, ed. Paul A. Scanlon (Peterborough, ON: Broadview Press, 2005).

byterian congregation. Publishes *A New Discovery of an Old Intreague,* a satire of city politics as the Whig radicalism of the 1680s was in irrevocable decline.

1692 First bankruptcy, purportedly for £17,000. Imprisoned for debt in Fleet Prison.

1693 Imprisoned for debt in the King's Bench prison, but negotiates terms with creditors. Begins to work for Thomas Neale as a manager trustee for Neale's private lotteries.

c. 1694 Sets up a brick and tile works at Tilbury.

1695 Adds "De" to his name, thereafter known as "DeFoe."

1697 Publishes *An Essay upon Projects,* begun in 1692 in which he offers specific advice about avoiding debt.

1697-1701
 Serves as an agent for William III in England and Scotland.

1698 *An Enquiry into the Occasional Conformity of Dissenters, The Poor Man's Plea.*

1699 *An Encomium upon a Parliament.*

1700 *The Pacificator,* a long verse essay in which Defoe takes on the theatrical debates of Jeremy Collier and others. In this piece Defoe rejects Collier's high didacticism as an aesthetic ideal.

1701 *The True-Born Englishman,* a verse satire that ridiculed those who resented King William for being Dutch and argued that the essence of English character had nothing to do with one's place of birth. It became one of the most popular poems of the century.

1702 *The Shortest-Way with Dissenters,* an ironic attack on Anglican extremism that invited High-Church partisans to examine the injustices to which Defoe believed Dissenters had been subjected. Conservative Anglicans within Queen Anne's government were not amused. A warrant is issued for his arrest.

1703 Convicted for seditious libel and confined to Newgate Prison for *The Shortest-Way,* Defoe is sentenced to stand in the pillory three times. During his imprisonment, his brick and tile works fail, precipitating a second bankruptcy. Defoe is released from Newgate when Robert Harley, close counselor to Queen Anne, intervenes on his behalf.

1703-14 Defoe serves both as Harley's confidential agent and

as a political journalist for Harley (1703-08), then
Godolphin (1708-10), and Harley again (1710-14).
During this latter period Defoe is joined in Tory writ-
ings by other luminaries of the early eighteenth
century, including Jonathan Swift and Delariviere
Manley.

1704 *The Storm*, a narrative about one the fiercest hurri-
canes to hit England, explores the relationship
between extraordinary events and providence.

1704-13 Writes *The Review*, a periodical mostly in support of
Harley's Tory government.

1709 *The History of the Union of Great Britain*, which
extolled the benefits of England's union with Scotland
and argued the union was providential.

1711 Publishes nearly twenty pamphlets on political and
economic issues of the day.

1713 *Memoirs of Count Tariff*. Defoe's satiric defense of the
Treaty of Commerce and Navigation and response to
Joseph Addison's *The Late Tryal and Conviction of
count Tariff*. Arrested and imprisoned twice for debt
and alleged treasonable writings.

1714-15 *The Secret History of the White Staff*, a three-part pamphlet defending Harley's shattered reputation.

1715 *The Family Instructor*, the first of Defoe's conduct
books. *An Appeal to Honour and Justice*, an apologia
for his own life. Defoe comes to terms with the new
Whig government, serving successive Whig ministries
until 1730, but sometimes still writes for Tory periodicals.

1716-20 *Mercurius Politicus*. A periodical Defoe wrote at the
request of Charles Townshend, a powerful Whig minister under George I. Townshend directed Defoe to
render the Tory press impotent.

1717 *Memoirs of the Church of Scotland*. A plea to Parliament
that they release the Scots from the Oath of Abjura-
tion, which required all Scottish clerics to bar
members of their own Church from the throne of
Great Britain.

1717-24 Contributes to Mist's *Weekly-Journal*, thus diluting its
radical Tory voice.

1719 *The Life and Strange Surprising Adventures of Robinson
Crusoe*, Defoe's first novel, followed by *The Farther
Adventures of Robinson Crusoe*, *The Anatomy of*

Exchange Alley, and other substantial pamphlets on trade and finance.

1720   *The King of Pirates, Memoirs of a Cavalier, Captain Singleton, Serious Reflections of Robinson Crusoe.*

1720-26   Contributes to the *Original Weekly Journal* (later called *Applebee's Original Weekly Journal*), designed primarily for entertainment, specializing in the lives and trials of pirates and felons. Scholars have long speculated that from these portraits, Defoe compiled his character Moll Flanders.

1722   *Moll Flanders, Religious Courtship, A Journal of the Plague Year, Colonel Jack.*

1724   *Roxana, The Great Law of Subordination Consider'd, A Tour thro' the Whole Island of Great Britain* (completed 1726), *The History of the Remarkable Life of John Sheppard, A New Voyage Round the World.* Court action taken against Defoe again for outstanding debt. This year concludes his five-year long experiment with fiction.

1725   *Every-body's Business is No-body's Business, The True and Genuine Account of the Life and Actions of the Late Jonathan Wild, The Complete English Tradesman.*

1726   *An Essay on Literature, Some Considerations upon Street-Walkers, The Political History of the Devil.*

1727   *Conjugal Lewdness, Parochial Tyranny, An Essay on the History and Reality of Apparitions.*

1728   *A Plan of English Commerce, Second Thoughts Are Best: Or, a Further Improvement of a Late Scheme to Prevent Street Robberies, Street-Robberies Consider'd.*

1729   *The Compleat English Gentleman* (not published until 1890).

1730   *A Brief State of the Inland or Home Trade,* a diatribe against hawkers and peddlers. Goes into hiding from his creditors.

1731   *An Effectual Scheme for the Immediate Preventing of Street Robberies.* Dies in lodgings in Ropemaker's Alley, London, and is buried in Bunhill Fields, the great Dissenting Cemetery.

1732   Defoe's wife of forty-seven years dies and is buried beside her husband.

Defoe's Times: A Brief Chronology[1]

1660   Charles II restored to the English throne.

1663   Mary Carleton, the self-styled "German Princess" to whom Roxana compares herself, is tried for bigamy but acquitted; she becomes thereby a notable Restoration celebrity.

1661-65 Clarendon Code, four pieces of legislation enacted over a four-year period, designed to exclude Dissenters from the public life of the nation. The Corporation Act (1661) excluded from municipal office those who refused to take sacraments in the Anglican Church; the Act of Conformity (1662) excluded Dissenters from church office; the Conventicle Act (1662) made all nonconformist meetings for worship illegal, including those held in private houses; and the Five-Mile Act (1665) sought to bar contact between expelled ministers and their former congregations by prohibiting them from coming within five miles of their former meetings.

1666   The last great outbreak of bubonic plague sweeps London, killing more than 70,000 people. The Great Fire rages through the old City for four days and four nights, destroying many landmarks and leaving thousands homeless.

1667   Milton publishes the ten-book version of *Paradise Lost*.

1668   Dryden becomes Poet Laureate.

1673   Charles II is forced by Parliament to withdraw the Declaration of Indulgence, issued the preceding year. The Test Act compels all holders of office—civil, military, or Crown—to take the Oath of Allegiance and communion in the Church of England. Mary Carleton is executed, having been convicted for theft and being an old offender.

1678   Popish Plot scare. Radical Protestants tried to persuade the King and Parliament that there was a

---

1   Adapted and modified from "Defoe's Times: A Brief Chronology," *Moll Flanders by Daniel Defoe*, ed. Paul A. Scanlon (Peterborough, ON: Broadview Press, 2005).

Catholic plot afoot to assassinate Charles II and return England to the Roman Catholic religion. The plot was exposed as a complete fabrication.

1679 The Exclusion Crisis begins as Parliament tries formally and informally to persuade and force the King to exclude his Catholic brother James from inheriting the throne upon Charles's death.

1683 The Rye House Plot is discovered wherein the Duke of Monmouth plotted to assassinate his father the King and his uncle at Rye. Algernon Sidney was executed for his role in the plot on flimsy evidence, but Monmouth escaped to the continent. *Quo warranto* proceedings are initiated against the City of London, resulting in the revocation of the City's charter, the cancellation of its elections, and the institution of Crown-appointed officers. *The Whores Rhetorick* and *The Politick Whore* are both published.

1685 Charles II dies. His brother James, Duke of York, is crowned James II. Several weeks later Monmouth stages his rebellion and is defeated.

1686 James II issues a general pardon, releasing many Dissenters from prison including those who participated in Monmouth's rebellion the preceding year.

1687 James II issues the Declaration of Indulgence granting freedom of worship to Dissenters and Roman Catholics. Nell Gwynn, Charles II's self-described "Protestant whore," dies. Newton publishes the *Principia Mathematica*.

1688 James II reissues the Declaration of Indulgence, which suspended penal laws against Dissenters and Catholics. William, Prince of Orange, lands at Torbay (the Glorious Revolution begins). James II flees the country.

1689 William III and Mary II crowned and rule England jointly. Bill of Rights enacted. Toleration Act allows freedom of worship to Protestant Dissenters. William forms the Grand Alliance with the United Provinces (Netherlands) and the Austrian Hapsbergs and begins a war with France to check Louis XIV's dynastic ambitions. Locke, *First Letter on Toleration*.

1690 William III defeats James II at the Battle of the Boyne. Locke publishes *Treatises of Government*.

1694 Bank of England established. Mary II dies, leaving

England to the sole government of her husband
William III.

1695   Licensing Act lapses.

1696   Navigation Act forbids American colonists to export
directly to Scotland or Ireland. John Dunton begins
publishing *The Nightwalker, or Evening Rambles in
Search after Lewd Women*, which is printed monthly
until 1697.

1698   British merchant vessels begin carrying slaves to the
West Indies. Ward publishes *The London-Spy*.

1700   Astell, *Some Reflections on Marriage*.

1701   James II dies. Louis XIV recognizes James Stuart
(James II's son) as the Pretender King of England.
War of the Spanish Succession begins in Europe.

1702   William III dies; Queen Anne ascends the throne.
England declares war on France.

1704   Swift, *Tale of a Tub*.

1707   The Act of Union is passed, formally uniting the governments of Scotland and England, in a country to be
called Great Britain.

1708   The French launch a Jacobite invasion in Scotland.

1709   Swift, *Project for the Advancement of Religion*; Manley,
The New Atalantis; Steele begins *The Tatler*. Charles
II's former mistress Barbara Palmer, Countess of
Castlemaine, dies.

1710   Parliament is dissolved; subsequent election gives
Tories a majority. Berkeley publishes *Principles of
Human Knowledge*.

1711   Peace preliminaries to end the war of Spanish Succession begin between Britain and France. Occasional
Conformity Bill passed. South Sea Company
launched. The rebuilding of St. Paul's Cathedral,
which had burned in the Great Fire of 1666, is completed. Pope, *Essay on Criticism*; Steel and Addison
collaborate to launch *The Spectator*.

1712   Stamp Act imposes duty on periodicals.

1713   Treaty of Utrecht ends the War of the Spanish Succession. South Sea Company acquires the *asiento*, a
monopoly on supplying African slaves to the Spanish
New World.

1714   Queen Anne dies; her second cousin is crowned
George I.

1715   First Jacobite Rebellion led by James Stuart the

Pretender. Bolingbroke and Harley, Defoe's patron, are impeached. Walpole becomes Chancellor of the Exchequer. Louis XIV dies.

1716   Execution of Jacobite leaders captured at Preston the previous year. Parliament passes the Septennial Act, mandating parliamentary elections every seven years.

1717   Walpole resigns as Chancellor of the Exchequer. Harley is acquitted of high treason.

1718   Quadruple Alliance formed against Spain. Transportation Act passed.

1719   Schism Act and Occasional Conformity Act repealed. Haywood publishes *Love in Excess*. Addison dies.

1720   South Sea Bubble scandal in which inflated stocks crashed, causing widespread financial distress.

1721   Walpole becomes the first minister to be known as Prime Minister.

1724   Swift, *Drapier's Letters*. Mandeville, *A Modest Defense of the Publick Stews*.

1726   John Wesley, Samuel Annesley's grandson, becomes a Fellow of Lincoln College, Oxford, and joins a group known as the Oxford Methodists. Rob Roy is imprisoned in Newgate. Swift publishes *Gulliver's Travels*. Thomson publishes *The Seasons*.

1727   George I dies; accession of his son George II. Spain attacks Gibraltar. Haywood publishes *Philadore and Placentia*.

1728   Gay publishes *The Beggar's Opera*.

1729   Swift publishes *A Modest Proposal*. Steele and Congreve die.

1730   Fielding publishes *The Author's Farce* and *Tom Thumb*.

1731   Lillo publishes *The London Merchant*; Hogarth publishes *The Harlot's Progress*.

A Note on the Text

This edition is based on the 1724 edition of *Roxana*, the only version published during Defoe's lifetime and thus the only authoritative text for the novel. I have retained Defoe's spelling, punctuation, and capitalization in the belief that they add to the reader's understanding for *Roxana* as an eighteenth-century novel with the following exceptions. I have silently corrected some obvious printer's misspellings in order to clarify meaning for the reader. Because the long S is no longer used in modern English, I have changed all such characters to the modern "s". All else here is as it appears in the 1724 edition.

Roxana

THE
FORTUNATE MISTRESS:
OR, A
HISTORY
OF THE
LIFE
AND
VAST VARIETY OF FORTUNES
OF
MADEMOISELLE DE BELEAU,
AFTERWARDS CALL'D
THE COUNTESS DE WINTSELSHEIM,
IN GERMANY.
BEING THE PERSON KNOWN BY THE NAME OF THE
LADY
ROXANA, IN THE TIME OF KING CHARLES II.

London:

Printed for T. Warner at the Black-Boy in Pater-Noster-Row; W. Meadows at the Angel in Cornhill; W. Pepper at the Crown in Maiden-Lane, Covent-Garden; S. Harding at the Post-House in St. Martin's Lane; and T. Edlin at the Prince's-Arms against Exeter-Exchange in the Strand.

THE PREFACE

The History of this Beautiful Lady, *is to speak for itself: If it is not as Beautiful as the Lady herself is reported to be; if it is not as diverting as the Reader can desire, and much more than he can reasonably expect; and if all the most diverting parts of it are not adapted to the Instruction and Improvement of the Reader, the* Relator *says, it must be from the Defect of his Performance; dressing up the Story in worse Cloaths than the* Lady, *whose Words he speaks, prepar'd it for the World.*

He takes the Liberty to say, That this Story *differs from most of the Modern Performances of this Kind, tho' some of them have met with a very good Reception in the World: I say, It differs from them in this Great and Essential Article,* Namely, *That the Foundation of this is laid in Truth of* Fact; *and so the Work is not a Story, but a History.*[1]

The Scene is laid so near the Place where the Main Part of it was transacted, that it was necessary to conceal Names and Persons; lest what cannot be yet entirely forgot in that Part of Town, shou'd be remembered, and the Facts trac'd back too plainly, by the many People yet living, who wou'd know the Persons by the Particulars.[2]

It is not always necessary that the Names of Persons shou'd be discover'd, tho' the History may be many Ways useful;[3] *and if we shou'd be always oblig'd to name the Persons, or not to relate the Story the consequence might be only this, That many a pleasant and delightful History wou'd be Buried in the Dark, and the World be depriv'd both of the Pleasure and the Profit of it.*

---

1 During the late seventeenth and early eighteenth centuries, it was common for writers to seek greater cultural validity for their works by claiming historical veracity for their fictions. "Stories" that were histories, rather than romances, were often thought to be more morally instructive than their fictional counterparts. For more on this, see Lincoln B. Faller, *Crime and Defoe: A New Kind of Writing* (Cambridge: Cambridge UP, 1993) and Robert Mayer, *History and the Early English Novel: Matters of Fact from Bacon to Defoe* (Cambridge: Cambridge UP, 1997).

2 Typically, scholars have understood this remark as Defoe's acknowledgement of his debt to the *roman à clefs* of the times. However, three years earlier he had offered his readers a similar gesture in *Moll Flanders*, which does not imply that it is a "secret history" of great people.

3 According to the 1378 statute of *scandalum magnatum*, "magnates" were afforded the right to sue in Courts of Common Law for slander. The original intent of the legislation was, according to J.H. Baker, to "prevent discord between classes." *An Introduction to English Legal History* (London, Butterworths: 1990) 497.

The Writer says, *He was particularly acquainted with this Lady's First Husband,* the Brewer, *and with his Father; and also, with his Bad Circumstances; and knows that first Part of the Story to be Truth.*

This may, he hopes, be a Pledge for the Credit of the rest, tho' the Latter Part of her History lay Abroad, and cou'd not so well be vouch'd as the First; yet, as she has told it herself, we have the less Reason to question the Truth of that Part also.

In the Manner she has told the Story, it is evident she does not insist upon her Justification in any one Part of it; much less does she recommend her Conduct, or indeed, any Part of it, except her Repentance to our Imitation: On the contrary, she makes frequent Excursions,[1] *in a just censuring and condemning her own Practice: How often does she reproach herself in the most passionate Manner; and guide us to just Reflections in the like Cases?*

It is true, She met with unexpected Success in all her wicked Courses; but even in the highest Elevations of her Prosperity, she makes frequent Acknowledgements, That the Pleasure of her Wickedness was not worth the Repentance; and that all the Satisfaction she had, all the Joy in the View of her Prosperity, no, nor all the Wealth she rowl'd in; the Gayety of her Appearance; the Equipages,[2] *and the Honours, she was attended with, cou'd quiet her Mind, abate the Reproaches of her Conscience, or procure her an Hour's Sleep, when just Reflections kept her waking.*

The Noble Inferences that are drawn from this one Part, are worth all the rest of the Story; and abundantly justifie (as they are the profess'd Design of) the Publication.

If there are any Parts in her Story, which being oblig'd to relate a wicked Action, seem to describe it too plainly, the Writer says, *all imaginable Care has been taken to keep clear of Indecencies, and immodest Expression; and 'tis hop'd you will find nothing to prompt a vicious Mind, but every-where much to discourage and expose it.*

Scenes of Crime can scarce be represented in such a Manner, but some may make a Criminal Use of them; but when Vice is painted in its Low-prized Colours, 'tis not to make People in love with it, but to expose it; and if the Reader makes a wrong Use of the Figures, the Wickedness is his own.

In the mean time, the Advantages of the present Work are so great, and the Virtuous Reader has room for so much Improvement, that we make no Question, the Story, however meanly told, will find a Passage to his best Hours; and be read both with Profit and Delight.

---

1 Comments to the reader.
2 Personal and or household accessories.

THE FORTUNATE MISTRESS:
OR, A HISTORY OF THE LIFE, &C.

I WAS BORN, *as my Friends told me*, at the City of POICTIERS, in the Province, or County of Poictou, in *France*,[1] from whence I was brought to *England* by my Parents, who fled for their Religion about the year 1683, when the Protestants were Banish'd from *France* by the Cruelty of their Persecutors.[2]

I, who knew little or nothing of what I was brought over hither for, was well-enough pleas'd with being here; *London*, a large and gay City, took with me mighty well, who, from my being a Child, lov'd a Crowd, and to see a great-many fine Folks.

I retain'd nothing of *France*, but the Language: My Father and Mother being People of better Fashion, than ordinarily the People call'd REFUGEES at that Time were; and having fled early, while it was easie to secure their Effects, had, before their coming over, remitted considerable Sums of Money, or, *as I remember*, a considerable Value in *French* Brandy, Paper, and other Goods; and these selling very much to Advantage here, my Father was in very good Circumstances at his coming over, so that he was far from applying to the rest of our Nation that were here, for his Countenance and Relief: On the contrary, he had his Door continually throng'd with miserable Objects of the poor starving Creatures, who at that Time fled hither for Shelter, on Account of Conscience, *or something else*.

I have indeed, heard my Father say, That he was pester'd with a great-many of those, who for any Religion they had, might e'en have stay'd where they were, but who flock'd over hither in Droves, for what they call in *English*, a Livelihood; hearing with what Open Arms the REFUGEES were receiv'd in *England*, and how

---

1 "Poictou": Poitou is a province in west-central France with a sizable Protestant population.
2 In thus situating Roxana and her parents, Defoe continues in the tradition of writers like Aphra Behn (*Love Letters Between a Nobleman and His Sister*) and John Dryden (*The Duke of Guise*) who compared the politics of 1680s' England with those of sixteenth- and seventeenth-century France. Roxana's family flees their native France in anticipation of Louis XIV's revocation of the Edict of Nantes (1598), which had afforded French Protestants both religious and civil liberties. Within a few years of the Edict's final revocation, nearly half a million Huguenots had emigrated either to other Protestant European countries or to Protestant colonies in the Americas.

they fell readily into Business, being, by the charitable Assistance of the People in *London*, encourag'd to Work in their Manufactures, in *Spittle-Fields*,[1] *Canterbury*, and other Places; and that they had a much better Price for their Work, than in *France, and the like*.

My Father, *I say*, told me, That he was more pester'd by the Clamours of these People, than of those who were truly Refugees, and fled in Distress, *merely for Conscience*.

I was about ten Years old when I was brought over hither, where, *as I have said*, my Father liv'd in very good Circumstances, and died in about eleven Years more; in which time, as I had accomplish'd myself for the sociable part of the World, so I had acquainted myself with some of our *English* Neighbours, as is the Custom in *London*; and as, while I was Young, I had pick'd-up three or four Play-Fellows and Companions, suitable to my Years; so as we grew bigger, we learnt to call one-another Intimates and Friends; and this forwarded very much the finishing me for Conversation, and the World.

I went to *English* Schools, and being young, I learnt the *English* Tongue perfectly well, with all the Customs of the *English* Young-Women; so that I retain'd nothing of the *French*, but the Speech; nor did I so much as keep any Remains of the *French* Language tagg'd to my Way of Speaking, *as most Foreigners do*, but spoke what we call Natural *English*, as if I had been born here.

Being to give my own Character, I must be excus'd to give it as impartially as possible, and as if I was speaking of another-body; *and the Sequel will lead you to judge whether I flatter myself or no.*

I was (*speaking of myself as about Fourteen Years of Age*) tall, and very well made; sharp as a Hawk in Matters of common Knowledge; quick and smart in Discourse; apt to be Satyrical; full of Repartee, and a little too forward in Conversation; or, as we call it in *English*, BOLD, tho' perfectly Modest in my Behaviour. Being *French* Born, I danc'd, *as some say*, naturally, lov'd it extremely, and sung well also, and so well, that, *as you will hear*, it was afterwards some Advantage to me: With all these things, I wanted neither Wit, Beauty, or Money. In this Manner I set out into the

---

1 Or "Spitalfields," is a neighborhood located just east of the Bishopgate section of the former London Wall, so named because it belonged to the priory and hospital or "spital" of St. Mary. As Roxana describes, Spittle-Fields became a textile center as large numbers of highly skilled French silk weavers settled there after fleeing persecution in France. Because Spittle-Fields lies beyond the city wall, it is also outside the jurisdiction of the London guilds.

World, having all the Advantages that any Young woman cou'd desire, to recommend me to others, and form a Prospect of happy Living to myself.

At about Fifteen Years of Age, my Father gave me, *as he call'd it in* French, 25000 Livres, *that is to say,* two Thousand Pounds Portion, and married me to an Eminent Brewer in the City;[1] *pardon me if I conceal his Name, for tho' he was the Foundation of my Ruin, I cannot take so severe a Revenge upon him.*

With this Thing call'd a Husband, I liv'd eight Years in good Fashion, and for some part of the Time, kept a Coach, *that is to say,* a kind of Mock-Coach; for all the Week the Horses were kept at Work in the Dray-Carts, but on Sunday I had the Privilege to go Abroad in my Chariot, either to Church, or otherways, as my Husband and I cou'd agree about it; which by the way, was not very often: But of that hereafter.

Before I proceed in the History of the Marry'd Part of my Life, you must allow me to give as impartial an Account of my Husband, as I have done of myself: He was a jolly, handsome Fellow, as any Woman need wish for a Companion; tall, and well made; rather a little too large, but not so as be ungentile;[2] he danc'd well, which, *I think*, was the first thing that brought us together: He had an old Father, who manag'd the Business carefully, so that he had little of that Part lay on him, but now-and-then to appear, and show himself; and he took Advantage of it, for he troubl'd himself very little about it, but went abroad, kept Company, hunted much, and lov'd it exceedingly.

After I have told you that he was a Handsome Man, and good

---

1 Among members of the commercial classes, where money rather than property was primarily an issue, it was common for fathers to settle a "portion" of their estates upon their daughters as part of a marriage settlement. Often the portion was a cash amount given directly to the future husband's father in guarantee that the future husband would settle a "jointure" or liveable estate on his wife upon his death. In some cases, as it seems to be for Roxana, the son-in-law received interest from his wife's portion upon marriage, rather than a lump-sum payment. As Roxana herself notes, her father decides to appoint her brother trustee for her portion because of misgivings he has about his daughter's marriage. Sadly, this trust in Roxana's brother proves to be misplaced as he loses all his money, including Roxana's portion, in misguided business dealings. For more on portion and its ability to ensure jointure, see Susan Staves, *Married Women's Separate Property in England, 1660-1833* (Cambridge: Harvard UP, 1990).

2 Awkward, ill-mannered.

Sportsman, I have, indeed, said all; and unhappy was I, like other young People of our Sex, I chose him for being a handsome, jolly Fellow, as I have said; for he was otherwise a weak, empty-headed, untaught Creature, as any Woman could ever desire to be coupled with: and here I must take the Liberty, whatever I have to reproach myself with in my after-Conduct, to turn to my Fellow-Creatures, the Young Ladies of this Country, and speak to them, by way of Precaution, If you have any Regard to your future Happiness; any View of living comfortably with a Husband; any Hope of preserving your Fortunes, or restoring them after any Disaster; Never Ladies, marry a Fool;[1] with some other Husbands you may be unhappy, but with a Fool you will be miserable; with another Husband you *may*, I say, be unhappy, but with a Fool you *must*; nay, if he wou'd, he cannot make you easie; every thing he does is so awkward, every thing he says is so empty, a Woman of any Sence cannot but be surfeited, and sick of him twenty times a-Day: What is more shocking, than for a Woman to bring a handsome, comely Fellow of a Husband, into Company, and then be oblig'd to Blush for him every time she hears him speak? To hear other Gentlemen talk Sence, and he able to say nothing? And so look like a Fool, or, which is worse, hear him talk Nonsence, and be laugh'd at for a Fool.

In the next Place, there are so many Sorts of Fools, such an infinite Variety of Fools, and so hard it is to know the Worst of the Kind, that I am oblig'd to say, No Fool, Ladies at all, no kind of Fool; whether a mad Fool, or a sober Fool, a wise Fool, or a silly Fool; take any thing but a Fool; nay, *be* any thing, be even an Old Maid, the worst of Nature's Curses, rather than take up with a Fool.

But to leave this a-while, for I shall have Occasion to speak of it again; my Case was particularly hard, for I had a Variety of foolish Things complicated in this unhappy Match.

First, and which I must confess, is very unsufferable, he was a

---

1 Defoe echoes this passage in *The Complete English Tradesman* (1725) when he reminds tradesmen who have fallen on hard times that "a Man that will lie still, should never hope to rise; he that will lie in a Ditch and pray, may depend upon it he shall lie in the Ditch and die" (I, 183). Roxana, too, reiterates her antipathy for her husband's foolishness later during her sojourn in France. For more on the parallels between *Roxana* and *The Complete English Tradesman*, see Bram Dijkstra, *Defoe and Economics: The Fortunes of* Roxana *in the History of Interpretation* (New York: St. Martin's Press, 1987).

conceited Fool, *Tout Opiniatre,*[1] everything he said, was Right, was Best, and was to the Purpose, whoever was in Company, and whatever was advanc'd by others, tho' with the greatest Modesty imaginable; and yet when he came to defend what he had said, by Argument and Reason, he would do it so weakly, so emptily, and so nothing to the Purpose, that it was enough to make anybody that heard him, sick and asham'd of him.

Secondly, He was positive and obstinate, and the most positive in the most simple and inconsistent Things, such as were intollerable to bear.

These two Articles, if there had been no more, qualified him to be a most unbearable Creature for a Husband; and so it may be suppos'd at first Sight, what a kind of Life I led with him: However, I did as well as I could, and held my Tongue, which was the only Victory I gain'd over him; for when he would talk after his own empty rattling Way with me, and I would not answer, or enter into Discourse with him on the Point he was upon, he would rise up in the greatest Passion imaginable, and go away; which was the cheapest Way I had to be deliver'd.

I could enlarge here much, upon the Method I took to make my Life passable and easie with the most incorrigible Temper in the World; but it is too long, and the Articles too trifling: I shall mention some of them as the Circumstances I am to relate, shall necessarily bring them in.

After I had been Married about four Years, my own Father died, my Mother having been dead before; he lik'd my Match so ill, and saw so little Room to be satisfied with the Conduct of my Husband, that tho' he left me 5000 Livres, and more at his Death,[2] yet he left it in the Hands of my Elder Brother, who running on too rashly in his Adventures, as a Merchant, fail'd, and lost not only what he had, but what he had for me too; as you shall hear presently.

Thus I lost the last Gift of my Father's Bounty, by having a Husband not fit to be trusted with it; there's one of the Benefits of marrying a Fool.

Within two Years after my own Father's Death, my Husband's Father also died, and, as I thought, left him a considerable Addition to his Estate, the whole Trade of the Brewhouse, which was a very good one, being now his own.

---

1 Opinionated.
2 This appears to be in addition to the 25000*l.* Livres Roxana receives as her marriage portion. [see p. 47]

But this Addition to his Stock was his Ruin, for he had no Genius to Business; he had no Knowledge of his Accounts; he bustled a little about it indeed, at first, and put on a Face of Business, but he soon grew slack; it was below him to inspect his Books, he committed all that to his Clerks and Book-Keepers; and while he found Money in Cash to pay the Malt-Man, and the Excise,[1] and put some in his Pocket, he was perfectly easie and indolent, let the main Chance go how it would.[2]

I foresaw the Consequence of this, and attempted several times to perswade him to apply himself to his Business; I put him in Mind how his Customers complain'd of the Neglect of his Servants on one hand, and how abundance Broke in his Debt, on the other hand, for want of the Clerk's Care to secure him, *and the like*; but he thrust me by, either with hard Words, or fraudulently, with representing the Cases otherwise than they were.

However, to cut short a dull Story, which ought not to be long, he began to find his Trade sunk, his Stock declin'd, and that, in short, he could not carry on his Business, and once or twice his Brewing Utensils were extended[3] for the Excise; and the last Time he was put to great Extremities to clear them.

This allarm'd him, and he resolv'd to lay down his Trade; which indeed, I was not sorry for; foreseeing that if he did not lay it down in Time, he would be forc'd to do it another Way, namely, as a Bankrupt.[4] Also I was willing he should draw out while he had something left, lest I should come to be stript at Home, and be turn'd out of Doors with my Children; for I had now five Children by him; the only Work (perhaps) that Fools are good for.

I thought myself happy when he got another Man to take his Brewhouse clear off his Hands; for paying down a large Sum of Money, my Husband found himself a clear Man, all his Debts paid, and with between Two and Three Thousand Pound in his

---

1 *OED*: The taxes levied under the name of Excise by the Ordinance of 1643 included certain duties imposed, in addition to the customs, on various foreign products.

2 In *The Complete English Tradesman*, Defoe warns tradesmen against committing their businesses to servants in the following way: "by giving up the shop, as it were, to [the servant], and indulging himself in being abroad, and absent from his business, the apprentice gets the mastery of the business, the fame of the shop, depends upon him; and when he sets up, certainly follows him" (101).

3 Pawned.

4 Defoe, himself, was twice imprisoned for bankruptcy, once in 1692 and again in 1703.

Pocket; and being now oblig'd to remove from the Brewhouse, we took a House at—, a village about two Miles out of Town; and happy I thought myself, all things consider'd, that I was got off clear, upon so good Terms, and had my handsome Fellow had but one Cap full of wit, I had been still well enough.

I propos'd to him either to buy some Place with the Money, or with Part of it, and offer'd to join my Part to it, which was then in Being, and might have been secur'd; so we might have liv'd tolerably, at least, during his Life. But as it is Part of a Fool to be void of Council, so he neglected it, liv'd on as he did before, kept his Horses and Men, rid every Day out to the Forest a Hunting, and nothing was done all this while; but the Money decrease'd apace, and I thought I saw my Ruine hastening on, without any possible Way to prevent it.

I was not wanting with all that Perswasions and Entreaties could perform, but it was all fruitless; representing to him how fast our Money wasted, and what would be our Condition when it was gone, made no Impression on him; but like one stupid, he went on, not valuing all that Tears and Lamentations could be suppos'd to do; nor did he abate his Figure or Equipage, his Horses or Servants, even to the last; till he had not a Hundred Pound left in the whole World.

It was not above three Years that all the Ready-Money was thus spending off; yet he spent it, as I may say, foolishly too, for he kept no valuable Company neither; but generally with Huntsmen and Horse-Coursers, and Men meaner than himself, which is another consequence of a Man's being a Fool; such can never take Delight in Men more wise and capable than themselves; and that makes them converse with Scoundrels, drink Belch[1] with porters, and Keep Company always below themselves.

This was my wretched Condition, when one Morning my Husband told me, he was sensible he was come to a miserable Condition, and he would go and seek his Fortune somewhere or other; he had said something to that Purpose several times before that, upon my pressing him to consider his Circumstances, and the Circumstances of his Family before it should be too late: But as I found he had no Meaning in anything of that Kind, as indeed, he had not much in any thing he ever said; so I thought they were but Words of Course now: When he said he wou'd be gone, I us'd to wish secretly, and even say in my Thoughts, *I wish you wou'd, for if you go on thus, you will starve us all.*

---

1 Cheap, poor-quality beer.

He staid, however, at home all that Day, and lay at home that Night; early the next Morning he gets out of Bed, goes to a Window which look'd out towards the Stables, and sounds his *French* Horn, as he call'd it; which was his usual Signal to call his Men to go out a hunting.

It was about the latter-end of *August*, and so was light yet at five a-Clock, and it was about that Time that I heard him and his two Men go out and shut the Yard-Gates after them. He said nothing to me more than as usual when he us'd to go out upon his Sport; neither did I rise, or say any thing to him that was material, but went to-sleep again after he was gone, for two Hours, or thereabouts.

It must be a little surprizing to the Reader to tell him at once, that after this, I never saw my Husband more; but to go farther, I not only never saw him more, but I never heard from him, or of him, neither of any or either of his two Servants, or of the Horses, either what became of them, where, or which Way they went, or what they did, or intended to do, no more than if the Ground had open'd and swallow'd them all up, and no-body had known it; except as hereafter.

I was not, for the first Night or two, at-all surpriz'd, no nor very much the first Week or two, believing that if anything Evil had befallen them, I should soon enough have heard of that; and also knowing that as he had two Servants and three Horses with him, it would be the strangest Thing in the World that any thing could befall them all, but that I must some time or other hear of them.

But you will easily allow, that as Time run on a Week, two Weeks, a Month, two Months, and so on, I was dreadfully frighted at last, and the more when I look'd into my own Circumstances, and consider'd the Condition which I was left; with five Children, and not one Farthing Subsistance for them, other than about seventy Pound in Money, and what few things of Value I had about me, which, tho' considerable in themselves, were yet nothing to feed a Family, and for a length of Time too.

What to do I knew not, nor to whom to have recourse; to keep in the House where I was, I could not, the Rent being too great; and to leave it without his Order, if my Husband should return, I could not think of that neither; so that I continued extremely perplex'd, melancholy, and discourag'd, to the last Degree.

I remain'd in this dejected Condition near a Twelvemonth. My Husband had two Sisters, who were married, and liv'd very well, and some other near Relations that I knew of, and I hop'd would do something for me; and I frequently sent to these, to know if they could give me any Account of my vagrant Creature; but they all declar'd to me in Answer, That they knew nothing about him; and after frequent sending, began to think me troublesome, and to let me know they thought so too, by their treating my Maid with very slight and unhandsome Returns to her Inquiries.

This grated hard, and added to my Affliction, but I had no recourse but to my Tears, for I had not a Friend of my own left me in the World: I should have observ'd, that it was about half a Year before this Elopement of my Husband, that the Disaster I mention'd above befel my Brother; who Broke,[1] and that in such bad Circumstances, that I had the Mortification to hear not only that he was in Prison, but that there would be little or nothing to be had by Way of Composition.[2]

Misfortunes seldom come alone: This was the Forerunner of my Husband's Flight; and as my Expectations were cut off on that Side, my Husband gone, and my Family of Children on my Hands, and nothing to subsist them, my Condition was the most deplorable that Words can express.

I had some Plate and some Jewels, as might be supposed, my Fortune and former Circumstances consider'd; and my Husband, who had never staid to be distress'd, had not been put to the Necessity of rifling me, as Husbands usually do in such Cases: But as I had seen an End of all the Ready-Money, during the long time I had liv'd in a State of Expectation for my Husband, so I began to make away[3] one thing after another, till those few Things of Value which I had, began to lessen apace, and I saw nothing but Misery and the utmost Distress before me, even to have my Children starve before my Face; I leave any one that is a Mother of Children, and has liv'd in Plenty and good Fashion, to consider and reflect, what must be my Condition: As to my Husband, I had now no Hope or Expectation of seeing him any more; and, indeed, if I had, he was the Man, of all the Men in the World, the least able to help me, or to have turn'd his hand to the gaining one Shilling towards lessening our Distress; he neither had the Capacity or the Inclination; he could have been no Clerk, for he scarce wrote a legible Hand; he was so far from being able to write Sence, that he could not make Sence of what others wrote; he was so far from understanding good *English*, that

---

1 Went bankrupt.
2 Residual money left from her brother's business either to pay his debts or to help Roxana.
3 Sell or pawn.

he could not spell good *English*: To be out of all Business was his Delight; and he wou'd stand leaning against a Post for half an Hour together, with a Pipe in his Mouth, with all the Tranquillity in the world, smoaking, like Dryden's *Countryman that Whistled as he went, for want of Thought*;[1] and this even when his Family was, as it were starving, that little he had wasting, and that we were all bleeding to Death; he not knowing, and as little considering, where to get another Shilling when the last was spent.

This being his Temper, and the Extent of his Capacity, I confess I did not see so much Loss in his parting with me, as at first I thought I did; tho' it was hard and cruel, to the last Degree in him, not giving me the least Notice of his Design; and, indeed, that which I was most astonished at, was, that seeing he must certainly have intended this Excursion some few Moments at least, before he put it in Practice, yet he did not come and take what little Stock of Money we had left; or at least, a Share of it, to bear his Expence for a little while, but he did not; and I am morally certain he had not five Guineas with him in the World, when he went away: All that I cou'd come to the Knowledge of, about him, was, that he left his Hunting-Horn, which he call'd the *French Horn*, in the Stable, and his Hunting Saddle, went away in a handsome Furniture,[2] as they call it, which he used sometimes to Travel with; having an embroidered Housing,[3] a Case of Pistols, and other things belonging to them; and one of his Servants had another Saddle with Pistols, though plain; and the other a long Gun; so that they did not go out as Sportsmen, but rather as Travellers: What Part of the World they went to, I never heard for many Years.

As I have said, I sent to his Relations, but they sent me short and surly Answers; nor did any one of them offer to come to see me, or to see the Children, or so much as to enquire after them, well perceiving that I was in a Condition that was likely to be soon troublesome to them:[4] But it was no Time now to dally with

---

1 From "Cymon and Iphigenia, from Boccace" ll. 84-5, *Fables Ancient and Modern* (1700).
2 Equipment.
3 Case.
4 Much of the family's response may be explained by the fact that extended families, particularly those that lived in the same parish where a child was born, retained primary responsibility for children who were orphaned. Only in cases where a poor orphaned child had no family capable of maintaining it did the child's natal parish assume its care.

them, or with the World; I left off sending to them, and went myself among them; laid my Circumstances open to them, told them my whole Case, and the Condition I was reduc'd to, begg'd they would advise me what Course to take, laid myself as low as they could desire, and intreated them to consider that I was not in a Condition to help myself, and that without some Assistance, we must all inevitably perish: I told them, that if I had had but one Child, or two Children, I would have done my Endeavour to have work'd for them with my Needle, and should only have come to them to beg them to help me to some Work, that I might get our Bread by my Labour;[1] but to think of one single Woman not bred to Work, and at a Loss where to get Employment, to get the Bread of five Children, that was not possible, some of my Children being young too, and none of them big enough to help one another.

It was all one, I receiv'd not one Farthing of Assistance from any-body, was hardly ask'd to sit down at the two Sisters Houses, nor offer'd to Eat or Drink at two more near Relations. The Fifth, an Ancient Gentlewoman, Aunt-in-Law to my Husband, a Widow, and the least able also of any of the rest, did, indeed, ask me to sit down, gave me a Dinner, and refresh'd me with a kinder Treatment than any of the rest; but added the melancholy Part, *viz.* That she would have help'd me, but that, indeed, she was not able; which, however, I was satisfied was very true.

Here I reliev'd myself with the constant Assistant of the Afflicted, I mean Tears; for, relating to her how I was received by the other of my Husband's Relations, it made me burst into Tears, and I cry'd vehemently for a great while together, till I made the good old Gentlewoman cry too several times.

However, I came home from them all without any Relief, and went on at home till I was reduc'd to such inexpressible Distress,

---

1 It is not entirely clear why Defoe insists on this point as women participated in several different aspects of textile work. The life of a seamstress
was arduous and offered only a meager existence. Indeed, many women
who made their living this way were subsidized by the parish. On the
other hand, women working as lace-makers did, at various points during
the period, make a respectable wage that allowed them to live independ-
ently. For more on this, see Bridget Hill, *Women, Work, and Sexual Politics
in Eighteenth-century England* (Montreal: McGill-Queen's UP, 1994) and
Pamela Sharpe, "Literally Spinsters: A New Interpretation of Local
Economy and Demography in Colyton in the Seventeenth and Eighteenth Centuries," *Economic History Review* 44.1 (1991): 46-65.

that it is not to be describ'd: I had been several times after this at the old Aunt's; for I prevail'd with her to promise me to go and talk with the other Relations; at least, that, if possible, she could bring some of them to take off the Children, or to contribute something towards their Maintenance; and, to do her Justice she did use her Endeavour with them, but all was to no Purpose, they would do nothing, at least that Way: I think, with much Entreaty, she obtain'd by a kind of Collection among them all, about eleven or twelve Shillings in Money; which tho' it was a present Comfort, was yet not to be nam'd as capable to deliver me from any Part of the Load that lay upon me.

There was a poor Woman that had been a kind of a Dependant upon our Family, and who I had often, among the rest of the Relations, been very kind to; my Maid put it into my Head one Morning to send to this poor Woman, and see whether she might not be able to help, in this dreadful Case.

I must remember it here, to the Praise of this poor Girl, my Maid, that tho' I was not able to give her any Wages, and had told her so, nay I was not able to pay her the Wages that I was in Arrears to her, yet she would not leave me; nay, and as long as she had any Money, when I had none, she would help me out of her own; for which, tho' I acknowledged her Kindness and Fidelity, yet it was but a bad Coin that she was paid in at last, as will appear in its Place.

Amy, (for that was her Name) put it into my Thoughts to send for this poor Woman to come to me, for I was now in great Distress, and I resolv'd to do so; but just the very Morning that I intended it, the old Aunt, with the poor Woman in her Company, came to see me; the good old Gentlewoman was, it seems, heartily concern'd for me, and had been talking again among those People, to see what she could do for me; but to very little Purpose.

You shall judge a little of my present Distress by the Posture she found me in: I had five little Children, the Eldest was under ten Years old, and I had not one Shilling in the House to buy them Victuals, but had sent *Amy* out with a Silver Spoon, to sell it, and bring home something from the Butcher's; and I was in a Parlour, sitting on the Ground, with a great Heap of old Rags, Linnen, and other things about me, looking them over, to see if I had any thing among them that would Sell or Pawn for a little Money, and had been crying ready to burst myself, to think what I should do next.

At this Juncture they knock'd at the Door, I thought it had been *Amy*, so I did not rise up, but one of the Children open'd the Door, and they came directly into the Room where I was, and where they found me in that Posture, and crying vehemently, as above; I was surpriz'd at their coming, you may be sure, especially seeing the Perosn I had but just before resolv'd to send for: But when they saw me; how I look'd, for my Eyes were swell'd with crying, and what a Condition I was in as to the House, and the Heaps of things that were about me, and especially when I told them what I was doing, and on what Occasion, they sat down like *Job*'s three Comforters,[1] and said not one Word to me for a great while, but both of them cry'd as fast, and as heartily as I did.

The Truth was, there was no Need of much Discourse in the Case, the Thing spoke of it self; they saw me in Rags and Dirt, who was but a little before riding in my Coach; thin, and looking almost like one Starv'd, who was before fat and beautiful: The House, that was before handsomely furnish'd with Pictures and Ornaments, Cabinets, Peir-Glasses,[2] and everything suitable, was now stripp'd and naked, most of the Goods having been seiz'd by the Landlord for Rent, or sold to buy Necessaries; in a word, all was Misery and Distress, the Face of Ruin was every where to be seen; we had eaten up almost every thing, and little remain'd, unless, like one of the pitiful Women of *Jerusalem*, I should eat up my very Children themselves.[3]

After these two good Creatures had sat, as I say, in Silence some time, and had then look'd about them, my Maid *Amy* came in, and brought with her a small Breast of Mutton, and two great Bunches of Turnips, which she intended to stew for our Dinner: As for me, my Heart was so overwhelm'd at seeing these two Friends, for such they were, tho' poor, and at their seeing me in

---

1   Job 2: 11-13. "Now when Job's three friends heard of all this evil that was come upon him, they came every one from his own place; Eliphaz the Temanite, and Bildad the Shuhite, and Zophar the Naamathite: for they had made an appointment together to come to mourn with him and to comfort him. And when they lifted up their eyes afar off, and knew him not, they lifted up their voice, and wept; and they rent everyone his mantle, and sprinkled dust upon their heads toward heaven. So they sat down with him upon the ground seven days and seven nights, and none spake a word unto him: for they saw that his grief was very great."

2   Mirrors.

3   Lamentations 2: 20. "Behold, O Lord; and consider to whom thou hast done this. Shall the women eat their fruit, and children of a span long? Shall the priest and the prophet be slain in the sanctuary of the Lord?"

such a Condition, that I fell into another violent Fit of Crying; so that, in short, I could not speak to them again for a great while longer.

During my being in such an Agony, they went to my Maid *Amy* at another Part of the same Room, and talk'd with her: *Amy* told them all my Circumstances, and set them forth in such moving Terms, and so to the Life, that I could not upon any Terms have done it like her myself, and in a Word, affected them both with it in such a manner, that the old Aunt came to me, and tho' hardly able to speak for Tears: Look ye, Cousin, said she, in a few Words, Things must not stand thus; some Course must be taken, and that forthwith; pray where were these Children born? I told her the Parish[1] where we liv'd before, that four of them were born there; and one in the House where I now was, where the Landlord, after having seiz'd my Goods for the Rent past, not then knowing my Circumstances, had now given me leave to live for a whole Year more without any Rent, being moved with Compassion; but that this Year was now almost expir'd.

Upon hearing this Account, they came to this Resolution: That the Children should be all carried by them to the Door of one of the Relations mention'd above, and be set down there by the Maid *Amy*, and that I the Mother, should remove for some Days, shut up the Doors, and be gone; that the People should be told, That if they did not think fit to take some Care of the Children, they might send for the Church-Wardens if they thought that better; for that they were born in that Parish, and there they must be provided for; as for the other Child which was born in the Parish of—, that was already taken Care of by the Parish-Officers there; for indeed, they were so sensible of the Distress of the Family, that they had, at first Word, done what was their Part to do.

This was what these good Women propos'd and bade me leave the rest to them. I was at first sadly afflicted at the Thoughts of parting with my Children, and especially at the terrible thing, their being taken into the Parish-keeping; and then a hundred terrible things came into my thoughts; *viz.* of Parish-Children being Starv'd at Nurse; of their being ruin'd, let grow crooked,

---

1 A parish was obligated to support anyone who was either born within it or had established a settlement of one year. Poor-relief varied significantly from parish to parish and depended on how many paupers constituted the poor-rate at any given time. For more on this, see Stephen Macfarlane, "Social Policy and the Poor in the Later Seventeenth Century," in *London 1500-1700: The Making of the Metropolis*, ed. A.L. Beier and Roger Finlay (London: Longman, 1986), 252-77.

lam'd, and the like, for want of being taken care of; and this sunk my very Heart within me.

But the Misery of my own Circumstances hardened my Heart against my own Flesh and Blood; and when I consider'd they must inevitably be Starv'd, and I too, if I continued to keep them about me, I began to be reconcil'd to parting with them all, any how, and any where, that I might be freed from the dreadful Necessity of seeing them all perish, and perishing with them myself: So I agreed to go away out of the House, and leave the Management of the whole Matter to my Maid *Amy*, and to them, and accordingly I did so; and the same Afternoon they carried them all away to one of their *Aunts*.

Amy, a resolute girl, knock'd at the Door, with the Children all with her, and bade the Eldest, as soon as the Door was open, run in, and the rest after her; she set them all down at the Door before she knock'd, and when she knock'd, she staid, till a Maid-Servant came to the Door; Sweetheart, said she, pray go in and tell your Mistress, here are her little Cousins come to see her from—, naming the Town where we liv'd, at which the Maid offer'd to go back: Here Child, says *Amy*, take one of 'em in your Hand, and I'll bring the rest; so she gives her the least, and the Wench goes in mighty innocently, with the Little One in her Hand, upon which *Amy* turns the rest in after her, shuts the Door softly, and marches off as fast as she could.

Just in the Interval of this, and even while the Maid and her Mistress were quarrelling, for the Mistress rav'd and scolded at her like a Mad-Woman, and had order'd her to go and stop the Maid *Amy*, and turn all the Children out of the Doors again; but she had been at the Door, and *Amy* was gone, and the Wench was out of her Wits, and the Mistress too: I say, just at this Juncture came the poor old Woman, not the Aunt, but the other of the two that had been with me, and knocks at the Door; the Aunt did not go, because she had pretended to Advocate for me, and they would have suspected her of some Contrivance; but as for the other Woman, they did not so much as know that she had kept up any Correspondence with me.

Amy and she had concerted this between them, and it was well enough contriv'd that they did so. When she came into the House, the Mistress was fuming and raging like one Distracted, and calling the Maid all the foolish Jades and Sluts that she could think of, and that she would take the Children and turn them all out into the Streets. The good poor Woman seeing her in such a Passion, turn'd about as if she would be gone again, and said, Madam, I'll come again another time, I see you are engag'd. No, no, Mrs.—, says the Mistress, I am not much engage'd, sit down: This senseless Creature here has brought in, my Fool of a Brother's whole House of Children upon me, and tells me, that a Wench brought them to the Door, and thrust them in, and bade her carry them to me; but it shall be no Disturbance to me, for I have order'd them to be set in the Street, without the Door, and so let the Church-Wardens take Care of them, or else make this dull Jade carry 'em back to— again, and let her that brought them into the World, look after them if she will; what does she send her Bratts to me for?

The last, indeed, had been the best of the two, says the Poor Woman, if it had been to be done, and that brings me to tell you my Errand, and the Occasion of my coming, for I came on purpose about this very Business, and to have prevented this being put upon you, if I could; but I see I am come too late.

How do you mean too late, says the Mistress? What, have you been concern'd in this Affair then? What, have you help'd bring this Family-Slur upon us? I hope you do not think such a thing of me Madam, says the poor Woman; but I went this Morning to—, to see my old Mistress and Benefactor, for she had been very kind to me, and when I came to the Door, I found all fast and lock'd and bolted, and the House looking as if nobody was at Home.

I knock'd at the Door, but no-body came, till at last some of the Neighbours' Servants call'd to me, and said, There's no-body lives there, Mistress, what do you knock for? I seem'd surpriz'd at that: What, no-body live there! *said I*, what d'ye mean! Does not Mrs.— live there? The Answer was, No, she is gone; at which I parly'd with the one of them, and ask'd her what was the Matter; Matter, says she, why 'tis Matter enough, the poor Gentlewoman has liv'd there all alone, and without anything to subsist her, a long time, and this Morning the Landlord turn'd her out of Doors.

Out of Doors! *says I*, what with all her Children, poor Lambs, what is become of them? Why truly, nothing worse, *said they*, can come to them than staying here, for they were almost starv'd with Hunger; so the Neighbours seeing the poor Lady in such Distress, for she stood crying, and wringing her Hands over her Children like one distracted, sent for the church-Wardens, to take care of the Children; and they, when they came, took the Youngest, which was born in this Parish, and have got it a very good Nurse, and taken Care of it; but as for the other four, they had sent them away to some of their Father's Relations, and who were very substantial People, and who besides that, liv'd in the Parish where they were born.

I was not so surpriz'd at this, as not presently to foresee that this Trouble would be brought upon you, or upon Mr.—, so I came immediately, to bring you word of it, that you might be prepar'd for it, and might not be surpriz'd, but I see they have been too nimble for me, so that I know not what to advise; the poor Woman, it seems, is turn'd out of Doors into the Street; and another of the Neighbours there told me, that when they took away her Children from her, she swoon'd away, and when they recover'd her out of that, she run distracted, and is put into a Mad-House by the Parish; for there is no-body else to take any Care of her.[1]

This was all acted to the Life by this good, kind, poor Creature; for tho' her Design was perfectly good and charitable, yet there was not one Word of it true in Fact; for I was not turn'd out of Doors by the Landlord, nor gone distracted; it was true, indeed, that at parting with my poor Children, I fainted, and was like one Mad when I came to myself and found they were gone; but I remain'd in the House a good while after that; as you shall hear.

While the poor Woman was telling this dismal Story, in came the Gentlewoman's Husband, and tho' her Heart was harden'd against all Pity, who was really and nearly related to the Children, for they were the Children of her own Brother; yet the good Man was quite soften'd with the dismal Relation of the Circumstances of the Family; and when the poor Woman had done, he said to his Wife, This is a dismal Case, my Dear, indeed, and something must be done: His Wife fell a raving at him, What *says she*, do you want to have four Children to keep? Have we not Children of our own? Would you have these Bratts come and eat up my Children's Bread? No, no, let'em go to the Parish, and let them take Care of them, I'll take Care of my own.

Come, come, my Dear, *says the Husband*, Charity is a Duty to the Poor, and *he that gives to the Poor, lends to the Lord* ;[2] let us lend our Heavenly Father a little of our Children's Bread, as you call

---

1 The model for madhouses was "Bedlem" or Bethlem Hospital which was given a royal charter in 1547 to serve the insane in the City of London.

2 This passage paraphrases *Proverbs* 19:17, which reads "He that hath pity upon the poor lendeth unto the Lord; And that which he hath given will he pay him again." It is not clear, however, that the Uncle represents Defoe's views on this matter. Defoe had vociferously opposed public alms in his diatribe *Giving Alms no Charity* (1704) in which he complained that subsidizing work of the idle was simply a policy of "enriching one poor man to starve another" (95).

it, it will be a Store well laid up for them, and will be the best Security that our Children shall never come to want Charity, or be turn'd out of Doors, as these poor innocent Creatures are. Don't tell me of Security, *says the Wife*; 'tis a good Security for our Children, to keep what we have together, and provide them, and then 'tis time enough to help keep other Folks Children; Charity begins at home.

Well, my Dear, *says he again*, I only talk of putting out a little Money to Interest, our Maker is a good Borrower, never fear making a bad Debt there, Child; I'll be Bound for it.

Don't banter me with your Charity, and your Allegories, *says the Wife angrily*, I tell you they are my Relations, not yours, and they shall not roost here, they shall go to the Parish.

All your Relations are my Relations now, *says the good Gentleman very calmly*, and I won't see your Relations in Distress and not pity them, any more than I would my own; indeed, my Dear, they shan't go to the Parish, I assure you none of my Wife's Relations shall come to the Parish, if I can help it.

What, will you take four Children to keep? s*ays the Wife*.

No, no, my Dear, *says he*, there's your Sister—, I'll go and talk with her, and your Uncle—, I'll send for him and the rest; I'll warrant you when we are all together we will find Ways and Means to keep four poor little Creatures from Beggary and Starving, or else it will be very hard; we are none of us in so bad Circumstances but we are able to spare a Mite for the Fatherless; don't shut up your Bowels of Compassion against your own Flesh and Blood: could you hear these poor innocent Children cry at your Door for Hunger and give them no Bread?

Prethee what need they cry at our Door? *says she*, 'tis the Business of the Parish to provide for them, they shan't cry at our Door; if they do, I'll give them nothing: Won't you, *says he*, but I will, remember that dreadful Scripture is directly against us, *Prov.* 21.13. *Whoso stoppeth his Ears at the Cry of the Poor, he also shall cry himself, but shall not be heard.*

Well, well, *says she*, you must do what you will, because you pretend to be Master; but if I had my Will, I would send them where they ought to be sent, I would send them from whence they came.

Then the poor Woman put in, and said, But, Madam, that is sending them to starve indeed; for the Parish has no Obligation to take Care of 'em, and so they would lie and perish in the Street.

Or be sent back again, *says the Husband*, to our Parish in a

Cripple-Cart,[1] by the Justice's Warrant, and so expose us and all the Relations to the last Degree, among our Neighbours, and among those who knew the good Old Gentleman their Grandfather, who liv'd and flourish'd in this Parish so many Years, and was so well belov'd among all People, and deserv'd it so well.

I don't value that one Farthing, not I, *says the Wife*, I'll keep none of them.

Well, my Dear, *says her Husband*, but I value it, for I won't have such a Blot lie upon the Family, and upon your Children; he was a worthy, ancient, and good Man, and his Name is respected among all his Neighbours; it will be a Reproach to you that are his Daughter, and to our children, that are his Grand-Children, that we should let your Brother's Children perish, or come to be a Charge to the Publick, in the very Place where your Family once flourish'd: Come, say no more, I'll see what can be done.

Upon this, he sends and gathers all the Relations together at a Tavern hard-by, and sent for the four little Children that they might see them; and they all, at first Word, agreed to have them taken Care of; and because his Wife was so furious that she would not suffer one of them to be kept at Home, they agreed to keep them all together for a-while; so they committed them to the poor Woman that had manag'd the Affair for them, and enter'd into Obligations to one another to supply the needful Sums for their Maintenance; and not to have one separated from the rest, they sent for the Youngest from the Parish where it was taken in, and had them all brought up together.

It would take up too long a Part of this Story to give a particular Account with what a charitable Tenderness this good Person, who was but Uncle-in-Law to them, manag'd that Affair; how careful he was of them; went constantly to see them, and to see that they were well provided for, cloath'd, put to School, and at last put out in the World for their Advantage; but 'tis enough to say he acted more like a Father to them, than an Uncle-in-Law, tho' all along much against his Wife's Consent, who was of a Disposition not so tender and compassionate as her Husband.

You may believe I heard this with the same Pleasure which I now feel at the relating it again; for I was terribly frighted at the Apprehensions of my Children being brought to Misery and Dis-

---

1 According to Charles II's 1661 proclamation, justices were empowered to have any idle poor found outside of their natal parish "openly whipped" and carted to their home.

tress, as those must be who have no Friends, but are left to Parish Benevolence.

I was now, however, entering on a new Scene of Life; I had a great House upon my Hands, and some Furniture left in it, but I was no more able to maintain myself and My Maid *Amy* in it, than I was my five Children; nor had I any thing to subsist with, but what I might get by working, and that was not a Town where much Work was to be had.

My Landlord had been very kind indeed, after he came to know my Circumstances, tho' before I was acquainted with that Part, he had gone so far as to seize my Goods, and to carry some of them off too.

But I had liv'd three Quarters of a Year in his House after that, and had paid him no Rent, and which was worse, I was in no Condition to pay him any; however, I observ'd he came oftner to see me, look'd kinder upon me, and spoke more friendly to me, than he us'd to do; particularly the last two or three times he had been there, he observ'd, *he said*, how poorly I liv'd, how low I was reduc'd, and the like, told me it griev'd him for my sake; and the last time of all he was kinder still, told me he came to Dine with me, and that I should give him leave to Treat me; so he call'd my Maid *Amy*, and sent her out to buy a Joint of Meat; he told her what she should buy, but naming two or three things, either of which she might take; the Maid, a cunning Wench, and faithful to me, as the Skin to my Back, did not buy any thing out-right, but brought the Butcher along with her, with both the things she had chosen, for him to please himself; the one was a large very good Leg of Veal; the other a Piece of the Fore-Ribs of Roasting Beef; he look'd at them, but bade me chaffer[1] with the Butcher for him, and I did so, and came back to him, and told him what the Butcher demanded for either of them, and what each of them came to; so he pulls out 11*s.* and 3*d.* which they came to together, and bade me take them both, and the rest, *he said*, would serve another time.

I was surpriz'd, you may be sure, at the Bounty of a Man that had but a little while ago been my Terror, and torn the Goods out of my House, like a Fury; but I consider'd that my Distresses had mollified his Temper, and that he had afterwards been so compassionate as to give me Leave to live Rent-free in the House a whole Year.

But now he put on the Face, not of a Man of Compassion only, but of a Man of Friendship and Kindness, and this was so

---

1 Bargain.

unexpected, that it was surprizing: We chatted together, and were, as I may call it, Chearful, which was more than I could say I had been for three Years before; he sent for Wine and Beer too, for I had none; poor *Amy* and I had drank nothing but Water for many Weeks, and indeed, I have often wonder'd at the faithful Temper of the poor Girl; for which I but ill requited her at last.

When *Amy* was come with the Wine, he made her fill a Glass to him, and with the Glass in his Hand, he came to me, and kiss'd me, which I was, I confess, a little surpriz'd at, but more at what follow'd; for he told me, That as the sad Condition which I was reduc'd to, had made him pity me, so my Conduct in it, and the Courage I bore it with, had given him a more than ordinary Respect for me, and made him very thoughtful for my Good; that he was resolv'd for the present to do something to relieve me, and to employ his Thoughts in the mean time, to see if he could, for the future, put me into a Way to support myself.

While he found me change Colour, and look surpriz'd at his Discourse, for so I did to be sure, he turns to my Maid *Amy*, and looking at her, he *says* to me, I say all this Madam, before your Maid, because both she and you shall know that I have no ill Design, and that I have, in meer Kindness, resolv'd to do something for you, if I can; and as I have been a Witness of the uncommon Honesty and Fidelity of Mrs.[1] *Amy* here, to you in all your Distresses, I know she may be trusted with so honest a Design as mine is; for, I assure you, I bear a proportion'd Regard to your Maid too, for her Affection to you.

Amy made him a Curtsie, and the poor Girl look'd so confounded with Joy, that she could not speak, but her Colour came and went, and every now and then she blush'd as red as Scarlet, and the next Minute look'd as pale as Death: Well, having said this, he sat down, made me sit down, and then drank to me, and made me drink two Glasses of Wine together; for, *says he*, you have Need of it, and so indeed I had: When he had done so, Come *Amy*, *says he*, with your Mistress's Leave, you shall have a Glass too, so he made her Drink two Glasses also, and then rising up; and now *Amy*, *says he*, go and get Dinner; and you, Madame, *says he* to me, go up and dress you, and come down and smile and be merry; adding, I'll make you easie, if I can; and in the mean time, *he said*, he would walk in the Garden.

---

1   In this case, "Mrs." indicates neither class nor marital status. Rather, the
     title is used here to indicate that Amy is a woman of marriageable age
     and thus no longer considered a juvenile female.

When he was gone, *Amy* chang'd her Countenance indeed, and look'd as merry as ever she did in her Life; Dear Madam! s*ays she*, what does this Gentleman mean? Nay, *Amy, said I*, he means to do us Good, you see, don't he? I know no other Meaning he can have, for he can get nothing by me: I warrant you, Madam, *says she*, he'll ask you a Favour by and by: No, no, you are mistaken, *Amy*, I dare say, *said I*; you heard what *he said*, didn't you? Ay, says *Amy*, it's no matter for that, you shall see what he will do after Dinner: Well, well, *Amy, says I*, you have hard Thoughts of him, I cannot be of your Opinion; I don't see any thing in him yet that looks like it: As to that, Madam, says *Amy*, I don't see any thing of it yet neither; but what should move a Gentleman to take Pity of us, as he does? Nay, *says I*, that's a hard thing too, that we should judge a Man to be wicked because he's charitable; and vicious because he's kind: O Madam, says *Amy*, there's abundance of Charity begins in that Vice, and he is not so unacquainted with things, as not to know, that Poverty is the strongest Incentive; a Temptation, against which no Virtue is powerful enough to stand out; he knows your Condition as well as you do:[1] Well, and what then? Why then he knows too that you are young and handsome, and he has the surest Bait in the World to take you with.

Well, *Amy, said I*, but he may find himself mistaken too in such a thing as that: Why, Madam, says *Amy*, I hope you won't deny him, if he should offer it.

What d'ye mean by that, *Hussy, said I*? No, I'd starve first.

I hope not, Madam, I hope you would be wiser; I'm sure if he will set you up, as he talks of, you ought to deny him nothing; and you will starve if you do not consent, that's certain.

What, consent to lye with him for Bread? *Amy, said I*, How can you talk so?

Nay, Madam, *says Amy*, I don't think you wou'd for any thing else; it would not be Lawful for any thing else, but for Bread, Madam; why nobody can starve, there's no bearing that, I'm sure.[2]

---

1 In *The Review* for 15 September 1711, Defoe wrote, "Poverty makes Thieves, as bare Walls makes giddy Housewives." The natural consequence of this, in his eyes, was that "Women whore for Bread."

2 Amy's argument, here, is indicative of shifting attitudes towards prostitution. The exchange of sex for money, per se, was not yet illegal. Women prosecuted for what modern readers would recognize as prostitution were usually charged either with vagrancy—a common law trans-

Ay, *says I*, but if he would give me an Estate to live on, he should not lye with me, I assure you.

Why look you, Madam, if he would but give you enough to live easie upon, he should lye with me for it with all my Heart.

That's a Token, *Amy*, of inimitable Kindness to me, *said I*, and I know how to value it; but there's more Friendship than Honesty in it, *Amy*.

O, Madam, says *Amy*, I'd do any thing to get you out of this sad Condition; as to Honesty, I think Honesty is out of the Question, when Starving is the Case; are not we almost starv'd to Death?

I am indeed, *said I*, and thou art for my sake; but to be a Whore, *Amy*! and there I stopt.

Dear Madam, says *Amy*, if I will starve for your sake, I will be a Whore, or any thing, for your sake; why I would die for you, if I were put to it.

Why that's an Excess of Affection, *Amy*, said I, I never met with before; I wish I may be ever in Condition to make you some Returns suitable: But however, *Amy*, you shall not be a Whore to him, to oblige him to be kind to me; no, *Amy*, nor I won't be Whore to him, if he would give me much more than he is able to give me, or do for me.

Why Madam, says *Amy*, I don't say I will go and ask him; but I say, if he should promise to do so and so for you, and the Condition was such, that he would not serve you unless I would let him lye with me, he should lye with me as often as he would, rather than you should not have his Assistance;[1] but this is but Talk, Madam, I don't see any need of such Discourse, and you are of Opinion that there will be no need of it.

Indeed so I am, *Amy*; but, *said I*, if there was, I tell you again,

---

gression—or fornication—a cannon law transgression. As such, through most of the late seventeenth century, prostitution was viewed as a consequence of idleness rather than a consequence of economic necessity. Amy's acknowledgement that many women were driven to prostitution as their only means of supporting themselves ("for Bread") registers an emergent belief that women might choose to avail themselves of other means of support if they were available.

1 Amy's arguments here use casuistry, a method for resolving difficult moral problems when specific contingencies seem to set themselves at odds with moral principle, e.g., Amy's claim that Roxana cannot be expected to starve for the sake of preserving her virtue. For more on this, see G.A. Starr, *Defoe and Casuistry* (Princeton: Princeton UP, 1971).

I'd die before I would consent or before you would consent for my sake.

Hitherto I had not only preserv'd the Virtue itself, but the virtuous Inclination and Resolution; and had I kept myself there, I had been happy, tho' I had perish'd of meer Hunger; for, without question, a Woman ought rather to die, than to prostitute her Virtue and Honour, let the Temptation be what it will.

But to return to my Story; he walk'd about the Garden; which was, indeed, all in Disorder, and over-run with Weeds, because I had not been able to hire a Gardener to do any thing to it, no not so much as to dig up Ground enough to sow a few Turnips and Carrots for Family-Use: After he had view'd it, he came in, and sent *Amy* to fetch a poor Man, a Gardener, that us'd to help our Man-Servant, and carry'd him into the Garden, and order'd him to do several things in it, to put it into a little Order; and this took him up near an Hour.

By this time I had dress'd me, as well as I could, for tho' I had good Linnen left still, yet I had but a poor Head-Dress, and no Knots,[1] but old Fragments; no Necklace, no Ear-Rings; all those things were gone long ago for meer Bread.

However, I was tight[2] and clean, and in better Plight than he had seen me in a great while, and he look'd extreamly pleas'd to see me so; for he said I look'd so disconsolate, and so afflicted before, that it griev'd him to see me; and he bade me pluck up a good Heart, for he hop'd to put me in a Condition to live in the World, and be beholden to nobody.

I told him that was impossible, for I must be beholden to him for it, for all the Friends I had in the World wou'd not, or cou'd not, do so much for me as that he spoke of. Well, *Widow, says he*, so he call'd me, and so indeed I was in the worst Sence that desolate Word cou'd be us'd in, if you are beholden to me, you shall be beholden to nobody else.

By this time Dinner was ready, and *Amy* came in to lay the Cloth, and indeed, it was happy there was none to Dine but he and I, for I had but six Plates left in the House, and but two Dishes; however, he knew how things were, and bade me make no Scruple about bringing out what I had, he hop'd to see me in a better Plight, he did not come, *he said*, to be Entertain'd, but to Entertain me, and Comfort and Encourage me: Thus he went on,

---

1 Ornamental ribbons.
2 Neat.

speaking so chearfully to me, and such chearful things, that it was a Cordial to my very Soul, to hear him speak.

Well, we went to Dinner, I'm sure I had not eat a good Meal hardly in a Twelvemonth, at least, not of such a Joint of Meat as the Loin of Veal was; I eat indeed very heartily, and so did he, and he made me drink three or four Glasses of Wine, so that, in short, my Spirits were lifted up to a Degree I had not been us'd to, and I was not only chearful, but merry, and so he press'd me to be.

I told him, I had a great deal of Reason to be merry, seeing he had been so kind to me, and had given me Hopes of recovering me from the worst Circumstances that ever Woman of any sort of Fortune, was sunk into; that he cou'd not but believe that what he had said to me, was like Life from the Dead; that it was like recovering one Sick from the Brink of the Grave; how I should ever make him a Return any way suitable, was what I had not yet had time to think of; I cou'd only say, that I should never forget it while I had Life, and shou'd be always ready to acknowledge it.

He said, That was all he desir'd of me, that his Reward would be, the Satisfaction of having rescued me from Misery; that he found he was obliging one that knew what Gratitude meant; that he would make it his Business to make me completely Easie, first or last, if it lay in his Power; and in the mean time, he bade me consider of any thing that I thought he might do for me, for my Advantage, and in order make me perfectly easie.

After we had talk'd thus, he bade me be chearful; come, says he, lay aside these melancholy things, and let us be merry; *Amy* waited at the Table, and she smil'd and laugh'd, and was so merry she could hardly contain it, for the Girl lov'd me to an Excess, hardly to be describ'd; and it was such an unexpected thing to hear anyone talk to her Mistress, that the Wench was besides herself almost, and as soon as Dinner was over, *Amy* went up-Stairs, and put on her Best Clothes too, and came down dress'd like a Gentlewoman.

We sat together talking of a Thousand things, of what had been, and what was to be, all the rest of the Day, and in the Evening he took his Leave of me, with a thousand Expressions of Kindness and Tenderness, and true Affection to me, but offer'd not the least of what my Maid *Amy* had suggested.

At his going away, he took me in his Arms, protested an honest Kindness to me; said a thousand kind things to me, which I cannot now recollect, and after kissing me twenty times, or thereabouts, put a Guinea[1] into my Hand; which, he said, was for my present Supply, and told me, that he would see me again, before 'twas out; also he gave *Amy* Half a Crown.[2]

When he was gone, Well, *Amy*, said *I*, are you convinc'd now that he is an honest as well as a true Friend, and that there has been nothing, not the least Appearance of any thing of what you imagin'd, in his Behaviour: Yes, says *Amy*, I am, but I admire at it; he is such a Friend as the World, sure, has not abundance of to show.

I am sure, *says I*, he is such a Friend as I have long wanted, and as I have as much Need of as any Creature in the World has, or ever had; and, in short, I was so overcome with the Comfort of it, that I sat down and cry'd for Joy a good-while, as I had formerly cry'd for Sorrow. *Amy* and I went to Bed that Night (for *Amy* lay with me) pretty early, but lay chatting almost all Night about it, and the Girl was so transported, that she got up two or three times in the Night, and danc'd about the room in her Shift; in short, the Girl was half distracted with the Joy of it; a Testimony still of her violent Affection for her Mistress, in which no Servant ever went beyond her.

We heard no more of him for two Days, but the third Day he came again; then he told me, with the same Kindness, that he had order'd me a Supply of Household-Goods for the furnishing the House; that in particular, he had sent me back all the Goods that he had seiz'd for Rent, which consisted, indeed, of the best of my former Furniture; and now, says he, I'll tell you what I have had in my Head for you, for your present Supply, and that is, *says he*, that the House being well furnish'd, you shall Let it out to Lodgings, for the Summer Gentry, *says he*, by which you will easily get a good comfortable Subsistance, especially seeing you shall pay

---

1 *OED*: An English gold coin, not coined since 1813, first struck in 1663 with the nominal value of 20*s*., but from 1717 until its disappearance circulating as legal tender at the rate of 21*s*. In 1663 the Royal Mint was authorized to coin gold pieces of the value of 20*s*. "in the name and for the use of the Company of Royal Adventurers of *England* trading with Africa"; these pieces were to bear for distinction the figure of a little elephant, and 44 of them were to contain 1 lb. troy of "our Crowne gold." The 20*s*. pieces of the African company received the popular name of *guineas* almost as soon as they were issued, as they were intended for use in the Guinea trade and were made of gold from Guinea; the name was extended to later coins of the same intrinsic value.

2 A silver-based coin with the value of 2 shillings six-pence.

me no Rent for two Years, nor after neither, unless you can afford it.[1]

This was the first View I had of living comfortably indeed, and it was a very probably Way, I must confess; seeing we had very good Conveniences, six Rooms on a Floor, and three Stories high: While he was laying down the Scheme of my management, came a Cart to the Door with a Load of Goods, and an Upholsterer's Man to put them up; they were chiefly the Furniture of two Rooms, which he had carried away for his two Years Rent, with two fine Cabinets, and some Peir-Glasses, out of the Parlour, and several other valuable things.

These were all restor'd to their Places, and he told me he gave them me freely, as a Satisfaction for the Cruelty he had us'd me with before; and the Furniture of one Room Being finish'd, and set up, he told me, he would furnish one Chamber for himself, and would come and be one of my Lodgers, if I would give him Leave.

I told him, he ought not to ask me Leave, who had so much Right to make himself welcome; so the House began to look in some tolerable Figure, and clean; the Garden also, in about a Fortnight's Work, began to look something less like a Wilderness than it us'd to do; and he order'd me to put up a Bill for Letting Rooms, reserving one for himself, to come to as he saw Occasion.

When all was done to his Mind, as to placing the Goods, he seem'd very well pleas'd, and we din'd together again of his own providing, and the Upholsterer's Man gone; after Dinner he took me by the Hand, Come, now Madam, *says he*, you must show me your House, (for he had a-Mind to see everything over again). No, Sir, *said I*, but I'll go show you your House, if you please; so we went up thro' all the Rooms, and in the Room which was appointed for himself, *Amy* was doing something; Well, *Amy*, says he, I intend to Lye with you to Morrow-Night; *To Night, if you please Sir*, says *Amy* very innocently, *your Room is quite ready*: Well *Amy says he*, I am glad you are so willing: No, says *Amy*, I mean your Chamber is ready to-Night, and away she run out of the Room asham'd enough; for the Girl meant no Harm, whatever she had said to me in private.

However, he said no more then; but when *Amy* was gone, he walk'd about the Room, and look'd at every thing, and taking me

---

1 The merchant's suggestion here, that Roxana transform herself into a landlady, is suggestive of her degradation, as bawds who ran the brothels often masqueraded as landladies.

by the Hand, he kiss'd me, and spoke a great many kind, affectionate things to me indeed; as of his Measures for my Advantage, and what he wou'd do to raise me again in the World; told me, that my Afflictions, and the Conduct I had shown in bearing them to such an Extremity, and so engag'd him to me, that he valued me infinitely above all the Women in the World; that tho' he was under such Engagements that he cou'd not Marry me, [his Wife and he had been parted, for some Reasons, which make too long a Story to intermix with mine][1] yet that he wou'd be every thing else that a Woman cou'd ask in a Husband, and with that he kiss'd me again, took me in his Arms, but offer'd not the least uncivil Action to me, and told me, he hop'd I would not deny him all the Favours he should ask, because he resolv'd to ask nothing of me but what it was fit for a Woman of Virtue and Modesty, for such he knew me to be, to yield.

I confess, the terrible Pressure of my former Misery, the Memory of which lay heavy upon my Mind, and the surprising Kindness with which he had deliver'd me, and withal, the Expectations of what he might still do for me, were powerful things, and made me have scarce the Power to deny him any thing he wou'd ask; however, I told him thus, with an Air of Tenderness too, that he had done so much for me, that I thought I ought to deny him nothing, only I hop'd, and depended upon him, that he wou'd not take the Advantage of the infinite Obligations I was under to him, to desire any thing of me, the yielding to which would lay me lower in his Esteem than I desir'd to be; that as I took him to be a Man of Honour, so I knew he could not like me the better for doing any thing that was below a Woman of Honesty and Good Manners to do.

He told me, that he had done all this for me, without so much as telling me what Kindness or real Affection he had for me; that I might not be under any Necessity of yielding to him in any thing, for want of Bread; and he would no more oppress my Gratitude now, than he would my Necessity before, nor ask any thing, supposing he would stop his Favours, or withdraw his Kindness, if he was deny'd; it was true, he said, he might tell me more freely

---

1 It was possible for estranged husbands and wives to live apart, protected from harassment by the other partner by one of two means: either they could negotiate what was called a separate maintenance contract, which indemnified the husband against the wife's debts; or they could obtain an ecclesiastical separation in church courts, which allowed both parties to live separately, but did not allow either partner to remarry.

his Mind now, than before, seeing I had let him see that I accepted his Assistance, and saw that he was sincere in his Design of serving me; that he had gone thus far to shew me that he was kind to me, but that now he would tell me, that he lov'd me, and yet wou'd demonstrate that his Love was both honourable, and that what he shou'd desire, was what he might honestly ask, and I might honestly grant.

I answer'd, that within those two Limitations, I was sure I ought to deny him nothing, and I should think myself not ungrateful only, but very unjust, if I shou'd; so he said no more, but I observ'd he kiss'd me more, and took me in his Arms in a kind of familiar Way, more than usual, and which once or twice put me in Mind of my Maid *Amy*'s Words; and yet, I must acknowledge I was so over-come with his Goodness to me in those many kind things he had done, that I not only was easie at what he did, and made no Resis-tance, but was inclin'd to do the like, whatever he had offer'd to do: But he went no farther than what I have said, nor did he offer so much as to sit down on the Bed-side with me, but took his Leave, said he lov'd me tenderly, and would convince me of it by such Demonstrations as should be to my Satisfaction: I told him, I had a great deal of Reason to believe him; that he was full Master of the whole House, and of me, as far as was within the Bounds we had spoken of, which I believ'd he would not break; and ask'd him if he wou'd not Lodge there that Night.

He said, he cou'd not well stay that Night, Business requiring him in *London*, but added, smiling, that he wou'd come the next Day, and take a Night's Lodging with me. I press'd him to stay that Night, and told him, I should be glad a Friend so valuable should be under the same Roof with me; and indeed, I began at that time not only to be much oblig'd to him, but to love him too, and that in a Manner that I had not been acquainted with myself.

O let no Woman slight the Temptation that being generously deliver'd from Trouble, is to any spirit furnish'd with Gratitude and just Principles: This Gentleman had freely and voluntarily deliver'd me from Misery, from Poverty, and Rags; he had made me what I was, and put me into a Way to be even more than I ever was, namely, to live happy and pleas'd, and on his Bounty I depended: What could I say to this Gentleman when he press'd me to yield to him, and argued the Lawfullness of it? But of that in its Place.

I press'd him again to stay that Night, and told him it was the first compleatly happy Night that I had ever had in the House in my Life, and I should be very sorry to have it be without his Company, who was the Cause and Foundation of it all; that we would be innocently merry, but that it could never be without him; and in short, I courted him so, that he said, he cou'd not deny me, but he wou'd take his Horse, and go to *London*, do the Business he had to do, which it seems was to pay a Foreign Bill[1] that was due that Night, and wou'd else be protested;[2] and that he would come back in three Hours at farthest, and Sup with me, but bade me get nothing there, for since I was resolv'd to be merry, which was what he desir'd above all things, he wou'd send me something from *London*, and we will make it a Wedding Supper, my Dear, *says he*, and with that Word, took me in his Arms; and kiss'd me so vehemently, that I made no question but he intended to do every thing else that *Amy* had talk'd of.

I started a little at the Word *Wedding*: What do ye mean? to call it by such a Name, *says I*; adding, We will have a Supper, but t'other is impossible, as well on your side as mine; he laugh'd, Well, says he, you shall call it what you will, but it may be the same thing, for I shall satisfie you, it is not so impossible, as you make it.

I don't understand you, said I, have not I a Husband, and you a Wife?

Well, well, says he, we will talk of that after Supper; so he rose up, gave me another Kiss, and took his Horse for *London*.

This kind of Discourse had fir'd my Blood, I confess, and I knew not what to think of it; it was plain now that he intended to lye with me, but how he would reconcile it to a legal thing, like a Marriage, that I cou'd not imagine: We had both of us us'd *Amy* with so much Intimacy, and trusted her with every thing, having such unexampled Instances of her Fidelity, that he made no Scruple to kiss me, and say all these things to me before her, nor had he car'd one Farthing if I would have let him Lay with me, to have had *Amy* there too all Night. When he was gone, Well, *Amy*, says I, what will all this come to now? I am all in a Sweat at him: Come to, Madam, says *Amy*, I see what it will come to, I must put you to-Bed to Night together: Why you wou'd not be so impudent, you Jade you, *says I*, wou'd you? Yes, I wou'd, says she, with all my Heart, and think you both as honest as ever you were in your Lives.

What ails the Slut to talk so? s*aid I*, Honest! how can it be honest? Why, I'll tell you, Madam, says *Amy*, I sounded[3] it as soon as I heard him speak, and it is very true too; he calls you

---

1 Debt to a foreign merchant.
2 Declared in default.
3 Figured it out.

Widow, and such, indeed, you are; for as my Master has left you so many Years, he is dead to be sure; at least he is dead to you; he is no Husband, you are, and ought to be free to marry who you will; and his Wife being gone from him, and refuses to lye with him, then he is a single Man again, as much as ever; and tho' you cannot bring the Laws of the Land to join you together, yet one refusing to do the Office of a Wife, and the other of a Husband, you may certainly take one another fairly.

Nay, *Amy, says I,* if I cou'd take him fairly, you may be sure I'd take him above all the Men in the World; it turn'd the very Heart within me, when I heard him say he lov'd me; how cou'd it do otherwise? When you know what a Condition I was in before; despis'd, and trampled on by all the World; I cou'd have took him in my Arms, and kiss'd him as freely as he did me, if it had not been for Shame,

Ay, and all the rest too, says *Amy,* at the first Word; I don't see how you can think of denying him any thing; has he not brought you out of the Devil's Clutches; brought you out of the blackest Misery that ever poor Lady was reduc'd to? Can a Woman deny such a Man any thing?

Nay, I don't know what to do, *Amy,* says I; I hope he won't desire any thing of that Kind of me, I hope he won't attempt it; if he does, I know not what to say to him.

Not ask you, says *Amy,* depend upon it, he will ask you, and you will grant it too; I'm sure my Mistress is no Fool; come, pray Madam, let me go air you a clean Shift; don't let him find you in foul Linnen the Wedding-Night.

But that I know you to be a very honest Girl, *Amy, says I,* you wou'd make me abhor you; why, you argue for the Devil, as if you were one of his Privy-Counsellors.

It's no matter for that, Madam, I say nothing but what I think; you own you love this Gentleman, and he has given you sufficient Testimony of his Affection to you; your Conditions are alike unhappy, and he is of the Opinion that he may take another Woman, his first Wife having broke her Honour, and living from him, and that, tho' the Laws of the Land will not allow him to marry formally, yet, that he may take another Woman into his Arms, provided he keeps true to the other woman as a Wife; nay he says it is usual to do so, and allow'd by the Custom of the Place, in several Countries abroad; and I must own, I'm of the same Mind; else 'tis in the Power of a Whore, after she has jilted and abandon'd her Husband, to confine him from the Pleasure as well as Convenience of a Woman all Days of his Life, which wou'd be very unreasonable; and as times go, not tolerable to all People; and the like on your side, Madam.

Had I now had my Sences about me, and had my Reason not been overcome by the powerful Attraction of so kind, so beneficent a Friend; had I consulted Conscience and Virtue, I shou'd have repell'd this *Amy*, however faithful and honest to me in other things, as a Viper, and Engine of the Devil; I ought to have remembred that neither he or I, either by the Laws of God or Man, cou'd come together, upon any other Terms than that of notorious Adultery: The ignorant Jade's Argument, That he had brought me out of the Hands of the Devil, by which she meant the Devil of Poverty and Distress, shou'd have been a powerful Motive to me, not to plunge myself into the Jaws of Hell, and into the Power of the real Devil, in Recompence for that Deliverance; I shou'd have look'd upon all the Good this Man had done for me, to have been the particular Work of the Goodness of Heaven; and that Goodness shou'd have mov'd me to a Return of Duty and humble Obedience; I shou'd have receiv'd the Mercy thankfully, and apply'd it soberly to the Praise and honour of my Maker; whereas by this wicked Course, all the Bounty and Kindness of this Gentleman, became a Snare to me, was meer Bait to the Devil's Hook; I receiv'd his Kindness at the dear Expence of Body and Soul, mortgaging Faith, Religion, Conscience and Modesty, for (as I may call it) a Morsel of Bread; or, if you will, ruin'd my Soul from a Principle of Gratitude, and gave myself up to the Devil, to shew myself grateful to my Benefactor: I must do the Gentleman that Justice, as to say, I verily believe that he did nothing but what he thought was Lawful; and I must do that Justice upon myself, as to say, I did what my own Conscience convinc'd me at the very Time I did it, was horribly unlawful, scandalous, and abominable.

But Poverty was my Snare; dreadful Poverty! the Misery I had been in, was great, such as wou'd make the Heart tremble at the Apprehensions of its Return; and I might appeal to any that has had any Experience of the World, whether one so entirely destitute as I was, of all manner of all Helps, or Friends, either to support me, or to assist me to support myself, could withstand the Proposal; not that I plead this as a Justification of my Conduct, but that it may move the Pity, even of those that abhor the Crime.

Besides this, I was young, handsome, and with all the Mortifications I had met with, was vain, and that not a little; and as it was a new thing, so it was a pleasant thing, to be courted, caress'd, embrac'd, and high Professions of Affection made to me by a Man so agreeable, and so able to do me good.

Add to this, that if I had ventur'd to disoblige the Gentleman, I had no Friend in the World to have Recourse to; I had no Prospect, no, not of a Bit of Bread; I had nothing before me, but to fall back into the same Misery that I had been in before.

Amy had but too much Rhetorick in this Cause; she represented all those Things in their proper Colours; she argued them all with her utmost Skill, and at last, the Merry Jade, when she came to Dress me, Look ye, Madam, said she, if you won't consent, tell him you'll do as *Rachael* did to *Jacob*,[1] when she could have no children, put her Maid to Bed to him; tell him you cannot comply with him, but there's *Amy*, he may ask her the question, she has promis'd me she won't deny you.

And wou'd you have me say so, *Amy? said I.*

No, Madam, but I wou'd really have you do so, besides you are undone if you do not; and if my doing it wou'd save you from being undone, as I said before, he shall if he will; if he asks me, I won't deny him, not I; Hang me if I do, *says Amy.*

Well, I know not what to do, *says I,* to *Amy.*

Do! *says Amy,* Your Choice is fair and plain; here you may have a handsome, charming Gentleman, be rich, live pleasantly, and in Plenty; or refuse him, and want a Dinner, go in Rags, live in Tears; in short, beg and starve; you know this is the Case, Madam, *says Amy,* I wonder how you can say you know not what to do.

Well, *Amy, says I,* the Case is as you say, and I think verily I must yield to him; but then, *said I, mov'd by Conscience,* don't talk any more of your Cant, of its being Lawful that I ought to Marry again, and that he ought to Marry again, and such Stuff as that; 'tis all Nonsence, *says I, Amy,* there's nothing in it, let me hear no more of that; for if I yield, 'tis in vain to mince the Matter, I am a Whore, *Amy,* neither better nor worse, I assure you.

I don't think so, Madam, by no means, *says Amy,* I wonder how you can talk so; and then she run on with her Argument of the Unreasonableness that a Woman should be oblig'd to live single, or a Man to live single in such Cases, as before: Well, *Amy, said I,* come let us dispute no more, for the longer I enter into that Part, the greater my Scruples will be; but if I let it alone, the Necessity of my present Circumstances is such that I believe I shall yield to him, if he should importune me much about it, but I should be glad he would not do it all, but leave me as I am.

---

1 Exodus 30: 1-5.

As to that, Madam, you may depend, *says Amy*, he expects to have you for his Bedfellow to Night; I saw plainly in his Management all Day, and at last he told you so too, as plain, I think, as he cou'd: Well, well, *Amy, said I*, I don't know what to say, if he will, he must, I think, I don't know how to resist such a Man, that has done so much for me: I don't know how you shou'd, *says Amy*.

Thus *Amy* and I canvass'd the Business between us; the Jade prompted the Crime, which I had but too much Inclination to commit; that is to say, not as a Crime, for I had nothing of the Vice in my Constitution; my Spirits were far from being high; my Blood had no Fire in it, to Kindle the Flame of Desire; but the Kindness and good Humour of the Man, and the Dread of my own Circumstances concurr'd to bring me to the Point, and I even resolv'd, before he ask'd, to give up my Virtue to him, whenever he should put it to the Question.

In this I was a double Offender, whatever he was, for I was resolv'd to commit the Crime, knowing and owning it to be a Crime; he, if it was true as he said, was fully perswaded it was Lawful, and in that Perswasion he took the Measures, and us'd all of the Circumlocutions which I am going to speak of.

About two Hours after he was gone, came a *Leaden-Hall*[1] Basket-woman, with a whole Load of good Things for the Mouth; the Particulars are not to the Purpose, and brought Orders to get Supper by Eight a-Clock; however I did not intend to begin to dress any thing, till I saw him; and he gave me time enough, for he came before Seven; so that *Amy*, who had gotten one to help her, got every thing ready in Time.

We sat down to Super about Eight, and were indeed, very merry; *Amy* made us some Sport, for she was a Girl of Spirit and Wit; and with her Talk she made us laugh very often, and yet the Jade manag'd her Wit with all the good Manners imaginable.

But to shorten the Story; after Supper, he took me up into his Chamber, where *Amy* had made a good Fire, and there he pull'd out a great many Papers, and spread them upon a little Table, and then took me by the Hand, and after kissing me very much, he enter'd into a Discourse of his Circumstances, and of mine, how they agreed in several things exactly; for Example, That I was abandon'd of a Husband in the Prime of my Youth and Vigour, and he of a Wife in his Middle-Age; how the End of Marriage was

---

1 At this time a poultry and game market in east London. Since the original burned in the great Fire of 1666, the market woman, here, plies her wares in the reconstructed market.

destroy'd by the Treatment we had either of us receiv'd; and it would be very hard that we should be ty'd by the Formality of the Contract, where the Essence of it was destroy'd: I interrupted him, and told him, There was a vast Difference between our Circumstances, and that in the most essential part; namely, that he was Rich, and I was Poor; that he was above the World, and I infinitely below it; that his Circumstances were very easie, mine miserable, and this was an Inequality the most essential that cou'd be imagin'd: As to that, my Dear, *says he*, I have taken such Measures as shall make an Equality still; and with that, he shew'd me a Contract in Writing, wherein he engag'd himself to me; to cohabit constantly with me; to provide for me in all Respects as a Wife; and repeating in the Preamble, a long Account of the Nature and Reason of our living together, and an Obligation in the Penalty of 7000*l*. never to abandon me; and at last, shew'd me a bond for 500*l*. to be paid to me, or to my Assigns,[1] within three Months after his Death.

He read over all these things to me, and then in a most moving, affectionate Manner, and in Words not to be answer'd, *he said*, Now, my Dear, is this not sufficient? Can you object any thing against it? If not, as I believe you will not, then let us debate this Matter no longer; with that, he pull'd out a silk Purse, which had three-score Guineas in it, and threw them into my Lap, and concluded all the rest of his Discourse with Kisses, and Protestations of his Love; of which indeed, I had abundant Proof.

Pity humane Frailty, you that read of a Woman reduc'd in her Youth, and prime, to the utmost Misery and Distress; and rais'd again, as above, by the unexpected and surprising Bounty of a Stranger; I say pity her if she was not able, after all these things, to make any more Resistance.

However, I stood out a little longer still, I ask'd him, how he cou'd expect that I cou'd come into a Proposal of such Consequence, the very first Time it was mov'd to me? and that I ought (if I consented to it) to captitulate with him, that he should never upbraid me with Easiness, and consenting too soon: *He said*, No; but on the contrary, he would take it as a Mark of the greatest Kindness I could show him; then he went on to give Reasons why there was no Occasion to use the ordinary Ceremony of Delay; or to wait a reasonable Time of Courtship, which was only to avoid Scandal; but, as this was private, it had nothing of that Nature in

1 Designated heirs.

it; that he had been courting me some time, by the best of Courtship, *viz.* doing Acts of Kindness to me; and that he had given Testimonies of his sincere Affection to me, by Deeds, not by flattering Trifles, and the usual Courtship of Words, which were often found to have very little Meaning; that he took me not as a Mistress, but as his Wife; and protested, it was clear to him he might lawfully do it, and that I was perfectly at Liberty; and assur'd me by all that it was possible for an Honest Man to say, that he would treat me as his Wife, as long as he liv'd; in a Word, he con-quer'd all the little Resistance I intended to make; he protested he lov'd me above all the World, and begg'd I would for once believe him; that he had never deceiv'd me, and never would, but would make it his Study to make my Life comfortable and happy, and to make me forget the Misery I had gone through: I stood still a-while, and said nothing, but seeing him eager for my Answer, I smil'd, and looking up at him; and must I then, *says I*, say Yes, at first asking? Must I depend upon your Promise? Why then, *said I*, upon the Faith of that Promise, and in the Sence of that inex-pressible Kindness you have shown me, you shall be oblig'd, and I will be wholly yours to the End of my Life; and with that, I took his Hand which held me by the Hand, and gave it a Kiss.

And thus in Gratitude for the Favours I receiv'd from a Man, was all Sence of Religion, and Duty to God, all Regard to Virtue and Honour, given up at once, and we were to call one another Man and Wife, who, in Sence of the Laws, both of God and our Country, were no more than two Adulterers, in short, a Whore and a Rogue; nor, as I have said above, was my Conscience silent in it, tho', it seems his was; for I sinn'd with open Eyes, and thereby had a double Guilt upon me; as I always said his Notions were of another Kind, and he either was before of the Opinion, or argued himself into it now, that we were both Free, and might lawfully Marry.

But I was quite of another Side, nay, and my Judgment was right, but my Circumstances were my Temptation; the Terrors behind me look'd blacker than the Terrors before me; and the dreadful Argument of wanting Bread, being run into the horrible Distresses I was in before, master'd all my Resolution, and I gave myself up, as above.

The rest of the Evening we spent very agreeably to me; he was perfectly good-humour'd, and was at that time very merry; then he made *Amy* dance with him, and I told him, I wou'd put *Amy* to Bed to him; *Amy* said, with all her Heart, she never had been a Bride in her Life; in short, he made the Girl so merry, that had he not been to lye with me the same Night, I believe he wou'd have play'd the Fool with *Amy* for half an Hour, and the Girl wou'd no more have refus'd him, than I intended to do; yet before, I had always found her a very modest Wench, as any I ever saw in all my Life; but, in short, the Mirth of that Night, and a few more such afterwards, ruin'd the Girl's Modesty for ever, as shall appear by and by, in its Place.

So far does fooling and toying sometimes go, that I know nothing a Woman has to be more cautious of; so far had this innocent Girl gone in jesting between her and I, and in talking that she would let him lye with her, if he would but be kinder to me, that at last she let him lye with her in earnest; and so empty was I now of all Principle, that I encourag'd the doing it almost before my Face.

I say but too justly, that I was empty of Principle, because, as above, I had yielded to him, not as deluded to believe it Lawful, but as overcome by his Kindness, and terrify'd at the Fear of my own Misery, if he shou'd leave me; so with my Eyes open, and with my Conscience, as I may say awake, I sinn'd, knowing it to be a Sin, but having no Power to resist; when this had thus made a Hole in my Heart, and I was come to such a height, as to transgress against the Light of my own Conscience, I was then fit for any Wickedness, and Conscience left off speaking, where it found it could not be heard.

But to return to our Story; having consented, as above, to his Proposal, we had not much more to do; he gave me my Writings, and the Bond for my Maintenance during his Life, and for 500*l.* after his Death; and so far was he from abating his Affection to me afterwards, that two Year after we were thus, as he call'd it Marry'd, he made his Will, and gave me a Thousand Pound more, and all my Household-Stuff, Plate, *&c.* which was considerable too.

Amy put us to-Bed, and my new Friend, I cannot call him Husband, was so well pleas'd with *Amy* for her Fidelity and Kindness to me, that he paid her all the Arrear of her Wages that I ow'd her, and gave her five Guineas over, and had it gone no farther, *Amy* had richly deserv'd what she had, for never was a Maid so true to a Mistress in such dreadful Circumstances as I was in; nor was what follow'd more her own Fault than mine, who led her almost into it at first, and quite into it at last; and this may be a farther Testimony what a hardness of Crime I was now arriv'd to, which was owing to the Conviction that was from the beginning, upon me, that I was a Whore, not a Wife; nor cou'd I ever frame my Mouth to call him Husband, or to say my Husband, when I was speaking of him.

We liv'd, surely, the most agreeable Life, the grand Exception only excepted, that ever Two liv'd together; he was the most obliging Gentlemanly Man, and the most tender of me, that ever Woman gave herself up to; nor was there ever the least interruption to our mutual Kindness, no, not to the last Day of his Life: But I must bring *Amy*'s Disaster in at once, that I may have done with her.

Amy was dressing me one Morning, for now I had two Maids, and *Amy* was my Chamber-Maid; Dear Madam, *says Amy*, what, a'n't you with-Child yet? No, *Amy*, *says I*, nor any Sign of it: *Law*, Madam, *says Amy*, what have you been doing? why you have been Marry'd a Year and a half, I warrant you, Master wou'd have got me with Child twice in that time: It may be so, *Amy*, *says I*, let him try, can't you: No, *says Amy*, you'll forbid it now; before I told you he shou'd with all my Heart, but I won't now, now he's all your own: O, *says I*, *Amy*, I'll freely give you my Consent, it will be nothing at-all to me; nay, I'll put you to-Bed to him myself one Night or other, if you are willing: No, Madam, no, *says Amy*, not now he's yours.

Why you Fool you, *says I*, don't I tell you I'll put you to Bed to him myself.

Nay, nay, *says Amy* if you put me to-Bed to him, that's another Case; I believe I shall not rise again very soon.

I'll venture that, *Amy*, *says I*.

After Supper, that Night, and before we were risen from Table, I said to him, *Amy* being by, Hark ye, Mr.—, do you know that you are to lye with *Amy* to-Night? No, not I, *says he*; but turns to *Amy*, Is it so, *Amy*, *says he*? No, Sir, *says she*; Nay, don't say no you Fool; Did not I promise to put you to-Bed to him? But the Girl said No still, and it pass'd off.

At Night, when we came to go to-Bed, *Amy* came into the Chamber to undress me, and her Master slipt into Bed first; then I began, and told him all that *Amy* had said about my not being with-Child, and of her being with-Child twice in that time: Ay, Mrs. *Amy*, *says he*, I believe so too, Come hither, and we'll try; but *Amy* did not go: Go, you Fool, *says I*, can't you, I freely give you both Leave; but *Amy* wou'd not go: Nay, you Whore, *says I*, you said, if I wou'd put you to-Bed, you wou'd with all your Heart: and with that I sat her down, pull'd off her Stockings and Shoes, and all her Cloaths, Piece by Piece, and led her to the Bed to him: *Here*, says I, *try what you can do with your Maid* Amy: She pull'd back a little, would not let me pull off her Cloaths at first, but it was hot Weather, and she had not many Cloaths on, and particularly, no Stays on; and at last, when she see I was in earnest, she let me do what I wou'd; so I fairly stript her, and then I threw open the Bed, and thrust her in.

I need say no more; this is enough to convince any-body that I did not think him my Husband, and that I had cast off all Principle, and all Modesty, and had effectually stifled Conscience.

Amy, I dare say, began now to repent, and wou'd fain have got out of Bed again; but *he said* to her, Nay, *Amy*, you see your Mistress has put you to-Bed, 'tis all her doing, you must blame her; so he held her fast, and the Wench being naked in the Bed with him, 'twas too late to look back, so she lay still, and let him do what he wou'd with her.

Had I look'd upon myself as a Wife, you cannot suppose I would have been willing to have let my Husband lye with my Maid, much less, before my Face, for I stood-by all the while; but as I thought myself a Whore, I cannot say but that it was something design'd in my Thoughts, that my Maid should be a Whore too, and should not reproach me with it.

Amy, however, less vicious than I, was grievously out of Sorts the next Morning, and cry'd and took-on most vehemently; that she was ruin'd and undone, and there was no pacifying her; she was a Whore, a Slut, and she was undone! undone! and cry'd almost all Day; I did all I could to pacify her: A Whore! says *I*, well, and am not I a Whore as well as you? No, no, *says Amy*, no, you are not, for you are Marry'd; not I, *Amy, says I*, I do not pretend to it; he may Marry you to-Morrow if he will, for any thing I cou'd do to hinder it, I am not Marry'd, I do not look upon it as any thing: Well, all did not pacify *Amy*, but she cry'd two or three Days about it; but it wore off by Degrees.

But the Case differ'd between *Amy* and her Master, exceedingly; for *Amy* retain'd the same kind Temper she always had; but on the contrary, he was quite alter'd, for he hated her heartily, and could, I believe, have kill'd her after it, and he told me so, for he thought this a vile Action; where as what he and I had done, he was perfectly easie in, thought it just, and esteem'd me as much his Wife as if we had been Marry'd from our Youth, and had neither of us known any other; nay, he lov'd me, I believe, as entirely, as if I had been the Wife of his Youth; nay he told me, it was true, in one Sence, that he had two Wives, but that I was the Wife of his Affection, the other, the Wife of his Aversion.

I was extremely concern'd at the Aversion he had taken to my Maid *Amy*, and us'd my utmost Skill to get it alter'd; for tho' he had indeed debauch'd the Wench, I knew that I was the principal Occasion of it; and as he was the best humour'd Man in the World, I never gave him over till I prevail'd with him to be easie with her, and as I was now become the Devil's Agent, to make others as wicked as myself, I brought him to lye with her again several times after that, till at last, as the poor Girl said, so it happen'd, and she was really with-Child.

She was terribly concern'd at it, and so was he too: Come, my Dear *says I*, when *Rachael* put her Handmaid to-Bed to *Jacob*, she took the Children as her own; don't be uneasie, I'll take the Child as my own; had not I a hand in the Frolick of putting her to-Bed to you? It was my Fault as much as yours; so I call'd *Amy*, and encourag'd her too, and told her that I wou'd take Care of the Child and her too, and added the same Argument to her; for, *says I, Amy*, it was all my Fault; did not I drag your Cloaths off of your Back, and put you to-Bed to him: Thus I that had, indeed, been the Cause of all the Wickedness between them, encourag'd them both, when they had any Remorse about it, and rather prompted them to go on with it, than to repent of it.

When *Amy* grew Big, she went to a Place I had provided for her, and the Neighbours knew nothing but that *Amy* and I was parted; she had a fine Child indeed, a Daughter, and we had it nurs'd, and *Amy* came again in about half a Year, to live with her old Mistress: but neither my Gentleman, or *Amy* either, car'd for playing that Game over again; for as he said, the Jade might bring him a House-full of Children to keep.

We liv'd as merrily, and as happily, after this, as cou'd be expected, considering our Circumstances; I mean as to the pretended Marriage &c. and as to that, my Gentleman had not the least Concern about him for it; but as much as I was harden'd, and that was as much, as I believe, ever any wicked Creature was, yet I could not help it; there was, and would be, Hours of Intervals, and of dark Reflections which came involuntarily in, and thrust in Sighs into the middle of all my Songs; and there would be, sometimes, a heaviness of Heart, which intermingl'd itself with all my Joy, and which would often fetch a Tear from my Eye; and let others pretend what they will, I believe it impossible to be otherwise with anybody; there can be no substantial Satisfaction in a Life of known Wickedness; Conscience will, and does, often break in upon them at particular times, let them do what they can to prevent it.

But I am not to preach, but to relate, and whatever loose Reflections were, and how often soever those dark Intervals came on, I did my utmost to conceal them from him; ay, and to suppress and smother them too in myself, and to outward Appearance we liv'd as chearfully, and as agreeably, as it was possible for any Couple in the World to live.

After I had thus liv'd with him something above two Year, truly, I found my-self with-Child too; my Gentleman was mightily pleas'd at it, and nothing could be kinder than he was in the Preparations he made for me, and for my Lying-in, which was, however, very private, because I car'd for as little Company as possible; nor had I kept up my neighbourly Acquaintance; so that I had no-body to invite upon such an Occasion.[1]

I was brought to-Bed very well, (of a Daughter too, as well as *Amy*) but the Child died at about six Weeks old, so all that Work was to do over again, that is to say, the Charge, the Expence, the Travel,[2] &c.

The next Year I made him amends, and brought him a Son, to his great Satisfaction; it was a charming Child, and did very well: After this, my Husband, as he call'd himself, came to me one Evening, and told me, he had a very difficult Thing happen'd to him, which he knew not what to do in, nor how to resolve about, unless I would make him easie; this was, that his Occasions[3] requir'd him to go over to *France* for about two Months.

Well, my Dear, *says I*, and how shall I make, you easie?

Why, by consenting to let me go, *says he*, upon which Condition, I'll tell you the Occasion of my going, that you may judge of the Necessity there is for it on my Side; then to make me easie in his going, he told me, he would make his Will before he went, which should be to my full Satisfaction.

I told him the last Part was so kind, that I could not decline the first Part, unless he would give me Leave to add, that if it was not for putting him to an extraordinary Expence, I would go over along with him.

He was so pleas'd with this Offer, that he told me, he would give me full Satisfaction for it, and accept of it too; so he took me to *London* with him the next Day, and there he made his Will, and shew'd it to me, and seal'd it before proper Witnesses, and then gave it to me to keep: In this Will he gave a thousand Pounds to

---

1 Women were customarily brought to witness the birth of a child and to safeguard against cases of infanticide. For more on this, see Laura Gowing, *Common Bodies: Women, Touch, and Power in Seventeenth-Century England* (New Haven: Yale UP, 2003).

2 Labor.

3 Business.

a person that we both knew very well, in Trust, to pay it, with the Interest from the Time of his Decease, to me, or my Assigns; then he Will'd the Payment of my Jointure,[1] as he call'd it, *viz.* his bond of a Hundred Pounds, after his Death; also he gave me all my Household-stuff, Plate, *&c.*

This was a most engaging thing for a Man to do to one under my Circumstances; and it would have been hard, as I told him, to deny him any thing, or to refuse to go with him any where; so we settled every thing as well as we cou'd; left *Amy* in Charge with the House; and for his other Business, which was in Jewels, he had two Men he entrusted, who he had good Security for, and who manag'd for him, and corresponded with him.

Things being thus concerted, we went away to *France*, arriv'd safe at *Calais*, and by easie Journeys, came in eight Days more to *Paris*, where we lodg'd in the House of an *English* Merchant of his Acquaintance, and was very courteously entertain'd.

My Gentleman's Business was with some Persons of First Rank, and to whom he had sold some Jewels of very good Value, and receiv'd a great Sum of Money in Specie,[2] and, as he told me privately, he gain'd 3000 Pistoles[3] by his Bargain, but would not suffer the most intimate Friend he had there, to know what he had receiv'd; for it is not so safe a thing in *Paris*, to have a great Sum of Money in keeping, as it might be in *London*.

We made this Journey much longer than we intended; and my Gentleman sent for one of his Managers in *London*, to come over to us to *Paris* with some Diamonds, and sent him back to *London* again, to fetch more; then other Business fell into his Hands so unexpectedly, that I began to think we should take up our constant Residence there, which I was not very averse to it, being my Native Country, and I spoke the Language perfectly well; so we took a good House in *Paris*, and liv'd very well there; and I sent for *Amy* to come over to me, for I liv'd gallantly, and my Gentleman was, two or three times, going to keep me a Coach, but I declin'd it, especially at *Paris*; but as they have those Conveniences by the Day there, at a certain Rate, I had an Equipage provided for me whenever I pleas'd, and I liv'd here in a very good Figure, and might have liv'd higher if I pleas'd.

---

1   *OED*: The holding of property to the joint use of a husband and wife for life or in tail, as a provision for the latter, in the event of her widowhood.

2   In return.

3   *OED*: A Spanish gold double-escudo dating from the 1530s and surviving into the nineteenth century; (also) any various coins derived from or resembling this from the seventeenth and eighteenth centuries.

But in the middle of all this Felicity, a dreadful Disaster befell me, which entirely unhing'd all my Affairs, and threw me back into the same state of Life that I was in before; with this one happy Exception however, that whereas before I was Poor, even to Misery, now I was not only provided for, but very Rich.

My Gentleman had the Name in *Paris*, for a very rich Man, and indeed, he was so, tho' not so immensely rich as People imagin'd; but that which was fatal to him, was, that he generally carried a shagreen[1] Case in his Pocket, especially when he went to Court, or to the Houses of any of the Princes of the Blood, in which he had Jewels of very great Value.

It happen'd one Day, that being to go to *Versailles*, to wait upon the Prince of—, he came up into my Chamber in the Morning, and laid out his Jewel-Case, because he was not going to show any Jewels, but to get a Foreign Bill accepted, which he had receiv'd from Amsterdam; so when he gave me the Case, *he said,* My Dear, I think I need not carry this with me, because, it may be, I may not come back till Night, and it is too much to venture; I return'd, then My Dear, you sha'n't go; Why? *says he*; because as they are too much for you, so you are too much for me to venture; and you shall not go, unless you will promise me not to stay so as to come back in the Night.

I hope there's no Danger, *said he,* seeing I have nothing about me of Value; and therefore, lest I should, take that too, *says he,* and gives me his Gold Watch, and a rich Diamond, which he had in a Ring, and always wore on his Finger.

Well, but *my Dear, says I,* you make me more uneasie now, than before; for if you apprehend no Danger, why do use this Caution? And if you apprehend there is Danger, why do you go at all?

There is no Danger, *says he,* if I do not stay late, and I do not design to do so.

Well, but promise me then, that you won't, *says I,* or else I cannot let you go.

I won't, indeed, my Dear, *says he,* unless I am oblig'd to it; I assure you I do not intend it; but if I shou'd, I am not worth robbing now; for I have nothing about me, but about six Pistoles in my little Purse, and that little Ring, showing me a small Diamond Ring, worth about ten or twelve Pistoles, which he put upon his Finger in the room of the rich one he usually wore.

---

1   *OED*: A species of untanned leather with a rough granular surface, pre-
pared from the skin of the horse, ass, etc., or of the shark, seal, etc., and
frequently dyed green. Also, an imitation of this.

I still press'd him not to stay late, and he said he wou'd not; but if I am kept late, *says he*, beyond my Expectation, I'll stay all Night, and come next Morning: This seem'd a very good Caution; but still my Mind was very uneasie about him, and I told him so, and entreated him not to go; I told him, I did not know what might be the reason, but that I had a strange Terror upon my Mind, about his going, and that if he did go, I was perswaded some Harm wou'd attend him; he smil'd, and return'd, Well, my Dear, if it should be so, you are now richly provided for; all that I have here, I give to you; and with that, he takes up the Casket, or Case, Here, *says he*, hold your Hand, there is a good Estate for you, in this Case; if any thing happens to me, 'tis all your own, I give it you for yourself; and with that, he put the Casket, the fine Ring, and his Gold Watch, all into my Hands, and the Key of his Scrutore[1] besides, adding, and in my Scrutore there is some Money, 'tis all your own.

I star'd at him, as if I was frighted, for I thought all his Face look'd like a Death's-Head; and then, immediately, I thought I perceiv'd his Head all Bloody; and then his Cloaths look'd Bloody too; and immediately it all went off, and he look'd as he really did; immediately I fell a-crying, and hung about him, My Dear *said I*, I am frighted to Death; you shall not go, depend upon it, some Mischief will befall you; I did not tell him how my vapourish Fancy had represented him to me, that I thought was not proper; besides he wou'd only have laugh'd at me, and wou'd have gone away with a Jest about it: But I press'd him seriously not to go that Day, or if he did, to promise me to come Home to *Paris* again by Day-light: He look'd a little graver then, than he did before; told me, he was not apprehensive of the least Danger; but if there was, he wou'd either take Care to come in the Day, or, as he had said before, wou'd stay all Night.

But all these Promises came to nothing; for he was set upon in the open Day, and robb'd, by three Men on Horseback, mask'd, as he went; and one of them, who, it seems, rifled him, while the rest stood to stop the Coach, stabb'd him into the Body with a Sword, so that he died immediately: He had a Footman behind the Coach, who they knock'd down with the Stock, or But-end of a Carabine:[2] they were suppos'd to kill him, because of the Disappointment they met with, in not getting his Case, or Casket of

---

1 Portable writing desk.

2 *OED*: A kind of fire-arm, shorter than the musket, used by the cavalry and other troops; "a kind of medium between the pistol and the musket."

Diamonds which they knew he carry'd about him; and this was suppos'd because after they had kill'd him, they made the Coachman drive out of the Road, a long-Way over the Heath,[1] till they came to a convenient Place, where they pull'd him out of the Coach, and search'd his Cloaths more narrowly, than they cou'd do while he was alive.

But they found nothing but his little Ring, six Pistoles, and the Value of about seven Livres in small Moneys.

This was a dreadful Blow to me; tho' I cannot say I was so surpriz'd as I should otherwise have been; for all the while he was gone, my Mind was oppress'd with the Weight of my own Thoughts; and I was as sure that I should never see him any more, that I think nothing could be like it; the Impression was so strong, that, I think, nothing could make so deep a Wound, that was imaginary; and I was so dejected, and disconsolate, that when I receiv'd the News of his Disaster, there was no room for any extraordinary Alteration in me: I had cry'd all that Day, eat nothing, and only waited, as I might say, to receive the dismal News, which I had brought to me about Five a-Clock in the Afternoon.

I was in a strange Country; and tho' I had a pretty many Acquaintances, had but very few Friends that I could consult on this Occasion; all possible Enquiry was made after the Rogues, that had been thus barbarous, but nothing could be heard of them; nor was it profitable, that the Footman could make any Discovery of them, by his Description; for they knock'd him down immediately, so that he knew nothing of what was done afterwards; the Coachman was the only Man that cou'd say any thing, and all his Account amounted to no more than this, that one of them had Soldiers' Cloaths, but he cou'd not remember the Particulars of his Mounting,[2] so as to know what Regiment he belong'd to; and as to their Faces, that he could know nothing of, because they had all of them Masks on.

I had him Buried as decently as the Place would permit a Protestant Stranger to be Buried, and made some of the Scruples and Difficulties on that Account,[3] easie, by the help of Money to a certain Person, who went impudently to the curate of the Parish St. *Sulpitius*, in *Paris*, and told him, that the Gentleman that was kill'd, was a Catholick; that the Thieves had taken from him a

---

1 *OED*: Open uncultivated ground; an extensive tract of waste land.
2 Uniform.
3 Protestant services had always been barred from Paris even under the Edict of Nantes. But when the Edict was revoked, such services would have been dangerous to solicit.

Cross of Gold, set with Diamonds, worth 6000 Livres; that his widow was a Catholick, and had sent by him 60 Crowns to the Church of—, for Masses to be said for the Repose of his Soul: Upon all which, *tho' not one Word of it was true*, he was Buried with all the Ceremonies of the *Roman* Church.

I think I almost cry'd myself to Death for him; for I abandon'd myself to all the Excesses of Grief; and indeed I lov'd him to a Degree inexpressible; and considering what Kindness he had shewn me at first, and how tenderly he had us'd me to the last, what cou'd I do less?

Then the Manner of his Death was terrible and frightful to me, and above all, the strange Notices I had of it: I had never pretended to the Second-Sight, or any thing of that Kind; but certainly, if any one ever had such a thing, I had it at this time; for I saw him as plainly in all those terrible Shapes, as above, First, as a Skeleton, not Dead only, but rotten and wasted; Secondly as kill'd, and his Face bloody; and Thirdly, his Cloaths bloody; and all within the Space of one Minute, or indeed, of a very few Moments.

These things amaz'd me, and I was a good-while as one stupid; however, after some time, I began to recover, and look into my Affairs; I had the Satisfaction not to be left in Distress, or in danger of Poverty; on the contrary, besides what he had put into my Hands fairly, in his Life-time, which amounted to a very considerable Value; I found above seven Hundred Pistoles in Gold, in his Scrutore, of which he had given me the Key; and found Foreign-Bills accepted, for about 12000 Livres; so that, in a Word, I found myself possess'd of almost ten Thousand Pounds Sterling, in a very few Days after the Disaster.

The first thing I did upon this Occasion, was, to send a Letter to my Maid, as I still call'd her, *Amy*; wherein I gave her an Account of my Disaster; how my Husband, as she call'd him (for I never call'd him so) was murther'd; and as I did not know how his relations, or his Wife's Friends, might act upon that Occasion, I order'd her to convey away all the Plate, Linnen, and other things of Value, and to secure them in a Person's Hands that I directed her to, and then to sell, or dispose the Furniture of the House, if she could; and so, without acquainting any-body with the Reason of her going, withdraw; sending Notice to his Head Manager at *London*, that the House was quitted by the Tennant, and they might come and take Possession of it for the Executors: *Amy* was so dextrous, and did her Work so nimbly, that she gutted the House, and sent the Key to the said Manager, almost as soon as he had Notice of the Misfortune that befell their Master.

Upon their receiving the surprising News of his Death, the Head Manager came over to *Paris*, and came to the House; I made no Scruple of calling myself Madam——, the widow of Monsieur——, the *English* Jeweller; and as I spoke *French* naturally, I did not let him know but that I was his wife, married in *France* and that I had not heard that he had any Wife in *England*; but pretended to be surpriz'd, and exclaim against him for so base an Action; and that I had good Friends in Poictou, where I was Born, who would take Care to have Justice done me in *England*, out of his Estate.

I should have observ'd, that as soon as the News was publick, of a Man being murther'd, and that he was a Jeweller, Fame did me the Favour as to publish presently, that he was robb'd of his Casket of Jewels, which he always carry'd about him; I confirm'd this, among my daily Lamentations for his Disaster, and added, that he had with him a fine Diamond Ring, which he was known to wear frequently about him, valued at 100 Pistoles, a Gold Watch, and a great Quantity of Diamonds of inestimable Value, in his Casket; which Jewels he was carrying to the Prince of——, to show some of them to him; and the Prince own'd, that he had spoken to him to bring some such Jewels, to let him see them. But I sorely repented this Part afterward, as you shall hear.

This Rumour put an End to all Enquiry after his Jewells, his Ring, or his Watch; and as for the 700 Pistoles, that I secur'd: For the Bills[1] which were in hand, I own'd I had them; but that, as *I said*, I brought my Husband 30000 Livres Portion, I claim'd the said Bills, which came to not above 12000 Livres, for my *Amende*;[2] and this, with the Plate, and the Household-Stuff, was the principal of all his Estate which they could come at; as the Foreign Bill, which he was going to Versailles to get accepted, it was really lost with him; but his Manager, who had remitted the Bill to him, by Way of *Amsterdam*, bringing over the second Bill,[3] the Money was sav'd, as they call'd it, which would, otherwise, have been also gone; the Thieves who robb'd and murther'd him, were, to be sure, afraid to send any-body to get the Bill accepted; for that would undoubtedly have discover'd them.[4]

By this time my Maid *Amy* was arriv'd, and she gave me an

---

1 Paper money.
2 Compensation.
3 A copy of the first.
4 In other words, if they presented the Bill—the modern equivalent of cashing a check—they would be caught and arrested.

Account of her Management, and how she had secur'd every-thing, and that she had quitted the House, and sent the Key to the Head-Manager of his Business; and let me know how much she had made of every thing, very punctually and honestly.

I should have observ'd in the Account of his dwelling with me so long at—, that he never pass'd for any thing there, but a Lodger in the House; and tho' he was Landlord, that did not alter the Case; so that at his Death, *Amy* coming to quit the House, and give them the Key, there was no affinity between that, and the Case of the Master who was newly kill'd.

I got good Advice at *Paris*, from an eminent Lawyer, a Coun-sellor of the Parliament there, and laying my Case before him, he directed me to make Process in Dower[1] upon the Estate, for making good my new Fortune upon Matrimony, which accord-ingly I did; and, upon the whole, the Manager went back to *England*, well satisfied, that he had gotten the unaccepted Bills of Exchange, which was for 2500*l.* with some other things, which together, amounted to 17000 Livres; and thus I got rid of him.

I was visited with great Civility on this sad Occasion, of the Loss of my Husband, as they thought him, by a great many Ladies of Quality; and the Prince of—, to whom it was reported he was carrying the Jewels, sent his Gentleman with a very hand-some Compliment of Condolance to me; and his Gentleman, whether with, or without Order, hinted, as if *his Highness* did intend to have visited me himself, but that some Accident, which he made along Story of, had prevented him.

By the Concourse of Ladies and others, that thus came to visit me, I began to be much known; and as I did not forget to set myself out with all possible Advantage, considering the Dress of a Widow, which in those Days was a most frightful thing; I say, as I did thus from my own Vanity, for I was not ignorant that I was very handsome; I say, on this Account, I was soon made very publick, and was known by the Name of *La Belle veufeu de Poictou*; or, The pretty Widow of *Poictou*: As I was very well pleas'd to see myself thus handsomly us'd in my Affliction, it soon dry'd up all my Tears; and tho' I appear'd as a Widow, yet, as we say in *England*, it was of a Widow comforted: I took Care to let the Ladies see, that I knew how to receive them; that I was not at a

---

1 It appears as though Roxana is trying to manipulate French and English law to her own advantage. When a woman agreed to jointure as part of her marriage settlement, she relinquished her right to dower, which enti-tled her to one-third of the total value of her husband's estate.

Loss how to Behave to any of them; and in short, I began to be very popular there; but I had an Occasion afterwards, which made me decline that kind of Management, as you shall hear presently.

About four Days after I had receiv'd the Compliments of Condolance from the Prince—, the same Gentleman he had sent before, came to tell me, that his Highness was coming to give me a Visit; I was indeed, surpriz'd at that, and perfectly at a Loss how to Behave: However, as there was no Remedy, I prepar'd to receive him as well as I cou'd; it was not many Minutes after, but he was at the Door, and came in, introduc'd by his own Gentleman, as above, and after, by my Woman, *Amy*.

He treated me with abundance of Civility, and condol'd handsomely the Loss of my Husband, and likewise the Manner of it; he told me, he understood he was coming to *Versailles*, to himself, to shew him some Jewels; that it was true, that he had discours'd with him about Jewels, but cou'd not imagine how any Villains shou'd hear of his coming at that time with them; that he had not order'd him to attend with them at *Versailles*, but told him, that he would come to *Paris* by such a Day, so that he was no way accessory to the Disaster: I told him gravely I knew very well that all *his Highness* had said of that Part was true; that these Villains knew his Profession, and knew, no doubt, that he always carry'd a Casket of Jewels about him, and that he always wore a Diamond Ring on his Finger, worth a hundred Pistoles, which Report had magnified to five Hundred; and that if he had been going to any other Place, it wou'd have been the same thing: After this, *his Highness* rise up to go, and told me, he had resolv'd however, to make me some Reparation; and with these Words, put a silk Purse into my Hand, with a hundred Pistoles, and told me, he would make me a farther Compliment of a small Pension, which his Gentleman would inform me of.

You may be sure I behav'd with a due Sence of so much Goodness, and offer'd to kneel to kiss his Hand, but he took me up, and saluted[1] me, and sat down again, (*tho' before, he made as if he was going away,*) making me sit down by him.

He then began to talk with me more familiarly; told me, he hop'd I was not left in bad Circumstances; that Mr.— was reputed to be very Rich, and that he had gain'd lately great Sums by some Jewels; and he hop'd *he said*, that I had still a Fortune agreeable to the Condition I had liv'd in before.

---

1 Greeted.

I reply'd with some Tears, which I confess, were a little forc'd, That I believ'd if Mr.— had liv'd, we shou'd have been out of Danger of Want; but that it was impossible to Estimate the Loss which I had sustain'd, besides that of the Life of my Husband; that by the Opinion of those that knew something of his Affairs, and of what Value the Jewels were which he intended to have shown *his Highness*, he could not have less about him, than the Value of a hundred Thousand Livres; that was a fatal Blow to me, and to his whole Family, especially that they should be lost in such a Manner.

His Highness return'd, with an Air of Concern, that he was very sorry for it; but he hop'd, if I settled in *Paris*, I might find Ways to restore my Fortune; at the same time he complimented me upon my being very handsome, *as he was pleas'd to call it*, that I could not fail of Admirers: I stood up, and humbly thank'd *his Highness*, but told him, I had no Expectations of that Kind; that I thought I should be oblig'd to go over to *England*, to look after my Husband's Effects there, which I was told, were considerable; but that I did not know what Justice a poor Stranger wou'd get among them; and as for *Paris*, my Fortune being so impair'd, I saw nothing before me, but to go back to Poictou, to my Friends, where some of my Relations, I hop'd, might do something for me, and added, that one of my Brothers was an *Abbot* at—, near *Poictiers*.

He stood up, and taking me by the Hand, led me to a large Looking-Glass, which made up the Peir in the Front of the Parlour; Look there, Madam, *said he*; Is it fit that Face, pointing to my Figure in the Glass, should go back to Poictou? No, Madam, *says he*, stay, and make some Gentleman of Quality happy, that may, in return, make you forget all your Sorrows; and with that, he took me in his Arms, and kissing me twice, told me he wou'd see me again, but with less Ceremony.

Some little time after this, but the same Day, his Gentleman came to me again, and with great Ceremony and Respect, deliver'd me a Black Box ty'd with a Scarlet Ribband, and seal'd with a noble Coat of Arms, which I suppose, was the Prince's; there was in it a Grant from *his Highness*, or an Assignment,[1] I know not which to call it, with a Warrant to his Banker to pay me two Thousand Livres a Year, during my Stay in *Paris* as Widow of Monsieur— the Jeweller, mentioning the horrid Murther of my late Husband, as the Occasion of it as above.

---

1 Gift.

I receiv'd it with great Submission, and Expressions of being infinitely oblig'd to his Master, and of my showing myself on all Occasions, *his Highness's* most obedient Servant; and after giving my most humble Duty to *his Highness*, with the utmost Acknowledgments of the Obligation, *&c.* I went to a little Cabinet, and taking out some Money, which made a little Sound in taking it out, offer'd to give him five Pistoles.

He drew back but with the greatest Respect, and told me, he humbly thank'd me, but that he durst not take a Farthing; that *his Highness* wou'd take it so ill of him he was sure, he would never see his Face more; but that he wou'd not fail to acquaint *his Highness* what Respect I had offer'd; and added, I assure you, Madam, you are more in the good Graces of my Master, the Prince of—, than you are aware of; and I believe you will hear more of him.

Now I began to understand him, and resolv'd, if *his Highness* did come again, he should see me under no Disadvantages, if I could help it: I told him, if *his Highness* did me the Honour to see me again, I hop'd he would not let me be so surpriz'd as I was before; that I would be glad to have some little Notice of it, and would be oblig'd to him, if he would procure it me; he told me, he was very sure, that when *his Highness* intended to visit me, he should be sent before, to give me Notice of it; and that he would give me as much Warning of it as possible.

He came several times after this, on the same Errand, that is, about the Settlement, the Grant, requiring several things yet to be done, for making it payable, without going every time to the Prince again for a fresh Warrant; the Particulars of this Part I did not understand; but as soon as it was finish'd, which was above two Months, the Gentleman came one Afternoon, and said, *his Highness* design'd to visit me in the Evening; but desir'd to be admitted without Ceremony.

I prepar'd not my Rooms only, but myself; and when he came in, there was no-body appear'd in the House but his Gentleman, and my Maid *Amy*; and of her I bid the Gentleman acquaint *his Highness*, that she was an *English* Woman; that she did not understand a Word of *French*; and that she was one also that might be trusted.

When he came into my Room, I fell down at his Feet, before he could come to salute me, and with Words that I had prepar'd, full of Duty and Respect, thank'd him for his bounty and Goodness to a poor desolate Woman, oppress'd under the Weight of so terrible a Disaster, and refus'd to rise till he would allow me the Honour to kiss his Hand.

Levez vous donc,[1] says the Prince, taking me in his Arms, I design more Favours for you, than this Trifle; and going on, he added, You shall, for the future, find a Friend, where you did not look for it; and I resolve to let you see how kind I can be, to one, who is to me the most agreeable Creature on Earth.

I was dress'd in a kind of half-Mourning,[2] had turn'd off my Weeds,[3] and my Head,[4] tho' *I had yet no Ribbands or Lace,* was so dress'd, as fail'd not to set me out with Advantage enough, for I began to understand his Meaning; and the Prince profess'd, I was the most beautiful Creature on Earth; *and where have I liv'd?* says he; *and how ill have I been serv'd, that I should never, till now, be shew'd the finest Woman in France?*

This was the Way, in all the World, the most likely to break in upon my Virtue, if I had been Mistress of any, for I was now become the vainest Creature upon Earth, and particularly, of my Beauty; which, as other People admir'd, so I became every Day more foolishly in Love with myself, than before.

He said some very kind things to me after this, and sat down with me, for an Hour, or more; when getting up, and calling his Gentleman, by his Name, he threw open the door, *Au Boir, says he*; upon which his Gentleman immediately brought up a little Table, cover'd with a fine Damask Cloth, the Table no Bigger than he cou'd bring in his two Hands; but upon it, was set two Decanters, one of Champaign, and the other of Water, six Silver Plates, and a Service of fine Sweet-Meats in fine *China* Dishes, on a Sett of Rings standing up about twenty Inches high, one above another; below, was three roasted Partriges, and a Quail; as soon as his Gentleman had set it all down, he order'd him to withdraw; now, *says the Prince,* I intend to Sup with you.

When he sent away his Gentleman, I stood up, and offer'd to wait on *his Highness* while he Eat, but he positively refus'd, and told me, No, To-Morrow you shall be the Widow of Monsieur— the Jeweller, but to-Night you shall be my Mistress; therefore sit here, *says he,* and Eat with me, or I will get up and serve.

I would then have call'd up my Woman, *Amy,* but I thought that would not be proper neither; so I made my Excuse, that since *his Highness* wou'd not let his own Servant wait, I wou'd not

---

1 Lift yourself up.
2 No longer dressed all in black.
3 Mourning dress.
4 Hair.

presume to let my Woman come up; but if he wou'd please to let me wait, it would be my Honour to fill *his Highness*'s Wine; but, as before, he would by no means allow me; so we sat and Eat together.

Now, Madam, *says the Prince*, give me leave to lay aside my Character; let us talk together with the Freedom of Equals; my Quality sets me at a Distance from you, and makes you ceremonious; your Beauty exalts you to more than an Equality, I must then treat you, as Lovers do their Mistresses, but I cannot speak the Language; 'tis enough to tell you, how agreeable you are to me; how I am surpriz'd at your Beauty, and resolve to make you happy, and to be happy with you.

I knew not what to say to him a good-while, but blush'd, and looking up towards him, said, I was already made happy, in the Favour of a Person of such Rank; and had nothing to ask of *his Highness*, but that he would believe me infinitely oblig'd.

After he had Eaten, he pour'd the Sweet-Meats into my Lap; and the Wine being out, he call'd his Gentleman again, to take away the Table, who, at first, only took the Cloth, and Remains of what was to Eat, away; and laying another Cloth, set the Table on one side of the Room, with a noble Service of Plate upon it, worth, at least, 200 Pistoles; then having set the two Decanters again upon the Table, fill'd, as before, he withdrew, for I found the Fellow understood his Business very well, and his Lord's Business too.

About half an Hour after, the Prince told me, that I offer'd to wait a little before; that if I would now take the Trouble, he would give me leave to give him some Wine; so I went to the Table, fill'd a Glass of Wine, and brought it to him, on a fine Salver, which the Glasses stood on, and brought the Bottle, or Decanter for Water, in my other hand, to mix it as he thought fit.

He smil'd, and bid me look on that Salver, which I did, and admir'd it much, for it was a very fine one, indeed: You may see, *says he*, I resolve to have more of your Company, for my Servant shall leave you that Plate, for my Use: I told him, I believ'd *his Highness* wou'd not take it ill, that I was not Furnish'd fit to Entertain a Person of his Rank; and that I would take great Care of it, and value myself infinitely upon the Honour of *his Highness*'s Visit.

It now began to grow late, and he began to take Notice of it; but, *says he*, I cannot leave you; have you not a spare Lodging, for one Night? I told him, I had but a homely Lodging to Entertain such a Guest; he said something exceeding kind on that Head, but not fit to repeat; adding, that my Company would make him amends.

About Midnight he sent his Gentleman of an Errand, after telling him, aloud, that he intended to stay here all Night; in a little time his Gentleman brought him a Night-Gown, Slippers, two Caps, a Neckcloth, and Shirt, which he gave me to carry into his chamber, and sent his Man home; and then turning to me, said, I shou'd do him the Honour to be his Chamberlain of the Household, and his Dresser also: I smil'd, and told him, I wou'd do myself the Honour to wait on him upon all Occasions.

About One in the Morning, while his Gentleman was yet with him, I begg'd Leave to withdraw, supposing he wou'd go to-Bed; but he took the Hint, and said, I'm not going to-Bed yet; pray let me see you again.

I took this time to undress me, and to come in a new Dress, which was, in a manner, *une Deshabile*,[1] but so fine, and all about me so clean, and so agreeable, that he seem'd surpriz'd: I thought, *says he*, you could not have dress'd to more Advantage, than you had done before; but now, *says he*, you Charm me a thousand times more, if that be possible.

It is only a loose Habit, My Lord, *said I*, that I may the better wait on *your Highness*; he pulls me to him; You are perfectly obliging, *says he*, and sitting on the Bed-side, *says he*, Now you shall be a Princess, and know what it is to oblige the gratefullest Man alive; and with that, he took me in his Arms,—I can go no farther in the Particulars of what pass'd at that time; but it ended in this, that, in short I lay with him all Night.

I have given you the whole Detail of this Story, to lay it down as a black Scheme of the Way how Unhappy Women are ruin'd by Great Men; for tho' Poverty and Want is an irresistible Temptation to the Poor, Vanity and Great Things are as irresistible to others; to be courted by a Prince, and by a Prince who was first a Benefactor, then an Admirer; to be call'd handsome, the finest Woman in *France*, and to be treated as a Woman fit for the Bed of a Prince; these are Things, a Woman must have no Vanity in her, nay, no Corruption in her, that is not overcome by it; and my Case was such, that, as before, I had enough of both.

I had now no Poverty attending me; on the contrary, I was Mistress of ten Thousand Pounds before the Prince did any thing for me; had I been Mistress of my Resolution; had I been less

---

1 A loose-fitting, casual dress, often an undergarment.

obliging, and rejected the first Attack, all had been safe; but my Virtue was lost before, and the Devil, who had found the Way to break-in upon me by one Temptation, easily master'd me now, by another; and I gave myself up to a Person, who, tho' a Man of high Dignity, was yet the most tempting and obliging, that ever I met with in my Life.

I had the same Particular to insist upon here with the Prince, that I had with my Gentleman before; I hesitated much at consenting, at first asking; but the Prince told me, Princes did not court like other Men; that they brought more powerful Arguments; and he very prettily added, that they were sooner repuls'd than other Men, and ought to be sooner comply'd with, intimating, tho' very genteely, that after a Woman had positively refus'd him once, he cou'd not, like other Men, wait with Importunities, and Stratagems, and laying long Sieges; but as such Men as he storm'd warmly, so, if repuls'd, they made no second Attacks, and indeed, it was but reasonable; for as it was below their Rank, to be long battering a Woman's Constancy, so they ran greater Hazards in being expos'd in their Amours, than other Men did.

I took this for a satisfactory Answer, and told *his Highness*, that I had the same Thoughts, in respect to the Manner of his Attacks, for that his person, and his Arguments, were irresistible; that a Person of his Rank, and a Munificence so unbounded, cou'd not be withstood; that no Virtue was Proof against him, except such, as was able to, to suffer Martyrdom; that I thought it impossible I cou'd be overcome, but that now I found it was impossible I shou'd not be overcome; that so much Goodness, join'd with so much Greatness, wou'd have conquer'd a Saint; and that I confess'd he had the Victory over me, by a Merit infinitely superior to the Conquest he had made.

He made me a most obliging Answer; told me, abundance of fine things, which still flatter'd my Vanity, till at last I began to have Pride enough to believe him, and fancy'd myself a fit Mistress for a Prince.

As I had thus given the Prince the Last Favour, and he had all the Freedom with me, that it was possible for me to grant, so he gave me Leave to use as much Freedom with him, another Way, and that was, to have every thing of him, I thought fit to command; and yet I did not ask of him with an Air of Avarice, as if I was greedily making a Penny of him; but I manag'd him with such Art, that he generally anticipated my Demands; he only requested of me, that I wou'd not think of taking another House, as I had intimated to *his Highness* that I had intended, not thinking it good enough to receive his Visits in; but, *he said,* my House was the most convenient that could possibly be found in all *Paris,* for an Amour, especially for him; having a Way out into Three Streets, and not overlook'd by any Neighbours, so that he could pass and repass, without Observation; for one of the Back-ways open'd into a narrow dark Alley, which Alley was a Thorow-fare, or Passage, out of one Street into another; and any Person that went in or out by the Door, had no more to do but to see, that there was no-body following him in the Alley, before he went in at the Door: This Request I knew was reasonable, and therefore I assur'd him, I wou'd not change my Dwelling, seeing *his Highness* did not think it too mean for me to receive him in.

He also desir'd me, that I wou'd not take any more Servants, or set up any Equipage, at least for the present; for that it would then be immediately concluded, I had been left very Rich, and then I shou'd be throng'd with the Impertinence of Admirers, who wou'd be attracted by the Money, as well as by the Beauty of a young Widow, and he shou'd be frequently interrupted in his Visits; or, that the world wou'd conclude I was maintain'd by somebody, and wou'd be indefatigable to find out the Person; so that he shou'd have Spies peeping at him, every time he went out or in, which it would be impossible to disappoint;[1] and that he shou'd presently have it talk'd over all the Toilets in *Paris,* that the Prince *de—* had got the Jeweller's Widow for a Mistress.

This was too just to oppose; and I made no Scruple to tell *his Highness,* that since he had stoop'd so low as to make me his own, he ought to have all the Satisfaction in the World, that I was all his own; that I would take all the Measures he should please to direct me, to avoid the impertinent Attacks of others; and that, if he thought fit, I would be wholly within-Doors, and have it given out, that I was oblig'd to go to *England* to solicit my Affairs there, after my Husband's Misfortune; and that I was not expected there again for at least a Year or two: This he lik'd very well, only, *he said,* that he would by no means have me confin'd; that it would injure my Health; and that I should then take a Country-House in some village, a good-way off of the City, where it should not be known who I was; and that I should be there sometimes, to divert me.

I made no Scruple of the Confinement, and told *his Highness,* no Place would be a Confinement, where I had such a Visiter;

---

1   I.e., the spies would discover his secret liaison with Roxana.

and so I put off the Country-House, which would have been to remove myself farther from him, and have less of his Company; so I made the House be, as it were, shut up; *Amy*, indeed, appear'd; and when any of the Neighbours and Servants enquir'd, she answer'd in broken *French*, that I was gone to *England*, to look after my Affairs; which presently went current thro' the Streets about us: For, you are to note, that the People of *Paris*, especially the Women, are the most busie and impertinent Enquirers into the Conduct of their Neighbours, especially that of a Single Woman, that are in the World; tho' there are no greater Intriguers in the Universe than themselves; and perhaps that may be the Reason of it; for it is an old, but a sure Rule; that

> When deep Intrigues are close and shy,
> The GUILTY are the first that spy.

Thus *his Highness* had the most easie, and yet the most undiscoverable Access to me, imaginable, and he seldom fail'd to come two or three Nights in a Week, and sometimes stay'd two or three Nights together: Once he told me, he was resolv'd I should be weary of his Company, and that he would learn to know what it was to be a Prisoner; so he gave out among his Servants, that he was gone to—, where he often went a-Hunting, and that he should not return under a Fortnight; and that Fortnight he stay'd wholly with me, and never went out of my Doors.

Never Woman, in such a Station, liv'd a Fortnight in so compleat a fullness of Humane Delight: for to have the entire Possession of one of the most accomplish'd Princes in the World, and of the politest, best bred Man; to converse with him all Day, and as he profess'd, charm him all Night; what could be more inexpressibly pleasing, and especially to a Woman of a vast deal of Pride, as I was?

To finish the Felicity of this Part, I must not forget, that the Devil had play'd a new Game with me, and prevail'd with me to satisfie myself with this Amour, as a lawful thing; that a Prince of such Grandeur, and Majesty; so infinitely superior to me; and one who had made such an Introduction by an unparalell'd Bounty, I could not resist; and therefore, that it was very Lawful for me to do it, being at that time perfectly single, and uningag'd to any other Man; as I was, most certainly, by the unaccountable Absence of my first Husband, and the Murther of my Gentleman, who went for my second.

It cannot be doubted but that I was the easier to perswade

myself of the Truth of such a Doctrine as this, when it was so much for my Ease, and for the Repose of my Mind, to have it be so.

In things we wish, 'tis easie to deceive;
What we would have, we willingly believe.

Besides I had no Casuists to resolve this Doubt; the same Devil that put this into my Head, bade me go to any of the *Romish* Clergy, and under the Pretence of Confession, state the Case exactly, and I should see they would either resolve it to be no Sin at all, or absolve me upon the easiest Pennance: This I had a strong Inclination to try, but I know not what Scruple put me off it, for I could never bring myself to like having to do with those Priests; and tho' it was strange that I, who had thus prostituted my Chastity, and given up all Sence of Virtue, in two such particular Cases, living a Life of open Adultery, should scruple any thing; yet so it was, I argued with myself, that I could not be a Cheat in any thing that was esteem'd Sacred; that I could not be of one Opinion, and pretend myself to be of another; nor could I go to Confession, who knew nothing of the Manner of it, and should betray myself to the Priest, to be a Hugonot, and then might come into Trouble; but, in short, tho' I was a Whore, yet I was a Protestant Whore, and could not act as if I was Popish, upon any Account whatsoever.[1]

But, I say, I satisfy'd myself with the surprising Occasion, that as it was all irresistible, so it was all lawful; for that Heaven would not suffer us to be punish'd for that which it was not possible for us to avoid; and with these Absurdities I kept Conscience from giving me any considerable Disturbance in all this Matter; and I was as perfectly easie as to the Lawfulness of it, as if I had been Marry'd to the Prince and had had no other Husband: so possible is it for us to roll ourselves up in Wickedness, till we grow invulnerable by Conscience; and that Centinel once doz'd, sleeps fast, not to be awaken'd while the Tide of Pleasure continues to flow, or till something dark and dreadful brings us to ourselves again.

I have, I confess, wonder'd at the Stupidity that my intellectual Part[2] was under all that while; what Lethargick Fumes doz'd the

---

1 Alison Conway has argued that Roxana's self-identification as a "Protestant Whore" here constitutes part of Defoe's critique of Charles II's court as the phrase echoes Nell Gwynn's admonition to a mob that they ought not to abuse her because she was the King's "Protestant Whore" and not one of his Catholic mistresses. "Defoe's Protestant Whore," *Eighteenth-Century Studies* 35.2 (2002): 215-33.

2 Her rational mind.

Soul; and how it was possible that I who in the Case before, where the Temptation was many ways more forcible, and the Arguments stronger, and more irrisistable, was yet under a continued Inquietude on account of the wicked Life I led, and could now live in the most profound Tranquility, and with an uninterrupted Peace, nay even rising up to Satisfaction, and Joy, and yet in a more palpable State of Adultery than before; for before, my Gentleman who call'd me Wife, had the Pretence of his Wife being parted from him, refusing to do the Duty of her Office as a Wife to him; as for me, my Circumstances were the same; but as for the Prince, as he had a fine and extraordinary Lady or Princess, of his own; so he had had two or three Mistresses more besides me, and made no Scruple of it at all.

However, I say, as to my own Part, I enjoy'd myself in perfect Tranquility; and as the Prince was the only Deity I worshipp'd, so I was really his Idol; and however it was with his Princess, I assure you, his other Mistresses found a sensible Difference; and tho' they could never find me out, yet I had good Intelligence, that they guess'd very well, that their Lord had got some new Favourite that robb'd them of his Company, and perhaps, some of his usual Bounty too: and now I must mention the Sacrifices he made to his Idol, and they were not a few, I assure you.

As he lov'd like a Prince, so he rewarded like a Prince; for tho' he declin'd my making a Figure, as above, he let me see, that he was above doing it for the saving the Expence of it, and so he told me, and that he would make it up in other things: First of all, he sent me a Toilet,[1] with all the Appurtenances of Silver, even so much as the Frame of the Table; and then, for the House, he gave me the Table, or Side-board of Plate I mention'd above, with all things belonging to it, of massy Silver; so that, in short, I could not for my Life, study to ask him for any thing of Plate which I had not.

He could then accommodate me in nothing more but Jewels and Cloaths, or Money for Cloaths; he sent his Gentleman to the Mercer's,[2] and bought me a Suit, or whole Piece, of the finest Brocaded Silk,[3] figur'd with Gold,[4] and another with Silver, and another of Crimson; so that I had three Suits of Cloaths, such as the Queen of *France* would not have disdain'd to have worn at

---

1 The Prince's gift not only includes what we might call a vanity or dressing table, edged in silver, but also brushes, mirrors, and combs.
2 Someone who deals in fine fabrics and accessories.
3 Cloth woven with a raised design.
4 I.e., embroidered with gold thread.

that time; yet I went out no-where; but as those were for me to put on, when I went out of Mourning, I dress'd myself in them, one after another, always when *his Highness* came to see me.

I had no less than five several Morning Dresses besides these, so that I need never be seen twice in the same Dress; to these he added several Parcels of fine Linnen, and of Lace, so much, that I had no room to ask for more, or indeed, for so much.

I took the Liberty once, in our Freedoms, to tell him, he was too Bountiful, and that I was too chargeable to him for a Mistress, and that I would be his faithful Servant, at less Expence to him; and that he not only left me no room to ask him for any thing, but that he supply'd me with such a Profusion of good things, that I scarce could wear them, or use them; unless I kept a great Equipage, which he knew was no way convenient for him, or for me; he smil'd; and took me in his Arms, and told me, he was resolv'd, while I was his, I should never be able to ask him for any-thing; but that he would be daily asking new Favours of me.

After we were up, for this Conference was in Bed, he desir'd I would dress me in the best Suit of Cloaths I had: It was a Day or two after the three Suits were made, and brought home; I told him, if he pleas'd, I would rather dress me in that Suit which I knew he lik'd best; he ask'd me, how I could know which he would like best before he had seen them? I told him I would presume, for once, to guess at his Fancy by my own; so I went away, and dress'd me in the second Suit, brocaded with Silver, and return'd in full Dress, with a Suit of Lace upon my Head which would have been worth in *England*, 200*l.* Sterling; and I was every Way set out as well as *Amy* could dress me, who was a very gentile[1] Dresser too: In this Figure I came to him, out of my Dressing-Room, which open'd with Folding Doors into his Bed-Chamber.

He sat as one astonish'd, a good-while, looking at me, without speaking a Word, till I came quite up to him, kneel'd on one Knee to him, and almost whether he would or no, kiss'd his Hand; he took me up, and stood up himself, but was surpriz'd when taking me in his Arms, he perceiv'd Tears to run down my Cheeks; My Dear, *says he*, aloud, what mean these Tears? My Lord, *said I*, after some little Check, for I cou'd not speak presently, I beseech you to believe me, they are not Tears of Sorrow, but Tears of Joy; it is impossible for me to see myself snatch'd from the Misery I was fallen into, and at once to be in the Arms of a Prince of such Goodness, such immense Bounty, and be treated in such a

---

1 I.e., genteel, well-mannered.

Manner; 'tis not possible, my Lord, *said I*, to contain the Satisfaction of it; and it will break out in an Excess in some measure proportion'd to your immense Bounty, and to the Affection which your Highness treats me with, who am so infinitely below you.

It wou'd look a little too much like a Romance here, to repeat all the kind things he said to me, on that Occasion; but I can't omit one Passage; as he saw the Tears drop down my Cheek, he pulls out a fine Cambrick Hankerchief,[1] and was going to wipe the Tears off, but check'd his Hand, as if he was afraid to deface something; I say, he check'd his Hand and toss'd the Handkerchief to me, to do it myself; I took the Hint immediately, and with a kind of pleasant Disdain, *How, my Lord*! said I, *Have you kiss'd me so often, and don't you know whether I am Painted,[2] or not? Pray let your Highness satisfie yourself, that you have no Cheats put upon you; for once let me be vain enough to say, I have not deceiv'd you with false Colours*: With this, I put a Handkerchief into his Hand, and taking his Hand into mine, I made him wipe my Face so hard, that he was unwilling to do it, for fear of hurting me.

He appear'd surpriz'd, more than ever, and swore, which was the first time that I had heard him swear, from my first knowing him, that he cou'd not have believ'd there was any such Skin, without Paint, in the World: *Well, my Lord*, said I, *Your Highness shall have a farther Demonstration than this; as to that which you are pleas'd to accept for Beauty, that it is the meer work of Nature*; and with that, I stept to the Door, and rung a little Bell, for my Woman, *Amy*, and bade her bring me a Cup-full of hot Water, which she did; and when it was come, I desir'd *his Highness* to feel if it was warm; which he did, and I immediately wash'd my Face all over with it, before him; this was, indeed, more than Satisfaction, that is to say, than Believing; for it was an undeniable Demonstration, and he kiss'd my Cheeks and Breasts a thousand times, the Expressions of the greatest Surprize imaginable.

Nor was I a very indifferent Figure as to Shape; tho' I had had two Children by my Gentleman, and six by my true Husband, I say, I was no despisable Shape; and my Prince (I must be allow'd the Vanity to call him so) was taking his View of me as I walk'd from one End of the Room to another, at last he leads me to the darkest Part of the Room, and standing behind me, bade me hold up my Head, when putting both his Hands round my Neck, as if he was spanning my Neck, to see how small it was, for it was long

---

1 A finely woven linen or cotton.
2 Wearing make-up.

and small; he held my Neck so long, and so hard, in his Hand that I complain'd he hurt me a little; what he did it for, I knew not, nor had I the least Suspicion but that he was spanning my Neck; but when I said he hurt me, he seem'd to let go, and in half a Minute more, led me to a Peir-Glass, and behold I saw my Neck clasp'd with a fine Necklace of Diamonds; whereas I felt no more what he was doing, than if he had really done nothing at-all, nor did I suspect it, in the least: If I had an Ounce of Blood in me, that did not fly up into my Face, Neck, and Breasts, it must be from some Interruption in the Vessels; I was all on fire with the Sight, and began to wonder what it was that was coming to me.

However, to let him see that I was not unqualified to receive Benefits; I turn'd about, My Lord, *says I*, Your Highness is resolv'd to conquer by your Bounty, the very Gratitude of your Servants; you will leave no room for any thing but Thanks, and make those Thanks useless too, by their being no Proportion to the Occasion.

I love, Child, *says he*, to see every thing suitable; a fine Gown and Petticoat; a fine lac'd Head; a fine Face and Neck, and no Necklace, would not have made the Object perfect: But why that Blush, my Dear, s*ays the Prince*? My Lord, *said I*, all your Gifts call for Blushes; but above all, I blush to receive what I am so ill able to merit, and may become so ill also.

Thus far I am a standing Mark of the Weakness of Great Men, in their Vice; that value not squandring away immense Wealth, upon the most worthless Creatures; or to sum it up in a Word, they raise the Value of the Object which they pretend to pitch upon, by their Fancy; I say, raise the Value of it, at their own Expence; give vast Presents for a ruinous Favour, which is so far from being equal to the Price, that nothing will, at last, prove more absurd, than the Cost Men are at to purchase their own Destruction.

I cou'd not, in the height of all this fine doings, I say, I cou'd not be without some just Reflection, tho' Conscience was, as I said, dumb as to any Disturbance it gave me in my Wickedness; my Vanity was fed up to such a height, that I had no room to give Way to such Reflections.

But I could not but sometimes look back, with Astonishment, at the Folly of Men of Quality, who immense in their Bounty, as in their Wealth, give to a Profusion, and without bounds, to the most scandalous of our Sex, for granting them the Liberty of abusing themselves, and ruining both.

I, that knew what this Carcass of mine had been but a few Years before; how overwhelm'd with Grief, drown'd in Tears, frighted with the Prospect of Beggery, and surrounded with Rags, and Fatherless Children; that was pawning and selling the Rags that cover'd me, for a Dinner, and sat on the Ground, despairing of Help, and expecting to be starv'd, till my Children were snatch'd from me, to be kept by the Parish; I, that was after this, a Whore for Bread, and abandoning Conscience and Virtue, liv'd with another Woman's Husband; I, that was despis'd by all my Relations, and my Husband's too; I, that was left so entirely desolate, friendless, and helpless, that I knew not how to get the least Help to keep me from starving; that I should be caress'd by a Prince, for the Honour of having the scandalous Use of my Prostituted Body, common before to his Inferiours; and perhaps wou'd not have denied one of his Footmen but a little while before, if I cou'd have got my Bread by it.[1]

I say, I cou'd not but reflect upon the Brutallity and Blindness of Mankind; that because Nature had given me a good Skin, and some agreeable Features, should suffer that Beauty to be such a Bait to Appetite, as to do such sordid, unaccountable things, to obtain the Possession of it.

It is for this Reason, that I have so largely set down the Particulars of the Caresses I was treated with by the Jeweller, and also by this Prince; not to make the Story an Incentive to the Vice, which I am now such a sorrowful Penitent for being guilty of, *God forbid any shou'd make so vile a Use of so good a Design*, but to draw the just Picture of a Man enslav'd to the Rage of his vicious Appetite; how he defaces the Image of God in his Soul; dethrones his Reason; causes Conscience to abdicate the Possession, and exalts Sence into the vacant Throne; how he deposes the Man, and exalts the Brute.

O! could we hear now, the Reproaches this Great Man afterwards loaded himself with, when he grew weary of this admir'd Creature, and became sick of his Vice! how printable would the Report of them be to the Reader of this Story; but had he himself also known the dirty History of my Actings upon the Stage of

---

1 Roxana's contemplation of her fate here alludes to the vernacular term for prostitute, "Common woman," so named because such women were socially indiscriminate in their choice of clients and like common lands were held in common by everyone. For more on the term, see Ruth Mazzo Karras, *Prostitution and Sexuality in Medieval England* (New York: Oxford UP, 1998).

Life, that little time I had been in the World, how much more severe would those Reproaches have been upon himself; but I shall come to this again.

I liv'd in this gay sort of Retirement almost three Years, in which time, no Amour of such a Kind,[1] sure, was ever carry'd up so high; the Prince knew no Bounds to his Munificence; he cou'd give me nothing, either for my wearing or using, or eating, or drinking, more than he had done from the Beginning.

His Presents were, after that, in Gold, and very frequent, and large; often a hundred Pistoles, never less than fifty, at a time; and I must do myself the Justice, that I seem'd rather backward to receive, than craving, and encroaching; not that I had not an avaricious Temper; nor was it, that I did not foresee that this was my Harvest, in which I was to gather up, and that it would not last long; but it was, that really his Bounty always anticipated my Expectations, and even my Wishes; and he gave me Money so fast, that he rather pour'd it in upon me, than left me room to ask it; so that, before I could spend fifty Pistoles, I had always a hundred to make it up.

After I had been near a Year and a half in his Arms, as above, or thereabouts, I prov'd with-Child; I did not take any Notice of it to him, till I was satisfied, that I was not deceiv'd; when one Morning early, when we were in Bed together, I said to him, My Lord, I doubt your Highness never gives yourself Leave to think, what the Case should be, if I should have the Honour to be with-Child by you: Why my Dear, *says he*, we are able to keep it, if such a thing should happen; I hope you are not concern'd about that: No, my Lord, *said I*, I should think myself very happy, if I could bring your Highness a Son, I should hope to see him a Lieutenant-General of the King's Armies, by the Interest of his Father, and by his own Merit.

Assure yourself, Child, *says he*, if it shou'd be so, I will not refuse owning him for my Son, tho' it be, as they call it, a Natural Son; and shall never slight or neglect him, for the sake of his Mother: Then he began to importune me, to know if it was so; but I positively denied it so long, till at last, I was able to give him the Satisfaction of knowing it himself, by the Motion of the Child within me.

He profess'd himself overjoy'd at the Discovery, but told me, that now it was absolutely necessary for me to quit the Confinement, which, *he said*, I had suffer'd for his sake, and to take a

---

1 Allusion to romances of the day.

House somewhere in the Country, in order for Health, as well as for Privacy, against my Lying-in: This was quite out of my Way; but the Prince, who was a Man of Pleasure, had, it seems, several Retreats of this Kind, which he had made use of, I suppose, upon like Occasions; and so leaving it, as it were, to his Gentleman, he provided a very convenient House, about four Miles south of *Paris*, at the Village of—, where I had very agreeable Lodgings, good Gardens, and all things very easie, to my Content; but one thing did not please me at all *viz.* that an Old Woman was provided, and put into the House to furnish every thing necessary to my Lying-in, and to assist at my Travel.[1]

I did not like this Old Woman at all; she look'd so like a Spy upon me, or, (as sometimes I was frighted to imagine) like one set privately to dispatch me out of the World, as might best suit with the Circumstance of my Lying-in; and when his Highness came the next time to see me, which was not many Days, I expostulated a little on the Subject of the Old Woman; and by the Management of my Tongue, as well as by the Strength of reasoning, I convinc'd him, that it would not be at all convenient; that it would be the greater Risque on his Side; and first, or last, it would certainly expose him, and me also; I assur'd him, that my Servant being an *English* Woman, never knew, to that Hour, who *his Highness* was; that I always call'd him the *Count de Clerac*; and that she new nothing else of him; nor ever should; that if he would give me leave to choose proper Persons for my Use, it shou'd be so order'd, that not one of them should know who he was, or perhaps, ever see his Face; and that for the reality of the Child that should be born, *his Highness*, who had alone been at the first of it, should, if he pleas'd, be present in the Room all the Time; so that he would need not Witnesses on that Account.

This Discourse fully satisfied him, so that he order'd his Gentleman to dismiss the Old Woman the same Day; and, without any Difficulty, I sent my Maid *Amy* to Callais, and thence to *Dover*, where she got an *English* Midwife, and an *English* Nurse, to come over, on purpose to attend an *English* Lady of Quality, as they stil'd me, for four Months certain: The Midwife, *Amy* had agreed to pay a hundred Guineas to, and bear her Charges to *Paris*, and back again to *Dover*; the poor Woman that was to be my

---

1 Midwives were often associated with infanticide and, as Roxana alludes to earlier, it was common practice to invite neighbors as well as midwives to attend the birth of a child in order to witness whether the child was born dead or alive.

Nurse, had twenty Pounds, and the same Terms for Charges, as the other.

I was very easie when *Amy* return'd, and the more, because she brought with the Midwife, a good Motherly sort of Woman, who was to be her Assistant, and would be very helpful on Occasion; and bespoke a Man-Midwife at *Paris* too, if there should be any Necessity for his Help: Having thus made Provision for every thing, the *Count,* for so we all call'd him in publick, came as often to see me, as I could expect, and continued exceeding kind, as he had always been; one Day conversing together, upon the Subject of my being with-Child, I told him how all things were in order; but that I had a strange Apprehension that I should die with that Child: He smil'd, *So all the Ladies say, my Dear*, says he, *when they are with-Child*: Well, however, my Lord, *said I,* it is but just, that Care should be taken, that what you have bestow'd in your Excess of Bounty upon me; should not be lost, and upon this, I pull'd a Paper out of my Bosom, folded up, but not seal'd, and I read it to him: Wherein I had left Order, that all the Plate and Jewels, and fine Furniture, which *his Highness* had give me, should be restor'd to him by my Woman, and the Keys be immediately deliver'd to his Gentleman, in case of Disaster.

Then I recommended my Woman, *Amy* to his Favour for a hundred Pistoles, on Condition she gave the Keys up, as above, to his Gentleman, and his Gentleman's Receipt for them; when he saw this, *My Dear Child,* said he, and took me in his Arms, *What have you been making your Will, and disposing your Effects? Pray who do you make your universal Heir?* So far as to do Justice to your Highness, in case of Mortality, I have, my Lord, *said I,* and who should I dispose the valuable things to, which I have had from your Hand, as Pledges of your Favour, and Testimonies of your Bounty, but to the Giver of them? If the Child should live, your Highness will, I don't question, act like yourself in that Part, and I shall have the utmost Satisfaction, that it will be well us'd by your Direction.

I cou'd see he took this very well: *I have forsaken all the Ladies in* Paris, says he, *for you; and I have liv'd every Day since I knew you, to see that you know how to merit all that a Man of Honour can do for you; be easie, Child, I hope you shall not die; and all you have is your own, to do what with it you please.*

I was then within about two Months of my time, and that soon wore off; when I found my Time was come, it fell out very happily, that he was in the House, and I entreated he would con-tinue a few hours in the House, which he agreed to; they call'd *his*

Highness to come into the Room, if he pleas'd, as I had offer'd, and as I desir'd him, and I sent Word, I would make as few Cries as possible, to prevent disturbing him; he came into the Room once and call'd to me, to be of good Courage, it wou'd soon be over, and then he withdrew again; and in about half an Hour more, *Amy* called him the news, that I was Deliver'd, and had brought him a charming Boy; he gave her ten Pistoles for her News, stay'd till they had adjusted things about me, and then came into the Room again, chear'd me, and spoke kindly to me, and look'd on the Child, then withdrew; and came again the next Day to visit me.

Since this, and when I have look'd back upon these things with Eyes unpossess'd with Crime, when the wicked Part has appear'd in its clearer Light, and I have seen it in its own natural Colours; when no more blinded with the glittering Appearances, which at that time deluded me, and, *as in like Cases, if I may guess at others by myself*; too much possess'd the Mind; I say, since this, I have often wonder'd, with what Pleasure, or Satisfaction, the Prince cou'd look upon the poor innocent Infant; which, tho' his own, and that he might that Way have some Attachment in his Affections to it, yet must always afterwards be a Remembrancer to him of his most early Crime; and which was worse, must bear upon itself, unmerited, an eternal Mark of Infamy, which should be spoken of, upon all Occasions, to its Reproach, from the Folly of its Father, and Wickedness of its Mother.

Great Men are, indeed, deliver'd from the Burthen of their Natural Children, or Bastards, as to their Maintenance: This is the main Affliction in other Cases, where there is not Substance sufficient, without breaking into the Fortunes of the Family; in those Cases, either a Man's legitimate Children suffer, which is very unnatural; or the unfortunate Mother of that illegitimate Birth, has a dreadful Affliction, either of being turn'd off with her Child, and be left to starve, *&c.* or of seeing the poor Infant pack'd off with a Piece of Money, to some of those She-Butchers,[1] who take Children off of their Hands, as 'tis call'd; that is to say, starve 'em, and in a Word, murther 'em.

Great Men, I say, are deliver'd from this Burthen, because they are always furnish'd to supply the Expence of their Out-of-the-Way Off-spring, by making little Assignments upon the Bank of

---

1 Midwives could sometimes be paid to take infants and put them to wet-nurse. By Defoe's time, however, people were increasingly aware that many infants died in these arrangements.

Lyons, or the Town-House of *Paris*, and settling those Sums, to be receiv'd for the Maintenance of such Expence as they see Cause.

Thus, in the Case of this Child of mine, while he and I convers'd, there was no need to make any Appointment, as an Appennage, or Maintenance for the Child, or its Nurse; for he supplied me more than sufficiently for all those things; but afterward when Time, and a particular Circumstance, put an End to our conversing together; as such things always meet with a Period, and generally break off abruptly; I say, after that, I found he appointed the Children a settled Allowance, by an Assignment of annual Rent, upon the Bank of *Lyons*, which was sufficient for Bringing them handsomely, tho' privately, up in the World; and that not in a Manner unworthy of their Father's Blood, tho' I came to be sunk and forgotten in the Case; nor did the Children ever know anything of their Mother, to this Day, other, than as you may have an Account hereafter.

But to look back to the particular Observation I was making, which, I hope may be of Use to those who read my Story; I say, it was something wonderful to me, to see this Person so exceedingly delighted at the Birth of this Child, and so pleas'd with it; for he would sit and look at it, and with an Air of Seriousness sometimes, a great while together; and particularly, I observ'd, he lov'd to look at it when it was asleep.

It was, indeed, a lovely, charming Child, and had a certain Vivacity in its Countenance, that is, far from being common to all Children so young; and he would often say to me, that he believ'd there was something extraordinary in the Child; and he did not doubt but he would come to be a Great Man.

I could never hear him say so, but tho' secretly it pleas'd me, yet it so closely touch'd me another Way, that I could not refrain Sighing, and sometimes Tears; and one time, in particular, it so affected me, that I could not conceal it from him; but when he saw Tears run down my Face, there was no concealing the Occasion from him; he was too importunate to be deny'd, in a thing of that Moment; so I frankly answer'd, It sensibly affects me, My Lord, *said I*, that whatever the Merit of this little Creature may be, he must always have a Bend on his Arms;[1] the Disaster of his Birth will be always, not a Blot only to his Honour, but a Bar to his Fortunes in the World; our Affection will be ever his Affliction, and his Mother's Crime be the Son's Reproach; the Blot can

---

1 Illegitimacy among members of the aristocracy was often represented by a bent arm in the family crest.

never be wip'd out by the most glorious Actions; nay, if it lives to raise a Family, *said I*, the Infamy must descend ever to its innocent Posterity.

He took the Thought, and sometimes told me afterwards, that it made a deeper Impression on him, than he discover'd to me at that time; but for the present, he put it off, with telling me, these things cou'd not be help'd; that they serv'd for a Spur to the Spirits of brave Men; inspir'd them with the Principles of Gallantry, and prompted them to brave Actions; that tho' it might be true, that the mention of Illegitimacy might attend the Name, yet that Personal virtue plac'd a Man of Honour above the Reproach of his Birth; that as he had no Share in the Offence, he would have no Concern at the Blot; when having by his own Merit plac'd himself out of the reach of Scandal, his Fame shou'd drown the Memory of his Beginning.

That as it was usual for Men of Quality to make such little Escapes,[1] so the Number of their Natural children were so great, and they generally took such good Care of their Education, that some of the greatest Men in the World had a Bend in their Coats of Arms, and that it was of no Consequence to them, especially when their Fame began to rise upon the Basis of their acquir'd Merit; and upon this, he began to reckon up to me some of the greatest Families in *France* and in *England* also.

This carry'd off our Discourse for a time; but I went farther with him once, removing the Discourse from the Part attending our Children, to the Reproach which those Children would be apt to throw upon us, their Originals; and when speaking a little too feelingly on the Subject, he began to receive the Impression a little deeper than I wish'd he had done; at last he told me, I had almost acted the Confessor to him; that I might, perhaps, preach a more dangerous Doctrine to him, than we should either of us like, or that I was aware of; for, *my Dear, says he*, if once we come to talk of Repentance, we must talk of parting.

If Tears were in my Eyes before, they flow'd too fast now to be restrain'd, and I gave him but too much Satisfaction by my Looks, that I had yet no Reflections upon my Mind, strong enough to go that Length, and that I could no more think of Parting, than he could.

He said a great many kind things, which were Great, like himself, and extenuating our Crime, intimated to me, that he cou'd no more part with me, than I cou'd with him; so we both,

---

1 I.e., to have affairs.

as I may say, even against our Light, and against our Conviction, concluded to SIN ON; indeed, his affection to the Child, was one great Tye to him, for he was extremely fond of it.

This Child liv'd to be a considerable Man: He was first, an Officer of the Guard *du Corps* of *France*; and afterwards Colonel of a Regiment of Dragoons, in *Italy*; and on many extraordinary Occasions, shew'd, that he was not unworthy such a Father, but many ways deserving a legitimate Birth, and a better Mother: Of which hereafter.

I think I may say now, that I liv'd indeed like a Queen; or if you will have me confess, that my Condition had still the Reproach of a *Whore*, I may say, I was sure, the Queen of Whores; for no Woman was ever more valued, or more caress'd by a Person of such Quality, only in the Station of a Mistress; I had, indeed, one Deficiency, which Women in such Circumstances seldom are chargeable with; namely I crav'd nothing of him; I never ask'd him for any thing in my Life; nor suffer'd myself to be made use of, as is too much the Custom of Mistresses, to ask Favours for others; his Bounty always prevented me in the first, and my strict concealing myself, in the last; which was no less to my Convenience, than his.

The only Favour I ever ask'd of him was, for his Gentleman, who he had long intrusted with the Secret of our Affair, and who had once so much offended him, by some Omissions in his Duty, that he found it very hard to make his Peace; he came and laid his Case before my Woman, *Amy*, and begg'd her to speak to me, to intercede for him; which I did, and on my Account, he was receiv'd again, and pardon'd; for which the grateful Dog requited me, by getting to-Bed his Benefactress, *Amy*; at which I was very angry; but *Amy* generously acknowledg'd, that it was her Fault as much as his; that she lov'd the Fellow so much, that she believ'd, if he had not ask'd her, she should have ask'd him; I say, this pacify'd me, and I only obtain'd of her, that she should not let him know, that I knew it.

I might have interspers'd this Part of my Story with a great many pleasant Parts, and Discourses, which happen'd between my Maid *Amy*, and I; but I omit them, on account of my own Story, which has been so extraordinary: However, I must mention something, as to *Amy*, and her Gentleman; I enquir'd of *Amy*, upon what Terms they came to be so intimate; but *Amy* seem'd backward to explain herself; I did not care to press her upon a Question of that Nature; knowing that she might have answer'd my Question with a Question, and said, Why, how did I and the Prince come to be so intimate? so I left off farther inquiring into it, till after some time, she told me all freely, of her own Accord, which, to cut it short, amounted to no more than this, that *like* Mistress, *like* Maid; as they had many leisure Hours together below, while they waited respectively, when his Lord and I were together above; I say, they could hardly avoid the usual Question one to another, namely, Why might not they do the same thing below, that we did above?

On that Account, indeed, as I said above, I could not find in my Heart to be angry with *Amy*; I was indeed, afraid the Girl would have been with-Child too, but that did not happen, and so there was no Hurt done; for *Amy* had been hansell'd[1] before, as well as her Mistress, and by the same Party too, *as you have heard*.

After I was up again, and my Child provided with a good Nurse, and withal, Winter coming on, it was proper to think of coming to *Paris* again, which I did; but as I had now a Coach and Horses, and some Servants to attend me, by my Lord's Allowance, I took the Liberty to have them come to *Paris* sometimes, and so to take a Tour into the Garden of the Tuilleries, and the other pleasant Places of the City: It happen'd one Day; that my Prince (if I may call him so) had a-Mind to give me some Diversion, and to take the Air with me; but that he might do it, and not be publickly known, he comes to me in a Coach of the Count *de*—, a great Officer of the Court, attended by his Liveries also; so that in a word, it was impossible to guess by the Equipage, who I was, or who I belong'd to; also, that I might be the more effectually conceal'd, he order'd me to be taken up at a Mantua-Maker's House,[2] where he sometimes came, whether upon other Amours, or not, was no Business of Mine to enquire: I knew nothing whither he intended to carry me; but when he was in the Coach with me, he told me, he had order'd his Servants to go to Court with me, and he would shew me some of the *Beau Monde*;[3] I told him, I car'd not where I went, while I had the Honour to have him with me; so he carried me to the fine Palace of *Meudon*, where the *Dauphine*[4] then was, where he had some particular Intimacy with one of the *Dauphine*'s Domesticks, who procur'd a Retreat for me in his Lodgings, while we stay'd there; which was three or four Days.

---

1 Literally, used, but here it means that Amy was already sexually active.
2 Mantuas were a kind of loose gown. Mantua-makers were often associated with prostitution.
3 Fashionable world.
4 Heir-apparent to the French throne.

While I was there, the KING happen'd to come thither, from *Versailles*, and making but a short Stay, visited Madam the *Dauphiness*, who was then living; the Prince was here *Incognito*, only because of his being with me; and therefore, when he heard, that the KING was in the Gardens, he kept close within the Lodgings; but the Gentleman, in whose Lodgings we were, with his Lady, and several others went out to see the KING, and I had the Honour to be ask'd to go with them.

After we had seen the KING, who did not stay long in the Gardens, we walk'd up the Broad Terrass, and crossing the Hall, towards the Great Stair-Case, I had a Sight, which confounded me at once, as I doubt not, it wou'd have done to any Woman in the world: The Horse-Guards, or what they call there the *Gens-d'arms*, had upon some Occasion, been either upon Duty, or been Review'd,[1] or something (I did not understand that Part) was the Matter, that occasion'd their being there, I know not what; but walking in the Guard-Chamber, and with his Jack-Boots on, and the whole Habit of the Troop, as it is worn; when our Horse-Guards are upon Duty, as they call it, at St. *James's*-Park; I say, there, to my inexpressible Confusion, I saw Mr.—, my first Husband, the Brewer.

I cou'd not be deceiv'd; I pass'd so near him, that I almost brush'd him with my Cloaths, and look'd him full in the Face, but having my Fan before my Face, so that he cou'd not know me; however, I knew him perfectly well, and I heard him speak, which was a second Way of knowing him; besides, *being you may be sure, astonish'd and surpriz'd at such a Sight*, I turn'd about after I had pass'd him some Steps, and pretending to ask the Lady that was with me some Questions, I stood as if I had view'd the Great Hall, the outer Guard-Chamber, and some other things; but I did it, to take a full View of his Dress, that I might farther inform myself.

While I stood thus amusing the Lady that was with me, with Questions, he walk'd, talking with another Man of the same Cloth, back again, just by me; and to my particular Satisfaction, or Dissatisfaction, take it which way you will, I heard him speak *English*, the other being, it seems an *Englishman*.

I then ask'd the Lady some other Questions; Pray, Madam, *says I* what are these Troopers, here? Are they the KING'S Guards? No, *says she*, they are the *Gensd'arms*; a small Detachment of them, I suppose, attended the KING to-Day, but they are not his

---

1 Paraded before the king.

Majesty's ordinary Guard; another Lady that was with her, said, No, Madam, it seems that is not the Case; for I heard them saying, the *Gensd'arms* were here to-Day by special Order, some of them being to march towards the *Rhine*,[1] and these attend for Orders; but they go back to-Morrow to *Orleans*,[2] where they are expected.

This satisfied me in Part, but I found Means after this, to enquire, whose particular Troop it was that the Gentlemen that were here, belong'd to; and with that, I heard, they would all be at *Paris* the Week after.

Two Days after this, we return'd for *Paris*, when I took Occasion to speak to my Lord, that I heard the *Gensd'arms* were to be in the City the next Week, and that I should be charm'd with seeing them March, if they came in a Body: He was so obliging in such things, that I need but just name a thing of that Kind, and it was done; so he order'd his Gentleman (I shou'd now call him *Amy*'s *Gentleman*,) to get me a Place in a certain House, where I might see them March.

As he did not appear with me on this Occasion, so I had the Liberty of taking my Woman, *Amy*, with me; and stood where we were very well accommodated for the Observation which I was to make: I told *Amy* what I had seen, and she was as forward to make the Discovery, as I was to have her, almost as much surpriz'd at the thing itself; in a Word, the *Gensd'arms* enter'd the City, as was expected, and made a most glorious show indeed, being new cloath'd and arm'd, and being to have their Standards bless'd by the Archbishop of *Paris*; on this Occasion, they indeed, look'd very gay; and as they march'd very leisurely, I had time to take as critical a View, and make as nice a Search among them, as I pleas'd: Here, in a particular Rank, eminent for one monstrous siz'd Man on the Right; here, I say, I saw my Gentleman again, and a very handsome jolly Fellow he was, as any in the Troop, tho' not so monstrous large as that great one I speak of, who it seems was however, a Gentleman of a good Family in *Gascogne*, and was call'd the *Giant of Gascogne*.

It was a kind of good Fortune to us, among the other Circumstances of it, that something caus'd the Troops to Halt in their March, a little before that particular Rank came right-against that Window which I stood in, so that then we had Occa-

---

1 A river that starts in eastern Switzerland and flows north mostly through Western Germany to the North Sea.
2 A city south of Paris on the Loire river.

sion to take our full View of him, at a small Distance, and so, as not to doubt of his being the same Person.

Amy, who thought she might on many Accounts, venture with more Safety to be particular, than I cou'd, ask'd her Gentleman, how a particular Man, who she saw there among the *Gensd'arms*, might be enquir'd after, and found out; she having seen an *Englishman* riding there, which was suppos'd to be dead in *England* for several Years before she came out of *London*, and that his Wife had marry'd again: It was a Question the Gentleman did not well understand how to answer; but another Person, that stood by, told her, if she wou'd tell him the Gentleman's Name, he wou'd endeavour to find him out for her, and ask'd jestingly, if he was her Lover? *Amy* put that off with a Laugh, but still continued her Enquiry, and in such a Manner, as the Gentleman easily perceiv'd she was in earnest; so he left bantering, and ask'd her in what Part of the Troop he rode; she foolishly told him his Name, which she should not have done; and pointing to the Cornet[1] that Troop carried, which was not then quite out of Sight, she let him easily know whereabouts he rode, only she cou'd not name the Captain; however, he gave her such Directions afterwards, that, in short, *Amy*, who was an indefatigable Girl, found him out; it seems he had not chang'd his Name, not supposing any Enquiry would be made after him here; but, I say, *Amy* found him out, and went boldly to his Quarters, ask'd for him, and he came out to her immediately.

I believe I was not more confounded at my first seeing him at *Meudon*, than he was at seeing *Amy*; he started, and turn'd pale as Death; *Amy* believ'd, if he had seen her at first, in any convenient Place for so villainous a Purpose, he would have murther'd her.

But he started, as I say above, and ask'd in *English*, with an Admiration,[2] What are you! *Sir*, says she, *don't you know me? Yes*, says he, *I knew you when you were alive, but what you are now, whether Ghost or Substance, I know not: Be not afraid, Sir, of that*, says Amy, *I am the same* Amy *that I was in your Service, and do not speak to you now for any Hurt, but that I saw you accidentally, Yesterday, ride among the Soldiers, I thought you might be glad to hear from your Friends at* London: Well, *Amy*, says he, *then*, having a little recover'd himself, *How does every-body do? What, is your Mistress here?* Thus they begun.

---

1 The standard or banner carried by the troops.
2 Astonishment.

Amy. My Mistress, Sir, alas! Not the Mistress you mean, poor Gentlewoman, you left her in a sad Condition.

Gent. Why, that's true, *Amy*, but it cou'd not be help'd; I was in a sad Condition myself.

Amy. I believe so, indeed, sir, or else you had not gone away as you did; for it was a very terrible Condition you left them all in, that I must say.

Gent. What did they do, after I was gone?

Amy. Do, Sir! very miserably, you may be sure; how could it be otherwise?

Gent. Well, that's true indeed; but you may tell me, *Amy*, what became of them, if you please; for tho' I went so away, it was not because I did not love them all very well, but because I could not bear to see the Poverty that was coming upon them, and which it was not in my Power to help; *what could I do?*

Amy. Nay, I believe so, indeed, and I have heard my Mistress say, many times, she did not doubt but your Affliction was as great as hers, almost, *wherever you were.*

Gent. Why, did she believe I was alive then?

Amy. Yes, Sir, she always said, she believ'd you were alive; because she thought she should have heard something of you, if you had been dead.

Gent. *Ay, ay*, my Perplexity was very great, indeed, or else I had never gone away.

Amy. It was very cruel tho', to the poor Lady, Sir, *my Mistress*; she almost broke her heart for you at first, for fear of what might befal you, and at last, because she cou'd not hear from you.

Gent. Alas, *Amy*! what cou'd I do? things were driven to the last Extremity before I went; I cou'd have done nothing, but help starve them all, if I had stay'd; and besides, I cou'd not bear to see it.

Amy. You know, Sir, I can say little to what pass'd before, but I am a melancholy Witness to the sad Distresses of my poor Mistress, as long as I stay'd with her, and which would grieve your Heart to hear them.

Here she tells my whole Story, to the Time that the Parish took off one of my Children, and which she perceiv'd very much affected him; and he shook his Head, and said some things very bitter, when he heard of the Cruelty of his own Relations, to me.

Gent. Well, *Amy*, I have heard enough so far; what did she do afterwards?

Amy. I can't give you any farther Account, Sir; my Mistress would not let me stay with her any longer; *she said*, she could neither pay me, or subsist me; I told her, I wou'd serve her without any Wages, but I cou'd not live without Victuals, you know; so I was forc'd to leave her, *poor Lady*, sore against my Will, and I heard afterwards, that the Landlord seiz'd her Goods, so she was, I suppose, turn'd out of Doors; for as I went by the Door, about a Month after, I saw the House shut up; and about a Fortnight after that, I found there were Workmen at work, fitting it up, as I suppose, for a new Tennant; but none of the Neighbours could tell me what was become of my poor Mistress, only that they said, she was so poor, that it was next to begging; that some of the neighbouring Gentlefolks had reliev'd her, or that else she must have starv'd; then she went on, and told him, that after that, they never heard any more of [*me*] her Mistress; but that she had been seen once or twice in the City, very shabby, and poor in Cloaths, and it was thought she work'd with her Needle, for her Bread: All this, the *Jade* said with so much Cunning, and manag'd and humour'd it so well, and wip'd her Eyes, and cry'd so artificially, that he took it all as it was intended he should, and once or twice she saw Tears in his Eyes too: He told her, it was a moving, melancholy Story, and it had almost broke his Heart at first; but that he was driven to the last Extremity, and cou'd do nothing, but stay and see 'em all starve, which he could not bear the Thoughts of, but shou'd have Pistol'd himself, if any such thing had happen'd while he was there; that he left [*me*,] his Wife, all the Money he had in the world, but 25*l.* which was as little as he could take with him, to seek his Fortune in the World; he cou'd not doubt but that his Relations, seeing they were all Rich, wou'd have taken the poor Children off, and not let them come to the Parish; and that his Wife was young and handsome, and, he thought, might Marry again, perhaps to her Advantage; and for that very Reason, he never wrote to her, or let her know he was alive, that she might, in a reasonable Term of Years, marry, and perhaps, mend her Fortunes: That he resolv'd never to claim her, because he should rejoice to hear, that she had settled to her Mind; and that he wish'd there had been a Law made to empower a Woman to marry, if her Husband was not heard of in so long time; which time, he thought shou'd not be above four Year, which was long enough to send Word in, to a Wife or Family, from any Part of the World.

Amy said, she cou'd say nothing to that; but this, that she was satisfied, her Mistress would marry no-body unless she had certain Intelligence that he had been dead, from somebody that saw him buried; but alas! s*ays Amy*, my Mistress was reduc'd to such dismal

Circumstance, that no-body wou'd be so foolish to think of her, unless it had been somebody to go a-begging with her.

Amy then seeing him so perfectly deluded, made a long and lamentable Outcry, how she had been deluded away, to marry a poor Footman; for he is no worse, or better, *says she*, tho' he calls himself a Lord's Gentleman; and here, *says Amy*, he has dragg'd me over into a strange Country, to make a Begger of me; and then she falls a howling again, and sniveling; which, by the way, was all Hypocrisie, but acted so to the Life, as perfectly deceiv'd him, and he gave entire Credit to every Word of it.

Why, *Amy*, *says he*, you are very well dress'd, you don't look as if you were in danger of being a Begger; *Ay*, hang him, *says Amy*, they love to have fine Cloaths here, if they have never a Sm–k under them; but I love to have Money in Cash, rather than a Chest full of fine Cloaths; besides, Sir, *says she*, most of the Cloaths I have, were given me in the last Place I had, when I went away from my Mistress.[1]

Upon the whole of the Discourse, *Amy* got out of him, what Condition he was in, and how he liv'd, upon her Promise to him, that if ever she came to *England*, and should see her old Mistress, she should not let her know that he was alive: *Alas!* Sir, *says Amy*, I may never come to see *England* again, as long as I live; and if I shou'd, it wou'd be ten Thousand to One, whether I shall see my old Mistress; for how shou'd I know which Way to look for her? Or what Part of *England* she may be in; not I, *says she*, I don't so much as know how to enquire for her; and if I shou'd, *says Amy*, ever be so happy as to see her, I would not do her so much Mischief as to tell her where you were, Sir, unless she was in a Condition to help herself and you too: This farther deluded him, and made him entirely open in his conversing with her: As to his own Circumstances, he told her, she saw him in the highest Preferment he had arriv'd to, or was ever like to arrive to; for having not Friends or Acquaintance in *France*, and which was worse, *no Money*, he never expected to rise; that he could have been made a Lieutenant to a Troop of Light-Horse but the Week before, by the Favour of an Officer in the *Gensd'arms*, who was his Friend;

---

1 Fabric in any form was an exceptionally valuable commodity. In 1670, for instance, it became impossible for individuals convicted of stealing cloth to invoke "benefit of clergy," an ancient practice that insulated convicted criminals from capital punishment if they could prove they could read on the grounds that literacy was a specialized skill usually acquired only by members of the clergy.

but that he must have found 8000 Livres to have paid for it, to the Gentleman who possess'd it, and had Leave given him to sell: *But where cou'd I get 8000 Livres*, says he, *that have never been Master of 500 Livres Ready-Money*, at a-time, *since I came into France?*

O Dear! *Sir, says Amy*, I am very sorry to hear you say so; I fancy if you once got up to some Preferment, you wou'd think of my old Mistress again, and do something for her; poor Lady, *says Amy*, she wants it, to be sure, and then she falls a-crying again; 'tis a sad thing, indeed *says she*, that you should be so hard put to it for Money, when you had got a Friend to recommend you, and shou'd lose it for want of Money; ay, so it was, *Amy*, indeed, *says he*; but what can a Stranger do, that has neither Money or Friends? Here *Amy* puts in again on my Account; well, *says she*, my poor Mistress had had the Loss, tho' she knows nothing of it; O dear! How happy it would have been, to be sure, Sir, you wou'd have help'd her all you cou'd; *Ay*, says he, *Amy, so I wou'd, with all my Heart*; and even as I am, *I wou'd send her some Relief, if I thought she wanted it; only, that then letting her know I was alive, might do her some Prejudice, in case of her settling, or marrying any-body.*

Alas! *says Amy*, Marry! who will marry her, in the poor Condition she is in? And so their Discourse ended for that Time.

All this was meer Talk on both Sides and Words of Course; for on farther Enquiry, *Amy* found, that he had no such Offer of a Lieutenant's Commission, or any thing like it; and that he rambled in his Discourse, from one thing to another: But of that in its Place.

You may be sure, that this Discourse, as *Amy* at first related it, was moving, to the last Degree, upon me; and I was once going to have sent him the 8000 Livres to purchase the Commission he had spoken of; but as I knew his Character better than any-body, I was willing to search a little farther into it; and so I set *Amy* to enquire of some other of the Troop, to see what character he had, and whether there was any-thing in the Story of a Lieutenant's Commission, or no.

But *Amy* soon came to a better Understanding of him; for she presently learnt, that he had a most scoundrel Character; that there was nothing of Weight in any thing he said; but that he was in short, a meer Sharper; one that would stick at nothing to get Money, and that there was no depending on any thing he said; and that, more especially, about the Lieutenant's Commission, she understood, that there was nothing at-all in it; but they told her, how he had often made use of *that Sham*, to borrow Money, and move Gentlemen to pity him, and lend him Money, in hopes to get him Preferment; that he had reported, that he had a Wife, and five Children, in *England*, who he maintain'd out of his Pay; and by these Shifts[1] had run into Debt in several Places; and upon several Complaints for such things, he had been threatened to be turn'd out of the *Gensd'arms*; and that, in short, he was not to be believ'd in any thing he said, or trusted on any Account.

Upon his Information, *Amy* began to cool in her farther meddling with him; and told me, it was not safe for me to attempt doing him any good, unless I resolv'd to put him upon Suspicions and Enquiries, which might be to my Ruin, in the Condition I was now in.

I was soon confirm'd in this Part of his Character; for the next time that *Amy* came to talk with him, he discover'd himself more effectually; for while she had put him in Hopes of procuring One to advance the Money for the Lieutenant's Commission for him upon easie Conditions, he by Degrees, dropt the Discourse, then pretended it was too late, and that he could not get it; and then descended to ask poor *Amy* to lend him 500 Pistoles.

Amy pretended Poverty; that her Circumstances were but mean; and that she cou'd not raise such a Sum; and this she did, to try him to the utmost; he descended to 300, then to 100, then to 50, then to a Pistole, which she lent him, and he never intending to pay it, play'd out of her Sight, as much as he cou'd; and thus being satisfi'd that he was the same worthless thing he had ever been, I threw off all Thoughts of him; whereas, had he been a Man of any Sence, and of any Principle of Honour, I had it in my thoughts to retire to *England* again, send for him over, and have liv'd honestly with him: But as a *Fool* is the worst of Husbands to do a Woman good, so a *Fool* is the worst Husband a Woman can do Good to: I wou'd willingly have done him Good, but he was not qualified to receive it, or make the best Use of it; had I sent him ten Thousand Crowns, instead of eight Thousand Livres, and sent it with the express Condition, that he should immediately have bought himself the Commission he talk'd of, with Part of the Money, and have sent some of it to relieve the Necessities of his poor miserable Wife at *London*, and to prevent his Children to be kept by the Parish, it was evident, he wou'd have been still but a private Trooper, and his Wife and Children should still have starv'd at *London*, or been kept of meer Charity, as, for ought he knew, they then were.

---

1 Obligations.

Seeing therefore, no Remedy, I was oblig'd to withdraw my Hand from him, that had been my first Destroyer, and reserve the Assistance that I intended to have given him, for another more desirable Opportunity; all that I had now to do, was to keep myself out of his Sight, which was not very difficult for me to do, considering in what Station he liv'd.

Amy and I had several Consultations then, upon the main Question, namely, how to be sure never to chop upon[1] him again, by Chance, and so be supriz'd into a Discovery; which would have been a fatal Discovery indeed: *Amy* propos'd, that we shou'd always take Care to know where the *Gensd'arms* were quarter'd, and thereby effectually avoid them; and this was one Way.

But this was not so as to be fully to my Satisfaction; no ordinary Way of enquiring where the *Gensd'arms* were quarter'd were sufficient to me; but I found out a Fellow, who was completely qualified for the Work of a Spy, (for *France* has Plenty of such People,) this Man I employ'd to be a constant and particular Attendant upon his Person and Motions; and he was especially employ'd and order'd to haunt him *as a Ghost*; that he should scarce let him be ever out of his Sight; he perform'd this to a Nicety, and fail'd not to give me a perfect Journal of all his Motions, from Day to Day; and whether for his Pleasures or his Business, was always at his Heels.

This was somewhat expensive, and such a Fellow merited to be well paid; but he did his Business so exquisitely punctual, that this poor Man scarce went out of the House, without my knowing the Way he went, the Company he kept, when he went Abroad, and when he stay'd at Home.

By this extraordinary Conduct I made myself safe, and so went out in publick, or stay'd at home, as I found he was, or was not, in a Possibility of being at *Paris*, at *Versailles*, or any Place I had Occasion to be at: This, tho' it was very chargeable,[2] yet as I found it absolutely necessary, so I took no Thought about the Expence of it; for I knew I cou'd not purchase my Safety too dear.

By this Management I found an Opportunity to see what a most insignificant, unthinking Life, the poor indolent Wretch, who by his unactive Temper had at first been my Ruin, now liv'd; how he only rose in the Morning, to go to-Bed at Night; that saving the necessary Motion of the Troops, which he was oblig'd

---

1 Stumble upon him by accident.
2 Inconvenient.

to attend, he was a meer motionless Animal, of no Consequence in the World; that he seem'd to be one, who, tho' he was indeed, alive, had no manner of Business in Life, but to stay to be call'd out of it; he neither kept any Company, minded any Sport, play'd at any Game, or indeed, did any thing of moment; but *in short*, saunter'd about, like one, that it was not two Livres Value whether he was dead or alive; that when he was gone, would leave no Remembrance behind him that ever he was here; that if ever he did any thing in the World to be talk'd of, it was, only to get[1] five Beggers, and starve his Wife: the Journal of his Life, which I had constantly sent me every Week, was the least significant of anything of its Kind, that was ever seen; as it had really nothing of Earnest in it, so it wou'd make no Jest, to relate it; it was not important enough, so much as to make the Reader merry withal; and for that Reason I omit it.

Yet this *Nothing-doing Wretch* was I oblig'd to watch and guard against, as against the only thing that was capable of doing me Hurt in the World, I was to shun him, as we wou'd shun a Spectre, or even the Devil, if he was actually in our Way; and it cost me after the Rate of a 150 Livres a Month, and very cheap too, to have this Creature constantly kept in View; that is to say, my Spy undertook never to let him be out of his Sight an Hour, but so as that he cou'd give an Account of him; which was much the easier to be done, considering his Way of Living; for he was sure, that for whole Weeks together, he wou'd be ten Hours of the Day, half asleep on a Bench at the Tavern-Door where he quarter'd, or drunk within the House.

Tho' this wicked Life he led, sometimes mov'd me to pity him, and to wonder how so well-bred, Gentlemanly a Man as he once was, could degenerate into such a useless thing, as he now appear'd; yet, at the same time, it gave me most contemptible Thoughts of him, and made me often say, I was a Warning for all the Ladies of Europe, against marrying of FOOLS; a Man of Sence falls in the World, and gets-up again, and a Woman has some Chance for herself; but with a FOOL! Once fall, and ever undone; once in the Ditch, and die in the Ditch; once poor, and sure to starve.

But 'tis time to have done with him; once I had nothing to hope for, but see him again; now my only Felicity was, if possible, never to see him, and, above all, to keep him from seeing me; which as above, I took effectual Care of.

---

1 Conceive.

I was now return'd to *Paris*; my little *Son of Honour*, as I call'd him was left at—, where my last country Seat then was, and I came to *Paris*, at the Prince's Request; thither he came to me as soon as I arriv'd, and told me, he came to give me Joy of my Return, and to make his Acknowledgments, for that I had given him a SON: I thought indeed, he had been going to give me a Present, and so he did the next Day, but in what he said then, he only jested with me: He gave me his Company all the Evening; Supp'd with me about Midnight, and did me the Honour, as I then call'd it, to lodge me in his Arms all the Night, telling me in jest, that the best Thanks for a Son born, was giving the Pledge for another.

But as I hinted, so it was, the next Morning he laid me down, on my Toilet, a Purse with 300 Pistoles: I saw him lay it down, and understood what he meant, but I took no Notice of it, till I came to it (as it were) casually; then I gave a great Cry-out, and fell a-scolding in my Way, for he gave me all possible Freedom of Speech, on such Occasions: I told him, he was unkind; that he would never give me an Opportunity to ask him for any thing; and that he forc'd me to Blush, by being too much oblig'd, *and the like*; all which I knew was very agreeable to him; for as he was Bountiful, beyond Measure, so he was infinitely oblig'd by my being so backward to ask any Favours; and I was even with him, for I never ask'd him for a Farthing in my Life.

Upon this rallying him, he told me, I had either perfectly studied the Art of Humour, or else, what was the greatest Difficulty to others, was Natural to me; adding, That nothing cou'd be more obliging to a Man of Honour, than not to be soliciting and craving.

I told him, nothing cou'd be craving upon him; that he left no room for it; that I hop'd he did not give, merely to avoid the Trouble of being importun'd; I told him, he might depend upon it, that I should be reduc'd very low indeed, before I offer'd to disturb him that Way.

He said, a Man of Honour ought always to know what he ought to do; and as he did nothing but what he knew was reasonable, he gave me Leave to be free with him, if I wanted any thing; that he had too much Value for me, to deny me any thing, if I ask'd; but that it was infinitely agreeable to him to hear me say, that what he did, was to my Satisfaction.

We strain'd Compliments thus a great while, and as he had me in his Arms most Part of the Time, so upon all my Expressions of his Bounty to me, he put a Stop to me with his Kisses, and wou'd admit me to go on no farther.

I should in this Place mention, that this Prince was not a Subject of *France* tho' at that Time he resided at *Paris*, and was much at Court, where, I suppose, he had or expected some considerable Employment: But I mention it on this Account; that a few Days after this, he came to me, and told me, he was come to bring me not the most welcome News that ever I heard from him in his Life; I look'd at him, a little surpriz'd; but he return'd, Do not be uneasie, it is as unpleasant to me, as to you, but I come to consult with you about it, and see if it cannot be made a little easie to us both.

I seem'd still more concern'd, and surpriz'd; at last he said, it was, that he believ'd he should be oblig'd to go into *Italy*; which tho' otherwise it was very agreeable to him, yet his parting with me, made it a very dull thing but to think of.

I sat mute, as one Thunder-struck, for a good-while; and it presently occur'd to me, that I was going to lose him, which, indeed, I cou'd but ill bear the Thoughts of; and as he told me, I turn'd pale: What's the Matter? *said he, hastily*; I have surpriz'd you, indeed; and stepping to the Side-Board, fills a Dram of Cordial-Water,[1] (which was of his own bringing) and comes to me, Be not surpriz'd, *said he*, I'll go no-where without you; adding several other things so kind, as nothing could exceed it.

I might, indeed, turn pale, for I was very much surpriz'd at first, believing that this was, as it often happens in such Cases, only a Project to drop me, and break off an Amour, which he had now carried on so long; and a thousand Thoughts whirl'd about my Head in the few Moments while I was kept in suspence; (for they were but a few) I say, I was indeed, surpriz'd, and might, perhaps, look pale; but I was not in any Danger of Fainting, that I knew of.

However, it not a little pleas'd me, to see him so concern'd and anxious about me; but I stopp'd a little, when he put the Cordial to my Mouth, and taking the Glass in my Hand, *I said*, My Lord, your Words are infinitely more of a Cordial to me, than this Citron;[2] for as nothing can be a greater Affliction, than to lose you, so nothing can be a greater Satisfaction than the Assurance, that I shall not have that Misfortune.

He made me sit down, and sat down by me, and after saying a thousand kind things to me; he turns upon me, with a Smile,

---

1 Alcohol.
2 Brandy flavored with lemon-peel.

Why, will you venture yourself to *Italy* with me? *says he*; I stopp'd a-while, and then answer'd, that I wonder'd he would ask me that Question; for I would go any-where in the World, or all over the World, wherever he shou'd desire me, and give me the Felicity of his Company.

Then he enter'd into a long Account of the Occasion of his Journey, and how the King had Engag'd him to go, and some other Circumstances, which are not proper to enter into here; it being by no means proper to say anything, that might lead the Reader into the least Guess at the Person.

But to cut short this Part of the Story, and the History of our Journey, and Stay abroad, which would almost fill up a Volume of itself, I say, we spent all that Evening in chearful Consultations about the Manner of our Travelling; the Equipage and Figure he shou'd go in; and in what Manner I shou'd go: Several Ways were propos'd, but none seem'd feasible; till, at last, I told him, I thought it wou'd be so troublesome, so expensive and so publick, that it wou'd be many Ways inconvenient to him; and tho' it was a kind of Death to me, to lose him, yet that rather than so very much perplex his Affairs, I would submit to any-thing.

At the next Visit I fill'd his Head with the same Difficulties, and then, at last, came over him with a Proposal, that I wou'd stay in *Paris*, or where else he shou'd direct; and when I heard of his safe Arrival, wou'd come away by myself, and place myself as near as I cou'd.

This gave him no Satisfaction at-all; nor wou'd he hear any more of it; but if I durst venture myself, as he call'd it, such a Journey, he wou'd not lose the Satisfaction of my Company; and as for the Expence, that was not to be nam'd, neither, indeed, was there room to name it; for I found, that he travell'd at the KING'S Expence, as well for himself, as for all his Equipage; being upon a Piece of secret Service of the last Importance.

But after several Debates between ourselves, he came to this Resolution, *viz.* that he wou'd travel *Incognito*, and so he shou'd avoid all publick Notice, either of himself, or of who went with him; and that then he shou'd not only carry me with him, but have a perfect Leisure of enjoying my agreeable Company, *(as he was pleas'd to call it)* all the Way.

This was so obliging, that nothing cou'd be more; so upon this Foot, he immediately set to Work to prepare things for his Journey; and by his Directions, so did I too: But now I had a terrible Difficulty upon me, and which way to get over it, I knew not; and that was, in what Manner to take Care of what I had to leave behind me; I was Rich, as I have said, very Rich, and what to do with it, I knew not, nor who to leave in Trust, I knew not; I had no-body but *Amy*, in the World, and to travel without *Amy*, was very uncomfortable; or to leave all I had in the World with her, and if she miscarried, be ruin'd at once, was still a frightful Thought; for *Amy* might die, and whose Hands things might fall into, I knew not: This gave me great Uneasiness, and I knew not what to do; for I could not mention it to the Prince, lest he should see that I was richer than he thought I was.

But the Prince made all this easie to me; for in concerting Measures for our Journey, he started the thing himself, and ask'd me merrily one Evening, who I wou'd trust with all my Wealth, in my Absence?

My Wealth, my Lord, *said I*, except what I owe to your Goodness, is but small; but yet, that little I have, I confess, causes some Thoughtfulness; because I have no Acquaintance in *Paris*, that I dare trust with it, not any-body but my Woman, to leave in the House; and how to do without her upon the Road, I do not well know.

As to the Road, be not concern'd, *says the Prince*, I'll provide you Servants to your Mind; and as for your Woman, if you can trust her, leave her here, and I'll put you in a Way how to secure things, as well as if you were at Home: I bow'd, and told him, I cou'd not be put into better hands, than his own, and that therefore, I wou'd govern all my Measures by his Directions; so we talk'd no more of it that Night.

The next Day he sent me in a great Iron Chest, so large, that it was as much as six lusty Fellows could get up the Steps, into the House; and in this I put, indeed, all my Wealth; and for my Safety, he order'd a good honest ancient Man and his Wife, to be in the House with her, to keep her Company, and a Maid-Servant, and Boy; so that there was a good Family, and *Amy* was Madam, the Mistress of the House.

Things being thus secur'd, we set out *Incog.* as he call'd it; but we had two Coaches and Six Horses; two Chaises; and about eight Men-Servants on Horseback all very well Arm'd.

Never was Woman better us'd in this World, that went upon no other Account than I did; I had three Women-Servants to wait on me, one whereof was an old Madam—, who thorowly understood her Business, and manag'd every thing, as if she had been *Major Domo*; so I had no Trouble; they had one Coach to themselves, and the Prince and I in the other; only that sometimes, where he knew it necessary, I went into their Coach; and one particular Gentleman of the Retinue rode with him.

I shall say no more of the Journey, than that when we came to those frightful Mountains, the *Alps*; there was no travelling in our Coaches, so he order'd a Horse-Litter, but carried by Mules, to be provided for me, and himself went on Horseback; the Coaches went some other Way back to *Lyons*; then we had Coaches hir'd at *Turin*, which met us at *Susa*; so that we were accommodated again, and went by easie Journeys afterwards, to *Rome*, where his Business, *wherever it was*, call'd him to stay some time; and from thence to *Venice*.

He was as good as his Word, indeed; for I had the Pleasure of his Company, and in a word, engross'd his Conversation almost all the Way: He took Delight in showing me everything that was to be seen, and particularly, in telling me something of the History of every thing he show'd me.

What valuable Pains were here thrown away upon One, who he was sure, at last, to abandon with Regret! How below himself, did a Man of Quality, and of a thousand Accomplishments, behave in all this! 'Tis one of my Reasons for entering into this Part, which otherwise wou'd not be worth relating: Had I been a Daughter, or a Wife, of whom it might be said, that he had a just Concern in their Instruction, or Improvement, it had been an admirable Step; but all this to a Whore! to one who he carried with him upon no Account, that could be rationally agreeable; and none but to gratifie the meanest of humane Frailties: This was the Wonder of it.

But such is the Power of a vicious Inclination; Whoring was, in a Word, his Darling Crime; the worst Excursion[1] he made; for he was otherwise, one of the most excellent Persons in the World; no Passions; no furious Excursions; no ostentatious Pride; the most humble, courteous, affable Person, in the World; not an Oath; not an indecent Word, or the least Blemish in Behaviour, was to seen in all his Conversation, except as before excepted; and it has given me Occasion for many dark Reflections since; to look back and think, that I should be the Snare of such a Person's Life; that I should influence him to so much Wickedness; and that I should be the Instrument in the Hand of the Devil, to do him so much Prejudice.

We were near two Year upon this *Grand Tour*, as it may be call'd, during most of which, I resided at *Rome*, or at *Venice*, having only been twice at *Florence*, and once at *Naples*: I made

---

1 Departure from his otherwise virtuous character.

some very diverting and Useful Observations in all these Places; and particularly, of the Conduct of the Ladies; for I had Opportunity to converse very much among them, by the Help of the old Witch that travell'd with us; she had been at *Naples*, and at *Venice* and had liv'd in the former, several Years, where, as I found, she had liv'd but a loose Life, as indeed, the Women of *Naples* generally do;[1] and, in short, I found she was fully acquainted with all the intriguing Arts of that Part of the World.

Here my Lord bought me a little Female *Turkish* Slave, who being Taken at Sea by a *Malthese* Man of War, was brought in there; and of her I learnt the *Turkish* Language; their Way of Dressing and Dancing, and some *Turkish*, or rather *Moorish* Songs, of which I made Use, to my Advantage, on an extraordinary Occasion, some Years after, as you shall hear in its Place. I need not say I learnt *Italian* too, for I got pretty well Mistress of that, before I had been there a Year; and as I had Leisure enough, and lov'd the Language, I read all the Italian Books I cou'd come at.

I began to be so in Love with *Italy*, expecially with *Naples* and *Venice*, that I cou'd have been very well satisfied to have sent for *Amy*, and have taken up my Residence there for Life.

As to *Rome*, I did not like it at-all: The swarms of Ecclesiasticks of all Kinds, on one side, and the scoundrel Rabbles of the Common People, on the other, make *Rome* the unpleasantest Place in the World, to live in; the innumerable Number of Valets, Lacqueys, and other Servants, is such, that they us'd to say, that there are very few of the Common People in *Rome*, but what have been Footmen, or Porters, or Grooms to Cardinals, or Foreign Ambassadors: In a Word, they have an Air of sharping and couzening,[2] quarelling and scolding, upon their general Behaviour; and when I was there, the Footmen made such a Broil between two Great Families in Rome, about which of their Coaches (the Ladies being in the Coaches on either side,) shou'd give Way to t'other; that there was above thirty People wounded on both Sides; five or six kill'd outright; and both the Ladies frighted almost to Death.

But I have no-Mind to write the History of my Travels on this side of the World, at least, not now; it would be too full of Variety.

I must not, however, omit, that the Prince continued in all this

---

1 During the Renaissance, prostitution was legal in Naples and the city became synonymous with sexual decadence.
2 Cheating, deceitful.

Journey, the most kind, obliging Person to me, in the World, and so constant, that tho' we were in a Country, where 'tis well known all manner of Liberties are taken, I am yet well assur'd, he neither took the Liberty he knew he might have, or so much as desir'd it.

I have often thought of this Noble Person, on that Account; had he been but half so true, so faithful and constant to the Best Lady in the World, I mean his Princess; how glorious a Virtue had it been in him? And how free had he been from those just Reflections which touch'd him, in her behalf, when it was too late.

We had some very agreeable Conversations upon this Subject: and once he told me, with a kind of more than ordinary Concern upon his Thoughts, that he was greatly beholden to me for taking this hazardous and difficult Journey; for that I had kept him Honest; I look'd up in his is Face, and colour'd red as Fire: Well, well, *says he*, do not let that surprise you; I do say, you have kept me Honest: My Lord, *said I*, 'tis not for me to explain your Words, but I wish I cou'd turn 'em my own Way; I hope, *says I*, and believe, we are both as Honest as we can be, in our Circumstances; ay, ay, *says he*, and honester than I doubt I shou'd have been, if you had not been with me; I cannot say but if you had not been here, I shou'd have wander'd among the gay World here, in *Naples* and in *Venice* too; for 'tis not such a Crime here, as 'tis in other Places; but I protest, *says he*, I have not touch'd a Woman in *Italy*, but yourself; and more than that, I have not so much as had any Desire to it; so that I say, you have kept me Honest.

I was silent, and was glad that he interrupted me, or kept me from speaking, with kissing me, for really I knew not what to say: I was once going to say that if his Lady the Princess, had been with him, she wou'd, doubtless, have had the same influence on his Virtue, with infinitely more Advantage to him; but I consider'd this might give him Offence; and besides, such things might have been dangerous to the Circumstance I stood in, so it pass'd off: But I must confess, I saw that he was quite another Man, as to Women, than I understood he had always been before; and it was a particular satisfaction to me, that I was thereby convinc'd that what he said, was true, and that he was, as I may say, all my Own.

I was with-Child again in this Journey, and Lay-in at *Venice*, but was not so happy as before; I brought him another Son, and a very fine Boy it was, but it liv'd not above two Months; nor, after the first Touches of Affection (which are usual, I believe, to all Mothers) were over, was I sorry the Child did not live, the necessary Difficulties attending it in our travelling, being consider'd.

After these several Perambulations, my Lord told me, his Business began to close, and we wou'd think of returning to *France*; which I was very glad of, but principally on Account of my Treasure I had there, which, as you have heard, was very considerable: It is true, I had Letters very frequently from my Maid *Amy*, with Accounts, that every thing was very safe, and that was very much to my Satisfaction: However, as the Prince's Negociations were at an End, and he was oblig'd to return, I was very glad to go; so we return'd from *Venice* to *Turin*; and in the Way, I saw the famous City of *Milan*; from *Turin*, we went over the Mountains again, as before, and our Coaches met us at *Pont a Voisin*, between *Chamberry* and *Lyons*; and so, by easie Journeys, we arriv'd safely at *Paris*, having been absent about two Years, wanting about eleven Days, as above.

I found the little Family we left, just as we left them; and *Amy* cry'd for Joy, when she saw me, and I almost did the same.

The Prince took his Leave of me the Night before; for as he told me, he knew he shou'd be met upon the Road by several Persons of Quality, and perhaps, by the Princess herself; so we lay at two different Inns that Night, lest some shou'd come quite to the Place, as indeed, it happen'd.

After this, I saw him not, for above twenty Days, being taken-up in his Family, and also with Business; but he sent me his Gentleman, to tell me the Reason of it; and bid me not be uneasie; and that satisfied me effectually.

In all this Affluence of my good Fortune, I did not forget that I had been Rich and Poor once already, alternately; and that I ought to know, that the Circumstances I was now in, were not to be expected to last always; that I had one Child, and expected another; and if I bred often, it wou'd something impair me in the Great Article that supported my Interest, I mean, what he call'd Beauty; that as that declin'd, I might expect the Fire wou'd abate, and the Warmth with which I was now so carress'd, wou'd cool, and in time, like the other Mistresses of Great Men, I might be dropt again; and that, therefore, it was my Business to take Care that I shou'd fall as softly as I cou'd.

I say, I did not forget, therefore, to make as good Provision for myself, as if I had had nothing to have subsisted on, but what I now gain'd; whereas I had not less than ten Thousand Pounds, as I said above, which I had amass'd, or secur'd, rather out of the Ruins of my faithful Friend, the Jeweller; and which, he little thinking of what was so near him when he went out, told me, tho' in a kind of a Jest, was all my own, if he was knock'd o' th' Head; and which, upon that Title, I took Care to preserve.

My greatest Difficulty now, was, how to secure my Wealth, and to keep what I had got; for I had greatly added to this Wealth, by the generous Bounty of the Prince—, and the more, by the private retir'd Manner of Living, which he had rather desir'd for Privacy, than Parsimony; for he supply'd me for a more magnificent Way of Life than I desir'd, if it had been proper.

I shall cut short the History of this prosperous Wickedness, with telling you I brought him a third Son, within little more than eleven Months after our Return from *Italy*; that now I liv'd a little more openly, and went by a particular Name which he gave me Abroad; but which I must omit; *viz.* the Countess *de*—, and had Coaches, and Servants, suitable to the Quality he had given me the Appearance of; and which is more than usually happens in such Cases, this held eight Years from the Beginning; during which Time, as I had been very faithful to him, so, I must say, as above, that I believe he was so separated[1] to me, that whereas he usually had two or three Women, which he kept privately, he had not in all that Time meddled with any of them, but that I had so perfectly engross'd him, that he dropt them all; not, perhaps, that he sav'd much by it, for I was a very chargeable Mistress to him, that I must acknowledge; but it was all owing to his particular Affection to me, not to my Extravagance; for, as I said, he never gave me leave to ask him for any thing, but pour'd in his Favours and Presents faster than I expected, and so fast, as I cou'd not have the Assurance to make the least Mention of desiring more.

Nor do I speak this of my own Guess, I mean, about his Constancy to me, and his quitting all other Women; but the old *Harradan*, as I may call her, who he made the Guide of our Travelling, and who was a strange old Creature, told me a Thousand Stories of his Gallantry, as she call'd it, and how, as he had no less than three Mistresses at one time, and as I found, all of her procuring,[2] he had of a sudden, dropt them all, and that he was entirely lost to both her and them; that they did believe he had fallen into some new Hands, but she could never hear who, or where, till he sent for her to go this Journey; and then the old Hag complimented me upon his Choice, That she did not wonder I had so engross'd him; so much Beauty, *&c.* and there she stopt.

Upon the whole, I found by her, what was, you may be sure, to my particular Satisfaction, *viz.* that, as above, I had him all my own.

But the highest Tide has its Ebb; and in all things of this Kind,

---

1 Devoted.

2 Defoe's choice of word here is telling. Procuring was what bawds were understood to do and a bawd was often called a "procuress."

there is a Reflux which sometimes also is more impetuously violent than the first Aggression: My Prince was a Man of a vast Fortune, tho' no Sovereign, and therefore there was no Probability that the Expence of keeping a Mistress could be injurious to him, as to his Estate; he had also several Employments, both out of *France*, as well as in it; for, as above, I say, he was not a Subject of *France*, tho' he liv'd in that Court: He had a Princess, a Wife, with whom he had liv'd several years, and a Woman *(so the Voice of Fame reported)* the most valuable of her Sex; of Birth equal to him, if not superiour, and Fortune proportionable; but in Beauty, Wit, and a thousand good Qualities, superiour not to most Women, but even to all her Sex; and as to her Virtue, the Character, which was most justly her due, was that of, not only the best of Princesses, but even the best of Women.

They liv'd in the utmost Harmony, as with such a Princess it was impossible to be otherwise; but yet the Princess was not insensible that her Lord had his *Foibles*; that he did make some Excursions; and particularly, that he had one Favourite Mistress which sometimes engross'd him more than she (the Princess) cou'd wish, or be easily satisfied with: However, she was so good, so generous, so truly kind a Wife, that she never gave him any Uneasiness on this Account; except so much as must arise from his Sence of her bearing the Affront of it with such Patience, and such a profound Respect for him, as was in itself enough to have reform'd him, and did sometimes shock his generous Mind, so as to keep him at Home, as I may call it, a great-while together; and it was not long before I not only perceiv'd it by his Absence, but really got a Knowledge of the Reason of it, and once or twice he even acknowleg'd it to me.

It was a Point that lay not in me to manage; I made a kind of Motion, once or twice, to him, to leave me, and keep himself to her, as he ought by the Laws and rites of Matrimony to do, and argued the Generosity of the Princess to him, to perswade him; but I was a Hypocrite; for had I prevail'd with him really to be honest, I had lost him, which I could not bear the Thoughts of; and he might easily see I was not in earnest; one time in particular, when I took upon me to talk at this rate, I found when I argued so much for the Virtue and Honour, the Birth, and above all, the generous Usage he found in the Person of the Princess, with respect to his private Amours, and how it should prevail upon him, *&c.* I found it began to affect him, and he return'd, *And do you indeed*, says he, *perswade me to leave you? Would you have me think you sincere?* I look'd up in his Face, smiling, *Not for* *any other Favourite,* my Lord, said I; *that wou'd break my Heart; but for Madam, the Princess!* said I, and then I could say no more, Tears follow'd, and I sat silent a-while: Well, *said he,* if ever I do leave you, it shall be on the Virtuous Account; it shall be for the Princess, I assure you it shall be for no other woman; *That's enough, my Lord,* said I, *There I ought to submit; and while I am assur'd it shall be for no other Mistress, I promise Your Highness, I will not repine;* or that, if I do, *it shall be a silent Grief, it shall not interrupt your Felicity.*

All this while I said I knew not what, and said what I was no more able to do, than he was able to leave me; which, at that time, he own'd he cou'd not do, no, not for the Princess herself.

But another Turn of Affairs determin'd this Matter; for the Princess was taken very ill, and in the Opinion of all her Physicians, very dangerously so; in her Sickness she desir'd to speak with her Lord, and to take her Leave of him: At this grievous Parting, she said so many passionate kind Things to him; lamented that she had left him no Children; she had had three, but they were dead; hinted to him, that it was one of the chief things which gave her Satisfaction in Death, as to this World; that she should leave him room to have Heirs to his Family, by some Princess that should supply her Place; with all Humility, but a Christian Earnestness, recommended to him to do Justice to such a Princess, whoever it should be, from whom, *to be sure,* he would expect Justice; that is to say, to keep to her singly, according to the solemnest Part of the Marriage-Covenant; humbly ask'd his Highness Pardon, if she had any way offended him; and appealing to Heaven, before whose Tribunal she was to appear, that she had never violated her Honour, or her Duty to him; and praying to Jesus, and the Blessed Virgin, for his Highness; and thus with the most moving, and most passionate Expressions of her Affection to him, took her last Leave of him, and died the next Day.

This Discourse from a Princess so valuable in herself, and so dear to him, and the Loss of her following so immediately after, made such deep Impressions on him, that he look'd back with Detestation upon the former Part of his Life; grew melancholy and reserv'd; chang'd his Society; and much of the general Conduct of his Life; resolv'd on a Life regulated most strictly by the Rules of Virtue, and Piety; and in a word, was quite another Man.

The first Part of his Reformation, was a Storm upon me; for about ten Days after the Princess's Funeral, he sent a Message to me by his Gentleman, intimating, tho' in very civil Terms, and with a Short Preamble, or Introduction, that he desir'd I wou'd not take it ill that he was oblig'd to let me know, that *he could see me no more*: His Gentleman told me a long Story of the new Regulation of Life his Lord had taken up, and that he had been so afflicted for the Loss of his Princess, that he thought it would either shorten his Life, or he wou'd retire into some Religious House, to end his Days in Solitude.

I need not direct any-body to suppose how I receiv'd this News; I was indeed, exceedingly surpriz'd at it, and had much a-do to support myself, when the first Part of it was deliver'd; tho' the Gentleman deliver'd his Errand with great Respect, and with all the Regard to me, that he was able, and with a great deal of Ceremony; also telling me how much he was concern'd to bring me such a Message.

But when I heard the Particulars of the Story at large, and especially, that of the Lady's Discourse to the Prince, a little before her Death, I was fully satisfied; I knew very well he had done nothing but what any Man must do, that had a true Sence upon him of the Justice of the Princess's Discourse to him, and of the Necessity there was of his altering his Course of Life, if he intended to be either a Christian, or an honest Man: I say, when I heard this, I was perfectly easie; I confess it was a Circumstance that it might be reasonably expected shou'd have wrought something also upon me: I that had so much to reflect upon more, than the Prince; that had now no more Temptation of Poverty, or of the powerful Motive, which *Amy* us'd with me, namely, *Comply and live; deny and starve*; I say, I that had no Poverty to introduce Vice, but was grown not only well supply'd but Rich and not only Rich, but was very Rich; in a word, richer than I knew how to think of; for the Truth of it was, that thinking of it sometimes almost distracted me, for want of knowing how to dispose of it, and for fear of losing it all again by some Cheat or Trick, not knowing any-body that I could commit the Trust of it to.

Besides I should add at the Close of this Affair, that the Prince did not, as I may say, turn me off rudely, and with Disgust; but with all the Decency and Goodness peculiar to himself, and that could consist with a Man reform'd, and struck with the Sence of his having abus'd so good a Lady as his late Princess had been; nor did he send me away empty, but did every thing like himself; and in particular, order'd his Gentleman to pay the Rent of the House, and all the Expence of his two Sons; and to tell me how they were taken Care of, and where; and also, that I might, at all times, inspect the Usage they had, and if I dislik'd any thing, it should be rectified; and having thus finish'd every thing, he retir'd to *Lorrain*, or somewhere that Way, where he had an Estate, and I never heard of him more, I mean, not as a Mistress.

Now I was at Liberty to go to any Part of the World, and take Care of my Money myself: The first thing that I resolv'd to do, was to go directly to *England*, for there, I thought, being among my Countryfolks, (for I esteem'd myself an *English-Woman*, tho' I was born in *France*,) but there I say, I thought I cou'd better manage things, than in *France*, at least, that I would be in less Danger of being circumvented and deceiv'd; but how to get away with such a Treasure as I had with me, was a difficult Point, and what I was greatly at a Loss about.

There was a *Dutch* Merchant in *Paris*, that was a Person of great Reputation for a Man of Substance, and of Honesty, but I had no manner of Acquaintance with him, nor did I know how to get acquainted with him, so as to discover my Circumstances to him; but at last I employ'd my Maid *Amy*, such I must be allow'd to call her, (notwithstanding what has been said of her) because she was in the Place of a Maid-Servant; I say, I employ'd my Maid *Amy* to go to him, and she got a Recommendation to him from somebody else, I knew not who; so that she got Access to him well enough.

But now was my Case as bad as before; for when I came to him, what cou'd I do? I had Money and Jewels, to a vast Value, and I might leave all those with him; that I might indeed, do; and so I might with several other Merchants in *Paris*, who wou'd give me Bills for it, payable at *London*, but then I ran a Hazard of my Money; and I had no-body at *London* to send the Bills to, and so to stay till I had an Account that they were accepted: for I had not one Friend in *London*, that I cou'd have recourse to, so that, indeed, I knew not what to do.

In this Case I had no Remedy, but that I must trust somebody; so I sent *Amy* to this *Dutch* Merchant, as I said above; he was a little surpriz'd when *Amy* came to him, and talk'd to him of remitting a Sum of about 12000 Pistoles to *England*, and began to think she came to put some cheat upon him; but when he found that *Amy* was but a Servant, and that I came to him myself, the Case was alter'd presently.

When I came to him myself, I presently saw such a plainness in his Dealing, and such Honesty in his Countenance, that I made no Scruple to tell him my whole Story, *viz.* That I was a Widow; that I had some Jewels to dispose of, and also some

Money, which I had a-mind to send to *England*, and to follow there myself; but being but a Woman, and having no Correspondence in *London*, or any-where else, I knew not what to do, or how to secure my Effects.

He dealt very candidly with me, but advis'd me, when he knew my Case so particularly, to take Bills upon *Amsterdam*, and to go that Way to *England*; for that I might lodge my Treasure in the Bank there, in the most secure Manner in the World; and that there he cou'd recommend me to a Man who perfectly understood Jewels, and would deal faithfully with me I the disposing them.

I thank'd him, but scrupled very much the travelling so far in a strange Country, and especially with such a Treasure about me; that whether known, or conceal'd, I did not know how to venture with it: Then he told me, he wou'd try to dispose of them there, that is, at *Paris*, and convert them into Money, and so get me Bills for the whole; and in a few Days he brought a *Jew* to me, who pretended[1] to buy the Jewels.

As soon as the *Jew* saw the Jewels, I saw my Folly; and it was ten thousand to one but I had been ruin'd, and perhaps, put to Death in as cruel a Manner as possible; and I was put in such a Fright by it, that I was once upon the Point of flying for my Life, and leaving the Jewels and Money too, in the Hands of the *Dutchman*, without any Bills, or any thing else; the Case was thus:

As soon as the *Jew* saw the Jewels, he falls a jabbering in *Dutch*, or *Portuguese*, to the Merchant, and I cou'd presently perceive that they were in some great Surprize, both of them; the *Jew* held up his Hands, look'd at me with some Horrour, then talk'd *Dutch* again, and put himself into a thousand Shapes, twisting his Body, and wringing up his Face this Way, and that Way, in his Discourse; stamping with his Feet, and throwing abroad his Hands, as if he was not in a Rage only, but in a meer Fury; then he wou'd turn, and give a Look at me, like the Devil; I thought I never saw anything so frightful in my Life.[2]

At length I put in a Word; Sir, *says I*, to the *Dutch* Merchant, What is all this Discourse to my Business? What is this Gentleman in all these Passions about? I wish, if he is to treat with me, he wou'd speak, that I may understand him; or if you have Busi-

---

1 Expressed interest in.
2 Roxana's descriptions here draw on ancient anti-semitic stereotypes of Jews as agents of the Devil, whose demonic affiliations were often thought to be visible in their physical appearances.

ness of your own between you, that is to be done first, let me withdraw, and I'll come again when you are at leisure.

No, no, Madam, *says the Dutchman*, very kindly, you must not go, all our Discourse is about you, and your Jewels, and you shall hear it presently, it concerns you very much, I assure you: Concern me, *says I*, what can it concern me so much, as to put this Gentleman into such Agonies? And what makes him give such Devil's Looks as he does? Why he looks as if he wou'd devour me.

The *Jew* understood me presently, continuing in a kind of Rage and spoke in *French*, Yes, Madam, it does concern you much, very much, very much, repeating the Words, shaking his Head, and then turning to the *Dutchman*, Sir, *says he*, pray tell her what is the Case; no, *says the Merchant*, not yet, let us talk a little farther of it by ourselves; upon which, they withdrew into another Room, where still they talk'd very high, but in a Language I did not understand: I began to be a little surpriz'd at what the *Jew* had said, you may be sure, and eager to know what he meant, and was very impatient till the *Dutch* Merchant came back, and that so impatient, that I call'd one of his Servants to let him know, I desir'd to speak with him; when he came in, I ask'd his Pardon for being so impatient, but told him, I cou'd not be easie, till he had told me what the Meaning of all this was: Why Madam, *says the Dutch Merchant*, in short, the Meaning is, what I am surpriz'd at too: This Man is a *Jew*, and understands Jewels perfectly well, and that was the Reason I sent for him, to dispose of them to him, for you; but as soon as he saw them, he knew the Jewels very distinctly, and flying out in a Passion, as you see he did; told me, in short, that they were the very Parcel of Jewels which the *English* Jeweller had about him, who was robb'd going to *Versailles*, (about eight Years ago) to show them the Prince *d'*—, and that it was for these very Jewels that the poor Gentleman was murther'd; and he is in all this Agony to make me ask you, how you came by them; and he says, you ought to be charg'd with the Robbery and Murther, and put to the Question,[1] to discover who were the Persons that did it, that they might be brought to Justice: While he said this, the *Jew* came impudently back, into the Room, without calling, which a little surpriz'd me again.

The Dutch Merchant spoke pretty good *English*, and he knew that the *Jew* did not understand *English* at-all; so he told me the latter Part, when the *Jew* came into the Room, in *English*; at which

---

1 Interrogated.

I smil'd, which put the *Jew* into his mad Fit again, and shaking his Head, and making his Devil's Faces again, he seem'd to threaten me for Laughing; saying in *French*, this was an Affair I shou'd have little Reason to laugh at, and the like; at this I laugh'd again, and flouted him, letting him see, that I scorn'd him; and turning to the *Dutch* Merchant, *Sir*, says I, *That those Jewels were belonging to Mr.—, the* English *Jeweller*, naming his Name readily, *in that*, says I, *this Person is right, but that I shou'd be question'd* how I came to have them, *is a Token of his Ignorance; which, however, he might have manag'd with a little more good Manners, till I had told him who I am; and both he, and you too, will be more easie in that Part, when I should tell you, that I am the unhappy Widow of that Mr.—, who was so barbarously murther'd going to* Versailles; *and that he was not robb'd of those Jewels, but of others; Mr.— having left those behind him, with me, lest he should be robb'd; had I, Sir, come otherwise by them, I should not have been weak enough to have expos'd them to Sale here, where the thing was done, but have carried them farther off.*

This was an agreeable Surprize to the *Dutch* Merchant, who being an honest Man himself, believ'd every thing I said, which indeed, being really and literally true, except the Deficiency of my Marriage, I spoke with such an unconcern'd Easiness, that it might plainly be seen, that I had no Guilt upon me, as the *Jew* suggested.

The *Jew* was confounded when he heard that I was the *Jeweller's Wife*; but as I had rais'd his Passion, with saying, he look'd at me with a Devil's Face, he studied Mischief in his Heart, and answer'd, *That should not serve my Turn*; so call'd the *Dutchman* out again, when he told him, that he resolv'd to prosecute this Matter farther.

There was one kind Chance in this Affair, which indeed, was my Deliverance, and that was, that the Fool cou'd not restrain his Passion, but must let it fly to the *Dutch* Merchant; to whom, when they withdrew a second time, as above, he told that he would bring a Process against me for the Murther; and that it should cost me dear, for using him at that rate; and *away he went*, desiring the *Dutch* Merchant to tell him when I wou'd be there again: Had he suspected, that the *Dutchman* wou'd have communicated the Particulars to me, he wou'd never have been so foolish as to have mention'd that Part to him.

But the Malice of his Thoughts anticipated him, and the *Dutch* Merchant was so good, as to give me an Account of his Design, which indeed, was wicked enough in its Nature; but to me it would have been worse, than otherwise it wou'd to another; for upon Examination, I cou'd not have prov'd myself to be the Wife of the Jeweller, so the Suspicion might have been carried on with the better Face; and then I shou'd also, have brought all his Relations in *England* upon me; who finding by the Proceedings, that I was not his Wife, but a Mistress, or in *English*, a Whore, wou'd immediately have laid Claim to the Jewels, as I had own'd them to be his.

This thought immediately rush'd into my Head, as soon as the *Dutch* merchant had told me, what wicked things were in the Head of that curs'd *Jew*; and the Villain *(for so I must call him)* convinc'd the *Dutch* Merchant that he was in earnest, by an Expression which shew'd the rest of his Design, and that was a Plot to get the rest of the Jewels into his Hand.

When first he hinted to the *Dutch*man, that the Jewels were such a Man's, meaning my Husband's, he made wonderful Explanations on account of their having been conceal'd so long; where must they have lain? And what was the Woman that brought them? And that she, meaning me, ought to be immediately apprehended, and put into the Hands of Justice; and this was the time that, as I said, he made such horrid Gestures, and look'd at me so like a Devil.

The Merchant hearing him talk at that rate, and seeing him in earnest, said to him, Hold your Tongue a little, this is a thing of Consequence; if it be so, let you and I go into the next Room and consider of it there; and so they withdrew, and left me.

Here, as before, I was uneasie and call'd him out, and having heard how it was, gave him that Answer, *that I was his Wife*, or Widow, which the malicious *Jew* said *shou'd not serve my turn*; and then it was, that the *Dutch*man call'd him out a again; and in this time of his withdrawing, the Merchant finding, as above, that he was really in earnest, counterfeited a little to be of his Mind, and enter'd into Proposals with him for the thing itself.

In this they agreed to go to an Advocate, or Council, for Directions how to proceed, and to meet again the next Day, against which time the Merchant was to appoint me to come again with the Jewels, in order to sell them: *No*, says the Merchant, *I will go farther with her than so; I will desire her to leave the Jewels with me, to show to another Person, in order get the better Price for them: That's right*, says the *Jew*, and *I'll engage she shall never be mistress of them again; they shall either be seiz'd by us*, says he, *in the King's Name, or she shall be glad to give them up to us, to prevent her being put to the Torture.*

The Merchant said Yes to every thing he offer'd, and they

agreed to meet the next Morning about it, and I was to be perswaded to leave the Jewels with him, and come to them the next
Day, at four a-Clock, in order to make a good Bargain for them;
and on these conditions they parted; but the honest *Dutchman*,
fill'd with Indignation at the barbarous Design, came directly to
me, and told me the whole Story; and now, madam, says he, *you
are to consider immediately what you have to do.*

I told him, if I was sure to have Justice, I would not fear all that
such a Rogue cou'd do to me; but how such things were carried
on in *France* I knew not; I told him the greatest Difficulty would
be to prove our Marriage, for that it was done in *England*, and in
a remote Part of *England* too, and which was worse, it would be
hard to produce authentick vouchers of it because we were
Married in Private: *But as to the Death of your Husband*, Madam,
what can be said to that? said he; *nay*, said I, *what can they say to
it?* In *England*, added I, if they wou'd offer such an Injury to any
one, they must prove the Fact, or give just Reason for their Suspicions; that my Husband was Murther'd, that everyone knows;
but that he was robb'd, or of what, or how much, that none
knows, no, not myself; and why was I not question'd for it then?
I have liv'd in *Paris* ever since, liv'd publickly, and no Man had yet
the Impudence to suggest such a thing of me.

I am fully satisfied of that, *says the Merchant*; but as this is a
Rogue, who will stick at nothing, what can we say? and who
knows what he may swear? Suppose he should swear, that he
knows your Husband had those particular Jewels with him the
Morning when he went out, and that he shew'd them to him, to
consider their Value, and what Price he should ask the Prince
de— for them.

Nay, by the same Rule, *said I*, he may swear, that I murther'd
my Husband, if he finds it for his Turn: That's true, *said he*; and
if he shou'd, I do not see what cou'd save you; but added, I have
found out his more immediate Design; his Design is to have you
carried to the *Chatellette*,[1] that the Suspicion may appear just; and
then to get the Jewels out of your Hands, if possible; then, at last,
to drop the Prosecution, on your consenting to quit the Jewels to
him; and how you will do to avoid this, is the Question, which I
would have you consider of.

My Misfortune Sir, *said I*, is, that I have no Time to consider,

---

1 A building housing both a prison and law courts, much like the Old
Bailey and Newgate.

and I have no Person to consider with, or advise about it; I find, that Innocence may be oppress'd by such an impudent Fellow as this; he that does not value a Perjury, has any Man's Life at his Mercy; but Sir, *said I*, is the Justice such here, that while I may be in the Hands of the Publick, and under Prosecution, he may get hold of my Effects, and get my Jewels into his Hands?

I don't know, *says he*, what may be done in that Case; but if not he, if the Court of Justice shou'd get hold of them, I do not know but you may find it as difficult to get them out of their Hands again, and, at least, it may cost you half as much as they are worth; so I think it would be a much better Way, to prevent their coming at them at-all.

But what Course can I take to do that, *says I*, now they have got Notice, that I have them? If they get me into their Hands, they will oblige me to produce them, or perhaps, sentence me to Prison till I do.

Nay, *says he*, as this Brute says too, put you to the Question, that is, to the Torture, on Pretence of making you confess who were the Murtherers of your Husband.

Confess! s*aid I*; how can I confess what I know nothing of?

If they come to have you to the Rack, *said he*, they will make you confess you did it yourself, whether you did it or no, and then you are as cast.[1]

The very word Rack frighted me to Death almost, and I had no Spirit left in me: Did it myself! s*aid I*; that's impossible!

No, Madam, *says he*, 'tis far from impossible; the most innocent People in the World have been forc'd to confess themselves Guilty of what they never heard of, much less, had any Hand it.

What then must I do? *said I*; what wou'd you advise me to?

Why, *says he*, I wou'd advise you to be gone; you intended to go away in four or five Days, and you may as well go in two Days; and if you can do so, I shall manage it so, that he shall not suspect your being gone, for several Days after: then he told me, how the Rogue wou'd have me order'd to bring the Jewels the next Day, for Sale; and that then he wou'd have me apprehended; how he had made the *Jew* believe he wou'd join with him in his Design; and that he [the Merchant] wou'd get the Jewels into his Hands: Now, *says the Merchant*, I shall give you Bills for the Money you desir'd, immediately, and such as shall not fail of being paid; take your Jewels with you, and go this very Evening to *St. Germains en*

---

1 Roxana's fate is sealed.

Lay; I'll send a Man thither with you, and from thence, he shall guide you to-Morrow, to *Roan*,[1] where there lies a Ship of mine, just ready to sail for *Rotterdam*; you shall have your Passage in that Ship, on my Account, and I will send Orders for him to sail as soon as you are on Board, and a Letter to my Friend at *Rotterdam*, to Entertain and take Care of you.

This was too kind an Offer for me, as things stood, not to be accepted, and be thankful for; and as to going away, I had prepar'd every thing for parting; so that I had little to do, but to go back, and take two or three Boxes and Bundles, and such things, and my Maid *Amy*, and be gone.

Then the Merchant told me the Measures he had resolv'd to take to delude the *Jew*, while I made my Escape, which were very well contriv'd indeed: FIRST, *said he*, when he come to-Morrow, I shall tell him, that I propos'd to you, to leave the Jewels with me, as we agreed; but that you said, you wou'd come and bring them in the Afternoon, so that we must stay for you till four a-Clock; but then, at that time, I will show a Letter from you, as if just come in, wherein you shall excuse your not coming; for that some Company came to visit you, and prevented you; but that you desire me to take Care that the Gentleman be ready to buy your Jewels; and that you will come to Morrow, at the same Hour, without fail.

When to-Morrow is come, we shall wait at the Time, but you not appearing, I shall seem most dissatisfied, and wonder what can be the Reason; and so we shall agree to go the next Day to get out a Process against you; but the next Day, in the Morning I'll send to give him Notice, that you have been at my House, but he not being there, have made another Appointment, and that I desire to speak with him; when he comes, I'll tell him, you appear perfectly blind, as to your Danger; and that you appear'd much disappointed that he did not come, tho' you cou'd not meet the Night before; and oblig'd me to have him here to-Morrow at three a-Clock; *when to-Morrow comes*, says he, *you shall send word, that you are taken so ill, that you cannot come out for that Day; but that you will not fail the next Day; and the next Day you shall neither come or send, nor let us ever hear any more of you; for by that time you shall be in* Holland, *if you please.*

I cou'd not but approve all his Measures, seeing they were so well contriv'd, and in so friendly a Manner, for my Benefit; and as he seem'd to be so very sincere, I resolv'd to put my Life in his

---

1 Rouen, a port city on France's northern coast.

Hands: Immediately I went to my Lodgings, and sent away *Amy* with such Bundles as I had prepar'd for my Travelling; I also sent several Parcels of my fine Furniture to the Merchant's House, to be laid up for me, and bringing the Key of the Lodgings with me, I came back to his House: Here we finish'd our Matters of Money; and I deliver'd into his Hands seven Thousand eight Hundred Pistoles in Bills and Money; a Copy of an Assignment on the Town-House in *Paris*, for 4000 Pistoles, at *3 per Cent.* Interest, attested; and a Procuration[1] for receiving the Interest half-yearly; but the Original I kept myself.

I cou'd have trusted all I had with him, for he was perfectly honest, and had not the least View of doing me any Wrong; indeed, after it was so apparent that he had, as it were, sav'd my Life, or at least, sav'd me from being expos'd and ruin'd; I say, after this, how cou'd I doubt him in any thing?

When I came to him, he had every-thing ready as I wanted, and as he had propos'd; as to my Money, he gave me first of all an accepted Bill, payable at *Rotterdam*, for 4000 Pistoles, and drawn from *Genoa* upon a Merchant at Rotterdam, payable to a Merchant at *Paris*, and endors'd by him to my Merchant; this he assur'd me wou'd be punctually paid, and so it was, to a Day; the rest I had in other Bills of Exchange, drawn by himself upon other Merchants in *Holland*: Having secur'd my Jewels too, as well as I cou'd, he sent me away the same Evening in a Friend's Coach, which he had procur'd for me, to *St. Germains*, and the next Morning to *Roan*; he also sent a Servant of his own, on Horseback, with me, who provided every thing for me and who carried his Orders to the Captain of the Ship, which lay about three Miles below *Roan*, in the River, and by his Directions I went immediately on Board: the third Day after I was on Board, the Ship went away, and we were out at Sea the next Day after that; and thus I took my leave of *France*, and got clear of an ugly Business, which, had it gone on, might have ruin'd me, and sent me back as Naked to *England*, as I was a little before I left it.

And now *Amy* and I were at Leisure to look upon the Mischiefs that we had escap'd; and had I had any Religion, or any Sence of a Supreme Power managing, directing, and governing, in both Causes and Events in this World, such a Case as this wou'd have given any-body room to have been very thankful to the Power who had not only put such a Treasure into my Hand,

---

1 Formal order that Roxana receive the interest she describes.

but given me such an Escape from the Ruin that threaten'd me; but I had none of those things about me; I had indeed, a grateful Sence upon my Mind of the generous Friendship of my Deliverer, the *Dutch* Merchant; by whom I was so faithfully serv'd, and by whom, as far as relates to second Causes, I was preserv'd from Destruction.

I say, I had a grateful Sence upon my Mind, of his Kindness and Faithfullness to me, and I resolv'd to show him some Testimony of it, as soon as I came to the end of my Rambles, for I was yet but in a State of Uncertainty, and sometimes that gave me a little Uneasiness too; I had Paper indeed, for my Money, and he had shew'd himself very good to me, in conveying me away, as above: But I had not seen the End of things yet; for unless the Bills were paid, I might still be a great Loser by my *Dutchman*, and he might, perhaps, have contriv'd all that Affair to the *Jew*, to put me into a Fright, and get me to run away, and that, as if it were to save my Life; that if the Bills should be refus'd, I was cheated, with a Witness, and the Like; but these were but surmises, and indeed, were perfectly without Cause; for the honest Man acted as honest Men always do; with an upright and disinterested Principle; and with a Sincerity not often to be found in the World; what Gain he made by the Exchange, was just, and was nothing but what was his Due, and was in the Way of his Business; but otherwise he made no Advantage of me at-all.

When I pass'd the Ship between *Dover* and *Calais*, and saw Beloved *England* once more under my View; *England*, which I counted my Native Country; being the Place where I was bred up in, tho' not born there; a strange kind of Joy possess'd my Mind, and I had such a longing Desire to be there, that I would have given the Master of the Ship twenty Pistoles to have stood-over, and set me on shore in the *Downs*; and when he told me he cou'd not do it, that is, that he durst not do it, if I wou'd have given him an hundred Pistoles, I secretly wish'd, that a Storm wou'd rise, that might drive the Ship over to the Coast of *England*, whether they wou'd or not, that I might be set on Shore any-where upon *English* Ground.

This wicked Wish had not been out of my Thoughts above two or three Hours, but the Master steering away to the North, as was his Course to do, we lost Sight of Land on that Side, and only had the *Flemish* Shore in View on our Right-hand, or as the Seamen call it, the Starboard-Side; and then with the Loss of the Sight, the Wish for Landing in *England*, abated; and I consider'd how foolish it was to wish myself out of the Way of my Business;

that if I had been on Shore in *England,* I must go back to *Holland,* on account of my Bills, which were so considerable, and I having no Correspondence there, that I cou'd not have manag'd it, without going myself: But we had not been out of Sight of *England* many Hours, before the Weather began to change, the Winds whistl'd, and made a Noise, and the Seamen said to one-another, that it wou'd Blow-hard at Night: It was then about two Hours before Sun-set, and we were pass'd by *Dunkirk,*[1] and I think they said we were in Sight of Ostend;[2] but then the Wind grew high, and the Sea swell'd, and all things look'd terrible, especially to us, that understood nothing but just what we saw before us; in short, Night came on, and very dark it was, the Wind freshen'd, and blew harder and harder, and about two Hours within Night, it blew a terrible Storm.

I was not quite a Stranger to the Sea, having come from *Rochelle* to *England,* when I was a Child, and gone from *London,* by the River *Thames,* to *France* afterward, as I have said: But I began to be alarm'd a little with the terrible Clamour of the Men over my Head, for I had never been in a Storm, and so had never seen the like, or heard it; and once, offering to look out at the Door of the Steerage, as they call'd it, it struck me with such Horrour, the darkness, the fierceness of the Wind, the dreadful height of the Waves, and the Hurry the *Dutch* Sailors were in, whose Language I did not understand one Word of; neither when they curs'd, or when they pray'd; I say, all these things together, fill'd me with Terror; and, in short, I began to be very much frighted.

When I was come back into the Great-Cabbin, there sat *Amy,* who was very Sea-sick, and I had a little before given her a Sup of Cordial-waters, to help her Stomach: When *Amy* saw me come back, and sit down without speaking, for so I did, she look'd two or three times up at me, at last she came running to me, Dear Madam! s*ays she,* what is the Matter? what makes you look so pale? why you an't well; what is the Matter? I said nothing still, but held up my hands two or three times; *Amy* doubl'd her Importunities; upon that, I said no more, but *step to the Steerage-Door, and look out, as I did;* so she went away immediately, and look'd too, as I had bidden her; but the poor Girl came back again in the greatest Amazement and Horrour, that ever I say any poor Creature in, wringing her Hands, and crying out she was

---

1 A city on the north coast of France.
2 A city on the north coast of Belgium.

undone! she was undone! she shou'd be drown'd! they were all lost! Thus she ran about the Cabin like a mad thing, and as perfectly out of her Senses, as any one in such a Case cou'd be suppos'd to be.

I was frighted myself; but when I saw the Girl in such a terrible Agony, it brought me a little to myself, and I began to talk to her, and put her in a little Hope; I told her, there was many a Ship in a Storm, that was not cast-away; and I hop'd we shou'd not be drown'd; and that it was true, the Storm was very dreadful, but I did not see that the Seamen were so much concern'd as we were; and so I talk'd to her as well as I cou'd, tho' my Heart was full enough of it, as well as *Amy*'s, and Death began to stare in my Face, ay, and something else too, that is to say, Conscience, and my Mind was very much disturb'd, but I had nobody to comfort me.

But *Amy* being in so much worse a Condition, that is to say, so much more terrify'd at the Storm than I was, I had something to do to comfort her; she was, as I have said, like one distracted, and went raving about the Cabbin, crying out, she was undone! undone! she shou'd be drown'd, and the like; and at last, the Ship giving a Jerk, by the Force, I suppose, of some violent Wave, it threw poor *Amy* quite down, for she was weak enough before, with being Sea-sick, and as it threw her forward, the poor Girl struck her Head against the Bulk-head, as the Seamen call it, of the Cabin, and laid her as dead as a Stone, upon the Floor, or Deck, that is to say, she was so to all Appearance.

I cry'd out for Help; but it had been all one, to have cry'd out on the top of a Mountain, where no-body had been within five Miles of me; for the Seamen were so engag'd, and made so much Noise, that no-body heard me, or came near me; I open'd the Great-Cabbin Door, and look'd into the Steerage, to cry for Help, but there, to encrease my Fight, was two Seamen on their Knees, at Prayers, and only one Man who steer'd, and he made a groaning Noise too, which I took to be saying his Prayers, but it seems it was answering to those above, when they call'd to him, to tell him which Way to steer.

Here was no Help for me, or for poor *Amy*, and there she lay still so, and in such a Condition, that I did not know whether she was dead or alive; in this Fright I went to her, and lifted her a little way up, setting her on the Deck, with her Back to the Boards of the Bulk-head, and I got a little Bottle out of my Pocket, and I held it to her Nose, and rubb'd her Temples, and what else I could do, but still *Amy* shew'd no Signs of Life, till I felt for her Pulse, but could hardly distinguish her to be alive; however, after a great while, she began to revive, and in about half an Hour she came to herself, but remember'd nothing at first of what had happen'd to her, for a good while more.

When she recover'd more fully, she ask'd me where she was? I told her, she was in the Ship yet, but God knows how long it might be; Why, Madam, *says she*, is not the Storm over? *No, no,* says I, *Amy*; *why, Madam*, says she, *it was calm just now*, (meaning when she was in the swooning Fit, occasion'd by her Fall,) *Calm* Amy, *says I, 'tis far from calm; it may be it will be calm-by-and-by, when we all drown'd, and gone to* HEAVEN.

HEAVEN! Madam, *says she*, what makes you talk so? HEAVEN! *No, no,* If I am drown'd, I am damn'd! *Don't you know what a wicked Creature I have been?* I have been a Whore to two Men, and have liv'd a wretched abominable Life of Vice and Wickedness for fourteen Years; O Madam, *you know it,* and GOD knows it; and *now I am to die; to be drown'd; O!* what will become of me? *I am undone for Ever!* ay, Madam, *for Ever! To all Eternity! O I am lost! I am lost! If I am drown'd, I am lost for Ever!*

All these, you will easily suppose, must be so many Stabs into the very Soul of one in my own Case; it immediately occur'd to me, *Poor* Amy! *what art thou, that I am not?* what hast thou been, that I have not been? Nay, I am guilty of my own Sin, and thine too: Then it came to my Remembrance, that I had not only been the same with *Amy*, but that I had been the Devil's Instrument, to make her wicked; that I had stripp'd her, and prostituted her to the very Man that I had been Naught with myself; that she had but follow'd me; I had been her wicked Example; and I had led her into all; and that as we had sinn'd together, now we were likely to sink together.

All this repeated itself to my Thoughts at that very Moment; and everyone of *Amy*'s Cries sounded thus in my Ears: I am the wicked Cause of it all; I have been thy[1] Ruin, *Amy*; I have brought thee to this, and now thou art to suffer for the Sin I have entic'd thee to; and if though art lost for ever, *what must I be?* what must be my Portion?

---

1 Roxana's use of the second person familiar (thee and thou) in this moment of repentance anticipates her life with the Quaker woman and her efforts to live a virtuous life towards the end of the novel. Quakers often disclosed their identities by their insistence on using the second person familiar, which was already archaic by the seventeenth century, as a manifestation of their belief that all individuals are equal in the eyes of God and that, therefore, no individual is entitled to by addressed in the second person formal.

It is true, this Difference was between us, that I said all these things within myself, and sigh'd, and mourn'd inwardly; but *Amy*, as her Temper was more violent, spoke aloud, and cry'd, and call'd out aloud, like one in an Agony.

I had but small Encouragement to give her, and indeed, cou'd say but very little; but I got her to compose herself a little, and not let any of the People of the Ship understand what she meant, or what she said; but even in her greatest Composure, she continued to express herself with the utmost Dread and Terror, on account of the wicked Life she had liv'd; and crying out, she shou'd be damn'd, and the like; and which was very terrible to me, who knew what Condition I was in myself.

Upon these serious Considerations, I was very Penitent too, for my former Sins, and cry'd out, *tho' softly*, two or three times, *Lord have Mercy upon me*; to this, I added abundance of Resolutions, of what a Life I wou'd live, if it should please God but to spare my Life but this one time; how I would live a single and virtuous Life, and spend a great deal of what I had thus wickedly got, in Acts of Charity, and doing Good.

Under these dreadful Apprehensions, I look'd back on the Life I had led, with the utmost Contempt and Abhorrence; I blush'd, and wonder'd at myself, how I cou'd act thus; how I cou'd divest myself of Modesty and Honour, and prostitute myself for Gain; and I thought, if ever it should please God to spare me this one time from Death, it wou'd not be possible that I should be the same Creature again.

Amy went farther; she pray'd, she resolv'd, she vow'd to lead a new Life, if God wou'd spare her but this time: It now began to be Day-light, for the Storm held all Night-long, and it was some Comfort to see the Light of another Day, which indeed, none of us expected; but the Sea went Mountains high, and the Noise of the Water was as frightful to us, as the Sight of the Waves; nor was any Land to be seen; nor did the Seamen know whereabout they were; at last, to our great Joy, they made Land, which was in *England*, and on the Coast of *Suffolk*; and the Ship being in the utmost Distress, they ran for the Shore, at all Hazards, and with great Difficulty, got into *Harwich*,[1] where they were safe, as to the Danger of Death; but the Ship was so full of Water, and so much damag'd, that if they had not laid her on Shore the same Day, she

---

1 The storm has blown Roxana's ship northwest from Dunkirk to Harwich across one of the widest parts of the English Channel.

wou'd have sunk before Night, according to the Opinion of the Seamen, and of the Workmen on Shore too, who were hir'd to assist them in stopping their Leaks.

Amy was reviv'd as soon as she heard they had espy'd Land, and went out upon the Deck, but she soon came in again to me, *O Madam*, says she, *there's the Land indeed, to be seen, it looks like a ridge of Clouds, and may be all a Cloud, for ought I know, but if it be Land, 'tis a great Way off; and the Sea is in such a Combustion, we shall all perish before we can reach it; 'tis the dreadfullest Sight, to look at the Waves, that ever was seen; why, they are as high as Mountains; we shall certainly be all swallow'd up for-all the Land is so near.*

I had conceiv'd some Hope, that if they saw Land, we should be deliver'd; and I told her, she did not understand things of that Nature; that she might be sure, if they saw Land, they would go directly towards it, and wou'd make into some Harbour; but it was, as *Amy* said a frightful Distance to it: The Land look'd like Clouds, and the Sea went as high as Mountains, so that no Hope appear'd in the seeing the Land; but we were in fear of foundring, before we cou'd reach it; this made *Amy* so desponding still; but as the Wind, which blew from the *East*, or that Way, drove us furiously towards the Land; so when, about half an Hour after, I stept to the Steerage-Door, and look'd-out, I saw the Land much nearer than *Amy* represented it; so I went in, and encourag'd *Amy* again, and indeed, was encourag'd myself.

In about an Hour, or something more, we see to our infinite Satisfaction, the open Harbour of *Harwich*, and the Vessel standing[1] directly towards it, and in a few Minutes more, the Ship was in smooth Water, to our inexpressible Comfort; and thus I had, tho' against my Will, and contrary to my true Interest, what I wish'd for, to be driven away to *England*, tho' it was by a Storm.

Nor did this Incident do either *Amy* or me much Service; for the Danger being over, the Fears of Death vanish'd with it; ay, and our Fear of what was beyond Death also; our Sence of the Life we had liv'd, went off, and with our return to Life, our wicked Taste of Life return'd, and we were both the same as before, if not worse: So certain is it, that the Repentance which is brought about by the meer Apprehensions of Death, wears off as those Apprehensions wear off; and Death-bed Repentance, or Storm-Repentance, which is much the same, is seldom true.

However, I do not tell you, that this was all at once, neither;

---

1 Heading for.

the Fright we had at Sea lasted a little while afterwards, at least the Impression was not quite blown off, as soon as the Storm; especially poor *Amy*, as soon as she set her Foot on Shore, she fell flat upon the Ground, and kiss'd it, and gave God thanks for her Deliverance from the Sea; and turning to me when she got up, I hope, Madam, *says she*, you will never go upon the Sea again.

I know not what ail'd me, not I; but *Amy* was much more penitent at Sea, and much more sensible of her Deliverance when she Landed, and was safe, than I was; I was in a kind of Stupidity, I know not well what to call it; I had a Mind full of Horrour in the time of the Storm, and saw Death before me, as plainly as *Amy*, but my thoughts got no Vent, as *Amy*'s did; I had a silent sullen kind of Grief, which cou'd not break out either in Words or Tears, and which was therefore, much the worse to bear.

I had a Terror upon me for my wicked Life past, and firmly believ'd I was going to the Bottom, launching into Death, where I was to give an Account of all my past Actions; and in this State, and on that Account, I look'd back upon my Wickedness with Abhorrence, as I have said above; but I had no Sence of Repentance, from the true Motive of Repentance; I saw nothing of the Corruption of Nature, the Sin of my Life, as an Offence against God; as a thing odious to the Holiness of his Being; as abusing his Mercy, and despising his Goodness; in short, I had no thorow effectual Repentance; no Sight of my Sins in their proper Shape; no View of a Redeemer, or Hope in him: I had only such a Repentance as a Criminal has at the Place of Execution, who is sorry, not that he has committed the Crime, as it is a Crime, but sorry *that he is to be Hang'd for it.*

It is true, *Amy*'s Repentance wore off too, as well as mine, but not so soon; however, we were both very grave for a time.

As soon as we could get a Boat from the Town, we went on Shore, and immediately went to a Publick-House in the Town of *Harwich*; where we were to consider seriously, what was to be done, and whether we should go up to *London*, or stay till the Ship was refitted, which they said, would be a Fortnight,[1] and then go for *Holland*, as we intended, and as Business requir'd.

Reason directed that I shou'd go to *Holland*, for there I had all my Money to receive, and there I had Persons of good Reputation, and Character, to apply to, having letters to them from the honest *Dutch* Merchant at *Paris*, and they might, perhaps, give me

---

1 Two weeks.

a Recommendation again, to Merchants in *London*, and so I should get Acquaintance with some People of Figure,[1] which was what I lov'd; whereas now I knew not one Creature in the whole City of *London*, or any-where else, that I cou'd go and make myself known to: Upon these Considerations, I resolv'd to go to *Holland*, whatever came on it.

But *Amy* cry'd and trembled, and was ready to fall into Fits, when I did but mention going upon the Sea again, and begg'd of me, not to go, or if I wou'd go, that I wou'd leave her behind, tho' I was to send her a-begging; the People in the Inn laugh'd at her, and jested with her; ask'd her, if she had any Sins to confess, that she was asham'd shou'd be heard of? And that she was troubled with an evil Conscience; told her, if she came to Sea, and to be in a Storm, if she had lain with her Master, she wou'd certainly tell her Mistress of it; and that it was a common thing for poor Maids to confess all the Young-Men they had lain with; that there was one poor Girl that went over with her Mistress, whose Husband was a —r, in—, the City of *London*, who confess'd, in the Terror of a Storm, that she had lain with her Master, and all the Apprentices so often, and in such and such Places, and made the poor Mistress, when she return'd to *London*, fly at her Husband, and make such a Stir, as was indeed, the Ruin of the whole Family: *Amy* cou'd bear all that well enough; for tho' she had indeed, lain with her Master, it was with her Mistress's Knowledge and Consent, and which was worse, was her Mistress's own doing; *I record it to the Reproach of my own Vice*, and to expose the Excesses of such Wickedness, as they deserve to be expos'd.[2]

I thought *Amy*'s Fear would have been over by that time the Ship would be gotten ready, but I found the Girl was rather worse and worse; and when I came to the Point, that we must go on Board, or lose the Passage, *Amy* was so terrified, that she fell into Fits, so the Ship went away without us.

But my going being absolutely necessary, as above, I was

---

1   People of influence and high social status.

2   The year following the publication of *Roxana*, Defoe published a pamphlet entitled *Everybody's Business is Nobody's Business,* which contained the following complaint about servant girls: "If she be tolerably handsome, and has any Share of Cunning, the Apprentice or her Master's son are enticed away and ruined by her. Thus many good Families are impoverished and disgraced by these pert Sluts, who taking the advantage of a young Man's Simplicity and unruly Desires, draw many heedless Youths, nay, some of good Estates into their Snares; and of this we have but too many Instances" (6).

oblig'd to go in the Packet-Boat some time after, and leave *Amy* behind, at *Harwich*, but with Directions to go to *London*, and stay there, to receive Letters and Orders from me what to do: Now I was become, from a Lady of Pleasure, a Woman of Business, and of great Business too, I assure you.

I got me a Servant at *Harwich*, to go over with me, who had been at *Rotterdam*, knew the Place, and spoke the Language, which was a great Help to me, and away I went; I had a very quick Passage, and pleasant Weather, and coming to *Rotterdam*, soon found out the Merchant to whom I was recommended, who receiv'd me with extraordinary Respect; and first he acknowledg'd the accepted Bill for 4000 Pistoles, which he afterwards paid punctually; other Bills that I had also payable at *Amsterdam*, he procur'd to be receiv'd for me; and whereas one of the Bills for a Thousand two Hundred Crowns, was protested at[1] *Amsterdam*, he paid it me himself, for the Honour of the Endorser, as he call'd it, which was my Friend, the Merchant at *Paris*.

There I enter'd into a Negociation, by his Means, for my Jewels, and he brought me several Jewellers, to look on them, and particularly one to Value them, and to tell me what every Particular was worth: This was a Man who had great Skill in Jewels, but did not Trade at that time; and he was desir'd by the Gentleman that I was with, to see that I might not be impos'd upon.

All this Work took me up near half a Year, and by managing my Business thus myself, and having large Sums to do with, I became as expert in it, as any She-Merchant of them all; I had Credit in the Bank for a large Sum of Money, and Bills and Notes for much more.

After I had been here about three Months, my Maid *Amy* writes me word, that she had receiv'd a Letter from her Friend, as she call'd him, that, *by the way*, was the Prince's Gentleman, that had been *Amy*'s extraordinary Friend indeed; for *Amy* own'd to me, he had lain with her a hundred times; that is to say, as often as he pleas'd; and perhaps, in the eight Year which that Affair lasted, it might be a great deal oftner: This was what she call'd her Friend, who she corresponded with upon this particular Subject; and among other things, sent her this particular News, that my extraordinary Friend, my real Husband, who rode in the *Gensd'arms*, was dead; that he was kill'd in a Rencounter, as they call it, or accidental Scuffle among the Troopers; and so the Jade congratulated me upon my being now a real Free-

---

1 Challenged.

woman; and now, Madam, *says she, at the End of her Letter*, you have nothing to do but to come hither, and set up a coach, and a good Equipage; and if Beauty and a good Fortune won't make you a Dutchess, nothing will; *but I had not fix'd my Measures yet*; I had no Inclination to be a Wife again, I had had such back Luck with my first Husband, I hated the Thoughts of it; I found, that a Wife is treated with Indifference, a Mistress with a strong Passion; a Wife is look'd upon, as but an Upper-Servant, a Mistress is a Sovereign; a Wife must give up all she has; have every Reserve she makes for herself, be thought hard of, and be upbraided with her very *Pin-Money*;[1] whereas a Mistress makes the Saying true, *that what the Man has*, is hers, and *what she has*, is her own; the Wife bears a thousand Insults, and is forc'd to sit still and bear it, or part and be undone; a Mistress insulted, helps herself immediately, and takes another.

These were my wicked Arguments for Whoring, for I never set against them the Difference another way, I may say every other way; how that, FIRST, A Wife appears boldly and honourably with her Husband; lives at Home, and possesses his House, his Servants, his Equipages, and has a Right to them all, and to call them her own; entertains his Friends, owns his Children, and has the return of Duty and Affection from them, as they are here her own, and claims upon his Estate, by the Custom of *England*, if he dies, and leaves her a Widow.

The Whore sculks about in Lodgings; is visited in the dark; disown'd upon all Occasions, before God and Man; is maintain'd indeed, for a time; but is certainly condemn'd to be abandon'd at last, and left to the Miseries of Fate, and her own just Disaster: If she has any Children, her Endeavour is to get rid of them, and not maintain them; and if she lives, she is certain to see them all hate her, and be asham'd of her; while the Vice rages, and the Man is in the Devil's Hand, *she has him*; and while she has him, she makes *a Prey of him*; but if he happens to fall Sick; if any Disaster befalls him, the Cause of all lies upon her; he is sure to lay

---

1 Susan Staves defines "pin-money" as "payments under contract by a husband to a wife during the couverture of a set annual sum. Often the contract was the marriage settlement, but sometimes husbands entered into other pre- and postnuptial agreements to pay pin money" (*Married Women's Separate Property in England*, 132-33). Staves goes on to note that "pin-money" became one species of a wife's separate property, establishable by contract, that evaded the prohibitions of common law against a wife owning separate property from her husband's.

all his Misfortunes at her Door; and if once he comes to Repentance, or makes but one Step towards a Reformation, he begins with her; leaves her; uses her as she deserves; hates her; abhors her; and sees her no more; and that with this never-failing Addition, namely, That the more sincere and unfeign'd his Repentance is, the more earnestly he looks up; and the more effectually he looks in, the more his Aversion to her encreases; and he curses her from the Bottom of his Soul; nay, it must be from a kind of Excess of Charity, if he so much as wishes God may forgive her.

The opposite Circumstances of a *Wife* and *Whore*, are such, and so many, and I have since seen the Difference with such Eyes, as I cou'd dwell upon the Subject a great-while; but my Business is History; I had a long Scene of Folly yet to run over; perhaps the Moral of all my Story may bring me back-again to this Part, and if it does, I shall speak of it fully.

While I continued in *Holland*, I receiv'd several Letters from my Friend, (so I had good Reason to call him) the Merchant in *Paris*; in which he gave me a farther Account of the Conduct of that Rogue, the *Jew*, and how he acted after I was gone; how Impatient he was while the said Merchant kept him in suspence, expecting me to come again; and how he rag'd when he found I came no more.

It seems after he found I did not come, he found out, by his unweary'd Enquiry, where I had liv'd; and that I had been kept as a Mistress, by some Great Person, but he cou'd never learn by who, except that, he learnt the Colour of his Livery; in Pursuit of this Enquiry, he guess'd at the right Person, but could not make it out or offer any positive Proof of it; but he found out the Prince's Gentleman, and talk'd so saucily to him of it, that the Gentleman treated him, as the *French* call it, *au Coup de Batton*; that is to say, Can'd him very severely, as he deserv'd; and that not satisfying him, or curing his Insolence, he was met one Night late, upon the *Pont Neuf* in *Paris*, by two Men, who muffling him up in a great Cloak, carried him into a more private Place, and cut off both his Ears, telling him, it was for talking impudently of his Superiors; adding that he shou'd take Care to govern his Tongue better, and behave with more Manners, or the next time they would cut his Tongue out of his Head.

This put a Check to his Sauciness that Way; but he comes back to the Merchant, and threatened to begin a Process against him, for corresponding with me, and being accessary to the Murther of the Jeweller, &c.

The Merchant found by his Discourse, that he suppos'd I was

protected by the said Prince *de*—, nay, the Rogue said, he was sure I was in his Lodgings at *Versailles*; *for he never had so much as the least Intimation of the Way I was really gone*; but that I was there, he was certain, and certain that the Merchant was privy to it: The Merchant bade him Defiance; however, he gave him a great deal of Trouble, and put him to a great Charge, and had like to have brought him in for a Party to my Escape, in which Case, he wou'd have been oblig'd to have produc'd me, and that in the Penalty of some capital Sum of Money.

But the Merchant was too-many for him another Way; for he brought an Information against him for a Cheat; wherein, laying down the whole Fact, How he intended falsely to accuse the Widow of the Jeweller, for the suppos'd Murther of her Husband; that he did it purely to get the Jewels from her; and that he offer'd to bring him [*the Merchant*] in, to be Confederate with him, and to share the Jewels between them; proving also, his Design to get the Jewels into his Hands and then to have dropp'd the Prosecution, upon Condition of my quitting the Jewels to him; upon this Charge, he got him laid by the Heels; so he was sent to the *Concergerie*, that is to say, to *Bridewell*,[1] and the Merchant clear'd: He got out of Jayl in a little-while, tho' not without the help of Money, and continued teizing[2] the Merchant a long while; and at last threatening to assassinate and murther him; so the Merchant, who having buried his wife about two Months before, was now a single Man, and not knowing what such a Villain might do, thought fit to quit *Paris*, and came away to *Holland* also.

It is more certain, that speaking of Originals, I was the Source and Spring of all that Trouble and Vexation to this honest Gentleman; and as it was afterwards in my Power to have made him full Satisfaction, and did not, I cannot say but I added Ingratitude to all the rest of my Follies; but of that I shall give a fuller Account presently.

I was surpriz'd one Morning, when being at the Merchant's House, who he had recommended me to, in *Rotterdam*, and being

---

1 Originally, a hospital chartered to the City of London by Edward VI in 1552 as part of an effort to reform the poor. By Defoe's day, the Hospital's most notorious inmates had become women arrested for sexual transgressions. Whether men or women, any one sent to Bridewell could expect that part of their punishment would likely consist in being put "to labour." Bridewell also became the prototype of reformatory workhouses throughout England.

2 Bothering.

busie in his Counting-House, managing my Bills, and preparing to write a Letter to him, to *Paris*, I heard a Noise of Horses at the Door; which is not very common in a City, where every-body passes by Water; but he had, it seems ferry'd over the *Maez* from *Williamstadt*, and so came to the very Door; and I looking towards the Door, upon hearing the Horses, saw a Gentleman alight, and come in at the Gate, I knew nothing, and expected nothing to be sure, of the Person; but as I say, was surpriz'd, when coming nearer to me, I saw it was my Merchant of *Paris*; my Benefactor; and indeed, my Deliverer.

I confess, it was an agreeable Surprize to me, and I was exceeding glad to see him, who was so honourable, and so kind to me, and who indeed, had sav'd my Life: As soon as he saw me, he run to me, took me in his Arms, and kiss'd me, with a Freedom that he never offer'd to take with me before; *Dear Madam*—, says he, *I am glad to see you safe in this Country; if you had stay'd two Days longer in* Paris, *you had been undone*: I was so glad to see him, that I cou'd not speak a good-while, and I burst out into Tears, without speaking a Word for a Minute; but I recover'd that Disorder, and said, *The more*, Sir, *is my Obligation to you, that sav'd my Life*; and added, *I am glad to see you here, that I may consider how to balance an Account, in which I am so much your Debtor.*

You and I will adjust the Matter easily, *says he*, now we are so near together; pray where do you Lodge? *says he.*

In a very honest good House, *said I*, where that Gentleman, your Friend, recommended me; pointing to the Merchant in whose House we then were.

And where you may Lodge too, Sir, *says the Gentleman*, if it suits with your Business, and your other Conveniency.

With-all my Heart, *says he*; then Madam, *adds he*, turning to me, I shall be near you, and have Time to tell you a Story, which will be very long, and yet many ways very pleasant to you, how troublesome that devilish Fellow, the *Jew*, has been to me, on your Account; and what a hellish Snare he had laid for you, if he cou'd have found you.

I shall have Leisure too, Sir, *said I*, to tell you all my Adventures since that; which have not been a few, I assure you.

In short, he took up his Lodgings in the same House where I lodg'd, and the Room he lay in, open'd as he was wishing it wou'd, just opposite to my Lodging-Room; so we cou'd almost call out of Bed to one another, and I was not at-all shy of him on that Score, for I believ'd him perfectly honest, and so indeed, he was; and if he had not, that Article was at present no Part of my Concern.

It was not till two or three Days, and after his first Hurries of Business were over, that we began to enter into the History of our Affairs on every side, but when we began, it took up all our Conversation, for almost a Fortnight: First, I gave him a particular Account of every thing that happen'd material upon my Voyage; and how we were driven into *Harwich* by a very terrible Storm; how I had left my Woman behind me, so frighted with the Danger she had been in, that she durst not venture to set her Foot into a Ship again, any more; and that I had not come myself, if the Bills I had of him, had not been payable in *Holland*; but that Money, he might see, wou'd make a Woman go any-where.

He seem'd to laugh at all our womanish Fears upon the Occasion of the Storm; telling me, it was nothing but what was very ordinary in those Seas; but that they had Harbours on every Coast so near, that they were seldom in Danger of being lost indeed; for, *says he*, if they cannot fetch one Coast, they can always stand away for another, and run afore it, *as he call'd it*, for one side or other: But when I came to tell him what a crazy Ship it was, and how, even when they got into *Harwich*, and into smooth Water, they were fain to run the Ship on Shore, or she wou'd have sunk in the very Harbour; and when I told him, that when I look'd out at the Cabin-Door, I saw the *Dutchmen*, one upon his Knees here, and another there, at their Prayers, then indeed, he acknowledg'd I had reason to be alarm'd; but smiling, *he added*, But you, Madam, *says he*, are so good a Lady, and so pious, you wou'd but have gone to Heaven a little the sooner, the Difference had not been much to you.

I confess, when he said this, it made all the Blood turn in my Veins, and I thought I shou'd have fainted; poor Gentleman! thought I, you know little of me; what wou'd I give to be really what you really think me to be! He perceiv'd the Disorder, but said nothing till I spoke; when shaking my head, *O Sir!* said I, *Death in any Shape has some Terror in it*; but in the frightful Figure of a Storm at Sea, and a sinking Ship, it comes with a double, a treble, and indeed, an inexpressible Horrour; and if I were that Saint you think me to be, which, God knows, I am not, 'tis still very dismal; I desire to die in a Calm, if I can: He said a great many good things, and very prettily order'd his Discourse, between serious Reflection and Compliment; but I had too much Guilt to relish it as it was meant, so I turn'd it off to something else, and talk'd of the necessity I had on me to come to *Holland*; but I wish'd myself safe on Shore in *England* again.

He told me, he was glad I had such an Obligation upon me to come over into *Holland*, however; but hinted, that he was so interested in my Wellfare, and besides, had such farther Designs upon me, that if I had not so happily been found in *Holland*, he was resolv'd to have gone to *England* to see me; and that it was one of the principal Reasons of his leaving *Paris*.

I told him, I was extremely oblig'd to him for so far interesting himself in my Affairs; but that I had been so far his Debtor before, that I knew not how any thing could encrease the Debt; for I ow'd my Life to him already, and I could not be in Debt for any-thing more valuable than that.

He answer'd in the most obliging Manner possible, that he wou'd put it in my Power to pay that Debt, and all the Obligations besides, that ever he had, or should be able to lay upon me.

I began to understand him now, and to see plainly, that he resolv'd to *make Love to me*; but I would by no means seem to take the Hint, and besides I knew that he had a Wife with him in *Paris*; and I had, *just then, at least*, no Gust[1] to any more intriguing; however, he surpriz'd me into a sudden Notice of the thing a little-while after, by saying something in his Discourse, that he did *as he said*, in his Wife's Days; I started at that Word; *What mean you by that?* Sir, said I; *Have you not a Wife at* Paris? No, Madam, indeed, *said he*, my Wife died the beginning of September last; which, it seems, was but a little after I came away.

We liv'd in the same House all this while; and as we lodg'd not far off of one-another, Opportunities were not wanting for as near an Acquaintance as we might desire; nor have such Opportunities the least Agency in vicious Minds, to bring to pass even what they might not intend at first.

However, tho' he courted so much at a distance, yet his Pretensions[2] were very honourable; and as I had before found him a most disinterested Friend, and perfectly honest in his Dealings, even when I trusted him with all I had; so now I found him strictly virtuous, till I made him otherwise myself, even almost, whether he wou'd or no; as you shall hear.

It was not long after our former Discourse, when he repeated what he had insinuated before, namely, that he had yet a Design to lay before me, which, if I wou'd agree to his Proposals, wou'd

---

1 Appetite or desire for.
2 Intentions.

more than balance all Accounts between us: I told him, I cou'd not reasonably deny him any-thing; and *except one thing, which I hop'd and believ'd he wou'd not think of,* I should think myself very ungrateful if I did not do every thing for him that lay in my Power.

He told me, what he should desire of me, wou'd be fully in my Power to grant, or else he should be very unfriendly to offer it, and still, all this while, he declin'd making the Proposal, *as he call'd it,* and so, for that time, we ended our Discourse, turning it off to other things; so that, in short, I began to think he might have met with some Disaster in his Business, and might have come away from *Paris* in some Discredit; or had had some Blow on his Affairs in general; and as really I had Kindness enough to have parted with a good Sum to have help'd him, and was in Gratitude, bound to have done so, *he having so effectually sav'd* to me *all I had*; so I resolv'd to make him the Offer, the first time I had an Opportunity, which, two or three Days after, offer'd itself, very much to my Satisfaction.

He had told me at large, *tho' on several Occasions,* the Treatment he had met with from the *Jew,* and what Expence he had put him to; how at length he had cast him, *as above,* and had recover'd good Damage of him, but that the Rogue was unable to make him any considerable Reparation; he had told me also, how the Prince *d'*—'s Gentleman had resented his Treatment of his Master; and how he had caus'd him to be us'd upon the *Pont Neuf, &c. as I have mention'd above*; which I laugh'd at most heartily.

It is pity, *said I,* that I should sit here, and make that Gentleman no Amends; if you wou'd direct me, Sir, *said I,* how to do it, I wou'd make him a handsome Present, and acknowledge the Justice he had done to me, as well as to the Prince, his Master: He said he wou'd do what I directed in it; so I told him, I would send him 500 Crowns; *that's too much,* said he, *for you are but half interested in the Usage of the* Jew; *it was on his Master's Account he corrected him, not on yours*: Well, however, we were oblig'd to do nothing in it, for neither of us knew how to direct a Letter to him, or to direct any-body to him; so I told him, I wou'd leave it till I came to *England,* for that my Woman, *Amy,* corresponded with him, and that he had made Love to her.

Well, but Sir, *said I,* as in requital for his generous Concern for me, I'm careful to think of him; it is but just, that what Expence you have been oblig'd to be at, which was all on my Account, shou'd be repaid you; and therefore, *said I,* let me see—*and there*

I paus'd, and began to reckon up what I had observ'd from his own Discourse, it had cost him in the Several Disputes, and Hearings, which he had with that *Dog* of a *Jew*, and I cast them up at something above 2130 Crowns; so I pull'd out some Bills which I had upon a Merchant in *Amsterdam*, and a particular Account in Bank, and was looking on them, in order to give them to him.

When he seeing evidently what I was going about, interrupted me with some Warmth, and told me, he wou'd have nothing of me on that Account, and desire'd I wou'd not pull out my Bills and papers on that Score; that he had not told me the Story on that Account, or with any such View; that it had been his Misfortune first to bring *that ugly Rogue to me*, which, tho' it was with a good Design, yet he wou'd punish himself with the Expence he had been at, for his being so unlucky to me; that I cou'd not think so hard of him, as to suppose he wou'd take Money of me, *a Widow*, for serving me, and doing Acts of Kindness to me in a strange Country, and in Distress too; but, *he said*, he wou'd repeat what he had said before, that he kept me for a deeper Reckoning, and that, as he had told me, he would put me in a Posture to Even all that Favour,[1] as I call'd it, *at once*, so we should talk it over another time, and balance all together.

Now I expected it wou'd come out, but still he put it off, as before, from whence I concluded, it cou'd not be Matter *of Love*, for that those things are not usually delay'd in such a manner and therefore it must be Matter of Money; upon which Thought, I broke the Silence, and told him, that as he knew I had, by Obligation, more Kindness for him, than to deny any Favour to him that I could grant, and that he seem'd backward to mention his Case; I begg'd Leave of him to give me Leave to ask him, whether any-thing lay upon his Mind, with respect to his Business and Effects in the World? That if it did, he knew what I had in the World, as well as I did; and that if he wanted Money, I wou'd let him have any Sum for this Occasion, as far as five or six Thousand Pistoles, and he shou'd pay me as his own Affairs wou'd permit; and that, if he never paid me, I wou'd assure him, that I wou'd never give him any Trouble for it.

He rise up with Ceremony, and gave me Thanks, in Terms that sufficiently told me, he had been bred among People more polite, and more courteous, than is esteem'd the ordinary Usage of the

---

1 Put Roxana in a position to pay him back.

Dutch;[1] and after his Compliment was over, he came nearer to me, and told me, that he was oblig'd to assure me, tho' with repeated Acknowledgements of my kind Offer, that he was not in any want of Money; that he had met with no Uneasiness in any of his Affairs, no not of any Kind whatever, except that of the Loss of his Wife, and one of his Children, which indeed, had troubled him much; but that this was no Part of what he had to offer to me, and by granting which, I shou'd balance all Obligations; but that, in short, it was that seeing Providence had (as it were for that Purpose) taken his Wife from him, I wou'd make up the Loss to him; and with that, he held me fast in his Arms, and kissing me, wou'd not give me Leave to say No, and hardly to Breathe.

At length, having got room to speak, I told him, that, as I had said before, I could deny him but one thing in the World; I was very sorry he shou'd propose *that thing only* that I cou'd not grant.

I cou'd not but smile however, to myself, that he shou'd make so many Circles, and round-about Motions, to come at a Discourse which had no such rarity at the Bottom of it, if he had known all: But there was another Reason why I resolv'd not to have him, when, at the same time, if he had courted me in a Manner less honest or virtuous, I believe I shou'd not have denied him; but I shall come to that Part presently.

He was, as I have said, long a-bringing it out, but when he had brought it out, he pursued it with such Importunities, as would admit of no Denial, *at least he intended they shou'd not*; but I resisted them obstinately, and yet with Expressions of the utmost Kindness and Respect for him that cou'd be imagin'd; often telling him, there was nothing else in the World that I cou'd deny him, and shewing him all the Respect, and upon all Occasions treating him with Intimacy and Freedom, as if he had been my Brother.

He tried all the Ways imaginable to bring his Design to pass, but I was inflexible; at last, he thought of a Way, which he flatter'd himself, wou'd not fail, nor would he have been mistaken perhaps, in any other Woman in the World *but me*; this was, to try if he cou'd take me at an Advantage, and get to-Bed to me, and then, *as was most rational to think*, I should willingly enough marry him afterwards.

We were so intimate together, that nothing but Man and Wife could, or at least ought to be, more; but still our Freedoms kept within the Bounds of Modesty and Decency: But one Evening, above all the rest, we were very merry, and I fancy'd he push'd the

---

1 Dutch custom.

Mirth to watch for his Advantage; and I resolv'd that I wou'd, at least feign to be as merry as he; and that, in short, if he offer'd any-thing, he shou'd have his Will easily enough.

About One a-Clock in the Morning, for so long we sat up together, I said, *Come, 'tis One a-Clock, I must go to-Bed; Well,* says he, I'll go with you; *No, No,* says I, *go to your own Chamber;* he said he wou'd go to-Bed with me: *Nay,* says I, *if you will,* I don't know what to say; *if I can't help it, you must:* However, I got from him, left him, and went into my Chamber, but did not shut the Door; and as he cou'd easily see that I was undressing myself, he steps to his own Room, which was but on the same Floor, and in a few Minutes undresses himself also, and returns to my Door in his Gown and Slippers.

I thought he had been gone indeed, so that he had been in jest; and by the way, thought either he had no-mind to the thing, or that he never intended it; so I shut my Door, that is, latch'd it, for I seldom lock'd or bolted it, and went to-Bed; I had not been in-Bed a Minute, but he comes in his Gown, to the Door, and opens it a little-way, but not enough to come in, or look in, and says softly, What are you really gone to-Bed? *Yes, yes,* says I, *get you gone:* No indeed, says he, *I shall not begone, you gave me Leave before, to come to-Bed, and you shan't say get you gone now:* So he comes into my room, and then turns about, and fastens the Door, and immediately comes to the Bed-side to me: I pretended to scold and struggle, and bid him begone, with more Warmth than before; but it was all one; he had not a Rag of Cloaths on, but his Gown and Slippers, and Shirt; so he throws off his Gown, and throws open the Bed, and came in at once.

I made a seeming Resistance, but it was no more indeed; for, *as above,* I resolv'd from the Beginning, he shou'd Lye with me if he wou'd, and for the rest, I left it to come after.

Well, he lay with me that Night, and the two next, and very merry we were all the three Days between; but the third Night he began to be a little more grave: now, my Dear, *says he,* tho' I have push'd this Matter farther than ever I intended; or than, I believe, you expected from me, who never made any Pretences to you but what were very honest; yet to heal it all up, and let you see how sincerely I meant at first, and how honest I will ever be to you, I am ready to marry you still, and desire you to let it be done to-Morrow Morning; and I will give you the same fair Conditions of Marriage as I wou'd have done before.

This, it must be own'd, was a Testimony that he was very honest, and that he lov'd me sincerely; but I construed it quite another Way, namely that he aim'd at the Money: But how surpriz'd did he look! and how was he confounded, when he found me receive his Proposal with Coldness and Indifference! and still tell him, that it was the only thing I cou'd not grant!

He was astonish'd! What, not take me now! *says he,* when I have been a-Bed with you! I answer'd coldly, tho' respectfully still, *It is true,* to my Shame be it spoken, says I, *that you have taken me by Surprize, and have had your Will of me: but I hope you will not take it ill that I cannot consent to Marry, for-all that; if I am with-Child,* said I, *Care must be taken to manage that as you shall direct; I hope you won't expose me, for my having expos'd myself to you, but I cannot go any farther;* and at that Point I stood, and wou'd hear of no Matrimony, by any means.

Now because this may seem a little odd, I shall state the Matter clearly, as I understood it myself; I knew that while I was a Mistress, it is customary for the Person kept, to receive from them that Keep; but if I shou'd be a Wife, all I had then, was given up to the Husband, and I was thenceforth to be under his Authority only; and as I had Money enough, and need not fear being what they call a cast-off Mistress, so I had no need to give him twenty Thousand Pound to marry me, which had been buying my Lodging too dear a great deal.

Thus his Project of coming to-Bed to me, was a Bite[1] upon himself, while he intended it for a Bite upon me; and he was no nearer his Aim of marrying me, than he was before; all his Arguments he could urge upon the Subject of Matrimony, were at an End, for I positively declin'd marrying him; and as he had refus'd the thousand Pistoles which I had offer'd him in Compensation for his Expences and Loss, at *Paris,* with the *Jew,* and had done it upon the Hopes he had of marrying me; so when he found his Way difficult still, he was amaz'd, and, I had some Reason to believe, repented that he had refus'd the Money.

But thus it is when Men run into wicked Measures, to bring their Designs about; I that was infinitely oblig'd to him before, began to talk to him, as if I had ballanc'd Accounts with him; and that the Favour of Lying with a Whore, was equal, not to the thousand Pistoles only, but to all the Debt I ow'd him, for saving my Life, and all my Effects.

But he drew himself into it, and tho' it was a dear Bargain, yet it was a Bargain of his own making; he cou'd not say I had trick'd him into it; but as he projected and drew me in to lye with him,

---

1 A trick.

depending that it was a sure Game in order to a Marriage, so I granted him the Favour, as he call'd it, to balance the Account of Favours receiv'd from, and keep the thousand Pistoles with good Grace.

He was extremely disappointed in this Article, and knew not how to manage for a great-while; and as I dare say, if he had not expected to have made it an Earnest for marrying me, he would never have attempted me the other way; so, I believ'd, if it had not been for the Money, which he knew I had, he wou'd never have desir'd to marry me after he had lain with me: For, where is the Man that cares to marry a Whore, tho' of his own making? And as I knew him to be no Fool, so I did him no Wrong, when I sup-pos'd that, but for the Money, he wou'd not have had any Thoughts of me that Way; especially after my yielding as I had done; in which it is to be remember'd, that I made no Capitula-tion for marrying him, when I yielded to him, but let him do just what he pleas'd, without any previous Bargain.

Well, hitherto we went upon Guesses at one-another's Designs; but as he continue'd to importune me to marry, tho' he had lain with me, and still did lye with me as often as he pleas'd, and I continued to refuse to marry him, tho' I let him lye with me whenever he desir'd it; I say, as these two Circumstances made up our Conversation, it cou'd not continue long thus, but we must come to an Explanation.

One Morning, in the middle of our unlawful Freedoms, that is to say, when we were in Bed together; he sigh'd, and told me, he desir'd my Leave to ask me one Question, and that I wou'd give him an Answer to it with the same ingenuous Freedom and Honesty, that I had us'd to treat him with; I told him I wou'd: Why then his Question was, why I wou'd not marry him, seeing I allow'd him all the Freedom of a Husband? *Or, says he,* my Dear, *since you have been so kind as to take me to your Bed, why will you not make me your Own, and take me for good-and-all,* that we may enjoy ourselves, *without any Reproach to one-another?*

I told him, that as I confess'd it was the only thing in all my Actions, that I could not give him a Reason for; that it was true, I had let him come to-Bed to me, which was suppos'd to be the greatest Favour a Woman could grant; but it was evident, and he might see it, that as I was sensible of the Obligation I was under to him, for saving me from the worst Circumstance it was possible for me to be brought to, I could deny him nothing; and if I had had any greater Favour to yield him, I should have done it, *that of Mat-rimony only excepted,* and he cou'd not but see that I lov'd him to an extraordinary Degree, in every Part of my Behavior to him; but that as to marrying, which was giving up my Liberty, it was what once he knew I had done, and he had seen how it had hurried me up and down in the World, and what it had expos'd me to; that I had an Aversion to it, and desir'd he wou'd not insist upon it; he might easily see I had no Aversion to him; and that if I was with-Child by him, he shou'd see a Testimony of my Kindness to the Father, for that I wou'd settle all I had in the World upon the Child.

He was mute a good-while; at last, *says he*, Come, my Dear, you are the first Woman in the World that ever lay with a Man, and then refus'd to marry him, and therefore there must be some other Reason for your Refusal; and I have therefore, one other Request, and that is, If I guess at the true Reason, and remove the Objection, will you then yield to me? I told him, if he remov'd the Objection, I must needs comply, for I shou'd certainly do everything that I had no Objection against.

Why then, my Dear, it must be, that either you are already engag'd and marry'd to some other Man, or you are not willing to dispose of your Money to me, and expect to advance yourself higher with your Fortune; no, if it be the first of these, my Mouth will be stopp'd, and I have no more to say; but if it be the last, I am prepar'd effectually to remove the Objection, and answer all you can say on that Subject.

I took him up short at the first of these; telling him, He must have base Thoughts of me indeed, to think that I could yield to him in such a Manner as I had done, and continue it with so much Freedom, as he found I did, if I had a Husband, or were engag'd to any other Man; and that he might depend upon it, that was not my Case, nor any Part of my Case.

Why then, *said he*, as to the other, I have an Offer to make to you, that shall take off all the Objection, *viz.* That I will not touch one Pistole of your Estate, more, than shall be with your own voluntary Consent; neither now, or at any other time, but you shall settle it as you please, for your Life, and upon who you please after your Death; that I shou'd see he was able to maintain me without it; and that it was not for that, that he follow'd me from *Paris*.

I was indeed, surpriz'd at that Part of his Offer, and he might easily perceive it; it was not only what I did not expect, but it was what I knew not what Answer to make to: He had indeed, remov'd my principal Objection, nay, all my Objections, and it was not possible for me to give any Answer; for if upon so generous an Offer I shou'd agree with him, I then did as good as confess, that it was upon the Account of my Money that I refus'd him; and that tho' I cou'd give up my Virtue, and expose myself, yet I wou'd not give up my Money, which, tho' it was true, yet was really too gross for me to acknowledge, and I cou'd not pretend to marry him upon that Principle neither; then as to having him, and make over all my Estate out of his Hands, so as not to give him the Management of what I had, I thought it would be not only a little Gothick and Inhumane, but would be always a foundation of Unkindness between us, and render us suspected one to another; so that, upon the whole, I was oblig'd to give a new Turn to it, and talk upon a kind of an elevated Strain, which really was not in my thoughts at first at-all; for I own, *as above*, the divesting myself of my Estate, and putting my Money out of my Hand, was the Sum of the Matter, that made me refuse to marry; but, I say, I gave it a new Turn, upon this Occasion, as follows:

I told him, I had, perhaps, differing Notions of Matrimony, from what the receiv'd Custom had given us of it; that I thought a Woman was a free Agent, as well as a Man, and born free, and cou'd she manage herself suitably, might enjoy that Liberty to as much Purpose as the Men do; that the Laws of Matrimony were indeed, otherwise, and Mankind at this time, acted quite upon other Principles; and those such, that a Woman gave herself entirely away from herself, in Marriage, and capitulated only to be, at best, but an Upper-Servant, and from the time she took the Man, she was no better or worse than the Servant among the Israelites, who had his Ears bor'd, that is nail'd to the Door-Post; who by that act, gave himself up to be a Servant during Life.

That the very Nature of the Marriage-Contract was, in short, nothing but giving up Liberty, Estate, Authority, and every-thing to the Man, and the Woman was indeed a meer Woman ever after, that is to say, a Slave.[1]

He reply'd, that tho' in some Respects it was as I had said, yet I ought to consider, that as an Equivalent to this, the Man had all the Care of things devolv'd upon him; that the Weight of Business lay upon his Shoulders, and as he had the Trust, so he had the

---

1 On one level Roxana is referring to the principles of common law that dominated marital relations at this time. According to those principles, married women were described as *femme covert*, that is, a woman under the cover of her husband. As such, all her property became the property of her husband's, she was not allowed to make contracts, nor was she allowed to testify against her husband under the assumption that mar-

[*over*

Toil of Life upon him, his was the Labour, his the Anxiety of Living; that the Woman had nothing to do, but to eat the Fat, and drink the Sweet; to sit still, and look round her; be waited on, and made much of; be serv'd, and lov'd, and made easie; *especially if the Husband acted as became him*; and that, in general, the Labour of the Man was appointed to make the Woman live quiet and unconcern'd in the World; that they had the Name of Subjection, without the Thing; and if in inferiour Families, they had the Drudgery of the House, and Care of the Provisions upon them; yet they had indeed, much the easier Part; for in general, the Women had only the Care of managing, that is, spending what their Husbands get; and that a Woman had the Name of Subjection indeed, but that they generally commanded not the Men only, but all they had; manag'd all for themselves, and where the man did his Duty, the Woman's Life was all Ease and Tranquility; and that she had nothing to do but to be easie, and to make all that were about her both easie and merry.

I return'd, that while a Woman was single, she was a Masculine in her politick Capacity; that she had then the full Command of what she had, and the full Direction of what she did; that she was a Man in her separated Capacity,[1] to all Intents and Purposes that a Man cou'd be so to himself; that she was controul'd by none, because accountable to none, and was in Subjection to none; so I sung these two Lines of Mr.— 's.

---

riage unified the partners as a single identity, that identity being the husband's. There were exceptions to these rules, and, as the Merchant suggests, married women could hold separate property if that control was stipulated in a contract that preceded the marriage itself. But as Roxana's earlier enumeration of the benefits wives accrued suggests, Defoe did not necessarily condemn the constraints women experienced under common law.

Roxana's commentary here also evokes satires from England's civil wars (1642-49) in which women were characterized as political opportunists for exploiting radical arguments about sovereign individualism and personal liberty to release themselves from a variety of marital obligations and responsibilities.

1 Unmarried state.

O! 'tis pleasant to be free,
The sweetest MISS is Liberty.[1]

I added, that whoever the Woman was, that had an Estate, and would give it up to be the Slave of a Great Man, that Woman was a Fool, and must be fit for nothing but a Beggar; that it was my Opinion, a Woman was as fit to govern and enjoy her own Estate, without a Man, as a Man was, without a Woman; and that, if she had a-mind to gratifie herself as to Sexes, she might entertain a Man, as a Man does a Mistress; that while she was thus single, she was her own, and if she gave away that Power, she merited to be as miserable as it was possible that any Creature cou'd be.

All he cou'd say, cou'd not answer the Force of this, as to Argument; only this, that the other Way was the ordinary Method that the World was guided by; that he had Reason to expect I shou'd be content with that which all the World was contented with; that he was of the Opinion, that a sincere Affection between a Man and his Wife, answer'd all the Objections that I had made about the being a Slave, a Servant, *and the like*; and where there was a mutual Love, there cou'd be no Bondage; but that there was but one Interest; one aim; one Design; and all conspir'd to make both very happy.

Ay, said I, *that is the Thing I complain of*; the Pretence of Affection, takes from a Woman every thing that can be call'd *herself*; she is to have no Interest; no Aim; no View; but all is the Interest, Aim, and View, of the Husband; she is to be the passive Creature you spoke of, *said I*; she is to lead a Life of perfect Indolence, and living by Faith (not in God, but) in her Husband, she sinks or swims, as he is either Fool or wise Man; unhappy or prosperous; and in the middle of what she thinks is her Happiness and Prosperity, she is ingulph'd in Misery and Beggary, which she had not the least Notice, Knowledge, or Suspicion of: How often have I seen a Woman living in all the Splendor that a plentiful Fortune ought to allow her? With her Coaches and Equipages; her Family, and rich Furniture; her Attendants and Friends; her Visiters, and good Company, all about her to-Day; to-Morrow surpriz'd with a Disaster; turn'd out of all by a Commission of Bankrupt; stripp'd to the Cloaths on her Back; her Jointure, *suppose she had it*, is sacrific'd to the Creditors, so long as her Husband liv'd, and she

---

1   Charles Cotton, "The Joys of Marriage," from *Poems on Several Occasions* (1689).

turn'd into the Street, and left to live on the Charity of her Friends, *if she has any*, or follow the Monarch, her Husband, into the Mint,[1] and live there on the Wreck of his Fortunes, till he is forc'd to run away from her, even there; and then she sees her Children starve; herself miserable; breaks her Heart; and cries herself to Death? This, *says I*, is the State of many a Lady that has had ten Thousand Pound to her Portion.

He did not know how feelingly I spoke this, and what Extremities I had gone thro' of this Kind; how near I was to the very last Article above, *viz. crying myself to Death*; and how I really starv'd for almost two Years together.

But he shook his Head, and said, Where had I liv'd? and what dreadful Families had I liv'd among, that had frighted me into such terrible Apprehensions of things? That these things indeed, might happen where Men run into hazardous things in Trade, and without Prudence or due consideration, launch'd their Fortunes in a Degree beyond their Strength, grasping at Adventures beyond their Stocks, *and the like*; but that, as he was stated in the World, if I wou'd embark with him, he had a Fortune equal with mine; that together, we should have no Occasion of engaging in Business any more; but that in any Part of the World where I had a-mind to live, whether *England, France, Holland*, or where I would, we might settle, and live as happily as the World could make any one live; that if I desir'd the Management of our Estate, when put together, if I wou'd not trust him with mine, he would trust me with his; that we wou'd be upon one Bottom, and I shou'd steer: Ay, *says I*, you'll allow me to steer, *that is*, hold the Helm, but you'll conn[2] the ship, *as they call it*; that is, as at Sea, a Boy serves to stand at the Helm, but he that gives him the Orders, is Pilot.

He laugh'd at my Simile; No, *says he*, you shall be Pilot then, you shall conn the Ship; ay, *says I*, as long as you please, but you

---

1　The Mint, located in Southwark, was one of several districts known as "liberties" in and around London, so called because, prior to Henry VIII, they had been governed by ecclesiastical authorities, but after England's break with Rome, they fell outside of most political and legal jurisdictions. Other liberties included the Clink, the Tower, and Lambeth Palace. The Mint, in particular, attracted debtors who fled to its confines to avoid their creditors. Once in the Mint, though, debtors often found themselves without any means to get themselves out of debt and trapped because they could not leave the region without risking arrest.

2　Command.

can take the Helm out of my Hand when you please, and bid me go spin: It is not you, *says I*, that I suspect, but the Laws of Matrimony puts the Power into your Hands; bids you do it; commands you to command; and binds me, forsooth, to obey; you that are now upon even Terms with me, and I with you, *says I*, are the next Hour set up upon the Throne, and the humble Wife plac'd at your Footstool; all the rest, all that you call Oneness of Interest, Mutual Affection, *and the like*, is Curtesie and Kindness then, and a Woman is indeed, infinitely oblig'd where she meets with it; but can't help herself where it fails.

Well, he did not give it over yet, but came to the serious Part, and there he thought he should be too many for me; he first hinted, that Marriage was decreed by Heaven; that it was the fix'd State of Life, which God had appointed for Man's Felicity, and for establishing a legal Posterity; that there cou'd be no legal Claim of Estates by Inheritance, but by Children born in Wedlock; that all the rest was sunk under Scandal and Illegitimacy; and very well he talk'd upon that Subject, indeed.

But it wou'd not do; I took him short there; Look you, Sir, *said I*; you have an Advantage of me there indeed, in my particular Case; but it wou'd not be generous to make use of it; I readily grant, that it were better for me to have marry'd you, than to admit you to the Liberty I have given you; but as I cou'd not reconcile my Judgment to Marriage, for the Reasons above, and had Kindness enough for you, and Obligation too much on me, to resist you, I suffer'd your Rudeness, and gave up my Virtue; but I have two things before me to heal up that Breach of Honour, without that desperate one of Marriage; and those are, Repentance for what is past, and putting an End to it for Time to come.

He seem'd to be concern'd, to think that I shou'd take him in that Manner; he assur'd me that I mis-understood him; that he had more Manners, as well as more Kindness for me; and more Justice, than to reproach me with what he had been the Aggressor in, and had surpriz'd me into; That what he spoke, refer'd to my Words above; that the Woman, if she thought fit, might entertain a Man, as the Man did a Mistress; and that I seem'd to mention that way of Living as justifiable, and setting it as a lawful thing, and in the Place of Matrimony.

Well, we strain'd some Compliments upon those Points, not worth repeating; and I added, I suppos'd when he got to-Bed to me, he thought himself sure of me; and indeed, in the ordinary Course of things, after he had lain with me, he ought to think so; but that, upon the same foot of Argument which I had discours'd with him upon, it was just the contrary; and when a Woman had been weak enough to yield up the last Point before Wedlock, it wou'd be adding one Weakness to another, to take the Man afterwards; to pin down the Shame of it upon herself all Days of her Life, and bind herself to live all her Time with the only Man that cou'd upbraid her with it; that in yielding at first, she must be a Fool, but to take the Man, is to be sure to be call'd Fool; that to resist a Man, is to act with Courage and Vigour, and to cast off the Reproach, which, in the Course of things, drops out of Knowledge, and dies; the Man goes one-way, and the Woman another, as Fate, and the Circumstances of Living direct; and if they keep one another's Council, the Folly is heard no more of; but to take the Man, *says I*, is the most preposterous thing in Nature, and (saving your Presence) is to befoul one's-self, and live always in the Smell of it; *No, no*, added I, after a Man has lain with me *as a Mistress*, he ought never to lye with me *as a Wife*; that's not only preserving the Crime in Memory, but it is recording it in the Family; if the Woman marries the Man afterwards, she bears the Reproach of it to the last Hour; if her Husband is not a Man of a hundred Thousand, he sometime or other upbraids her with it; if he has Children, they fail not one way or other, to hear of it; if they are wicked, they give her the Mortification of doing the like, and giving her for the Example: On the other-hand, if the Man and the Woman part, there is an End of the Crime, and an End of the Clamour; Time wears out the Memory of it; or a Woman may remove but a few Streets, and she soon out-lives it, and hears no more of it.

He was confounded at this Discourse, and told me, he cou'd not say but I was right in the Main; that as to that Part relating to managing Estates, it was arguing *a la Cavalier;*[1] it was in some Sence, right, if the Women were able to carry it on so, but that in general, the Sex were not capable of it; their Heads were not turn'd for it, and they had better choose a Person capable, and honest, that knew how to do them Justice, as Women, as well as to love them; and that then the Trouble was all taken off their Hands. I told him, it was a dear Way of purchasing their Ease; for very often when the Trouble was taken off of their Hands, so was their Money too; and that I thought it was far safer for the Sex not to be afraid of the Trouble, but to be really afraid of their Money; that if no-body was trusted, no-body wou'd be deceiv'd; and the Staff in their own Hands, was the best Security in the World.

---

1 Whimsically, without reference to reality.

He reply'd, that I had started a new thing in the World; that however I might support it by subtle reasoning, yet it was a way of arguing that was contrary to the general Practice, and that he confess'd he was much disappointed in it; that had he known I wou'd have made such a Use of it, he wou'd never have attempted what he did, which he had no wicked Design in, resolving to make me Reparation, and that he was very sorry he had been so unhappy; that he was very sure he shou'd never upbraid me with it hereafter, and had so good an Opinion of me, as to believe I did not suspect him; but seeing I was positive in refusing him, notwithstanding what had pass'd, he had nothing to do but to secure me from Reproach, by going back again to *Paris*, that so, according to my own way of arguing, it might die out of Memory, and I might never meet with it again to my Disadvantage.

I was not pleas'd with this Part at-all, for I had no-mind to let him go neither; and yet I had no-mind to give him such hold of me as he wou'd have had; and thus I was in a kind of suspence, irresolute, and doubtful what Course to take.

I was in the House with him, as I have observ'd, and I saw evidently that he was preparing to go back to *Paris*; and particularly, I found he was remitting Money to *Paris*, which was, as I understood afterwards, to pay for some Wines which he had given Order to have bought for him, at *Troyes* in *Champagne*; and I knew not what Course to take; and besides that, I was very loth to part with him; I found also, that I was with-Child by him, which was what I had not yet told him of; and sometimes I thought not to tell him of it at-all; but I was in a strange Place, and had no Acquaintance, tho' I had a great deal of Substance, which indeed, having no Friends there, was the more dangerous to me.

This oblig'd me to take him one Morning, when I saw him, as I thought, a little anxious about his going, and irresolute; *says I* to him, *I fancy you can hardly find in your Heart to leave me now:* The more *unkind is it in you*, said he, *severely unkind, to refuse a Man that knows not how to part with you.*

I am so far from being unkind to you, *said I*, that I will go all over the World with you, if you desir'd me, except to *Paris*, where you know I can't go.

It is pity so much Love, said he, on both Sides, shou'd ever separate.

Why then, *said I*, do you go away from me?

Because, *said he*, you won't take me.

But if I won't take you, *said I*, you may take me, any-where, but to *Paris*.

He was very loth to go any-where, *he said*, without me; but he must go to *Paris*, or to the *East-Indies*.

I told him I did not use to court,[1] but I durst venture myself to the *East-Indies* with him, if there was a Necessity of his going.

He told me, God be thank'd, he was in no Necessity of going any-where, but that he had a tempting Invitation to go to the *Indies*.

I answer'd, I wou'd say nothing to that; but that I desir'd he wou'd go any-where but to *Paris*; because there he knew I must not go.

He said he had no Remedy, but to go where I cou'd not go; for he cou'd not bear to see me, if he must not have me.

I told him, that was the unkindest thing he cou'd say of me, and that I ought to take it very ill, seeing I knew how very well to oblige him to stay, without yielding to what he knew I cou'd not yield to.

This amaz'd him, and he told me, I was pleas'd to be mysterious; but, that he was sure it was in no-body's Power to hinder him going, if he resolv'd upon it, except me; who had Influence enough upon him to make him do any-thing.

Yes, *I told him*, I cou'd hinder him, because I knew he cou'd no more do an unkind thing by me, than he cou'd do an unjust one; and to put him out of his Pain, I told him I was with-Child.

He came to me, and taking me in his Arms, and kissing me a Thousand times almost, said, Why wou'd I be so unkind, not to tell him that before?

I told him, 'twas hard, that, to have him stay, I shou'd be forc'd to do as Criminals do to avoid the Gallows, *plead my Belly*;[2] and that I thought I had given him Testimonies enough of an Affection equal to that of a Wife; if I had not only lain with him; been with-Child by him; shewn myself unwilling to part with him; but offer'd to go to the *East-Indies* with him; and except One Thing that I cou'd not grant, what cou'd he ask more?

---

1 Unaccustomed to initiating proposals.
2 It was possible for women convicted of crimes to defer their sentences and sometimes receive a reprieve if they could prove they were pregnant. Final determination of this plea usually resided with a midwife who would determine whether the fetus was "quick," that is, moving. At this point, the child was determined to have a nominal identity separate from its mother. Justices were then barred from executing the mother, under the assumption that to do so would make the state a murderer as well as an executioner.

He stood mute a good-while; but afterwards told me, he had a great-deal more to say, if I cou'd assure him, that I wou'd not take ill whatever Freedom he might use with me in his Discourse.

I told him, he might use any Freedom in Words with me; for a Woman who had given Leave to such other Freedoms, as I had done, had left herself no room to take any-thing ill, let it be what it wou'd.

Why then, *he said*, I hope you believe, Madam, I was born a Christian, and that I have some Sence of Sacred Things upon my Mind; when I first broke-in upon my own Virtue, and assaulted yours; when I surpriz'd, and as it were, forc'd you to that which neither you intended, or I design'd, but a few Hours before, it was upon a Presumption that you wou'd certainly marry me, if once I cou'd go that Length with you; and it was with an honest Resolution to make you my Wife.

But I have been surpriz'd with such a Denial, that no Woman in such Circumstances ever gave to a Man; for certainly it was never known, that any Woman refus'd to marry a Man that had first lain with her, much less a Man that had gotten her with-Child; but you go upon different Notions from all the World; and tho' you reason upon it so strongly, that a Man knows hardly what to answer, yet I must own, there is something in it shocking to Nature, and something very unkind to yourself; but above all, it is unkind to the Child that is yet unborn; who, if we marry, will come into the World with Advantage enough, but if not, is ruin'd before it is born; must bear the eternal Reproach of what it is not guilty of; must be branded from its Cradle with a Mark of Infamy; be loaded with the Crimes and Follies of its Parents and suffer for Sins that it never committed; This I take to be very hard, and indeed cruel to the poor Infant not yet born, who you cannot think of, with any Patience, if you have the common Affection of a Mother, and not do that for it, which shou'd at once place it on a Level with the rest of the World; and not leave it to curse its Parents for what also we ought to be asham'd of: I cannot, therefore, *says he*, but beg and intreat you, as you are a Christian, and a Mother, not to let the innocent Lamb you go with, be ruin'd before it is born, and leave it to curse and reproach us hereafter, for what may be so easily avoided.

Then, dear Madam, *said he*, with a World of Tenderness, (and I thought I saw Tears in his Eyes) allow me to repeat it, that I am a Christian, and consequently I do not allow what I have rashly, and with due Consideration, done; I say, I do not approve of it as lawful; and therefore tho' I did, with a View I have mention'd, one unjustifiable Action, I cannot say, that I cou'd satisfie myself to live in a continual Practice of what, in Judgement, we must both condemn; and tho' I love you above all the Women in the World, and have done enough to convince you of it, by resolving to marry you after what has pass'd between us, and by offering to quit all Pretensions to any Part of your Estate, so that I shou'd, as it were, take a Wife after I had lain with her, and without a Farthing Portion; which, as my Circumstances are, I need not do; I say, notwithstanding my Affection to you, which is inexpressible, yet I cannot give up Soul as well as Body, the Interest of this World, and the hopes of another; and you cannot call this my Disrespect to you.

If ever any Man in the world was truly valuable for the strictest honesty of Intention, *this was the Man*; and if ever Woman in her Senses rejected a Man of Merit, on so trivial and frivolous a Pretence, *I was the Woman*; but surely it was the most preposterous thing that ever Woman did.

He would have taken me as a Wife, but would not entertain me as a Whore; was ever Woman angry with any Gentleman on that head? And was ever Woman so stupid to choose to be a Whore, where she might have been an honest Wife? But Infatuations are next to being possess'd of the Devil; I was inflexible, and pretended to argue upon the Point of a Woman's Liberty, as before; but he took me short and with more Warmth than he had yet us'd with me, tho' with the utmost Respect; reply'd Dear Madam, you argue for Liberty at the same time that you restrain yourself from that Liberty, which God and Nature has directed you to take; and to supply the Deficiency, propose a viscous Liberty, which is neither honourable or religious; will you propose Liberty at the Expense of Modesty?

I return'd, that he mistook me; I did not propose it; I only said, that those that cou'd not be content without concerning the Sexes in that Affair, might do so indeed; might entertain a Man as Men do a Mistress, if they thought fit, but he did not hear me say I wou'd do so; and tho', by what had pass'd, he might well censure me in that Part, yet he should find, for the future, that I should freely converse with him without any Inclination that way.

He told me, he cou'd not promise that for himself, and thought he ought not to trust himself with the Opportunity; for that, as he had fail'd already, he was loth to *lead himself into the Temptation* of offending again; and that this was the true Reason of his resolving to go back to *Paris*; not that he cou'd willingly leave me, and would be very far from wanting my Invitation; but if he cou'd not stay upon Terms that became him, either as an honest Man, or a Christian, what cou'd he do? and he hop'd, *he said*, I cou'd not blame him, that he was unwilling any thing that was to call him Father, shou'd upbraid him with leaving him in the World, to be call'd Bastard; adding, that he was astonished to think how I could satisfie myself to be so cruel to an innocent Infant, not yet born; profess'd he cou'd neither bear the Thoughts of it, much less bear to see it, and hop'd I wou'd not take it ill that he cou'd not stay to see me Deliver'd, for that very Reason.

I saw he spoke this with a disturb'd Mind, and that it was with some Difficulty that he restrain'd his Passion; so I declin'd any farther Discourse upon it; only said, I hop'd he wou'd consider of it: *O Madam!* says he, *Do not bid me consider, 'tis for you to consider;* and with that he went out of the Room, in a strange kind of Confusion, as was easie to be seen in his Countenance.

If I had not been one of the foolishest, as well as the wickedest Creatures upon Earth, I cou'd never have acted thus; I had one of the honestest compleatest Gentlemen on Earth, at my hand; he had in one Sence sav'd my Life, but he had sav'd that Life from Ruin in a Most remarkable Manner; he lov'd me even to Distraction, and had come from *Paris* to *Rotterdam*, on purpose to seek me; he had offer'd me Marriage, even after I was with-Child by him, and had offer'd to quit all his Pretensions to my Estate, and give it up to my own Management, having a plentiful Estate of his own: here I might have settled myself out of the reach even of Disaster itself; his Estate and mine, wou'd have purchas'd even then above two Thousand Pounds a Year, and I might have liv'd like a Queen, nay, far more happy than a Queen; and which was above all, I had now an Opportunity to have quitted a Life of Crime and Debauchery, which I had been given up to for several Years, and to have sat down quiet in Plenty and Honour, and to have set myself apart to the Great Work, which I have since seen so much Necessity of, and Occasion for; I mean that of Repentance.

But my Measure of Wickedness was not yet full; I continue'd obstinate against Matrimony, and yet I cou'd not bear the Thoughts of his going away neither; as to the Child, I was not very anxious about it; I told him, I wou'd promise him that it shou'd never come to him to upbraid him with its being illegitimate; that if it was a Boy, I wou'd breed it up like the Son of a Gentleman, and use it well for his sake; and after a little more such Talk as this, and seeing him resolv'd to go, I retir'd, but cou'd not help letting him see the Tears run down my Cheeks; he came to me, and kiss'd me, entreated me, conjur'd me by the Kindness he had shewn me in my Distress; by the Justice he had done me in my Bills and Money-Affairs; by the Respect which made him refuse a Thousand Pistoles from me for his Expences with that Traytor, the *Jew*; by the Pledge of our Misfortunes, so he call'd it, which I carry'd with me; and by all that the sincerest Affection cou'd propose to do, that I wou'd not drive him away.

But it wou'd not do; I was stupid and senceless, deaf to all his Importunities, and continued so to the last; so we parted, only desiring me to promise him that I would write him word when I was Deliver'd, and how he might give me an Answer; and this I engag'd my Word I would do; and upon his desiring to be inform'd which Way I intended to dispose myself, I told him, I resolv'd to go directly to *England*, and to *London*, where I propos'd to Lye-in; but since he resolv'd to leave me, I told him, I suppos'd it wou'd be of no Consequence to him, what became of me.

He lay in his Lodgings that Night, but went away early in the Morning, leaving me a Letter, in which he repeated all he had said; recommended the Care of the Child, and desir'd of me, that as he had remitted to me the Offer of a Thousand Pistoles, which I wou'd have given him for the Recompense of his charges and Trouble with the *Jew*, and had given it me back; so he desir'd I wou'd allow him to oblige me to set apart that Thousand Pistoles, with its Improvement, for the Child, and for its Education; earnestly pressing me to secure that little Portion for the abandon'd Orphan, when I shou'd think fit, *as he was sure I wou'd*, to throw away the rest upon something as worthless as my sincere Friend at *Paris*; he concluded with moving me to reflect with the same Regret as he did, on our Follies we had committed together; ask'd me Forgiveness for being the Aggressor in the Fact; and forgave me every-thing, *he said*, but the Cruelty of refusing him, which he own'd he cou'd not forgive me so heartily as he shou'd do, because he was satisfied it was an Injury to myself; would be an Introduction to my Ruin; and that I wou'd seriously repent of it; he foretold some fatal things, which, *he said*, he was well assur'd I shou'd fall into; and that, at last I wou'd be ruin'd by a bad Husband; bid me be the more wary, that I might render him a False Prophet; but to remember, that if ever I came into Distress, I had a fast-Friend at *Paris*, who wou'd not upbraid me with the unkind things past, but wou'd be always ready to return me Good for Evil.

This Letter stunn'd me; I cou'd not think it possible for any-one, that had not dealt with the Devil to write such a Letter; for he spoke of some particular things which afterwards were to befall me, with such an Assurance that it frighted me beforehand; and when those things did come to pass, I was perswaded he had some more than humane Knowledge; in a word, his Advices to me to repent, were very affectionate; his Warnings of Evil to happen to me, were very kind; and his Promise of Assistance, if I wanted him, were so generous, that I have seldom seen the like; and tho' I did not at first set much by that Part, because I look'd upon them as what might not happen, and as what was improbable to happen at that time; yet all the rest of his Letter was so moving, that it left me very melancholy, and I cry'd four and twenty Hours after, almost, without ceasing, about it; and yet, even all this while, whatever it was that bewitch'd me, I had not one serious Wish that I had taken him; I wish'd heartily indeed, that I cou'd have kept him with me; but I had a mortal Aversion to marrying him, or indeed, anybody else; but form'd a thousand wild Notions in my Head, that I was yet gay enough, and young, and handsome enough to please a Man of Quality; and that I wou'd try my Fortune at *London*, come of it what wou'd.

Thus blinded by my own Vanity, I threw away the only Opportunity I then had, to have effectually settl'd my Fortunes, and secur'd them for this World; and I am a Memorial to all that shall read my Story; a standing Monument of the Madness and Distraction which Pride and Infatuations from Hell runs us into; how ill our Passions guide us; and how dangerously we act, when we follow the Dictates of an ambitious Mind.

I was rich, beautiful, and agreeable, and not yet old; I had known something of the Influence I had had upon the Fancies of Men, even of the highest Rank; I never forgot that the Prince *de—* had said with an Extasie, that I was the finest Woman in *France*; I knew I cou'd make a Figure at *London*; I was not at a Loss how to behave, and having already been ador'd by Princes, I thought of nothing less than of being Mistress to the King himself: But I go back to my immediate Circumstances at that time.

I got over the Absence of my honest Merchant but slowly at first; it was with infinite Regret that I let him go at-all; and when I read the Letter he left, I was quite confounded; as soon as he was out of Call, and irrecoverable, I wou'd have given half I had in the World, for him back again; my Notions of things chang'd in an Instant, and I call'd myself a thousand Fools, for casting myself upon a Life of Scandal and Hazard; when after the Shipwreck of Virtue, Honour, and Principle, and sailing at the utmost

Risque in the stormy Seas of Crime, and abominable Levity, I had a safe Harbour presented, and no Heart to cast-Anchor in it.

His Predictions terrify'd me; his Promises of Kindness if I came to Distress, melted me into Tears, but frighted me with Apprehensions of ever coming into such Distress, and fill'd my Head with a thousand Anxieties and Thoughts, how it shou'd be possible for me, who had now such a Fortune, to sink again into Misery.

Then the dreadful Scene of my Life, when I was left with my five Children, &c. as I have related, represented itself again to me, and I sat considering what Measures I might take to bring myself to such a State of Desolation again, and how I shou'd act to avoid it.

But these things wore off gradually; as to my Friend, the Merchant, he was gone, and gone irrecoverably, for I durst not follow him to *Paris*, for the Reasons mention'd above; again, I was afraid to write to him to return, lest he shou'd have refus'd, as I verily believ'd he wou'd; so I sat and cry'd intolerably, for some Days, nay, I may say, for some Weeks; but I say, it wore off gradually; and as I had a pretty deal of Business for managing my Effects, the Hurry of that particular Part, serv'd to divert my thoughts, and in part to wear out the Impressions which had been made upon my Mind.

I had sold my Jewels; all but the fine Diamond Ring, which my Gentleman, the Jeweller, us'd to wear; and this, at proper times, I wore myself; as also the Diamond Necklace, which the Prince had given me, and a Pair of extraordinary Ear-Rings, worth about 600 Pistoles; the other, which was a fine Casket, he left with me at his going to *Versailles*, and a small Case with some Rubies and Emeralds, &c. I say, I sold them at the *Hague* for 7600 Pistoles; I had receiv'd all the Bills which the Merchant had help'd me to at *Paris*, and with the Money I brought with me, they made up 13900 Pistoles more; so that I had Ready-Money, and in Account in the Bank at *Amsterdam*, above One and twenty thousand Pistoles, besides Jewels; and how to get this Treasure to *England*, was my next Care.

The Business I had had now with a great many People, for receiving such large Sums, and selling Jewels of such considerable Value, gave me Opportunity to know and converse with several of the best Merchants of the Place; so that I wanted no Direction now, how to get my Money remitted to *England*; applying therefore, to several Merchants, that I might neither risque it all on the Credit of one Merchant, nor suffer any single Man to know the quantity of Money I had; I say, applying myself to several Merchants, I got Bills of Exchange, payable in *London*, for all my Money; the first Bills I took with me; the second Bills I left in Trust, (in case of any Disaster at Sea) in the Hands of the first Merchant, him to whom I was recommended by my Friend from *Paris*.

Having thus spent nine Months in *Holland*; refus'd the best Offer ever Woman in my Circumstances had; parted unkindly, and indeed, barbarously with the best Friend, and honestest Man in the World; got all my Money in my Pocket, and a Bastard in my Belly, I took Shipping at the *Briel*, in the Packet-Boat, and arriv'd safe at *Harwich*, where my Woman, *Amy*, was come, by my Direction, to meet me.

I wou'd willingly have given ten Thousand Pounds of my Money, to have been rid of the Burthen I had in my Belly, as above; but it cou'd not be; so I was oblig'd to bear with that Part, and get rid of it by the ordinary Method of Patience, and a hard Travel.[1]

I was above the comtemptible usage that Women in my Circumstances oftentimes meet with; I had consider'd all that before-hand; and having sent *Amy* before-hand, and remitted her Money to do it, she had taken me a very handsome House, in— *Street*, near *Charing-Cross*; had hir'd me two Maids, and a Footman, who she had put in a good Livery, and having hir'd a Glass-Coach[2] and four Horses, she came with them and the Man-Servant, to *Harwich*, to meet me, and had been there near a Week before I came; so I had nothing to do, but to go-away to *London*, to my own House, where I arriv'd in very good Health, and where I pass'd for a *French* Lady, by the Title of—.

My first Business was, to get all my Bills accepted; which, to cut the Story short, was all both accepted, and currently paid; and I then resolv'd to take me a Country-Lodging somewhere near the Town, to be *Incognito*, till I was brought-to-Bed; which, appearing in such a Figure, and having such an Equipage, I easily manag'd, without any-body's offering the usual Insults of Parish-Enquiries:[3] I did not appear in my new House for some time; and afterwards I thought fit, for particular Reasons, to quit that House, and not come to it at-all, but take handsome large Apart-

---

1 Labour.
2 A private coach with glass windows.
3 Parish officials checking to be sure the child was not illegitimate.

ments in the *Pall-mall*,[1] in a House, out of which was a private Door into the King's Garden, by the Permission of the Chief Gardener, who had liv'd in the House.

I had now all my Effects secur'd; but my Money being my great Concern at that time, I found it a Difficulty how to dispose of it, so as to bring me in an annual Interest; however, in some time I got a substantial safe Mortgage for 14000 Pound, by the Assistance of the famous Sir *Robert Clayton*,[2] for which, I had an Estate of 1800 Pounds a Year bound to me; and had 700 Pounds *per Annum* Interest for it.

This, with some other Securities, made me a very handsome Estate, of above a Thousand Pounds a Year; enough, one wou'd think, to keep any Woman in *England* from being a Whore.

I Lay-in at—, about four Miles from *London*, and brought a fine Boy into the World; and according to my Promise sent an Account of it to my Friend at *Paris*, the Father of it; and in the Letter, told him how sorry I was for his going away, and did as good as intimate, that if he wou'd come once more to see me, I should use him better than I had done: He gave me a very kind and obliging Answer, but took not the least Notice of what I had said *of his coming Over*, so I found my Interest lost there for ever: He gave me Joy of the Child, and hinted, that he hop'd I wou'd make good what he had begg'd for the poor Infant, as I had promis'd; and I sent him word again, that I wou'd fullfil his Order

---

1   Pall Mall is a major thoroughfare in Westminster and runs parallel to the Mall from St. James Street to the Haymarket. St. James' Palace is located on the south side of the western end. Roxana's description of her apartments as adjacent to the palace suggests that she lived at this point on the road. Pall Mall, like the Mall, is so named because it was one of the long, straight, alley-like stretches along which the croquet-like game of the same name was played.

2   Robert Clayton is an extremely ambiguous figure in this novel. He is the only historic character in *Roxana*, and his presence evokes a time of significant political upheaval. Clayton was born in 1629 and apprenticed as a scrivener. While serving his apprenticeship, he and a fellow apprentice, John Morris, conducted a successful business lending money. Clayton entered London politics in the 1670s, first as Sherriff (1670-83), then as Alderman (1689-1707). Clayton, along with other Whigs, was purged from the aldermanic bench in 1683 during the *quo warranto* proceedings. When he returned to City politics, he worked vigorously along with other Whig radicals to convince William III to expand the City's franchise. When this plan failed, Clayton seems to have cast his lot with the Whig financiers who supported the Crown.

to a Title;[1] and such a Fool, and so weak I was in this last Letter, notwithstanding what I have said of his not taking notice of my Invitation, as to ask his Pardon almost, for the Usage I gave him at *Rotterdam*, and stoop'd so low, as to expostulate with him for not taking Notice of my inviting him to come to me again, as I had done; and which was still more, went so far as to make a second sort of an Offer to him, telling him almost in plain Words, that if he wou'd come Over now, I wou'd have him; but he never gave me the least Reply to it at-all, which was as absolute a Denial to me, as he was ever able to give; so I sat down, I cannot say contented, but vex'd heartily that I had made the Offer at-all; for he had, as I may say, his full Revenge of me, in scorning to answer, and to let me twice ask that of him, which he with so much Importunity begg'd of me before.

I was now up again,[2] and soon came to my City Lodging, in the *Pall-mall*; and there I began to make a Figure suitable to my Estate, which was very great; and I shall give you an Account of my Equipage in a few Words, and of myself too.

I paid 60*l.* a Year for my new Apartments, for I took them by the Year; but then, they were handsome Lodgings indeed, and very richly furnished; I kept my own Servants to clean and look after them; found my own Kitchen-Ware, and Firing;[3] my Equipage was handsome, but not very great: I had a Coach, a Coachman, a Footman, my Woman, *Amy*, who I now dress'd like a Gentlewoman, and made her my Companion, and three Maids; and thus I liv'd for a time: I dress'd to the height of every Mode; went extremely rich in Cloaths; and as for Jewels, I wanted none; I gave a very good Livery lac'd with Silver, and as rich as any-body below the Nobility, cou'd be seen with: And thus I appear'd, leaving the World to guess who or what I was, without offering to put myself forward.

I walk'd sometimes in the *Mall* with my Woman *Amy*; but I kept no company, and made no Acquaintances, only made as gay a Show as I was able to do, and that upon all Occasions: I found however, the World was not altogether so unconcern'd about me, as I seem'd to be about them; and first, I understood that the Neighbours begun to be mighty inquisitive about me; as who I was? And what my Circumstances were?

Amy was the only Person that cou'd answer their Curiosity, or

---

1 Grant every detail of his request.
2 Recovered from childbirth.
3 Fuel.

give any Account of me, and she a tattling Woman, and a true Gossip, took Care to do that with all the Art that she was Mistress of; she let them know, that I was the Widow of a Person of Quality in *France*; that I was very rich; that I came over hither to look after an Estate that fell to me by some of my Relations who died here; that I was worth 4000*l*. all in my own Hands, *and the like*.

This was all wrong in *Amy*, and in me too, tho' we did not see it at first; for this recommended me indeed, to those sort of Gentlemen they call *Fortune-Hunters*, and who always besieg'd Ladies, *as they call'd it*, on purpose to take them Prisoners, *as I call'd it*; that is to say, to marry the Women, and have the spending of their Money: But if I was wrong in refusing the honourable Proposals of the *Dutch Merchant*, who offer'd me the Disposal of my whole Estate, and had as much of his own to maintain me with; I was right now, in refusing those Offers which came generally from Gentlemen of good Families, and good Estates, but who living to the Extent of them, were always needy and necessitous, and wanted a Sum of Money to make themselves easie, *as they call it*; that is to say, to pay off Incumbrances, Sisters' Portions, *and the like*; and then the Woman is Prisoner for Life, and may live as they please to give her Leave: This Life I had seen into clearly enough, and therefore I was not to be catch'd that way; however, as I said, the Reputation of my Money brought several of those sort of Gentry about me, and they found means, by one Stratagem or other, to get access to my Ladyship; but in short, I answer'd them all well enough; *that I liv'd single, and was happy; that as I had no Occasion to change my Condition for an Estate,* so I did not see, *that by the best Offer that any of them cou'd make me, I cou'd mend my Fortune; that I might be honour'd with* Titles indeed, and in time rank on publick Occasions with the Peeresses; I mention that, because one that offer'd at me, was the eldest Son of a Peer: *But that I was as well without the Title,* as long as *I had the Estate; and while I had 2000l. a Year of my own, I was happier than I cou'd be in being Prisoner of State to a Nobleman*; for I took the Ladies of that Rank to be little better.

As I have mention'd Sir *Robert Clayton*, with whom I had the good Fortune to become acquainted, on account of the Mortgage which he help'd me to, it is necessary to take Notice, that I had much Advantage in my ordinary Affairs, by his Advice, and therefore I call it my good Fortune; for as he paid me so considerable an annual Income as 700*l*. a Year, so I am to acknowledge myself much a Debtor, not only to the Justice of his Dealings with me, but to the Prudence and Conduct which he guided me to, by his Advice, for the Management of my Estate; and as he found I was not inclin'd to marry, he frequently took Occasion to hint, how soon I might raise my Fortune to a prodigious Height, if I wou'd but order my Family-Oeconomy so far within my Revenue, as to lay-up every Year something, to add to the Capital.

I was convinc'd of the Truth of what he said, and agreed to the Advantages of it; you are to take it as you go, that Sir *Robert* suppos'd by my own Discourse, and especially, by my Woman, *Amy*, that I had 2000*l.* a Year Income; he judg'd, as he said, by my way of Living, that I cou'd not spend above one Thousand; and so, he added, I might prudently lay-by 1000*l.* every Year, to add to the Capital; and by adding every Year the additional Interest, or Income of the Money to the Capital, he prov'd to me, that in ten Year I shou'd double the 1000*l. per Annum*, that I laid by; and he drew me out a Table, as he call'd it, of the Encrease, for me to judge by; and by which, he said, if the Gentlemen of *England* wou'd but act so, every Family of them wou'd encrease their Fortunes to a great Degree, just as Merchants do by Trade; whereas now, *says* Sir *Robert*, by Humour of living up to the Extent of their Fortunes, and rather beyond, the Gentlemen, *says he*, ay, and the Nobility too, are, almost all of them, Borrowers, and all in necessitous Circumstances.

As Sir *Robert* frequently visited me, and was (if I may say so from his own Mouth) very well pleas'd with my way of conversing with him, for he knew nothing, nor so much as guess'd at what I had been; I say, as he came often to see me, so he always entertain'd me with this Scheme of Frugality; and one time he brought another Paper, wherein he shew'd me, much to the same Purpose as the former, to what Degree I shou'd encrease my Estate, if I wou'd come into this Method of contracting my Expences; and by this Scheme of his, it appear'd, that laying up a thousand Pounds a Year, and every Year adding the Interest to it, I shou'd in twelve Years time have in Bank, One and twenty Thousand, and Fifty eight Pounds; after which, I might lay-up two Thousand Pounds a Year.

I objected, that I was a young Woman; that I had been us'd to live plentifully, and with a good Appearance; and that I knew not how to be a Miser.

He told me, that if I thought I had enough, it was well; but if I desir'd to have more, this was the Way; that in another twelve Year, I shou'd be too rich, so that I shou'd not know what to do with it.

Ay Sir; *says I*, you are contriving how to make me a rich Old

Woman, but that won't answer my End; I had rather have 20000*l.* now, than 60000*l.* when I am fifty Year old.

Then, Madam, says he, *I suppose your Honour has no Children?*

None, Sir *Robert*, said I, *but what are provided for*; so I left him in the dark, as much as I found him: However, I consider'd his Scheme very well, tho' I said no more to him at that time, and I resolv'd, tho' I would make a very good Figure, I say, I resolv'd to abate a little of my Expence, and draw in, live closer, and save something, if not so much as he propos'd to me: It was near the End of the Year that Sir *Robert* made this Proposal to me, and when the Year was up, I went to his House in the City, and there I told him, I came to thank him for his Scheme of Frugality; that I had been studying much upon it; and tho' I had not been able to mortifie myself so much as to lay-up a thousand Pounds a Year; yet, as I had not come to him for my Interest half-yearly, as was usual, I was now come to let him know, that I had resolv'd to lay-up that seven Hundred Pound a Year, and never use a Penny of it; desiring him to help me to put it out to Advantage.

Sir *Robert*, a Man thorowly vers'd in Arts of improving Money, but thorowly honest, *said to me*, Madam, I am glad you approve of the Method that I propos'd to you; but you have begun wrong; you shou'd have come for your Interest at Half-Year, and then you had had the Money to put out; now you have lost half a Year's Interest of 350*l.* which is 9*l.* for I had but 5 *per Cent.* on the Mortgage.

Well, well, Sir, *says I*, can you put this out for me now?

Let it lie, Madam, *says he*, till the next Year, and then I'll put out your 1400*l.* together, and in the mean time I'll pay you Interest for the 700*l.* so he gave me his Bill for the Money, which he told me shou'd be no less than 6*l. per Cent.* Sir *Robert Clayton*'s Bill was what no-body wou'd refuse; so I thank'd him, and let it lie; and next Year I did the same; and the third Year Sir *Robert* got me a good Mortgage for 2200*l.* at 6 *per Cent.* Interest: So I had 132*l.* a Year added to my Income; which was a very satisfying Article.[1]

But I return to my History: As I have said, I found that my Measures were all wrong, the Posture I set up in, expos'd me to innumberable Visiters of the Kind I have mention'd above; I was cry'd up for a vast Fortune, and one that Sir *Robert Clayton* manag'd for; and Sir *Robert* Clayton was courted for me, as much as I was for myself: But I had given Sir *Robert* his Cue; I had told

---

1 Roxana is describing here the business of land mortgages for which Clayton was most famous and in which he had made his own fortune.

him my Opinion of Matrimony, in just the same Terms as I had done my Merchant, and he came into it presently; he own'd that my Observation was just, and that, if I valued my Liberty, as I knew my Fortune, and that it was in my own Hands, I was to blame, if I gave it away to any-one.

But Sir *Robert* knew nothing of my Design; that I aim'd at being a kept Mistress, and to have a handsome Maintenance; and that I was still for getting Money, *and laying it up too*, as much as he cou'd desire me, only by a worse Way.

However, Sir *Robert* came seriously to me one Day, and told me, he had an Offer of Matrimony to make to me, that was beyond all that he had heard had offer'd themselves, and this was a Merchant; Sir *Robert* and I agreed exactly in our Notions of a Merchant; Sir *Robert* said, and I found it to be true, that a true-bred Merchant is the best Gentleman in the Nation; that in Knowledge, in Manners, in Judgment of things, the Merchant out-did many of the Nobility; that having once master'd the World, and being above the Demand of Business tho' no real Estate,[1] they were then superior to most Gentlemen, even in Estate; that a Merchant in flush Business, and a capital Stock, is able to spend more Money than a Gentleman of 5000*l.* a year Estate; that while a Merchant spent, he only spent what he got, and not that; and that he laid up great Sums every Year.

That an Estate is a Pond; but that a Trade was Spring; that if the first is once mortgag'd, it seldom gets clear, but embarrass'd the Person for ever; but the Merchant had his Estate continually flowing; and upon this, he nam'd me Merchants who liv'd in more real Splendor, and spent more Money than most of the Noblemen in *England* cou'd singly expend, and that they still grew immensely rich.[2]

He went on to tell me, that even the Tradesmen in London, speaking of the better sort of Trades, cou'd spend more Money in their Families, and yet give better Fortunes to their Children, than generally speaking, the Gentry of *England* from 1000*l.* a Year downward, cou'd do, and yet grow rich too.

The Upshot of all this was, to recommend to me, rather the bestowing my Fortune upon some eminent Merchant, who liv'd already in the first Figure of Merchant, and who not being in

---

1 A merchant's wealth lay in capital and moveable goods rather than in "real" estate, or property.

2 Clayton himself was among these merchants.

Want or Scarcity of Money, but having a flourishing Business, and flowing Case, wou'd at the first word, settle all my Fortune on myself and Children, and maintain me like a Queen.

This was certainly right; and had I taken his Advice, I had been really happy; but my Heart was bent upon an Independency of Fortune; and I told him, I knew no State of Matrimony, but what was, at best, a State of Inferiority, if not of Bondage; that I had no Notion of it; that I liv'd a Life of absolute Liberty now; was free as I was born, and having a plentiful Fortune, I did not understand what Coherence the Words *Honour* and *Obey* had with the Liberty of a *Free Woman*; that I knew no Reason the Men had to engross the whole Liberty of the Race, and make Women, notwithstanding any disparity of Fortune, be subject to the Laws of Marriage, of their own making; that it was my Misfortune to be a Woman, but I was resolv'd it shou'd not be made worse by the Sex; and seeing Liberty seem'd to be the Men's Property, I wou'd be a *Man-Woman*; for I was born free, I wou'd die so.

Sir *Robert* smil'd, and told me, I talk'd a kind of *Amazonian*[1] Language; that he found few Women of my Mind, or that if they were, they wanted Resolution to go on with it; that notwithstanding all my Notions, which he could not but say had some Weight in them, yet he understood I had broke-in upon them, and had been marry'd; I answer'd, I had so, but he did not hear me say, that I had any Encouragement from what was past, to make a second Venture; that I was got well out of the Toil, and if I came in again, I shou'd have no-body to blame but myself.

Sir *Robert* laugh'd heartily at me, but gave over offering any more Arguments, only told me he had pointed me out for some of the best Merchants in *London*, but since I forbad him, he wou'd give me no Disturbance of that Kind; he applauded my Way of managing my Money, and told me, I shou'd soon be monstrous rich; but he neither knew, or mistrusted, that with all this Wealth, I was yet a Whore, and was not averse to adding to my Estate at the farther Expence of my Virtue.

But to go on with my Story as to my ways of living; I found, as above, that my living as I did, wou'd not answer; that it only brought the *Fortune-Hunters* and Bites[2] about me, as I have said before, to make a Prey of me and my Money; and in short, I was harrass'd

---

1 Amazons were a mythical race of women warriors who lived in a matriarchal culture and dominated their male counterparts.
2 Swindlers.

with Lovers, *Beaus*, and *Fops* of Quality, in abundance; but it wou'd not do, I aim'd at other things, and was possess'd with so vain an Opinion of my own Beauty, that nothing less than the KING himself was in my Eye; and this Vanity was rais'd by some Words *let fall* by a Person I convers'd with, who was, perhaps, likely enough to have brought such a thing to pass, had it been sooner; *but that Game began to be pretty well over at Court:* However, he having mention'd such a thing, it seems, a little too publickly, it brought abundance of People about me, upon a Wicked Account too.

And now I began to act in a new Sphere; the Court was exceeding gay and fine, tho' fuller of Men than of Women, the Queen not affecting to be very much in publick; on the other hand, it is no Slander upon the Courtiers, *to say*, they were as wicked as any-body in reason cou'd desire them: The KING had several Mistresses, who were prodigious fine, and there was a glorious Show on that Side indeed: If the Sovereign gave himself a Loose,[1] it cou'd not be expected the rest of the Court shou'd be all Saints; so far was it from that, tho' I wou'd not make it worse than it was, that a Woman that had any-thing agreeable in her Appearance, cou'd never want Followers.

I soon found myself throng'd with Admirers, and I receiv'd Visits from some Persons of very great Figure, who always introduc'd themselves by the help of an old Lady or two, who were now become my Intimates; and one of them, I understood afterwards, was set to-work on purpose to get into my Favour, in order to introduce what follow'd.

The Conversation we had, was generally courtly, but civil; at length, some Gentleman propos'd to Play,[2] and made what they call'd, a Party; this it seems, was a Contrivance of one of my Female hangers-on, *for as I said, I had two of them,* who thought this was the way to introduce People as often as she pleas'd, and so indeed it was: They play'd high, and stay'd late, but begg'd my Pardon, only ask'd Leave to make an Appointment for the next Night; I was as gay, and as well-pleas'd as any of them, and one Night told one of the Gentlemen, my Lord—, that seeing they were doing me the Honour of diverting themselves at my Apartment, and desire'd to be there sometimes, I did not keep a Gaming Table, but I wou'd give them a little Ball the next Day, if they pleas'd; which they accepted very willingly.

Accordingly, in the Evening the Gentlemen began to come,

---

1 Unrestrained freedom.
2 Gamble.

where I let them see, that I understood very well what such things meant: I had a large Dining-Room in my Apartments, with five other Rooms on the same Floor, all which I made Drawing-Rooms for the Occasion, having all the Beds taken down for the Day; in three of these I had Tables plac'd, cover'd with Wine and Sweet-Meats; the fourth had a green Table for Play, and the fifth was my own Room, where I sat, and where I receiv'd all the Company that came to pay their Compliments to me: I was dress'd, you may be sure, to all the Advantage possible, and had all the Jewels on, that I was Mistress of: My Lord—, to whom I had made the Invitation, sent me a Sett of fine Musick from the Play-House,[1] and the Ladies danc'd, and we began to be very merry; when about eleven a-Clock I had Notice given me, that there were some Gentlemen coming in Masquerade.

I seem'd a little surpriz'd, and began to apprehend some Disturbance; when my Lord— perceiving it, spoke to me to be easie, for that there was a Party of the Guards at the Door, which shou'd be ready to prevent any Rudeness; and another Gentleman gave me a Hint, as if the KING was among the Masks; I colour'd as red as Blood itself cou'd make a Face look, and express'd a great Surprize; however, there was no going back; so I kept my Station in my Drawing-Room, but with the Folding-Doors wide open.

A-while after, the Masks came in, and began with a Dance *a la Comique*, performing wonderfully indeed; while they were dancing, I withdrew, and left a Lady to answer for me, that I wou'd return immediately; in less than half an Hour I return'd immediately; in less than half an Hour I return'd, dress'd in the Habit of a *Turkish Princess*;[2] the Habit I got at *Leghorn*, when my *Foreign Prince* bought me a *Turkish* Slave, as I have said; the *Malthese* Man of War had, it seems, taken a *Turkish* Vessel going

---

1 A group of musicians who would have accompanied theatrical performances.

2 As Laura Brown points out, "The dress is the counterpart of the slave, and in this passage indistinguishable from her, and both are made available through the agency of imperialist aggression, here the unofficial imperialist rivalry of piracy. Indeed the outfitting of the English female body in the complete and gorgeous costume of an exotic and exploited other is one dimension of the powerful motif of female dressing that characterizes eighteenth-century ideology." *Ends of Empire: Women and Ideology in Early Eighteenth-Century English Literature* (Ithaca: Cornell UP, 1993) 148.

from *Constantinople* to *Alexandria*, in which were some Ladies bound for *Grand Cairo* in *Egypt*; and as the Ladies were made Slaves, so their fine Cloaths were thus expos'd; and with this Turkish Slave, I bought the rich Cloaths too: The dress was extraordinary fine indeed, I had bought it as a Curiosity, having never seen the like; the robe was a fine *Persian*, or *India* Damask; the Ground white, and the Flowers blue and gold, and the Train held five Yards; the Dress under it, was a Vest of the same, embroider'd with Gold, and set with some Pearl in the Work, and some *Turquois* Stones; to the Vest, was a Girdle five or six Inches wide, after the *Turkish* Mode; and on both Ends where it join'd or hook'd, was set with Diamonds for eight Inches either way, only they were not true Diamonds; but no-body knew that but myself.

The Turban, or Head-Dress, had a Pinacle on the top, but not above five Inches, with a Piece of loose Sarcenet[1] hanging from it; and on the front, just over the Forehead, was a good Jewel, which I had added to it.

This Habit, as above, cost me about sixty Pistoles in *Italy*, but cost much more in the Country from whence it came; and little did I think, when I bought it, that I shou'd put it to such a Use as this; tho' I had dress'd myself in it many times, by the help of my little *Turk*, and afterwards between *Amy* and I, only to see how I look'd in it: I had sent her up before, to get it ready, and when I came up, I had nothing to do, but slip it on, and was down in my Drawing-Room in a little more than a quarter of an Hour; when I came there, the room was full of Company, but I order'd the Folding-Doors to be shut for a Minute or two, till I had receiv'd the Compliments of the Ladies that were in the Room, and had given them a full view of my Dress.

But my Lord—, who happen'd to be in the room, slipp'd out at another Door, and brought back with him one of the Masks, a tall well-shap'd Person, but who had no Name, *being all Mask'd*, nor would it have been allow'd to ask any Person's Name on such an Occasion;[2] the Person spoke in *French* to me, that it was the finest Dress he had ever seen; and ask'd me, if he shou'd have the Honour to dance with me? I bow'd, as giving my Consent, but said, As I had been a *Mahometan*,[3] I cou'd not dance after the Manner of this Country; I suppos'd their Musick wou'd not play *a la Moresque*; he answer'd merrily, I had a Christian's Face, and

---

1 A fine soft, silk cloth.
2 I.e., while in masquerade.
3 A Muslim.

he'd venture it, that I cou'd dance like a Christian; adding, that so much Beauty cou'd not be *Mahometan*: Immediately the Folding-Doors were flung open, and he led me into the Room: the Company were under the greatest Surprize imaginable; the very Musick stopp'd a-while to gaze; for the Dress was indeed, exceedingly surprizing, perfectly new, very agreeable, and wonderful rich.

The Gentleman, *whoever he was*, for I never knew, led me only a Courant,[1] and then ask'd me, if I had a-mind to dance an Antick,[2] that is to say, whether I wou'd dance the Antick as they had danc'd in Masquerade, or any-thing by myself; I told him, anything else rather, if he pleas'd; so we danc'd only two *French* Dances, and he led me to the Drawing-Room door, when he retir'd to the rest of the Masks: When he left me at the Drawing-Room Door, I did not go in, as he thought I wou'd have done, but turn'd about, and show'd myself to the whole Room, and calling my Woman to me, gave her some Directions to the Musick, by which the Company presently understood that I would give them a Dance by myself: Immediately all the House rose up, and paid me a kind of Compliment, by removing back every way to make me room, for the Place was exceeding full; the Musick did not at first hit the Tune that I directed, which was a *French* Tune, so I was forc'd to send my Woman to 'em again, standing all the while at my Drawing-Room Door; but as soon as my Woman spoke to them again, they play'd it right; and I, to let them see it was so, stepp'd forward to the middle of the Room; then they began it again, and I danc'd by myself a Figure which I learnt in *France*, when the Prince *de*— desir'd I wou'd dance for his Diversion; it was indeed, a very fine Figure, invented by a famous Master at *Paris*, for a Lady or a Gentleman to dance single; but being perfectly new, it pleas'd the Company exceedingly, and they all thought it had been Turkish; nay, one Gentleman had the Folly to expose himself so much, as to say, and I think swore too, that he had see it danc'd at *Constantinople*; which was ridiculous enough.

At the finishing the Dance, the Company clapp'd, and almost shouted; and one of the Gentlemen cry'd out, *Roxana!*

---

1   A seventeenth-century French dance, characterized by running and gliding steps to an accompaniment in triple time.
2   A grotesque or comic dance.

Roxana![1] By—, with an Oath; upon which foolish Accident I had the Name of *Roxana* presently fix'd upon me all over the Court End of Town, as Effectually as if I had been Christen'd *Roxana*: I had, it seems the Felicity of pleasing every-body that Night, to an Extreme; and my Ball, but especially my Dress, was the Chat of the Town for that Week, and so the Name *Roxana* was the Toast at, and about the Court; no other Health was to be nam'd with it.

Now things began to work as I wou'd have them, and I began to be very popular, as much as I cou'd desire: The Ball held till (as well as I was pleas'd with the Show) I was sick of the Night; the Gentlemen mask'd, went off about three a-Clock in the Morning; the other Gentlemen sat down to Play; the Musick held it out; and some of the Ladies were dancing at Six in the Morning.

But I was mighty eager to know who it was danc'd with me; some of the Lords went so far as to tell me, I was very much honour'd in my Company; one of them spoke so broad, as almost to say it was the KING, but I was convinc'd afterwards, it was not; and another reply'd, If he had been His Majesty, he shou'd have thought it no Dishonour to Lead-up a *Roxana*; but to this Hour I never knew positively who it was; and by his Behaviour I thought he was too young, His Majesty being at that time in an Age that might be discover'd from a young Person, even in his Dancing,

Be that as it wou'd, I had 500 Guineas sent me the next Morning, and the Messenger was order'd to tell me, that the Persons who sent it, desir'd a Ball again at my Lodging on the next *Tuesday*, but that they wou'd have my Leave to give the Entertainment themselves: I was mighty well pleas'd with this, (to be sure) but very inquisitive to know who the Money came from; but the Messenger was silent as Death, as to that Point; and bowing always at my Enquiries, begg'd me to ask no Questions which he cou'd not give an obliging Answer to.

I forgot to mention that the Gentlemen that play'd, gave a Hundred Guineas to the Box,[2] *as they call'd it*, and at the End of their Play, they ask'd my Gentlewoman of the Bed-Chamber, as

---

1 Defoe's exact source for this name has been the subject of considerable speculation. However, virtually all critics agree that versions of Roxana were fairly common in Restoration drama, and most characters who bore the name were Asian or Middle Eastern in origin and sexually available women.

2 Tipped the establishment, in this case Roxana's house.

they call'd her, (Mrs. *Amy*, forsooth) and gave it her; and gave twenty Guineas more among the Servants.

This Magnificent Doings equally both pleas'd and surpriz'd me, and I hardly knew where I was; but especially, that Notion of the KING being the Person that danc'd with me puff'd me up to that Degree, that I not only did not know anybody else, but indeed, was very far from knowing myself.

I had now the next *Tuesday* to provide for the like Company; but alas! it was all taken out of my Hand; three Gentlemen, who yet were, it seems, but Servants, came on the *Saturday*, and bringing sufficient Testimonies that they were right, for one was the same who brought the five hundred Guineas; I say, three of them came, and brought Bottles of all sorts of Wines, and Hampers of Sweet-Meats to such a Quantity, it appear'd they design'd to hold the Trade on more than once, and that they wou'd furnish everything to a Profusion.

However, as I found a Deficiency in two things, I made Provision of about twelve Dozen of fine Damask Napkins, with Table-cloaths of the same, sufficient to cover all the Tables, with three Table-cloaths upon every Table, and Side-boards in Proportion; also I bought a handsome Quantity of Plate, necessary to have serv'd all the Side-boards, but the Gentlemen would not suffer any of it to be us'd; telling me, they had bought fine *China* Dishes and Plates for the whole Service; and that in such publick Places[1] they cou'd not be answerable for the Plate; so it was set all up in a large Glass-Cupboard in the Room I sat in, where it made a very good Show indeed.

On *Tuesday* there came such an Appearance of Gentlemen and Ladies, that my Apartments were by no means able to receive them; and those who in particular appear'd as Principals, gave Order below, to let no more Company come up; the Street was full of Coaches with Coronets, and fine Glass-Chairs; and in short, it was impossible to receive the Company; I kept my little Room, as before, and the Dancers fill'd the great Room; all the Drawing-Rooms also were fill'd, and three Rooms below-Stairs, which were not mine.

It was very well that there was a strong Party of the Guards brought to keep the Door, for without that, there had been such

---

1 The servant's characterization of Roxana's house as "public" is telling. Public places—fairs, inns, theaters, etc.—were generally thought to be places of low morals and dissolute activities. That Roxana's private residence seems nonetheless public to the servant is indicative of the activities he understands to be ongoing there.

a promiscuous Crowd, and some of them scandalous too, that we shou'd have been all Disorder and Confusion; but the three Head-Servants manag'd all that, and had a word to admit all the Company by.

It was uncertain to me, and is to this Day, who it was that danc'd with me the *Wednesday* before, when the Ball was my own; but that the K— was at this Assembly, was out of Question with me, by Circumstances that I suppose I cou'd not be deceiv'd in; and particularly, that there were five Person who were not Mask'd, three of them had blue Garters,[1] and they appear'd not to me till I came out to dance.

This Meeting was manag'd just as the first, tho' with much more Magnificence, because of the Company; I plac'd myself (exceedingly rich in Cloaths and Jewels) in the middle of my little Room, as before, and made my Compliment to all the Company, as they pass'd me, as I did before; but my Lord—, who had spoken openly to me the first Night, came to me, and unmasking, told me the Company had order'd him to tell me, they hop'd they shou'd see me in the Dress I had appear'd in the first Day, which had been so acceptable, that it had been the Occasion of this new Meeting; and Madam, *says he*, there are some in this Assembly, who it is worth your while to oblige.

I bow'd to my Lord—, and immediately withdrew: while I was above, a-dressing in my new Habit, two Ladies, perfectly unknown to me, were convey'd into my Apartment below, by the Order of a Noble Person, who, with his Family, had been in *Persia*; and here indeed, I thought I shou'd have been out-done, or perhaps, baulk'd.

One of the Ladies was dress'd most exquisitely fine indeed, in the Habit of a Virgin Lady of Quality of *Georgia*, and the other in the same Habit of *Armenia*, with each of them a Woman-Slave to attend them.

The Ladies had their Petticoats short, to their Ancles, but pleated all round, and before them short Aprons, but of the finest Point[2] that cou'd be seen; their Gowns were made with long antick Sleeves[3] hanging down behind, and a Train let down; they

---

1 Blue Garters were worn by Knights of the Garter, an extremely select group consisting of no more than 25 members including the sovereign at any given time. Appointment was made exclusively at the sovereign's discretion.

2 Lace.

3 Old-fashioned sleeves.

had no Jewels; but their Heads and Breasts were dress'd up with Flowers, and they both came in veil'd.

Their Slaves were *bare-headed*; but their long black Hair was breeded in Locks hanging down behind, to their Wastes, and tied up with Ribbands; they were dress'd exceeding rich, and were as beautiful as their Mistresses; for none of them had any Masks on: They waited in my Room till I came down, and all paid their Respects to me after the *Persian* Manner and sat down on a *Safra*, that is to say, almost cross-legg'd on a Couch made up of Cushions laid on the Ground.

This was admirably fine, and I was indeed, startled at it; they made their compliment to me in *French*, and I reply'd in the same Language; when the Doors were open'd, they walk'd into the Dancing-Room, and danc'd such a Dance, as indeed, no-body there had ever seen, and to an Instrument like a Guittar, with a small low-sounding Trumpet, which indeed, was very fine, and which my Lord— had provided.

They danc'd three times all-alone, for no-body indeed, cou'd dance with them: The Novelty pleas'd, truly, but yet there was something wild and *Bizarre* in it, because they really acted to the Life the barbarous Country whence they came; but as mine had the *French* Behaviour under *Mahometan* Dress, it was every way as new, and pleas'd much better, indeed.

As soon as they had shewn their *Georgian* and *Armenian* Shapes, and danc'd, as I have said, three times, they withdrew, paid their Compliment to me, (for I was Queen of the Day) and went off to undress.

Some Gentlemen then danc'd with Ladies all in Masks, and when they stopp'd, no-body rose up to dance, but all call'd out *Roxana, Roxana*; in the Interval, my Lord— had brought another mask'd Person into my room, who I knew not, only that I cou'd discern it was not the same Person that led me out before: this noble Person (for I afterwards understood it was the Duke of—) after a short Compliment, led me out into the middle of the Room.

I was dress'd in the same Vest and Girdle as before; but the Robe had a Mantle over it, which is usual in the *Turkish* Habit, and it was of Crimson and Green; the Green brocaded with Gold; and my *Tyhiaai*, or Head-Dress, vary'd a little from that I had before, as it stood higher, and had some Jewels about the rising Part; which made it look like a Turban crown'd.

I had no Mask, neither did I Paint; and yet I had the Day of all the Ladies that appear'd at the Ball, I mean, of those that appear'd with Faces on; as for those Mask'd, nothing cou'd be said of them, no doubt there might be many finer than I was; it must be confess'd, that the Habit was infinitely advantageous to me, and every-body look'd at me with a kind of Pleasure, which gave me great Advantage too.

After I had danc'd with that noble Person, I did not offer to dance by myself, as I had before; but they all call'd out *Roxana* again; and two of the Gentlemen came into the Drawing-Room, to intreat me to give them the Turkish Dance, which I yielded to, readily; so I came out and danc'd, just as at first.

While I was dancing, I perceiv'd five Persons standing all together, and among them, one only with his Hat on;[1] it was an immediate Hint to me who it was, and had at first, almost put me into some Disorder; but I went on, receiv'd the Applause of the House, as before, and retir'd into my own room; when I was there, the five Gentlemen came cross the Room to my Side, and coming in, follow'd by a Throng of Great Persons, the Person with his Hat on, said Madam *Roxana* you *perform to Admiration*; I was prepar'd, and offer'd to kneel to kiss his Hand, but he declin'd it, and saluted me, and so passing back again thro' the Great Room, went away.

I do not say here, who this was, but I say, I came afterwards to know something more plainly; I wou'd have withdrawn, and disrob'd, being somewhat too thin in that Dress, unlac'd, and open-breasted, as if I had been in my Shift; but it cou'd not be, and I was oblig'd to dance afterwards with six or eight Gentlemen, most, if not all of them, of the *First Rank*; and I was told afterwards, that one of them was the *D— of M—th.*[2]

---

1 The gentleman's failure to remove his hat indicates that he is of the highest social rank, either nobility or royalty.

2 Defoe suggests here that Roxana's partner is the Duke of Monmouth, Charles II's illegitimate, but nonetheless Protestant, son. During the Exclusion Crisis, Whig partisans aimed to exclude Charles II's Catholic brother James from inheriting the throne. The Earl of Shaftesbury and others vigorously promoted Monmouth as the viable Protestant heir. Monmouth, however, was forced to flee England in 1683, the year of Roxana's arrival, when he was discovered to have plotted to assassinate his father and uncle on their way to the horse races at Newmarket. Five years later, he attempted to mount an invasion force and overthrow his uncle, who had, in fact, been crowned king. Defoe participated in what is known as Monmouth's Rebellion. Monmouth, himself, was captured, tried for treason, and executed, a fate Defoe himself narrowly escaped.

About two or three a-Clock in the Morning, the Company began to decrease, the Number of women especially, dropp'd away Home, some and some at a time; and the Gentlemen retir'd down Stairs, where they unmask'd, and went to Play.

Amy waited at the Room where they Play'd; sat up all-Night to attend them; and in the Morning, when they broke-up, they swept the Box into her Lap, when she counted out to me, sixty two Guineas and a half; and the other Servants got very well too: *Amy* came to me when they were all gone, *Law— Madam*, says *Amy*, with a long gaping Cry, what shall I do with all this Money? And indeed, the poor Creature was half-mad with Joy.

I was now in my Element; I was as much talk'd of as any-body cou'd desire, and I did not doubt but something or other wou'd come of it; but the Report of my being so rich, rather was a Baulk to my View, than any-thing else; for the Gentlemen that wou'd, perhaps, have been troublesome enough otherwise, seem'd to be kept off; for Roxana was too high for them.

There is a Scene which came in here, which I must cover from humane Eyes or Ears; for three Years and about a Month, *Roxana* liv'd retir'd, having been oblig'd to make an Excursion, in a Manner, and with a Person, which Duty, and private Vows, obliges her not to reveal, at least, not yet.

At the End of this Time I appear'd again; but I must add, that as I had in the Time of Retreat, *made Hay*, &c.—so I did not come Abroad again with the same Lustre, or shine with so much Advantage as before; for as some People had got at least, a Suspicion of where I had been, and who had had me all the while, it began to be publick, that *Roxana* was, in short, a meer *Roxana*, neither better nor worse; and not that Woman of Honour and Virtue that was at first suppos'd.

You are now to suppose me about seven years come to Town, and that I had not only suffer'd the old Revenue, which I hinted was manag'd by Sir *Robert Clayton*, to grow, as was mention'd before; but I had laid-up an incredible Wealth, the time consider'd; and had I yet had the least Thought of reforming, I had all the Opportunity to do it with Advantage, that ever Woman had; for the common Vice of all Whores, I mean Money, was out of the Question, nay, even Avarice itself seem'd to be glutted; for, including what I had sav'd in reserving the Interest of 14000*l.* which as above, I had left to grow; and including some very good Presents I had made to me, in meer Compliment, upon those shining masquerading Meetings, which I held up for about two Years, and what I made of three Years of the most glorious

Retreat, *as I call it*, that ever Woman had, I had fully doubled my first Substance, and had near 5000 Pounds in Money, which I kept at-home; besides abundance of Plate, and Jewels, which I had either given me, or had bought to set myself out for Publick Days.

In a word, I had now five and thirty Thousand Pounds Estate; and as I found Ways to live without wasting either Prinicpal or Interest, I laid-up 2000*l.* every Year, at least, out of the meer Interest, adding it to the Principal; and thus I went on.

After the End of what I call my Retreat, and out of which I brought a great deal of Money, I appear'd again, but I seem'd like an old Piece of Plate that had been hoarded up some Years, and comes out tarnish'd and discolour'd; so I came out blown,[1] and look'd like *a cast-off Mistress*, nor indeed, was I any better; tho' I was not at-all impair'd in Beauty, except that I was a little fatter than I was formerly, and always granting that I was four Years older.

However, I preserv'd the Youth of my Temper; was always bright, pleasant in Company, and agreeable to every-body, or else every-body flatter'd me; and in this Condition I came Abroad to the World again; and tho' I was not so popular as before, and indeed, did not seek it, because I knew it cou'd not be; yet I was far from being without Company, and that of the greatest Quality, *of Subjects I mean*, who frequently visited me, and sometimes we had Meetings for Mirth, and Play, at my Apartments, where I fail'd not to divert them in the most agreeable Manner possible.

Nor cou'd any of them make the least particular Application to me, from the Notion they had of my excessive Wealth, which, as they thought, plac'd me above the meanness of a Maintenance; and so left no room to come easily about me.

But at last I was very handsomely attack'd by a Person of Honour, and (which recommended him particularly to me) a Person of a very great Estate; he made a long Introduction to me upon the Subject of my Wealth: Ignorant Creature! *said I to myself*, considering him as a LORD; was there ever Woman in the World that cou'd stoop to the Baseness of being a Whore, and was above taking the Reward of her Vice! *No, no, depend upon it, if your Lordship obtains any-thing of me, you must pay for it; and the Notion of my being so rich, serves only to make it cost you the dearer, seeing you cannot offer a small Matter to a Woman of 2000l. a Year Estate.*

---

1 When a flower blossom has faded and fallen off, past its peak.

After he had harangu'd upon that Subject a good-while, and had assur'd me he had no Design upon me; that he did not come to make a Prize of me, or to pick my Pocket, which (by the way) I was in no fear of, for I took too much Care of my Money, to part with any of it that way; he then turn'd his Discourse to the Subject of Love; a Point so ridiculous to me, without the main thing, I mean the Money, that I had no Patience to hear him make so long a Story of it.

I receiv'd him civilly, and let him see I cou'd bear to hear a wicked Proposal, without being affronted, and yet I was not to be brought into it too easily: He visited me a long-while, and in short, courted me as closely and assiduously, as if he had been wooing me to Matrimony; he made me several valuable Presents, which I suffer'd myself to be prevail'd with to accept, but not without great Difficulty.

Gradually I suffer'd also his other Importunities, and when he made a Proposal of a Compliment, or Appointment to me, for a Settlement, *he said,* That tho' I was rich, yet there was not the less due from him, to acknowledge the Favours he receiv'd; and that if I was to be his, I shou'd not live at my own Expence, *cost what it wou'd:* I told him I was far from being Extravagant, and yet I did not live at the Expence of less than 500*l.* a Year out of my own Pocket; that however, I was not covetous of settled Allowances, for I look'd upon that as a kind of *Golden Chain,* something like Matrimony; that tho' I knew how to be true to a Man of Honour, as I knew his Lordship to be, yet I had a kind of Aversion to the Bonds; and tho' I was not so rich as the World talk'd me up to be, yet I was not so poor as to bind myself to Hardships, for a Pension.

He told me, he expected to make my Life perfectly easie, and intended it so; that he knew of no Bondage there cou'd be in a private Engagement between us; that the Bonds of Honour he knew I wou'd be ty'd by, and think them no Burthen, and for other Obligations, he scorn'd to expect any-thing from me, but what he knew, as a Woman of Honour, I cou'd grant; then, as to Maintenance, he told me, he wou'd soon show me that he valued me infinitely above 500*l.* a Year; and upon this foot we began.

I seem'd kinder to him after this Discourse; and as Time and Private Conversation made us very intimate, we began to come nearer to the main Article, namely, the 500*l.* a Year; he offer'd that at first Word; and to acknowledge it as in infinite Favour to have it be accepted of; and I, that thought it was too much by all the Money, suffer'd myself to be master'd, or prevail'd with, to yield, even on but a bare Engagement upon Parole.

When he had obtain'd his End that way, I told him my Mind: Now you see, my Lord, *said I*, how weakly I have acted, *namely*, to yield to you without any Capitulation, or any-thing secur'd to me, but that which you may cease to allow, when you please; if I am the less valued for such a Confidence, I shall be injur'd in a Manner that I will endeavour not to deserve.

He told me, that he wou'd make it evident to me, that he did not seek me by way of Bargain, as such things were often done; that as I had treated him with a generous Confidence, so I shou'd find I was in the Hands of a Man of Honour, and one that knew how to value the Obligation; and upon this, he pull'd out a Goldsmith's Bill[1] for 300*l.* which, putting into my Hand, he said he gave me as a Pledge, that I shou'd not be a Loser by my not having made a Bargain with him.

This was engaging indeed, and gave me a good Idea of our future Correspondence; and in short, as I cou'd not refrain treating him with more Kindness than I had done before, so one thing begetting another, I gave him several Testimonies that I was entirely his own, by Inclination, as well as by the common Obligation of a Mistress; and this pleas'd him exceedingly.

Soon after this private Engagement, I began to consider, whether it were not more suitable to the Manner of Life I now led, to be a little less publick; and as I told my Lord, it wou'd rid me of the Importunities of others, and of continual Visits from a sort of People who he knew of, and who, by the way, having now got the Notion of me which I really deserv'd, began to talk of the old Game, Love and Gallantry, and to offer at what was rude enough; things as nauceous to me now, as if I had been married, and as virtuous as other People: The Visits of these People began indeed, to be uneasie to me, and particularly, as they were always very tedious and impertinent; nor cou'd my Lord— be pleas'd with them at-all, if they had gone on: It wou'd be diverting to set down here, in what manner I repuls'd these sort of People; how in some I resented it as an Affront, and told them, that I was sorry they shou'd oblige me to vindicate myself from the Scandal of such Suggestions, by telling them, that *I cou'd see them no more*, and be desiring them not to give themselves the trouble of visiting me, who, tho' I was not willing to be uncivil, yet thought myself oblig'd never to receive any Visit from any Gentleman, after he had made such Proposals as those to me: But these things wou'd be too tedious to bring in here; it was on this

---

1 A check to be drawn on the Goldsmith's Company.

Account I propos'd to his Lordship my taking new Lodgings for Privacy; besides I consider'd that as I might live very handsomely, and yet not so publickly, so I needed not spend so much Money, by a great deal; and if I made 500*l.* a Year of this generous Person, it was more than I had any Occasion to spend, by a great deal.

My Lord came readily into this Proposal, and went farther than I expected; for he found out a Lodging for me in a very handsome House, where yet he was not known; I suppose he had employ'd somebody to find it out for him; and where he had a convenient Way to come into the Garden, by a Door that open'd into the Park;[1] a thing very rarely allow'd in those Times.

By this Key he cou'd come in at what time of the Night or Day he pleas'd; and as we had also a little Door in the lower Part of the House, which was always left upon a Lock, and his was the Master-Key, so if it was twelve, one, or two a-Clock at Night, he cou'd come directly into my Bed-Chamber. *N.B.* I was not afraid I shou'd be found a-Bed with any-body else, for, in a word, I convers'd with no-body at-all.

It happen'd pleasantly enough one Night; his Lordship had staid late, and I not expecting him that Night, had taken *Amy* to-Bed with me, and when my Lord came into the Chamber, we were both fast asleep, I think it was near three a-Clock when he came in, and a little merry, but not at-all fuddl'd, or what they call in Drink; and he came at once into the Room.

Amy was frighted out of her Wits, and cry'd out; I said calmly, indeed my Lord, I did not expect you to-Night, and we have been a little frighted to-Night with Fire: O! *says he*, I see you have got a Bedfellow with you; I began to make an Apology, *No, no, says my Lord*, you need not Excuse, 'tis not a Man-Bedfellow I see; but then talking merrily enough, he catch'd his Words back; but hark-ye, *says he*, now I think on't, how shall I be satisfied it is not a Man-Bedfellow? O, *says I*, I dare say your Lordship is satisfy'd 'tis poor *Amy*; yes, *says he*, 'tis Mrs. *Amy*, but how do I know what *Amy* is? It may be Mr. *Amy*, for ought I know; I hope you'll give me Leave to be satisfy'd: I told him, Yes, by all means I wou'd have his Lordship satisfy'd, but I suppos'd he knew who she was.

Well, he fell foul of poor *Amy*, and indeed, I thought once he wou'd have carry'd the Jest on before my Face, as was once done in a like Case; but his Lordship was not so hot neither; but he wou'd know whether *Amy* was Mr. *Amy*, or Mrs. *Amy*, and so I suppose he did; and then being satisfy'd in that doubtful Case, he

---

1 An enclosed tract of land for hunting game held by royal grant.

walk'd to the farther-end of the Room, and went into a little Closet, and sat down.

In the mean time *Amy* and I got up, and I bid her run and make the Bed in another Chamber for my Lord, and I gave her Sheets to put into it; which she did immediately, and put my Lord to-Bed there; and when I had done, at his Desire, went to-Bed to him, and made my Excuse, because I had been in-Bed with *Amy*, and had not shifted me,[1] but he was past those Niceties at that time; and as long as he was sure it was Mrs. *Amy*, and not Mr. *Amy*, he was very well satisfy'd, and so the Jest pass'd over; but *Amy* appear'd no more all that Night, or the next Day, and when she did, my Lord was so merry with her upon his *Ecclairissement*,[2] as he call'd it, that *Amy* did not know what to do with herself.

Not that *Amy* was such a nice Lady in the main, if she had been fairly dealt with, as has appear'd in the former Part of this Work; but now she was surpriz'd, and a little hurried, that she scarce knew where she was; and besides, she was, as to his Lord-ship, as nice a Lady as any in the World, and for any-thing he knew of her, she appear'd as such; the rest was to us only that knew of it.

I held this wicked Scene of Life out eight Years, reckoning from my first coming to *England*; and tho' my Lord found no Fault, yet I found, without much examining, that any-one who look'd in my Face, might see I was above twenty Years old, and yet, without flattering myself, I carried my Age, which was above Fifty, very well too.

I venture to say, that no Woman ever liv'd a Life like me of six and twenty Years of Wickedness, without the least Signals of Remorse; without any Signs of Repentance; or without so much as a Wish to put an End to it; I had so long habituated myself to a Life of Vice, that really it appear'd to be no Vice to me; I went on smooth and pleasant; I wallow'd in Wealth, and it flow'd in upon me at such a Rate, having taken the frugal Measures that the good Knight directed; so that I had at the End of the eight Years, two Thousand eight Hundred Pounds coming Yearly in, of which I did not spend one Penny, being maintain'd by my Allowance from my Lord—, and more than maintain'd, by above 200*l. per Annum*; for tho' he did not contract for 500*l.* a Year, as I

---

1 Had not yet changed her clothes.
2 Clarification.

made dumb Signs to have it be, yet he gave me Money so often, and that in such large Parcels, that I had seldom so little as seven to eight Hundred Pounds a Year of him, one Year with another.

I must go back here, after telling openly the wicked things I did, to mention something, which however, had the Face of doing good; I remember'd, that when I went from *England*, which was fifteen years before, I had left five little Children, turn'd out, as it were, to the wide World, and to the charity of their Father's Relations; the Eldest was not six Years old, for we had not been marry'd full seven Years when their Father went away.

After my coming to *England*, I was greatly desirous to hear how things stood with them; and whether they were all alive or not; and in what Manner they had been maintain'd; and yet I resolv'd not to discover myself to them, in the least; or to let any of the People that had the breeding of them up, know that there was such a-body left in the World, as their Mother.

Amy was the only-body I cou'd trust with such a Commission, and I sent her into *Spittle-Fields*, to the old Aunt, and to the poor Woman, that were so instrumental in disposing the Relations to take some Care of the Children, but they were both gone, dead and buried some Years; the next Enquiry she made, was at the House where she carry'd the poor Children, and turn'd them in at the Door; when she came there, she found the House inhabited by other People, so that she cou'd make little or nothing of her Enquiries, and came back with an Answer, that indeed, was no Answer to me, for it gave me no Satisfaction at-all: I sent her back to enquire in the Neighbourhood, what was become of the Family that liv'd in that House? And if they were remov'd, where they liv'd? and what Circumstances they were in? and withal, if she cou'd, what became of the poor Children, and how they liv'd, and where? how they had been treated? *and the like.*

She brought me back word, upon this second going, that she heard as to the Family, that the Husband, who tho' but Uncle-in-Law to the Children, had yet been kindest to them, was dead; and that the Widow was left but in mean Circumstances, that is to say, she did not want, but that she was not so well in the World as she was thought to be when her Husband was alive.

That as to the poor Children, two of them it seems, had been kept by her, that is to say, by her Husband, while he liv'd, for that it was against her Will, that we all knew; but the honest Neighbours pity'd the poor Children, they said, heartily; for that their Aunt us'd them barbarously, and made them little better than

Servants in the House, to wait upon her and her Children, and scarce allow'd them Cloaths fit to wear.

These were it seems my Eldest and Third, which were Daughters; the Second was a Son; the Fourth a Daughter; and the Youngest a Son.

To finish the melancholy Part of this History of my two unhappy Girls, she brought me word, that as soon as they were able to go out, and get any Work, they went from her; and some said, she had turn'd them out of Doors; but it seems she had not done so, but she us'd them so cruelly that they left her; and one of them went to Service to a Neighbour's a little-way off, who knew her, an honest substantial Weaver's Wife, to whom she was a Chamber-Maid, and in a little time she took her Sister out of the *Bridewell* of her Aunt's house, and got her Place too.

This was all melancholy and dull; I sent her then to the Weaver's House, where the Eldest had liv'd, but found that her Mistress being dead, she was gone, and no-body knew there, whither she went; only that they heard she had liv'd with a great Lady at the other-end of the Town; but they did not know who that Lady was.

These Enquiries took us up three or four Weeks, and I was not one Jot the better for it, for I cou'd hear nothing to my Satisfaction; I sent her next to find out the honest Man, who, as in the Beginning of my Story I observ'd made them be entertain'd, and caus'd the Youngest to be fetch'd from the Town where we liv'd, and where the Parish-Officers had taken Care of him: this Gentleman was still alive; and there she heard that my youngest Daughter and eldest Son was dead also; but that my youngest Son was alive, and was at that time, about 17 Years old; and that he was put out Apprentice, by the Kindness and Charity of his Uncle, but to a Mean Trade, and at which he was oblig'd to work very hard.

Amy was so curious in this Part, that she went immediately to see him, and found him all-dirty, and hard at-work; she had no rememberance at-all of the Youth, for she had not seen him since he was about two Years old; and it was evident he cou'd have no Knowledge of her.

However, she talk'd with him, and found him a good sensible mannerly Youth; that he knew little of the Story of his Father or Mother, and had no View of any-thing, but to work hard for his Living; and she did not think fit to put any great things into his Head, lest it shou'd take him off his Business, and perhaps, make him turn giddy-headed, and be good for nothing; but she went and found out that Kind Man, his Benefactor, who had put him out; and finding him a plain well-meaning, honest, and kind-hearted Man, she open'd her Tale to him the easier: She made a long Story, how she had a prodigious Kindness for the Child, because she had the same for his Father and Mother; told him, that she was the Servant-Maid that brought all of them to their Aunt's Door, and run away and left them; that their poor Mother wanted Bread; and what came to her after, she wou'd have been glad to know; she added, that her Circumstances had happen'd to mend in the world; and that, as she was in Condition, so she was dispos'd to shew some Kindness to the Children, if she cou'd find them out.

He receiv'd her with all the Civility that so kind a Proposal demanded; gave her an Account what he had done for the Child; how he had maintain'd him, fed and cloath'd him; put him to School, and at last, put him out to a Trade; she said, he had indeed, been a Father to the Child; but Sir, says she, 'tis a very laborious hard-working Trade, and he is but a thin weak Boy; that's true, says he, but the Boy chose the Trade, and I assure you, I gave 20l. with him, and am to find him Cloaths all his Apprenticeship; and as to its being a hard Trade, says he, that's the Fate of his Circumstances, poor Boy; I cou'd not well do better for him.

Well, Sir, as you did all for him in charity, says she, it was exceeding well; but as my Resolution is to do something for him, I desire you will, if possible, take him away again, from that Place, where he works so hard, for I cannot bear to see the Child work so very hard for his Bread, and I will do something for him, that shall make him live without such hard Labour.

He smil'd at that; I can indeed, says he, take him away, but then I must lose my 20l. that I gave with him.

Well Sir, said Amy, I'll enable you to lose that 20l. immediately, and so put her Hand in her Pocket, and pulls out her Purse.

He begun to be a little amaz'd at her, and look'd her hard in the Face, and that so very much, that she took Notice of it, and said, Sir, I Fancy by your looking at me, you think you know me, but I am assur'd you do not, for I never saw your Face before; I think you have done enough for the Child, and that you ought to be acknowledg'd as a Father to him, but you ought not to lose by your Kindness to him, more than the Kindness of bringing him up obliges you to; and therefore there's the twenty Pound, added she, and pray let him be fetch'd away.

Well, Madam, says he, I will thank you for the Boy, as well as for my self; but will you please to tell me, what I must do with him.

Sir, *says Amy*, as you have been so Kind to keep him so many Years, I beg you will take him home again one Year more, and I'll bring you an hundred Pound more, which I will desire you to lay-out in Schooling and Cloathes for him, and to pay you for his Board; perhaps I may put him in a Condition to return your Kindness.

He look'd pleas'd, but surpriz'd very much, and enquir'd of *Amy*, but with very great Respect, what he should go to School to learn? And what Trade she would please to put him out to?

Amy said, he should put him to learn a little *Latin*, and then Merchants-Accounts; and to write a good Hand, for she would have him be put to a *Turkey*-Merchant.[1]

Madam, *says he*, I am glad for his sake, to hear you talk so; but do you know that a *Turkey*-Merchant will not take him under 4 or 500 pounds?

Yes Sir, *says Amy*, I know very well.

And, *says he*, that it will require as many Thousands to set him up?

Yes Sir, *says Amy*, I know that very well too; and resolving to talk very big, *she added*, I have no Children of my own, and I resolve to make him my Heir; and if ten Thousand Pounds be requir'd to set him up, he shall not want it; I was but his Mother's Servant when he was born, and I mourn'd heartily for the Disaster of the Family; and I always said, if ever I was worth anything in the World, I wou'd take the Child for my own, and I'll be as good as my Word now, tho' I did not then foresee that it wou'd be with me, as it has been since: And so *Amy* told him a long Story how she was troubled for me; and what she wou'd give to hear whether I was dead or alive, and what Circumstances I was in; that if she cou'd but find me, if I was ever so poor, she wou'd take Care of me, and make a Gentlewoman of me again.

He told her, That as to the Child's Mother, she had been reduc'd to the last Extremity, and was oblig'd (as he suppos'd she knew) to send the Children all among her Husband's Friends; and if it had not been for him, they had all been sent to the Parish; but that he oblig'd the other Relations to share the charge among them; that he had taken two, whereof he had lost the eldest, who died of the Small-Pox; but that he had been as careful of this, as of his own, and had made very little Difference in their breeding up; only that when he came to put him out, he thought it was best for the Boy, to put him to a Trade which he might set-up in, without

---

1 A merchant who traded with Turkey.

a Stock; for otherwise his Time wou'd be lost; and that as to his Mother, he had never been able to hear one Word of her, no, not tho' he had made the utmost Enquiry after her; that there went a Report, that she had drown'd herself; but that he cou'd never meet with any-body that cou'd give him a certain Account of it.

Amy counterfeited a Cry for her poor Mistress; told him, she wou'd give anything in the World to see her, if she was alive; and a great deal more such-like Talk they had about that; then they return'd to speak of the Boy.

He enquir'd of her, why she did not seek after the Child before, that he might have been brought up from a younger Age, suitable to what she design'd to do for him.

She told him, she had been out of *England*, and was but newly return'd from the *East-Indies*; that she had been out of *England*, and was but newly return'd, was true; but the latter was false, and was put in to blind him, and provide against farther Enquiries; for it was not a strange thing for young Women to go away poor to the *East-Indies*, and come home vastly Rich; so she went on with Directions about him; and both agreed in this, that the Boy should by no means be told what was intended for him, but only that he should be taken home again to his Uncle's; that his Uncle thought the Trade too hard for him, *and the like.*

About three Days after this, *Amy* goes again, and carry'd him the hundred Pound she promis'd him, but then *Amy* made quite another Figure than she did before; for she went in my Coach, with two Footmen after her, and dress'd very fine also, with Jewels and a Gold Watch; and there was indeed, no great Difficulty to make *Amy* look like a Lady, for she was a very handsome well-shap'd Woman, and genteel enough; and the Coachman and Servants were particularly order'd to show her the same Respect as they wou'd to me, and to call her Madam *Collins*, if they were ask'd any Questions about her.

When the Gentleman saw what a Figure she made, it added to the former Surprize, and he entertain'd her in the most respectful Manner possible; congratulated her Advancement in Fortune, and particularly rejoyc'd that it should fall to the poor Child's Lot to be so provided for, contrary to all Expectation.

Well, *Amy* talk'd big, but very free and familiar; told them she had no Pride in her good-Fortune; (and that was true enough for to give *Amy* her due, she was far from it, and was as good-humour'd a Creature as ever liv'd) that she was the same as ever, and that she always lov'd this Boy, and was resolv'd to do something extraordinary for him.

Then she pull'd out her Money, and paid him down an hundred and twenty Pounds, which she said, she paid him, that he might be sure that he should be no Loser by taking him Home again, and she would come and see him again, and talk farther about things with him, that so all might be settled for him, in such a Manner, as the Accidents, such as Mortality, or any-thing else, should make no Alteration to the Child's Prejudice.

At this meeting, the Uncle brought his Wife out, a good motherly, comely, grave Woman who spoke very tenderly of the Youth, and as it appear'd, had been very good to him, tho' she had several Children of her own: After a long Discourse, she put in a Word of her own; Madam, *says she*, I am heartily glad of the good Intentions you have for this poor Orphan, and I rejoice sincerely in it, for his sake; but Madam, you know, (I suppose) that there are two Sisters alive too, may we not speak a Word for them? *Poor Girls, says she*, they have not been so kindly us'd, as he has; and are turn'd out to the wide World.

Where are they, Madam? *says, Amy*.

Poor Creatures, *says the Gentlewoman*, they are out at Service; no-body knows where but themselves; their Case is very hard.

Well, Madam, *says Amy*, tho', if I cou'd find them, I would assist them; yet my Concern is for the Boy, *as I call him*, and I will put him into a Condition to take Care of his Sisters.

But Madam, *says the good compassionate Creature*, he may not be so charitable perhaps, by his own Inclination, for Brothers are not Fathers; and they have been cruelly us'd already, poor Girls; we have often reliev'd them, both with Victuals and Cloaths too, even while they were pretended to be kept by their barbarous Aunt.

Well, Madam, *says Amy*, what can I do for them; they are gone, it seems, and cannot be heard of? When I see them, 'tis time enough.

She press'd *Amy* then, to oblige their Brother, out of the Plentiful Fortune he was like to have, to do something for his Sisters, when he should be able.

Amy spoke coldly of that still, but said, she would consider of it; and so they parted for that time; they had several Meetings after this, for *Amy* went to see her adopted Son, and order'd his Schooling, Cloaths, and other things, but enjoin'd them not to tell the Young-Man any-thing, but that they thought the Trade he was at, too hard for him, and they wou'd keep him at-home a little longer, and give him some Schooling, to fit him for better Business; and *Amy* appear'd to him as she did before, only as one that had known his Mother, and had some Kindness for him.

Thus this Matter pass'd on for near a Twelve-month, when it happen'd, that one of my Maid-Servants having ask'd *Amy* Leave, for *Amy* was Mistress of the Servants, and too, and put-out such as she pleas'd; I say, having ask'd Leave to go into the City, to see her Friends, came Home crying bitterly, and in a most grievous Agony she was, and continued so several Days, till *Amy* perceiving the Excess, and that the Maid wou'd certainly cry herself Sick; she took an Opportunity with her, and examin'd her about it.

The Maid told her a long Story, that she had been to see her Brother, the only Brother she had in the World; and that she knew he was put-out Apprentice to a—; but there had come a Lady in a Coach, to his Uncle—, who had brought him up, and made him take him Home again; and so the Wench run-on with the whole Story, just as 'tis told above, till she came to that part that belong'd to herself; and there, *says she*, I had not let them know where I liv'd; and the Lady wou'd have taken me, and they say, wou'd have provided for me too, as she has done for my Brother, but no-body cou'd tell where to find me, and so I have lost it all, and all Hopes of being any-thing, but a poor Servant all my Days; and then the Girl fell a-crying again.

Amy said, what's all this Story? Who cou'd this Lady be? It must be some Trick sure? No, s*he said*, it was not a Trick, for she had made them take her Brother home from Apprentice, and bought him new Cloaths, and put him to have more Learning; and the Gentlewoman said she wou'd make him her Heir.

Her Heir! *says Amy*; what does that amount to; it may be she had nothing to leave him; she might make any-body her Heir.

No, no, *says the Girl*, she came in a fine Coach and Horses, and I don't know how-many Footmen to attend her, and brought a great Bag of Gold, and gave it to my Uncle—, he that brought up my Brother, to buy him Cloaths, and to pay for his Schooling and Board.

He that brought up your Brother? *Says Amy*, why did not he bring you up too, as well as your Brother? Pray who brought you up then?

Here the poor Girl told a melancholly Story, how an Aunt had brought-up her and her Sister, and how barbarously she had us'd them, as we have heard.

By this time *Amy* had her Head full enough, and her Heart too; and did not know how to hold it, or what to do, for she was satisfied that this was no other than my own Daughter; for she told her all the History of her Father and Mother; and how she was carried by their Maid, to her Aunt's Door, just as is related in the beginning of my Story.

Amy did not tell me this Story for a great-while; nor did she well know what Course to take in it; but as she had Authority to manage everything in the Family, she took Occasion some time after, without letting me know any thing of it, to find some Fault with the Maid, and turn her away.

Her Reasons were good, tho' at first I was not pleas'd when I heard of it, but I was convinc'd afterwards, that she was in the right; for if she had told me of it, I shou'd have been in great Perplexity between the Difficulty of concealing myself from my own Child, and the Inconvenience of having my Way of Living be known among my First Husband's Relations, and even to my Husband himself; for as to his being dead at *Paris, Amy* seeing me resolv'd against marrying any-more, had told me, that she had form'd that Story only to make me easie, when I was in *Holland*, if any-thing should offer to my liking.

However, I was too tender a Mother still, notwithstanding what I had done, to let this poor Girl go about the World drudging, as it were, for Bread, and slaving at the Fire and in the Kitchin, as a Cook-Maid; besides it came into my Head, that she might, perhaps, marry some poor Devil of a Footman, or a Coachman, or some such thing, and be undone that way; or, which was worse, be drawn in to lie with some of that course cursed Kind, and be with-Child, and be utterly ruin'd that way; and in the midst of all my Prosperity this gave me great Uneasiness.

As to sending *Amy* to her, there was no doing that now; for as she had been Servant in the House, she knew *Amy*, as well as *Amy* knew me; and no doubt, tho' I was much out of her Sight, yet she might have had the Curiosity to have peep'd at me, and seen me enough to know me again, if I had discover'd myself to her; so that in short, there was nothing to be done that way.

However, *Amy*, a diligent and indefatigable Creature, found out another Woman, and gave her her Errand, and sent her to the honest Man's House in *Spittle-Fields*, whither she suppos'd the Girl wou'd go, after she was out of her Place; and bade her talk with her, and tell her at a distance, that as something had been done for her Brother, so something wou'd be done for her too; and that she shou'd not be discourag'd, she carried her 20*l.* to buy her Cloaths, and bid her not go to Service any-more, but think of other things; that she shou'd take a Lodging in some good Family, and that she shou'd soon hear farther.

The Girl was over joy'd with this News, you may be sure, and at first a little too much elevated with it, and dress'd herself very handsomely indeed, and as soon as she had done so, came and paid a Visit to Madam *Amy* to let her see how fine she was: *Amy* congratulated her, and wish'd it might be all as she expected; but admonish'd her not to be elevated with it too much; told her, Humility was the best Ornament for a Gentlewoman; and a great deal of good Advice she gave her, but discover'd nothing.

All this was acted in the first years of my setting-up my new Figure here in Town, and while the Masks and Balls were in Agitation;[1] and *Amy* carried on the Affair of setting-out my Son into the World, which we were assisted in by the sage Advice of my faithful Counsellor, Sir *Robert Clayton*,[2] who procur'd us a Master for him, by whom he was afterwards sent Abroad to *Italy*, as you shall hear in its Place; and *Amy* manag'd my Daughter too, very well, tho' by a third hand.

My Amour with my Lord— began now to draw to an end, and indeed, notwithstanding his Money, it had lasted so long, that I was much more sick of his Lordship, than he cou'd be of me; he grew old, and fretful, and captious, and I must add, which made the Vice itself begin to grow surfeiting and nauseous to me, he grew worse and wickeder the older he grew, and that to such Degree, as is not fit to write of; and made me so weary of him, that upon one of his capricious Humours, which he often took Occasion to trouble me with, I took Occasion to be much less complaisant to him than I us'd to be; and as I knew him to be hasty, I first took care to put him into a little Passion, and then to resent it, and this brought us to Words; in which I told him, I thought he grew sick of me; and he answer'd, in a heat, that *truly so he was*; I answer'd, that I found his Lordship was endeavouring to *make me sick too*; that I had met with several such Rubs from him of late; and that he did not use me as he us'd to do; and I begg'd his Lordship, he wou'd make himself easie: This I spoke with an Air of Coldness and Indifference such as I knew he cou'd not bear, but I did not downright quarrel with him, and tell him *I was sick of him too*, and desire him to quit me, for I knew that wou'd come of itself; besides I had receiv'd a great-deal of hand-

---

1 Literally, in motion or ongoing.
2 Clayton was, in fact, dedicated to helping poor boys seek a gainful living and entered into several philanthropic projects for workhouses with the great social reformer Thomas Firmin. From 1692 until his death, Clayton served as president of St. Thomas's Hospital.

some Usage from him, and I was loth to have the Breach be on my Side, that he might not be able to say I was ungrateful.

But he put the Occasion into my Hands, for he came no more to me for two Months; indeed I expected a Fit of Absence, for such I had had several times before, but not for above a Fortnight or three-Weeks at most: But after I had staid a Month, which was longer than ever he kept away yet, I took a new Method with him, for I was resolv'd now it shou'd be in my Power to continue, or not, as I thought fit; at the end of a Month therefore, I remov'd, and took Lodgings at *Kensington Gravel-Pitts*,[1] and that Part next to the Road to *Acton*, and left no-body in my Lodgings but *Amy* and a Footman; with proper Instructions how to behave, when his Lordship being come to himself, shou'd think fit to come again, which I knew he wou'd.

About the end of two Months, he came in the Dusk of the Evening, as usual, the Footman answer'd him, and told him, his Lady was not at home, but there was Mrs. *Amy* above; so he did not order her to be call'd down, but went up-Stairs into the Dining-Room, and Mrs. *Amy* came to him; he ask'd where I was? My Lord, *said she*, my Mistress has been remov'd a good-while, from hence, and lives at *Kensington*: Ay, Mrs. *Amy*! how come you to be here then? My Lord, *said she*, we are here till the Quarter-Day,[2] because the Goods are not remov'd, and to give Answers, if any comes to ask for my Lady: Well, and what answer are you to give to me? Indeed, my Lord, *says Amy*, I have no particular Answer to your Lordship, but to tell you, and every-body else, where my Lady lives, that they may not think she's run away: No Mrs. *Amy*, *says he*, I don't think she's run away, but indeed, I can't go after her so far as that; *Amy* said nothing to that, but made a Curtsie, and said, she believ'd I wou'd be there again for a Week or two, in a little time: How little time, Mrs. *Amy*? *says my Lord*: She comes next *Tuesday*, says *Amy*: Very well, *says my Lord*, I'll call and see her then; and so he went away.

---

1 The north part of Kensington. In the eighteenth century, this became Kensington Gardens.

2 *OED*: One of the four days fixed by custom as marking off the quarters of the year, on which tenancy of houses usually begins and ends, and the payment of rent and other quarterly charges falls due. In England and Ireland the quarter-days are Lady Day (March 25), Midsummer Day (June 24), Michaelmas (Sept. 29), and Christmas (Dec. 25). The name is also sometimes applied to the Scottish terms of Candlemas (Feb. 2), Whit-sunday (May 15), Lammas (Aug. 1), and Martinmas (Nov. 11).

Accordingly I came on the *Tuesday*, and staid a Fortnight, but he came not; so I went back to *Kensington*, and after that, I had very few of his Lordship's Visits, which I was very glad of, and in a little time after was more glad of it, than I was at first, and upon a far better Account too.

For now I began not to be sick of his Lordship only, but really I began to be sick of the Vice; and as I had good Leisure now to divert and enjoy myself in the World, as much as it was possible for any Woman to do, that ever liv'd in it; so I found that my Judgment began to prevail upon me to fix my Delight upon nobler Objects than I had formerly done; and the very beginning of this brought some just Reflections upon me, relating to things past, and to the former Manner of my living; and tho' there was not the least Hint in all this, from what may be call'd Religion or Conscience, and far from any-thing of Repentance, or any-thing that was a-kin to it, especially at first; yet the Sence of things, and the Knowledge I had of the World, and the vast Variety of Scenes that I had acted my Part in, began to work upon my Sences, and it came so very strong upon my Mind one Morning, when I had been lying awake some time in my Bed, as if somebody had ask'd me the Question, *What was I a Whore for now?* It occurr'd naturally upon this Enquiry, that at first I yielded to the Importunity of my Circumstances, the Misery of which, the Devil dismally aggravated, to draw me to comply; for I confess, I had strong Natural Aversions to the Crime at first, partly owing to a virtuous Education, and partly to a Sence of Religion; but the Devil, and that greater Devil of Poverty, prevail'd; and the Person who laid Siege to me, did it in such an obliging, and I may almost say, irresistible Manner, all still manag'd by the Evil Spirit; for I must be allow'd to believe, that he has a Share in all such things, if not the whole Management of them: But, I say, it was carried on by that Person, in such an irresistible Manner, that, (as I said when I related the Fact) there was no withstanding it: These Circumstances, I say, the Devil manag'd, not only to bring me to comply, but he continued them as Arguments to fortifie my Mind against all Reflection, and to keep me in that horrid Course I had engag'd in, as if it were honest and lawful.

But not to dwell upon that now; this was a Pretence, and here was something to be said, tho' I acknowledge, it ought not to have been sufficient to me at all; but, I say, to leave that, all this was out of Doors; the Devil himself cou'd not form one Argument, or put one Reason into my Head *now*, that cou'd serve for an Answer, no, not so much as a pretended Answer to this Question, *Why I shou'd be a Whore now?*

It had for a-while been a little kind of Excuse to me, that I was engag'd with this wicked old Lord, and that I cou'd not, in Honour, forsake him; but how foolish and absurd did it look, to repeat the Word Honour on so vile an Occasion? As if a Woman shou'd prostitute her Honour in Point of Honour; horrid Inconsistency; Honour call'd upon me to detest the Crime and the Man too, and to have resisted all the Attacks which from the beginning had been made upon my Virtue; and Honour, had it been consulted, wou'd have preserv'd me honest from the Beginning.

For HONESTY and HONOUR, are the same.[1]

This, however, shews us with what faint Excuses, and with what Trifles we pretend to satisfie ourselves, and suppress the Attempts of Conscience in the Pursuit of agreeable Crime, and in the possessing those Pleasures which we are loth to part with.

But this Objection wou'd now serve no longer; for my Lord had, in some sort, broke his Engagements (*I won't call it Honour again*) with me, and had so far slighted me, as fairly to justifie my entire quitting of him now; and so, as the Objection was fully answer'd, the Question remain'd still unanswer'd, *Why am I a Whore now?* Nor indeed, had I any-thing to say for myself *even to myself*; I cou'd not without blushing, as wicked as I was, answer, that I lov'd it for the sake of the Vice, and that I delighted in being a Whore, *as such*; I say, I cou'd not say this, even to myself, *and all alone*, nor indeed, wou'd it have been true; I was never able in Justice, and with Truth, to say I was so wicked as that; but as Necessity first debauch'd me, and Poverty made me a Whore at the beginning; so excess of Avarice for getting Money, and excess of Vanity, continued me in the Crime, not being able to resist the Flatteries of Great Persons; being call'd the finest Woman in *France*; being caress'd by a Prince; and afterwards I had Pride enough to expect, and Folly enough to believe, tho' indeed, without ground, by a Great Monarch: These were my Baits, these the Chains by which the Devil held me bound; and by which I was indeed, too fast held for any Reasoning that I was then Mistress of, to deliver me from.

But this was all over now; Avarice cou'd have no Pretence; I was out of reach of all that Fate cou'd be suppos'd to do to reduce me; now I was so far from Poor, or the Danger of it, that I had fifty Thousand Pounds in my Pocket at least; nay, I had the

---

1 From Defoe's "The Character of the Late Mr. Samuel Annesley, By way of Elegy." Annesley was a famous non-conformist minister and led the congregation in the church where Defoe's family worshipped.

Income of fifty Thousand Pounds; for I had 2500*l.* a Year coming in, upon very good Land-Security, besides 3 or 4000*l.* in Money, which I kept by me for ordinary Occasions, and besides Jewels and Plate, and Goods, which were worth near 5600*l.* more; these put together, when I ruminated on it all in my Thoughts, as you may be sure I did often, added Weight still to the Question, as above, and it sounded continually in my Head, what's next? *What am I a Whore for now?*

It is true, this was, as I say, seldom out of my Thoughts, but yet it made no Impressions upon me of that Kind which might be expected from a Reflection of so important a Nature, and which had so much of Substance and Seriousness in it.

But however, it was not without some little Consequences, even at that time, and which gave a little Turn to my Way of Living at first, as you shall hear in its Place.

But one particular thing interven'd besides this, which gave me some Uneasiness at this time, and made way for other things that follow'd: I have mention'd in several little Digressions, the Concern I had upon me for my Children, and in what Manner I had direct'd that Affair; I must go on a little with that Part, in order to bring the subsequent Parts of my Story together.

My Boy, the only Son I had left, that I had a legal right to call my Son, was, as I have said, rescued from the unhappy Circumstances of being apprentice to a Mechanick, and was brought-up upon a new foot; but tho' this was infinitely to his Advantage, yet it put him back near three Years in his coming into the World, for he had been near a Year at the Drudgery he was first put to and it took up two Year more to form him for what he had Hopes given him he shou'd hereafter be, so that he was full 19 Years old, or rather 20 Years, before he came to be put-out[1] as I intended; at the end of which time, I put him to a very flourishing *Italian* Merchant, and he again sent him to *Messina*, in the Island of *Sicily*; and a little before the Juncture I am now speaking of, I had Letters from him, that is to say, Mrs. *Amy* had letters from him, intimating, that he was out of his Time,[2] and that he had an Opportunity to be taken in to an *English* House there, on very good Terms, if his Support from hence might answer what he was bid to hope for; and so begg'd, that what wou'd be done for him, might be so order'd, that he might have it for his present Advancement, referring for the Particulars to his Master, the

---

1 Sent to be an apprentice.
2 The term of his apprenticeship was over.

Merchant in *London*, who he had been put Apprentice to here; who, to cut the Story short, gave such a satisfactory Account of it, and of my Young-Man, to my steddy and faithful Counsellor, Sir *Robert Clayton*, that I made no Scruple to pay 4000*l.* which was 1000*l.* more than he demanded, or rather propos'd, that he might have Encouragement to enter into the World better than he expected.

His Master remitted the Money very faithfully to him, and finding by Sir *Robert Clayton*, that the young Gentleman, for so he call'd him, was well supported, wrote such Letters on his Account, as gave him Credit at *Messina*, equal in Value to the Money itself.

I cou'd not digest it very well, that I shou'd all this while conceal myself thus from my own Child, and make all this Favour due, in his Opinion, to a Stranger; and yet I cou'd not find in my Heart to let my Son know what a Mother he had, and what a Life she liv'd; when at the same time that he must think himself infinitely oblig'd to me, he must be oblig'd, if he was a Man of Virtue, to hate his Mother, and abhor the Way of Living, by which all the Bounty he enjoy'd, was rais'd.

This is the Reason of mentioning this Part of my Son's Story, which is otherwise no ways concern'd in my History, but as it put me upon thinking how to put an End to that wicked Course I was in, that my own Child, when he shou'd afterwards come to *England* in a good Figure, and with the Appearance of a merchant, shou'd not be asham'd to own me.

But there was another Difficulty, which lay heavier upon me a great-deal, and that was, my Daughter; who, as before, I had reliev'd by the Hands of another Instrument, which *Amy* had procur'd: The Girl, as I have mention'd, was directed to put herself into a good Garb, take Lodgings, and entertain a Maid to wait upon her, and to give herself some Breeding, that is to say, to learn to Dance, and fit herself to appear as a Gentlewoman; being made to hope, that she shou'd, sometime or other, find that she shou'd be put into a Condition to support her Character, and to make herself amends for all her former Troubles; she was only charg'd not to be drawn into Matrimony, till she was secur'd of a Fortune that might assist to dispose of herself suitable not to what she then was, but what she was to be.

The Girl was too sensible of her Circumstances, not to give all possible Satisfaction of that Kind, and indeed, she was Mistress of too much Understanding, not to see how much she shou'd be oblig'd to that Part, for her own Interest.

It was not long after this, but being well-equipp'd, and in every-thing well set-out, as she was directed, she came, as I have related above, and paid a Visit to Mrs. *Amy*, and to tell her of her good Fortune: *Amy* pretended to be much surpriz'd at the Alteration, and overjoy'd for her sake, and began to treat her very well, entertain'd her handsomely, and when she wou'd have gone away, pretended to ask my Leave, and sent my Coach home with her; and in short, learning from her where she lodg'd, which was in the City, *Amy* promis'd to return her Visit, and did so; and in a word, *Amy* and Susan, (for she was my own Name) began an intimate Acquaintance together.

There was an inexpressible Difficulty in the poor Girl's way, or else I shou'd not have been able to have forborn discovering myself to her, and this was, her having been a Servant in my particular Family; and I cou'd by no means think of ever letting the Children know what kind of Creature they own'd their Being to, or giving them an Occasion to upbraid their Mother with her scandalous Life, much less to justifie the like Practice from my Example.

Thus it was with me; and thus, no doubt, considering Parents always find it, that their own Children are a Restraint to them in their worst courses, when the Sence of a Superiour Power has not the same Influence: *But of that hereafter.*

There happen'd however, one good Circumstance in the Case of this poor Girl, which brought about a Discovery sooner than otherwise it wou'd have been; and it was thus: After she and *Amy* had been intimate for some time, and had exchang'd several Visits, the Girl now grown to a Woman, talking to *Amy* of the gay things that us'd to fall-out when she was Servant in my Family, spoke of it with a kind of Concern, that she cou'd not see [me] her Lady; and at the last she adds, *'twas very strange*: Madam, *says she* to *Amy*, but tho' I liv'd near two Years in the House, I never saw my Mistress in my Life, except it was that publick Night when she danc'd in the fine Turkish Habit, and then she was so disguis'd, that I knew nothing of her afterwards.

Amy was glad to hear this: but as she was a cunning Girl from the beginning, she was not to be Bit, and so she laid no Stress upon that, at first, but gave me an Account of it; and, I must confess, it gave me a secret Joy, to think that I was not known to her; and that, by virtue of that only Accident, I might, when other Circumstances made room for it, discover myself to her, and let her know she had a Mother in a Condition fit to be own'd.

It was a dreadful Restraint to me before, and this gave me some very sad Reflections, and made way for the great Question

I have mention'd above; and by how much the Circumstance was bitter to me, by so much the more agreeable it was, to understand that the Girl had never seen me, and consequently, did not know me again, if she was to be told who I was.

However, the next time she came to visit *Amy*, I was resolv'd to put it to a Tryal, and to come into the Room, and let her see me, and to see by that, whether she knew me or no; but *Amy* put me by, lest indeed, as there was reason enough to question, I shou'd not be able to contain, or forbear discovering myself to her; so it went off for that time.

But both these Circumstances, and that is the reason of mentioning them, brought me to consider of the Life I liv'd, and to resolve to put myself into some Figure of Life, in which I might not be scandalous to my own Family, and be afraid to make myself known to my own Children, who were my own Flesh and Blood.

There was another Daughter I had, which, with all our Enquiries we cou'd not hear of, high nor low, for several Years after the first: But I return to my own Story.

Being now in part remov'd from my old Station, I seem'd to be in a fair Way of retiring from my old Acquaintances, and consequently from the vile abominable Trade I had driven so long; so that the Door seem'd to be, as it were, particularly open'd to my Reformation, if I had any-mind to it in earnest; but for all that, some of my old Friends as I had us'd to call them, enquir'd me out, and came to visit me at *Kensington*, and that more frequently than I wish'd they would do; but it being once known where I was, there was no avoiding it, unless I wou'd have downright refus'd and affronted them; and I was not yet in Earnest enough with my Resolutions, to go that length.

The best of it was, my old lewd Favourite, who I now heartily hated, entirely dropp'd me; he came once to visit me, but I caus'd *Amy* to deny me, and say I was gone out; she did it so oddly too, that when his Lordship went away, *he said* coldly to her, Well, well, Mrs. *Amy*, I find your Mistress does not desire to be seen; tell her I won't trouble her *any-more*, repeating the Words *any-more* two or three times over, just at his going away.

I reflected a little on it at first, as unkind to him, having had so many considerable Presents from him; but, *as I have said*, I was sick of him, and that on some Accounts, which, if I cou'd suffer myself to publish them, wou'd fully justifie my Conduct; but that Part of the Story will not bear telling; so I must leave it, and proceed.

I had begun a little, *as I have said above*, to reflect upon my Manner of Living, and to think of putting a new Face upon it; and nothing mov'd me to it more, than the Consideration of my having three Children, who were now grown up; and yet, that while I was in that Station of Life, I cou'd not converse with them, or make myself known to them; and this gave me a great-deal of Uneasiness; at last I enter'd into Talk on this Part of it, with my Woman, *Amy.*

We liv'd at *Kensington, as I have said,* and though I had done with my old wicked L—, as above, yet I was frequently visited, *as I said,* by some others, so that, in a word, I began to be known in the Town, not by my Name only, but by my Character too, which was worse.

It was one Morning when *Amy* was in-Bed with me, and I had some of my dullest Thoughts about me, that *Amy* hearing me sigh pretty often, ask'd me if I was not well? Yes, *Amy,* I am well enough, *says I,* but my Mind is oppress'd with heavy Thoughts, and has been so a good-while; and then I told her how it griev'd me what I cou'd not make myself known to my own Children, or form any Acquaintances in the World: Why so? S*ays Amy*; Why prethee *Amy, says I,* what will my Children say to themselves, and to one another, when they find their Mother, however rich she may be, is at best but a Whore, a common Whore? And as for Acquaintance, prethee *Amy,* what sober Lady, or what Family of any character will visit or be acquainted with a Whore?

Why, all that's true, Madam, *says Amy*; but how can it be rem-edy'd now? 'tis true *Amy, said I,* the thing cannot be remedy'd now, but the Scandal of it, I fancy, may be thrown off.

Truly, *says Amy* I do not see how, unless you will go Abroad again, and live in some other Nation, where no-body has known us, or seen us, so that they cannot say they ever saw us before.

That very Thought of *Amy* put what follows into my Head; and I return'd, Why *Amy, says I,* is it not possible for me to shift my Being from this Part of the Town, and go and live in another Part of the City, or another Part of the Country, and be as entirely conceal'd as if I had never been known?

Yes, *says Amy,* I believe it might: but then you must put-off all your Equipages, and Servants, and Coaches, and Horses; change your Liveries, nay, your own Cloaths, and if it was possible, your very Face.

Well, *says I,* and that's the way *Amy,* and that I'll do, and that forthwith; for I am not able to live in this Manner any longer: *Amy* came into this with a kind of Pleasure particular to herself, that is to say, with an Eagerness not to be resisted; for *Amy* was apt to be precipitant in her Motions, and was for doing it immediately: Well, *says I*, *Amy*, as soon as you will, but what Course must we take to do it? We cannot put off Servants, and Coach and Horses, and every-thing; leave off House-keeping, and transform ourselves into a new Shape, all in a Moment; Servants must have Warning, and the Goods must be sold off, and a thousand things, and this began to perplex us, and in particular, took us up two or three Days Consideration.

At last, *Amy*, who was a clever Manager in such Cases, came to me with a Scheme, as she call'd it; I have found it out, Madam, *says she*; I have found a Scheme how you shall, if you have a-mind to it, begin and finish a perfect entire Change of your Figure and Circumstances, in one Day; and shall be as much unknown, Madam, in twenty-four Hours, as you wou'd be in so many Years.

Come *Amy*, *says I*, let us hear it, for you please me mightily with the Thoughts of it: Why then, *says Amy*, let me go into the City this Afternoon, and I'll enquire out some honest, plain, sober Family, where I will take Lodgings for you, as for a Country-Gentlewoman that desires to be in *London* for about half a Year, and to Board yourself and a Kinswoman, that is half a Servant, half a Companion, meaning myself; and so agree with them by the Month.

To this Lodging (if I hit upon one to your Mind) you may go to-Morrow Morning, in a Hackney-Coach, with no-body but me, and leave such Cloaths and Linnen as you think fit; but to be sure, the plainest you have, and then you are remov'd at once, you need never so much as set your Foot in this House again, (meaning where we then were) or see any-body belonging to it; in the mean time I'll let the Servants know, that you are going over to *Holland* upon extraordinary Business, and will leave off your Equipages, and so I'll give them Warning, or, if they will accept of it, give them a Month's Wages; then I'll sell off your Furniture as well as I can; as to your Coach, it is but having it new-painted, and the Lining chang'd, and getting new Harness and Hammer-Cloths,[1] and you may keep it still, or dispose of it, as you think fit; and only take care to let this Lodging be in some remote Part of the Town, and you may be perfectly unknown, as if you had never been in *England* in your Life.

This was *Amy*'s Scheme; and it pleas'd me so well, that I resolv'd not only to let her go, but was resolv'd to go with her

---

1 A cloth to cover the driver's seat in a coach.

myself; but *Amy* put me off of that, because, s*he said*, she shou'd have Occasion to hurry up-and-down so long, that if I was with her, it wou'd rather hinder than farther her; so I wav'd it.

In a word, *Amy* went, and was gone five long Hours; but when she came back, I cou'd see by her Countenance, that her Success had been suitable to her Pains; for she came laughing and gaping, O Madam! s*ays she*, I have pleas'd you to the Life; and with that, she tells me how she had fix'd upon a House in a Court in the *Minories*;[1] that she was directed to it merely by Accident; that it was a Female Family, the Master of the House being gone to *New-England*; and that the Woman had four Children; kept two Maids, and liv'd very handsomely, but wanted Company to divert her; and that on that very account, she had agreed to take Boarders.

Amy agreed for a good handsome Price, because she was resolv'd I shou'd be us'd as well; so she bargain'd to give her 35*l*. for the Half-Year, and 50*l*. if we took a Maid, leaving that to my Choice; and that we might be satisfied we shou'd meet with nothing very gay; the People were QUAKERS,[2] and I lik'd them the better.

I was so pleas'd, that I resolv'd to go with *Amy* the next Day to see the Lodgings, and to see the Woman of the House, and see how I lik'd them; but if I was pleas'd with the general, I was much more pleas'd with the particulars; for the Gentlewoman, I must call her so, tho' she was a QUAKER, was a most courteous, obliging mannerly Person; perfectly well-bred, and perfectly well-

---

1   An area of London down by the Tower.
2   Originally, a derogatory name given to the Religious Society of Friends founded by George Fox in 1648. The Quakers did (and continue to) emphasize non-hierarchical forms of decision-making and religious worship. They believed, as did several other radical sects of the time, that all individuals were created in the image of God, and that, therefore, all individuals were equal. They rejected sacraments, ministers, and liturgical forms of worship, preferring a meditative form of worship in which individual members of a meeting focused on the "inner light" of God, and topics of worship and discussion at meeting were guided by that light. Quaker decision-making was consensual and relied heavily on public debate. No meeting or other deliberative body could issue a statement or change in policy unless every member endorsed the decision. Quakers have long refused to serve in combat roles during military conflicts, partly because of a commitment to non-violence, but also in the belief that neither governments nor individuals can command a person to jeopardize his or her God-given life.

humour'd, and in short, the most agreeable Conversation that ever I met with; and which was worth all, so grave, and yet so pleasant and so merry, that 'tis scarce possible for me to express how I was pleas'd and delighted with her Company; and particularly, I was so pleas'd, that I wou'd go away no more; so I e'en took up my Lodging there the very first Night.

In the mean time, tho' it took up *Amy* almost a Month so entirely, to put off all the Appearances of House-keeping, as above; it need take me up no Time to relate it; 'tis enough to say, that *Amy* quitted all that Part of the World, and came Pack and Package to me, and here we took up our Abode.

I was now in a perfect Retreat indeed; remote from the Eyes of all that ever had seen me, and as much out of the way of being ever seen or heard-of by any of the Gang that us'd to follow me, as if I had been among the Mountains in *Lancashire*; for when did a Blue Garter, or a Coach-and-Six come into a little narrow Passage in the *Minories*, or *Goodman's-Fields?* And as there was no Fear of them, so really I had no Desire to see them, or so much as to hear from them any-more, as long as I liv'd.

I seem'd in a little Hurry while *Amy* came and went, so every-Day, at first; but when that was over, I liv'd here perfectly retir'd, and with a most pleasant and agreeable Lady; I must call her so, for tho' a QUAKER, she had a full Share of good Breeding, sufficient to her, if she had been a Dutchess; in a word, she was the most agreeable Creature in her Conversation, *as I said before*, that ever I met with.

I pretended, after I had been there some time, to be extreamly in Love with the Dress of the QUAKERS,[1] and this pleas'd her so much, that she wou'd needs dress me up one Day in a Suit of her own Cloaths; but my real Design was, to see whether it wou'd pass upon me for a Disguise.

Amy was struck with the Novelty, tho' I had not mention'd my Design to her, and when the QUAKER was gone out of the Room, *says Amy*, I guess your Meaning; it is a perfect Disguise for you; why you look quite another-body, I should not have known you myself; nay, *says Amy*, more than that, it makes you look ten Years younger than you did.

Nothing cou'd please me better than that; and when *Amy* repeated it, I was so fond of it, that I ask'd my QUAKER, (I won't call her Landlady, 'tis indeed too course a Word for her, and she deserv'd a much better) I say, I ask'd her if she wou'd sell it; I told

---

1 Quakers were known for their modest, plain, and sober dress.

her, I was so fond of it, that I wou'd give her enough to buy her a better Suit; she declin'd it at first, but I soon perceiv'd that it was chiefly in good Manners, because I shou'd not dishonour myself, as she call'd it, to put on her old Cloaths; but if I pleas'd to accept of them, she wou'd give me them for my dressing-Cloaths, and go with me, and buy a Suit for me, that might be better-worth my wearing.

But as I convers'd in a very frank open Manner with her, I bid her do the like with me; that I made no Scruples of such things; but that if she wou'd let me have them, I wou'd satisfie her; so she let me know what they cost, and to make her amends, I gave her three Guineas more than they cost her.

This good (tho' unhappy) QUAKER had the Misfortune to have had a bad Husband, and he was gone beyond-Sea; she had a good House, and well-furnish'd, and had some Jointure of her own Estate, which supported her and her Children, so that she did not want; but she was not at-all above such a Help, as my being there was to her; so she was as glad of me, as I was of her.

However, as I knew there was no way to fix this new Acquaintance, like making myself a Friend to her, I began with making her some handsome Presents, and the like to her Children; and first, opening my Bundles one Day in my Chamber, I heard her in another Room, and call'd her in, with a kind of familiar way; there I show'd her some of my fine Cloaths, and having among the rest of my things, a Piece of very fine new Holland,[1] which I had bought a little before, worth about 9s. an Ell,[2] I pull'd it out, *Here, my Friend*, says I, *I will make you a Present, if you will accept of it*; and with that I laid the Piece of Holland in her Lap.

I cou'd see she was surpriz'd, and that she cou'd hardly speak; *What dost thou mean?* says she; *indeed I cannot have the Face to accept so fine a Present as this*; adding, *'Tis fit for thy own Use, but 'tis above my Wear, indeed*: I thought she had meant she must not wear it so fine, because she was a QUAKER; so I return'd, Why, do not you QUAKERs wear fine Linnen neither? Yes, *says she*, we wear fine Linnen when we can afford it, but this is too good for me: However, I made her take it, and she was very thankful too; but my End was answer'd another Way; for by this I engag'd her so, that as I found her a Woman of Understanding, and of Honesty too, I might, upon any Occasion, have a Confidence in her, which was indeed, what I very much wanted.

---

1 Linen.
2 45 inches.

By accustoming myself to converse with her, I had not only learn'd to dress like a QUAKER, but so us'd myself to Thee and Thou, that I talk'd like a QUAKER too, as readily and naturally as if I had been born among them; and, in a word, I pass'd for a QUAKER among all People that did not know me; I went but little Abroad, but I had been so us'd to a Coach, that I knew not how well to go without one; besides, I thought it wou'd be a farther Disguise to me, so I told my Quaker-Friend one Day, that I thought I liv'd too close; that I wanted Air; she propos'd taking a Hackney-Coach sometimes, or a Boat; but I told her, I had always had a Coach of my own, till now, and I cou'd find in my Heart to have one again.

She seem'd to think it strange at first, considering how close I liv'd, but had nothing to say when she found I did not value the Expence; so in short, I resolv'd I wou'd have a Coach: When we came to talk of Equipages; she extoll'd the having all things plain; I said so too; so I left it to her Direction, and a Coach-Maker was sent for, and he provided me a plain Coach, no gilding or painting, lin'd with a light-grey Cloath, and my Coachman had a coat of the same, and no Lace on his Hat.

When all was ready, I dress'd myself in the Dress I bought of her, *and said*, Come, I'll be a QUAKER to-Day, and you and I'll go Abroad; which we did, and there was not a QUAKER in the Town look'd less like a Counterfeit than I did: But all this was my particular Plot to be the more completely conceal'd, and that I might depend upon being not known, and yet need not be confin'd like a Prisoner, and be always in Fear; so that all the rest was Grimace.[1]

We liv'd here very easie and quiet, and yet I cannot say I was so in my Mind; I was like a Fish out of Water; I was as gay, and as young in my Disposition, as I was at five and twenty; and as I had always been courted, flatter'd, and us'd to love it, so I miss'd in my Conversation; and this put me many times, upon looking-back upon things past.

I had very few Moments in my Life, which in their Reflection, afforded me any-thing but Regret; but of all the foolish Actions I had to look back upon in my Life, none look'd so preposterous, and so like Distraction, nor left so much Melancholly on my Mind, as my Parting with my Friend, the *Merchant of Paris*, and the refusing him upon such honourable and just Conditions as he had offer'd; and tho' on his just (which I call'd unkind) rejecting my Invitation to come to him again, I had look'd on him with

---

1 Affectation.

some Disgust, yet now my Mind run upon him continually, and the ridiculous Conduct of my refusing him, and I cou'd never be satisfied about him; I flatter'd myself, that if I cou'd but see him, I cou'd yet Master him, and that he wou'd presently forget all that had pass'd, that might be thought unkind; but as there was no room to imagine any-thing like that to be possible, I threw those Thoughts off again as much as I cou'd.

However, they continually return'd, and I had no Rest Night or Day, for thinking of him, who I had forgot above eleven Years. I told *Amy* of it, and we talk'd it over sometimes in-Bed, almost whole Nights together; at last, *Amy* started a thing of her own Head, which put it in a Way of Management, tho' a wild one too: *You are so uneasie Madam,* says she, a*bout this Mr.—, the Merchant at* Paris; *Come,* says she, *if you'll give me Leave, I'll go over, and see what's become of him.*

Not for ten Thousand Pounds, *said I*; no, nor if you met him in the Street, not to offer to speak to him on my Account: No, *says Amy,* I wou'd not speak to him at-all, or if I did, I warrant you it shall not look to be upon your Account: I'll only enquire after him, and if he is in Being, you shall hear of him; if not, you shall hear of him still, and that may be enough.

Why, *says I*, if you will promise me not to enter into any-thing relating to me, with him; nor to begin any Discourse at-all, unless he begins it with you, I cou'd almost, be perswaded to let you go and try.

Amy promis'd me all that I desir'd; and, in a word, to cut the Story short, I let her go; but ty'd her up to so many Particulars, that it was almost impossible, her going cou'd signifie any-thing; and had she intended to observe them, she might as well have staid at-home as have gone; for I charg'd her, if she came to see him, she shou'd not so much as take Notice that she knew him again; and if he spoke to her, she shou'd tell him, she was come away from me a great-many Years ago, and knew nothing what was become of me; that she had been come-over to *France* six Years ago, and was marry'd there, and liv'd at *Calais,* or to that Purpose.

Amy promis'd me nothing indeed; for as s*he said,* it was impossible for her to resolve what wou'd be fit to do, or not to do, till she was there, upon the Spot, and had found out the Gentleman, or heard of him; but that then, if I wou'd trust her, as I had always done, she wou'd answer for it, that she wou'd do nothing but what shou'd be for my Interest, and what she wou'd hope I shou'd be very well pleas'd with.

With this general Commission, *Amy,* notwithstanding she had been so frighted at the Sea, ventur'd her Carcass once more by Water, and away she goes to *France*; she had four Articles of Confidence in Charge to enquire after, for me; and as I found by her, she had one for herself; I say, four for me, because tho' her *first* and principal Errand was, to inform herself of my *Dutch* Merchant, yet I gave her in Charge to enquire, 2. After my Husband, who I left a Trooper in the *Gensd'arms*. 3. After that Rogue of a *Jew*, whose very Name I hated, and of whose Face I had such a frightful *Idea*, that *Sathan* himself cou'd not counterfeit a worse: and *Lastly*, After my Foreign Prince: And she discharg'd herself very well of them all, tho' not so successful as I wish'd.

Amy had a very good Passage over the Sea, and I had a Letter from her, from *Calais*, in three Days after she went from *London*: When she came to *Paris*, she wrote me an Account, that as to her first and most important Enquiry, which was after the *Dutch* Merchant; her Account was, That he had return'd to *Paris*; liv'd three Years there, and quitting that City, went to live at *Roan*: So away goes *Amy* for *Roan*.

But as she was going to bespeak a Place in the Coach to *Roan*, she meets very accidentally in the Street with her Gentleman, *as I call'd him*; that is to say, the Prince de—'s Gentleman, who had been her Favourite, *as above.*

You may be sure there were several other kind Things happen'd between *Amy* and him, as you shall hear afterwards: But the two main things were, 1. That *Amy* enquir'd about his Lord, and had a full Account of him; of which presently; and in the next Place, telling him whither she was going, and for what; he bade her not go yet, for that he wou'd have a particular Account of it the next Day, from a Merchant that knew him; and accordingly he brought her word the next Day, that he had been for six Years before that, gone for *Holland*, and that he liv'd there still.

This, *I say*, was the first News from *Amy*, for some time, *I mean*, about my Merchant: In the mean time, *Amy*, as I have said, enquir'd about the other Persons she had in her Instructions: As for the Prince, the Gentleman told her, he was gone into *Germany*, where his Estate lay, and that he liv'd there; that he had made great Enquiry after me; that he (his Gentleman) had made all the Search he had been able, for me; but that he cou'd not hear of me; that he believ'd if his Lord had known I had been in *England*, he wou'd have gone over to me; but that, after long Enquiry, he was oblig'd to give it over; but that he verily believ'd, if he cou'd have found me, he cou'd have married me; and that he was extremely concern'd that he cou'd hear nothing of me.

I was not at-all satisfied with *Amy's* Account, but order'd her to go to *Roan* herself; which she did, and there with much Difficulty, (the Person she was directed to being dead) I say, with much Difficulty, she came to be inform'd, that my Merchant had liv'd there two Years, or something more; but that having met with a very great Misfortune, he had gone back to *Holland, as the* French *Merchant said,* where he had staid two Years; but with this Addition, *viz.* that he came back again to *Roan,* and liv'd in good Reputation there another Year; and afterwards, he was gone to *England;* and that he liv'd in *London:* But *Amy* cou'd by no means learn how to write to him there, till by great Accident, an old *Dutch* Skipper, who had formerly serv'd him, coming to *Roan, Amy* was told of it; and he told her, that he lodg'd in St. *Lawrence Pountney's-Lane,* in *London;* but was to be seen every Day upon the Exchange, in the *French* Walk.

This *Amy* thought it was time enough to tell me of, when she came over; and besides she did not find this *Dutch* Skipper, till she had spent four or five Months, and been again at *Paris,* and then come back to *Roan* for farther information: But in the mean time she wrote me from *Paris,* that he was not to be found by any means; that he had been gone from *Paris* seven or eight Years; that she was told he had liv'd at *Roan,* and she was a-going thither to enquire, but that she had heard afterward, that he was gone also from thence to *Holland,* so she did not go.

This, I say, was *Amy's* first Account; and I not satisfied with it, had sent her an Order to go to *Roan,* to enquire there also, *as above.*

While this was negociating, and I received these Accounts from *Amy* at several times, a strange Adventure happen'd to me, which I must mention just here; I had been Abroad to take the Air, as usual, with my QUAKER, as far as *Epping-Forest,* and we were driving back towards *London;* when on the road between *Bow* and *Mile-End,* two Gentlemen on Horseback came riding-by, having over-taken the Coach, and pass'd it, and went forwards towards *London.*

They did not ride apace, tho' they pass'd the Coach, for we went very softly, nor did they look into the Coach at-all, but rode side by side, earnestly talking to one another, and inclining their Faces side-ways a little towards one another, he that went nearest the Coach, with his Face from it, and he that was farthest from the Coach, with his Face towards it, and passing in the very next Tract to the coach, I cou'd hear them talk *Dutch* very distinctly; but it is impossible to describe the Confusion I was in, when I plainly saw that the farthest of the two, him whose Face look'd towards the Coach, was my Friend, the *Dutch* Merchant of *Paris*.

If it had been possible to conceal my Disorder from my Friend, the QUAKER, I would have done it, but I found she was too well acquainted with such things, not to take the Hint; dost Thou understand *Dutch? said she; Why? said I; Why, says she,* 'tis easie to suppose that Thou art a little concern'd at somewhat those Men say; I suppose they are talking of Thee: Indeed my good Friend, *said I,* thou art mistaken this time, for I know very well what they are talking of, but 'tis all about Ships, and Trading Affairs: Well, *says she,* then one of them is a Man-Friend of Thine, or somewhat is the Case; for tho' thy Tongue will not confess it, thy Face does.

I was going to have told a bold Lye, and said, I knew nothing of them, but I found it was impossible to conceal it, *so I said,* indeed, I think I know the farthest of them; but I have neither spoken to him, or so much as seen him for above 11 Years: Well then, *says she,* Thou hast seen him with more than common Eyes, when thou did'st see him; or else seeing him now would not be such a Surprize to Thee: Indeed, *said I,* 'tis true I am a little sur-priz'd at seeing him just now, for I thought he had been in quite another Part of the World; and I can assure you, I never saw him in *England* in my Life: Well then, 'tis the more likely he is come over now on purpose to seek Thee: No, no, *said I,* Knight-Errantry is over, Women are not so hard to come at, that Men should not be able to please themselves without running from one Kingdom to another: Well, well, *says she,* I would have him see Thee for-all that, as plainly as Thou hast seen him; No, but he shan't, *says I,* for I am sure he don't know me in this Dress, and I'll take Care he shan't see my Face, if I can help it; so I held up my Fan before my Face, and she saw me resolute in that, so she press'd me no farther.

We had several Discourses upon the Subject, but still I let her know I was resolv'd he should not know me: but, at last, I con-fess'd so much, that tho' I would not let him know who I was, or where I liv'd, I did not care if I knew where he liv'd, and how I might enquire about him: She took the Hint immediately, and her Servant being behind the Coach, she call'd him to the Coach-side, and bade him keep his Eye upon that Gentleman, and as soon as the Coach came to the End of *White-Chappel,* he should get down, and follow him closely, so as to see where he put up his Horse, and then to go into the Inn, and enquire, if he could, who he was, and where he liv'd.

The Fellow follow'd diligently to the Gate of an Inn in *Bishop-gate-Street*, and seeing him go in, made no doubt but he had him fast, but was confounded, when upon Enquiry he found the Inn was a Thorowfare into another Street, and that the two Gentlemen had only rode thorow the Inn, as the Way to the Street where they were going, and so, in short, came back no wiser than he went.

My kind QUAKER was more vex'd at the Disappointment, at least apparently so, than I was; and asking the Fellow, if he was sure he knew the Gentlemen again if he saw him; the Fellow said, he had follow'd him so close, and took so much Notice of him, in order to do his Errand as it ought to be done, that he was very sure he should know him again; and that besides, he was sure he shou'd know his Horse.

This Part was, indeed, likely enough; and the kind QUAKER, without telling me any-thing of the Matter, caus'd her Man to place himself just at the corner of *Whitechappel-Church-Wall* every *Saturday* in the Afternoon, that being the Day when the Citizens chiefly ride Abroad to take the Air; and there to watch all the Afternoon, and look for him.

It was not till the fifth Saturday, that her Man came, with a great deal of Joy, and gave her an Account, that he had found out the Gentleman; that he was a *Dutchman*, but a *French* Merchant; that he came from *Roan*, and his Name was—; and that he lodg'd at Mr.— on *Lawrence Pountney's-Hill*: I was surpriz'd, you may be sure, when she came and told me one Evening, all the Particulars, except that of having set her Man to watch; I have found out thy *Dutch* Friend, *says she*, and can tell THEE how to find him too; I colour'd again as red as Fire: then THOU has dealt with the Evil One, Friend, *said I very gravely*: No, no, *says she*, I have no Familiar;[1] but I tell Thee, I have found him for Thee, and his Name is so and so; and he lives as above recited.

I was surpriz'd again at this, not being able to imagine how she shou'd come to know all this: However, to put me out of Pain, she told me what she had done; well, *said I*, Thou art very kind, but this is not worth thy Pains; for now I know it, 'tis only to satisfie my Curiosity, for I shall not send to him upon any Account: Be that as thou wilt, *says she*; besides, added she, Thou art in the right to say so to me; for, why shou'd I be trusted with it? Tho' if I were, *I assure thee*, I shou'd not betray thee; That is very kind,

---

1   An agent, someone to act on her behalf.

said I and I believe thee; and assure Thy-self, if I do send to him, Thou shalt know it, and be trusted with it too.

During this Interval of five Weeks, I suffer'd a hundred Thousand Perplexities of Mind; I was thorowly convinc'd I was right as to the Person, that it was the Man; I knew him so well, and saw him so plain, I cou'd not be deceiv'd: I drove out again in the Coach, (*on Pretence of Air*) almost every-Day, in hopes of seeing him again, but was never so lucky as to see him; and now I had made the Discovery, I was as far to seek what Measures to take, as I was before.

To send to him, or speak to him first, if I shou'd see him so as to be known to him, that I resolv'd not to do, if I dy'd for it; to watch him about his Lodging, that was as much below my Spirit as the other; so that, *in a word*, I was at a perfect Loss how to act, or what to do.

At length came *Amy's* Letter, with the last Account which she had at *Roan*, from the *Dutch* Skipper, which confirming the other, left me out of Doubt that this was my Man; but still, no humane Invention cou'd bring me to the Speech of him, in such a manner as wou'd suit with my Resolutions; for, after all, how did I know what his Circumstances were? Whether marry'd or single? And if he had a Wife, I know he was so honest a Man, he wou'd not so much as converse with me, or so much as know me, if he met me in the Street.

In the next Place, as he had entirely neglected me, which in short, is the worst Way of slighting a Woman, and had given no Answer to my Letters, I did not know but he might be the same Man still; so I resolv'd, that I cou'd do nothing in it, unless some fairer Opportunity presented, which might make my Way clearer to me; for I was determin'd he shou'd have no room to put any more Slights upon me.

In these Thoughts I pass'd away near three Months; till at last, (being impatient) I resolv'd to send for *Amy* to come Over, and tell her how things stood, and that I wou'd do nothing till she came; *Amy* in Answer sent me word, she wou'd come away with all speed, but begg'd of me, that I wou'd enter into no Engagement with him, or any-body, till she arriv'd; but still keeping me in the dark, as to the thing itself, which she had to say, at which I was heartily vex'd, for many Reasons.

But while all these things were transacting, and Letters and Answers pass'd between *Amy* and I a little slower than usual, at which I was not so well pleas'd as I us'd to be with *Amy's* Dispatch; *I say*, in this time the following Scene open'd.

It was one Afternoon, about four a-Clock, my Friendly QUAKER and I sitting in her Chamber up-stairs, and very chearful, chatting together, (*for she was the best Company in the World*) when somebody ringing hastily at the Door, and no Servant just then in the way, she ran down *herself*, to the Door; when a Gentleman appears with a Footman attending, and making some Apologies, which she did not thorowly understand, he speaking but broken *English*; he ask'd to speak with me, by the very same Name that I went by in her House; which, *by the way*, was not the Name that he had known me by.

She, with very civil Language, *in her way*, brought him into a very handsome Parlour below-stairs, *and said*, she wou'd go and see whether the Person who lodg'd in her House own'd that Name, and he shou'd hear farther.

I was a little surpriz'd, even before I knew anything of who it was, my Mind foreboding the thing as it happen'd; (*whence that arises, let the Naturalists*[1] *explain to us*) but I was frighted, and ready to die, when my QUAKER came up all gay, and crowing; *There*, says she, *is the* Dutch French *Merchant come to see Thee*: I cou'd not speak one Word to her, nor stir off of my Chair, but sat as motionless as a Statue: She talk'd a thousand pleasant things to me, but they made no Impression on me; at last she pull'd me, and teiz'd me, *Come, come*, says she, *be thy self, and rouze up*, I must go down again to him; what shall I say to him? Say, *said I*, that you have no such-body in the House. That I cannot do, *says she, because it is not the Truth*; besides, I have own'd Thou art above, *Come, come, go down with me*; not for a thousand Guineas, *said I*; well, *says she*, I'll go and tell him Thou wilt come quickly; so, without giving me Time to answer her, away she goes.

A Million of Thoughts circulated in my Head while she was gone, and what to do I cou'd not tell; I saw no Remedy but I must speak with him, but wou'd have give 500*l*. to have shun'd it; yet, had I shun'd it, perhaps then, I wou'd have given 500*l*. again, that I had seen him: Thus fluctuating, and unconcluding, were my Thoughts; what I so earnestly desir'd, I declin'd when it offer'd itself; and what now I pretended to decline, was nothing but what I had been at the Expence of 40 or 50*l*. to send *Amy* to *France* for; and even without any View, or indeed, any rational Expectation of bringing it to pass; and what, for half a Year before, I was so uneasie about that I cou'd not be quiet Night or Day, till *Amy* propos'd to go over to enquire after him: In short, my Thoughts

---

1 Scientists.

were all confus'd and in the utmost Disorder; I had once refus'd and rejected him, and I repented it heartily; then I had taken ill his Silence, and in my Mind rejected him again, but had repented that too: Now I had stoop'd so low as to send after him into *France*, which if he had known, perhaps, he had never come after me; and shou'd I reject him a third time! On the other-hand, he had repented too in his Turn, perhaps, and not knowing how I had acted, either in stooping to send a Search after him, or in the wickeder Part of my Life, was come over hither to seek me again; and I might take him perhaps, with the same Advantages as I might have done before, and wou'd I now be backward to see him! Well, while I was in this Hurry, my Friend the QUAKER, comes up again, and perceiving the Confusion I was in, she runs to her Closet, and fetch'd me a little pleasant Cordial, *but I wou'd not taste it*: O says she, *I understand Thee, be not uneasie, I'll give thee something shall take off all the Smell of it; if he kisses Thee a thousand times, he shall be no wiser*; I thought with myself, Thou art perfectly acquainted with Affairs of this Nature, I think you must govern me now, so I began to incline to go down with her; upon that, I took the Cordial, and she gave me a kind of spicey Preserve after it, whose Flavour was so strong, and yet so deliciously pleasant, that it wou'd cheat the nicest Smelling, and it left not the least taint of the Cordial on the Breath.

Well, after this, (*tho' with some Hesitation still*) I went down a Pair of Back-stairs with her, and into a Dining-Room, next to the Parlour in which he was; but there I halted, and desir'd she wou'd let me consider of it a little: *Well, do so*, says she, and left me with more readiness than she did before; *do, consider, and I'll come to Thee again.*

Tho' I hung back with an awkwardness that was really unfeign'd, yet when she so readily left me, I thought it was not so kind, and I began to think she should have press'd me still on to it; so foolishly backward are we, to the thing, which of all the World we most desire; mocking our selves with a feign'd Reluctance, when the Negative wou'd be Death to us; but she was too cunning for me, for while I, as it were, blam'd her in my Mind, for not carrying me to him, tho' at the same time I appear'd backward to see him; on a sudden she unlocks the Folding-Doors, which look'd into the next Parlour, and throwing them open, *There*, says she, (ushering him in) *is the Person, who, I suppose, thou enquirest for*; and the same moment, with a kind Decency she retire'd, and that so swift, that she wou'd not give us leave, hardly, to know which Way she went.

I stood up, but was confounded with a sudden Enquiry in my Thoughts, how I shou'd receive him? And with Resolution as swift as Lightning, in Answer to it, *said to myself*, It shall be COLDLY; so, on a sudden, I put on an Air of Stiffness and Ceremony, and held it for about two Minutes; but it was with great Difficulty.

He restrain'd himself too, on the other-hand, came towards me gravely, and saluted me in Form;[1] but it was, it seems, upon his supposing the QUAKER was behind him, whereas she, *as I said*, understood things too well, and had retir'd, as if she had vanish'd, that we might have full Freedom; for, as s*he said afterwards*, she suppos'd we had seen one-another before, tho' it might have been a great-while ago.

Whatever Stiffness I had put on my Behaviour to him, I was surpriz'd in my Mind, and angry at his, and began to wonder what kind of a ceremonious Meeting it was to be: However, after he perceiv'd the Woman was gone, he made a kind of a Hesitation, looking a little round him; *Indeed*, said he, *I thought the Gentlewoman was not withdrawn*, and with that, he took me in his Arms, and kiss'd me three or four times; but I that was prejudic'd to the last Degree, with the coldness of his first Salutes, when I did not know the Cause of it, cou'd not be thorowly clear'd of the Prejudice, tho' I did know the Cause; and thought that even his return, and taking me in his Arms, did not seem to have the same Ardour with which he us'd to receive me, and this made me behave to him awkwardly, *and I know not how*, for a good-while; *but this by the way*.

He began with a kind of an Extasie upon the Subject of his finding me out; how it was possible that he shou'd have been four Years in *England*, and had us'd all the Ways imaginable, and cou'd never so much as have the least Intimation of me, or of any-one like me; and that it was now above two Years that he had despair'd of it, and had given over all Enquiry; and that now he shou'd chop upon me,[2] as it were, unlook'd and unsought-for.

I cou'd easily have accounted for his not finding me, if I had but set down the Detail of my real Retirement; but I gave it a new, and indeed, a truly hypocritical Turn; I told him, that any-one that knew the manner of Life I led, might account for his not finding me; that the Retreat I had taken up, wou'd have render'd it a hundred Thousand to one odds that he ever found me at-all;

---

1   Reserved and sober, formally.
2   Stumble upon.

that as I had abandon'd all Conversation;[1] taken up anther Name; liv'd remote from *London*, and had not preserv'd one Acquaintance in it; it was no wonder he had not met with me; that even my Dress wou'd let him see, that I did not desire to be known by any-body.

Then he ask'd if I had not receiv'd some Letters from him? I told him, No, he had not thought fit to give me the Civility of an Answer to the last I wrote to him; and he cou'd not suppose I shou'd expect a Return, after a Silence in a Case where I had laid myself so low, and expos'd myself in a Manner I had never been us'd to; that indeed, I had never sent for any Letters after that, to the Place where I had order'd his to be directed; and that being so justly, as I thought, punish'd for my Weakness, I had nothing to do, but to repent of being a Fool, after I had strictly adher'd to a just Principle before: That however, as what I did was rather from Motions of Gratitude, than from real Weakness, however it might be construed by him, I had the Satisfaction in myself of having fully discharg'd the Debt: *I added*, that I had not wanted Occasions of all the seeming Advancements which the pretended Felicity of a Marriage-Life was usually set-off with, and might have been what I desir'd not to name; but that, however, low I had stoop'd to him, I had maintain'd the Dignity of Female Liberty, against all the Attacks, either of Pride or Avarice; and that I had been infinitely oblig'd to him for giving me an Opportunity to discharge the only Obligation that endanger'd me, without subjecting me to the Consequence; and that I hop'd he was satisfied I had paid the Debt, by offering myself to be chain'd; but was infinitely Debtor to him another way, for letting me remain free.

He was so confounded at this Discourse, that he knew not what to say, and for a good-while he stood mute indeed; but recovering himself a little, *he said*, I run-out into a Discourse he hop'd was over, and forgotten, and he did not intend to revive it; that he knew I had not had his Letters, for that, when he first came to *England*, he had been at the Place to which they were directed; and found them all lying here, but one; and that the People had not known how to deliver them; that he thought to have had a Direction there, how to find me, but had the Mortification to be told, that they did not so much as know who I was; that he was under a great Disappointment, and that I ought to know, *in answer to all my Resentments*, that he had done a long, and

---

1 Social appearances.

(he hop'd) a sufficient Pennance for the Slight *that I had suppos'd* he had put upon me; that it was true, (*and I cou'd not suppose any other*) that upon the Repulse I had given him in a Case so circumstanc'd as his was, and after such earnest Entreaties, and such Offers as he had made me, he went away with a Mind heartily griev'd, and full of Resentment; that he had look'd back on the Crime he had committed, with some Regret, but on the Cruelty of my Treatment of the poor Infant I went with at that time, with the utmost Detestation; and that this made him unable to send an agreeable Answer to me: for which Reason he had sent none at-all for some time; but that in about six or seven Months those Resentments wearing off by the return of his Affection to me, and his Concern in the poor Child—*there he stopp'd, and indeed, Tears stood in his Eyes, while in a Parenthesis,* he only added, *and to this Minute he did not know whether it was dead or alive;* he then went on, those Resentments wearing off, he sent me several Letters, *I think he said,* seven or eight, but receiv'd no Answer; that then his Business obliging him to go to *Holland,* he came to *England,* as in his Way, but found, *as above,* that his Letters had not been call'd for, but that he left them at the House after paying the Postage of them; and going then back to *France,* he was yet uneasie, and cou'd not refrain the *Knight-Errantry* of coming to *England* again to seek me, tho' he knew neither where, or of who, to enquire for me, being disappointed in all his Enquiries before: That he had yet taken up his Residence here, firmly believing, that one-time or other he shou'd meet me, or hear of me, and that some kind Chance wou'd at last throw him in my Way; that he had liv'd thus above four Years, and tho' his Hopes were vanish'd, yet he had not any Thoughts of removing any more in the World, unless it shou'd be at last, as it is with other old Men, he might have some Inclination to go Home, to die in his own Country; but that he had no thought of it yet; that if I wou'd consider all these Steps, I wou'd find some Reasons to forget his first Resentments, and to think that Pennance, *as he call'd it,* which he had undergone in search of me, an *Amende Honorable,* in Reparation of the Affront give to the kindness of my Letter of Invitation; and that we might at last make ourselves some Satisfaction on both sides, for the Mortifications past.

I confess I cou'd not hear all this without being mov'd very much, and yet I continued a little stiff and formal too, a good-while: *I told him,* that before I cou'd give him any Reply to the rest of his Discourse, I ought to give him the Satisfaction of telling him, *that his Son was alive;* and that indeed since I saw him so concern'd about it, and mention it with such Affection, I was sorry that I had not found out some Way or other to let him know it sooner; but that I thought, after his slighting the Mother, *as above,* he had summ'd up his Affection to the Child, in the letter he had wrote to me about providing for it; and that he had, as other Fathers often do, look'd upon it as a Birth, *which being out of the Way,* was to be forgotten, as its Beginning was to be repented of; that in providing sufficiently for it, he had done more than all such Fathers us'd to do, and might be well satisfied with it.

He answer'd me, that he shou'd have been very glad if I had been so good, but to have given him the Satisfaction of knowing the poor unfortunate Creature was yet alive, and he wou'd have taken some Care of it upon himself, and particularly, by owning it for a legitimate Child, which, where nobody had known the contrary, wou'd have taken off the Infamy which wou'd otherwise cleave to it; and so the Child shou'd not, itself, have known anything of its own Disaster; but that he fear'd it was now too late.

He added, that I might see by all his Conduct since that, what unhappy Mistake drew him into the thing at first; and that he wou'd have been very far from doing the Injury to me, or being instrumental to add *Une Miserable,* (that was his Word) to the World, if he had not been drawn into it, by the Hopes he had of making me his own; but that, if it was possible to rescue the Child from the Consequences of its unhappy Birth, he hop'd I wou'd give him leave to do it, and he wou'd let me see that he had both Means and Affection still to do it; and that, notwithstanding all the Misfortunes that had befallen him, nothing that belong'd to him, especially by a Mother he had such a Concern for, as he had for me, should ever want what he was in a Condition to do for it.

I cou'd not hear this without being sensibly touch'd with it; I was asham'd that he shou'd show that he had more real affection for the Child, tho' he had never seen it in his Life, than I that bore it; for indeed, I did not love the Child, nor love to see it; and tho' I had provided for it, yet I did it by *Amy's* Hand, and had not seen it above twice in four Years; being privately resolv'd that when it grew up, it shou'd not be able to call me Mother.

However, *I told him,* the Child was taken Care of, and that he need not be anxious about it, unless he suspected, that I had less affection for it than he, that had never seen it in his Life; that he knew what I had promis'd him to do for it, *namely,* to give it the Thousand Pistoles which I had offer'd him, and which he had declin'd; that, *I assur'd him,* I had made my Will, and that I had left it 5000*l.* and the Interest of it till he shou'd come of Age, if I died before that time; that I wou'd still be as good as that to it; but if he had a-mind to take it from me, into his Government, I wou'd not be against it; and to satisfie him that I wou'd perform what I said, I wou'd cause the Child to be deliver'd to him, and the 5000*l.* also for its Support; depending upon it, that he wou'd show himself a Father to it, by what I saw of his Affection to it, now.

I had observ'd that he had hinted two or three times in his Discourse, his having had *Misfortunes in the World*, and I was a little surpriz'd at the Expression, especially at the repeating it so often, but I took no Notice of that Part yet.

He thank'd me for my Kindness to the Child, with a Tenderness which shew'd the Sincerity of all he had said before; and which encreas'd the Regret with which, *as I said*, I look'd back on the little Affection I had shew'd to the poor Child; *he told me*, he did not desire to take him from me, but so as to introduce him into the World as his own; which he cou'd still do, having liv'd absent from his other Children (for he had two Sons and a Daughter which were brought up at *Nimeugen* in *Holland*, with a Sister of his) so long, that he might very well send another Son of ten Years old to be bred up with them; and suppose his Mother to be dead or alive, as he found Occasion; and that as I had resolv'd to do so handsomely for the Child, he wou'd add to it something considerable, tho' having had some great Disappointments, (*repeating the Words*) he cou'd not do for it as he wou'd otherwise have done.

I then thought myself oblig'd to take Notice his having so often mention'd his having *met with Disappointments*; I told him, I was very sorry to hear he had met with any-thing afflicting to him in the World; that I wou'd not have any-thing belonging to me, add to his Loss, or weaken him in what he might do for his other Children; and that I wou'd not agree to his having the Child away, *tho' the Proposal was infinitely to the Child's Advantage*, unless he wou'd promise me, that the whole Expence shou'd be mine; and that if he did not think 5000*l.* enough for the Child, I wou'd give it more.

We had so much Discourse upon this, *and the old Affairs*, that it took up all our Time at his first Visit; I was a little importunate with him, to tell me how he came to find me out, but he put it off for that time; and only obtaining my Leave to visit me again, he went away; and indeed, my Heart was so full with what he had said already, that I was glad when he went away; sometimes I was full of Tenderness and Affection for him, especially, when he express'd himself so earnestly and passionately about the Child; other-times I was crowded with Doubts about his Circumstances; sometimes I was terrify'd with Apprehensions, lest if I shou'd come into a close Correspondence with him, he shou'd any-way come to hear what kind of Life I had led at *Pall-mall*, and in other Places, and it might make me miserable afterwards; from which last Thought I concluded, that I had better repulse him again, than receive him: All these Thoughts, and many more, crowded in so fast, I say, upon me, that I wanted to give Vent to them, and get rid of him, and was very glad when he was gone away.

We had several Meetings after this, in which still we had so many Preliminaries to go through, that we scarce ever border'd upon the main Subject; once indeed, he said something of it, and I put it off with a kind of Jest; alas! *says I,* those things are out of Question now; 'tis almost two Ages since those things were talk'd between us, *says I;* you see I am grown *an Old-Woman* since that: another time he gave a little Push at it again, and I laugh'd again; *Why what dost thou talk of,* said I, in a formal way, *Dost thou not see I am turn'd* QUAKER? *I cannot speak of those things now: Why,* says he, the QUAKERS marry as well as other People, and love one-another as well; besides, *says he,* the QUAKERS Dress does not ill-become you, and so jested with me again, and so it went off for a third time; *however,* I began to be kind to him in process of time, *as they call it,* and we grew very intimate; and if the following Accident had not unluckily interven'd, I had certainly married him, or consented to marry him, the very next time he had ask'd me.

I had long waited for a Letter from *Amy,* who it seems, was just at that time gone to *Roan* the second time, to make her Enquiries about him; and I recei'vd a letter from her at this unhappy Juncture, which gave me the following Account of my Business.

I. That for *my Gentleman,* who I had now, *as I may say,* in my Arms; *she said,* he had been gone from *Paris, as I have hinted,* having met with some great Losses and Misfortunes; that he had been in *Holland* on that very Account, whither he had also carried his Children; that he was after that, settl'd for some time, at *Roan;* that she had been at *Roan,* and found there, (by a meer accident) from a *Dutch* Skipper, that he was at *London,* had been there above three Years; that he was to be found upon the *Exchange,* on the *French* Walk; and that he lodg'd at St.

Lawrence Pountney's-Lane, and the like; so *Amy* said she suppos'd I might soon find him out; but that she doubted[1] he was
poor, and not worth looking-after: this she did because of the
next Clause, which the Jade had most mind-to, on many
Accounts.

II. That as to the Prince—, that, *as above,* he was gone into
Germany, where his Estate lay; that he had quitted the *French*
Service, and liv'd retir'd; that she had seen his Gentleman,
who remain'd at *Paris,* to solicit his Arrears,[2] *&c.* That he had
given her an Account how his Lord had employ'd him, to
enquire for me, and find me out, *as above,* and told her what
Pains he had taken to find me; that he had understood that I
had gone to *England;* that he once had Orders to go to *England*
to find me; that his Lord had resolv'd, if he cou'd have found
me, to have call'd me a Countess, and so have marry'd me, and
have carry'd me into *Germany* with him; and that his Commission was still to assure me, that the Prince wou'd marry
me, if I wou'd come to him; and that he wou'd send him an
Account that he had found me, and did not doubt but he
wou'd have Orders to come over to *England* to attend me, in a
Figure suitable to my Quality.

Amy, an ambitious Jade, who knew my weakest Part, namely,
that I lov'd great things, and that I lov'd to be flatter'd and
courted; said abundance of kind things upon this Occasion,
which she knew were suitable to me, and wou'd prompt my
Vanity; and talk'd big of the Prince's Gentleman having Orders to
come over to me, with a Procuration to marry me by Proxy,[3] (*as
Princes usually do in like Cases*) and to furnish me with an
Equipage, and I know not how many fine things; but told me
withal, that she had not yet let him know that she belong'd to me
still, or that she knew where to find me, or to write to me; because
she was willing to see the Bottom of it, and whether it was a
Reality, or a *Gasconade;*[4] she had indeed, told him, that if he had
any such Commission, she wou'd endeavour to find me out; but
no more.

---

1 Amy is certain that he is poor.
2 Pay his debts.
3 The Prince's gentleman would stand in for the Prince at the marriage
  ceremony, which would legally marry Roxana to the Prince.
4 A farce.

III. For *the Jew*, she assur'd me, that she had not been able to come at a Certainty what was become of him, or in what Part of the World he was; but that thus much she had learn'd from good-hands, that he had committed a Crime, in being concern'd in a Design to rob a rich Banker at *Paris*; and that he was fled, and had not been heard-of there for above six Years.

IV. For that of *my Husband the Brewer*, she learn'd, that being commanded into the Field upon an Occasion of some Action in *Flanders*, he was wounded at the Battle of *Mons*,[1] and died of his Wounds in the Hospital of the Invalids;[2] so there was an End of my four Enquiries, which I sent her over to make.

This Account of the Prince, and the return of his Affection to me, with all the flattering great things which seem'd to come along with it; and especially, as they came gilded, and set-out by my Maid *Amy*; *I say*, this Account of the Prince came to me in a very unlucky Hour, and in the very Crisis of my Affair.

The Merchant and I had enter'd into close Conferences upon the grand Affair; I had left off talking my Platonicks,[3] and of my Independency, and being a *Free Woman*, as before; and he having clear'd up my Doubts too, as to his Circumstances, and the Misfortunes he had spoken of, I had gone so far, that we had begun to consider where we shou'd live, and in what Figure; what Equipage; what House, *and the like*.

I had made some Harangues upon the delightful Retirement of Country-Life, and how we might enjoy ourselves so effectually, without the Incumbrances of Business, and the World; but all this was *Grimace*, and purely because I was afraid to make any publick Appearance in the World, for fear some impertinent Person of Quality shou'd chop upon again, and cry out, *Roxana, Roxana*, by— with an Oath, *as had been done before*.

My Merchant, bred to Business, and us'd to converse among Men of Business, cou'd hardly tell how to live without it; at least, it appear'd he shou'd be like a Fish out of Water, uneasie and dying; but however, he join'd with me, only argued, that we might live as near *London* as we cou'd; that he might sometimes come

---

1 A battle fought between the French and the English in the War of the Spanish Succession in 1709.
2 A famous hospital in Paris.
3 Ideals.

to *Change*,[1] and hear how the World shou'd go Abroad, and how it far'd with his Friends, and his Children.

I answer'd, that if he chose still to embarrass himself with Business, I suppos'd it wou'd be more to his Satisfaction to be in his own Country, and where his Family was so well known, and where his Children also were.

He smil'd at the thoughts of that, *and let me know*, that he shou'd be very willing to embrace such an Offer, but that he wou'd not expect it of me, to whom *England* was, *to be sure*, so naturaliz'd now, as that it wou'd be carrying me out of my native Country, which he wou'd not desire by any means, however agreeable it might be to him.

I told him, he was mistaken in me; that as I had told him so much of a Married State being a Captivity, and the family being a House of Bondage; that when I married, I expected to be but an Upper Servant; so if I did, notwithstanding, submit to it, I hop'd he shou'd see I knew how to act the Servant's Part, and do every-thing to oblige my Master; that if I did not resolve to go with him wherever he desir'd to go, he might depend I wou'd never have him; *and did I not*, said I, *offer myself to go with you to the* East-Indies?

All this while, this was indeed, but a Copy of my Countenance;[2] for as my Circumstances wou'd not admit my stay in *London*, at least, not so as to appear publickly; I resolv'd if I took him, to live remote in the Country, or go out of *England* with him.

But in *an evil Hour*, just now came *Amy*'s Letter; in the very middle of all these Discourses; and the fine things she had said about *the Prince*, began to make strange Work with me; the Notion of being *a Princess*, and going over to live where all that had happen'd here, wou'd have been quite sunk out of Knowledge, as well as out of Memory, (*Conscience excepted*) was mighty taking; the Thoughts of being surrounded with Domesticks; honour'd with Titles; be call'd HER HIGHNESS; and live in all the Splendor of a Court; and, *which was still more*, in the Arms of a Man of such Rank, and who I knew lov'd and valued me; all this, *in a word*, dazzl'd my Eyes; turn'd my Head; and I was as truly craz'd and distracted for about a Fortnight, as most of the People in *Bedlam*, tho' perhaps, not quite so far gone.

---

1 The Exchange, the banking center of seventeenth-century London.
2 Roxana claims to be deceiving the Dutch merchant about her true motives.

When my Gentleman came to me the next time, I had no Notion of him;[1] I wish'd I had never receiv'd him at-all; *in short*, I resolv'd to have no more to say to him; so I feign'd myself indispos'd; and tho' I did come down to him, and speak to him a little, yet I let him see that I was so ill, that I was (*as we say*) no Company, and that it wou'd be kind in him to give me Leave to quit him for that time.

The next Morning he sent a Footman to enquire how I did; and I let him know, I had a violent Cold, and was very ill with it; two Days after, he came again, and I let him see me again, but feign'd myself so hoarse, that I cou'd not speak to be heard; and that it was painful to me but to whisper; and, *in a word*, I held him in this suspence near three Weeks.

During this time, I had a strange Elevation upon my Mind; and the Prince, *or the Spirit of him*, had such a Possession of me, that I spent most of this Time in the realizing all the Great Things of *a Life with the Prince*, to my Mind; pleasing my Fancy with the Grandeur I was supposing myself to enjoy; and withal, wickedly studying in what Manner to put off this Gentleman, and be rid of him for-ever.

I cannot but say, that sometimes the Baseness of the Action stuck hard with me; the Honour and Sincerity with which he had always treated me; and, *above all*, the Fidelity he had shew'd me at *Paris*, and that I ow'd my Life to him; *I say*, all these star'd in my Face; and I frequently argued with myself upon the Obligation I was under, to him; and how base wou'd it be, *now too, after so many Obligations and Engagements*, to cast him off?

But the Title of *Highness*, and of a *Princess*, and all those fine things, as they came in, weigh'd down all this; *and the Sence of Gratitude vanish'd, as if it had been a Shadow.*

At other times, I consider'd the Wealth I was Mistress of; that I was able to live like a Princess, tho' not a Princess; and that my Merchant (*for he had told me all the Affair of his Misfortunes*) was far from being poor, or even mean; that together, we were able to make up an Estate of between three and four Thousand Pounds a Year, which was in itself, equal to some Princes abroad: But tho' this was true, yet the Name of *Princess*, and the flutter of it, *in a word*, the Pride weigh'd 'em down; and all these Arguings generally ended to the Disadvantage of my Merchant; so that, *in short*, I resolv'd to drop him, and give him a final Answer, at his next coming; *namely*, That something had happen'd in my Affairs,

---

1   She could not think about him.

which had caus'd me to alter my Measures, unexpectedly; and, *in a word*, to desire him to trouble himself no farther.

I think verily, this rude Treatment of him, was for sometime, the Effect of a violent Fermentation in my Blood;[1] for the very Motion which the steddy Contemplation of my fancy'd Greatness had put my Spirits into, had thrown me into a kind of Fever, and I scarce knew what I did.

I have wonder'd since, that it did not make me Mad; nor do I now think it strange, to hear of those, who have been quite *Lunatick* with their Pride; that fancy'd themselves Queens, and Empresses, and have made their Attendants serve them upon the Knee; given Visitors their Hand to kiss, *and the like*; for certainly, if Pride will not turn the Brain, nothing can.

However, the next time my Gentleman came, I had not courage enough, *or not Ill-Nature enough*, to treat him in the rude Manner I had resolv'd to do; and it was very well I did not; for soon after, I had another Letter from *Amy*, in which was the mortifying News, and indeed, surprising to me, that my Prince (*as I with a secret Pleasure had call'd him*) was very much hurt by a Bruise he had receiv'd in hunting (and engaging with) a wild Boar; a cruel and desperate Sport, which the Noblemen of *Germany*, it seems, much delight in.

This alarm'd me indeed, and the more, because *Amy* wrote me word, that his Gentleman was gone away Express to him, not without Apprehensions, that he shou'd find his Master was dead, before his coming home; but that he [*the Gentleman*] had promis'd her, that as soon as he arriv'd, he wou'd send back the same Courier to her, with an Account of his Master's Health, and of the main Affair; and that he had oblig'd *Amy* to stay at *Paris* fourteen Days for his Return; she having promis'd him before, to make it her Business to go to *England*, and to find me out for his Lord, if he sent her such Orders; and he was to send her a Bill for fifty Pistoles, for her Journey: So *Amy* told me she waited for the Answer.

This was a Blow to me several Ways; for *first*, I was in a State of Uncertainty as to his Person, whether he was alive or dead; and I was not unconcern'd in that Part, I assure you; for I had an inexpressible Affection remaining for his Person, besides the Degree to which it was reviv'd by the View of a firmer Interest in him; *but this was not all*; for in losing him, I for-ever lost the

---

1 Changes in psychological conditions were sometimes still understood in the eighteenth century as disorders of the blood.

Prospect of all the Gayety and Glory, that had made such an Impression upon my Imagination.

In this State of Uncertainty, *I say*, by *Amy*'s Letter, I was like still, to remain another Fortnight; and had I now continued the Resolution of using my Merchant in the rude Manner I once intended, I had made, perhaps, a sorry Piece of Work of it indeed, and it was very well my Heart fail'd me, *as it did*.

However, I treated him with a great-many Shuffles, and feign'd Stories, to keep him off from any closer Conferences than we had already had, that I might act afterwards as Occasion might offer, one way or other: But that which mortified me most, was, that *Amy* did not write, tho' the fourteen Days was expir'd; at last, to my great Surprize, when I was, with the utmost Impatience, looking out at the Window, expecting the Postman, that usually brought the Foreign Letters; *I say*, I was agreeably surpriz'd to see a Coach come to the Yard-Gate where we liv'd, and my Woman, *Amy*, alight out of it, and come towards the Door, having the Coachman bringing several Bundles after her.

I flew like Lightning down-stairs, to speak to her; but was soon damp'd with her News: Is the Prince alive or dead, *Amy*? says I: She spoke coldly and slightly: *He is alive, Madam*, said she, *but it is not much Matter, I had as lief he had been dead*; so we went upstairs again to my Chamber, and there we began a serious Discourse of the whole Matter.

First, *she told me a long Story* of his being hurt by a Wild-Boar; and of the Condition he was reduc'd to, so that every-one expected he shou'd die, the Anguish of the Wound having thrown him into a Fever; with abundance of Circumstances, too long to relate here; how he recover'd of that extreme Danger, but continued very weak; how the Gentleman had been *Homme de Parole*,[1] and had sent back the Courier, as punctually as if it had been to the KING; that he had give a long Account of his Lord, and of his Illness and Recovery; but the sum of the Matter, *as to me*, was, That as to the Lady, his Lord was turn'd Penitent; was under some Vows for his Recovery, and cou'd not think any-more on that Affair; and especially, the Lady being gone, and that it had not been offer'd to her, so there was no Breach of Honour; but that his Lord was sensible of the good Offices of Mrs. *Amy*, and had sent her the fifty Pistoles for her Trouble, as if she had really gone the Journey.

---

1 A servant who is empowered to speak on behalf of his master.

I was, *I confess*, hardly able to bear the first Surprize of this Disappointment; *Amy*, saw it, and gapes out, *(as was her way)* *Law'd Madam*! never be concern'd at it; you see he is gotten among the Priests; and I suppose, they have saucily impos'd some Pennance upon him; and, it may-be sent him of an Errand bare-foot, to some *Madonna* or *Nosterdame* or other; and he is off of his Amours for the present; I'll warrant you, he'll be as wicked again as ever he was, when he is got throrow-well, and gets but out of their Hands again; I hate this out-o'-Season Repentance; what Occasion had he, in his Repentance, to be off of taking a good Wife? I shou'd have been glad to see you have been a Princess, *and all that*; but if it can't be, never afflict yourself; you are rich enough to be a Princess to yourself; you don't want him, that's the best of it:

Well, I cry'd for-all that, and was heartily vex'd, and that a great-while; but as *Amy* was always at my Elbow, and always jogging it out of my Head, with her Mirth, and her Wit, it wore off again.

Then I told *Amy* all the Story of my Merchant, and how he had found me out, when I was in such a Concern to find him; how it was true, that he lodg'd in St. *Lawrence Pountney's-Lane*; and how I had had all the Story of his Misfortune, which she had heard of, in which he had lost above 8000*l*. Sterling; and that he had told me frankly of it, before she had sent me any Account of it, or, at least, before I had taken any Notice that I had heard of it.

Amy was very joyful at that Part; Well, Madam then, *says Amy*, what need you value the Story of the Prince? and going I know not whether into *Germany*, to lay your Bones in another World, and learn the Devil's Language, call'd HIGH-DUTCH?[1] You are better here, by-half, *says Amy*: Law'd Madam, *says she*, why are not you as rich as *Crassus*?[2]

Well, it was a great-while still, before I cou'd bring myself off of this fancy'd Sovereignty; and I that was so willing once to be Mistress to a KING, was now ten thousand times more fond of being Wife to a Prince.

So fast a hold has Pride and Ambition upon our Minds, that when once it gets Admission, nothing is so chimerical, but under this Possession we can form *Ideas* of, in our Fancy, and realize to our Imagination: Nothing can be so ridiculous as the simple Steps we take in such Cases; a Man or a Woman becomes a meer

---

1   Aristocratic German.
2   Croesus was the fabled king of Lydia, renowned for his great wealth.

Malade Imaginaire,[1] and I believe, may as easily die with Grief, or run-mad with Joy, (as the Affair in his Fancy appears right or wrong) as if all was real, and actually under the Management of the Person.

I had indeed, two Assistants to deliver me from this snare, and these were, *first*, Amy, who knew my Disease, but was able do nothing as to the Remedy; the *second*, the Merchant, who really brought the Remedy, but knew nothing of the Distemper.

I remember, when all these Disorders were upon my Thoughts, in one of the Visits my Friend the Merchant made me, he took Notice, that he perceiv'd I was under some unusual Disorder; he believ'd, *he said*, that my Distemper, *whatever it was*, lay much in my Head, and it being Summer-Weather, and very hot, propos'd to me to go a little-way into the Air.

I started at his Expression; what *says I*, do you think then, that *I am craz'd*? you shou'd then propose a Mad-House for my Cure: no, no, *says he*, I do not mean any-thing like that, I hope the Head may be distemper'd, and not the Brain: Well, I was too sensible that he was right, for I knew I had acted a strange wild kind of Part with him; but he insisted upon it, and press'd me to go into the country; *I took him short again*, What need you, *says I*, send me out of your Way? It is in your Power to be less troubled with, and with less Inconvenience, to us both.

He took that ill, and told me I us'd to have a better Opinion of his Sincerity; and desire'd to know what he had done to forfeit my Charity: I mention this, only to let you see how far I had gone in my Measures of quitting him, *that is to say*, how near I was of shewing him how base, ungrateful, and vilely I cou'd act; But I found I had carried the Jest far enough, and that a little Matter might have made him sick of me again, as he was before, so I began, by little and little to change my way of talking to him, and to come to Discourse to the Purpose again, as we had done before.

A while after this, when we were very merry, and talking familiarly together, he call'd me with an Air of particular Satisfaction, *his Princess*; I colour'd at the Word, *for it indeed touch'd me to the quick*; but he knew nothing of the Reason of my being touch'd with it: What d'ye mean by that, *said I*? Nay, *says he*, I mean nothing, but that you are a Princess to me: Well, *says I*, as to that, I am content; and yet I cou'd tell you, I might have been a Princess if I wou'd have quitted you, and believe I cou'd be so still: It is not in my Power to make you a Princess, *says he*, but I

---

1 Literally someone with a "sick imagination," mentally ill.

can easily make you a Lady, here in *England*, and a Countess too, if you will go out of it.

I heard both with a great deal of Satisfaction, for my Pride remain'd, tho' it had been baulk'd, and I thought *with myself*, that this Proposal wou'd make me some Amends for the Loss of the Title that had so tickl'd my Imagination another-way; and I was impatient to understand what he meant; but I wou'd not ask him by any-means; so it pass'd off for that time.

When he was gone, I told *Amy* what he had said, and *Amy* was as impatient to know the Manner, how it cou'd be, as I was; but the next time, (*perfectly unexpected to me*) he told me, that he had accidentally mention'd a thing to me, last time he was with me, having not the least Thought of the thing itself; but not knowing but such a thing might be of some Weight to me, and that it might bring me Respect among People where I might appear, had he thought since of it, and was resolv'd to ask me about it.

I made light of it, and told him, that as he knew I had chosen a retir'd Life, it was of no Value to me to be call'd LADY, or COUNTESS either, but that if he intended to drag me, *as I might call it*, into the World again, perhaps it might be agreeable to him; but, *besides that*, I cou'd not judge of the thing, because I did not understand how either of them was to be done.

He told me, that Money purchas'd Titles of Honour in almost all Parts of the World; tho' Money cou'd not give Principles of Honour, they must come by Birth and Blood; that however, Titles sometimes assist to elevate the Soul, and to infuse generous Principles into the Mind, and especially, where there was a good Foundation laid in the Persons; that he hop'd we shou'd neither of us misbehave, if we came to it; and that as we knew how to wear a Title without undue Elevations, so it might sit as well upon us, as on another; that as to *England*, he had nothing to do, but to get an Act of *Naturalization*[1] in his Favour, and he knew where to purchase a Patent for BARONET, *that is to say*, to have the Honour and Title transferr'd to him; but if I intended to go Abroad with him, he had a Nephew, the son of his Elder Brother, who had the Title of COUNT, with the Estate annex'd,[2] which was but small; and that he had frequently offer'd to make it over to him for a thousand Pistoles, which was not a great-deal

---

1 An act of Parliament that would declare the Dutch merchant a naturalized citizen of England.
2 Property attached.

of Money; and considering it was in the Family already, he wou'd, upon my willing, purchase it immediately.

I told him, I lik'd the last best; but then, I wou'd not let him buy it, unless he wou'd let me pay the thousand Pistoles: No, No, *says he*, I refus'd a thousand Pistoles that I had more right to have accepted, than that, and you shall not be at so much Expence now: Yes, *says I*, you did refuse it, and perhaps, repented it afterwards: I never complain'd, *says he*: but I did, *says I*, and often repented it for you: I do not understand you, *says he*: Why, *says I*, I repented that I suffer'd you to refuse it: Well, well, *said he*, we may talk of that hereafter, when you shall resolve which Part of the World you will make your settl'd Residence in: here he talk'd very handsomely to me, and for a good-while together; how it had been his Lot to live all his Days out of his Native Country, and to be often shifting and changing the Situation of his Affairs; and that I myself had not always had a fix'd Abode; but that now, as neither of us was very Young, he fancy'd I wou'd be for taking-up our Abode, where, *if possible*, we might remove no more; that as to his Part, he was of that Opinion entirely, only with this Exception, that the Choice of the Place shou'd be mine; for, that all Places in the World were alike to him; only with this single Addition, namely, that I was with him.

I heard him with a great-deal of Pleasure, *as well* for his being willing to give me the Choice, as for that I resolv'd to live Abroad, for the Reason I have mention'd already, *namely*, lest I shou'd at any-time be known in *England*, and all that Story of Roxana, and the Balls, shou'd come out; as also I was not a little tickl'd with the Satisfaction of being still a *Countess*, tho' I cou'd not be a *Princess*.

I told *Amy* all this Story, for she was still my Privy-Counsellor; but when I ask'd her Opinion, she made me laugh heartily: *Now, which of the two shall I take*, Amy? *said I*; shall I be a Lady, *that is*, a Baronet's Lady in *England*, or a Countess in *Holland?* the ready-witted Jade, that knew the Pride of my Temper too, almost as well as did myself, answer'd, (without the least Hesitation) *both Madam*; which of them! *says she*, (repeating the Words) why not both of them? And then you will be really *a Princess*; for sure, to be a Lady in *English*, and a Countess in *Dutch*, may make a Princess in *High-Dutch*: Upon the whole, tho' *Amy* was in jest, she put the Thought into my Head, and I resolv'd, that, *in short*, I wou'd be both of them; which I manag'd as you shall hear.

First, I seem'd to resolve that I wou'd live and settle in *England*, only with this Condition, *namely*, that I wou'd not live in

London; I pretended that it wou'd choak me up; that I wanted Breath when I was in *London*; but that any-where else I wou'd be satisfied; and then I ask'd him, whether any Sea-Port Town in *England* wou'd not suit him? because I knew, tho' he seem'd to leave off, he wou'd always love to be among Business, and conversing with Men of Business; and I nam'd several Places, either nearest for Business with *France*, or with *Holland*; as *Dover*, or *Southhampton* for the first; and *Ipswich*, or *Yarmouth*, or *Hull*, for the *last*; but I took care that we wou'd resolve upon nothing; only by this it seem'd to be certain, that we shou'd live in *England*.

It was time now, to bring things to Conclusion, and so in about six Weeks time more, we settl'd all our Preliminaries; and among the rest, he let me know, that he sho'd have the Bill for his *Naturalization* pass'd time enough; so that he wou'd be, (*as he call'd it*) an *Englishman*, before we *marry'd*: That was soon perfected, the Parliament being then sitting, and several other Foreigners joining in the said Bill, to save the Expence.

It was not above three or four Days after, but that, without giving me the least Notice that he had so much as been about the Patent for *Baronet*, he brought it me in a fine embroider'd Bag; and saluting me by the Name of my Lady— (*joining his own Sirname to it*) presented it to me, with his Picture set with Diamonds; and at the same time, gave me a Breast-Jewel worth a thousand Pistoles, and the next Morning we were marry'd; thus I put an End to all the intrieguing Part of my Life; a Life full of prosperous Wickedness; the Reflections upon which, were so much the more afflicting, as the time had been spent in the grossest Crimes, which the more I look'd back upon, the more black and horrid they appear'd, effectually drinking up all the Comfort and Satisfaction which I might otherwise have taken in that Part of Life which was still before me.

The first Satisfaction, however, that I took in the new Condition I was in, was in reflecting, that at length the Life of Crime was over; and that I was like a Passenger coming back from the *Indies*, who having, after many Years Fatigues and Hurry in Business, gotten a good Estate, with innumerable Difficulties and Hazards, is arriv'd safe at *London* with all his Effects, and has the Pleasure of saying, he shall never venture upon the Seas any-more.

When we were marry'd, we came back immediately to my Lodgings, (*for the Church was but just-by*) and we were so privately marry'd, that, none but *Amy* and my Friend the QUAKER, was acquainted with it: As soon as we came into the House, he took me in his Arms, and kissing me, *Now you are my Own*, says he; O!

that you had been so good to have done this eleven Years ago: Then, *said I*, you *perhaps, wou'd have been tir'd of me long ago*; 'tis much better now; for now all our happy Days are to come; besides, *said I*, I should not have been half so rich; but that I said to myself, for there was no letting him into the Reason of it: O! *says he*, I shou'd not been tir'd of you; but besides having the Satisfaction of your Company, it had sav'd me that unlucky Blow at *Paris*, which was a dead Loss to me, of above 8000 Pistoles, and all the Fatigues of so many Years Hurry and Business; and then *he added*, but I'll make you pay for it all, now I have you: I started a little at the Words: *Ay, said I, do you threaten already?* Pray what d'ye mean by that? *and began to look a little grave.*

I'll tell you, *says he*, very plainly what I mean, and still he held me fast in his Arms; I intend from this time, never to trouble myself with any-more Business; so I shall never get one Shilling for you, more than I have already; all that you will lose one way; *next*, I intend not to trouble myself with any of the Care or Trouble of managing what either you have for me, or what I have to add to it; but you shall e'en take it all upon yourself, as the Wives do in *Holland*,[1] so you will pay for it that way too; for all the Drudgery shall be yours; *thirdly*, I intend to condemn you to the constant Bondage of my impertinent Company, for I shall tie you like a Pedlar's Pack, at my Back, I shall scarce ever be from you; for, I am sure, I can take Delight in nothing else in this World: Very well, *says I* , but I am pretty heavy, I hope you'll set me down sometimes, when you are aweary; as for that, *says he*, tire me if you can.

This was all Jest and Allegory; but it was all true, in the Moral of the Fable, as you shall hear in its Place: We were very merry the rest of the Day, but without Noise, or Clutter; for he brought not one of his Acquaintances, or Friends, either *English*, or Foreigner: The honest QUAKER provided us a very noble Dinner indeed, considering how few we were to eat it; and every Day that Week she did the like, and wou'd, at last, have it be all at her own charge, which I was utterly averse to; *first*, because I knew her Circumstances not to be very great, tho' not very low; *and next*, because she had been so true a Friend, and so cheerful a Comforter to me, *ay, and Counsellor too*, in all this Affair, that I had resolv'd to make her a Present, that shou'd be some Help to her when all was over.

---

1 Wives in Holland were reputed to be extraordinarily adept household managers.

But to return to the Circumstances of our Wedding; after being very merry, as I have told you, *Amy* and the QUAKER, put us to-Bed, the honest QUAKER little-thinking we had been *a-Bed together* eleven Years before; nay, that was a Secret which, *as it happen'd, Amy* herself did not know: *Amy* grinn'd, and made Faces, as if she had been pleas'd; but it came out in so many Words, when he was not by, the Sum of her mumbling and muttering was, that this shou'd have been done ten or a dozen Years before; that it wou'd signifie little now; *that was to say, in short,* that her Mistress was pretty near Fifty, and too old to have any Children; I chid her; the QUAKER laugh'd; complimented me upon my not being so old as *Amy* pretended; that I cou'd not be above Forty, and might have a Housefull of Children yet; but *Amy* and I too, knew better than she, how it was; for, *in short,* I was old enough to have done breeding, however I look'd; but I made her hold her Tongue.

In the Morning my QUAKER-Landlady came and visited us, before we were up, and made us eat Cakes, and drink Chocolate in-Bed; and then left us again, and bid us take a Nap upon it, which I believe we did; *in short,* she treated us so handsomely, and with such an agreeable Chearfulness, as well as Plenty, as made it appear to me, that QUAKERS may, and that this QUAKER did, understand Good-Manners, as well as any other People.

I resisted her Offer, *however,* of treating us for the whole Week; and I oppos'd it so long, that I saw evidently that she took it ill, and wou'd have thought herself slighted, if we had not accepted it; so I said no more, but let her go on, only told her, I wou'd be even with her, *and so I was:* However, for that Week she treated us, *as she said she wou'd,* and did it so very fine, and with such a Profussion of all sorts of good things, that the greatest Burthen to her was, how to dispose of things that were left; for she never let any-thing, how dainty, or however large, be so much as seen twice among us.

I had some Servants indeed, which help'd her off a little; *that is to say,* two Maids, for *Amy* was now a Woman of Business, not a Servant, and eat always with us; I had also a Coachman, and a Boy; my QUAKER had a Man-Servant too, but had but one Maid; but she borrow'd two more of some of her Friends, for the Occasion; and had a Man-Cook for dressing the Victuals.

She was only at a loss for Plate, which she gave me a Whisper of; and I made *Amy* fetch a large strong Box, which I had lodg'd in a safe Hand, in which was all the fine Plate, which I had provided on a worse Occasion, *as is mention'd before*; and I put it into the QUAKER's Hand, obliging her not to use it as mine, but as her own, for a Reason I shall mention presently.

I was now my LADY——, and I must own, I was exceedingly pleas'd with it; 'twas so Big, and so Great, to hear myself call'd *Her Ladyship*, and *Your Ladyship, and the like*, that I was like the *Indian* King at *Virginia*, who having a House built for him by the *English*, and a Lock put upon the Door, wou'd sit whole Days together, with the Key in his Hand, locking and unlocking, and double-locking the Door, with an unaccountable Pleasure at the Novelty; so I cou'd have sat a whole Day together, to hear *Amy* talk to me, and call me *Your Ladyship* at every word; but after a while the Novelty wore off, and the Pride of it abated; till at last, truly, I wanted the other Title as much as I did that of *Ladyship* before.

We liv'd this Week in all the Innocent Mirth imaginable; and our good-humour'd QUAKER was so pleasant in her Way, that it was particularly entertaining to us: We had no Musick at-all, or Dancing; only I now and then sung a *French* Song, to divert my Spouse, who desir'd it, and the Privacy of our Mirth, greatly added to the Pleasure of it: I did not make many Cloaths for my Wedding, having always a great-many rich Cloaths by me, which with a little altering for the Fashion, were perfectly new: The next Day he press'd me to dress tho' we had no Company; at last, jesting with him, I told him, I believ'd I was able to dress me so, in one kind of Dress that I had by me, that he wou'd not know his Wife when he saw her, especially if any-body else was by: *No!* he said, *that was impossible*; he long'd to see that Dress; *I told him*, I wou'd dress me in it, if he wou'd promise me never to desire me to appear in it before Company; he promis'd he wou'd not, but wanted to know *why* too; as Husbands, you know, are inquisitive Creatures, and love to enquire after any-thing they think is kept from them; but I had an Answer ready for him; because, *said I*, it is not a decent Dress in this Country, and wou'd not look modest; neither indeed, wou'd it, for it was but one Degree off, from appearing in one's Shift; but was the usual Wear in the Country where they were used: He was satisfy'd with my Answer, and gave me his Promise, never to ask me to be seen in it before Company: I then withdrew, taking only *Amy* and the QUAKER with me; and *Amy* dress'd me in my old *Turkish Habit* which I danc'd in formerly, *&c. as before*: The QUAKER was charm'd with the Dress, *and merrily said*, That if such a Dress shou'd come to be worn here, she shou'd not know what to do: she shou'd be tempted not to dress in the QUAKERS Way any-more.

When all the Dress was put on, I loaded it with Jewels, and in particular, I plac'd the large Breast-Jewel which he had given me, of a thousand Pistoles, upon the Front of the *Tyhaia*, or Head-Dress; where it made a most glorious Show indeed; I had my own Diamond-Necklace on, and my Hair was *Tout Brilliant*, all glittering with Jewels.

His Picture set with Diamonds, I had plac'd stitch'd to my Vest, just, *as might be suppos'd*, upon my Heart, (which is the Compliment in such Cases among the *Eastern* People) and all being open at the Breast, there was no room for any-thing of a Jewel there: In this Figure, *Amy* holding the Train of my Robe, I came down to him: He was surpriz'd, and perfectly astonish'd; he knew me, *to be sure*, because I had prepar'd him, and because there was no-body else there, but the QUAKER and *Amy*; but he by no means knew *Amy*; for she had dress'd herself in the Habit of a *Turkish* Slave, being the Garb of my *little Turk*, which I had at *Naples, as I have said*; she had her Neck and Arms bare; was bareheaded, and her Hair breeded[1] in a long Tossel hanging down her Back; but the Jade cou'd neither hold her Countenance, or her chattering Tongue, so as to be conceal'd long.

Well, he was so charm'd with this Dress, that he wou'd have me sit and dine in it; but it was so thin and so open before, and the Weather being also sharp, that I was afraid of taking Cold; however, the Fire being enlarg'd, and the Doors kept shut, I sat to oblige him; and he profess'd, he never saw so fine a Dress in his Life: I afterwards told him, that my Husband (so he call'd the Jeweller *that was kill'd*) bought it for me, at *Leghorn*, with a young *Turkish* Slave, which I parted with at *Paris*; and that it was by the help of that Slave that I learn'd how to dress in it, and how everything was to be worn, and many of the *Turkish* Customs also, with some of their Language; this Story agreeing with the Fact, only changing the Person, was very natural, and so it went off with him; but there was good Reason why I shou'd not receive any Company in this Dress, *that is to say*, not in *England*; *I need not repeat it; you will hear more of it.*

But when I came Abroad, I frequently put it on, and upon two or three Occasions danc'd in it, but always at his Request.

We continued at the QUAKER's Lodgings for above a Year; for now making as tho' it was difficult to determine where to settle in *England* to his Satisfaction, unless in *London*, which was not to mine; I pretended to make him an Offer, that to oblige him, I

---

1 Braided.

began to incline to go and live Abroad with him; that I knew nothing could be more agreeable to him, and that as to me, every Place was alike; that as I had liv'd Abroad without a Husband so many Years, it cou'd be no Burthen to me to live Abroad again, *especially with him*; then we fell to straining our Courtesies upon one-another; he told me, he was perfectly easie at living in *England*, and had squar'd all his Affairs, accordingly; for that, as he had told me he intended to give over all Business in the World, as well the Care of managing it, as the Concern about it; seeing we were both in Condition, neither to want it, or to have it be worth our while; so I might see it was his Intention, by his getting himself Naturaliz'd, and getting the Patent of Baronet, *&c.* Well, for-all that, I told him, I accepted his Compliment, but I cou'd not but know that his Native Country, where his Children were breeding up, must be most agreeable to him, and that if I was of such Value to him, I wou'd be there then, to enhance the rate of his Satisfaction; that wherever he was, wou'd be a Home to me; and any Place in the World wou'd be *England* to me, if he was with me; and thus, *in short*, I brought him to give me leave to oblige him with going to live Abroad; when in truth, I cou'd not have been perfectly easie at living in *England*, unless I had kept constantly within-doors: lest some time or other, the dissolute Life I had liv'd here, shou'd have come to be known; and all those wicked things have been known too, which I now began to be very much asham'd of.

When we clos'd up our Wedding-Week, in which our QUAKER had been so very handsome to us, I told him how much I thought we were oblig'd to her for her generous Carriage[1] to us; how she had acted the kindest Part thro' the whole, and how faithful a Friend she had been to me, upon all Occasions; and the letting him know a little of her Family Unhappiness, I propos'd, that I thought I not only ought to be grateful to her, but really to do something extraordinary for her, towards making her easie in her Affairs; *and I added*, that I had no hangers-on, that shou'd trouble him; that there was no-body belong'd to me, but what was thorowly provided for; and that if I did something for this honest Woman, that was considerable, it shou'd be the last Gift I wou'd give to any-body in the World, *but Amy*; and as for her, we was not a-going to turn her adrift, but whenever any-thing offer'd, for her, we wou'd do as we saw Cause; that *in the mean time, Amy* was not poor; that she had sav'd together between

---

1 Attitude towards, treatment of.

seven and eight Hundred Pounds; *by the way, I did not tell him how, and by what wicked Ways she had got it*; but *that she had it*; and that was enough to let him know she wou'd never be in want of us.

My Spouse was exceedingly pleas'd with my Discourse about the QUAKER, made a kind of a Speech to me upon the Subject of Gratitude; told me it was one of the brightest Parts of a Gentlewoman; that it was so twisted with Honesty, *nay*, and even with Religion too, that he question'd whether either of them cou'd be found, where Gratitude was not to be found; that in this Act there was not only Gratitude, but Charity; and that to make the Charity still more Christian-like, the Object too had real Merit to attract it; he therefore agreed to the thing with all his Heart, only wou'd have had me let him pay it out of his Effects.

I told him, *as for that*, I did not design, *whatever I had said formerly*, that we shou'd have *two Pockets*; and that tho' I had talk'd to him of being a Free Woman, and an Independent, *and the like*, and he had offer'd and promis'd that I shou'd keep all my own Estate in my own Hands; yet, that since I had taken him, I wou'd e'en do as other *honest Wives* did, where I thought fit to give myself, I shou'd give what I had too; that if I reserv'd any-thing, it shou'd be only in case of Mortality, and that I might give it to his Children afterwards, *as my own Gift*; and that, *in short*, if he thought fit to join Stocks, we wou'd see to Morrow Morning, what Strength we cou'd both make up in the World, and bringing it all together, consider before we resolv'd upon the Place of removing, how we shou'd dispose of what we had, as well as of ourselves: This Discourse was too obliging, and he too much a Man of Sence, not to receive it, as it was meant; *he only answer'd*, We wou'd do in that, as we shou'd both agree; but the thing under our present Care, was to shew not Gratitude only, but Charity and Affection too, to our kind Friend the QUAKER; and the first Word he spoke of, was to settle a thousand Pounds upon her, *for her Life, that is to say*, sixty Pounds a Year; but in such a manner, as not to be in the Power of any Person to reach, but herself: This was a great thing, and indeed shew'd the generous Principles of my Husband, and for that reason I mention it; but I thought that a little too much too, and particularly, because I had another thing in View for her, about the Plate; so I told him, I thought if he gave her a Purse with a Hundred Guineas as a Present *first*, and then made her a Compliment of 40*l. per Annum* for her Life, secur'd any such Way as she shou'd desire, it wou'd be very handsome.

He agreed to that; and the same Day, in the Evening, when we were just going to-Bed, he took my QUAKER by the Hand, and with a Kiss, told her, That we had been very kindly treated by her from the beginning of this Affair, and his Wife before, as she, (*meaning me*) had inform'd him; and that he thought himself bound to let her see, that she had oblig'd Friends who knew how to be grateful; that for his Part of the Obligation, he desir'd she wou'd accept of *that*, for an Acknowledgement in Part only, (*putting the Gold into her Hand*) and that his Wife wou'd talk with her about what farther he had to say to her; and upon that, not giving her time hardly to say *thank ye*, away he went up-Stairs, into our Bed-Chamber, leaving her confus'd, and not knowing what to say.

When he was gone, she began to make very handsome and obliging Representations of her Good-will to us both, but that it was without Expectation of Reward; that I had given her several valuable Presents before and so indeed I had; for, besides the Piece of Linnen which I had given her *at first*, I had given her a Suit of Damask *Table-Linnen*,[1] of the Linnen I had bought for my Balls, *viz.* Three Table-cloths, and three Dozen of Napkins; and at another time, I gave her a little Necklace of Gold Beads, *and the like*; but that is *by the way*; but she mention'd them, *I say*; and how she was oblig'd by me, on many other Occasions; that she was not in Condition to show her Gratitude any other way, not being able to make a suitable Return; and that now we took from her all Opportunity to balance my former Friendship, and left her more in Debt than she was before: She spoke this in a very good kind of a Manner, *in her own way*, but which was very agreeable indeed, and had as much apparent Sincerity, and I verily believe as real, as was possible to be express'd; but I put a Stop to it, and bid her say no more, but accept of what my Spouse had given her, which was but in Part, as she had heard him say; and *put it up,* says I, *and come and sit down here, and give me Leave to say something else to you, on the same Head, which my Spouse and I have settled between ourselves, in your Behalf:* What dost Thee mean, *says she?* and blush'd, and look'd surpriz'd, but did not stir; she was going to speak again, but I interrupted her, and told her, she shou'd make no more Apologies of any kind whatever, for I had better things than all this, to talk to her of; so I went on, and told her, That as she had been so friendly and kind to us on every

---

1 Damask is a type of fabric with a raised pattern. Roxana describes a set
  of table linens, table cloth and napkins made of Damask.

Occasion; and that her House was the lucky Place where we came together; and that she knew I was from her own Mouth, acquainted in Part, with her Circumstances, we were resolv'd she shou'd be the better for us, as long as she liv'd: Then I told her what we had resolv'd to do for her; and that she had nothing more to do, but to consult with me, how it shou'd be effectually secur'd for her, distinct form any of the Effects which were her Husband's; and that if her Husband did so supply her, that she cou'd live comfortably, and not want it for Bread, or other Necessaries, she shou'd not make Use of it, but lay up the Income of it, and add it every Year to the Prinicpal, so to encrease the Annual Payment,[1] which in time, and perhaps before she might come to want it, might double itself, that we were very willing whatever she shou'd so lay up, shou'd be to herself, and whoever she thought fit after her; but that the forty Pound a-Year, must return to our Family, after her Life; which we both wish'd might be long and happy.

Let no Reader wonder at my extraordinary Concern for this poor Woman; or at my giving my Bounty to her a Place in this Account; it is not, *I assure you*, to make a Pageantry of my Charity, or to value myself upon the Greatness of my Soul, that shou'd give in so profuse a Manner as this, which was above my Figure, if my Wealth had been twice as much as it was; but there was another Spring from whence all flow'd, and 'tis on that Account I speak of it: Was it possible I cou'd think of a poor desolate Woman with four Children, and her Husband gone from her, *and perhaps good for little if he had stay'd; I say*, was I, that had tasted so deep of the Sorrows of such a kind of Widowhood, able to look on her, and think of her Circumstances, and not be touch'd in an uncommon Manner? No, No, I never look'd on her, and her Family, tho' she was not left so helpless and friendless as I had been, without remembering my own Condition; when *Amy* was sent out to pawn or sell my *Pair of Stays*, to buy a Breast of Mutton, and a Bunch of Turnips; nor cou'd I look on her poor Children, tho' not poor and perishing, like mine, without Tears; reflecting on the dreadful Condition that mine were reduc'd to, when poor *Amy* sent them all into their Aunt's in *Spittle-Fields*, and run away from them: these were the Original Springs, or Fountain-Head, from whence my Affectionate Thoughts were mov'd to assist this poor Woman.

---

1 Roxana is repeating the advice she herself received from Robert Clayton and successfully employed to increase her own wealth.

When a poor Debtor, having lain long in the *Compter*, or *Ludgate*, or the *Kings-Bench*,[1] for Debt, afterwards gets out, rises again in the World, and grows rich; such an one is a certain Benefactor to the Prisoners there, and perhaps to every Prison he passes by, as long as he lives; for he remembers the dark Days of his own Sorrow; and even those who never had the Experience of such Sorrows to stir up their Minds to Acts of Charity, would have the same charitable good Disposition, did they as sensibly remember what it is, that distinguishes them from others, by a more favourable and merciful Providence.

This, I say, was however, the Spring of my Concern for this honest friendly and grateful QUAKER, and as I had so plentiful a Fortune in the World, I resolv'd she shou'd taste the Fruit of her kind Usage to me, in a manner that she cou'd not expect.

All the while I talk'd to her, I saw the Disorder of her Mind; the sudden Joy was too much for her, and she colour'd, trembled, chang'd, and at last grew pale, and was indeed near fainting; when she hastily rung a little Bell for her Maid, who coming in immediately, she beckon'd to her, *for speak she cou'd not*, to fill her a Glass of Wine, but she had no Breath to take it in, and was almost choak'd with that which she took in her Mouth; I saw she was ill, and assisted her what I cou'd, and with Spirits and things to smell too, just kept her from Fainting, when she beckon'd to her Maid to withdraw, and immediately burst out in crying, and that reliev'd her; when she recover'd herself a little, she flew to me, and throwing her Arms about my Neck, O! *says she, thou hast almost kill'd me*; and there she hung, laying her Head in my Neck for half a quarter of an Hour, not able to speak, but sobbing like a Child that had been whipp'd,

I was very sorry, that I did not stop a little, in the middle of my Discourse, and make her drink a Glass of Wine, before it had put her Spirits into such a violent Motion; but it was too late, and it was ten to one odds, but that it had kill'd her.

But she came to herself at last, and began to say some very good things in return for my Kindness; I would not let her go on, but *told her*, I had more to say to her still, than all this, but that I would let it alone till another time; my meaning was, about the Box of Plate, good part of which I gave her, and some I gave to *Amy*, for I had so much Plate, and some so large, that I thought

---

1 Three of several prisons in and around London to which debtors could be committed, though their clienteles were not exclusively composed of debtors.

if I let my Husband see it, he might be apt to wonder what Occasion I cou'd ever have for so much, and for Plate of such a kind too; as particularly, a great Cistern for Bottles,[1] which cost a hundred and twenty Pound, and some large Candlesticks, too big, for any ordinary Use: These I caus'd *Amy* to sell; *in short, Amy* sold above three hundred Pound's-worth of Plate; what I gave the QUAKER, was worth above sixty Pounds, and I gave *Amy* above thirty Pound's-worth, and yet I had a great-deal left for my Husband.

Nor did our Kindness to the QUAKER end with the forty Pound a Year, for we were always, while we stay'd with her, which was above ten Months, giving her one good thing or another; and, *in a word*, instead of Lodging with her, she Boarded with us, for I kept the House, and she and all her Family eat and drank with us, and yet we paid her the Rent of the House too; *in short,* I remember'd *my Widowhood*,[2] and I made this Widow's Heart glad many a Day the more, upon that Account.

And now my Spouse and I began to think of going over to *Holland*, where I had propos'd to him to live, and in order to settle all the Preliminaries of our future Manner of Living, I began to draw in my Effects, so as to have them all at Command, upon whatever Occasion we thought fit; after which, *one Morning* I call'd my Spouse up to me; hark ye, Sir, *said I to him*, I have two very weighty Questions to ask of you; I don't know what Answer you will give to the *first*, but I doubt you will be able to give but a sorry Answer to the *other*, and yet, *I assure you*, it is of the last Importance to yourself, and towards the future Part of your Life, wherever it is to be.

He did not seem to be much alarm'd because he could see I was speaking in a kind of merry way, *Let's hear your Questions*, my Dear, *says he, and I'll give the best Answer I can to them*: Why first, *says I*,

I. You have marry'd a Wife here, made her a *Lady*, and put her in Expectation of being something else still, when she comes Abroad; pray have you examin'd whether you are able to supply all her extravagant Demands when she comes Abroad; and maintain an expensive *Englishwoman* in all her Pride, and

---

1 It was customary to keep liquor bottles in a case that could be locked.
2 Roxana's euphemism for the period during which her husband had abandoned her and before her liaison with the Jeweller.

Vanity? *In short,* have you enquir'd whether you are able to keep her?

II. You have marry'd a Wife here, and given her a great many fine things, and you maintain her like a *Princess,* and sometimes call her *so;* pray what Portion have you had with her? What Fortune has she been to you? And where does her Estate lie, that you keep her so fine? I am afraid you keep her in a Figure a great-deal above her Estate, *at least,* above all that you have seen of it yet? Are you sure you ha'n't got a *Bite?* And that you have not made a Beggar a *Lady?*

Well, *says he,* have you any more Questions to ask? let's have them all together, perhaps they may be all answer'd in a few Words, as well as these two: No, *says I,* these are the two grand Questions, at least, for the present: Why then, *says he,* I'll answer you in a few Words, That I am fully master of my own Circumstances, and without farther Enquiry, can let my Wife you speak of, know, that as I have made her a *Lady,* I can maintain her *as a Lady,* wherever she goes with me; and this, whether I have one Pistole of her Portion, or whether she has any Portion or no: And as I have not enquir'd whether she has any Portion or not, so she shall not have the less Respect shew'd her from me, or be oblig'd to live meaner, or be any-ways straiten'd on that Account; on the contrary, if she goes Abroad to live with me in my own Country, I will make her more than a *Lady* and support the Expence of it too, without meddling with any-thing she has; and this I suppose, *says he,* contains an Answer to both your Questions together.

He spoke this with a great deal more Earnestness in his Countenance, than I had when I propos'd my Questions; and said a great-many kind things upon it, as the consequence of former Discourses, so that I was oblig'd to be in earnest too; My Dear, *says I,* I was but in jest in my Questions; but they were propos'd to introduce what I am going to say to you in earnest; *namely,* that if I am to go Abroad, 'tis time I shou'd let you know how things stand, and what I have to bring you, with your Wife; how it is to be dispos'd, and secur'd, *and the like;* and therefore come, *says I,* sit down, and let me show you your Bargain here; I hope you will find, that you have not got a Wife without a Fortune.

He told me then, that since he found I was in earnest, he desir'd that I wou'd adjourn it till to-Morrow, and then we wou'd do as the poor People do after they Marry, feel in their Pockets, and see how much Money they can bring together in the World;

well *says I*, with all my Heart; and so we ended our Talk for that time.

As this was in the Morning, my Spouse went out after Dinner to his Goldsmith's,[1] as *he said*, and about three Hours after, returns with a Porter and two large Boxes, with him; and his Servant brought another Box, which I observ'd was almost as heavy as the two that the Porter brought, and made the poor Fellow sweat heartily; he dismiss'd the Porter, and in a little-while after went out again with his Man, and returning at Night, brought another Porter with more Boxes and Bundles, and all was carried up, and put into a Chamber, next to our Bed-Chamber, and in the Morning he call'd for a pretty large round Table, and began to unpack.

When the Boxes were open'd, I found they were chiefly full of Books, and Papers and Parchments, *I mean*, Books of Accompts, and Writings, *and such things*, as were in themselves of no Moment to me, because I understood them not; but I perceiv'd he took them all out, and spread them about him, upon the Table, and Chairs, and began to be very busie with them; so I withdrew, and left him; and he was indeed, so busie among them, that he never miss'd me, till I had been gone a good-while; but when he had gone thro' all his Papers, and come to open a little Box, he call'd for me again; Now, *says he*, and call'd me *his Countess*, I am ready to answer your first Question; if you will sit down till I have open'd this Box, we will see how it stands.

So we open'd the Box; there was in it indeed, what I did not expect, for I thought he had sunk his Estate, rather than rais'd it; but he produc'd me, in Goldsmith's Bills, and Stock in the *English East-India Company*,[2] about sixteen thousand Pounds Sterling; then he gave into my Hands, nine Assignments upon the Bank of *Lyons* in *France*, and two upon the Rents of the Town-House in *Paris*, amounting in the whole to 5800 Crowns *per Annum*, or annual Rent, *as 'tis call'd there*; and *lastly*, the Sum of 30000 *Rix-dollars*[3] in the Bank of *Amsterdam*; besides some Jewels and Gold in the Box, to the Value of about 15 or 1600*l*. among which was a very good Necklace of Pearl, of about 200*l*. Value; and that he

---

1 It was common for Goldsmiths to serve as bankers of assets other than land during the late seventeenth century.
2 One of the major joint stock companies of the period. The English East-India Company was heavily involved in governing England's holdings in the near and far east.
3 The currency of Holland.

pull'd out, and ty'd about my Neck; telling me, That shou'd not be reckon'd into the Account.

I was equally pleas'd and surpriz'd; and it was with an inexpressible Joy, that I saw him so rich: You might well tell me, *said I*, that you were able to make me *Countess*, and maintain me as such: *In short*, he was immensely rich; for besides all this, he shew'd me, which was the Reason of his being so busie among the Books, *I say*, he shew'd me several Adventures he had Abroad, in the Business of Merchandize; as particularly, an eighth Share in an *East-India* Ship then Abroad; an Account-Courant with a Merchant, at *Cadiz* in *Spain*; about 3000*l.* let upon *Bottomtree*,[1] upon Ships gone to the Indies; and a large Cargo of Goods in a Merchant's Hands, for Sale, at *Lisbon* in *Portugal*; so that in his Books there was about 12000*l.*, more; all which put together, made about 27000*l.* Sterling, and 1320*l.* a Year.

I stood amaz'd at this Account, *as well I might*, and said nothing to him for a good-while, and the rather, because I saw him still busie, looking over his Books: After a-while, as I was going to express my Wonder; *Hold*, my Dear, *says he*, this is not all neither; then he pull'd me out some old Seals, and small Parchment-Rolls, which I did not understand; *but he told me* they were a Right Reversion[2] which he had to a Paternal Estate in his Family, and a Mortgage of 14000 *Rixdollars*, which he had upon it, in the Hands of the Present Possessor; so that was about 3000*l.* more.

But now hold again, *says he*, for I must pay my Debts out of all this, and they are very great, *I assure you*; and the *first, he said*, was a black Article of 8000 Pistoles, which he had a Law-Suit about, at *Paris*, but had it awarded against him, which was the Loss he had told me of, and which made him leave *Paris* in Disgust; that in other Accounts he ow'd about 5300*l.* Sterling; but after all this, upon the whole, he had still 17000*l.* clear Stock in Money, and 1320*l.* a-Year in Rent.

---

1 *OED*: A species of contract of the nature of a mortgage, whereby the owner of a ship, or the master as his agent, borrows money to enable him to carry on or complete a voyage, and pledges the ship as security for repayment of the money. If the ship is lost, the lender loses his money; but if it arrives safe, he receives the principal together with the interest or premium stipulated, "however it may exceed the usual or legal rate of interest."

2 A particular form of title to an estate. In this case, the estate will revert to the Dutch merchant upon the current occupant's death.

After some Pause, it came to my Turn to speak; Well, *says I*, 'tis very hard a Gentleman with such a Fortune as this, shou'd come over to *England*, and marry a Wife with *Nothing*; it shall never, *says I*, be said, but what I have, I'll bring into the Publick Stock; so I began to produce.

First, I pull'd out the Mortgage which good Sir *Robert* had procur'd for me, the annual Rent 700*l. per Annum*; the principal Money 14000*l.*

Secondly, I pull'd out another Mortgage upon Land, procur'd by the same faithful Friend, which at three times, had advanc'd 12000*l.*

Thirdly, I pull'd him out a Parcel of little Securities, procur'd by several Hands, by Fee-Farm Rents,[1] and such Petty Mortgages as those Times afforded, amounting to 10800*l.* principal Money, and paying six hundred and thirty six Pounds a-Year; so that in the while, there was two thousand fifty Pounds a-Year, Ready-Money, constantly coming in.

When I had shewn him all these, I laid them upon the Table, and bade him take them, that he might be able to give me an Answer to the *second Question, viz. What Fortune he had with his Wife?* And laugh'd a little at it.

He look'd at them a-while, and then handed them all back again to me; I will not touch them, *says he*, nor one of them, till they are all settl'd in Trustees Hands, for your own Use, and the Management wholly your own.

I cannot omit what happen'd to me while all this was acting, tho' it was chearful Work in the main, yet I trembled every Joint of me, worse for ought I know, than ever *Belshazzer* did at the Hand-writing on the Wall,[2] and the Occasion was every way as just: *Unhappy Wretch*, said I to myself, *shall my ill-got Wealth, the Product of prosperous Lust, and of a vile and vicious Life* of Whoredom and Adultery, *be intermingled with the honest well-gotten Estate of this innocent Gentleman, to be a Moth and a Caterpiller among it,*[3] *and bring the Judgments of Heaven upon him, and upon what he has, for my sake! Shall my Wickedness blast his Comforts! Shall I* be Fire in his Flax! *and be a Means to provoke Heaven to curse his Blessings!* God forbid! *I'll keep them asunder, if it be possible.*

---

1 The rent or income from tenant farms, which the renter used for the duration of his life.
2 *Daniel* 5:5-7. Belshazzar is an ancient king of Babylon, whose doom is foretold by handwriting on a wall, that he himself cannot read.
3 To destroy as moths do wool.

This is the true Reason why I have been so particular in the Account of my vast acquir'd Stock; and how his Estate, which was perhaps, the Product of many Years' fortunate Industry; and which was equal, if not superior, to mine, at best, was *at my Request*, kept apart from mine, *as is mention'd above.*

I have told you how he gave back all my Writings into my own Hands again: *Well, says I,* seeing you will have it be kept apart, *it shall be so,* upon one Condition, which I have to propose, and no other; and what is the Condition, *says he?* why, *says I,* all the Pretence[1] I can have for the making-over my own Estate to me, is that in Case of your Mortallity, I may have it reserv'd for me, if I out-live you; well, *says he,* that is true: But then, *said I,* the Annual Income is always receiv'd by the Husband, during his Life, as 'tis suppos'd for the mutual Subsistance of the Family; now, *says I,* here is 2000*l.* a Year, which I believe is as much as we shall spend, and I desire none of it may be sav'd; and all the Income of your own Estate, the Interest of the 17000*l.* and the 1320*l.* a Year may be constantly laid by for the Encrease of your Estate, and so, added I, by joining the Interest every year to the Capital, you will perhaps grow as rich as you would do, if you were to Trade with it all, if you were oblig'd to keep House out of it too.

He lik'd the Proposal very well, *and said* it should be so; and this way I, in some Measure, satisfied myself, that I should not bring my Husband under the Blast of a just Providence, for mingling my cursed ill-gotten Wealth with his honest Estate: This was occasion'd by the Reflections which at some certain Intervals of time, came into my Thoughts, of the Justice of Heaven, which I had reason to expect would sometime or other still fall upon me or my Effects, for the dreadful Life I had liv'd.

And let no-body conclude from the strange Success I met with in all my wicked Doings, and the vast Estate which I had rais'd by it, that therefore I either was happy or easie: No, no, there was a Dart struck into the Liver;[2] there was a secret Hell within, even all the while, when our Joy was at the highest; but more especially *now*, after it was all over, and when according to all appearance, I was one of the happiest Women upon Earth, all this while, *I say,* I had such a constant Terror upon my Mind, as gave me every now and then very terrible Shocks, and which made me expect something very Frightful upon every Accident of Life.

---

1 Claim.
2 A vital organ, understood at this time to be equally as important as the heart and brain.

In a word, it never Lightn'd or Thunder'd, but I expected the next Flash wou'd penetrate my Vitals, and melt the Sword [*Soul*] in this Scabbord of Flesh; it never blew a Storm of Wind, but I expected the Fall of some Stack of Chimneys, or some Part of the House, wou'd bury me in its Ruins; and so of other things.

But I shall perhaps, have Occasion to speak of all these things again by-and-by; the Case before us was in a manner settl'd; we had full four thousand Pounds *per Annum* for our future Subsistence, besides a vast Sum in Jewels and Plate; and besides this, I had about eight thousand Pounds reserv'd in Money, which I kept back from him, to provided for my two Daughters; of whom I have yet much to say.

With this Estate, settl'd as you have heard, and with the best Husband in the World, I left *England* again; I had not only in humane Prudence, and by the Nature of the thing, *being now marry'd and settl'd in so glorious a Manner*, I say, I had not only abandon'd all the gay and wicked Course which I had gone throrow before, but I began to look back upon it with that Horror, and that Detestation, which is the certain Companion, if not the Forerunner, of Repentance.

Sometimes the Wonders of my present Circumstances wou'd work upon me, and I shou'd have some Raptures upon my Soul, upon the Subject of my coming so smoothly out of the Arms of Hell, that I was not ingulph'd in Ruin, as most who lead such Lives are, first or last; but this was a Flight too high for me; I was not come to that Repentance that is rais'd from a Sence of Heaven's Goodness; I repented of the Crime, but it was of another and lower kind of Repentance, and rather mov'd by my Fears of Vengeance, than from a Sense of being spar'd from being punish'd, and landed safe after a Storm.

The first thing which happen'd after our coming to the *Hague*, (where we lodg'd for a-while) was, that my Spouse saluted me one Morning with the Title of *Countess*; as *he said* he intended to do, by having the Inheritance to which the Honour was annex'd, made over to him; it is true, it was a Reversion, but it soon fell, and in the mean time, as all the Brothers of a *Count* are call'd *Counts*, so I had the Title by Courtesie, about three years before I had it in reality.

I was agreeably surpiz'd at this coming so soon, and wou'd have had my Spouse have taken the Money which it cost him, out of my Stock, but he laugh'd at me, and went on.

I was now in the height of my Glory and Prosperity, and I was call'd the *Countess de*—; for I had obtain'd that unlook'd for, which I secretly aim'd at, and was really the main Reason of my coming Abroad: I took now more Servants; liv'd in a kind of Magnificence that I had not been acquainted with; was call'd *Your Honour* at every word, and had a *Coronet* behind my Coach; tho' at the same time I knew little or nothing of my new Pedigree.

The first thing that my Spouse took upon him to manage, was to declare ourselves marry'd eleven Years before our arriving in *Holland*; and consequently to acknowledge our little Son, who was yet in *England*, to be legitimate; order him to be brought over, and added to his Family, and acknowledge him to be our own.

This was done by giving Notice to his People at *Nimeguen*, where his Children (which were two Sons and a Daughter) were brought-up; that he was come over from *England*; and that he was arriv'd at the *Hague*, with his Wife, and shou'd reside there some time; and that he wou'd have his two Sons brought down to see him, which accordingly was done, and where I entertain'd them with all the Kindness and Tenderness that they cou'd expect from their Mother-in-Law; and who pretended to be so ever since they were two or three Years old.

This, supposing as to have been so long marry'd, was not difficult at-all, in a Country where we had been seen together about that time, *viz.* eleven Years and a half before; and where we had never been seen afterwards, till we now return'd together; this being seen together was also openly own'd, and acknowledg'd of course, by our Friend, the Merchant at *Rotterdam*; and also by the People in the House where we both lodg'd, in the same City, and where our first Intimacies began, and who, as it happen'd were all alive; and therefore to make it the more publick we made a Tour to *Rotterdam* again, lodg'd in the same House, and was visited there by our Friend the Merchant; and afterwards invited frequently to his House, where he treated us very handsomely.

This Conduct of my Spouse, and which he manag'd very cleverly, was indeed, a Testimony of a wonderful Degree of Honesty and Affection to our little Son; for it was done purely for the sake of the Child.

I call it an honest Affection, because it was from a Principle of Honesty that he so earnestly concern'd himself, to prevent the Scandal which wou'd otherwise have fallen upon the Child, *who was itself innocent*; and as it was from this Principle of Justice that he so earnestly solicited me, and conjur'd[1] me by the natural

---

1 Cajoled, attempted to persuade.

Affections of a Mother, to marry him, when it was yet young within me, and unborn, that the Child might not suffer for the Sin of its Father and Mother; so tho' at the same time, he really lov'd me very well, yet I had reason to believe, that it was from his Principle of Justice to the Child, that he came to *England* again to seek me, with design to marry me, and, *as he call'd it*, save the innocent Lamb from an Infamy worse than Death.

It is with a just Reproach to myself, that I must repeat it again, that I had not the same Concern for it, tho' it was the Child of my own Body; nor had I ever the hearty affectionate Love to the Child, that he had; what the reason of it was, I cannot tell; and indeed, I had shown a general Neglect of the Child, thro' all the gay Years of my *London* Revels; except that I sent *Amy* to look upon it now and then, and to pay for its Nursing; as for me, I scarce saw it four times in the first four Years of its Life, and often wish'd it wou'd go quietly out of the World; whereas a Son which I had by the Jeweller, I took a different Care of, and shew'd a differing Concern for, tho' I did not let him know me; for I provided very well for him; had him put out very well to School; and when he came to Years fit for it, let him go over with a Person of Honesty and good Business, to the *Indies*; and after he had liv'd there some time, and began to act for himself, sent him over the Value of 2000*l.* at several times, with which he traded, and grew rich; and, *as 'tis to be hop'd*, may at last come over again with forty or fifty Thousand Pounds in his Pocket, as many do who have not such Encouragement at their Beginning.

I also sent him over a Wife; a beautiful young Lady, well-bred, an exceeding good-natur'd pleasant Creature; but the nice young Fellow did not like her, and had the Impudence to write to me, *that is, to the Person I employ'd to correspond with him*, to send him another; and promis'd, that he wou'd marry her I had sent him, to a Friend of his, who lik'd her better than he did; but I took it so ill, that I wou'd not send him another, and withal, stopp'd another Article of 1000*l.* which I had appointed to send him: He consider'd of it afterwards, and offer'd to take her; but then truly she took so ill the first Affront he put upon her, that she wou'd not have him, and I sent him word, that I thought she was very much in the right: However, after courting her two Years, and some Friends interposing, she took him, and made him an excellent Wife, as I knew she wou'd; but I never sent him the thousand Pound Cargo, so that he lost that Money for misusing me, and took the Lady at last without it.

My new Spouse and I, liv'd a very regular contemplative Life, and in itself certainly a Life fill'd with all humane Felicity: But if I look'd upon my present Situation with Satisfaction, as I certainly did, so in Proportion I on all Occasions look'd back on former things with Detestation, and with the utmost Affliction; and now indeed, and not till now, those Reflections began to prey upon my Comforts, and lessen the Sweets of my other Enjoyments: They might be said to have gnaw'd a Hole in my Heart before; but now they made a Hole quite thro' it; now they eat into all my pleasant things; made bitter every Sweet, and mix'd my Sighs with every Smile.

Not all the Affluence of a plentiful Fortune, not a hundred Thousand Pounds Estate; (for between us we had little less) not Honour and Titles, Attendants and Equipages; *in a word*, not all the things we call Pleasure, cou'd give me any relish, or sweeten the Taste of things to me; *at least*, not so much, but I grew sad, heavy, pensive, and melancholy; slept little, and eat little; dream'd continually of the most frightful and terrible things imaginable: Nothing but Apparitions of Devils and Monsters; falling into Gulphs, and off from steep and high Precipices, *and the like*; so that in the Morning, when I shou'd rise, and be refresh'd with the Blessing of Rest, I was *Hag-ridden*[1] with Frights, and terrible things, form'd meerly in the Imagination; and was either tir'd and wanted Sleep, or over-run with Vapours, and not fit for conversing with my Family, or any-one else.

My Husband, the tenderest Creature in the World, and particularly so to me, was in great Concern for me, and did every-thing that lay in his Power, to comfort and restore me; strove to reason me out of it; then tried all the Ways possible to divert me; but it was all to no purpose, or to but very little.

My only Relief was, sometimes to unbosom myself to poor *Amy*, when she and I was alone' and she did all she cou'd to comfort me, but all was to little Effect there; for tho' *Amy* was the better Penitent before, when we had been in the Storm; *Amy* was just where she us'd to be, *now*, a wild, gay, loose Wretch, and not much the graver for her Age; for *Amy* was between forty and fifty by this time too.

But to go on with my own Story; as I had no Comforter, so I had no Counsellor; it was well, *as I often thought*, that I was not a

---

1 Haunted and harassed as if by a witch.

Roman-Catholick; for what a piece of Work shou'd I have made, to have gone to a Priest with such a History as I had to tell him? And what Pennance wou'd any *Father-Confessor* have oblig'd me to perform? especially if he had been honest and true to his Office.

However, as I had none of the recourse, so I had none of the Absolution, by which the Criminal confessing, goes away comforted; but I went about with a Heart loaded with Crime, and altogether in the dark, as to what I was to do; and in this Condition I languish'd near two Years; I may well call it languishing, for if Providence had not reliev'd me, I shou'd have died in little time: *But of that hereafter.*

I must now go back to another Scene, and join it to this End of my Story, which will compleat all my concern with *England*, *at least*, all that I shall bring into this Account. I have hinted at large, what I had done for my two Sons, one at *Messina*, and the other in the *Indies*.

But I have not gone thorow the Story of my two Daughters: I was so in danger of being known by one of them, that I durst not see her, so as to let her know who I was; and for the other, I cou'd not well know how to see her, and own her, and let her see me, because she must then know that I wou'd not let her Sister know me, which wou'd look strange; so that upon the whole, I resolv'd to see neither of them at-all, but *Amy* manag'd all that for me; and when she had made Gentlewomen of them both, by giving them a good tho' late Education, she had like to have blown up the whole Case, and herself and me too, by an unhappy Discovery of herself to the last of them, *that is*, to her who was our Cookmaid, and who, *as I said before*, *Amy* had been oblig'd to turn away, for fear of the very Discovery which now happen'd: I have oberv'd already in what Manner *Amy* manag'd her by a third Person; and how the Girl, when she was set up for a Lady, *as above*, came and visited *Amy* at my Lodgings; after which, *Amy* going, as was her Custom, to see the Girl's Brother, (my Son) at the honest Man's House in *Spittle-Fields*; both the Girls were there, meerly by accident, at the same time, and the other Girl unawares discover'd the Secret; *namely*, that this was the Lady that had done all this for them.

Amy was greatly surpriz'd at it, but as she saw there was no Remedy, she made a Jest of it; and so after that, convers'd openly, being still satisfied that neither of them cou'd make much of it, as long as they knew nothing of me: So she took them together one time, and told them the History, *as she call'd it, of their Mother*; beginning at the miserable carrying them to their Aunt's; she own'd she was not their Mother, herself, but describ'd her to them: However, when she said *she was not their Mother*, one of them express'd herself very much surpriz'd, for the Girl had taken up a strong Fancy that *Amy* was really her Mother; and that she had for some particular Reasons, conceal'd it from her; and therefore when she told her frankly that she was not her Mother, the Girl fell a-crying, and *Amy* had much ado to keep Life in her: This was the Girl who was at first my Cook-maid in the *Pall-mall*; when *Amy* had brought her to again a little, and she had recover'd her first Disorder, *Amy* ask'd what ail'd her? the poor Girl hung about her, and kiss'd her, and was in such a Passion still, tho' she was a great Wench of Nineteen or Twenty Years old, that she cou'd not be brought to speak a great-while; at last having recover'd her Speech, she said still, *But O do not say you a'n't my Mother! I'm sure you are my Mother*; and then the Girl cry'd again like to kill herself: *Amy* cou'd not tell what to do with her a good-while; she was loth to say again, *she was not her Mother*, because she wou'd not throw her into a Fit of crying again; but she went round about a little with her: Why Child, *says she*, why wou'd you have me be your Mother? If it be because I am so kind to you, be easie, my Dear, *says Amy*, I'll be as kind to you still, as if I was your Mother.

Ay but, *says the Girl*, I am sure you are my Mother too; and what have I done that you won't own me, and that you will not be call'd my Mother? Tho' I am poor, you have made me a Gentlewoman, *says she*, and I won't do any-thing to disgrace you; besides, *adds she*, I can keep a Secret too, especially for my own Mother, sure; then she calls *Amy* her *Dear Mother*, and hung about her Neck again, crying still vehemently.

This last Part of the Girl's Words alarm'd *Amy*, and, *as she told me*, frighted her terribly; nay, she was so confounded with it, that she was not able to govern herself, or to conceal her Disorder from the Girl herself, *as you shall hear*: *Amy* was at a full Stop, and confus'd to the last Degree; and the Girl, a sharp Jade, turn'd it upon her: My dear Mother, *says she*, do not be uneasie about it; I know it all; but do not be uneasie, I won't let my Sister know a word of it, or my Brother either, without you give me leave; but don't disown me now you have found me; don't hide yourself from me any longer; I can't bear that, *says she*, it will break my Heart.

I think the Girl's mad, *says Amy*; why Child, I tell thee, if I was thy Mother I wou'd not disown thee; don't you see I am as kind to you as if I was your Mother? *Amy* might as well have sung a Song to a Kettle-Drum, as talk to her: Yes, *says the Girl*, you are very good to me indeed; and that was enough to make any-body believe she was her Mother too; but however that was not the Case, she had other Reasons to believe, and to know that she was her Mother; and it was a sad thing she wou'd not let her call her Mother, who was her own Child.

Amy was so Heart-full with the Disturbance of it, that she did not enter farther with her into the Enquiry, as she wou'd other-wise have done; I mean, as to what made the Girl so positive, but comes away, and tells me the whole Story.

I was Thunder-struck with the Story at first, and much more afterwards, *as you shall hear*; but, *I say*, I was Thunder-struck at first, and amaz'd, and said to *Amy*, There must be something or other in it more than we know of; but having examin'd farther into it, I found the Girl had no Notion of any-body, but of *Amy*; and glad I was that I was not concern'd in the Pretence, and that the Girl had no Notion of me in it: But even this Easiness did not continue long, for the next time *Amy* went to see her, she was the same thing, and rather more violent with *Amy* than she was before: *Amy* endeavour'd to pacifie her by all the Ways imagina-ble; *first*, she told her, she took it ill that she wou'd not believe her; *and told her*, if she wou'd not give over such a foolish Whimsie, she wou'd leave her to the wide World, as she found her.

This put the Girl into Fits, and she cry'd ready to kill herself, and hung about *Amy* again, like a Child: Why, *says Amy*, why can you not be easie with me then, and compose yourself, and let me go on to do you good, and show you Kindness, as I wou'd do, and as I intend to do? Can you think that if I was your Mother, I wou'd not tell you so? What Whimsie is this that possesses your Mind? s*ays Amy*: Well, the Girl told her in a few Words, but those few such as frighted *Amy* out of her Wits, and me too: That she knew well enough how it was; I know, *says she*, when you left—, *naming the Village*, where I liv'd when my Father went away from us all, that you went over to *France*, I know that too, and who you went with, *says the Girl*; did not my Lady *Roxana* come back again with you? I know it all well enough, tho' I was but a Child, I have heard it all. And thus she run on with such Discourse, as put *Amy* out of all Temper again; and she rav'd at her like a

Bedlam,[1] and *told her*, she wou'd never come near her any more; she might go a-begging again if she wou'd; she'd have nothing to do with her: The Girl, a passionate Wench, *told her*, she knew the worst of it, she cou'd go to Service again, and if she wou'd not own her own Child, she must do as she pleas'd; then she fell into a Passion of crying again, as if she wou'd kill herself.

In short, this Girl's Conduct terrify'd *Amy* to the last Degree, and me too, and was it not that we knew the Girl was quite wrong in some things, she was yet so right in some other, that it gave me a great-deal of Perplexity; but that which put *Amy* the most to it, was, that the Girl (*my Daughter*) told her, that she (*meaning me her Mother*) had gone away with the *Jeweller*, and into *France* too; she did not call him *the Jeweller*, but with the Landlord of the House; who, after her Mother fell into Distress, and that *Amy* had taken all the Children from her, made much of her, and afterwards marry'd her.

In short, it was plain the Girl had but a broken Account of things, but yet, that she had receiv'd some Accounts that had a reality in the Bottom of them; so that it seems our first Measures and the Amour with the *Jeweller*, were not so conceal'd as I thought they had been; and it seems, came in a broken manner to my Sister-in-Law, who *Amy* carry'd the Children to, and she made some Bustle it seems, about it; but as good-luck was, it was too late, and I was remov'd, and gone, none knew whither; or else she wou'd have sent all the Children home to me again, *to be sure*.

This we pick'd out of the Girl's Discourse, *that is to say*, *Amy* did, at several times; but it all consisted of broken Fragments of Stories, such as the Girl herself had heard so long ago, that she herself cou'd make very little of it; only that in the main, that her Mother had play'd the Whore; had gone away with the Gentleman that was Landlord of the House; that he married her; that she went into *France*; and as she had learn'd in my Family, where she was a Servant, that Mrs. *Amy* and her Lady *Roxana* had been in *France* together; so she put all these things together, and joining them with the great Kindness that *Amy* now shew'd her, possess'd the Creature that *Amy* was really her Mother; nor was it possible for *Amy* to conquer it for a long time.

But this, after I had search'd into it as far as by *Amy*'s relation, I cou'd get an Account of it, did not disquiet me half so much, as that the young Slut had got the name of *Roxana* by the end; and

---

1 An inmate of Bethlehem Hospital for the insane.

that she knew who her Lady *Roxana* was, *and the like*; tho' this neither, did not hang together, for then she wou'd not have fix'd upon *Amy* for her Mother: But sometime after, when *Amy* had almost perswaded her out of it, and that the Girl began to be so confounded in her Discourses of it, that they made neither Head nor Tail; at last, the passionate Creature flew out in a kind of Rage, *and said to* Amy, That if she was not her Mother, Madam *Roxana* was her Mother then, for one of them, *she was sure*, was her Mother; and then all this that *Amy* had done for her, was by Madam *Roxana*'s Order; and I am sure, *says she*, it was my Lady *Roxana*'s Coach that brought the Gentlewoman (whoever it was) to my Uncle's in *Spittle-Fields*; for the Coachman told me so: *Amy* fell a-laughing at her aloud, *as was her usual way*; but as *Amy* told me, it was but on one side of her Mouth; for she was so confounded at her Discourse, that she was ready to sink into the Ground; and so was I too, when she told it me.

However, *Amy* brazen'd her out of it all; *told her*, Well, since you are so high-born, as to be my Lady *Roxana*'s Daughter, you may go to her and claim your Kindred, can't you? I suppose, *says Amy*, you know where to find her? *She said*, she did not question to find her, for she knew where she was gone to live privately; but tho' she might be remov'd again, for I know how it is, *says she*, with a kind of a Smile, or a Grin; I know how it all is, well enough.

Amy was so provok'd, that she told me, *in short*, she began to think it wou'd be absolutely necessary to murther her: That Expression fill'd me with Horror; all my Blood ran chill in my Veins, and a Fit of trembling seiz'd me, that I cou'd not speak a good-while; at last, What is the Devil in you, *Amy*, said I? Nay, nay, *says she*, let it be the Devil, or not the Devil, if I thought she knew one tittle of your History, I wou'd dispatch her if she were my own Daughter a thousand times; and I, *says I in a Rage*, as well as I love you, wou'd be the first that shou'd put the Halter about your Neck, and see you hang'd, with more Satisfaction than ever I saw you in my Life; nay, *says I*, you wou'd not live to be hang'd, *I believe*, I shou'd cut your Throat with my own Hand; I am almost ready to do it, *said I*, as 'tis , for your but naming the thing; with that, I call'd her cursed Devil, and bade her get out of the Room.

I think it was the first time that ever I was angry with *Amy* in all my Life; and when all was done, tho' she was a devilish Jade in having such a Thought, yet it was all of it the Effect of her Excess of Affection and Fidelity to me.

But this thing gave me a terrible Shock, for it happen'd just after I was marry'd, and serv'd to hasten my going over to *Holland*; for I wou'd not have been seen, so as to be known by the Name of *Roxana*, no, not for ten Thousand Pounds; it wou'd have been enough to have ruin'd me to all Intents and Purposes with my Husband, and every body else too; I might as well have been the *German Princess*.[1]

Well, I set *Amy* to-work; and give *Amy* her due, she set all her Wits to-work, to find out which way this Girl had her Knowledge; but more particularly, how much Knowledge she had, *that is to say*, what she really knew, and what she did not know; for this was the main thing with me; how she cou'd say she knew who Madam *Roxana* was, and what Notions she had of that Affair was very mysterious to me; for 'twas certain she cou'd not have a right Notion of me, because she wou'd have it be, that *Amy* was her Mother.

I scolded heartily at *Amy*, for letting the Girl ever know her, *that is to say*, know her in this Affair; for that she knew her, cou'd not be hid, because she, *as I might say*, serv'd *Amy*, or rather under *Amy*, in my Family, *as is said before*; but she (*Amy*) talk'd with her at first by another Person, and not by herself; and that Secret came out by an Accident, *as I have said above*.

Amy was concern'd at it as well as I, but cou'd not help it; and tho' it gave us great Uneasiness, yet as there was no Remedy, we were bound to make as little Noise of it as we cou'd, that it might go no farther: I bade *Amy* punish the Girl for it, *and she did so*, for she parted with her in a Huff, *and told her*, she shou'd see, she was not her Mother, for that she cou'd leave her just where she found her; and seeing she cou'd not be content to be serv'd by the Kindness of a Friend, but that she wou'd needs make a Mother of her,

---

1 In 1663, a woman named Mary Carleton, carried out a con against a man named John Carleton and his family. Born in Canterbury, Mary Carleton came to London masquerading as Maria de Wolway, a member of the German aristocracy; she later was known as the German Princess. The Carletons, socially ambitious and eager to see their children marry "up," were taken in by Mary's performance. In their turn the Carletons represented themselves as wealthy and their son as a worthy match for the "German Princess." After John and Mary were married, the Carletons discovered that, on the contrary, she was little more than a petty thief. They tried to prosecute her for bigamy but were unsuccessful. For more on this, see Elizabeth Spearing's introduction to *The Case of Mary Carleton* in *Counterfeit Ladies*, ed. Janet Todd and Elizabeth Spearing (New York: NYU Press, 1994).

she wou'd for the future, be neither Mother or Friend; and so bid her go to Service again, and be a Drudge, as she was before.

The poor Girl cry'd most lamentably, but wou'd not be beaten out of it still; but that which dumbfounded *Amy* more than all the rest, was, that when she had rated the poor Girl a long time, and cou'd not beat her out of it, and had, *as I have observ'd*, threaten'd to leave her; the Girl kept to what *she said* before, and put this Turn to it again; that she was sure, if *Amy* wa'n't, my Lady *Roxana* was, her Mother; and that she wou'd go find her out; adding, that she made no doubt but she cou'd do it, for she knew where to enquire the Name of her new Husband.

Amy came home with this Piece of News in her Mouth, to me; I cou'd easily perceive when she came in, that she was mad in her Mind, and in a Rage at something or other, and was in great Pain to get it out; for when she came first in, my Husband was in the Room; however, *Amy* going up to undress her, I soon made an Excuse to follow her, and coming into the Room; What the D—l is the Matter, *Amy? says I*; I am sure you have some bad News: News, *says Amy, aloud,* ay, so I have; I think the D—l is in that young Wench, she'll ruin us all, and herself too, there's no quieting her: So she went on, and told me all the Particulars; but sure nothing was so astonish'd as I was, when she told me that the Girl knew I was marry'd; that she knew my Husband's Name, and wou'd endeavour to find me out; I thought I shou'd have sunk down at the very Words; in the middle of all my Amazement, *Amy* starts up, and runs about the Room like a distracted body; I'll put an End to it, that I will; I can't bear it; I must murther her; I'll kill her B—, *and swears by her Maker, in the most serious Tone in the World*; and then repeated it over three or four times, walking to-and-again in the Room; I will, *in short,* I will kill her, if there was not another Wench in the World.

Prethee hold thy Tongue, *Amy, says I,* why thou art mad; ay, so I am, *says she,* stark-mad, but I'll be the Death of her for-all that, and then I shall be sober again: But you shan't, *says I,* you shan't hurt a Hair of her Head; why you ought to be hang'd for what you have done already; for having resolv'd on it, is doing it, as to the Guilt of the Fact; you are a Murtherer already, as much as if you had done it already.

I know that, *says Amy,* and it can be no worse; I'll put you out of your Pain, and her too; she shall never challenge you for her Mother in this World, whatever she may in the next: Well, well, *says I,* be quiet, and do not talk thus, I can't bear it; so she grew a little soberer after a-while.

I must acknowledge, the Notion of being discover'd, carried with it so many frightful *Ideas*, and hurry'd my Thoughts so much, that I was scarce myself, any more than *Amy*, so dreadful a thing is a Load of Guilt upon the Mind.

And yet when *Amy* began the second time, to talk thus abominably of killing the poor Child, of murthering her, and swore by her Maker that she wou'd, so that I began to see that she was in earnest, I was farther terrified a great deal, and it help'd to bring me to myself again in other Cases.

We laid our Heads together then, to see if it was possible to discover by what means she had learn'd to talk so, and how she (*I mean my Girl*) came to know that her Mother had marry'd a Husband; but it wou'd not do, the Girl wou'd acknowledge nothing, and gave but a very imperfect Account of things still, being Disgusted to the last Degree with *Amy's* leaving her so abruptly as she did.

Well, *Amy* went to the House where the Boy was, but it was all one; there they had only heard a confus'd Story of the Lady *somebody*, they knew not who, which this same Wench had told them, but they gave no heed to it at-all: *Amy* told them how foolishly the Girl had acted; and how she had carry'd on the Whimsie so far, in spight of all they cou'd say to her; that she had taken it so ill, she wou'd see her no more, and so she might e'en go to Service again if she wou'd, for she (*Amy*) wou'd have nothing to do with her, unless she humbl'd herself, and chang'd her Note, and that quickly too.

The good old Gentleman who had been the Benefactor to them all, was greatly concern'd at it, and the good Woman his Wife was griev'd beyond all expressing, and begg'd her Ladyship, *meaning Amy*, not to resent it, they promis'd too, they wou'd talk with her about it; and the old Gentlewoman added, *with some Astonishment*, Sure she cannot be such a Fool but she will be prevail'd with to hold her Tongue, when she has it from your own Mouth, that you are not her Mother, and sees that it disobliges your Ladyship to have her insist upon it; and so *Amy* came away, with some Expectation that it wou'd be stopp'd here.

But the Girl was such a Fool for all that, and persisted in it obstinately, notwithstanding all they cou'd say to her; nay, her Sister begg'd and intreated her not to play the Fool, for that it wou'd ruin her too; and that the Lady (*meaning Amy*) wou'd abandon them both.

Well, notwithstanding this, she insisted, *I say*, upon it, and which was worse, the longer it lasted, the more she began to drop

Amy's Ladyship, and wou'd have it, that the Lady *Roxana* was her Mother; and that she had made some Enquiries about it, and did not doubt but she shou'd find her out.

When it was come to this, and we found there was nothing to be done with the Girl, but that she was so obstinately bent upon the Search after me, that she ventur'd to forfeit all she had in view; *I say*, when I found it was come to this, I began to be more serious in my Preparations of my going beyond-Sea; and particularly, it gave me some reason to fear that there was something in it; but the following Accident put me beside all my Measures, and struck me into the greatest Confusion that ever I was in, in my Life.

I was so near going Abroad, that my Spouse and I had taken Measures for our going-off; and because I wou'd be sure not to go too publick, but so as to take away all Possibility of being seen, I had made some Exception to my Spouse against going in the ordinary publick Passage-Boats; my Pretence to him, was, the promiscuous[1] Crowds in those Vessels; want of Convenience, *and the like*; so he took the Hint, and found me out an *English* Merchant-Ship, which was bound for *Rotterdam*, and getting soon acquainted with the Master, he hir'd his whole Ship, *that is to say*, his Great-Cabin, for I do not mean his Ship for Freight; that so we had all the Conveniences possible, for our Passage; and all things being near ready, he brought home the Captain one Day to Dinner with him, that I might see him, and be acquainted a little with him; so we came, after Dinner, to talk of the Ship, and the Conveniences on-board, and the Captain press'd me earnestly to come on-board, and see the Ship, intimating, That he wou'd treat us as well as he cou'd; and in Discourse I happen'd to say, I hop'd he had no other Passengers; *he said*, No, he had not; but *he said*, his Wife had courted him a good-while to let her go over to *Holland* with him, for he always us'd that Trade, but he never cou'd think of venturing all he had in one Bottom; but if I went with him, he thought to take her and her Kinswoman along with him this Voyage, that they might both wait upon me; *and so added*, that if we wou'd do him the Honour to Dine on-board the next Day, he wou'd bring his Wife on-board, the better to make us welcome.

Who now cou'd have believ'd the Devil had any Snare at the Bottom of all this? or that I was in any Danger on such an Occasion, so remote and out of the way as this was? But the Event was

---

1 Socially mixed.

the oddest that cou'd be thought of : As it happen'd, *Amy* was not at-home when we accepted this Invitation, and so she was left out of the Company; but instead of *Amy*, we took our honest, good-humour'd, never-to-be-omitted Friend the QUAKER, one of the best Creatures *that ever liv'd*, sure; and who, besides a thousand good Qualities unmix'd with one bad one, was particularly Excellent for being the best Company in the World; tho' I think I had carry'd *Amy* too, if she had not been engag'd in this unhappy Girl's Affair; for on a sudden the Girl was lost, and no News was to be heard of her, and *Amy* had hunted her to every Place she cou'd think of, that it was likely to find her in, but all the News she cou'd hear of her, was, that she was gone to an old Comerade's House of hers, which she call'd Sister, and who was marry'd to a Master of a Ship who liv'd in *Redriff*,[1] and even this the Jade never told me: It seems when this Girl was directed by *Amy* to get her some Breeding, go to the Boarding-School, and the like, she was recommended to a Boarding-School at *Camberwell*;[2] and there she contracted an Acquaintance with a young Lady (*so they are all call'd*) her Bedfellow, that they call'd Sisters, and promis'd never to break off their Acquaintance.

But judge you what an unaccountable Surprize I must be in, when I came on-board the Ship, and was brought into the Captain's Cabbin, or, *what they call it*, the Great-Cabbin of the Ship, to see his Lady or Wife, and another young Person with her, who, when I came to see her near-hand, was my old Cook-Maid in the *Pall-mall*, and as appear'd by the Sequel of the Story, was neither more or less, than my own Daughter; that I knew her, was out of Doubt; for tho' she had not had Opportunity to see me very often, yet I had often seen her, *as I must needs*, being in my own Family so long.

If ever I had need of Courage, and a full Presence of Mind, it was now; it was the only valuable Secret in the World to me; all depended upon this Occasion; if the Girl knew me, I was undone; and to discover any Surprize or Disorder, had been to make her know me, or guess it, and discover herself.

I was once going to feign a swooning, and faint-away, and so falling on the Ground, or Floor, put them all into a Hurry and Fright, and by that means get an Opportunity to be continually

---

1 Rotherhithe, an historic shipping district in Southwark located opposite the Tower Liberties.
2 Camberwell is part of the borough of Southwark, which sits opposite the City of London across the Thames.

holding something to my Nose to smell to, and so hold my Hand, or my Handkerchief, or both, before my Mouth; then pretend I cou'd not bear the Smell of the Ship, or the closeness of the Cabbin; but that wou'd have been only to remove into a clearer Air upon the Quarter-Deck, where we shou'd with it, have had a clearer Light too; and if I had pretended the Smell of the Ship, it wou'd have serv'd only to have carry'd us all on-Shoar, to the Captain's House, which was hard-by; for the Ship lay so close to the Shore, that we only walk'd over a Plank to go on-board, and over another Ship which lay within her;[1] so this not appearing feasible, and the Thought not being two Minutes old, there was no time; for the two Ladies rise up, and we saluted, so that I was bound to come so near *my Girl*, as to kiss her, which I wou'd not have done, had it been possible to have avoided it; but there was no room to escape.

I cannot but take Notice here, that notwithstanding there was a secret Horror upon my Mind, and I was ready to sink when I came close to her, to salute her; yet it was a secret inconceivable Pleasure to me when I kiss'd her, to know that I kiss'd my own Child; my own Flesh and Blood, born of my Body; and who I had never kiss'd since I took the fatal Farewell of them all, with a Million of Tears and a Heart almost dead with Grief, when *Amy* and the Good Woman took them all away, and went with them to *Spittle-Fields*; No Pen can describe, no Words can express, *I say*, the strange Impression which this thing made upon my Spirits; I felt something shoot thro' my Blood; my Heart flutter'd; my Head flash'd, and was dizzy, and all within me, *as I thought*, turn'd about, and much ado I had, not to abandon myself to an Excess of Passion at the first Sight of her, much more when my Lips touch'd her Face; I thought I must have taken her in my Arms, and kiss'd her again a thousand times, whether I wou'd or no.

But I rous'd up my Judgment, and shook it off, and with infinite Uneasiness in my Mind, I sat down: You will not wonder, if upon this Surprize I was not conversible for some Minutes, and that the Disorder had almost discover'd itself; I had a Complication of severe things upon me: I cou'd not conceal my Disorder without the utmost Difficulty; and yet upon my concealing it, depended the whole of my Prosperity; so I us'd all manner of Violence with myself, to prevent the Mischief which was at the Door.

---

1 Over one other ship that lay between the ship on which they expect to sail and the shore.

Well, I saluted her; but as I went first forward to the Captain's Lady, who was at the farther-end of the Cabbin, towards the Light, I had the Occasion offer'd, to stand with my Back to the Light, when I turn'd about to her, who stood more on my Left-hand, so that she had not a fair Sight of me, tho' I was so near her; I trembled, and knew neither what I did, or said; I was in the utmost Extremity, between so many particular Circumstances as lay upon me; for I was to conceal my Disorder from every-body, at the utmost Peril, and at the same time expected every-body wou'd discern it; I was to expect she wou'd discover that she knew me, and yet was, by all means possible, to prevent it; I was to conceal myself, if possible, and yet had not the least room to do any-thing towards it; *in short*, there was no retreat; no shifting any-thing off; no avoiding or preventing her having a full Sight of me; nor was there any counterfeiting my Voice, for then my Husband wou'd have perceiv'd it; *in short*, there was not the least Circumstance that offer'd me any Assistance, or any favourable thing to help me in this Exigence.

After I had been upon the Rack for near half an Hour, during which, I appear'd stiff and reserv'd, and a little too formal; my Spouse and the Captain fell into Discourses about the Ship, and the Sea, and Business remote from us Women, and by-and-by the Captain carry'd him out upon the Quarter-Deck, and left us all by ourselves, in the Great-Cabbin: Then we began to be a little freer one with another, and I began to be a little reviv'd, by a sudden Fancy of my own, *namely*, I thought I perceiv'd that the Girl did not know me; and the chief Reason of my having such a Notion, was, because I did not perceive the least Disorder in her Countenance, or the least Change in her Carriage; no Confusion, no Hesitation in her Discourse; nor, which I had my Eye partic-ularly upon, did I observe that she fix'd her Eyes much upon me, that is to say, not singling me out to look steddily at me, as I thought wou'd have been the Case; but that she rather singl'd out my Friend the QUAKER, and chatted with her on several things; but I observd' too, that it was all about indifferent Matters.

This greatly encourag'd me, and I began to be a little chearful; but I was knock'd down again as with a Thunder-Clap, when turning to the Captain's Wife, and discoursing of me, s*he said to her*, Sister, I cannot but think (*my Lady*) to be very much like such a Person, *then she nam'd the Person*; and the Captain's Wife said, *she thought so too*; the Girl reply'd again, *she was sure she had seen me before, but she cou'd not recollect where*; I answer'd, (tho' her Speech was not directed to me) *That I fancy'd she had not seen me* *before, in* England, but ask'd, if she had liv'd in *Holland, She said, No, no, she had never been out of* England; and I added, *That she cou'd not then have known me in* England, *unless it was very lately, for I had liv'd at* Rotterdam *a great while*: This carry'd me out of that Part of the Broil, pretty well; and to make it go off the better, when a little *Dutch* Boy came into the Cabbin, who belong'd to the Captain, and who I easily perceiv'd to be *Dutch*, I jested, and talk'd *Dutch* to him, and was merry about the Boy, that is to say, as merry as the Consternation I was still in, wou'd let me be.

However, I began to be thorowly convinc'd by this time, that the Girl did not know me, which was an infinite Satisfaction to me; or, *at least*, that tho' she had some Notion of me, yet that she did not think any-thing about my being who I was, and which perhaps, she wou'd have been as glad to have known, as I wou'd have been surpriz'd if she had; indeed it was evident, that had she suspected any-thing of the Truth, she would not have been able to have conceal'd it.

Thus this Meeting went off, and, *you may be sure*, I was resolv'd, if once I got off of it, she should never see me again, to revive her Fancy; but I was mistaken there too, *as you shall hear*. After we had been on-board, the Captain's Lady carry'd us home to her House, which was but just on-shore, and treated us there again, very handsomely, and made us promise that we wou'd come again and see her before we went, to concert our Affairs for the Voyage, *and the like*; for she assur'd us, that both she and her Sister went the Voyage at that time, for our Company; and I thought to myself, *Then you'll never go the Voyage at-all*; for I saw from that Moment, that it wou'd be no way convenient for *my Ladyship* to go with them; for that frequent Conversation might bring me to her Mind, and she wou'd certainly claim her Kindred to me in a few Days, as indeed, wou'd have been the Case.

It is hardly possible for me to conceive what wou'd have been our Part in this Affair, had my Woman *Amy* gone with me on-board this Ship; it had certainly blown-up the whole Affair, and I must for-ever after have been this Girl's Vassal, *that is to say*, have let her into the Secret, and trusted to her keeping it too, or have been expos'd, and undone; *the very Thought fill'd me with Horror*.

But I was not so unhappy neither, as it fell out, for *Amy* was not with us, and that was my Deliverance indeed; yet we had another Chance to get over still: As I resolv'd to put off the Voyage, so I resolv'd to put off the Visit, *you may be sure*; going upon this Principle, *namely*, that I was fix'd in it, that the Girl had seen her last of me, and shou'd never see me more.

However, to bring myself well off, and withal to see (if I cou'd) a little farther into the Matter, I sent my Friend, the QUAKER, to the Captain's Lady, to make the Visit promis'd, and to make my Excuse that I cou'd not possibly wait on her, for that I was very much out of Order; and in the end of the Discourse, I bade her insinuate to them, that she was afraid I shou'd not be able to get ready to go the Voyage, so soon as the Captain wou'd be oblig'd to go; and that perhaps we might put it off to his next Voyage: I did not let the QUAKER into any other Reason for it, than that I was indispos'd; and not knowing what other Face to put upon that Part, I made her believe that I thought I was a-breeding.

It was easie to put that into her Head, and she of course hinted to the Captain's Lady, that she found me so very ill, that she was afraid I wou'd miscarry; and then, *to be sure*, I cou'd not think of going.

She went, and she manag'd that Part very dexterously, *as I knew she wou'd*, tho' she knew not a word of the grand Reason of my Indisposition; but I was all sunk, and dead-hearted again, when she told me, She cou'd not understand the Meaning of one thing in her Visit, *namely*, That the young Woman, *as she call'd her*, that was with the Captain's Lady, and who she call'd Sister, was most impertinently inquisitive into things; as who I was? How long I had been in *England?* Where I had liv'd? *and the like*; and that, *above all the rest*, she enquir'd if I did not live once at the other end of the Town.

I thought her Enquiries so out of the Way, *says the honest* QUAKER, that I gave her not the least Satisfaction; but as I saw by *thy* Answers on-board the Ship, when she talk'd of *thee*, that *thou* did'st not incline to let her be acquainted with *thee*, so I was resolv'd that she shou'd not be much the wiser for me; and when she ask'd me if *thou* ever liv'dst *here* or *there*, I always said *No*; but that *thou* wast a *Dutch* Lady, and was going home again to *thy* Family, and liv'd Abroad.

I thank'd her very heartily for that Part, and indeed, she serv'd me in it more than I let her know she did; *in a word*, she thwarted the Girl so cleverly, that if she had known the whole Affair, she cou'd not have done it better.

But I must acknowledge, all this put me upon the Rack again, and I was quite discourag'd not at-all doubting but that the Jade had a right Scent of things, and that she knew and remember'd my Face, but had artfully conceal'd her Knowledge of me, till she might perhaps, do it more to my Disadvantage: I told all this to *Amy, for she was all the Relief I had*: The poor Soul (*Amy*) was ready to hang herself, that, *as she said,* she had been the Occasion of it all; and that if I was ruin'd, (*which was the word I always us'd to her*) she had ruin'd me; and she tormented herself about it so much, that I was sometimes fain to comfort her and myself too.

What *Amy* vex'd herself at, was chiefly, that she shou'd be surpriz'd so by the Girl, *as she call'd her,* I mean surpriz'd into a Discovery of herself to the Girl; which indeed, was a false Step of *Amy*'s, and so I had often told her; but 'twas to no Purpose to talk of that now; the Business was, how to get clear of the Girl's Suspicions, and of the Girl too, for it look'd more threatning every Day, than other; and if I was uneasie at what *Amy* had told me of her rambling and rattling to her, (*Amy*) I had a thousand times as much reason to be uneasie *now*, when she had chopp'd upon me so unhappily as this; and not only had seen my Face, but knew too where I liv'd; what Name I went by, *and the like.*

And I am not come to the worst of it yet neither; for a few Days after my Friend the QUAKER had made her Visit, and excus'd me on the account of Indisposition; as if they had done it in over and above Kindness, because they had been told I was not well, they comes both directly to my Lodgings, to visit me; the Captain's Wife, and my Daughter, (*who she call'd Sister*) and the Captain to show them the Place; the Captain only brought them to the Door, put them in, and went away upon some Business.

Had not the kind QUAKER, in a lucky Moment, come running in before them, they had not only clapp'd in upon me, in the Parlour, *as it had been a Surprize*; but which wou'd have been a thousand times worse, had seen *Amy* with me; I think if that had happen'd, I had had no Remedy, but to take the Girl by herself, and have made myself known to her, which wou'd have been all Distraction.

But the QUAKER, a lucky Creature to me, happen'd to see them come to the Door, before they rung the Bell, and instead of going to let them in, came running in, with some Confusion in her Countenance, and told me who was a-coming; at which, *Amy* run first, and I after her, and bid the QUAKER come up as soon as she had let them in.

I was going to bid her deny me, but it came into my Thoughts, that having been represented so much out of Order, it wou'd have look'd very odd; besides, I knew the honest QUAKER, tho' she wou'd do any-thing else for me, wou'd not LYE for me, and it wou'd have been hard to have desir'd it of her.

After she had let them in, and brought them into the Parlour, she came up to *Amy* and I, who were hardly out of the Fright, and yet were congratulating one another, that *Amy* was not surpriz'd again.

They paid their Visit in Form, and I receiv'd them as formally; but took Occasion two or three times to hint, that I was so ill that I was afraid I shou'd not be able to go to *Holland, at least,* not so soon as the Captain must go off; and made my Compliment, how sorry I was to be disappointed of the Advantage of their Company and Assistance in the Voyage; and sometimes I talk'd as if I thought I might stay till the Captain return'd, and wou'd be ready to go again; then the QUAKER put in, That then I might be too far gone, *meaning with-Child,* that I shou'd not venture at-all; and then (*as if she shou'd be pleas'd with it*) *added,* She hop'd I wou'd stay and Lye-in at her House; so as this carried its own Face with[1] it, *'twas well enough.*

But it was now high-time to talk of this to my Husband, which however was not the greatest Difficulty before me: For after this and another Chat had taken up some time, the young Fool began her Tattle again; and two or three times she brought it in, That I was so like a Lady that she had the Honour to know at the other end of the Town, that she cou'd not put that Lady out of her Mind, *when I was by*; and once or twice I fancy'd the Girl was ready to cry; by-and-by she was at it again; and at last, I plainly saw Tears in her Eyes; upon which, *I ask'd her if the Lady was dead, because she seem'd to be in some Concern for her*; she made me much easier by her Answer, than ever she did before: S*he said, She did not really know, but she believ'd she was dead.*

This, *I say,* a little reliev'd my Thoughts, but I was soon down again; for after some time, the Jade began to grow Talkative; and as it was plain that she had told all that her Head cou'd retain of *Roxana,* and Days of Joy which I had spent at that Part of the Town, another Accident had like to have blown us all up again.

I was in a kind of *Dishabille* when they came, having on a loose Robe, like a Morning-Gown, but much after the *Italian* Way; and I had not alter'd it when I went up, only dress'd my Head[2] a little; and as I had been represented as having been lately very ill, so the Dress was becoming enough for a Chamber.

This Morning-Vest, or Robe, *call it as you please,* was more shap'd to the Body, than we wear them since, showing the Body in its true Shape, and perhaps, a little two plainly, if it had been to be worn where any Men were to come; but among ourselves it

---

1 Self-evidently legitimate.
2 Arranged her hair.

was well enough, especially for hot Weather; the Colour was green, figur'd; and the Stuff a *French* Damask, very rich.

This Gown, or Vest, put the Girl's Tongue a-running again, and her Sister, *as she call'd her*, prompted it; for as they both admir'd my Vest, and were taken up much about the Beauty of the Dress; the charming Damask; the noble Trimming, *and the like*; my Girl puts in a Word to the Sister, (*Captain's Wife*) This is just such a Thing as I told you, *says she*, the Lady danc'd in: What, *says the Captain's Wife*, the Lady *Roxana* that you told me of? O! that's a charming Story, *says she*; tell it *my Lady*; I cou'd not avoid saying so too, tho' from my Soul I wish'd her in Heaven for but naming it; *nay*, I won't say but if she had been carried t'other Way, it had been much at one[1] to me, if I cou'd but have been rid of her, and her Story too; for when she came to describe the *Turkish* Dress, it was impossible but the QUAKER, who was a sharp penetrating Creature, shou'd receive the Impression in a more dangerous Manner, than the Girl; only that indeed, she was not so dangerous a Person; for if she had known it all, I cou'd more freely have trusted her, than I cou'd the Girl, by a great-deal; *nay*, I shou'd have been perfectly easie in her.

However, *as I have said*, her Talk made me dreadfully uneasie, and the more when the Captain's Wife mention'd but the Name of *Roxana*; what my Face might do towards betraying me, I know not, because I cou'd not see myself, but my Heart beat as if it wou'd have jump'd out at my Mouth; and my Passion was so great, that for want of Vent, I thought I shou'd have burst: *In a word*, I was in a kind of a silent Rage; for the Force I was under of restraining my Passion, was such, as I never felt the like of: I had no Vent; no-body to open myself to, or to make a Complaint to for my Relief; I durst not leave the Room by any means, for then she wou'd have told all the Story in my Absence, and I shou'd have been perpetually uneasie to know what she had said, or had not said; so that, *in a word*, I was oblig'd to sit and hear her tell all the Story of *Roxana*, *that is to say*, of myself, and not know at the same time, whether she knew me or no; or, *in short*, whether I was to be expos'd, or not expos'd.

She began only in general, with telling where she liv'd; what a Place she had of it; how gallant a Company her Lady had always had in the House; how they us'd to sit up all-Night in the House, gaming and dancing; what a fine Lady her Mistress was; and what a vast deal of Money the upper Servants got; as for her, *she*

---

1 All the same.

said, her whole Business was in the next House, so that she got but little; except one Night, that there was twenty Guineas given to be divided among the Servants, when, s*he said*, she got two Guineas and a half for her Share.

She went on, and told them how many Servants there was, and how they were order'd; but, s*he said*, there was one Mrs. *Amy*, who was over them all; and that she being the Lady's Favourite, got a great-deal; she did not know, s*he said*, whether *Amy* was her Christian Name, or her Sir-Name, but she suppos'd it was her Sir-Name; that they were told, she got threescore Pieces of Gold at one time, being the same Night that the rest of the Servants had the twenty Guineas divided among them.

I put in at that Word, *and said*, 'twas a vast deal to give away; why, *says I*, 'twas a Portion for a Servant: O Madam! *says she*, it was nothing to what she got afterwards; we that were Servants, hated her heartily for it, *that is to say*, we wish'd it had been our Lott, in her stead: *Then I said, again*, Why, it was enough to get her a good Husband, and settle her for the World, if she had Sence to manage it: So it might, *to be sure*, Madam, *says she*; for we were told, she laid up above 500*l*. But *I suppose*, Mrs. *Amy* was too sensible that her Character would require a good Portion to put her off.

O, *said I*, if that was the Case, 'twas another thing.

Nay, *says she*, I don't know, but they talk'd very much of a young Lord that was very great[1] with her.

And pray what came of her at last? s*aid I*; for I was willing to hear a little (*seeing she wou'd talk of it*) what she had to say, as well of *Amy*, as of myself.

I don't know, Madam, *said she*, I never heard of her for several Years, till t'other Day I happen'd to see her.

Did you indeed ! *says I*; (*and made mighty strange of it*) what, and in Rags, it may be, *said I*, that's often the End of such Creatures.

Just the contrary, Madam, *says she*, She came to visit an Acquaintance of mine, little thinking, *I suppose*, to see me, and, *I assure you*, she came in her Coach.

In her Coach! s*aid I*; upon my word she had made her Market then: I suppose *she made Hay while the Sun shone*; was she marry'd, pray?

I believe she had been marry'd, Madam, *says she*, but it seems she had been at the *East-Indies*, and if she was marry'd,

---

1 Taken with, attracted to.

it was there, to be sure; I think *she said* she had good luck in the *Indies*.

That is, I suppose, *said I*, had buried her Husband there.

I understand it so, Madam, *says she*, and that she had got his Estate.

Was that her good Luck? *said I*; it might be good to her, as to the Money indeed, but it was but the Part of a Jade, to call it good Luck.

Thus far our Discourse of Mrs. *Amy* went; and no farther, for she knew no more of her; but then the QUAKER unhappily, tho' undesignedly, put in a Question, which the honest good-humour'd Creature wou'd have been far from doing, if she had known that I had carry'd on the Discourse of *Amy*, on purpose to drop *Roxana* out of the Conversation.

But I was not to be made easie too soon: The QUAKER put in, But I think *thou* said'st, something was behind of *thy* Mistress;[1] what did'st thou call her, *Roxana*, was it not? Pray what became of her?

Ay, ay, *Roxana, says the Captain's Wife*; pray Sister let's hear the Story of *Roxana*; it will divert *my* Lady, I'm sure.

That's a damn'd Lye, *said I to myself*; if you knew how little 'twou'd divert me, you wou'd have too much Advantage over me: Well, I saw no Remedy, but the Story must come on, so I prepar'd to hear the worst of it.

Roxana! says she; I know not what to say of her; she was so much above us, and so seldom seen, that we cou'd know little of her, but by Report, but we did sometimes see her too; she was a charming Woman indeed; and the Footmen us'd to say, that she was to be sent for to Court.

To Court, *said I*, why she was at Court, wa'n't she? The *Pall-mall* is not far from *Whitehall*.

Yes, Madam, *says she*, but I mean another way.

I understand thee, *says the* QUAKER; Thou mean'st, I suppose, to be Mistress to the KING; yes, Madam, *says she*.

I cannot help confessing what a Reserve of Pride still was left in me; and tho' I dreaded the Sequel of the Story, yet when she talk'd how handsome and how fine a Lady this *Roxana* was, I cou'd not help being pleas'd and tickl'd with it; and put in Questions two or three times, of how handsome she was? and was she really so fine a Woman as they talk'd of? *and the like*, on purpose

---

1 Still to come.

to hear her repeat what the People's Opinion of me was, and how I had behav'd.

Indeed, *says she at last*, she was a most beautiful Creature, as ever I saw in my Life: But then, *said I*, you never had the Opportunity to see her, but when she was set-out to the best Advantage.

Yes, yes, Madam, *says she*, I have seen her several times in her *Dishabille*, and I can assure you, she was a very fine Woman; and that which was more still, every-body said she did not paint.

This was still very agreeable to me one way; but there was a devilish Sting in the Tail of it all, and this last Article was one; wherein s*he said*, she had seen me several times in my *Dishabille*: this put me in Mind, that then she must certainly know me, and it wou'd come out at last; which was Death to me but to think of.

Well, but Sister, *says the Captain's Wife*, tell my Lady about the Ball, that's the best of all the Story; and of *Roxana's* dancing in a fine Outlandish Dress.

That's one of the brightest Parts of her Story indeed, *says the Girl*; the Case was this: We had Balls and Meetings in her Ladyship's Apartments, every Week almost; but one time my Lady invited all the Nobles to come such a time, and she wou'd give them a Ball; and there was a vast Crowd indeed, *says she*.

I think you said, the KING was there, Sister, didn't you?

No, Madam, *says she*, that was the second time, when they said the KING had heard how finely the *Turkish* Lady danc'd, and that he was there to see her; but the KING, if His Majesty was there, came disguis'd.

That is what they call *Incog.* says my Friend the QUAKER; thou can'st not think the KING wou'd disguise himself; yes, *says the Girl*, it was so, he did not come in Publick, with his Guards, but we all knew which was the KING, well enough; *that is to say*, which they said was the KING.

Well, *says the Captain's Wife*, about the *Turkish* Dress; pray let us hear that: Why, *says she*, my Lady sat in a fine little Drawing-Room, which open'd into the Great Room, and where she receiv'd the Compliments of the Company; and when the Dancing began, a great Lord, *says she, I forget who they call'd him*, (but he was a very great Lord or Duke, I don't know which) took her out, and danc'd with her; but after a-while, *my Lady* on a sudden shut the Drawing-Room, and run up-stairs with her Woman, Mrs. *Amy*, and tho' she did not stay long, (*for I suppose she had contriv'd it all before-hand*) she came down dress'd in the strangest Figure that ever I say in my Life; but it was exceeding fine.

Here she went on to describe the Dress, as I have done already; but did it so exactly, that I was surpriz'd at the Manner of her telling it; there was not a Circumstance of it left out.

I was now under a new Perplexity; for this young Slut gave so compleat an Account of everything in the Dress, that my Friend the QUAKER colour'd at it, and look'd two or three times at me, to see if I did not do so too; for (*as she told me afterwards*) she immediately perceiv'd it was the same Dress that she had seen me have on, *as I have said before*: However, as she saw I took no Notice of it, she kept her Thoughts private to herself; and I did so too, as well as I cou'd.

I put in two or three times, that she had a good Memory, that cou'd be so particular in every Part of such a thing.

O Madam! *says she*, we that were Servants, stood by ourselves in a Corner, but so, as we cou'd see more than some Strangers; besides, *says she*, it was all our Conversations for several Days in the Family, and what one did not observe, another did: Why, *says I* to her, this was no *Persian* Dress; only, *I suppose*, your Lady was some *French* Comedian, *that is to say*, a Stage Amazon, that put on a counterfeit Dress to please the Company, such as they us'd in the Play of Tamerlane,[1] at *Paris*, or some such.

No indeed, Madam, *says she*, I assure you, my Lady was no Actress; she was a fine modest Lady, fit to be a Princess; everybody said, If she was a Mistress she was fit to be a Mistress to none but the KING; and they talk'd her up for the KING, as if it had really been so: Besides, Madam, *says she*, my Lady danc'd a *Turkish* Dance, all the Lords and Gentry said it was so; and one of them swore, *he had seen it danc'd in* Turkey *himself*; so that it cou'd not come from the Theatre in *Paris*; and then the Name *Roxana*, *says she*, was a *Turkish* Name.

Well, *said I*, but that was not your Lady's Name, *I suppose*.

No, no, Madam, *said she*, I know that; I know my Lady's Name and Family very well; *Roxana* was not her Name, that's true indeed.

Here she run me a-ground again, for I durst not ask her what was *Roxana*'s real Name, lest she had really dealt with the Devil, and had boldly given my own Name in for Answer: So that I was still more and more afraid that the Girl had really gotten the

---

1   Tamerlane was a Tartar conqueror whose name was synonymous with tyranny. Tamerlane was the title character in plays by both Christopher Marlowe (1586) and Nicholas Rowe (1702).

Secret somewhere or other; tho' I cou'd not imagine neither, how that cou'd be.

In a word, I was sick of the Discourse, and endeavour'd many ways to put an End to it, but it was impossible; for the Captain's Wife, *who call'd her Sister*, prompted her, and press'd her to tell it, most ignorantly thinking, that it wou'd be a pleasant Tale to all of us.

Two or three times the QUAKER put in, That this Lady *Roxana* had a good Stock of Assurance; and that 'twas likely, if she had been in *Turkey*, she had liv'd with, or been kept by, some Great *Bassa*[1] there: But still she wou'd break-in upon all such Discourse, and fly-out into the most extravagant Praises of her Mistress, the fam'd *Roxana*: I run her down, as some scandalous Woman; that it was not possible to be otherwise; but she wou'd not hear of it; her Lady was a Person of such and such Qualifications; that nothing but an Angel was like her, *to be sure*; and yet, *after all she cou'd say*, her own Account brought her down to this, That, *in short*, her Lady kept little less than a Gaming-Ordinary; or, *as it wou'd be call'd in the Times since that*, an Assembly for Gallantry and Play.

All this while I was very uneasie, *as I said before*, and yet the whole Story went off again without any Discovery, only that I seem'd a little concern'd, that she shou'd liken me to this gay Lady, whose Character I pretended to run down very much, even upon the foot of her own Relation.[2]

But I was not at the End of my Mortifications yet neither; for now my innocent QUAKER threw out an unhappy Expression, which put me upon the Tenters[3] again: *Says she to me*, This Lady's Habit, *I fancy*, is just such a-one as thine, by the Description of it; *and then turning to the Captain's Wife*, says she, *I fancy*, my Friend has a finer *Turkish* or *Persian* Dress, a great-deal: O! *says the Girl*, 'tis impossible to be finer; my Lady's, *says she*, was all cover'd with Gold, and Diamonds; her Hair and Head-Dress, *I forgot the Name they gave it, said she*, shone like the Stars, there was so many Jewels in it.

I never wish'd my good Friend the QUAKER out of my Company before now; but indeed, I wou'd have given some Guineas to have been rid of her *just now*; for beginning to be curious in the comparing the two Dresses, she innocently began

---

1 High-ranking official.
2 Right in front of her own relative.
3 Made Roxana apprehensive.

a Description of *mine*; and nothing terrify'd me so much, as the Apprehension lest she shou'd importune me to show it, which I was resolv'd I wou'd never agree to.

But before it came to this, she press'd my Girl to describe the *Tyhaia*, or Head-dress; which she did so cleverly, that the QUAKER cou'd not help saying, *Mine was just such a-one*; and after several other Similitudes, all very vexatious to me, out comes the kind Motion to me, to let the Ladies see my Dress; and they join'd their eager Desires of it, even to Importunity.

I desir'd to be excus'd; tho' I had little to say at first, why I declin'd it; but at last, it came into my Head to say, *It was pack'd up with my other Cloaths that I had least Occasion for, in order to be sent on-board the Captain's Ship*; but that if we liv'd to come to *Holland* together, (which, *by the way*, I resolv'd shou'd never happen) then, *I told them*, at unpacking my Cloaths, they shou'd see me dress'd in it; but they must not expect I shou'd dance in it, like the Lady *Roxana*, in all her fine things.

This carry'd it off pretty well; and getting over this, got over most of the rest, and I began to be easie again; and *in a word*, that I may dismiss the Story too, as soon as may be, I got-rid at last, of my Visitors, who I had wish'd gone two Hours sooner than they intended it.

As soon as they were gone, I run up to *Amy*, and gave Vent to my Passions, by telling her the whole Story, and letting her see what Mischiefs one false Step of hers had like, unluckily, to have involv'd us all in, more perhaps, than we cou'd ever have liv'd to get through: *Amy* was sensible of it enough, and was just giving her Wrath a Vent another way, *viz.* by calling the poor Girl all the damn'd Jades and Fools, (*and sometimes worse Names*) that she cou'd think of; in the middle of which, up comes my honest good QUAKER, and put an end to our Discourse: The QUAKER came in smiling, (for she was always soberly chearful) *Well*, says she, *Thou art deliver'd at last; I come to joy thee of it; I perceiv'd thou wer't tir'd grievously of thy Visitors.*

Indeed, says I, *so I was*; that foolish young Girl held us all in a *Canterbury Story*,[1] I thought she wou'd never have done with it: Why truly, I thought she was very careful to let *thee* know she was but a Cookmaid: Ay, *says I*, and at a Gaming-House, or Gaming-Ordinary, and at t'other-end of the Town too; all which (*by the*

---

1 A tall tale originally told by pilgrims on their way to Canterbury to entertain one another, as in Chaucer's *Canterbury Tales*.

way) she might know, wou'd add very little to her Good-Name among us Citizens.

I can't think, *says the* QUAKER, but she had some other Drift in that long Discourse; there's something else in her Head, *says she,* I am satisfy'd of that: *Thought I,* are you satisfy'd of it? I am sure I am the less satisfy'd for that; *at least,* 'tis but small Satisfaction to me, to hear you say so: What can this be? *says I;* and when will my Uneasiness have an end? *But this was silent, and to myself, you may be sure*: But in Answer to my Friend the QUAKER, I return'd, by asking her a Question or two about it: As what she thought was in it? and why she thought there was any-thing in it? For, *says I,* she can have nothing in it relating to me.

Nay, *says the kind* QUAKER, if she had any View toward *thee,* that's no Business of mine; and I sho'd be far from desiring *thee* to inform me.

This allarm'd me again; not that I fear'd trusting the good-humour'd Creature with it, if there had been any-thing of just Suspicion in her; but this Affair was a Secret I car'd not to communicate to any-body: However, *I say,* this allarm'd me a little; for as I had conceal'd every-thing from her, I was willing to do so still; but as she cou'd not but gather up abundance of things from the Girl's Discourse, which look'd towards me, so she was too penetrating to be put-off with such Answers, as might stop another's Mouth: Only there was this double Felicity in it: *first,* that she was not Inquisitive to know, or find any-thing out; and not dangerous, if she had known the whole Story: But, *as I say,* she cou'd not but gather up several Circumstances from the Girl's Discourse; as particularly, the Name of *Amy;* and the several Descriptions of the *Turkish* Dress, which my Friend the QUAKER, had seen, and taken so much Notice of, *as I have said above.*

As for that, I might have turn'd it off by jesting with *Amy,* and asking her, who she liv'd with before she came to live with me? But that wou'd not do; for we had unhappily anticipated that way of talking, by having often talk'd how long *Amy* had liv'd with me; and which was still worse, by having own'd formerly, that I had had Lodgings in the *Pall-mall;* so that all those things corresponded too well: there was only one thing that help'd me out with the QUAKER, and that was, the Girl's having reported how rich Mrs. *Amy* was grown, and that she kept her Coach; now as there might be many more Mrs. *Amy*'s besides *mine,* so it was not likely to be my *Amy,* because she was far from such a Figure as keeping her Coach; and this carry'd it off from the Suspicions which the good Friendly QUAKER might have in her Head.

But as to what she imagin'd *the Girl* had in her Head, there lay more real Difficulty in that Part, a great-deal; and I was allarm'd at it very much; for my Friend the QUAKER, *told me*, She observ'd that the *Girl* was in a great Passion when she talk'd of the Habit, and more when I had been importun'd to show her mine, but declin'd it: S*he said*, She several times perceiv'd her to be in Disorder, and to restrain herself with great Difficulty; and once or twice she mutter'd to herself, that *she had found it out*, or, that *she wou'd find it out*, she cou'd not tell whether; and that she often saw Tears in her Eyes; that when I said my Suit of *Turkish* Cloaths was put up, but that she shou'd see it when we arriv'd in *Holland*, she heard her say softly, *She wou'd go over on purpose then.*

After she had ended her Observations, *I added*, I observ'd too, that *the Girl* talk'd and look'd oddly, and that she was mighty Inquisitive, but I cou'd not imagine what it was she aim'd at: Aim'd at, *says the* QUAKER, 'tis plain to me what she aims at; she believes thou art the same Lady *Roxana* that danc'd in the *Turkish* Vest, but she is not certain: does she believe so! *says I*; If I had thought that, I wou'd have put her out of her Pain: Believe so! *Says the* QUAKER, Yes; and I began to believe so too, and shou'd have believ'd so still, if *thou* hadst not satisfy'd me to the contrary, by *thy* taking no Notice of it, and by what *thou* hast said since: Shou'd you have believ'd so? *said I, warmly*, I am very sorry for that; why, wou'd you have taken me for an *Actress*, or a *French Stage-Player*? No, *says the good kind Creature, thou* carry'st it too far; as soon as *thou* mad'st *thy* Reflections upon her, I knew it cou'd not be; but who cou'd think any other, when she describ'd the *Turkish* Dress which *thou* hast here, with the Head-Tire and Jewels; and she nam'd *thy* Maid *Amy* too, and several other Circumstances concurring? I shou'd certainly have believ'd it, *said she*, if *thou* had'st not contradicted it; but as soon as I heard *thee* speak, I concluded it was otherwise: That was very kind, *said I*, and I am oblig'd to you for doing me so much Justice; 'tis more it seems, than that young talking Creature does: Nay, *says the* QUAKER, indeed she does not do *thee* Justice; for she as certainly believes it still, as ever she did: Does she, *said I*? Ay, *says the* QUAKER, and I warrant *thee* she'll make *thee* another Visit about it: Will she, *says I*? then I believe I shall downright affront her: No, *thou* shalt not affront her, *says she*, (full of her good-humour and Temper) I'll take that Part off thy hands, for I'll affront her for *thee*, and not let her see *thee*: I thought that was a very kind Offer, but was at a Loss how she wou'd be able to do it; and the Thought of seeing her there again, half distracted me; not knowing what Temper she wou'd come in, much less what Manner to receive her in; but my fast Friend, and constant Comforter, the QUAKER, said, she perceiv'd the *Girl* was impertinent, and that I had no Inclination to converse with her; and she was resolv'd I sho'd not be troubled with her: But I shall have Occasion to say more of this presently; for this *Girl* went farther yet, than I thought she had.

It was now time, *as I said before*, to take Measures with my Husband, in order to put-off my Voyage; so I fell into Talk with him one Morning as he was dressing, and while I was in-Bed; I pretended I was very ill; and as I had but too easie a Way to impose upon him, because he so absolutely believ'd every-thing I said; so I manag'd my Discourse so, as that he shou'd understand by it, I was a-breeding, tho' I did not tell him so.

However, I brought it about so handsomely, that before he went out of the Room, he came and sat down by my Bed-side, and began to talk very seriously to me, upon the Subject of my being so every-Day ill; and that, as he hop'd I was with-Child, he wou'd have me consider well of it, whether I had not best alter my Thoughts of the Voyage to *Holland*; for that being Sea-sick, and which was worse, if a Storm shou'd happen, might be very dangerous to me; and after saying abundance of the kindest things that the kindest of Husbands in the World cou'd say, he concluded, That it was his Request to me, that I wou'd not think any-more of going, till after all shou'd be over; but that I wou'd, *on the contrary*, prepare to Lye-in where I was, and where I knew as well as he, I cou'd be very well provided, and very well assisted.

This was just what I wanted; for I had, *as you have heard*, a thousand good Reasons why I shou'd put off the Voyage, *especially*, with that Creature in Company, but I had a-mind the putting it off shou'd be at his Motion, not my own; and he came into it of himself, just as I wou'd have had it: this gave me an Opportunity to hang-back a little, and to seem as if I was unwilling; *I told him*, I cou'd not abide to put him to Difficulties and Perplexities in his Business; that now he had hir'd the Great-Cabbin in the Ship, and perhaps, paid some of the Money, and, *it may be*, taken Freight of Goods; and to make him break it all off again, wou'd be a needless Charge to him, *or perhaps*, a Damage to the Captain.

As to that, *he said*, it was not to be nam'd, and he wou'd not allow it to be any Consideration at-all; that he cou'd easily pacifie the Captain of the Ship, by telling him the Reason of it; and that if he did make him some Satisfaction of the Disappointment, it shou'd not be much.

But my Dear, *says I*, you ha'n't heard me say I am with-Child, neither can I say so; and if it shou'd not be so at last, then I shall have made a fine Piece of Work of it indeed; besides, *says I*, the two Ladies, the Captain's Wife and her Sister, they depend upon our going over, and have made great Preparations, and all in Compliment to me; what must I say to them?

Well, my Dear, *says he*, if you shou'd not be with-Child, tho' I hope you are, yet there is no harm done; the staying three or four Months longer in *England* will be no Damage to me, and we can go when we please, when we are sure you are not with-Child, or when it appearing that you are with-Child, you shall be down and up again; and as for the Captain's Wife and Sister, leave that Part to me, I'll answer for it, there shall be no Quarrel rais'd upon that Subject; I'll make your Excuse to them by the Captain himself; so all will be well enough there, I'll warrant you.

This was much as I cou'd desire; and thus it rested for a-while: I had indeed, some anxious Thoughts about this impertinent Girl, but believ'd that putting off the Voyage wou'd have put an End to it all; so I began to be pretty easie; but I found myself mistaken, for I was brought to the Point of Destruction by her again, and that in the most unaccountable Manner imaginable.

My Husband, as he and I had agreed, meeting the Captain of the Ship, took the Freedom to tell him, That he was afraid he must disappoint him, for that something had fallen out, which had oblig'd him to alter his Measures, and that his Family cou'd not be ready to go, time enough for him.

I know the Occasion, Sir, *says the Captain*; I hear your Lady has got a Daughter more than she expected; I give you Joy of it: What do you mean by that? *says my Spouse*: Nay, nothing, *says the Captain*, but what I hear the Women tattle over the Tea-Table; I know nothing, but that you don't go the Voyage upon it, which I am sorry for; but you know your own Affairs, *added the Captain*, that's no Business of mine.

Well but, *says my Husband*, I must make you some Satisfaction for the Disappointment, and so pulls out his Money: No, no, *says the Captain*, and so they fell to straining their Compliments one upon another; but, *in short*, my Spouse gave him three or four Guineas, and made him take it; and so the first Discourse went off again, and they had no more of it.

But it did not go off so easily with me; for now, *in a word*, the

Clouds began to thicken about me, and I had Allarms on every side: My Husband told me what the Captain had said; but very happily took it, that the Captain had brought a Tale by-halves,[1] and having heard it one way had told it another; and that neither cou'd he understand the Captain, neither did the Captain understand himself; so he contented himself to tell me, *he said*, word for word, as the Captain deliver'd it.

How I kept my Husband from discovering my Disorder, *you shall hear presently*; but let it suffice to say just now, that if my Husband did not understand the Captain, nor the Captain understand himself, yet I understood them both very well; and to tell the Truth, it was a worse Shock than ever I had had yet: Invention supply'd me indeed, with a sudden Motion to avoid showing my Surprize; for as my Spouse and I was sitting by a little Table, near the Fire, I reach'd out my Hand, as if I had intended to take a Spoon which lay on the other side, and threw one of the Candles off the Table; and then snatching it up, started up upon my Feet, and stoop'd to the Lap of my Gown, and took it in my Hand; O! *says I*, my Gown's spoil'd; the Candle has greas'd[2] it prodigiously: This furnish'd me with an Excuse to my Spouse, to break off the Discourse for the present, and call *Amy* down; and *Amy* not coming presently, *I said to him*, My Dear, I must run upstairs, and put it off, and let *Amy* clean it a-little; so my Husband rise up too, and went into a Closet, where he kept his Papers and Books, and fetch'd a Book out, and sat down by himself, to read.

Glad I was that I had got away; and up I run to *Amy*, who, as it happen'd, was alone; O *Amy*! *says I*, we are all utterly undone; and with that I burst out a-crying, and cou'd not speak a Word for a great-while.

I cannot help saying, that some very good Reflections offer'd themselves upon this Head; it presently occurr'd, What a glorious Testimony it is to the Justice of Providence, and to the Concern Providence has in guiding all the Affairs of Men, (*even the least, as well as the greatest*) that the most secret Crimes are, by the most unforeseen Accidents, brought to light, and discover'd.

Another Reflection was, How just it is, that Sin and Shame follow one-another so constantly at the Heels, that they are not like Attendants only, but like Cause and Consequence, necessarily connected one with another; that the Crime going before, the

---

1 Incomplete.
2 At this time, candles were typically made with tallow or animal fat.

Scandal is certain to follow; and that 'tis not in the Power of humane Nature to conceal the first, or avoid the last.

What shall I do? *Amy*, said, I, *as soon as I cou'd speak*; and what will become of me? And then I cry'd again so vehemently, that I cou'd say no more a great-while; *Amy* was frighted almost out of her Wits, but knew nothing what the Matter was; but she begg'd to know, and perswaded me to compose myself, and not cry so: Why Madam, if my Master shou'd come up now, *says she*, he will see what a Disorder you are in; he will know you have been crying, and then he will want to know the Cause of it; with that I broke-out again, O! he knows it already, *Amy, says I*; he knows all! 'tis all discover'd! and we are undone! *Amy* was Thunder-struck now indeed: Nay, *says Amy*, if that be true, we are undone indeed; but that can never be; that's impossible, I'm sure.

No, no, says I, 'tis far from impossible, for I tell you 'tis so; and by this time being a little recover'd, I told her what Discourse my Husband and the Captain had had together, and what the Captain had said: This put *Amy* into such a Hurry that she cry'd; she rav'd; she swore and curs'd like a Mad-thing; then she upbraided me, that I wou'd not let her kill the Girl when she wou'd have done it; and that it was all my own doing, *and the like*: Well however, I was not for killing the Girl yet, I cou'd not bear the Thoughts of that neither.

We spent half an Hour in these Extravagances, and brought nothing out of them neither; for indeed, we cou'd do nothing, or say nothing, that was to the Purpose; for if any-thing was to come out-of-the-way,[1] there was no hindring it, nor help for it; so after thus giving a Vent to myself by crying, I began to reflect how I had left my Spouse below, and what I had pretended to come up for; so I chang'd my Gown that I pretended the Candle fell upon, and put on another, and went down.

When I had been down a good-while, and found my Spouse did not fall into the Story again, as I expected, I took-heart, and call'd for it: My Dear, *said I*, the Fall of the Candle put you out of your History; won't you go on with it? What History? *says he*: Why, *says I*, about the Captain: O! *says he*, I had done with it; I know no more, than that the Captain told a broken Piece of News that he had heard by halves, and told more by halves than he heard it; *namely*, of your being with-Child, and that you cou'd not go the Voyage.

---

1 Look out of the ordinary.

I perceiv'd my Husband enter'd not into the thing at-all, but took it for a Story, which being told two or three times over, was puzzl'd, and come to nothing; and that all that was meant by it was, what he knew, or thought he knew already, *viz.* that I was with-Child, which he wish'd might be true.

His Ignorance was a Cordial to my Soul; and I curs'd them in my thoughts, that shou'd ever undeceive him; and as I saw him willing to have the Story end there, as not worth being farther mention'd, I clos'd it too; *and said*, I suppos'd the Captain had it from his Wife; she might have found somebody else to make her Remarks upon, so it pass'd off with my Husband well enough, and I was still safe there, where I thought myself in the most Danger; but I had two Uneasinesses still; *the first* was, lest the Captain and my Spouse shou'd meet again, and enter into farther Discourse about it; and *the second* was, lest the busie impertinent Girl shou'd come again, and when she came, how to prevent her seeing *Amy*, which was an Article as material as any of the rest; for seeing *Amy*, wou'd have been as fatal to me, as her knowing all the rest.

As to the *first* of these, I knew the Captain cou'd not stay in Town above a Week; but that his Ship being already full of Goods, and fallen down the River,[1] he must soon follow; so I contriv'd to carry my Husband somewhere out of Town for a few Days, that they might be sure not to meet.

My greatest Concern was, where we shou'd go; at last I fix'd upon *North-Hall*; not, I said, that I wou'd drink the Waters, but that, I thought the Air was good, and might be for my Advantage: He who did every-thing upon the Foundation of obliging me, readily came into it, and the Coach was appointed to be ready the next Morning; but as we were settling Matters, he put in an ugly Word that Thwarted all my Design; and that was, That he had rather I wou'd stay till Afternoon, for that he shou'd speak to the Captain next Morning, if he cou'd to give him some Letters; which he cou'd do, and be back-again about Twelve a-Clock.

I said, Ay, by all means; but it was but a Cheat on him, and my Voice and my Heart differ'd; for I resolv'd, *if possible*, he shou'd not come near the Captain, nor see him, whatever came of it.

In the Evening therefore, a little before we went to-Bed, I pretended to have alter'd my Mind, and that I wou'd not go to *North-Hall*, but I had a-mind to go another-way, *but I told him*, I was afraid his Business wou'd not permit him; he wanted to know where it was? *I told him, smiling*, I wou'd not tell him, lest it shou'd oblige him

---

1 Taken down the river, ready to sail.

to hinder his Business: *He answer'd*, with the same Temper, *but with infinitely more Sincerity*, That he had no Business of so much Consequence, as to hinder him going with me any-where that I had a-mind to go: *Yes*, says I, *you want to speak with the Captain before he goes away*: Why that's true, *say he, so I do*, and paus'd a-while; and *then added*, But I'll write a Note to a Man that does Business for me, to go to him; 'tis only to get some Bills of Loading sign'd, and he can do it: When I saw I had gain'd my Point, I seem'd to hang back a little; my Dear, *says I*, don't hinder an Hour's Business for me; I can put it off for a Week or two, rather than you shall do yourself any Prejudice: *No, no, says he*, you shall not put it off an Hour for me, for I can do my Business by Proxy with any-body, *but my* WIFE; *and then he took me in his Arms and kiss'd me*: How did my Blood flush up into my Face! when I reflected how sincerely how affectionately this good-humour'd Gentleman embrac'd the most cursed Piece of Hypocrasie that ever came into the Arms of an honest Man? His was all Tenderness, all Kindness, and the utmost Sincerity; Mine all Grimace and Deceit; a Piece of meer Manage, and fram'd Conduct, to conceal a pass'd Life of Wickedness, and prevent his discovering, that he had in his Arms a She-Devil, whose whole Conversation[1] for twenty five Years had been black as Hell, a Complication of Crime;[2] and for which, had he been let into it, he must have abhor'd me, and the very mention of my Name: But there was no help for me in it; all I had to satisfie myself was, that it was my Business to be what I was, and conceal what I had been; that all the Satisfaction I cou'd make him, was to live virtuously for the Time to come, not being able to retrieve what had been in Time past; and this I resolv'd upon, tho' had the great Temptation offer'd as it did afterwards, I had reason to question my Stability: *But of that hereafter.*

After my Husband had kindly thus given up his Measures to mine, we resolv'd to set-out in the Morning early; I told him, that my Project, if he lik'd it, was, to go to *Tunbridge*; and he, being entirely passive in the thing, agreed to it with the greatest willingness; *but said*, If I had not nam'd *Tunbridge*, he wou'd have nam'd *Newmarket*;[3] *(there being a great Court there, and abundance*

---

1 Life and interactions.
2 Roxana's deceptions have made her crimes and sins worse.
3 Newmarket was a favorite watering-hole of the aristocracy and nobility, partly because of the races held there. It was also the town from which Charles II and his brother were returning when the Rye-House Plot to assassinate them (in which the Duke of Monmouth was implicated) was discovered.

of fine things to be seen) I offer'd him another Piece of Hypocrisie here, for I pretended to be willing to go thither, *as the Place of his Choice,* but indeed, I wou'd not have gone for a Thousand Pounds; for the COURT being there at that time, I durst not run the Hazard of being known at a Place where there were so many Eyes that had seen me before: So that, *after some time,* I told my Husband, that I thought *Newmarket* was so full of People at that time, that we shou'd get no Accommodation; that seeing the COURT, and the Crowd, was no Entertainment at-all to me, unless as it might be so to him; that if he thought fit, we wou'd rather put it off to another time; and that if, when he went to *Holland,* we shou'd go by *Harwich,* we might take a round by *Newmarket* and *Bury,* and so come down to *Ipswich,* and go from thence to the Sea-side: He was easily put-off from this, as he was from anything else, that I did not approve; and so with all imaginable Facility he appointed to be ready early in the Morning, to go with me for *Tunbridge.*

I had a double Design in this, *viz. First,* To get away my Spouse from seeing the Captain any-more; and *secondly,* To be out of the way myself, in case this impertinent Girl, *who was now my Plague,* shou'd offer to come again, *as my Friend* the QUAKER *believ'd she wou'd;* and as indeed, happen'd within two or three Days afterwards.

Having thus secur'd my going away the next Day, I had nothing to do, but to furnish my faithful Agent, the QUAKER, with some Instructions what to say to this *Tormentor,* (for such she prov'd afterwards) and how to manage her, if she made any-more Visits than ordinary.

I had a great-mind to leave *Amy* behind too, as an Assistant, because she understood so perfectly well, what to advise upon any Emergence;[1] and *Amy* importun'd me to do so; but I know not what secret Impulse prevail'd over my Thoughts, against it, I cou'd not do it, for fear the wicked Jade shou'd make her away, which my very Soul abhorr'd the Thoughts of; which however, *Amy* found Means to bring to pass afterwards; *as I may in time relate more particularly.*

It is true, I wanted as much to be deliver'd from her, as ever a Sick-Man did from a Third-Day Ague;[2] and had she dropp'd into the Grave by any fair Way, *as I may call it;* I mean had she died by any ordinary Distemper, I shou'd have shed but very few Tears for

1 Emergency.
2 The flu.

her: But I was not arriv'd to such a Pitch of obstinate Wickedness, as to commit Murther, especially such, as to murther my own Child, or so much as to harbour a Thought so barbarous, in my Mind: But, *as I said, Amy* effected all afterwards, without my Knowledge, for which I gave her my hearty Curse, tho' I cou'd do little more; for to have fall'n upon *Amy*, had been to have murther'd myself: But this Tragedy requires a longer Story than I have room for here: *I return to my Journey.*

My dear Friend, the QUAKER, was kind, and yet honest, and wou'd do any-thing that was just and upright, to serve me, but nothing wicked, or dishonourable; that she might be able to say boldly to the Creature, if she came, she did not know where I was gone, she desir'd I wou'd not let her know; and to make her Ignorance the more absolutely safe to herself, and likewise to me, I allow'd her to say, that she heard us talk of going to *Newmarket, &c.* She lik'd that Part, and I left all the rest to her, to act as she thought fit, only charg'd her, that if the Girl enter'd into the Story of the *Pall-mall*, she shou'd not entertain much Talk about it; but let her understand, that we all thought she spoke of it a little too particularly; and that the Lady, *meaning me*, took it a little ill, to be so liken'd to a publick Mistress, or a Stage-Player, *and the like*; and so to bring her, *if possible* to say no more of it: However, tho' I did not tell my Friend the QUAKER, how to write to me, or where I was, yet I left a seal'd Paper with her Maid to give her, in which I gave her a Direction how to write to *Amy*, and so in effect, to myself.

It was but a few Days after I was gone, but the impatient Girl came to my Lodgings, on Pretence to see how I did, and to hear if I intended to go the Voyage, *and the like*: My trusty Agent was at-home, and receiv'd her coldly at the Door; *but told her,* That the Lady, *which she suppos'd she meant, was gone from her House.*

This was a full Stop to all she cou'd say for a good-while; but as she stood musing some time at the Door, considering what to begin a Talk upon, she perceiv'd my Friend the QUAKER, look'd a little uneasie, as if she wanted to go in, and shut the Door, which stung her to the quick; and the wary QUAKER had not so much as ask'd her to come in; for seeing her alone, she expected she wou'd be very Impertinent; and concluded, that I did not care how coldly she receiv'd her.

But she was not to be put off so: *She said*, If the Lady—was not to be spoke with, she desir'd to speak two or three Words with her, *meaning my Friend. the* QUAKER: Upon that, the QUAKER civilly, *but coldly*, ask'd her to walk in, which was what she wanted:

Note, She did not carry her into her best Parlour, *as formerly*, but into a little outer-Room, where the Servants usually waited.

By the first of her Discourse she did not stick to insinuate, as if she believ'd I was in the House, but was unwilling to be seen; and press'd earnestly that she might speak but two Words with me; to which she added earnest Entreaties, and at last, Tears.

I am sorry, *says my good Creature the* QUAKER, *thou* hast so ill an Opinion of me, as to think I wou'd tell *thee* an Untruth, and say, that the Lady— was gone from my House, if she was not? I assure *thee* I do not use any such Method; nor does the Lady— desire any such kind of Service from me, as I know of: If she had been in the House, I shou'd have told *thee* so.

She said little to that, but said, It was Business of the utmost Importance that she desir'd to speak with me about; *and then cry'd again very much.*

Thou seem'st to be sorely afflicted, *says the* QUAKER, I wish I cou'd give *thee* any Relief; but if nothing will comfort *thee* but seeing the Lady—, it is not in my Power.

I hope it is, *says she again*; to be sure it is of great Consequence to me, so much, that I am undone without it.

Thou troubl'st me very much, to hear *thee* say so, *says the* QUAKER; but why then did'st *thou* not speak to her apart, when *thou* wast here before?

I had no Opportunity, *says she*, to speak to her alone, and I cou'd not do it in Company; if I cou'd have spoken but two Words to her alone, I wou'd have thrown myself at her Foot, and ask'd her Blessing.

I am surpriz'd at *thee*; I do not understand *thee*, *says the* QUAKER.

O! *says she*, stand my Friend, if you have any Charity, or if you have any Compassion for the Miserable; for I am utterly undone!

Thou terrify'st me, *says the* QUAKER, with such passionate Expressions; for *verily* I cannot comprehend *thee*.

O! *says she*, She is my Mother; She is my Mother; and she does not own me.

Thy Mother! *says the* QUAKER, and began to be greatly mov'd indeed; I am astonish'd at *thee*; what do'st *thou* mean?

I mean nothing but what I say, *says she, I say again*, She is my Mother! and will not own me; *and with that she stopp'd, with a Flood of Tears.*

Not own *thee*! s*ays the* QUAKER; and the tender, good Creature wept too; why, she says, she does not know *thee*, and never saw *thee* before.

No, *says the Girl*, I believe she does not know me, but I know her; and I know that she is my Mother.

It's impossible! *Thou* talk'st Mystery, *says the* QUAKER; wilt *thou* explain *thyself* a little to me?

Yes, Yes, says she, I can explain it well enough; I am sure she is my Mother, and I have broke my Heart to search for her; and now to lose her again, when I was so sure I had found her, will break my Heart more effectually.

Well, but if she be *thy* Mother, *says the* QUAKER, How can it be, that she shou'd not know *thee*?

Alas! *says she*, I have been lost to her ever since I was a Child: She has never seen me.

And hast *thou* never seen her? *says the* QUAKER.

Yes, *says she*, I have seen her, often enough, I saw her; for when she was the Lady *Roxana*, I was her House-maid, *being a Servant*, but I did not know her then, nor she me, but it has all come out since; has she not a Maid nam'd *Amy*? [*Note, the honest* QUAKER *was nonpluss'd, and greatly surpriz'd at that Question.*]

Truly, *says she*, the Lady— has several Women-Servants, but I do not know all their Names.

But her Woman, her Favourite, *adds the Girl*; is not her Name *Amy*?

Why, truly, *says the* QUAKER, *with a very happy turn of Wit*, I do not like to be examin'd; but lest *thou* should'st take up any Mistakes, by reason of my backwardness to speak, I will answer *thee* for once, That what her Woman's Name is, I know not; but they call her *Cherry*.

N.B. *My Husband gave her that Name in jest, on our Wedding-Day, and we had call'd her by it ever after; so that she spoke literally true at that time.*

The Girl reply'd very modestly, That she was sorry if she gave her any Offence in asking; that she did not design to be rude to her, or pretend to examine her; but that she was in such an Agony at this Disaster, that she knew not what she did or said; and that she shou'd be very sorry to disoblige her; but begg'd of her again, as she was a Christian, and a Woman, and had been a Mother of Children, that she wou'd take Pity on her, and, *if possible*, assist her, so that she might but come to me, and speak a few Words to me.

The tender-hearted QUAKER told me, the Girl spoke this with such moving Eloquence, that it forc'd Tears from her; but she was oblig'd to say, That she neither knew where I was gone, or how to write to me; but that if she did ever see me again, she wou'd not fail to give me an Account of all she had said to her, or that she shou'd yet think fit to say; and to take my Answer to it, if I thought fit to give any.

Then the QUAKER took the Freedom to ask a few Particulars about this wonderful Story, *as she call'd it*; at which, the Girl beginning at the first Distresses of my Life, *and indeed, of her own*, went thro' all the History of her miserable Education; her Service under the Lady *Roxana, as she call'd me*, and her Relief by Mrs. *Amy*; with the Reasons she had to believe, that as Amy own'd herself to be the same that liv'd with her Mother, *and especially*, that *Amy* was the lady *Roxana's* Maid too, and came out of *France* with her, She was by those Circumstances, and several others in her Conversation, as fully convinc'd, that the Lady *Roxana* was her Mother, as she was that the Lady— at her House [*the* QUAKER's] was the very same *Roxana* that she had been Servant too.

My good Friend the QUAKER, tho' terribly shock'd at the Story, and not well-knowing what to say, yet was too much my Friend to seem convinc'd in a Thing, which she did not know to be true, and which, if it was true, she cou'd see plainly I had a-mind shou'd not be known; so she turn'd her Discourse to argue the Girl out of it: she insisted upon the slender Evidence she had of the Fact itself, and the Rudeness of claiming so near a Relation of one so much above her, and of whose concern in it she had no Knowledge, *at least*, no sufficient Proof; that as the Lady at her House was a Person above any Disguises, so she cou'd not believe that she wou'd deny her being her Daughter, if she was really her Mother; that she was able sufficiently to have provided for her, if she had not a-mind to have her known; and therefore, seeing she had heard all she had said of the Lady *Roxana*, and was so far from owning herself to be the Person, so she had censur'd that Sham-Lady as a Cheat, and a Common Woman;[1] and that 'twas certain she cou'd never be brought to own a Name and Character she had so justly expos'd.

Beside, *she told her*, that her Lodger, *meaning me*, was not a Sham-Lady, but the real Wife of a Knight Baronet; and that she knew her to be honestly such, and far above such a Person as she had describ'd: *She then added*, that she had another Reason why it was not very possible to be true, *and that is, says she, Thy* Age is in the way; for *thou* acknowledgest, that *thou* art four and

---

1 Whore.

twenty Years old; and that *thou* was the Youngest[1] of three of *thy* Mother's Children; so that, by thy Account, *thy* Mother must be extremely young, or this Lady cannot be *thy* Mother; for *thou* seest, *says she,* and any one may see, she is but a young Woman now, and cannot be suppos'd to be above Forty Years old, if she is so much, and is now big with-Child at her going in to the Country; so that I cannot give any Credit to *thy* Notion of her being *thy* Mother; and if I might counsel *thee,* it shou'd be to give-over that Thought, as an improbable Story that does but serve to disorder *thee,* and disturb *thy* Head; for, added she, I perceive *thou* art much disturb'd indeed.

But this was all nothing: She cou'd be satisfy'd with nothing but seeing me; but the QUAKER defended herself very well, and insisted on it, that she cou'd not give her any Account of me; and finding her still importunate, she affected at last, being a little disgusted that she shou'd not believe her, *and added,* That indeed, if she had known where I was gone, she wou'd not have given any-one an Account of it, unless I had given her Orders to do so; but seeing she has not acquainted me, *says she,* where she is gone, 'tis an Intimation to me, she was not desirous it shou'd be publickly known; and with this she rise up, which was as plain a desiring her to rise up too, and be gone, as cou'd be express'd, except the downright showing her the Door.

Well, the Girl rejected all this, *and told her,* She cou'd not indeed expect that she (*the* QUAKER) shou'd be affected with the Story she had told her, however moving; or that she shou'd take any Pity on her: That it was her Misfortune, that when she was at the House before, and in the Room with me, she did not beg to speak a Word with me in private, or throw herself upon the Floor, at my Feet, and claim what the Affection of a Mother wou'd have done for her; but since she had slipp'd her Opportunity, she wou'd wait for another; that she found by her (*the QUAKER's*) Talk, that she had not quite left her Lodgings, but was gone into the Country, *she suppos'd,* for the Air; and she was resolv'd she wou'd take so much *Knight-Errantry* upon her, that she wou'd visit all the Airing-Places in the Nation, and even all the Kingdom over, ay, and *Holland* too, but she wou'd find me; for she was satisfy'd she cou'd so convince me that she was my own Child, that I wou'd not deny it; and she was sure I was so tender and compas-

---

1 This contradicts Roxana's earlier claim that the daughter in question, Susan, is the eldest of her children and also her namesake.

sionate, I wou'd not let her perish after I was convinc'd that she was my own Flesh and Blood; and in saying she wou'd visit all the Airing-Places in *England*, she reckon'd them all up by Name, and began with *Tunbridge*, the very Place I was gone to; then reckoning up *Epsom, North-Hall, Barnet, Newmarket, Bury*, and at last, the *Bath*: And with this she took her Leave.

My faithful Agent the QUAKER, fail'd not to write to me immediately; but as she was a cunning, as well as an honest Woman, it presently occurr'd to her, that this was a Story, which, whether True or False, was not very fit to come to my Husband's Knowledge; that as she did not know what I might have been, or might have been call'd in former Times, and how far there might have been *something* or *nothing* in it, so she thought if it was a Secret, I ought to have the telling it myself; and if it was not, it might as well be publick afterwards, as now; and that, *at least*, she ought to leave it where she found it, and not hand it forwards to any-body without my Consent: These prudent Measures were inexpressibly kind, as well as seasonable; for it had been likely enough that her Letter might have come publickly to me, and tho' my Husband wou'd not have open'd it, yet it wou'd have look'd a little odd that I shou'd conceal its Contents from him, when I had pretended so much to communicate all my Affairs.

In Consequence of this wise Caution, my good Friend only wrote me in a few Words, That the impertinent Young-Woman had been with her, as she expected she wou'd; and that she thought it wou'd be very convenient that, if I cou'd spare *Cherry*, I wou'd send her up, (meaning *Amy*) because she found there might be some Occasion for her.

As it happen'd, this Letter was enclos'd to *Amy* herself, and not sent by the Way I had at first order'd; but it came safe to my Hands; and tho' I was allarm'd a little at it, yet I was not acquainted with the Danger I was in of an immediate Visit from this teizing[1] Creature, till afterwards; and I run a greater Risque indeed, than ordinary, in that I did not send *Amy* up under thirteen or fourteen Days, believing myself as much conceal'd at *Tunbridge*, as if I had been at *Vienna*.

But the Concern my faithful SPY, (*for such my* QUAKER *was now, upon the meer foot of her own Sagacity*) I say, her concern for me, was my Safety in this Exigence, when I was, *as it were*,

---

1 Pestering.

keeping no Guard for myself; for finding *Amy* not come up, and that she did not know how soon this wild Thing might put her design'd Ramble in Practice, she sent a Messenger to the Captain's Wife's House, where she lodg'd, to tell her that she wanted to speak with her: She was at the Heels of the Messenger, and came eager for some News; and hop'd, *she said*, the Lady, (*meaning me*) had been come to Town.

The QUAKER, with as much Caution as she was Mistress of, *not to tell a downright Lye*, made her believe she expected to hear of me very quickly; and frequently *by the by*, speaking of being Abroad to take the Air, talk'd of the Country about *Bury*, how pleasant it was; how wholesome; and how fine an Air: How the *Downs*[1] about *Newmarket* were exceeding fine; and what a vast deal of Company there was, now the *Court* was there; till at last, the Girl began to conclude, that *my Ladyship* was gone thither; for, *she said*, She knew I lov'd to see a great-deal of Company.

Nay, *says my Friend*, *thou* tak'st me wrong, I did not suggest, *says she*, that the Person *thou* enquir'st after, is gone thither, neither do I believe she is, *I assure thee*: Well, the Girl smil'd, and let her know, that she believ'd it for-all that; so, to clench it fast, Verily *says she*, *with great Seriousness*, *Thou* do'st not do well, for *thou* suspectest every-thing, and believest nothing: I speak solemnly to *thee*, that I do not believe they are gone that Way; so if *thou* giv'st *thyself* the Trouble to go that Way, and art disappointed, do not say that I have deceiv'd *thee*: She knew well enough, that if this did abate her Suspicion, it wou'd not remove it; and that it wou'd do little more than amuse[2] her; but by this she kept her in suspence till *Amy* came up, and that was enough.

When *Amy* came up, she was quite confounded, to hear the Relation which the QUAKER gave her, and found means to acquaint me of it; only letting me know, to my great Satisfaction, that she wou'd not come to *Tunbridge* first; but that she wou'd certainly go to *Newmarket* or *Bury* first.

However, it gave me very great Uneasiness; for as she resolv'd to ramble in search after me, over the whole Country, I was safe no-where, no, not in *Holland* itself; so indeed, I did not know what to do with her: And thus I had a *Bitter* in all my *Sweet*, for I was continually perpelx'd with this Hussy, and thought she haunted me like an Evil Spirit.

---

1 *OED*: An open expanse of elevated land; an extensive piece of waste-land.
2 Distract.

In the mean time, *Amy* was next-door to stark-mad about her; she durst not see her at my Lodgings, for her Life; and she went Days without Number, to *Spittle-Fields*, where she us'd to come, and to her former Lodging, and cou'd never meet with her; *at length*, she took up a mad Resolution, that she wou'd go directly to the Captain's House in *Redriff*, and speak with her; it was a mad Step, *that's true*, but, *as* Amy *said*, she was mad, so nothing she cou'd do, cou'd be otherwise: For if *Amy* had found her at *Redriff*, she (*the Girl*) wou'd have concluded presently, that the QUAKER had given her Notice, and so that we were all of a Knot,[1] and that, *in short*, all she had said was right: But as it happen'd, things came to hit better[2] than we expected; for that *Amy* going out of a Coach, to take Water at *Tower-Wharf*,[3] meets *the Girl* just come on-Shoar, having cross'd the Water from *Redriff*: *Amy* made as if she wou'd have pass'd by her, tho' they met so full that she did not pretend she did not see her, for she look'd fairly upon her first; but then turning her Head away, with a Slight, offer'd to go from her; but the Girl stopp'd, and spoke first, and made some Manners[4] to her.

Amy spoke coldly to her, and a little angry; and after some Words, standing in the Street, or Passage, *the Girl saying*, she seem'd to be angry, and wou'd not have spoken to her: *Why*, says Amy, *How can you expect I shou'd have any-more to say to you, after I had done so much for you, and you have behav'd so to me?* The Girl seem'd to take no Notice of that now, but answer'd, *I was going to wait on you now;* Wait on me! says *Amy*; what do you mean by that? Why, *says she again, with a kind of Familiarity,* I was going to your Lodgings.

Amy was provok'd to the last Degree at her, and yet she thought it was not her time to resent, because she had a more fatal and wicked Design in her Head, against her; which indeed, I never knew till after it was executed, nor durst *Amy* ever communicate it to me; for as I had always express'd myself vehemently against hurting a Hair of her Head, so she was resolv'd to take her own Measures, without consulting me any-more.

In order to this, *Amy* gave her good Words, and conceal'd her Resentment as much as she cou'd; and when she talk'd of going to her Lodging, *Amy* smil'd, and said nothing, but call'd for a Pair

---

1 In collusion.
2 Turned out better.
3 To take a water-taxi.
4 Was courteous.

of Oars to go to *Greenwich*; and ask'd her, seeing s*he said* she was going to her Lodging, to go along with her, for she was going Home, and was all-alone.

Amy did this with such a Stock of Assurance, that the Girl was confounded, and knew not what to say; but the more she hesitated, the more *Amy* press'd her to go; and talking very kindly to her, *told her*, If she did not go to see her Lodgings, she might go to keep her Company, and she wou'd pay a Boat to bring her back-again; so, *in a word, Amy* prevail'd on her to go into the Boat with her, and carry'd her down to *Greenwich*.

'Tis certain, that *Amy* had no more Business at *Greenwich* than I had; nor was she going thither; but we were all hamper'd to the last Degree, with the Impertinence of this Creature; and in particular, I was horribly perplex'd with it.

As they were in the Boat, *Amy* began to reproach her with Ingratitude, in treating her so rudely, who had done so much for her, and been so kind to her; and to ask her what she had got by it? Or what she expected to get? Then came in my Share, the Lady *Roxana*; *Amy* jested with that, and banter'd her a little; *and ask'd her*, if she had found her yet?

But *Amy* was both surpriz'd and enrag'd, when the Girl told her roundly, That she thank'd her for what she had done for her; but that she wou'd not have her think she was so ignorant, as not to know that what she [*Amy*] had done, was by her Mother's Order; and who she was beholden to for it: That she cou'd never make Instruments pass for Principals, and pay the Debt to the Agent, when the Obligation was all to the Original: That she knew well enough who she was, and who she was employ'd by: that she knew the Lady— very well, (*naming the Name that I now went by*) which was my Husband's true Name, and by which she might know whether she had found out her Mother or no.

Amy wish'd her at the Bottom of the *Thames*; and had there been no Watermen in the Boat, and no-body in sight, *she swore to me*, she wou'd have thrown her into the River: I was horribly disturb'd when she told me this Story, and began to think this wou'd, at last, all end in my Ruin; but when *Amy* spoke of throwing her into the River, and drowning her, I was so provok'd at her, that all my Rage turn'd against *Amy*, and I fell thorowly out with her: I had now kept *Amy* almost thirty Year, and found her, on all Occasions, the faithfulest Creature to me, that ever Woman had; *I say*, faithful to me; for however wicked she was, still she was true to me; and even this Rage of hers was all upon my Account, and for fear any Mischief shou'd befall me.

But be that how it wou'd, I cou'd not bear the Mention of her Murthering the poor Girl, and it put me so beside myself, that I rise up in a Rage, and bade her get out of my Sight, and out of my House; *told her*, I had kept her too long, and that I wou'd never see her Face more; I had before told her, That she was a Murtherer, and a bloody-minded Creature; that she cou'd not but know that I cou'd not bear the Thought of it, much less the Mention of it; and that it was the impudentest Thing that ever was known, to make such a Proposal to me, when she knew that I was really the Mother of this Girl, and that she was my own Child; that it was wicked enough in her; but that she must conclude I was ten times wickeder than herself, if I cou'd come into it: That the Girl was in the right, and I had nothing to blame her for; but that it was owing to the Wickedness of my Life, that made it necessary for me to keep her from a Discovery, but that I wou'd not murther my Child, tho' I was otherwise to be ruin'd by it: *Amy* reply'd somewhat rough and short, Would I not, but she wou'd, *she said*, if she had an Opportunity: And upon these Words it was that I bade her get out of my Sight, and out of my House; and it went so far, that *Amy* pack'd up her Alls, and march'd off, and was gone for almost good-and-all: *But of that in its Order; I must go back to her Relation of the Voyage which they made to* Greenwich *together.*

They held on the Wrangle[1] all-the-way by Water; the Girl insisted upon her knowing that I was her Mother, and told her all the History of my Life in the *Pall-mall*, as well after her being turn'd away, as before; and of my Marriage since: and which was worse, not only who my present Husband was, but where he had liv'd, *viz.* at *Roan* in *France*; she knew nothing of *Paris*, or of where we was going to live, *Namely* at *Nimuegen*; *but told her in so many Words,* That if she cou'd not find me here, she wou'd go to *Holland* after me.

They landed at *Greenwich*, and *Amy* carried her into the Park with her, and they walk'd above two Hours there, in the farthest and remotest Walks; which *Amy* did, because as they talk'd with great heat, it was apparent they were quarrelling, and the People took Notice of it.

They walk'd till they came almost to the Wilderness, at the *South* side of the Park; but *the Girl* perceiving *Amy* offer'd to go in there, among the Woods, and Trees, stopp'd short there, and wou'd go no farther; *but said,* She wou'd not go in there.

---

1 They continued to argue angrily.

Amy smil'd, and ask'd her what was the Matter? *She replied short*, She did not know where she was, nor where she was going to carry her, and she wou'd go no farther; and without any more Ceremony, turns back, and walks apace away from her: *Amy* own'd she was surpriz'd, and came back too, and call'd to her; upon which the Girl stopt, and *Amy* coming up to her, ask'd her, what she meant?

The Girl boldly replied, She did not know but she might murther her; and that, *in short*, She wou'd not trust herself with her; and never wou'd come into her Company again, alone.

It was very provoking; but, however, *Amy* kept her Temper, with much Difficulty, and bore it, knowing that much might depend upon it; so she mock'd her foolish Jealousie, *and told her*, She need not be uneasie for her, she wou'd do her no Harm, and wou'd have done her Good, if she wou'd have let her; but since she was of such a refractory Humour, she shou'd not trouble herself, for she shou'd never come into her Company again; and that neither she, or her Brother, or Sister, shou'd ever hear from her, or see her any-more; and so she shou'd have the Satisfaction of being the Ruin of her Brother and Sister, as well as of herself.

The Girl seem'd a little mollifi'd at that, *and said*, That for herself, she knew the worst of it, she cou'd seek her Fortune; but 'twas hard her Brother and Sister shou'd suffer on her Score; and said something that was tender, and well enough, on that Account: *But* Amy *told her*, It was for her to take that into Consideration; for she wou'd let her see, that it was all her own; that she wou'd have done them all Good, but that having been us'd thus, she wou'd do no more for any of them; and that she shou'd not need to be afraid to come into her Company again, for she wou'd never give her Occasion for it any-more; *by the way*, was false in *the Girl* too, for she did venture into *Amy*'s Company again after that, *once too much; as I shall relate by itself.*

They grew cooler however, afterwards, and *Amy* carry'd her into a House[1] at *Greenwich*, where she was acquainted, and took an Occasion to leave *the Girl* in a Room a-while, to speak to the People in the House; and then going in to her again, *told her*, There she lodg'd, if she had a-mind to find her out; of if any-body else had any-thing to say to her; and so *Amy* dismiss'd her, and got rid of her again; and finding an empty Hackney-Coach in the Town, came away by Land to *London*; and the Girl going down to the Water-side, came by Boat.

---

1 A "Public House," "Pub," or Inn.

This Conversation did not answer *Amy*'s End at-all, because it did not secure the Girl from pursuing her Design of hunting me out; and tho' my indefatigable Friend the QUAKER, amus'd her three or four Days, yet I had such Notice of it at last, that I thought fit to come away from *Tunbridge* upon it, and where to go, I knew not; but, *in short*, I went to a little Village upon *Epping-Forest*, call'd *Woodford*, and took Lodgings in a Private House, where I liv'd retir'd about six Weeks, till I thought she might be tir'd of her Search, and have given me over.

Here I receiv'd an Account from my trusty QUAKER, that *the Wench* had really been at *Tunbridge*; had found out my Lodgings; and had told her Tale there in a most dismal Tone; that she had follow'd us as she thought to London; but the QUAKER had answer'd her, That she knew nothing of it, which was indeed true; and had admonish'd her to be easie, and not hunt after People of such Fashion as we were, as if we were Thieves; that she might be assur'd, that since I was not willing to see her, I wou'd not be forc'd to it; and treating me thus wou'd effectually disoblige me: And with such Discourses as these she quieted her; and she (*the* QUAKER) *added*, that she hop'd I shou'd not be troubl'd much more with her.

It was in this time that *Amy* gave me the History of her *Greenwich* Voyage, when she spoke of drowning and killing the Girl, in so serious a manner, and with such an apparent Resolution of doing it, that, *as I said*, put me in a Rage with her, so that I effectually turn'd her away from me, *as I have said above*; and she was gone; nor did she so much as tell me whither, or which Way she was gone; on the other-hand, when I came to reflect it, that now I had neither Assistant or Confident to speak to, or receive the least information from, *my Friend the* QUAKER *excepted*, it made me very uneasie.

I waited, and expected, and wonder'd from Day to Day, still thinking *Amy* wou'd one time or other, think a little, and come again, or *at least*, let me hear of her; but for ten Days together I heard nothing of her; I was so impatient, that I got neither Rest by Day, or Sleep by Night, and what to do I knew not; I durst not go to Town to the QUAKER's for fear of meeting that vexatious Creature, *my Girl*, and I cou'd get no Intelligence, where I was; so I got my Spouse, upon Pretence of wanting her Company, to take the Coach one Day, and fetch my good QUAKER to me.

When I had her, I durst ask her no Questions nor hardly knew which End of the Business to begin to talk of; but of her own accord *she told me*, that the Girl had been three or four times

haunting her, for News from me; and that she had been so troublesome, that she had been oblig'd to show herself a little angry
with her, and *at last, told her plainly,* that she need give herself no
Trouble in searching after me, by her means; for she (*the*
QUAKER) wou'd not tell her, if she knew; upon which she refrain'd
a-while: But on the other-hand, *she told me,* it was not safe for me
to send my own Coach for her to come in; for she had some
Reason to believe, that *she, (my Daughter)* watch'd her Door
Night and Day, *nay,* and watch'd her too every time she went in
and out; for she was so bent upon a Discovery, that she spar'd no
Pains; and she believ'd she had taken a Lodging very near their
House, for that Purpose.

I cou'd hardly give her a Hearing of all this, for my Eagerness
to ask for *Amy*; but I was confounded when she told me she had
heard nothing of her; 'tis impossible to express the anxious
Thoughts that rowl'd[1] about in my Mind, and continually per-
plex'd me about her; particularly, I reproach'd myself with my
Rashness, in turning away so faithful a Creature, that for so many
Years had not only been a Servant, but an Agent; and not only an
Agent, but a Friend, and a faithful Friend too.

Then I consider'd too, that *Amy* knew all the Secret History of
my Life; and had been in all the Intriegues of it, and been a Party
in both Evil and Good, and at best, there was no Policy in it; that
as it was very ungenerous and unkind, to run Things to such an
Extremity with her, and for an Occasion too, in which all the
Fault she was guilty of, was owing to her Excess of Care for my
Safety; *so* it must be only her steddy Kindness to me, and an
excess of Generous Friendship for me, that shou'd keep her from
ill-using me in return for it; which ill-using me was enough in her
Power, and might be my utter Undoing.

These Thoughts perplex'd me exceedingly; and what Course
to take, I really did not know; I began indeed, to give *Amy* quite
over, for she had now been gone above a Fortnight; and as she
had taken away all her Cloaths, and her Money too, *which was not
a little,* and so had no Occasion of that kind, to come any-more,
so she had not left any word where she was gone, or to which Part
of the World I might send to hear of her.

And I was troubl'd on another Account too, *viz.* That my
Spouse and I too had resolv'd to do very handsomely for *Amy*,
without considering what she might have got another way at-all;
but we had said nothing of it to her; and so I thought, as she had

---

1 Rolled around.

not known what was likely to fall in her way, she had not the Influence of that Expectation to make her come back.

Upon the Whole, the Perplexity of this Girl, who hunted me, as if, *like a Hound*, she had had a hot Scent, but was now at a Fault; *I say*, that Perplexity, and this other Part, of *Amy* being gone, issued in this, I resolv'd to be gone, and go over to *Holland*; there I believ'd, I shou'd be at rest: So I took Occasion one-Day to tell my Spouse, that I was afraid he might take it ill that I had amus'd him thus long, and that, *at last*, I doubted I was with-Child; and that since it was so, our Things being pack'd-up, and all in order for going to *Holland*, I wou'd go away now, when he pleas'd.

My Spouse, who was perfectly easie, whether in going or staying, left it all entirely to me; so I consider'd of it, and began to prepare again for my Voyage; but alas! I was irresolute to the last Degree; I was, for want of *Amy*, destitute; I had lost my Right-hand; she was my Steward, gather'd my Rents, *I mean my Interest-Money*, and kept my Accompts, and, *in a word*, did all my Business; and without her, *indeed*, I knew not how to go away, nor how to stay: But an Accident thrust itself in here, and that even in *Amy*'s Conduct too, which frighted me away, and without her too, in the utmost Horror and Confusion.

I have related how my faithful Friend the QUAKER, was come to me, and what Account she gave of her being continually haunted by my Daughter; and that, *as she said*, she watch'd her very Door, Night and Day; *the Truth was*, she had set a SPY to watch so effectually, that she (*the* QUAKER) neither went in or out, but *she* had Notice of it.

This was too evident, when the next Morning after she came to me, (*for I kept her all-Night*) to my unspeakable Surprize, I saw a Hackney-Coach stop at the Door where I lodg'd, and saw her (*my Daughter*) in the Coach all-alone: It was a very good Chance in the middle of a bad one, that my Husband had taken out the Coach that very Morning, and was gone to *London*; as for me, I had neither Life or Soul left in me; I was so confounded, I knew not what to do, or to say.

My *happy Visitor* had more Presence of Mind than I; *and ask'd me*, If I had made no Acquaintance among the Neighbours? I told her, Yes, there was a Lady lodg'd two Doors off, that I was very intimate with; but hast *thou* no Way out backward to go to her? *says she*: Now it happen'd there was a Back-Door in the Garden, by which we usually went and came to and from the House; so I told her of it: *Well, well*, says she, *Go out and make a Visit then, and leave the rest to me:* Away I run; told the Lady, (for I was very free there) that I was a Widow to-Day, my Spouse being gone to *London*, so I came not to visit her, but to dwell with her that Day; because also, our Landlady had got Strangers come from *London*: So having fram'd this orderly Lye, I pull'd some Work out of my Pocket, *and added*, I did not come to be Idle.

As I went out one-way, my Friend the QUAKER went the other, to receive this unwelcome Guest: The Girl made but little Ceremony; but having bid the Coachman ring at the Gate, gets down, out of the Coach, and comes to the Door; a Country-Girl going to the Door, (belonging to the House) for the QUAKER forbid any of my Maids going: *Madam* ask'd for my QUAKER by Name; and the Girl ask'd her to walk in.

Upon this, my QUAKER seeing there was no hanging back, goes immediately, but put on all the Gravity upon her Countenance, that she was Mistress of; and that was not a little indeed.

When *she* (*the* QUAKER) came into the Room, (*for they had show'd my Daughter into a little Parlour*) she kept her grave Countenance, but said not a Word; nor did *my Daughter* speak a goodwhile; but after some time, *my Girl* began, *and said*, I suppose you know me, Madam.

Yes, *says the* QUAKER, I know *thee*; and so the Dialogue went on.

Girl. Then you know my Business too.

QUAKER. No verily, I do not know any Business *thou* can'st have here with me.

Girl. Indeed my Business is not chiefly with you.

Qu. Why then do'st *thou* come after me thus far?

Girl. You know who I seek. [*And with that she cry'd.*]

Qu. But why should'st *thou* follow me for her, since *thou* know'st, that I assur'd *thee* more than once, that I knew not where *she* was?

Girl. But hop'd you cou'd.

Qu. Then *thou* must hope that I did not speak Truth; which wou'd be very wicked.

Girl. I doubt not but *she* is in this House.

Qu. If those be *thy* Thoughts, *thou* may'st enquire in the House; so *thou* hast no more Business with me; Farewell. [*Offers to go.*]

Girl. I wou'd not be uncivil; I beg you let me see her.

Qu. I am here to visit some of my Friends, and I think *thou* art not very civil in following me hither.

Girl. I came in hopes of a Discovery in my great Affair, which you know of.

Qu. *Thou* cam'st wildly indeed; I counsel *thee* to go back-again, and be easy; I shall keep my Word with *thee*, that I wou'd not meddle in it, or give *thee* any Account, if I knew it, unless I had her Orders.

Girl. If you knew my Distress, you cou'd not be so cruel.

Qu. *Thou* hast told me all *thy* Story, and I think it might be more Cruelty to tell *thee*, than not to tell *thee*; for I understand *she* is resolv'd not to see *thee*, and declares *she* is not Mother: Will'st *thou* be own'd, where *thou* hast no Relation.

Girl. O! if I cou'd but speak to her, I wou'd prove my Relation to her, so that *she* could not deny it any-longer.

Qu. Well, but *thou* can'st not come to speak with her, it seems.

Girl. I hope you will tell me if *she* is here; I had a good Account that you were come out to see her, and that *she* sent for you.

Qu. I much wonder how *thou* cou'dst have such an Account; if I had come out to see her, *thou* hast happen'd to miss the House; for I assure *thee*, *she* is not to be found in this House.

Here the Girl importun'd her again, with the utmost Earnestness, and cry'd bitterly; insomuch, that my poor QUAKER was soften'd with it, and began to perswade me to consider of it, and if it might consist with my Affairs, to see her, and hear what she had to say; but this was afterwards: *I return to the Discourse.*

The QUAKER was perplex'd with her a long time; she talk'd of sending back the Coach, and lying in the Town all-Night: This my Friend knew wou'd be very uneasie to me, but she durst not speak a Word against it; but on a sudden Thought, she offer'd a bold Stroke, which tho' dangerous if it had happen'd wrong, had its desir'd Effect.

She told her, That as for dismissing her Coach, that was as she pleas'd; she believ'd, she wou'd not easily get a Lodging in the Town; but that as she was in a strange Place, she wou'd so much befriend her, that she wou'd speak to the People of the House, that if they had room, she might have a Lodging there for one Night, rather than be forc'd back to London, before she was free to go.

This was a cunning, tho' a dangerous Step, and it succeeded accordingly, for it amus'd the Creature entirely, and she presently concluded, that really I cou'd not be there then; otherwise she wou'd never have ask'd her to lie in the House: So she grew cold again presently, as to her lodging there; *and said, No,* since it was so, She wou'd go back that Afternoon, but she wou'd come again in two or three Days, and search that, and all the Towns round, in an effectual Manner, if she stay'd a Week or two to do it; for, *in short,* if I was in *England* or *Holland,* she wou'd find me.

In Truth, *says the* QUAKER, *thou* wilt make me very hurtful to *thee*, then: Why so, *says she?* Because wherever I go, *thou* wilt put *thyself* to great Expence, and the Country to a great-deal of unnecessary Trouble: Not unnecessary, *says she*: Yes truly, *says the* QUAKER, it must be unnecessary, because 'twill be to no Purpose; I think I must abide in my own House, to save *thee* that Charge and Trouble.

She said little to that, except that, s*he said*, she wou'd give her as little Trouble as possible; but she was afraid she shou'd sometime be uneasie to her, which she hop'd she wou'd excuse: My QUAKER *told her*, She wou'd much rather excuse her, if she wou'd forbear; for that, if she wou'd believe her, she wou'd assure her, she shou'd never get any Intelligence of me, by her.

That set her into Tears again; but after a-while recovering herself, *she told her*, Perhaps she might be mistaken; and she (*the* QUAKER) shou'd watch herself, very narrowly; or she might one time or other get some Intelligence from her, whether she wou'd or no; and she was satisfy'd she had gain'd some of her by this Journey; for that if I was not in the House, I was not far off; and if I did not remove very quickly, she wou'd find me out: Very well, *says my* QUAKER; then if the Lady is not willing to see *thee*, *thou* giv'st me Notice to tell her, that she may get out of *thy* Way.

She flew out in a Rage at that, *and told my Friend*, that if she did, a Curse wou'd follow her, and her Children after her; and denounc'd[1] such horrid things upon her, as frighted the poor tender-hearted QUAKER strangely, and put her more out of Temper, than ever I saw her before; so that she resolv'd to go home the next Morning; and I, that was ten times more uneasie than she, resolv'd to follow her, and go to *London* too; which however, upon second Thoughts, I did not; but took effectual Measures not to be seen or own'd, if she came any-more; but I heard no more of her for some time.

I stay'd there about a Fortnight, and in all that time I heard no more of her, or of my QUAKER about her; but after about two Days more, I had a letter from my QUAKER, intimating that she had something of moment to say, that she cou'd not communicate by a Letter, but wish'd I wou'd give myself the Trouble to come up; directing me to come with the Coach into *Goodman's-Fields*,[2] and then walk to her Back-Door on-foot, which being left

---

1 Pronounced.
2 An area of east London.

open on purpose, the watchful Lady, if she had any Spies, could not well see me.

My Thoughts had for so long time been kept as it were, waking, that almost every-thing gave me the Allarm, and this especially, so that I· was very uneasie; but I cou'd not bring Matters to bear, to make my coming to *London* so clear to my Husband as I wou'd have done; for he lik'd the Place, and had a-mind, *he said*, to stay a little longer, if it was not against my Inclination; so I wrote my Friend the· QUAKER, Word, *That I cou'd not come to Town yet*; and that besides, I cou'd not think of being there under Spies, and afraid to look out-of-Doors; and so, *in short*, I put off going for near a Fortnight more.

At the end of that Time she wrote again, *in which she told me*, That she had not lately seen *the Impertinent Visitor*, which had been so troublesome; but that she had seen my *Trusty Agent*, *Amy*, who told her, she had cry'd for six Weeks, without Intermission; that *Amy* had given her an Account how troublesome the Creature had been; and to what Straits and Perplexities I was driven, by her hunting after, and following me from Place to Place: upon which, *Amy* had said, That notwithstanding I was angry with her, and had us'd her so hardly, for saying something about her of the same kind; yet there was an absolute Necessity of securing her, and removing her out-of-the-way; and that, *in short*, without asking my Leave, or any-body's Leave, she wou'd take Care she shou'd trouble her Mistress (*meaning me*) no more; and that after *Amy* had said so, she had indeed, never heard any-more of the Girl; so that she suppos'd *Amy* had manag'd it so well, as to put an End to it.

The innocent well-meaning Creature, my QUAKER, who was all Kindness, and Goodness, in herself, *and particularly to me*, saw nothing in this, but she thought *Amy* had found some Way to perswade her to be quiet and easie, and to give over teizing and following me, and rejoic'd in it, for my sake; as she thought nothing of any Evil herself, so she suspected none in any-body else, and was exceeding glad of having such good News to write to me: but my Thoughts of it run otherwise.

I was struck as with a Blast from Heaven, at the reading her Letter; I fell into a Fit of trembling, from Head to Foot; and I ran raving about the Room like a Mad-Woman; I had nobody to speak a Word to, to give Vent to my Passion; nor did I speak a Word for a good-while, till after it had almost overcome me: I threw myself on the Bed, and cry'd out, *Lord be merciful to me, she has murther'd my Child*; and with that, a Flood of Tears burst out, and I cry'd vehemently for above an Hour.

My Husband was very happily gone out a-hunting, so that I had the Opportunity of being alone, and to give my Passions some Vent, by which I a little recover'd myself: But after my Crying was over, then I fell in a new Rage at *Amy*; I call'd her a thousand Devils, and Monsters, and hard-hearted Tygers; I reproach'd her with her knowing that I abhor'd it, and had let her know it sufficiently, in that I had, *as it were,* kick'd her out of Doors, after so many Years Friendship and Service, only for naming it to me.

Well, after some time my Spouse came in from his Sport, and I put on the best Looks I cou'd to deceive him; but he did not take so little Notice of me, as not to see I had been crying, and that something troubl'd me; and he press'd me to tell him; I seem'd to bring it out with Reluctance, *but told him,* My Back-wardness was, more because I was asham'd that such a Trifle shou'd have any Effect upon me, than for any Weight that was in it: So *I told him,* I had been vexing myself about my Woman *Amy's* not coming again; that she might have known me better, than not believe I shou'd have been Friends with her again, *and the like*; and that, *in short,* I had lost the best Servant by my Rashness, that ever Woman had.

Well, well, *says he*, if that be all your Grief I hope you will soon shake it off; I'll warrant you, in a little-while we shall hear of Mrs. *Amy* again; and so it went off for that time: But it did not go off with me; for I was uneasie, and terrified to the last Degree, and wanted to get some farther Account of the thing: So I went away to my sure and certain Comforter the QUAKER, and there I had the whole Story of it; and the good innocent QUAKER gave me Joy of my being rid of such an unsufferable Tormentor.

Rid of her! Ay, *says I*, if I was rid of her fairly and honourably; but I don't know what *Amy* may have done; sure she ha'n't made her away: O fie! *says my* QUAKER, how can'st *thou* entertain such a Notion? *No, no,* made her away! *Amy* didn't talk like that; I dare say, *thou* may'st be easie in that, *Amy* has nothing of that in her Head, I dare say, *says she*; and so threw it, *as it were,* out of my Thoughts.

But it wou'd not do; it run in my Head continually, Night and Day I cou'd think of nothing else; and it fix'd such a Horrour of the Fact upon my Spirits, and such a Detestation of *Amy*, who I look'd upon as the Murtherer, that, *as for her*, I believe, if I cou'd have seen her, I shou'd certainly have sent her to *Newgate*, or to a worse Place, upon Suspicion; *indeed*, I think I cou'd have kill'd her with my own Hands.

As for the poor Girl herself, she was ever before my Eyes; I saw her by-Night, and by-Day; she haunted my Imagination, if she did not haunt the House; my Fancy show'd her me in a hundred Shapes and Postures; sleeping or waking, she was with me: Sometimes I thought I saw her with her Throat cut; sometimes with her Head cut, and her Brains knock'd-out; other-times hang'd up upon a Beam; another time drown'd in the Great Pond in *Camberwell*: And all these Appearances were terrifying to the last Degree; and that which was still worse, I cou'd really hear nothing of her: I sent to the Captain's Wife in *Redriff, and she answer'd me*, She was gone to her Relations in *Spittle-Fields*; I sent thither, *and they said*, she was there about three Weeks ago, but that she went out in a Coach with the Gentlewoman that us'd to be so kind to her, but whither she was gone, they knew not; for she had not been there since; I sent back the Messenger for a Description of the Woman she went out with; and they describ'd her so perfectly, that I knew it to be *Amy*, and none but *Amy*.

I sent word again, That Mrs. *Amy*, who she went out with, left her in two or three Hours; and that they shou'd search for her, for I had reason to fear she was Murther'd: This frighted them all intolerably; they believ'd *Amy* had carry'd her to pay her a Sum of Money, and that somebody had watch'd her after her having receiv'd it, and had Robb'd and Murther'd her.

I believ'd nothing of that Part; but I believ'd as it was, That whatever was done, *Amy* had done it; and that, *in short, Amy* had made her away; and I believ'd it the more, because *Amy* came no more near me, but confirm'd her Guilt by her Absence.

Upon the whole, I mourn'd thus for her, for above a Month; but finding *Amy* still come not near me, and that I must put my Affairs in a Posture that I might go to *Holland*, I open'd all my Affairs to my dear trusty Friend, the QUAKER, and plac'd her, in Matters of Trust, in the room of *Amy*, and with a heavy, bleeding Heart for my poor Girl, I embark'd with my Spouse, and all our Equipage and Goods, on-board another *Holland's-Trader*, not a Packet-Boat, and went over to *Holland*; where I arriv'd as I have said.

I must put in a Caution however, here, that you must not understand me as if I let my Friend the QUAKER into any Part of the Secret History of my former Life; nor did I commit the Grand reserv'd Article of all, to her, *viz.* That I was really the Girl's Mother, and the Lady *Roxana*; there was no need of that Part being expos'd; and it was always a Maxim with me, *That Secrets shou'd never be open'd without evident Utility*: It cou'd be of no manner of Use to me, or her to communicate that Part to her, besides she was too honest herself, to make it safe to me; for tho' she lov'd me very sincerely, and it was plain, by many Circumstances, that she did so, yet she wou'd not Lye for me upon Occasion, as *Amy* wou'd, and therefore it was not advisable on any Terms to communicate that Part; for if the Girl, or any one else, shou'd have come to her afterwards, and put it home to her, Whether she knew that I was the Girl's Mother or not; or was the same as the Lady *Roxana*, or not, she either wou'd not have denied it, or wou'd have done it with so ill a Grace, such Blushing, such Hesitations, and Faultrings in her Answers, as wou'd have put the Matter out of doubt, and betray'd herself and the Secret too.

For this Reason, *I say*, I did not discover anything of that kind to her; but I plac'd her, *as I have said*, in *Amy*'s stead, in the other Affairs of receiving Money, Interests, Rents, and the like, and she was as faithful as *Amy* cou'd be, and as diligent.

But there fell out a great Difficulty here, which I knew not how to get over; and this was, how to convey the usual Supply, or Provision and Money, to the Uncle and the other Sister, who depended, especially the Sister, upon the said Supply, for her Support; and indeed, tho' *Amy* had said rashly, that she wou'd not take any more Notice of the Sister, and wou'd leave her to perish, *as above*, yet it was neither in my Nature, or *Amy*'s either, much less was it in my Design; and therefore I resolv'd to leave the Management of what I had reserv'd for that Work, with my faithful QUAKER, but how to direct her to manage them, was the great Difficulty.

Amy had told them in so many Words, That she was not their Mother, but that she was the Maid *Amy*, that carried them to their Aunt's; that she and their Mother went over to the *East-Indies* to seek their Fortune, and that their Mother was very rich and happy; that she (*Amy*) had married in the *Indies*, but being now a Widow, and resolving to come over to *England*, their Mother had oblig'd her to enquire them out, and do for them as she had done; and that now she was resolv'd to go back to the *Indies* again; but that she had Orders from their Mother to do very handsomely by them; and, *in a word*, told them, She had 2000*l*. a-piece for them, upon Condition that they prov'd sober, and married suitably to themselves, and did not throw themselves away upon Scoundrels.

The good Family in whose Care they had been, I had resolv'd to take more than ordinary Notice of; and *Amy*, by my Order, had acquainted them with it, and oblig'd my Daughters to promise to submit to their Government, as formerly, and to be rul'd by the honest Man, as by a Father and Counsellor; and engag'd him to treat them as his Children; and to oblige him effectually to take Care of them, and to make his Old-Age comfortable both to him and his Wife, who had been so good to the Orphans: I had order'd her to settle the other 2000*l. that is to say*, the Interest of it, which was 120*l.* a Year, upon them; to be theirs for both their Lives; but to come to my two Daughters after them: This was so just, and was so prudently manag'd by *Amy*, that nothing she ever did for me, pleas'd me better: And in this Posture, leaving my two Daughters with their ancient Friend, and so coming away to me, (*as they thought to the* East Indies) she had prepar'd everything in order to her going over with me to *Holland*; and in this Posture that Matter stood when that unhappy Girl, *who I have said so much of*, broke in upon all our Measures, *as you have heard*; and by an Obstinancy never to be conquer'd or pacify'd, either with Threats or Perswasions, pursu'd her Search after me (her Mother) as I have said, till she brought me even to the Brink of Destruction, and wou'd, in all Probability, have trac'd me out at last, if *Amy* had not by the Violence of her Passion, and by a Way which I had no Knowledge of and indeed abhorr'd, put a Stop to her; of which I cannot enter into the Particulars here.

However, notwithstanding this, I cou'd not think of going away, and leaving this Work so unfinish'd as *Amy* had threatn'd to do, and for the Folly of one Child, to leave the other to starve; or to stop my determin'd Bounty to the Family I have mention'd: So, *in a word*, I committed the finishing it all, to my Faithful Friend the QUAKER, to whom I communicated as much of the old Story, as was needful to empower her to perform what *Amy* had promis'd; and to make her talk so much to the Purpose, as one employ'd more remotely than *Amy* had been, needed to do.

To this Purpose, she had first of all a full Possession of the Money; and went first to the Honest Man and his Wife, and settl'd all the Matter with them; when she talk'd of Mrs. *Amy*, she talk'd of her as one that had been empower'd by the Mother of the Girls, in the *Indies*, but was oblig'd to go back to the *Indies*, and had settl'd all sooner, if she had not been hinder'd by the obstinate Humour of the other Daughter; that she had left Instructions with her for the rest; but that the other had affronted her so much, that she was gone away without doing any-thing for her; and that now, if any-thing was done, it must be by fresh Orders from the *East-Indies*.

I need not say how punctually my new Agent acted; but which was more, she brought the Old-Man and his Wife, and my other Daughter, several times to her House, by which I had an Opportunity, being there only as a Lodger, and a Stranger, to see my other Girl, which I had never done before, since she was a little Child.

The Day I contriv'd to see them, I was dress'd-up in a QUAKER's Habit, and look'd so like a QUAKER, that it was impossible for them, who had never seen me before, to suppose I had ever been anything else; also my Way of talking was suitable enough to it, for I had learn'd that long before.

I have not Time here to take Notice what a Surprize it was to me, to see my Child; how it work'd upon my Affections; with what infinite Struggle I master'd a strong Inclination that I had to discover myself to her; how the Girl was the very Counterpart of myself, only much handsomer; and how sweetly and modestly she behav'd; how on that Occasion I resolv'd to do more for her, than I had appointed by *Amy, and the like.*

'Tis enough to mention here, that as the settling this Affair made Way for my going on-board, notwithstanding the Absence of my old Agent *Amy*; so however, I left some Hints for *Amy* too, for I did not yet despair of my hearing from her; and that if my good QUAKER shou'd ever see her again, she should let her see them; wherein particularly ordering her to leave the Affair of *Spittle-Fields* just as I had done, in the Hands of my Friend, she shou'd come away to me, upon this Condition nevertheless, that she gave full Satisfaction to my Friend the QUAKER, that she had not murther'd my Child; for if she had, *I told her,* I wou'd never see her Face more: How, notwithstanding this, she came over afterwards, without giving my Friend any of that Satisfaction, or any Account that she intended to come over.

I can say no more, but that, *as above,* being arriv'd in *Holland,* with my Spouse and his Son, *formerly mention'd,* I appear'd there with all the Splendor and Equipage suitable to our new Prospect, *as I have already observ'd.*

Here after some few Years of flourishing, and outwardly happy Circumstances, I fell into a dreadful Course of Calamities, and *Amy* also; the very Reverse of our former Good Days; the Blast of Heaven seem'd to follow the Injury done the poor Girl, by us both; and I was brought so low again, that my Repentance seem'd to be only the Consequence of my Misery, as my Misery was of my Crime.

FINIS.

Appendix A: Roxana's Shifting Identity and the Tradition of Whore Biography

[Defoe's portrait of Roxana and the fears he hopes to inspire thereby draw heavily from the tradition of whore biography that had been established during the Restoration and the remainder of the late Stuart period.]

1. From *The Lawyer's Clarke Trappan'd*[1] *by the Crafty Whore of Canterbury. Or, a True Relation of the Whole Life of Mary Mauders* (1663)[2]

After she had a little recruited her self, and was in some handsome apparel, she came to London, and took her Lodging at the Exchange-Tavern near the Stocks where she met with a Lawyers Clark, who she so sweetened on, that he soon became a Suiter to her, she telling him of her Birth and Parentage.

First, she acquainted him, that her Name was Henrietta Maria de Vulva,[3] Daughter to a Great Prince in Germany, and that when she was Two years old, she was put in a Nunnery, where she had left as many Cloaths as was worth 3000 pound.

Thence she came to her own Country in Germany, and some of the princes there would have perswaded her to marry an Old Man; which she would not do, lest her Estate (if she dyed without Issue) should go to the Nunnery; from whence (to prevent all danger) she came over to this Country, and had in her keeping as

---

1 Tricked.

2 Mary Mauders, more commonly known as Mary Carleton, created a tremendous stir in 1663 when her husband, John Carleton, charged her with bigamy. Carleton had arrived in London earlier that year masquerading as the "German Princess" Henrietta Maria de Vulva. Both Carleton and his family were ambitious and greedy. They sought to take advantage of the apparent princess's vulnerability and lure her into marriage, thus gaining for themselves aristocratic status and great wealth. When the Carletons discovered they had been conned, they were furious and charged Mary Carleton with bigamy, a capital offense. However, because the Carletons were unable to produce Mary's previous husband, she was acquitted. It is with considerable chagrin that Roxana acknowledges the parallels between her own life and that of Mary Carleton.

3 Actually, Maria de Wolway. This version of Carleton's pseudonym is obviously a snide allusion to her sexual promiscuity.

many Jewels as were judg'd by a Gold-Smith (whom they sent for) to be worth three thousand pound.

She also told him, That she had a Coach and six Flanders Mares coming over, with store of her Money, her Estate being ten or twelve thousand pounds per annum: and the better to carry on her Design, she said she had a Steward in Germany, to whom she fram'd a Letter which was sent by the Post, and an Answer return'd to this effect, viz.

Madam, The money you sent for is not yet ready, but I have gathered three thousand pounds, which shall come by the next Ship; and also your Coach and six Horses with it, which made the story so plain, as many wise Heads (besides the fresh-water[1] Lad) believed it to be truth. Hereupon his Friends made up the Match, and upon Easter-Day their Nuptual was solemnized of this young Lord and Lady; for which purpose a gown was bought her of fifty five pound, besides other Necessaries the young Lord having the Lackey to wait on him, all things being performed in a noble manner, to the admiration of all his old Acquaintance.

The Wedding being done, they provided Coaches for their Friends; and went to Barnet,[2] where they continued making merry till Tuesday following; spending in so high a nature, as some will repent their Acquaintance with this new German Lady, who spake Dutch so exactly, that she deceived many, and but little English, which was so profuse, and in such a broken manner, as they could hardly understand her.

Tuesday she came back and pretending she had great friends at Court, her young Lord desired to accompany her thither; but she refused that proposition, till her own Coach and Horses came.

Her Deportment was very noble, and her Heart open, for passing by New-Gate, (the old castle of her safety[3]) she gave her Lackey half a Crown to put into the Prisoners Bag.

Since this, one Clark a Porter, (who plyes at Warwick-Lane end) carried her a Letter, which she gave notice he should come up to her Bed-Chamber, where she askt what he would have for the Letter, eight pence Madam, and shall please you; her Lady-ship answer'd that was too little and gave him 12d, asking him to drink her Lords health, which he accepted of; upon which she call'd for a Bottle of Sack,[4] & after he had drank that, made him

---

1 Naïve.

2 An outer borough, now on the northwest edge of London.

3 Newgate was a prison.

4 Wine, imported from Spain or the Canary Islands.

drink her health till the bottle was out and the poor Porter went reeling home.

The Nuptual being past, and all things concluded, she was designed to make her pack and be gone; but a Shoe-maker coming in, who had formerly wrought with her Husband in Canterbury, seeing her, said to some of the House, She was a Whore: They replyed, He had best have a care what he said, for she was a person of Honour, But he still persisted and said she was a Whore, and he'd prov'd her a whore: With which being brought to the Room, he look'd in her face, and said she was the same person he took her for, and that he wrought with her Husband who was a Shoe-maker in Canterbury, and that she had another Fidler,[1] who is a Souldier in Dover Castle.

Hereupon she was carried before a Justice and examined, and her Jewels and Rings were all found Counterfeit; upon which she was committed to the Gate-House,[2] from whence (if her first Husband appear) she will be transported to her old Quarter at New-Gate, and finish her course at Paddington, if she do not Cheat Squire Dun of his right and Title; which is just Doom for all such Impudent Pieces of Iniquity.

2. From *The London Jilt: Or, The Politick Whore. Shewing All the Artifices and Strategems which the Ladies of Pleasure make use of for the Intriguing and Decoying of Men; Interwoven with several Pleasant Stories of the Misses Ingenious Performances* **(1683)**

To the Reader.
Courteous Reader,

Notwithstanding the many Discoveries that have been made by several Authors in Pieces of this Nature, of the Subtilties and Cheats that the Misses of this Town put upon Men, yet we still dayly see that they find Cullyes[3] enough to be imposed upon, to the decay and ruine both of their Health, their Fortune and Reputation. Wherefore a Mirrour of their damned Wheadling Arts, and Cursed Devices, cannot be too often set before the Eyes of Mankind, that so the easy Fops themselves may take a warning, and be diverted from falling into their Destructive Snare. For thou hast here, Reader, the Jilt displayed in her true

---

1 Slang for another lover.
2 A prison.
3 Gullible targets.

Colours, all her Wheadling and Treacherous Decoys laid open. And in short, thou hast not only the Bulcker[1] but the fine London Misses Picture drawn to the Life. Shee is here set before thee as a Beacon to warn thee of the Shoales and Quick-sands, on which thou wilt of necessity Shipwrack thy All, if thou blindly and willfully continuest and perseverest in steering that Course of Female Debauchery, which will inevitably prove at length thy utter Destruction. This perhaps will be allowed to be no small Piece of Service, if it may be a means of dissuading, but some few from that Roving, Libertine, Lascivious Course of Life, and contribute but to the making Men be upon their Guard against all Female Ambauscdoes.[2] And indeed what greater Folly can there be than to venture one's All in such rotten Bottoms, and at length become the Horrour and Detestation of all the World, only for a Momentary Pleasure, and which in truth cannot well be termed Pleasure, considering what filthy, nasty, and stinking Carcasses, are the best and finest of our Common Whores? A Whore is but a Close-stool[3] to Man, or a Common-shoar[4] that receives all manners of Filth, she's like a Barber's Chair, no sooner one's out, but t'others in, or as another has likened 'em to Sampson's Foxes, who carry fire in their Tails to burn the standing Corn.[5] And though the danger does so vastly surpass the Delight that can be had in the Conversation and Enjoyment of the most charming of 'em all, yet we see foolish silly Men such easy Fops, as to be lured by their False Attractions into that bitter Trap of theirs, which is ever followed or attended with all manner of Diseases, both Mind and Body. Thus sure the Publick cannot blame or Condemn a Man, for drawing his Pen in so necessary an occasion, expecially at this time, when the Trade of Jilting is grown so ripe, that Warnings of this kind cannot be too often repeated, nor instances of their Devilish Pranks and Practices too frequently proclaim'd, that so Men may be as it were teiz'd[6] into good sense and their own security. Not that this Piece had the Dullness and Gravity of a Sermon. It shows you the Miss revelling in her Culley's[7] Arms, it shows her displaying all her Arts to entice, seduce and ensnare Mankind, and what thou thoughtest fondness of thy Person, thou wilt find only a damn'd unbounded self-interest, and an insatiable Avidity of Money; thou wilt discover her giving

---

1 A low-life person, petty thief, street-walker, whore.
2 Misspelled. Ambuscado, someone who sets traps, ambushes.
3 A stool on which to hang clothes.
4 Idiosyncratic spelling of shore.
5 A mutant strain of red fox that lacks the long guard hairs of the dominant form and has a tightly curled undercoat.
6 Persuaded.
7 A love or client who is cheated by a whore.

everyone Entertainment suitable to the largeness of their Purses, and the Extravagances of their Expences. But when the weak and Credulous Fop has spent his All upon her, thou wilt see him shee so much before Cherish'd and Indulg'd shut out of Door, scorn'd and despis'd by her, and treated with all manner of Infamy and Contempt. Thus all her Carriage[1] *that was so tender and endearing while that thou lavish'd thy Stock and Fortune upon her, when this once begins to fail, thou wilt find her Favours and Affection decay and languish at the same time. Wherefore Reader, take this seasonable Advice, leave off in time that lewd Course of Life, and be not bubled*[2] *by Detestable Creatures, that are so little worthy of thy Amusement and Application. Avoid all their Cursed Allurement, and be mindful that Snake lies concealed under such bewitching Appearances, and how beautiful and attractive soever the outside of the Apple may be, that it is Rotten and Pestilent at Core. But it is time* Reader, *that thou seest our Jilt exposed naked in all her Deformities, that it may so create a horrour in thee for what thou before so eagerly pursuedst, and so fondly adoredst. Not but that this Narrative of her Stratagems and Artifices will afford thee a peculiar delight and satisfaction, being agreeably interwoven with Pleasant Stories of her Wiles and Juggles, and in short, a perfect account of her Performances in the Art of winning others and her self. If this undertaking prove but as beneficial in curbing the bad and unlawful inclinations of Men, as the Author design'd it, the Pains will be sufficiently rewarded, that have been taken for thy Good, thy Diversion and Service.*

Farewel.

★★★

London is the place of my Birth, where my Father, or at least the Man my Mother was pleased to honour with that Title, had been a Merchant until the Age of thirty two Years; but his fortune taking an other bias[3] about that time, the good Man found himself obliged, that he might not be oppress'd with Poverty, after he had been for a while in the *Fryars*,[4] and had Compounded with his Creditors, to set up a Tipling House.[5]

---

1 Demeanor.
2 Cheated or deceived.
3 Direction.
4 Likely an area of London where debtors could take refuge from their creditors.
5 A place where alcohol was served.

Of these two Persons so full of Probity, was I the only Daughter, and for that reason, I was brought up in some sort of Libertinism; for to be an only Child, and to be rendred wanton, are two things which cannot be well separated. I was about five years old, when my Father was transformed from a Merchant into a Victualler, and I was sent to School to write and learn *French*, as also to Dance; and for that purpose, I can assure you, that my Parents strain'd their Purse, but were nevertheless well enough satisfied since it flatter'd their Ambition.[1]

★★★

Tho that my Territory was so frequently cultivated by five Men; and that by this Reason it seem'd there could not arise any Fruit, but by reason that I figured to my self, that the too great abundance of Humidity would be capable of stifling it in its Birth. Nevertheless, after having led this Life six Months, I began to perceive I was with Child. It is certain that I was not over-joyed; for I imagine, that this would not come out so commodiously, nor so easily as it went in; and that my Beauty, which I was provided with after a reasonable passable manner, would receive great Injury thereby: But since such was the State of Affairs, and that I could not hinder the Progress but by wicked and unlawful means, I resolved to make use of it to my best Advantage; and as soon as *Valere* came to my Lodging, I let him know how things stood with me. This poor Man, really imagining that he had got the Child, was so transported with Joy, that he hardly knew what he did: He hung about my Neck, and having given me at least a thousand Kisses, he opened his Purse of Gold, and gave me Fifteen Guinneys,[2] for me to begin with preparing Clouts[3] and Necessaries for my Child; and 'tis certain this was only a Beginning; for this Appanage[4] cost him afterwards thrice that Sum, by reason there was not a Clout but was of the finest Cloth, and besides garnished with Laces.

Besides this Sum, I did what I could to get twice as much from my other Lovers: For as the one knew nothing of the other, I found it no difficult matter to make each of them believe that he

---

1 The jilt's description of her early education bears a striking resemblance to Roxana's description of her early education.

2 Guineas.

3 Clothes.

4 Gift.

had got at least half the Child, and by Consequence was obliged to buy something towards the Appanage of the Child. I endeavoured also to make them believe, that *Valere* could not contribute much thereto; and though they seemed not to believe me in this, yet I could easily perceive by their Looks, that they were not displeased at this Discourse; Thus are these young men so easie and credulous in point of getting Children....

At length the Term of *Lying in* being come, I fell into Labour one *Wednesday* Noon with such dreadful Pains, as if I had had my Entrails torn out of my Body, which made me curse the Hours and Day that I suffer'd that unruly Member to rummage my Body, just as a Number of silly women do in such like Occasions.

I was in this lamentable Condition, crying and groaning until the *Saturday* following at which time I was delivered of a dead Child; which by reason of the Compressions and Contorsions of my Body, seem'd so blew and deformed, that one could hardly perceive it had the Form of a humane Figure. I lay aside its resembling *Valere*, who fancied himself the Father of it; but it very much resembled me so well in one part, except the difference there was in Bigness and Length; but without doubt, with Time and frequent use of it, there would have been wrought great Alterations.

Valere was very sad upon the Death of his little imaginary Girle; so that he was hardly to be comforted; for my part, I pretended likewise to be very much afflicted, that I might please him, tho' indeed I was over-joyed; For I easily foresaw, that it was not very convenient for a Maiden of my Circumstances to have Children; and besides, I do not believe that there is a Miss in all this City, who will say, that I am mistaken in this Matter, by reason that this young Baggage gives so much trouble, and is attended with so many Inconveniences, that most of our time is lost upon it; and we must abandon our own Affairs.

3. From *The Whores Rhetorick, Calculated to the Meridian of London; And Conformed to the Rules of Art* (1683)[1]

M.C. The Regular Priests of the *Romish* Church[2] do seemingly take three Vows of Chastity, Poverty, and Obedience; but instead of these they wisely devote themselves to Luxury, and avarice, and Dissimulation; in like manner you must put on a seeming modesty, even when you exercise the most essential parts of your Profession: you must pretend at contempt of money, that your amorous caresses are purely the effects of love; and a counterfeit humility, as oft as the occasion may require: when in the mean time, your main, and indeed sole aim must be to impose on all men, never to stick at anything how licentious soever, that may forward your designs or interest: your avarice must be insatiable, you must therefore never fly[3] any occasion of increasing your stock; and your whole life must be one continued act of dissimulation.

Dor. I will obey you.

M.C. On these foundations I intend to superstruct my subsequent discourse; and will for the most part, confine my self to those Doctrines, that may seem to animate a young handsome Lady in this Trade, such as I have chose for a Disciple: without regarding the married Women, Widow, or superficial Maid; who do not obey the dictates of interest, but prostitute themselves merely to gratifie their libidinous appetites. Neither is this discourse directed to Whores, that have already spent some considerable time in the exercise of their Function. To those whom either years, or some personal blemish had made less agreeable, I give only this general caution, to conceal with all possible industry their particular imperfections; and to supply their wants as far as is possible, with abundance of good Chat, rich Cloaths, Flattery, endearing Expressions, and some particular Dexterities to please their Lovers: after all, they will be forced to submit to harder terms than I shall ever suffer you to comply with.

---

1 Published in the same year that Roxana claims to have arrived in England, *The Whores Rhetorick* dramatizes a conversation between the imaginary character Dorothea and the real-life bawd, Madam Cresswell. Cresswell was a notorious Whig partisan during the Restoration and aligned herself politically with men like Sir Thomas Player and Sir Robert Clayton, Roxana's financial advisor. Cresswell's advice to Dorothea closely parallels Roxana's own justifications for rejecting marriage.

2 Roman Catholic Church.

3 Flee.

Dor. I thank you good Mother, in that you are so sensible of my interest as to square your Discourse to my particular necessities; but I am confident your instructions, though directed to me, may be likewise profitable to the cunningest, and most experienced Whore living.

M.C. There is a mighty necessity, Daughter, that you in all points conform yourself to those obligations your Profession will impose upon you in ways far different from the ordinary artifices of our Sex. We are all, it is true, naturally inclined to weave fraudulent webs, and to be likewise overjoyed at the success of our experiments: but a Whore ought to exceed others of her Sex in these undertakings; as many degrees as her opportunities of knowledge are greater, and her necessities of living by such subtleties may seem to require. She moves in a higher sphere, than the rest of Women; and her actions ought to seem publick-spirited; though Statesman-like, she should contrive them all to meet in the centre of her own particular advantage: You must be furnished with great variety of words, and even those that are most familiar and trivial, to enable you to entertain your Lovers on all subjects: still complying in the choice of the matter with their various tempers. This part of Rhetorick is necessary to fit you all occasions, to use ambiguous expressions, and for ornament sometimes, synonymous terms; to equivocate, vary and double, according to your fancy and the present circumstances: all which do extreamly enhaunce the value of your words; and add a particular gallantry to your discourse. A Whores language in the lascivious dialect, is ever to please the present lover; who always coming to feed on the same dish, ought to enjoy the variety of discourse, in such sort that he be not cloyed with his fare, and by consequence she lose efficacy and main end of her eloquence. You must seem altogether insatiable in pleasing your lover; and in multiplying his delight; ever pretending to receive therein your self particular satisfaction; if his experience has taught him divers forms in the enjoyment, gratifie him in condescending to his humour therein: provided his particular generosity challenge this particular treatment. During these ravishing minutes be not wanting to afford him a multiplicity of strict imbraces: let your caresses, and ecstasies be sometimes inclining to a violent, sometimes slow and remiss; but still such as may seem natural, without any artificial constraint, that so he may believe you ravished beyond your self: and be thought, not only to feed him with your body, but to have given likewise your very Soul. Let this be attended with some dying words, soft murmering sighs, as may be just overheard by your lover. Redoubling the knots of hands and feet, let the Comedy end with some sweet kisses, in which let your tongue gently glide within his lips; that you may seem to have transmitted your Soul that way; whilst he infuses his, in return, at another door. After the disjunction, be very industrious to drive away that repentance, or melancholy rather, which naturally succeeds fruition: to hinder him from nauseating those delights, even for the space of one minute: on which depend the main force of all your perswasions. It will not be amiss, during this interval, to divert him with an aery Song, or some jocular, and facetious Novel, that may remove all marks of sadness, and prepare him for a second assault. When he is ready to depart, has payed for his pleasure (for I still suppose) and you expect no more of his liberality for that time, be sure to dismiss him with some extraordinary Epilogue, that may soon enforce a return; let your kisses be on this occasion more savory than usual, and your dalliances so exquisite as may create in him strong, and invincible desires, to buy more of your fruit, tho' you should be so cruel as to raise the price. Those are still esteemed the choicest, and are ever the dearest cakes, which do not cloy the Stomach; but only whet its edge, and prepare it for a new meal. Promise him the next time greater satisfaction, and more delicious fare; make him believe the pleasures you disperse are so refined and spiritualized, that they will always improve by a repetition, and increase in proportion, as they become familiar by frequent practice. Give him to understand your Treasure is inexhaustible, and that you will never want sufficient reserves; being thus intangled in the net, he will fancy himself always a Prisoner, but when your soft hands loose the knot, and make him free; he will believe every Hour an Age till he may satiate his longing appetite, and revive his Soul with the delicacies of the same repast. Men are oft of opinion, that Women were made only for their enjoyment; so by consequence they will too frequently despise them when the pleasure is over, as they do meat on a full Stomach. Consider then how nearly it concerns you to know some extraordinary arts to engage your Lovers, and make them indivisibly yours (if I may so say) even after the act of separation. Your graces must be strong, and your charms irresistible to oblige them to continue their conversation; which must after a time redound[1] to your profit and advantage. Use all men and at all times with terms of highest civility, a feigned kindness, and a pretended affection can suggest:

---

1 Overflow.

unless some particular disobligation may require the contrary; and then let your resentments be shewed in a stately and scornful contempt; but this I will only allow, when all hopes of further gain are taken away; when your Votary has hardened his heart, not to be reclaimed by reason, nor dissolved by tears. With those that are familiar and constant Customers you must learn a particular deportment. When you find your Minion imparadised in pleasure, drowned in excess of love, and now scarce able to bear the weight of the joy, it will be then fit you should experiment the vertue of your well regulated note, insinuate some considerable request, for the which you must never want some plausible pretence: at one time you shall feign that some of your moveables of value are pawned for a sum of money (which must be proportioned to his temper and ability) which if not redeemed by a certain day, then at hand, will be irrecoverably lost; at another time, give him to believe the loss of a Pendant, Ring, or such like utensil, for which you have a singular value, not for the thing it self, but lest you should be thought careless of the Donors favour who must be some particular relation, whom you would by no means disoblige. You may sometimes complain of an obligation that lyes upon you, to pay a debt at such a day; seem sensible of your present disability, and the damage your credit will receive thereby, your creditor being one of your main benefactors. At another opportunity you must put on a borrowing face, but with a firm intent to make no restitution. If your lover have a retentive faculty, abound with protestations of good will, and excuse with impotence, the contrariety of effects; put him fairly to it by way of being security: and be sure never to want a friend on those occasions, that will lend money, having a hint before hand, of the stanchness of the person he is to have as surety; with these and the like inventions, you must strive to keep your Purse, and supply the contingencies of any extraordinary charge: for all these purposes take care your Maid be wisely pre-instructed to shew her Mistress wholly disinterested, who, she is sure, would not stoop beneath her *decorum*,[1] to make any such request, were not her kindness and familiarity the occasions of it. It will be necessary your Servant should on occasion to act the buffoon, or at least many capricious and pleasant humours: that so under the notion of burlesque, all things being permitted her, she may by way of jest, use her earnest endeavors to fleece the Rivals: her desires must be either moderate, or more exorbitant, according to

---

1 Beneath her dignity.

the discretion of the amorous guest. Some are pretty well, or perniciously rather, armed against Whores wit: and dare be so hardy, to resist all the shocks of her importunities: but much the greater number, are prone to yield in all these points if discreetly managed; and not a few so weak, as to be imposed on by the Legerdemains[1] of a Servant. Above all things see that your snares be not detected, before you have caught the Woodcock; for if the net be foreseen, even those shallow Animals can avoid the danger. Whatever is acquired by these means may be reckoned as clear gain, in regard the purchase comes in without trouble; so it is trying mens generosity and good nature: when ever a repulse happens in the way, step lightly over it without any apparent regard, or the least trip. There is incertainty in all traffick; one that will build on no less than infallibility, wants faith, and must never expect any considerable return: but she that can run the risque, who can look danger in the face, with a favourable gale, may arrive at some degree of eminence, and come off with multiplyed gain. The Documents are good, but yet the rules of commerce are voluble: in as much as there are variety of contracts with the like variety of Persons, it is impossible to meet at all times, one and the same humour: however Daughter, be sure to trade in the bank of subtilty, that so your cast may still increase, and your profit advance agreeably to your own desires.

Dor. What do I hear! I had thoughts to interrupt you several times before you came to this period, but my ears were so busie, I could not make use of my Tongue.

M.C. You must look on it as the great business of your life, to please others, and enrich your self. Fancy your self subjugated by an inevitable decree to satisfie any the most lascivious appetite, provided he comes with Gold in his Purse, and is willing to purchase at your rates. You must forget the distinction of Gentleman, and Mechanick;[2] but let men be divided in your Books under the names of Poor, Rich, Liberal, and Niggardly. I would indeed have you only seen with first rate Gallants, in the face of the Sun, and in publick places, but under the shelter of darkness, and covert of the night, lower your Sail, and condescend to the embraces of inferiour persons, who have oft-times a larger Fond,[3] and are easier induced to comply with a Ladies humour. The Emperour that raised a Tax from Piss, to confute one that thought it beneath

---

1 Persuasions.
2 Someone who works with their hands.
3 Fund.

and inconsistent with the dignity of a Prince, produced a heap of Gold that came into his Treasury by that Imposition; *Does this,* says he, *stink of the excrement whence it was drained?* Thereby shewing, that money removes all stench, from the meanest action, by virtue of its purging quality. Carry yourself at all times with a superficial stateliness, to gain respect, and avoid contempt: but remember to bate some degrees of this gravity, if it either may offend, or be discovered by a discerning Lover. You must in your Cloaths appear beyond all measure rich and magnificent. Young sparks (nay and some that have arrived at years of discretion) do judge of one anothers Wit and Parts, by their dress and garb: so they ever conclude a Woman's attractives to increase, with the glittering of fine Cloaths, and sumptuous Lodgings. Though I am sure the Coxcombs[1] are almost equally astray in both particulars: I would have your Cloaths rather seem grave than gawdy, yet such as may in their splendour shew something of the fantastical, and notwithstanding preserve a *decorum.* Those Whores are very ill advised, and do ever in short time become crack't and bankrupt in their reputation, who for the humour of strutting about, and to be thought frolicsome, brisk, and gay, do deviate from the strict rules of sobriety, they ought to observe, into a contrary excess of lewdness and obscenity: they hereby precipitate themselves into open danger, and lose their aim, which was thereby to gain upon their amorous Servants, by falling into open contempt, because impudence was of the same stamp. She ever sells most Ware, and at the best rate, who can handsomely shew its worth, but does not seem too fond of the Buyer. Men will be sure to respect those most, who set a high value on themselves, and their own goods. They deal with Women as they do with their Habberdashers; let the Shop be in a gentile[2] part of the Town, have a fair outside, let the Seller be well stored with Shop-Rhetorick, and then he that asks most, is certainly esteemed to vend the best Commodities. But on a seeming veneration for Piety and Religion, especially before Strangers, whereby you will be ever valued even by those that have themselves laid aside those considerations; but much more by Men of generous and free thoughts. By no means give your self the liberty of Swearing or drinking to excess; unless on some particular occasion, a young Bubble[3] may encourage you thereto, who is free of his money, and in love with

---

1 Arrogant young men.
2 Genteel.
3 Client.

those insipid and unprofitable vices. As to the various modes of fine dressing, Singing, Niceties to be observed in Eating, and Drinking, Behaviour and Conversation; I have already told you, that some time is to be laid aside for the learning of these, before you can safely begin the World, all which you must be instructed in at another School.... For that, Daughter, I must tell you: a Whore is a Whore, but Whore is not a Woman; as being obliged to relinquish all those frailties that render the Sex weak and contemptible. A Whore ought not to think of her own pleasure, but how to gratifie her Bedfellow in his sensitive desires: She must mind her interest not her sport; the Lovers sport, the ruine of his interest and the emptying his Purse. The unthinking part of Women place all their worldly happiness in the centre of venereal Pastimes,[1] and they are *Mahometans*[2] so far as to wish a continuance of them in the world to come; though all these things are enjoyed by Wolves, Bears, Cats, Dogs and Rats, in an equal if not a larger measure than what we can pretend to.

---

1 Pleasures of the flesh.
2 Muslims.

Appendix B: Women's Work

[One of the questions raised by *Roxana* is why her *modus vivendi*—method of living—is not viewed as legitimate work. Part of the answer lies in the way women of the commonality,[1] who worked either as hawkers, artisans, or servants, were vilified in late seventeenth-century England.]

1. *A True Copie of the Petition of the Gentlewomen, and Tradesmens-Wives, in and About the City of London* (1641)[2]

To the Honourable Knights, Citizens and Burgesses, of the House of Commons assembled in Parliament.

The most humble Petition of the Gentlewomen, Tradesmens wives, and many others of the Female Sex, all Inhabitants of the Citie of London, and the Suburbs thereof.
With lowest submission shewing,

That we also with all thankfull humility acknowledging the unwearied paines, care and great charge, besides hazard of health and life, which you the noble worthies of this honourable and renowned Assembly have undergone, for the safety both of Church and Commonwealth, for a long time already past; for which not only we your humble Petitioners, and all well affected in this Kingdome, but also all other good Christians are bound now and at all times to acknowledge; yet not withstanding that many worthy deeds have been done by you, great danger and feare do still attend us, & will, as long as Popish Lords & and

---

1 The phrase "commonality" referred specifically to anyone in English society who did not belong to the aristocracy or the church.

2 The revolutionary years (1640-59) were times of great economic hardship for the citizens of England, and it was not uncommon for women to address Parliament for relief. However, the Petition of tradesmen's wives is one of the rare non-satirical documents during the seventeenth century to identify women by their occupation. Here, non-elite women ask Parliament to intervene and continue to purge the country of the influence of Catholics, to which they attribute their difficulties, including threats to their children, loss of their husbands, and threats of sexual violence. The sense of political entitlement here was often viewed as the root of women's non-compliance during the later seventeenth century.

superstitious Bishops are suffered to have their voice in the House of Peers, and that accursed and abominable Idole of the Masse suffered in the Kingdome,[1] and that Arch-enemy of our prosperity and Reformation lyeth in the Tower, yet not receiving his deserved punishment.

All these under correction, gives us great cause to suspect, that God is angry with us, and to be the chiefe causes why your pious indeavours for a further Reformation proceedeth not with that successe as you desire, and is most earnestly prayed for of all that wish well to true Religion, and the florishing estate both of King and Kingdome; the insolencies of the Papists and their abbettors, raiseth a just feare and suspicion of sowing sedition, and breaking out into bloody persecution in this Kingdome, as they have done in Ireland,[2] the thoughts of which sad and barbarous events, maketh our tender hearts to melt within us, forcing us humbly to Petition to this honourable Assembly, to make safe provision for your selves and us, before it be too late. And whereas we, whose hearts have joyned cheerefully with all those Petitions which have been exhibited unto you in the behalfe of the purity of Religion, and the liberty of our Husbands persons and estates, recounting our selves to have an interest in the common priviledges with them, doe with the same confidence assure our selves to finde the same gracious acceptance with you, for easing of those greivances, which in regard of our fraile condition, do more neerly concerne us, and do deeply terrifie our soules: our Domesticall[3] dangers with which this Kingdome is so much distracted, especially growing on us from those treacherous and wicked attempts already are such, as we finde our selves to have as deepe a share as any other.

We cannot but tremble at the very thoughts of the horrid and hideous facts which modesty forbids us now to name, occasioned by the bloody Warres in Germany, his Majesties late Northern Army, how often did it affright our hearts, whilst their violence began to break out so furiously upon the persons of those, whose Husbands or Parents were not able to rescue: we wish we had no cause to speake of those insolencies, and savage usage and un-

---

1 Probably a reference to Archbishop William Laud who persecuted Puritans and was viewed as a crypto-Catholic. Laud was tried by the House of Commons and executed in 1645.

2 In October 1641 Irish Catholics rose up against English Protestant settlers and massacred them.

3 Civil War.

heard of rapes, exercised upon our Sex in Ireland, and have we not just cause to feare they will prove the forerunners of our ruine, except Almighty God by the wisdome and care of this Parliament be pleased to succor us, our Husbands and Children, which are as deere and tender unto us, as the lives and blood of our hearts, to see them murthered and mangled and cut in pieces before our eyes, to see our Children dashed against the stones, and the Mothers milk mingled with the Infants blood, running down the streets; to see our Houses on flaming fire over our heads: oh how dreadfull would this be! we thought it misery enough (though nothing to that we have just cause to feare) but few yeares since for some of our Sex, by unjust divisions from their bosome comforts, to be rendred in a manner Widdowes, and the children Fatherlesse, Husbands were Imprisoned from the Society of their wives, even against the Lawes of God and Nature; and little Infants suffered in their Fathers' banishments: thousands of our deerest friends have been compelled to fly from Episcopall persecutions[1] into desert places amongst wilde Beasts, there finding more favour then in their native soyle,[2] and in the midst of all their sorrowes, such hath the pity of the Prelates[3] been, that our cries could never enter into their eares or hearts, nor yet through multitudes of obstructions could never have accesse or come nigh to those Royall mercies of our most gracious Soveraigne, which we confidently hope, would have relieved us: but after all these pressures ended, we humbly signifie, that our present feares are, that unlesse the blood-thirsty faction of the Papists and Prelates be hindered in their designes, our selves here in England as well as they in Ireland, shall be exposed to that misery which is more intollerable then that which is already past, as namely to the rage not of men alone, but of Divel's incarnate, (as we may so say) besides the thraldome of our soules and consciences in matters concerning God, which of all things are most deare unto us.

Now the remembrance of all these fearfell accidents aforementioned, do strongly move us from the example of the woman of Tekoa[4] to fall submissively at the feete of his Majestie, our

---

1 Many Puritans and sectarians were singled out for persecution by the Anglican church in the years just before the civil wars.

2 Soil.

3 Church leaders.

4 A reference to 2 *Samuel* 14:1-20, referring to women who petitioned David for redress of wrongs committed against their family.

dread Soveraigne, and cry Helpe O King, helpe o ye the noble Worthies now sitting in Parliament: And we humbly beseech you, that you will be a meanes to his Majestie and the House of Peeres,[1] that they will be pleased to take our heart breaking grievances into timely consideration, and to adde strength & incouragement to your noble indeavours, and further that you would move his Majesty with our humble requests, that he would be graciously pleased according to the example of the good King Asa,[2] to purge both the Court and Kingdome of that great Idolatrous Service of the Masse, which is tollerated in the Queenes Court, this sinne (as we conceive) is able to draw downe a greater curse upon the whole Kingdome, then all your noble and pious indeavours can prevent, which was the cause that the good and pious King Asa would not suffer Idolatry in his own Mother, whose example if it shall please his Majesties gracious goodnesse to follow, in puting downe Popery and Idolatry both in great and small, in Court and in the Kingdome throughout, to subdue the Papists and their abetters, and by taking away the power of the Prelates, whose government by long and wofull experience we have found to be against the liberty of our conscience and the freedome of the Gospell, and the sincere profession and practice thereof, then shall our feares be removed, and we may expect that God will power downe his blessings in abundance both upon his Majesty, and upon this Honourable Assembly, and upon the whole Land.

For which your new Petitioners shall pray affectionately.

The Reasons follow.

It may be thought strange, and unbeseeming our sex to shew our selves by way of Petition to this Honourable Assembly: but the matter being rightly considered, of the right and interest we have in the common and publique cause of the Church, it will, as we conceive (under correction) be found a duty commanded and required.

First, because Christ hath purchased us at as deare a rate as he hath done Men, and therfore requireth the like obedience for the same mercy as of men.

Secondly, because in the free enjoying of Christ in his own Laws, and a flourishing estate of the Church and Commonwealth, consisteth the happinesse of Women as well as Men.

---

1 House of Lords.
2 An ancient Hebrew king who destroyed idols. 1 *Kings* 15.

Thirdly, because Women are sharers in the common Calamities that accompany both Church and Common-Wealth, when oppression is exercised over the Church or Kingdome wherein they live; and an unlimited power have been given to Prelates to exercise authority over the Consciences of Women, as well as Men; witnesse Newgate, Smithfield, and other places of persecution,[1] wherein Women as well as Men have felt the smart of their fury.

Neither are we left without example in Scripture, for when the state of the Church, in the time of King Ahasuerus was by the bloody enemies thereof sought to be utterly destroyed, we find that Ester the Queen[2] and her Mayds fasted and prayed, and that Ester petitioned to the King in the behalfe of the Church: and though she enterprised this duty with the hazard of her own life, being contrary to the Law to appeare before the King before she were sent for, yet her love to the Church carryed her thorow all difficulties, to the performance of that duty.

On which grounds we were imboldned to present our humble Petition into this Honourable Assembly, not weighing the reproaches which may and are by many cast upon us, who (not well weighing the premisses) scoffe and deride our good intent. We doe it not out of any selfe conceit, or pride of heart, as seeking to equall ourselves with Men, either in Authority or wisdome: But according to our places to discharge that duty we owe to God, and the cause of the Church, as farre as lyeth in us, following herein the example of the Men, which have gone in this duty before us.

A relation of the manner how it was delivered, with their Answer, sent by Mr. Pym.[3]

This Petition, with their Reasons, was delivered the 4th of Feb. 1641 by Mris[4] Anne Stagg, a Gentlewoman and Brewers Wife, and many others with her of like rank and quality, which when they had delivered it, after some time spent in reading of it, the Honourable Assembly sent them an Answer by Mr Pym, which was performed in this manner.

---

1 Places where Protestant martyrs had been executed under Mary I.
2 Esther was the Jewish wife of the Persian king Ahasuerus (Xerxes I) who had ordered the annihilation of all Jews in ancient Persia. Esther interceded and persuaded her husband to lift the order.
3 John Pym was a prominent member of Parliament and architect of Parliament's victory over Charles I.
4 Abbreviation for Mistress.

Mr Pym came to the Commons doore, and called for the Women, and spake unto them in these words: Good Women, your Petition and the Reasons have been read in the House; and is very thankfully accepted of, and is come in a seasonable time: You shall (God Willing) receive from us all the satisfaction which we can possibly give to your just and lawfull desires. We intreat you to repaire to your Houses, and turne your Petition which you have delivered here, into Prayeres at home for us; for we have been, are, and shall be (to our utmost power) ready to believe you, your Husbands, and Children, and to perform the trust committed unto us, towards God, our King and Countrey, as becometh faithfull Christians and Loyall Subjects.

2. Mary Collier, *The Woman's Labour: An Epistle to Mr. Stephen Duck* (1739)[1]

> Immortal Bard! Thou Fav'rite of the Nine!
> Enrich'd by Peers, advanc'd by CAROLINE[2]
> Deign to look down on One that's poor and Low,
> Remembring you yourself was lately so;
> Accept these Lines: Alas! what can you have
> From her, who ever was, and's still a Slave?
> No Learning ever was bestow'd on me;
> My Life was always spent in Drudgery:
> And not alone; alas! with Grief I find,
> It is the Portion of poor Woman-kind.
> Oft have I thought as on my Bed I lay,
> Eas'd from the tiresome Labours of the Day,
> Our first Extraction from a mass refin'd,
> Could never be Slavery design'd;
> Till Time and Custom by degrees destroy'd
> That happy State our Sex at first enjoy'd.
> When Men had us'd their utmost Care and Toil,
> Their Recompence was but a Female Smile;
> When they by Arts or Arms were render'd Great,
> They laid their Trophies at a Woman's Feet;

---

1 According to Donna Landry, Mary Collier was the "first published laboring-class woman poet in England." *Muses of Resistance: Laboring Class Women's Poetry in Britain, 1739-1796* (Cambridge: Cambridge UP, 1990). *As* Collier indicates, *The Woman's Labour* was written in answer to *The Thresher's Labour* (1736), a poem by Stephen Duck about the laboring class.

2 Queen Caroline, consort of George II, died 1737.

They in those Days, unto our Sex did bring
Their Hearts, there All, a Free-will Offering;
And as from us their Being they derive,
They back again should all due Homage give.

JOVE once descending from the Clouds did drop
In Show'rs of Gold on Lovely *Danae's* Lap;
The sweet-tongu'd Poets, in those generous Days,
Unto our Shrine still offer'd up their Lays:
But now, alas! that Golden Age is past,
We are the Objects of your Scorn at last.
And you, great DUCK, upon whose happy Brow
The Muses seem to fix the Garland now,
In your late *Poem* boldly did declaire
Alcides' Labours[1] can't with yours compare;
And of your annual Task have much to say,
Of Threshing, Reaping, Mowing, Corn and Hay;
Boasting your daily Toil, and nightly Dream,
But can't conclude your never-dying theme,
And let our hapless Sex in Silence lie
Forgotten, and in dark Oblivion die;
But on your abject State you throw your Scorn,
And Women wrong, your Verses to adorn.
You of Hay-making speak a Word or two,
As if our Sex but little Work could do:
This makes the honest Farmer smiling say,
He'll seek for Women still to make his Hay;
For if his Back be turn'd, their Work they mind
As well as Men, as far as he can find.

For my own Part, I many a *Summer's* Day
Have spent in throwing, turning, making Hay;
But ne'er could see, what you have lately found,
Our Wages paid for sitting on the Ground.
'Tis true, that when our Morning's Work is done,
And all our Grass expos'd unto the Sun,
While that his scorching Beams do on it shine,
As well as you, we have a Time to dine:
I hope, that since we freely toil and sweat
To earn our Bread, you'll give us Time to eat.

---

1   Hercules was a hero of ancient Greek mythology famous for his feats of
super-human strength.

That over, soon we must get up again,
And nimbly turn our Hay upon the Plain;
Nay, rake and prow[1] it in, the Case is clear;
Or how should Cocks in equal rows appear?
But if you'd have what you have wrote believ'd,
I find, that you to hear us talk are griev'd:
In this, I hope, you do not speak your Mind,
For none but *Turks*, that ever I could find,
Have Mutes to serve them, or did e'er deny
Their Slaves, at Work, to chat it merrily.
Since you have Liberty to speak your Mind,
And are to talk, as well as we, inclin'd,
Why should you thus repine, because that we,
Like you, enjoy that pleasing Liberty?
What would you lord it quite, and take away
The only Privelege our Sex enjoy.

WHEN Ev'ning does approach, we homeward hie,
And our domestic Toils incessant ply:
Against your coming Home prepare to get
Our work all done, our House in order set;
Bacon and *Dumpling* in the Pot we boil,
Our Beds we make, our Swine we feed the while;
Then wait at Door to see you coming Home,
And set the Table out against you come:
Early next Morning we on you attend;
Our Children dress and feed, their Cloaths we mend;
And in the Field our daily Task renew,
Soon as the rising Sun has dry'd the Dew.
When Harvest comes, into the Field we go,
And help to reap the Wheat as well as you;
Or else we go the Ears of Corn to glean;
No Labour scorning, be it e'er so mean;
But in the Work we freely bear a part,
And what we can, perform with all our Heart.
To get a Living we so willing are,
Our tender Babes into the Field we bear,
And wrap them in our Cloaths to keep them warm,
While round we gather up the Corn;
And often unto them our course do bend,
To keep them safe, that nothing them offend:

---

1   Plough.

Our children that are able, bear a share
In gleaning Corn, such is our frugal Care.
When Night comes on, unto our Home we go,
Our Corn we carry, and our Infant too;
Weary, alas! but 'tis not worth our while
Once to complain, or *rest at every Stile*;[1]
We must make haste, for when we Home are come,
Alas we find our Work but just begun;
So many things for our Attendance call,
Had we ten Hands, we could employ them all.
Our children put to Bed, with greatest Care
We all Things for your coming Home prepare:
You sup, and go to Bed without delay,
And rest yourselves till the ensuing Day;
While we, alas! but little Sleep can have,
Because our froward[2] Children cry and rave;
Yet, without fail, soon as Day-light doth spring,
We in the Field again our Work begin,
And there, with all our Strength, our Toil renew,
Till *Titan*'s[3] golden Rays have dry'd the Dew;
Then home we go unto our Children dear,
Dress, feed, and bring them to the Field with care.
Were this your Case, you justly might complain
That Day nor Night you are secure from Pain;
Those mighty Troubles which perplex your Mind,
(*Thistles* before, and *Females* come behind)
Would vanish soon, and quickly disappear,
Were you, like us, encomber'd thus with Care.
What you would have of us we do not know:
We oft' take up the Corn that you do mow;
We cut the Peas, and always ready are
In ev'ry Work to take our proper Share;
And from the Time that Harvest doth begin,
Until the Corn be cut and carry'd in,
Our Toil and Labour's daily so extreme,
That we have hardly ever *Time to dream*.

---

1 Something the men do in Duck's poem and for Collier a sign that the
   men are not as hardy as they claim.
2 Discontented.
3 The sun.

THE Harvest ended, Respite none we find;
The hardest of our Toil is still behind:
Hard Labour we most cheerfully pursue,
And out, abroad, a Charing[1] often go:
Of which I now will briefly tell in part,
What fully to declare is past my Art;
So many Hardships daily we go through,
I boldly say, the like *you* never knew.

When bright *Orion* glitters in the Skies
In *Winter* Nights, then early we must rise;
The Weather ne'er so bad, Wind, Rain, or Snow,
Our Work appointed, we must rise and go;
While you on easy Beds may lie and sleep,
Till Light does thro' your Chamber-windows peep.
When to the House we come where we should go,
How to get in, alas! we do not know:
The Maid quite tir'd with Work the Day before,
O'ercome with Sleep; we standing at the Door
Oppress'd with Cold, and often call in vain,
E're to our Work we can Admittance gain:
But when from Wind and Weather we get in,
Briskly with Courage we our Work begin;
Heaps of fine Linen we before us view,
Whereon to lay our Strength and Patience too;
Cambricks and Muslins, which our Ladies wear,
Laces and Edgings, constantly, fine and rare,
Which must be wash'd with utmost Skill and Care;

With Holland Shirts, Ruffles and Fringes too,
Fashions which our Fore-fathers never knew.
For several Hours here we work and slave,
Before we can one Glimpse of Day-light have;
We labour hard before the Morning's past,
Because we fear the Time runs on too fast.

AT length bright *Sol*[2] illuminates the Skies,
And summons drowsy Mortals to arise;
Then comes our Mistress to us without fail,
And in her Hand, *perhaps*, a Mug of Ale

---

1 To help at other people's houses, though not a servant.
2 The sun.

To cheer our Hearts, and also to inform
Herself, what Work is done that very Morn;
Lays her Commands upon us, that we mind
Her Linen well, nor *leave the Dirt behind*:
Not this alone, but also to take care
We don't her Cambricks nor her Ruffles tear;
And *these* most strictly does of us require,
To save her Soap, and sparing be of Fire;
Tell us her charge is great, nay furthermore,
Her cloaths are fewer than the Time before.
Now we drive on, resolvd' our Strength to try,
And what we can, we do most willingly;
Until with Heat and work, 'tis often known,
Not only Sweat, but Blood runs trickling down
Our Wrists and Fingers; still our Work demands
The constant Action of our lab'ring Hands.

NOW Night comes on, from whence you have Relief,
But that, alas! does but increase our Grief;
With heavy Hearts we often view the Sun,
Fearing he'll set before our Work is done;
For either in the Morning, or at Night,
We piece the *Summer*'s Day with Candle-light.
Tho' we all Day with Care our work attend,
Such is our Fate, we know not when 'twill end:

When Ev'ning's come, you Homeward take your Way,
WE, till our Work is done, are forc'd to stay;
And after all our Toil and Labour past,
Six-pence or Eight-pence pays us off at last;
For all our Pains, no Prospect can we see
Attend us, but *Old Age* and *Poverty*.

THE *Washing* is not all we have to do;
We oft change Work for Work as well as you.
Our Mistress of her Pewter doth complain,
And 'tis our Part to make it clean again.
This Work, tho' very hard and tiresome too,
Is not the worst we hapless Females do:
When Night comes on, and we quite weary are,
We scarce can count what falls unto our Share;

Pots, Kettles, Sauce-pans, Skillets, we may see,
Skimmers and Ladles, and such Trumpery,

Brought in to make complete our Slavery.
Tho' early in the Morning 'tis begun,
'Tis often very late before we've done;
Alas our Labours never know an End;
On Brass and Iron we our Strength must spend;
Our tender Hands and fingers scratch and tear:
All this, and more, with Patience we must bear.
Colour'd with Dirt and Filth we now appear;
Your threshing *sooty Peas*[1] will not come near.
All the Perfections Woman once could boast,
Are quite obscur'd, and altogether lost.

Once more our Mistress sends to let us know
She wants our Help, because the Beer runs low:
Then in much hast for Brewing we prepare,
The vessels clean, and scald with greatest Care;
Often at Midnight, from our Bed we rise
At other Times, ev'n that will not suffice;
Our Work at Ev'ning oft we do begin,
And 'ere we've done, the Night comes on again.
Water we pump, the Copper[2] we must fill,
Or tend the Fire; for if we e'er stand still,
Like you, when threshing, we a Watch must keep,
Our Work boils over if we dare to sleep.

BUT to rehearse all Labour is in vain,
Of which we very justly might complain:
For us, you see, but little Rest is found;
Our Toil increases as the Year runs round.
While you to *Sysiphus*[3] your selves compare,
With *Danaus' Daughters*[4] we may claim a Share;
For while *he* labours hard against the Hill,
Bottomless Tubs of Water *they* must fill.

---

1 Moldy.

2 Water-carrying vessels made from copper.

3 In Greek mythology, Sysiphus was condemned to push a boulder up a
hill for eternity. Everytime he neared the top, the boulder rolled back
down to the bottom of the hill.

4 Danaus's daughters murdered their husbands at their father's request.
As punishment for their sins, they were condemned forever to fill a
water vessel that had no bottom.

SO the industrious Bees do hourly strive
To bring their Loads of Honey to the Hive;
Their sordid[1] Owners always reap the Gains,
And poorly recompense their Toil and Pains.

---

1 Greedy.

Appendix C: Court Culture

[When Charles II returned to England in 1660, his court brought back a renewed interest in and commitment to the trappings of wealth and status. Though in many ways the Caroline court patronized a cultural renaissance, it also came to be viewed as a repository of moral decadence and corruption, as those who were members of the court and the aristocracy felt themselves to be above the conventions and rules that governed the lives of ordinary citizens.]

1. ***Poor-Whores Petition. The most Splendid, Illustrious, Serene and Emminent Lady of Pleasure, the Countess of CASTLEMAYNE, &c. The Humble Petition of the Undone Company of poore distressed Whores, Bawds, Pimps and Panders, &c. (1668)***[1]

Humbly sheweth,
That Your Petitioners having been for a long time connived at, and countenanced in the practice of our Venerial pleasures (a Trade Wherein your Lady ship hath great Experience, and for your diligence there in, have arrived to a hight and Eminent Advancement for these late years), But now, We, through the Rage and Malice of a Company of London-Apprentices, and other malicious and very bad persons, being mechanick, rude and ill-bred Boys, have sustained the loss of our Habitations Trades and Employments; And many of us, that have had foul play in the Court and Sport of Venus, being full of Ulcers, but were in a hopeful way of Recovery, have our Cures retarded through this Barbarous and Un-Venus-like Usage, and all of us exposed to very hard shifts, being made uncapable of giving that Entertainment, as the Honour and dignity of such persons as frequented our Houses doth call for, as your Lady ship by your own practice hath experienced the knowledge of.

---

1 On Easter Monday, 1668, mobs, apparently led by London's apprentices, rose up and destroyed many of the brothels then located in London's east end. The events sparked a minor "pamphlet war" in which blame was cast in a variety of quarters, among them the court of Charles II. Here and in the following selections, the London's most prominent bawds are represented petitioning the Countess of Castlemaine, one of Charles II's many mistresses, for help in the unrest.

We therefore being moved by the imminent danger now impending, and the great sense of our present speedy Relief may be afforded us, to prevent our Utter Ruine and Undoing. And that such a sure Course may be taken with the Ringleaders and Abetters of these evil-disposed persons, that a stop may be put unto them before they come to your Honours Pallace,[1] and bring contempt upon your worshipping of Venus, the great Goddess whom we all adore.

Wherefore in our Devotion (your Honour being eminently concerned with us) We humbly judge it meet, that you procure the French, Irish, and English Hectors,[2] being our approved Friends, to be our Guard, Aid, and Protectors, and to free us from these ill home-bred slaves, that threaten your destruction as well as ours; that so your Lady ship may escape our present Calamity, Else we know not how soon it may be your Honours Own Case: for should your eminency but once fall into these Rough hands, you may expect no more Favour then they have shewn unto us poor Inferious[3] Whores.

Will your Eminency therefore be pleased to consider how highly it concerns you to restore us to your former practice with Honour, Freedom and Safety; for which we shall oblige our selves by as many Oaths as you please, To contribute to Your Lady ship, (as our Sisters do at Rome & Venice to his Holiness the Pope) that we may have your Protection in the Exercise of all our Venerial pleasures. And we shall endeavour, as our bounded duty, the promoting of your Great Name, and the preservation of your Honour, Safety and Interest, with the hazard of our Lives, Fortunes and Honesty.

And your Petition shall (as by custom bound) Evermore Play—

Signed by Us, Madam Cresswell and Damaris Page, in the behalf of our Sisters and Fellow-Sufferers (in this day of our Calamity) in Dog and Bitch Yard, Lukeners Lane, Saffron-Hill, Moor-fields, Chiswell-Street, Rosemary-Lane, Nightingale-Lane, Ratcliffe-Highway, Well-close, Church-Lane, East-Smithfield, &c. this present 25th day of March 1668.

---

1 The mobs had threatened to tear down the palace at Whitehall where Castlemaine had chambers adjacent to the King's.

2 Braggarts or bullies.

3 Inferior.

2. The Gracious ANSWER *of the most Illustrious* Lady *of* Pleasure, *the* Countess *of* Castlem—*To the Poor-Whores Petition* (1668)

Right Trusty and Well-beloved Madam *Cresswell* and *Damaris Page* with the rest of the suffering Sister-hood in *Dog and Bitch Yard, Lukeners Lane, Saffron Hill, Moor-fields, Ratcliff-Highway, &c.* We greet you well, in giving you to understand our Noble Mind, by returning our Thanks, which you are worthy of, in rendring us our Titles of Honour, which are but our Due. For on *Shrove-Tuesday* last, Splendidly did we appear upon the Theatre at W.H.[1] being to amazement wonderfully deck'd with Jewels and Diamonds, which the (abhorred and to be undone) Subjects of this Kingdom have payed for. We have been also Serene and illustrious ever since the Day that *Mars* was so instrumental to restore our Goddess *Venus* to her Temple and Worship; where, by special Grant, we quickly became a Famous Lady: And as a Reward of our Devotion, soon created Right Honourable, the Countess of *Castlemaine.*[2] And as a further addition to our Illustrious Serenity, according to the ancient Rules and laudable Customs of our Order, we have *cum privilegio*[3] always (without our Husband) satisfied our self with the Delights of *Venus*; and in our Husbands absence have had a Numerous Off-spring, (who are beautifully and Nobly provided for). Which Practice hath Episcopal Allowance[4] also, according to the Principles of *Seer Shelden,*[5] *&c. If Women have not Children by their own Husbands, they are bound to try by using the* means *with other men*: Which wholesome and pleasing Doctrine did for sometime hold me fast to his Religion. But since this Seer hath shewn more Cowardize, than Principles or Policy, in fearing to declare the Church of *Rome* to be the True, Ancient, Uniform, Universal and most Holy Mother Church; Therefore we tell you (with all the Sisterhood) That we are now no longer of the Church of *England* which is like a Brazen-Bacon tied to a Barbers wooden Pole,[6] (*viz.*) Protestant Doctrine and Order tied by Parliamentary Power to Roman Catholick Foun-

---

1 Whitehall, where Charles II had his palace.
2 Barbara Villiers, nee Palmer, was created Countess of Castlemaine in 1661.
3 According to custom.
4 Permission from the Church.
5 Gilbert Sheldon, Archbishop of Canterbury (1663-77).
6 The Church of England has become simply figure-head for Parliamentary will.

dations, Constitutions, and rights, *&c.* And are become a Convert to, and professed Member of the Church of *Rome*; where the worthy Fathers and Confessors, as *Durandus Gentianus*, with multitudes of others, (who were not, neither are, of the Protestant, Puritanical, and Fanatical Conventicling Opinion) do declare *That Venerial Pleasures, accompanied with Looseness, Debauchery, and Prophaneness, are not such heinous Crimes and crying Sins, but rather* (as the old Woman of *Loven* said) *they do mortify the Flesh.* And the general Opinion of Holy Mother Church, is *That Venerial Pleasures, in the strictest sence are but Venial sins, which confessors of the meanest Order can forgive.* So that the Adoring of *Venus*, is by the Allowance of Great Authority, Desirable, Honourable and Profitable.

But when we understood in your Address, the Barbarity of those Rude Apprentices, and the cruel Sufferings that the Sisterhood was exposed unto; especially those which were in a hopeful way of Recovery, and others that were disabled from giving Accommodation to their Right Honourable Devotaries, with the danger which you convinc'd us our own Person was in, together with the remembrance of our two New Cotivals with *Little Miss*: We were for many hours swallowed up with sorrow, and almost drown'd in Tears, and could not at all be comforted, until the sweet sound of the Report came to our Ears, *That L.C.J.K.*[1] *and his Brethren, with our Counsel Learned in the Law, had Commission and Instruction given to frame a Bill of Indictment against those Trayterous and Rebellious Boys, and to select a Jury of Gentlemen that should shew them no favour:* At which our Noble Spirit revived and presently we consulted how we might express our Grace and Compassion towards you, and also seasonably provide for the future safety of your Practice and exercise our Revenge upon those that so grossly abused you, and therein offered such an insufferable Affront to our Eminency, these we cannot bear without great indignation.

Imprimus, We engage to contribute to your Losses, either out of the Annual Rents which we have begged, or out of the next Moneys which shall come to your hands by our own Practice, or as soon as our *standing* Revenue shall be established: For should we part with a hundred thousand pounds worth of our Jewels, since so much English Money had cross'd the Narrow Seas, we fear that our Goldsmiths will not be able to raise it upon them.

---

1 Lord Chief Justice Keyling, who presided over the King's Bench trial at which the leaders of the Bawdy House riots were charged with and convicted of high treason.

Item. For your Safety, we do conjure all *French, Irish, and English Hectors* to be a Guard to the whole Sisterhood, and to take up their Quarters with them for their better security; and if they want Money for their subsistence, let them put on Courage and take it up on the High-ways;[1] and if any of them should be taken in the Fact, we shall upon our Honour, procure them pardons: Or else let them cheat and couzen, and they shall have Protection.

Item. For your Honour, doubt not of having what countenance Authority of holy Mother Church can give you. And for the increase of our Practice, the Master of our Revels shall give License for the setting up as many Play-houses as his Holiness the Pope hath Holidays in his Kalendar, that the Civil Youth of the City may be Debauch'd and trained upon in Loosness and Ignorance, whereby the Roman Religion may with ease be established in Court, Church, City, and Nation, the most effectual means for the accomplishment of our Designs.

Item. We have taken special care that our Sisterhood, and the whole Corporation, may be restored by Charter to all their former Liberties, Priviledges, and Immunities whatsoever.

Item. That Sir—*Berkenhead*[2] and Sir—*Charlton*,[3] two worthy Patriots, together with Sr. *W.M.* lately become zealously tender of our Honour, be appointed to bring in a Bill upon *Wednesday* next, for a full Toleration of all Bawdy-houses, Playhouses, Whorehouses, &c. that all the Adorers of *Venus* may come to their Worship without Molestation: And at this Proviso may be inserted, *That all Preaching, Printing, Private Meetings, Conventicles,* &c. *may be forthwith suppressed; except those that are connived at as members of Holy Mother Church.*

Item. We have appointed the Right Reverend Seer of *Canterbury* and other Reverend Seers, (*viz.*) the B. of *Rochester*, the B. of *Gloucester*, and Dean *Hardy*, B. of *Loutherdale*, Mr. *Brounkerd*, and *Bab May*,[4] or any three of them, to be a close *Committee* to consult the Grievances of the Sisterhood, and to remove all things that may hinder their happy Restauration with all Freedom, Safety, and Honour.

---

1 Probably solicit on behalf of the prostitutes out in the street.
2 John Birkenhead, arch-royalist and licenser of the press from 1660-63.
3 Job Charlton, Member of Parliament from Ludlow, who played a leading role in carving out the Restoration settlement and bringing back the monarchy in 1660.
4 Bab, or Baptist May, was one of Charles II's most trusted courtiers and servants.

Item. That all Members of *Parliament*, of our Religion, during this Session, and no longer, may use their *Priviledge*, in sending for such of our Sisterhood to their Chambers, as they have a Mind to upon their own terms, considering they have so Freely and Unanimously Voted Taxes, till their Own Revenues will not maintain them: That the Ingenuity and Gentility of the Sisterhood may appear to all the World, that we are better bred, than to slight those that have so Nobly provided for us.

Item. We charge that none of the Sisterhood take any more *Cirsingles* or *Cassocks* to pawn, of any *Churchmen* either Romish or English, when they reel into their Quarters, because they turn not to Accompt.

Item. That if any Alderman will Eat Flesh in *Lent* or deal in prohibited Commodities, Our pleasure is, That they pay and be paid soundly for it, least they build *London* again; contrary to the intent of those that burnt it: Only let Sir *T.B.* That would Piss out the Fire, and Lieut. Col. *Rouswell* [1] with their Brethren, that took care, *That the Fire should be quenched*, and also withstood the *Common Council*, in sending their Petition to the Parliament, (when such full and pregnant proof was made), that the City was burnt by the Good *Roman Catholicks* have all the courtesie Immaginable. But above all, We desire them to be kind to those, who have (to this day, out of their good affection to the *Roman* Interest) prevented by several Artifices, the putting of the aforesaid Petition into the Hands of Sir *Thomas Allen*, that *Fanatick Zealot*, who was appointed by the Court of *Common Council* to deliver it to the Parliament, who now (to our great Joy) will be Prorogued before they can do any thing in it. Neither let those Worthies be forgotten who (in despite of the Importunities of several busie Citizens) have till now hindred the preparing of the most necessary Additional Bill, for the Rebuilding of *London*: Which Work it is hoped will now cease, there being no time before the end of this Session, to carry that Bill through all the Formalities of Parliament.

Item. That the same Kindness be shewed to all Officers, both Civil and Military, that came to the Relief of the Sisterhood in the time of their necessity. And let those *Papists* which are now drawing from all parts of *England* and *Wales* to this Place, be acquainted with the Habitations of the Sisterhood, and delight themselves together and console the weighty Affairs now in hand.

---

1 Possibly Thomas Roswell; initially a royalist and always a Presbyterian, he was tried for high treason in 1684.

But for our Adversaries, with the Rebellious citizens, Let them look to it when the *French* are ready (who do yet drop in by small Parties, and lie *incognito* with the rest of the *Catholicks*) we shall deal with them as we did their Brethren in *Ireland*.

Item. to any other then here directed, give no Entertainment without Ready Money, lest you suffer Loss. For had we not been careful in that particular, we had neither gained Honour nor Rewards, which are now (as you know) both conferred upon Us.

3. **John Dunton,** *The Night-Walker: Or, Evening Rambles*
   In search after Lewd Women, With the Conferences Held
   with them, &c. To be publish'd Monthly, 'till a Discovery
   be made of all the chief Prostitutes in England, from
   the Pensionary Miss, down to the Common Strumpet.
   This for September 1696. Dedicated to the Whore-
   Masters of London and Westminster

***

To the Whore-Masters of London and Westminster.

Gentlemen,
Whatever Respect may be due to your *Numbers*, you cannot claim any as due to your *Characters*; and tho' too many of you are not ashamed to make your boasts of the Thing, yet you would take it as an Affront to be call'd by the *Name; Whence it's* plain, Gentlemen, that you *Glory in your Shame.* By the *Laws of God* you are excluded from heaven, and by the *Laws of the Land* you are entitled to Punishment and Disgrace; so that God and Man do both Condemn you, and the Devil, who doth now tempt, will at last accuse and torment you, if Repentence don't prevent it. Such of you as are *Married* would be very ill pleas'd to have your Wives follow your own Examples, and such of you as are not would take it for a Reproach to have your Mothers, or your Sisters *accounted Whores*; which is a plain Demonstration that you hate that Vice in others, which you indulge in your selves: Then where, in the mean time, is *Common Justice?* Some of you value your selves as being the *Representations* of Ancient and Noble Families; but by the Methods which you take you will deprive your Posterity of those Pretentions, for you give your Ladies occasion to repay you in your own Coin; and as you make bold with their *Waiting-women, Chamber-maids, and your Pensionary-mistresses*, they to quit you as good a

Common,[1] will make bold with your *Gentlemen, Valet de Chambres, or some Sparkish Gallants*; and by this means your Estates and Honours shall be Inherited by a spurious Brood and the Ancient Honour and Gallantry of the *English Nobility* and *Gentry* miserably tarnisht. Nay, Gentlemen, if this *abominable Trade go on*, we shall have the Sons of debaucht Comedians, *brawny Coachmen, and sweaty Footmen*, pawn'd upon us, instead of *Dukes, Earls, Lords, and Knights*: And how unlikely such a degenerate Off-spring are to maintain the Honour of *Old England*, we leave it to your selves to be judges. Certainly our *Nobility and Gentry* would take it very ill to be accounted the *Race of such an Ignoble Crew*, but if those of them that are Guilty of those dissolute Practices don't reform their own Lives, we would fain know of them what reason they have to think that *their Wives and Daughters* will not be infected with their bad Examples. And seeing it is also plain from Experience, that the Practice of the Great ones have always an Influence upon those of the Commons, if these Enormities be not Reformed the whole Nation, in time, will become Vile and Despicable in the Eyes of God and Man.

The Judgments which the Sin of Uncleanness hath brought upon particular Persons and Nations, is so frequently Exemplified both in Divine and Prophane Records, that it is amazing to consider that so many should be Ship-wreck'd upon the same Shelves, where there are so many *Beacons* erected to give them Warning of their *Danger—Sodom and Gomorrah, Admah and Zeboim, the Children of Schechem, and the Tribe of Benjamin*[2] *are noted Instances* of this sad Truth, as to the Judgments brought upon People by that horrid Abomination; and that it hath not only left an eternal Blot upon the Reputation of some of the greatest Saints mentioned in Scripture, but hath also been fatal to themselves, or their Posterity, there's no Man can be Ignorant who hath ever heard of *Lot, Sampson, David, Solomon*, &c. If we look into *Profane History*, we shall not only find this Sin of Uncleanness reckoned amongst the greatest Deformities, which make up the Characters of those Monsters of Men and Princes *Tiberius* and *Nero*, but that it hath also fixt an Indelible Stain upon the Memories of *Julius Caeser* and *Augustus*, who had oth-

---

1 The women treat their aristocratic husbands with as much disdain as they would treat a commoner.

2 Biblical examples of people whom God punished for their decadence and iniquity.

erwise many Commendable Qualities, and were Two of the greatest Men that ever Governed the *Roman* Empire. How contemptible is the name of *Sardanapalus*,[1] because of his *Goatish Lustfulness*: And who is it that doth not condemn the Folly of *Mark Anthony*, for being so far bewitcht with the *Charms of Cleopatra*.

Then if we look into the History of our own Nation, we shall find that the *Saxon Invasion* happened in the Reign of *Vortigern*, a lustful Prince, *Whose inordinate Affection to* Hengist*'s Daughter, gave the Saxons the first Opportunity of settling in* Kent, *and then of usurping the whole Kingdom. We shall likewise find that a Rape gave the first Occasion to the Invasion of the* Danes, *and of that Ignominy under which the Nation suffered by having those barbarous Heathens become Masters of their Wives and Daughters; and not long after we became the Conquest of* William *the* Norman, *a Bastard, as if Heaven intended that we should read our Sin in our Punishment.*

But there's no need of going so far back. That Deluge of Uncleanness which overflowed the Kingdom by the bad Example of *Charles* II did enervate our Strength, and lessen our Reputation, so that the Nation became the *Hire of a Harlot*; the Glory, Trade, and Naval Strength of *England*, were made a Sacrifice to that Prince's *Impure Pleasures*, and those of his Brother: And as a Consummation of our Misery, and proper Punishment, we were like to have been given up to the *Spiritual Uncleanness, and to be made a Prey to the Whore of Rome.*

Perhaps, Gentlemen, these publick Instances may have but small Weight with you, and therefore we would intreat you to retire a little into your *own Bosoms*, and consider what are the Fruits you reap by your Debauches: And as many of you as pretend to be Men of Honour, Answer impartially whether the natural Consequences of your *lewd Practices* be not a reproaching Conscience, the *ruine of your Health, Estates and Reputations*, accompanied with the breach of the Peace of your Families. Some of you are mighty Pretenders to impartial Justice, and zealous Asserters of *Liberty and Property*; but how will you reconcile those Principles with defiling your Neighbour's Bed, *debauching of poor Maids*, and exposing of 'em, and spurious Issue by them, to Poverty, Reproach and Punishment. Do you really, when you allow your selves liberty of Thought, think it worth your whiles to purchase *some moments of brutish Pleasure* at such a rate? Take but a view of *Death and Judgment*, and consider how those

---

1 Transvestite king of ancient Assyria.

impure diversions will relish with you when you are on the brink of the Grave, and for ought you know of Damnation. Set before your Eyes the Example of the *late Lord Rochester*,[1] who had wallowed in such Impurities, and had more Wit to defend or palliate his lewd Practices, than some Hundreds of you: And tho' his Quality set him above the ordinary Methods of Prosecution before Men, yet he was forc'd to *arraign and condemn Himself* at the Bar of Conscience and Heaven, and became a *glorious Conquest of Truth over Atheism and Profanity.*

★★★

The *First Night* I travers'd the *Pall-mall*, and read the Face of every unmask'd Lady I met; and if mask'd, I started some Question that still gave me an Indication of their Temper, endeavouring to light upon as *refin'd* yet *modest piece of Wickedness* as I could: At last having made (as I thought) the *best of the Market*, away we walk'd to drink upon the Bargain: So, after several Glasses, and some little insignificant Prittle-prattle, I fix'd my Eyes upon her, and said, *Madam, methinks I read some Lines and Characters of Goodness in your Face, which are not yet absolutely defac'd: Your Education, I am confident, has not been unhappy: Pray be free, and tell me, Are you yet Proof against the Lashes of your Conscience?* Sir, (said she) your Design I know not, but I dare not believe it to be ill, you having made such an inquisitive Prologue. No indeed (reply'd I) my Request proceeds purely from a generous Pity at your Misfortunes, which are sufficiently slavish. Alas Sir! (said she and sigh'd) 'tis a slavish *Riddle to chuse what I hate*; I have repeated those Actions, but never without regret and self-abhorrency for such a Folly:—. This I had peculiar to myself, that I never was Mercenary, thinking it a greater baseness to *sell* my Heaven, than *give* it; I was first betray'd by keeping company with a Lady that was not *over-modest*, but not thinking to engage myself, till one of her Gallants weaken'd my Resolves, and at last—I know not what; but I was ruin'd, for all my Resolves are now too weak to resist, never being able to hold out a quarter of a year together; but *secure my Honour for this once by Secrecy*, and not tatching me to my Lodgings: And I hope the Novelty of this Enterprize may have new Effects upon me, and keep me from doing such Actions as must be repented of, or I am undone.

---

1 John Wilmot, 2nd Earl of Rochester, was a poet and courtier who led a notorious dissolute life and died at the age of 33.

The next attack was a *City Madam*, with a melancholy Air in her Face, which put me upon acting as follows: After having drank a Glass or two, she began to draw a little too near me; whereupon I rose up, and with as severe a Look as I could affect, I said, *Madam, keep off, you think I'm flesh and Blood, and I doubt not but that I imitate it near enough to deceive your Eyes; assure your self I am not what I appear: reclaim your Whoredoms, or you are lost; you have but a little time left, make good use of it; if you are otherwise resolv'd, view these Features, and expect me to be a Witness against you at the Day of Judgment.* Here she waxed pale, and swooned away, and as soon as she came to her self again I left her; and enquiring the next day about her, I heard she took me for a Spirit, and was resolv'd to follow the Advice of her strange Monitor.

The third was a *Savoy-Bird*,[1] well skill'd in *Confidence* and the *depth of Pockets*, but so simple and foolish in all her Answers, that I think nothing can *reclaim* her but *Afflictions*. Such Wretches perhaps may deserve a particular way of treating in the new measures of Reformation.

The next Enterprize was an old Friend, a *Companion of mine*, whom I overtook caressing a Lady near the *Maypole* in the *Strand*, but being not certain, I kept behind 'em till they came to *S— lane*, where seeing 'em turn down, I made a halt, and they came up again presently into the *Strand*; so resolving to be satisfied, I made up to 'em, and by asking *What is't a Clock?* discover'd the truth of the matter: The lady finding my acquaintance with my Friend, scowred[2] off; and he feeling himself discovered, *begg'd my silence*, and promis'd a Reformation, which I hope he has kept to ever since, having given me such satisfaction as argues his Sincerity in this Affair.

The *fifth Engagement* occasion'd this Confession, That she had an easie tender Education, but her Brother grew extravagant, and instead of paying hers and her Sisters Portions, he spent all; and she having no way left to get her Bread, and *not being able* to work, took up *this Course* which (said she) at first was very afflicting and uneasie to my Conscience but has worn off by degrees; tho' after all, I wish I had begg'd rather than lived thus dissatisfied; for I have lost my Credit, *am asham'd of my Friends, afraid of my Enemies*, and which is yet worse, see no probability of living under better Circumstances all my life, and must die without hopes of mending it in the other World.

---

1 Flighty, untamed.
2 Snuck away furtively.

The *sixth Enterprize* was so like the Story of *Paphnutiae*'s converting a *Harlot*, that I shall tell that only, perhaps not yet known to every body: He put on the Habit of a Soldier, and went to an infamous House, and choosing his woman, he desir'd to go with her into a private Room, where none might see him; she brought him into a Chamber, which he objects against, as not private enough; she brings him into another, against which he also objects; at last she brings him into the most private Room in the House; he looks about every way, and asks if they were secure there, and if none saw 'em; she answer'd, *None but GOD or the Devil.* And believest thou (saith he) that there is a God? She answer'd, *Yes.* And believest thou that he is everywhere present, and seeth all things? She answer'd, *she did believe it.* And shall we, said he, sin so shamefully under the Eye of the most *Just Judge,* that seeth all things? Hereupon she had nothing to say for herself, but fetched a deep sigh, being asham'd of her wicked Life, liv'd afterwards on Bread and Water, and not daring to take the Name of God into her Mouth, but frequently repeated these words. *Thou who hast made me, have mercy on me*; and so she continued three years, died.

To this Conviction our *present* Instance agrees; and we are not without hopes of like effects in the rest.

Reader, if the Time and Money's spent in these *Six Nights Rambles*, may reclaim or hinder the Debauchery of one single Person, I shall think it all worth my Labour.

The Night-Walker, October, 1696, "Epistle Dedicatory"

To the Dutches of —[1]
Madam,
The Bounty of a Certain Prince, who was taken with your Charms, has made it familiar to you for many years, to be accosted with the usual Compliment of may it please your Grace: But most people are of opinion, that how good soever your Title may be to the Name, you were never actually possessed of the Thing: It's impossible Madam, that those who have any Regard to Virtue, can ever think the forfeiture of that which is the greatest Honour of the Fair-Sex, can be the true way to raise any person Honour. The very Heathens had a juster Notion of this, when they made the Temple of Virtue the entrance to the Temple of Honour; and whatever the Favour of Princes, or the Flattery of the

---

1   Dunton is referring here to Barbara Villiers, Countess of Castlemaine and Duchess of Cleveland.

People can advance to the contrary, the Christian Religion teaches us that Marriage is Honourable, and the Bed undefiled, but Whoremongers and Adulterers God will punish; so that it's plain Madam, you are so far from having any just claim to Honour, either by the Laws of natural or revealed Religion, that you are condemned to Ignominy by both, and tho you may carry your Title of Grace to your Grave, yet when you come before the Bar of the King of Kings you will find it to be a badge of your Disgrace, and an Evidence of your having dishonoured your Body, and defiled the Marriage Bed.

Madam, the Ruines of your former Beauty (which was the Ruine of your self and of those whom it ensnared) and the Furrows which time hath now drawn upon your Forehead, are so many warnings that your Day of Accounts draws nigh, and tho the Power and Authority of one who was your Companion in Iniquity protected you from being brought to Justice before men, There's nothing that can secure you from the fierce Wrath of the almighty, but the Merits of Jesus Christ applied by Faith, which 'tis in vain for you to pretend to so long as you continue without having repented of your impure course of Life.

Madam, consider what a heavy Charge will be brought against you, as being the first after the Re—,[1] who in an avowed and daring manner polluted this Nation by your bad Example. It had been a greater Instance of your Loyalty, to have rejected the unchaste Embraces of than to have compli'd with him, in turning the Grace of God towards him in to Wantonness, and infecting other Ladies by your Example.

Consider Madam, how Justice has found you out already in some measure, and how it order'd matters, so as you became Comtemptible in the Eyes of him, to be whose Paramour you accounted your greatest Honour. It was a mighty downfall from being the darling of a M—ch[2] to become the Mistress of a Com—n,[3] for that in you Madam, is verified what the Wiseman tells us in the 6th of the Proverbs, that those who commit Adultery get a Wound and Dishonour, and their reproach shall not be wiped away. You cannot but know Madam, that the people in General entertain mean thoughts of you, notwithstanding your Gaudy Title, and that persons of Quality who have any regard to Virtue, are shy of conversing with you: Then, Madam, is it possible you can think your self fit for the Conversation of Saints and Angels in Heaven, when your crimes have made you despicable In the eyes of all those who are Virtuous and Modest upon Earth. It's in vain for Great

---

1 Restoration.

2 Monarch.

3 Common.

persons to think that their Grandeur will be able to save their Good Name, if they act such things as are inconsistent with it, for tho people may be afraid to speak truth to them, they will never refrain from speaking truth of 'em, the Higher the Station, the Greater is the Guilt, and the more taken notice of; and when Infamous persons of a meaner Rank perish in their wickedness their Memory perishes with them; but the names of as have been Companions in Impurity to Lustful Princes are handed down to Posterity, in the Records of Nations, with notes of disgrace. The names of a Jezebel and Herodias are recorded in Sacred History, to their perpetual infamy; whereas the names of their Sisters in Impurity whom Solomon describes to be lying in Wait at the Corner of every Street, in the Evening and Twilight are buried in Oblivion; But not to oppress your Memory with 100 Influences, we shall only put you in mind of one, viz. of Jane Shore, who tho but a Tradesman's Wife, yet her Whoredom and Infamy is handed down to Posterity, because she was Paramour to King Ed. the IV. whereas the Lascivious and Wanton practices of many other City Dames, is buried in Oblivion with themselves. You may assure yourself Madam, that those who Record the Proceedings of the present Age, will not miss to take notice of your self; N G. and the D—s of P.[1] as having been Companions In Debauchery to a certain P—[2] now gone to his place; and there's no way left for you to retrieve your Honour, but by a publick Repentance, and leaving a Testimony behind you to the World, that you abominate your former Course of Life; and Madam, for your encouragement consider the Instance of Mary Magdalen, whose former infamy of having been once posses't with Seven unclean Devils, is sufficiently washt off by her becoming a Saint at last, which is the worst we wish your Ladiship, that so we might without any scruple, join with the Vulgar in giving you the Title of Grace.

---

1 Nell Gwyn and the Duchess of Portsmouth.

2 Prince. Both women were Charles II's mistresses.

Appendix D: City Culture

[As the Caroline court was viewed as a source of moral corruption, so too was the City of London. The City and the people who populated it were often characterized as having a willingness to sacrifice moral probity for profit.]

1. *The Character of a Town-Miss* (1680)

A Miss is a new Name, which the *Civility* of this Age bestows on *one*, that our *unmannerly* Ancestors call'd *Whore* and *Strumpet*. A certain Help meet for a Gentleman, instead of a Wife; Serving either for prevention of the Sin of *Marrying*, or else as a little Side *Pillow*, to render the Yoke of *Matrimony* more easie. She is an excellent *Conveniency* for those that have more *Money* than *Wit*, to spend their *Estates* upon; and the most that can be said in her *Commendation*, Is, that she will infallibly bring a Man to *Repentance*. Yet you may call her an *honest Cortezan*, or at least a *Common Inclos'd*; for though she is an *Out-lier*, yet she seems to be confined within the *Pall*, and differs from your ordinary *Prostitute*, as *Whole-sale* men from *Retailers*; one perhaps has an *hundred* Customers, and to these but *Two* or *Three*, and yet *this* gets most by her *Trade*. Indeed she may well *thrive*, seeing she always carries her *Stock* above her and every man is desirous to deal in her Commodity: For she is a Gallant *business*, a Citizens *Recreation*, a Lawyers *Estate in Fee-tail*,[1] a Young Doctors *Necessary Experiment*, and a Patrons *comfortable importance*.

The Royal Preacher calls her a *Strange* Woman, but we actually term her a *Common* Woman and have reason so to do, for sins that were *strange* in Solomons day, are *common* in ours. She is a Caterpillar that destroys many a hopeful Young Gentleman in the Blossom, a *Lady Syren* far more dangerous than they in the Sea: For he that falls into her hands, runs a *threefold* hazard of Shipwracking *Soul, Body, and Estate*.

She talks high of her *Family*, and tells a large story how they were Ruined by the late *Wars*. But the true History of her Life, is generally to this Effect. She is only the *Cub* of a *Bumkin*, lickt into a Genteel form by *Town*.... She was scarce *thirteen* when her

---

1 In common law, the hereditary right of successive generations to become the tenants of a lord's fief and thus serve the resident lord.

Father *Plow-man*, and the *Squire* their Landlord (the veryer[1] *Clown* of the *two*) went Joint Tenants to her *Coppy-hold*,[2] but proving with Child, she had the wit to lay it to the *Last*, who for his Credit, dispatcht her *Incognito*, with a sum of Money on a Carriers Pack, to be distburthen'd at *London*, the goodliest Forest in *England*, to shelter a great *Belly*. There the *Birthing* was exposed to the Tuition of the *Parish* in a Handbasket, and the Charitable *Midwife* of who counts *pleasuring* in a civil way, a necessary part of her Office, soon brought her acquainted with a *third Rate Gentlewoman*, who took her a Lodging in a Garret, and allow'd her *six Shillings* a Week. But making a Sally abroad one Night, pickt up *a Drunken Cully*,[3] and at a Tavern (whilest he was no less *pleasantly* imployed) pict his pocket of a *Gold Watch*, and some straggling *Guinnies*, and left him to pawn his *Sword* and *Perriwig* for the Reckoning. After this lucky Adventure, she discards *Monsieur Shabby* (her former Customer) and her *Lofty* Lodging; puts her self in a good *garb*, gets a *Maid* (forgive me, for I Lye, I mean a *She-servant*) whom she teaches to call her *Madam*, and your *Honour*, and hires Noble Rooms richly Furnished, about *Covent garden*; there she takes State upon her, and practices every day four hours in the *Glass*, how *Greatness* will become her. Her first business is to make her self to be taken notice of, to which purpose like *Dinah*, she walks the Streets; sometimes like *Jael*, she stands at the Door; and sometimes like *Jezabel*, she looks out at the Window: But her main *Market-place* is the *Balcony*, which she frequents as constantly as any Lady in a *Romance*; and the Language of her Eyes is, *What do you lack Sir?* By which she at last attracts a Wealthy *Gallant*, who with a little *Address* obtains the mighty Honour of her *Acquaintance*, but she seems extreme Nice, Reserv'd and Modest, protests she would not go to a *Tavern* for a World, when the whole business is, she is only afraid of being *Pawn'd* there. In brief, she *Manages* him so discreetly that she *Ghents*[4] him into Love *Insensibly*, like a *Taylors Bill*, wherein a man sees himself *Rooks* abominably, yet knows not where to find fault. Having thus got the *Woodcock* into the Pit-fall, she resolves to *Pluck* him: When he importunes her for the *Great Kindness*, she talks of *Honour* and *Conscience*, and vows she will never *stain* her Reputation but for *valuable Considerations*: this brings them to

---

1 Truer.
2 Copy-hold is a piece of land where someone is a tenant at will.
3 Dupe.
4 Lures him into love without him being aware.

Articles, he promises to allow her a *Hundred and fifty pounds* a Year, and she Swears a thousand dissembling Oaths, how infinitly she loves him, and that she will prove constant and true to him alone, and never be concern'd with any other man in the World, and the silly Fop is so fatally bewitcht as to believe her; And continues a long time in that fools Paradice of *Dotage*, whilst in the mean time she drives a *Trade* privately, with two or three more. For the *Concealing* of which from the first, 'tis the whole Imploy of the little *Harlotry*, her Chamber-Maid, to study Lyes, Pretences and *Excuses*, and she makes them pay her even to *Extortion*; to quicken her *Invention*; Sometimes she is gone abroad in her *Aunts Coach*; Sometimes one of her Cozens, a Linen Draper's Wife in the City is Sick, and she must *Visit* her. Nor is *Madam* herself less full of Plot and *Intrigue* to *Bubble* her *Gallant*. Sometimes having *pleased* him well, she begs the best *Ring* he has on his finger, or pretends herself to be in *Debt*; and that unless he will suffer her to be [?] with an *Arrest*, *Bound* he must be for her to one of her *Confederates* (you may be sure) for fifty pound and the *everlasting Changling* cannot find in his heart to deny her: At other times she shall purposely given him reason to be *Jealous*, and when he has *Rav'd* and *Swore*, and *Curs'd* and *Ranted* for two hours, as if he had been *posses't* by a hundred and fifty Devils. she shall *cleverly* wipe off the Suspition, upbraid his Jealous *Coxcombship*; fall a *Sniviling*, and call her self the most *unfortunate* of Women, to love a man with so much *Passion*, that thus *abuses* her: Then he *submits*, begs her Pardon on his Knees, and *Coakses* her with all imaginable kindness, but still she *pouts*, looks *Sullen*, and will not let him have a bit of *that same* till he has given her a *New Gown, or a Necklace of Pearl*, for Atonement, and Reconcilation.

But in time, his Appetite being *Cloy'd*, his Purse *exhausted*, or his Eyes *enlightened*, he begins to withdraw, and she soon finds out another, a *verrier Fool* than he; but for Security, will not Trade, unless he *settle* an *Annuity of 300l* a Year on her *Life*; which being firmly done by an able *Conveyancer* in *Sheep-skins*,[1] half as *large* as the *Premises*: Within *one* Month she *Abandons* him for a more *Noble* and *Strenuous Gallant*. And now being arrived at the *Zenith* of her *Glory*, she has her Boys in *Livery*, her *House* splendidly furnisht, and scorns to stir abroad without a *Coach and six Horses*: She glitters in the *Boxes* at the *Play house* and draws all Eyes after her in the Street, to the shame and Confusion of all *honest* Women, and Encouragement of each *pretty Girle* that loves

---

1 A formal legal document, written by a lawyer on parchment.

fine Cloaths, good *Chear*, and *Idleness*, to turn *Harlot*, in Imitation of such a *thriving Example*.

She hath always two necessary Implements about her, a *Blackmore*,[1] and a little *Dog*; for without these, she would be neither *Fair* nor *Sweet*: The rest of her Retinue consists of her *She-Secretary*, that keeps the Box of her Teeth, her Hair, and her Painting. An Old *Trot*,[2] that understands the Town, and goes between *Party* and *Party*, and a *French Merchant* to supply her with *Dildo's*; or in default of those, she makes her Gallants Purse maintain two able *Stallions*[3] (that she loves better than him) for performance of points wherein he is *Defective*. Her Skin is much Cleerer than her *Conscience*, which makes her go with her *Neck* and *Shoulders Bare*; and she has reason; for her upper Parts are the *shop* of *Cupid*, and those below, his *Warehouse*: But all that you are like to buy there, is *Damnation*, and *Diseases*. She is a very *Butcher*, that exposes her own Flesh to Sale by the *Stone*; or if you please, a *Cook* that is Dressing her self all day with *poinant*[4] *Sauces*, to be tasted with the better Appetite at Night. Like a Disabled *Frigot*, that has received many Shots between *Wind* and *Water*, She is forc'd once a year to put in at Tunbridge or Epsom to *Wash* and *Tallow*, and *Refit* her *Leaky* Bottom; after which she *Cruises* up and down the Town as briskly as ever; till *Age* spoyle her Sayling, and ingraves *Wrinkles*, where she once Painted *Roses*: Then her former *Adorers* despise her, the World *hates* her, and she becomes a *Loathsome* thing, too unclean to enter into *Heaven*; too *Diseased* to continue long upon Earth; and too foul to be *toucht* with anything but a *Pen* or a pair of *Tongs*: And therefore 'tis time to *Leave* her—For *Foh how she sinks*.

2. *Auction of Whores, or, The Bawds Bill of Sale, For Bartholomew-Fair, Held in the Cloysters, near Smithfiled. Worth the reading of all Single Men and Batchelours* (1691)

On Tuesday the 25th of this Instant August, will be exposed to Saile, by Auction, a curious Collection of painted Whores, Cracks, Night-Walkers, Newgate-Nappers, Bridewell-Workers,[5]

---

1 An African servant.
2 An insulting name for an old woman.
3 Lovers.
4 Arousing.
5 A napper is a thief. Prostitutes were routinely sentenced to Bridewell Hospital where they were put to work beating hemp.

Ladies of Pleasure, Cart-Dancers; with other such dissembling Pick-pocket Cheats, some Pox'd, some Clap'd and some quite rotten and ready to fall in pieces: Some whereof will smile in your faces, and yet be ready, behind your backs, to cut your Throats for Sixpence. Others will chuck you under the chin, with the Left-hand, and with their Right be picking your pockets. Some will be so drunk, when you carry them to the Tavern, that they will p— on your knees, and hug and kiss you at so damnable a rate, that the stink of their breath will be ready to smother you, and force you to spew. Others will put one hand in your Cod-piece, and another in your Watch pocket. Others will keep you in discourse, till their Partners carry away your Hat, Cloak, Cane and Gloves. Some will spew in your face, when you are busy with them, whilst you are already half stifled by the stink of their breath. Who can but buy and love such pretty profitable, and well accomplish'd Ladies? Wherein so many such Qualities are concentrated.

There will be great variety bothe of Whores and Tricks, more than I can well inform you of at present. But for the satisfaction of the young Sparks, who yearly frequent the place, I give this account that followeth.

A List of the whores of Bartholomew Fair, with the rates, whereat they have commonly hitherto been Sold.

	Price per piece
From St. James's Park 10 Whores, in gorgeous apparel, and well drest, price	01 01 06[1]
From Westminster, 16 Whores, at Six pence per piece	00 00 06
From Covent Garden, 30 Whores troubled with the Gout	00 02 06
From Holbourn 21, whereof several are Rag-wenches[2]	00 00 03
From the Temple, Grays-Inn, Lincolns-Inn, and other Inns of Court, 173	00 01 03
From Bull and Mouth meeting-house, who kiss with discretion 4	00 00 06

---

1 The numbers here represent the prices of various whores. The first column denotes pounds, the second column denotes shillings, and the third column denotes pence, So the price for the first whore is $1l. 1s. 6p.$

2 Girls who made their living selling second-hand clothes or rags.

From the royal Exchange 13, with loafty Commodes and Top-knots, curiously painted by a careful hand, Price	00 10 00
From Cheapside, 13 brisk and active Whores, who pass for Maids, and yet bestowed their Maiden-heads on their Masters Apprentices	00 00 09
From Lombard-street, a little, short, black, dirty Whore	00 00 02
From Cornhill 1, who bestowed her Maiden-head on her Master, when her Mistress lay in[1]	00 05 00
From Wood-street a Cook-maid, but of a good Complexion	00 00 06
From St. Katherines 2, One old, and the other young, both brazenfac'd impudent Whores	00 00 01
From St. Martin le Grand, an ugly nasty, stinking, impudent Whore	00 00 02
From White Chappel, Bishopsgate-Street, Shore-ditch, Spittle-fields, Stepney, Popular and Wapping, in old torn Crape Gowns, without Smocks, who look as if they were half starv'd 575	00 00 02
From St. John-street, Islington, Newington, Aldersgate street 421	00 00 03

From Salubury Court, Neutler's Lane and Black-Mary's Hole 2399 Whores, wereof are pox'd 1398, lost their Noses 392, at several Prices.
From Southwark, Deptford, Greenwich, and other adjacent places 2133, at several Prices.

There are a great many more, whom you may see at the place of Auction, whom I cannot conveniently mention here, such as, Country Whores, Ubiquitarian[2] Whores, Journey women Whores, and Whores from all parts of England, besides Out-landish Whores, a multitude of Spanish, French, Dutch, High German Whores, and Country Jones,[3] in their night Cloaths, with Whores of all sorts and sizes, where you may pick and choose, and please your selves. As we can best conjecture our Number will be about 65000.

---

1 Gave birth.
2 A whore who is everywhere.
3 Whores who pretended to be from the country and without pretense.

Note, That the Sale is to continue, during the whole time of the Fair, beginning at one a Clock every morning, and lasting till 12 at night. Lifts may be had in all Booksellers Shops, and Coffee-houses, for a penny a piece.

POSTSCRIPT

Be sure to bring Money with, and I'll secure you shall carry none home.

Appendix E: The Great Debate on the Poor

[The driving force behind Roxana's accumulation of wealth is her deep fear of poverty. During the late seventeenth and eighteenth centuries a vigorous debate emerged on how England might best keep its neediest citizens out of poverty and put them into productive labor.]

1. From Matthew Hale, *A Discourse Touching Provision for the Poor* (1683)

The Preface

A *Due care for the Relief of the Poor is an act 1. of great Piety towards Almighty God who requires it of us: He hath left the Poor as his Pupils, and the Rich as his Stewards to provide for them: It is one of those great Tributes that he justly requires from the rest of Mankind; which, because they cannot pay to him, he hath scattered the Poor among the rest of Mankind as his Substitutes and Receivers.*

2. It is an act of greatest Humanity among men. Mercy and Benignity is due to the very Beasts that serve us, much more to those that are partakers of the same common nature with us.

3. It is an act of great Civil Prudence and Political Wisdom: for Poverty in it self is apt to Emasculate the minds of men, or at least it makes men tumultuous and unquiet. Where there are many very Poor, the Rich cannot long or safely continue such; necessity renders men of Phlegmatique[1] *and dull natures stupid and indisciplinable; And men of more fiery or active constitutions rapacious, and desperate.*

At this day it seems to me that the English Nation is more deficient in their prudent Provision for the Poor than any other cultivated and Christian State; at least that have so many opportunities and advantages to supply them.

In some other Countries a Beggar is a rare sight; Those that are unable to maintain themselves by Age or Impotency are relieved. And those that are able to supply their wants by their Labour are furnished with Imployments suitable to their condition.

And by this means there is not only a good and orderly Education and a decent face of the publique; But the more populous the State or Country is, the Richer and the more wealthy it is.

---

1 Sluggish.

But with us in England *for want of a due regulation of things the more Populous we are the Poorer we are; so that, that wherein the Strength and Wealth of a Kingdom conflicts, renders us the weaker and the poorer.*

And which is yet worse, Poor Families which daily multiply in the Kingdom for want of a due order for their Imployment in an honest course of life whereby they may gain subsistence for them and their Children do unavoidably bring up their Children either in a Trade of Begging or Stealing, or such other Idle course, which again they propagate over to their Children, and so there is a successive multiplication of hurtful or at least unprofitable People, neither capable of Discipline nor beneficial Imployment.

It is true we have severe Laws against Begging the very giver being in some cases subject to a penalty by the Statute of 1 Jac. Cap. 17. *But it takes little Effect. And indeed as the case stands with us it is no reason it should: for what man that is of ability can have the conscience to deny an Alms, or to bring a Wanderer to the punishment directed by that Statute, and the Statute of* 39 Eliz. *when he cannot choose but know that there is not that due course provided, or at least used, that Persons necessitous, and able to work may have it; Indeed were there a clear means practised for the Imploying of poor Persons, It were an uncharitable action to relieve them in a course of Idleness. But when I do not know that there is such a Provision, I dare not deny my relief, because I know not whether without it he may be starved with hunger, without his own default.*

We have also very severe Laws against Theft, possibly more severe than most other Nations, yea, and than the Offense in it self simply considered deserves; And there is little to be said in the defence of the severity of the Law herein, but the multitude of the Offenders and the design of the Law rather to terrify than to punish, ut metus in omnes, poena in paucos: *But it is most apparent that the Law is frustrated of its design therein; for although more suffer at one Sessions a* Newgate *for Stealing and Breaking up Houses, and Picking of Pockets, and such other Larcenies out of the protection of Clergy;[1] than suffer in some other Countries for all Offences in three years, yet the Goals[2] are never the Emptier: Necessity, and Poverty, and want of a due Provision for Imployment of Indigent Persons, and the custom of a*

---

1 Under common law, clergy were exempted from capital punishment and remanded to church courts. By the time Firmin is writing, one only had to prove that one could "read" in order to be exempted from capital punishment.

2 Jails.

loose and Idle life, daily supply with advantage the number of those who are taken off by the Sentence of the Law: And doubtless as the multitude of the Poor, and necessitous, and uneducated Persons, increase, the multitude of Malefactors will increase, notwithstanding the Examples of Severity.

So that upon the whole account the prudence of prevention, as it is more Christian, so it will be more Effectual than the Prudence of remedy: The prevention of Poverty, Idleness, and a loose and disorderly Education, Even of poor Children, would do more good to the Kingdom than all the Gibbets, and Cauterizations,[1] and Whipping Posts, and Goals in this Kingdom, and would render these kind of Disciplines less necessary and less frequent.

But hitherto I am in generals, which rarely prosper into Action of Conviction: I therefore shall consider principally these things:

1. What Provisions there are already settled by Laws in force for the Relief and Imployment of the Poor.

2. Wherein the Defects are, in relation to those Laws, or Provisions, and the Consequences thereof.

3. What may be thought a convenient Supply of those Defects and the Consequences of such Supplies.

CHAP. I

Touching the Laws at present in force for the Relief and Imployment of the Poor.

The Laws relating to the Poor are of two kinds, viz. 1. Such as concern the relief of the Aged, and Impotent, that are not able by their labour to maintain themselves. 2. Such as concern the imployment and setting of work, of such as are able. And this latter as shall be shewn, is the more comprehensive & beneficial charity, although both are necessary and become us, both as men and as Christians; much more Touching the former of these. *viz.* the relief of the impotent Poor, the Laws of *England* have provided a double remedy. First, by giving great incouragement to voluntary undertakings of good and liberal minds in this kind. 2. by Compulsary means upon all.

Again as touching the former of these, the Statute of 39 *Eliz. Cap.* 5 hath given a great incouragement to such as shall Erect Hospitals, Houses of Correction and *Maisons de Dieu.*[2] And the

---

1 Brandings.
2 Home for the poor.

Statutes of 39. *Eliz. Cap.* 6. *and* 43. *Eliz. Cap.* 4. have taken special care for the due implement of gifts to charitable uses. And certainly such voluntary assignations argue an Excellent and Charitable mind in those that shall so voluntarily give; And the Statutes have given a fair Incouragement to the Charities of men in this kind. But this provision doth but little in order to relief. For 1. for the most part such Hospitals, Extend but to a few aged Persons limited to some particular Town, unless it be in the large Hospitals, in *London,* where there is some provision more Extensive in respect both of number and age, as St. *Thomas* Hospital, *Christ-Church* Hospital and some others. 2. But besides this those are but Voluntary and not Compulsary; although there may be some that may be charitably minded, yet for the most part men are backward in works of Charity; Self love, Covetousness, distrust of the Truth and Providence of God keeps most from overflowing Charity or Building or Endowing Hospitals.

2. Therefore there was a Compulsary laid upon men for the relief of the Poor within their respective Parishes, *viz..* the Statute of 43. *Eliz. Cap.* 2. being the first compulsory Law that I remember of that kind: And indeed it now became necessary to be done by a Compulsary means which before that time was left more arbitrary, because the Kingdom became then much more Populous than in former time and with it the Poor also greatly increased, and besides many of those methods of their voluntary relief was then much abated; which Statute Enables the Church-Wardens and Overseers, &c. to do these things:

1. To take order for setting to work the Children of those whose Parents are not able to maintain their Children.

2. To take order to set those to work as such, having no means to maintain themselves, use no ordinary trade. But provides not sufficient Compulsaries to make them work.

3. To raise weekly by Taxation a convenient stock of Flax, Hemp, &c. to set the Poor on work: But no means at the first, before the return of the Manufacture to pay them wages in Express words, but is supplied by the latter general clause. (*And to do and Execute all other things, as well for the disposing of the said Stock, or otherwise concerning the premises as to them shall seem convenient.*)

4. To raise competent sums of Money for the impotent Poor not able to work.

5. Also for the putting of Poor Children Apprentices but no Compulsary for any to receive them:

Among all these Provisions the 4th concerns the relief of the

Poor by Taxation, and Contributions to such as are impotent, the four other particulars concern their Imployment, and of such as are able to work, which is the far greater number. And although the relief of the Impotent Poor seems to be a Charity of more immediate Exigence yet the Imployment of the Poor is a Charity of greater Extent, and of very great and important Consequence to the publique Wealth, and Peace of the Kingdom as also to the Benefit and Advantage of the Poor.

I therefore come to that second Business relating to the Poor, *viz.* the setting the Poor on Work.

The Laws that concern that Business of the Imployment of the Poor are of two kinds; *viz.* that which contains a Compulsary means of providing work for the Poor which is the Statute of 43. *Eliz.* And secondly those Laws which are in some kind of Compulsary to force Persons to work; and there are two kinds, *viz.*

1. Those that concern Children And the Binding of them Apprentices, *viz.* the Clause of the Statute 43. *Eliz. Cap.* 4. before mentioned and the Statute 7. *Jac. Cap.* 1. which makes fair Provision for the raising of Money to bind them, and directs the manner of its Imployment. But as before is observed, hath not any sufficient Compulsary for Persons to take them, & perchance there might be fit to have some such qualifications in that Compulsary which might not leave it too arbitrary in the Justices of Peace to compell whom they please, to take whom they please: But this is not the Business, I drive at, perchance the general Provision which I design may make this at least not so frequently necessary.

2. In reference to Rogues, Vagabonds and Idle & disorderly Persons, the Statute 7. *Jac. Cap.* 4 gives power to the Justices of Peace to send them to the House of Correction, which they are thereby required to cause to be Erected. 2. Power to the Master of such House of Correction to keep them to work.

But even in this particular there are defects. 1. It is not general for all Persons, but at most Idle and disorderly Persons. 2. That description is very uncertain in reference to such Persons, and leaves the Justices either too great or too little power. 3. For want of a convenient Stock to be raised[1] for such Houses of Correction, and advantageous ways for such work, it either leaves such as are sent without an Imployment or renders their Imployment ungrateful in respect of the smallness of the wages, and rather makes People hate Imployment as a hell than to Entertain it as a

---

1 Sufficient funds.

means of a comfortable support; which though it may be well enough as a punishment for disorderly persons that refuse to work, yet it is not applicable to those that are only idle, it may be, because they have no work: 4. It is a difficult thing to determine who shall be said an Idle Person, it is a reasonable answer to that, they are Idle for want of such work as they are able to do, or for want of such wages as might give them a reasonable support; For there is no power given, nor is it reasonable it should, to compel Persons to set them on work, or to set them on work at convenient wages. 5. And lastly, it is not universal; many Persons are not within that Law which would work if they might: or if they might at reasonable rates, whereby they might live. There is need, therefore of some such provision that might be as ample as the occasion, and without which indeed all the Laws already made are either weak and ineffectual to their Ends, and the generality of the Poor left destitute of a convenient support and provision.

CHAP. II

Touching the Power by the Law settled for the general Provision for the Poor, and their defects.

Upon the consideration of the Statutes for the Poor the only Statute that provides universally is that of 43. *Eliz.* which generally makes two Provisions.

1. For the Impotent Poor, that are not able to work: And it is true is a good and Effectual Provision for such, if duly Executed. But as I said before, the Plaister[1] is not so large as the sore, there are many Poor that are able to work if they had it, and had it at reasonable wages, whereby they might support themselves and their Families, which oftentimes are many. These are not within the Provision of the Law and if they come for Exhibitions,[2] they are denied, or at least have but very small,[3] and such as cannot support them and their Families. And indeed if they should have sufficient Exhibition for the support of them and their Families, the Parishes where they live were not able to supply them in a proportion answerable to their necessities, or answerable to that supply which a full Imployment would afford them; For instance a Poor Man and his Wife though able to work, may have four Children, two of them possibly

---

1 A medicinal substance spread over a wound.
2 A way of supporting the poor with food and money.
3 They are given only a small amount of support.

able to work, two not able: The Father and the Mother are not able to maintain themselves and their Family in Meat, Drink, Cloathing and House rent under ten Shillings *per* Week, and so much they might probably get if imployed; This amounts to 26*l. per Annum*, if there were forty such Families in a great Parish, and they lived upon this Exhibition collected by rates, it would arise to above 800*l. per Annum*, which in many Parishes Exceeds the yearly Value of their Lands or Rents, yet when these Persons are kept on work thus much must be gotten by them, and without a supply Equivalent to this they must live by Begging, or Stealing, or Starve: Therefore the second Provision is,

2. For those Poor that are able to work, and in reference to them it gives power to raise Stocks by rateing the Parishioners, and setting the Poor on work.

The defects of this Provision are,

1. In the Execution of the Law already made; for let any look over most of the Populous Parishes in England, indeed there are rates made for the relief of the Impotent Poor, and it may be the same relief also given in a narrow measure unto some others, that have great Families, and upon this they live miserably and at best from Hand to Mouth, and if they cannot get work to make out their livelihood they and their Children set up a trade of Begging at best. But it is rare to see any Provision of a Stock in any Parish for the relief of the Poor. And the reasons are principally there: 1. The Generality of People that are able yet unwilling to Exceed the present necessary charge, they do choose to live for an hour rather than project for the future; and although possibly trebling their Exhibition in one gross sum at the beginning of the year, to raise a Stock might in all probability render their future years altogether less by half or two thirds, than what must be without it, yet they had rather continue on their yearly Payments, year after year, though it Exhaust them in time, and make the Poor nothing the better at the years End. 2. Because those places, where there are most Poor, consist for the most part of Tradesmen, whose Estates lye principally in their Stocks, which they will not endure to be searched into to make them contributory to raise any considerable Stock for the Poor, nor indeed so much as to the ordinary Contributions: But they lay all the rates to the Poor upon the Rents of Lands and Houses, which alone without the help of the Stocks are not able to raise a Stock for the Poor, although it is very plain that Stocks are as well by Law rateable as Lands, both to the relief, and raising a Stock for the Poor: 3. Because the Church-Wardens and Overseers, to whom this

power is given, are Inhabitants of the same Parish, and are either unwilling to charge themselves, or displease their Neighbours in Charging more than they needs must towards the Poor: And although it were to be wished and hoped that the Justices of Peace would be forwardly to Enforce them if they might, though it may concern them also in point of present profit, yet if they would do any thing herein they are not impowered to compel the Church-Wardens and Overseers to do it, who most certainly will never go about it to burden as they think, themselves, and displease their Neighbours unless some Compulsary power were not only lodged by Law, but also executed in some that may have a power over them to inforce it, or to do it, if they do it not, and to do it effectually, if they do it either partially or too sparingly: 4. Because People do not consider the inconvenience that will in time grow to themselves by this neglect, and the benefit that would in a little time accrue to them by putting it in practice if they would have but a little patience, as shall be shewn hereafter.

2. The second Defect is in the Law itself; which are these:

1. No power in the Justices of Peace, or some Superintendent power to compel the raising of a Stock where the Church-Wardens and Overseers neglect it.

2. The act chargeth every Parish apart where it may be they are able to do little towards it, neither would it be so effectual as if three, four, five or more contiguous Parishes did contribute towards the raising of a Stock proportionable to their Poor respectively.

3. There is no power for the hiring or erecting a common House, or place for their common Work-House, which may be in some respects, and upon some occasions, useful and necessary, as shall be shewn.

2. From Thomas Firman, *Some Proposals for the imployment of the Poor, and For the prevention of Idleness and the Consequence thereof, Begging* (1681)

Sir,

It is now above four years since I erected my Work-House in *Little Britain* for the Imployment of the Poor in the Linnen Manufacture, which hath proved so great a Help, and afforded such Relief to many Hundreds of poor Families, that I never did, nor I fear ever shall do an Action more to my own satisfaction, nor to the good and benefit of the Poor.

[T]here being nothing so necessary for the prevention of Poverty and the consequence thereof, Begging, as to provide some Imployment for our Poor People, whereby to prevent Idleness, the Mother and Nurse of all Mischief, and one of those sins for which God destroyed *Sodom* with fire and Brimstone form heaven, as the Holy Scripture informs us.

To the end therefore that Poverty, together with that wicked Trade of Begging (which so many thousands of late years have taken up, to the dishonour of Almighty god, and the great scandal of the Government of the Nation) may be prevented, I shall humbly propose a few things, which being put in practice, may with God's Blessing, prove effectual to the ends designed.

And the first is this, That every Parish that abounds with Poor People, would set up a School in the nature of a Workhouse, to teach their poor Children to work in, who for want thereof, now wander up and down the Parish and parts adjacent, and between Begging and Stealing, get a sorry living; but never bring any thing to their poor Parents, nor earn one Farthing towards their own maintenance, or good of the Nation.

This, in a short time, would be found very advantageous, not only to the poor Children themselves, who by this means, whilst young should be inured to labour, and taught to get their own Livings, but also to their Parents, who should hereby both be freed from the Charge of keeping them, and in time, be helpt by their Labours, as it is in other places; and moreover the Parish should be freed from much Charge which many times they are at, to keep such poor children, or at least which they are necessitated to allow their Parents towards it.

Nothing being accounted a better Argument for a large Pension, than that a Man or Woman hath six or seven small children, whereas unless they were all born at a time, or came faster into the World than ordinarily so many Children do, it is very hard if some them are not able to work for themselves. I my self have at this time many poor children, not above five or six years old, that can earn two pence a day, and others but a little older, three pence or four pence, by spinning flax which will go very far towards the maintenance of any poor Child. Not that I would have these Schools confined only to Spinning, but left at liberty to take in any other work that the Children shall be capable of, as knitting of Stockings, winding of Silk, making of Lace or plain Work, or the like: For it matters not so much what you employ these poor children in, as that you do employ them in some thing, to prevent an idle, lazy, kind of Life, which if once they get the habit of, they will hardly leave; but on the contrary, if you train up a Child in the way that he should go, when he is old, he will not depart from it. If it be said that their children are not maintained so well, nor learnt so much as generally our Children in Hospitals are; I answer, 'Tis so much the better, for why should poor Children that must be put out to poor Trades, where they must work hard, and fare hardly, be fed with white Bread, or taught farther than is necessary for such Trades? Is not this to make them too big for their Business, which is always for the worse? Why, I pray, must a poor Boy that is designed for a Mason, bricklayer, Shoemaker, or the like honest and necessary Trade, be taught to write as if he were designed for a Master in that Art; or so far in Arithmetick, as if he were designed for a Merchant? It is not enough that such Children are taught to read the Bible, and so much of Arithmetick and Writing, as may fit them for such Trades and Employments, as they are intended to be put into? And must Children be kept from seven to fifteen Years old, to learn so much when two hours a day would be more than enough to effect it? And all the rest of their Time might be spent in doing something or other that might help to keep them, and be by degrees, inured to the Work and Business for which they are designed and intended. This in a very short time, however it may seem hard at first, would be much more pleasant to the Children themselves, than sitting eight or ten hours in a day under a severe School-Master, who many times shall whip a poor Child for not remembering or else for mistaking a few words, as severely as a Rogue in Bridewell, for picking a Pocket or cutting a Purse.

3. **From Daniel Defoe, *The Poor Man's Plea To all the Proclamations, Declarations, Acts of Parliament, &v. Which Have been, or shall be made, or publish'd, for a Reformation of Manners, and suppressing Immorality in the Nation. The Second Edition Corrected. Printed for A. Baldwin, near the Oxford-Arms in Warwick-Lane* (1698)**

The Preface

Reformation of Manners is a Work so Honourable, and at This Time so absolutely necessary, that, like the Reform of our Money, it can be no longer delayed.

The Ways by which the present Torrent of Vice has been let in upon the Nation, and by which it maintains the Tyranny it has usurp'd on the Lives of the Inhabitants, are too plain to be hid. The following Sheets aim at the Work, by leading to the most direct means, Viz. Reformation by Example. Laws are, in Terrorem Punishments,[1] and *Magistrates compel and put a Force upon Mens Minds; but Example is Persuasive and Gentle, and draws by a Secret, Invisible, and almost Involuntary Power.*

If there can be any Remedies proposed more proper to bring it to pass, they that know them would do well to bring them forth. In the mean time the Author thinks Conscience in the Minds of Men Impartially Consulted, will give a Probatum[2] *to the following Proposal; and to that Judgement he refers all those who Object against it.*

★★★

[W]e of the *Plebeii*[3] find our selves justly aggriev'd in all this Work of Reformation; and the Partiality of this Reforming Rigor makes the real Work impossible: Wherefore we find our selves forced to seek Redress of our Grievances in the old honest way of Petitioning Heaven to relieve us: And in the mean time, we solemnly Enter our Protestation against all the Vicious Part of the Nobility and Gentry of the Nation; as follows:

First, We Protest, That we do not find impartially enquiring into the matter, and speaking of Moral Goodness, that you are one jot better than we are, *your Dignities, Estates and Quality excepted.* 'Tis true, we are all bad enough, and we are willing in good Manners to agree, that we are as wicked as you; but we cannot find on the exact Scrutiny, but that in the Commonwealth of Vice, the Devil has taken care to level Poor and Rich into one Class, and is fairly going on to make us all Graduates in the last degree of Immorality.

Secondly, We do not find that all the Proclamations, Declarations, and Acts of Parliament yet made, have any *effective Power* to punish *you* for your immoralities as they do us. Now while *you* make Laws to punish *us,* and let *your selves* go free, though guilty of the same Vices and Immoralities, those Laws are unjust and unequal in themselves.

'Tis true, the Laws do not express a Liberty to *you* and Punishment to *us*; and therefore the King and Parliament are free, as King and Parliament, from this our Appeal; but the Gentry and

---

1 Earthly punishments.
2 Due consideration.
3 Common people.

Magistrates of the Kingdom, while they execute those Laws upon us the poor Commons, and themselves practicing the same Crimes, in defiance of the Laws both of God and Man, go unpunish'd; *This* is the Grievance we protest against, as unjust and unequal.

Wherefore, till the Nobility, Gentry, Justices of the Peace, and Clergy, will be pleased wither to reform their own Manners, and suppress their own Immoralities, or find out some Method and Power impartially to punish themselves when guilty, we humbly crave leave to object against setting any Poor Man in the Stocks, or sending them to the House of Correction for Immoralities, as the most unequal and unjust way of proceeding in the World.

4. **From Daniel Defoe, *Every-Body's Business is No-Body's Business; Or, Private Abuses, Public Grievances. Exemplified in the Pride, Insolence, and Exorbitant Wages of our Women-Servants, Footmen, &c. With a Proposal for Amendment of the same: As also, for clearing the Streets of those Vermin called Shoe-Cleaners, and substituting in their stead many Thousands Poor now ready to starve. With divers other Hints, of great Use to the Publick* (1725)**

The *Romans* had a Law, called *Jus Trium Liberorum*, by which every Man who had been the Father of three Children had particular Honours and Privileges. This incited the Youth to quit a dissolute single Life, and become Fathers of Families, to the Support and Glory of the Empire.

In Imitation of this most excellent Law, I would have such Servants who should continue many Years in one Service, meet with singular Esteem and Reward.

The Apparel of Women-servants should be next regulated, that we may know the Mistress from the Maid. I remember I was once put very much to the blush; being at a Friend's House, and by him required to salute the Ladies, I kissed the Chamber-maid into the Bargain, for she was as well dressed as the best. But I was soon undeceived by a general Titter, which gave me the utmost Confusion; nor can I believe myself the only Person who has made such a Mistake.

Things of this Nature would be easily avoided, if Servant-maids were to wear Liveries, as our Footmen do; or obliged to go in a Dress suitable to their Station. What should ail them but a

Jacket and Petticoat of good Yard-wide Stuff, or Callimanco,[1] might keep them decent and warm.

Our Charity Children are distinguished by their Dress; why then may not our Women-servants? Why may they not be made frugal by Force, and not suffered to put all on their Backs, but obliged to save something against a rainy Day? I am therefore entirely gainst any Servants wearing of Silks, Laces, and other superfluous Finery; it sets them above themselves, and makes their Mistresses contemptible in their Eyes. "I am handsomer than my Mistress," says a young prinkt-up Baggage, "what pity it is I should be her Servant: I go as well drest, or better, than she." This makes the Girl take the first Offer to be made a Whore, and there is a good Servant spoiled: whereas, were her Dress suitable to her Condition, it would teach her Humility, and put her in mind of her Duty.

5. From Bernard Mandeville, *Modest Defense of the Publick Stews* (1724)

That long course of Experience which most of these *Gentlemen* have had in the world, and which is of so great Use in other Cases, may probably occasion their Mistake in this; for Age is very liable to forget the violence of youthful Passions, and consequently, apt to think them easier curb'd: whereas if we consider the true Source of Whoring, and the strong Impulse of Nature that way, we shall find, it is a Thing not to be too violently restrain'd; lest, like a Stream diverted out of its proper Channel, it should break in and overflow the neighbouring *Enclosures....*

Publick Whoring consists in lying with a certain Set of women, who have shook off all Pretence to Modesty, and for such a Sum of Money, more or less, profess themselves always in Readiness to be enjoy'd. The Mischief a Man does in this Case is entirely to himself; for with respect to the Woman, he does a laudable Action, in furnishing her with the Means of Subsistence, in the only, or at least most innocent way that she is capable of procuring it. The Damage he does to himself, is either with regard to his Health, or the Expence of Money, and may be consider'd under the same View as Drinking, with this considerable Advantage, that it restores us to that cool Exercise of our Reason, which Drinking tends to deprive us of. Indeed, was there a Probability

---

1 Callico.

of a Woman's Amendment, and of her gaining a Livelihood by some honester Method, there might be some Crime in encouraging her to follow such a Profession: But the Minds of Women are observ'd to be so much corrupted by the Loss of Chastity, or rather by the Reproach they suffer upon that Loss, that they seldom or never change that Course of Life for the better; and if they should, they can never recover that good Name, which is so absolutely necessary to their getting a Maintenance in any honest Way whatever; and that nothing but meer Necessity obliges them to continue in that Course, is plain from this, That they themselves in Reality utter abhor it: And indeed there appears nothing in it so very alluring and bewitching, especially to People who have that Inclination to Lewdness intirely extinguish'd, which is the only thing could possibly make it supportable.

The other Branch of Whoring, viz. *Private*, is of much worse Consequence and a Man's Crime in this Case, increases in proportion to the different Degree of Mischief done, if you consider his Crime with regard to the *Society*; for as to personal Guilt, Allowance ought to be made for the Increase of Temptation, which is very considerable in the Case of debauching *Married Women*; upon account of the Safety to the Agressor, either with Respect to his Health, or the Charge, and if that affects him, the Scandal of having a Bastard. On the other hand, the Injury done, is very considerable, as such an Action tends to corrupt a Woman's Mind, and destroys that mutual Love and Affection between Man and Wife, which is so necessary to both their Happiness. Besides the Risque run of a Discovery, which at least ruins a Woman's Reputation, and destroys the Husband's Quiet; nay, where Virtue does not intirely give way, if it warps but by so little, the Consequence is shockingly fatal: for tho' the good Man, suspicious of the Gallant's Constancy, and the Gallant of the Husband's Watchfulness, by being a Check upon each other, may keep the Gate of Virtue shut; yet then even all Parties must be attended with a never ceasing Misery, not to be imagin'd, but by those who too fatally *feel it*....

Female Honour, therefore being so nearly ally'd and closely annex'd to worldly Interest, we must confine this Class of Women to two Sorts: First, those whose Fortunes are independent, and above being influenc'd by the Censure of the World; and secondly, those who are so far below the World, that they either escape its Censure, or else are incapable of being hurt by it. The first Sort lie under this Disadvantage, that let their natural Chastity be ever so great, the smallest part of Desire is capable of being blown up and rais'd to a considerable Pitch; whereas, when a Woman is once arriv'd to Maturity, that Portion of Honour which she has acquir'd, is with Difficulty preserv'd, and at the best is incapable of any Improvement. The second Sort are equally liable to have their Passions rais'd, however low they may be naturally, and besides like under this farther Disadvantage, that tho' they can't promote their Interest by preserving their Chastity, yet, if they have the least Spark of Beauty, they will find their Account sufficiently in parting with it. The Virtue indeed, of this Class of Women, seems chiefly to depend upon the Degree of Beauty which they stand possess'd of; for if they have Charms sufficient to provoke young Men to be at any tolerable Pains and Cost, their Chastity can never hold out long, but must infallibly surrender....

6. **From Daniel Defoe,** *Some Considerations Upon Street-Walkers. With a Proposal for lessening the present Number of them. In Two Letters to a Member of Parliament* (1726)

I cannot but on this Occasion give you, Sir, a genuine Letter from One of the unhappy Persons I have troubled you about, and who was afterwards executed for picking a Gentleman's Pocket, to Mrs.—, who kept a noted Bawdy-House in Great P—ney-street; by which the miserable Condition of these Creatures will more fully appear, and consequently, the great Necessity there is to suppress them.

Madam,

The forlorn Condition I am in, the many unmerited Injuries I have suffer'd from you, and the great Use I have formerly been of to you, I thought might be sufficient to incite you to afford me a little charitable Assistance; but in vain: that you reduce me to the unhappy Necessity of reminding you of the Miseries of my past Life, not a few of which were owing to you, and which if you have not joined a sear'd Conscience to a hardened Heart, must extort from you that Compassion I call for.

You know Madam, my Father, who was by his Rank a Gentleman, was by his Fortune unable to make any other Provision for me, than by giving me an Education suitable to that Rank; which Education has been my greatest Curse, as it has enabled me to feel more bitterly the Ills which I have undergone. The want of

Means to support my Character, soon after his Death laid me open to the Sollicitations of Sir James —, whose great Fortune made it proper to me to bear with the first Insolence of his Proposals, rather than by shocking him, destroy the Hopes I had form'd of making him like me in an honourable Way. But why do I say this to you? Alas, Madam, I am distracted! I like what I was, tho' I feel with Bitterness what I am.

The History of his Triumph, his forsaking and deceiving me concerning the Maintenance which he promis'd and pretended to secure for me, are but too well known to you; they were the Means of my Acquaintance with you. I know not how you and he had concerted Matters before-hand; but when he brought me to your House, he represented it to me as a new Lodging which he had taken for me: after having gutted and sent away all the Goods and Furniture I had in the former, which I thought to find with you, but never heard of since. The necessitous Condition which I found my self reduc'd to by this new Villainy of his, soon made me compliant with your Requests. What and how much Shame I have suffered for your Benefit, I can't bear to think of: I say, for your Benefit; for so you manag'd it, that almost all my Wages of Sin were Diseases. Oh, would to God that, according to the Scripture, they had been instant Death.

Those Maladies, which Intemperance as well as Incontinence contributed to, soon render'd me unfit for your Purpose; the little Beauty which recommended me to you was fled, and I was no longer a Temptation to Sin. You therefore, cruel Women, turn'd me out of Doors, poorer than you receiv'd me. I had Cloaths when I came to you splendid enough to adorn Beauty; when I left you, scarce Rags to cover it. In this sad Condition, I fell into more and new Vices, which I think of with Horror; I grew harden'd to Shame, and therefore forgot all Thoughts of Sin. Drunkenness, which was at first a Relief, now became an incurable Disease; and all the little Gains that my shameful Occupation brought me in, were laid out upon intoxicating vulgar Drams. Work-Houses and Whippings have been employ'd in vain upon me; still as I was released, my Wants threw me into my old Ways; till at last, oh Shame to think of! by frequent Converse with Thieves and Pickpockets, I learn'd their Arts; and, intic'd by their Gains, practiced them. I stand at present committed to this Place for picking a Gentleman's Pocket. I am now awaken'd from my Sins, and wish for that Death which I am told attends me: but such is my miserable Condition, that I can't prepare properly for it without your Assistance. I have no Friends to apply to; they all forsook me before I came to you; you are the only Person I deserve any thing from on Earth; what I deserve from Heaven, distracting Thought!—But I may repent, and assuredly shall, if the want of due Relief drives me not to Despair. Farewell, Madam; I am the same that you knew me in nothing but the Name of,

Your, &c.

Newgate &c.

Appendix F: Women and Marriage

[Partly because England was seeking to augment its colonial expansions abroad, it sought to stabilize its social relations at home. The result was an important debate about women's roles within the context of marriage.]

1. From Mary Astell, *Some Considerations on Marriage* (1700/1706)

Monsieur Mazarine[1] is not to be justified, nor Madam his Spouse excus'd. It is no question which is most Criminal, the having no Sense, or the abuse of a liberal Portion; nor any hard matter to determine who is most to be pity'd, he whom Nature never qualify'd for great things, who therefore can't be very sensible of great Misfortunes; or she, who being capable of every thing, must therefore suffer more and be the more lamented. To be yok'd for Life to a disagreeable Person and Temper; to have Folly and Ignorance tyrannize over Wit and Sense; to be contradicted in every thing one does or says, and bore down not by Reason but Authority; to be denied one's most innocent desires, for no other cause but the Will and Pleasure of an absolute Lord and Master, whose Follies a Woman with all her Prudence cannot hide, and whose Commands she cannot but despise at the same time she obeys them; is a misery none can have a just Idea of, but those who have felt it....

Women, it's true, ought to be treated with Civility; for since a little Ceremony and out-side Respect is all their Guard, all the privilege that's allow'd them, it were barbarous to deprive them of it; and because I would treat them civilly, I would not express my Civility at the usual Rate. I would not under pretence of honouring and paying a mighty Deference to the Ladies, call them fools to their faces; for what are all the fine Speeches and Submissions that are made, but an abusing them in a well-bred way? She must be a Fool with a witness, who can believe a Man, Proud and Vain as he is, will lay his boasted Authority, the Dignity and Prerogative of his Sex, one Moment at her Feet, but in prospect of taking it up again to more advantage; he may call himself her Slave a few days, but it is only in order to make her his all the rest of his Life.

---

1 The Duchess of Mazarine was one of Charles II's mistresses. Here, Astell addresses the Duchess's aggrieved husband.

A Man enters into Articles very readily before Marriage, and so he may, for he performs no more of them afterwards than he thinks fit. A Wife must never dispute with her Husband, his Reasons are now no doubt on't better than hers, whatever they were before; he is sure to perswade her out of her Agreement, and bring her, it must be suppos'd, Willingly, to give up what she did vainly hope to obtain, and what she thought had been made sure to her. And if she shews any Refractoriness, there are ways enough to humble her; so that by right or wrong the Husband gains his Will. For Covenants betwixt Husband and Wife, like Laws in an Arbitrary Government, are of little Force, the Will of the Sovereign is all in all. Thus it is in Matter of Fact, I will not answer for the Right of it; for if the Woman's Reasons upon which those Agreements are grounded are not Just and Good, why did he consent to them? Was it because there was no other way to obtain his Suit, and with an intention to Annul them when it shall be in his Power? Where then is his Sincerity? But if her Reasons are good, where is his Justice in obliging her to quit them? He neither way acts like an equitable or honest Man.

But when a Woman Marrys unequally and beneath her self, there is almost Demonstration that the Man is Sordid and Unfair, that instead of Loving her he only Loves himself, trapans[1] and ruines her to serve his own Ends. For if he had not a mighty Opinion of himself, (which temper is like to make an admirable Husband,) he cou'd never imagine that his Person and good Qualities should make compensation for all the advantages she quits on his account. If he had a real Esteem for her or valu'd her Reputation, he wou'd not expose it, nor have her Discretion call'd in Question for his sake; and if he truly Lov'd her he wou'd not reduce her to Straits and a narrow Fortune, nor so much as lessen her way of Living to better his own. For since GOD has plac'd different Ranks in the World, put some in a higher and some in a lower Station, for Order and Beauty's sake, and for many good Reasons; tho' it is both our Wisdom and Duty not only to submit with Patience, but to be Thankful and well-satisfied when by his Providence we are brought low, yet there is no manner of Reason for us to Degrade our selves; on the contrary, much why we ought not. The better our Lot is in this World and the more we have of it, the greater is our leisure to prepare for the next; we have the more opportunity to exercise that God-like Quality, to taste that Divine Pleasure, Doing good to the Bodies

---

1 Tricks.

and Souls of those beneath us. Is it not then ill Manners to Heaven, and an irreligious contempt of its Favours, for a Woman to slight that nobler Employment, to which it has assign'd her, and thrust her self down to a meaner Drudgery, to what is in the very literal Sense a caring for the things of the World, a caring not only to please, but to Maintain a Husband?

And a Husband so chosen will not at all abate of his Authority and right to Govern, whatever fair Promises he might make before. She has made him her Head, and he thinks himself as well qualify'd as the best to Act accordingly, nor has she given him any such Evidence of her Prudence as may dispose him to make an Act of Grace in her Favour. Besides, great Obligations are what Superiors cannot bear, they are more than can be return'd; to acknowledge, were only to reproach themselves with ingratitude, and therefore the readiest way is not to own but overlook them, or rather, as too many do, to repay them with Affronts and Injuries.

2. From Daniel Defoe, *Conjugal Lewdness* (1727)

Marriage is an *honourable State* or Station of Life, but it is not a thoughtless, idle, unemployed State, even where the Concerns of the Family are easy, where Plenty flows, and the World smiles; yet a married Life has its Cares, its Anxieties, it Embarassments, which the young Lady knew nothing of in her Father's House, where she liv'd without Care, without Disturbance, slept without Fear, and wak'd without Sorrows. But married, she is a Mistress, she is a Mother, she is a Wife, every one of which Relations has its little addenda of Incumbrance, and perhaps of Uneasiness too, be her Circumstances as good otherwise as she can or would suppose them to be.

We have an English saying, they that marry in haste repent at leisure. Now though my Design is not to run down the married State, and raise frightful Ideas in the Minds of those that are to enter into it, so as to prevent them their marrying; yet, I hope, I may hint to them, that they should look before they take this leap in the Dark, that they should consider all the Circumstances that are before them, that they may have no Reason to repent when they shall be sure to have no Room for it....

A— B— was a Gentleman of Figure and Fortune; in his Coach and four, and with a suitable Equipage: He made his Addresses to a wealthy Citizen, and Proposals of suitable Settlement, for his Consent to court his Daughter. Nothing appeared but what was fair and honourable; he is accepted; the young Lady, virtuous,

modest, beautiful, finely bred, in the Bloom of her Youth, whee-
dled with his Tongue, and deceived with the appearance of a fine
Gentleman, and Lover, yields to the Proposals, and throws her
self in to the Arms of the worst of Monsters....

Appendix G: Alternate Endings of Roxana

[*Roxana* underwent only one printing during Defoe's lifetime. Beginning in the 1730s, however, editions of the novel began to appear with some regularity. All of these posthumous versions altered the ending of the novel.]

1. **Daniel Defoe, *The fortunate mistress; or, a history of the life and vast variety of fortunes of Mademoiselle de Beleau, afterwards call'd the Countess de Wintselsheim, in Germany. Being the person known by the name of the Lady Roxana* (1740)**

Having sent away these Letters to my Son at times, as I wrote them; he came one Day into my Study, to tell me all Things were now ready; that is to say the Building finished, my Coach and Horses come, &c. I therefore proceeded to the main Design of making myself known to my Son and this one Daughter, I had not yet received any farther Account, what became of my other Daughter (who had formerly been so troublesome to me) since the Account which *Amy* had given me of her, the last Time of her coming to *Holland*; so that I believed what *Amy* had said of her to be Truth. But to proceed.

A few Days after this, I dressed myself in a new Suit of black Padusoy Silk,[1] and plain Linnen (but not quite after the *Quakers* Mode) for two Reasons; First, that I would not give any the least occasion of Offence to my Son, who was not of that persuasion, and well knew that neither he nor his Sister had their Education as such. *Second*, That as my Daughter had thought fit to change her Religion, I was in wise willing to give her the least Suspicion, but that I had always lived a chaste sober Life. Add to this that it was the most becoming Habit with respect to my Age, and the retired Life I now lived.

Thus equipp'd, with my plain Coach, &c. I made a Visit to my Son, who received me with all the Demonstration of Affection possible, entertaining me in the hansomest Manner.—At this Interview he returned me his Most hearty Thanks for my foregoing Letters of Advice, assuring me they were so acceptable to

---

1 Slightly corded or embossed silk.

him, that he would make it his chief Study to practice the Rules therein laid down to him—He then told me all the particular Steps taken, in respect to the proposal of marrying his Master's Niece; assuring me, he should have somewhat rashly entered into Matrimony, had it not been for my seasonable Advice, which had caused him to consider much better of that Holy Ordinance than he should otherwise have done; adding, he would do nothing more in that grand Affair without my Advice and Concurrence; notwithstanding he thought all things would be adjusted to his Satisfaction, and he might appoint the Day of Solemnization when he pleased; at the same Time desiring my Company as his chiefest Guest and best Friend—I invited him home with me that Evening, which he accepting of, hindered my visiting my Daughter at that Time, as I at first intended.

That Evening I presented my Son with a handsome Service of Plate, which I had still left by me, against his Wedding, worth about five hundred Pounds Sterling; and finding him in a very agreeable Humour, after some previous Discourse I asked him, if his Mother would not accompany him at his Wedding? He said, his Mother being dead, he should always esteem me as such, in her stead, for my Care of, and Goodness towards him and his Sister. I examined him strictly as to the Time and Circumstances of his Mother's Death; which he could give no farther Account of than his Sister had done (as before related) only he heartily wished she were living; adding, with a particular Emphasis, that upon Condition he would be assured his dear Mother was living, he would willingly part with half he had in the World to see her.

Not being able to constrain himself longer, he burst into Tears, and after venting his Passion a little, said, were his Mother but living at this time, he should be completely Happy.

This touched me so to the Quick, that (though I had determined to break the Affair to my Daughter first) I could not but reflect on his tender Affection, and the Hardship we all had labour'd under so long, which the Words, *I am She*, would now remove. This drew Tears from my Eyes in more abundance than I had shed for some Years; he was astonished at this, and endeavoured all he could to pacify me, and wiped the Tears off my Cheecks; upon this I had not Power to contain myself any longer, but flinging my Arms round his Neck, bursting again into Tears, whisper'd thus to him, *My dear—I can no longer forbear telling you, I am your own Mother, and am ready to convince you of it.*

At this my Son started from me, and stood like one Thunderstruck looking passionately in my Face for some Time; at last,

Silence broke, *And are you Madam* (said he) *the Person to whom I owe my Being?* I answering in the Affirmative, we clasp'd our Arms about each others Neck, and mingled our Tears of Joy together.

The first transport of Passion being a little over, we debated the Matter, and I thoroughly satisfied him I was the very Person—we then consulted in what Manner I should discover myself to my Daughter; he intreated me to let him have the Management of that by reason she was big with Child, and therefore it required to be brought out by Degrees, lest a too hasty excess of Joy might endanger her or the Child's Life, if not both.

This was so modest a Request that I had not any thing to say against it; so we spent the remainder of the Evening in my giving him an Account as I thought proper of my past Life, how I went Abroad, in what Parts I had lived, and the like, with which he was fully satisfied.

Next Morning he took his Leave of me for that Time, promising to let me know every Evening how he proceeded in the Affair with his Sister, and that he would bring her to me as soon as he possibly could, to pay her Duty.

While he was busy with his Sister, I looked over all my Papers, and burnt all *Amy's* Letters to me, and the Copies of mine to her, with all other Writings that could give the least Intimation of my former Gallantry, and wicked Course of Life, that they might not bring anything to light.

My Son managed the Matter much better and more discreetly than I should have done, and with such Expedition, that the fourth Day he brought his Sister to me, fully satisfied that I was really her Mother; and in respect to the Sex, and the Condition she was in, left us together for the Space of two Hours, in which time we were perfectly reconciled in all Things; only she thought it strange I had not made myself known before, so many Opportunities as I had with her.

This Affair over, I now lived as happy as my Heart could wish, enjoying the sweet Consolation of my own Children, which I had been deprived of so many Years. This Comfort I enjoyed for seven Years, bless'd with a tolerable good State of Health. At last, finding Infirmities begin to creep on me, I settled all my worldly Affairs, made my Will, leaving only a few Legacies, among some distant Relations, and all the rest, which was still something Valuable, between my Son and Daughter and their Children.

About three Months after this, Madam ROXANA was taken Sick, and though it was the Opinion of her Phisicians, that her Distemper was Mortal, she was not in the least dismayed, but freely resigned her Soul to the Mercy of him who gave it, dying in Charity with all the World.

She was buried according to her own Desire, in a private Manner, in Hornsey Church-Yard.

2. **Daniel Defoe, *The history of Mademoiselle de Beleau; or, the new Roxana, the fortunate mistress: afterwards Countess of Wintselsheim. Published by Mr. Daniel De Foe. And from papers found, since his decease, it appears was greatly altered by himself* (London 1775)**

Five women in one family, each to get a good husband, is a happiness seldom to be found, and what is more rare, myself, my two daughters, Amy, and the Quaker, each thinking she has the best, and indeed, they are all deserving men.

Notwithstanding the manifold blessings which I have received, and the most endearing usage from the best of husbands, yet there is a something corroding at my heart, which gives me great uneasiness; the life I had formerly led, for several years in adultery, disturbs me now in my serious moments; and I find by experience the splendor of this world, though it may lull and compose us for a time, will not in the end, without a thorough repentance, heal an unquiet and disturbed mind.

It was in one of these solemn and important fits, my husband observed a tear steal down my cheek, and tenderly questioning me the occasion, I revealed to him that part of my corrupt and vicious life, with others, which, though the reader has been already acquainted with it, he my husband, was an utter stranger to before.

"My dear, do not possess your mind with ideas so afflictive; you have been an unexceptionable and a virtuous wife to me, which I doubt not will atone for follies past; and my love is so unbounded, so unlimited towards you, to see you thus renders me miserable."

"Oh! my love, you are too good, too kind to such a wretch as me; had I no other than the crime which, long since we ourselves together committed, I could not bear it now; and, though you never have reproached me with it, I have a monitor within me, that will not let me rest; and, fearful I am, I shall never know comfort more."

"My dear, do not indulge such melancholy thoughts, let us cheerfully return thanks to the Almighty for his goodness towards us; let us earnestly do unto others what we would have other do unto us; and we have an assurance from him, who never failed in his promise, of our receiving a happy reward hereafter."

Such were the cordial drops, my kind and loving husband ever endeavoured to relieve me, nor has he failed in his applications— My thoughts are more serene—I have not that tempest in my mind as heretofore—I rely on the father of all mercies, and he has given me ease—blessed be his name—now and forevermore—

Here the conclusion is left for me to relate, as I had it from Mr. Worthy himself. He told me, his dear and affectionate wife, for such he assured me she was to him, being sensibly touched with the remembrance of her former follies, and stedfastly relying, and frequently calling upon her Redeemer, had for several months past been truly a penitent, had no sooner pronounced the last sentence, than she, dropping her pen, reclined her head upon his bosom, fainted and expired.

Appendix H: Defoe, Roxana, and Posterity

[As it did during his own lifetime, Defoe's literary reputation has drifted in and out of currency.]

1. From Charles Gildon, *The Life and Strange Surprizing Adventures of Mr. Daniel Defoe* (1719)

If his Works should happen to live to the next Age, there would in all probability be a greater Strife among the several Parties, whose he really was, than among the seven Græcian Cities, to which of them Homer belong'd: The Dissenters first would claim him as theirs, the Whigs in general as theirs, the Tories as theirs, the Non-jurors[1] as theirs, the Papists as theirs, the Atheists as theirs, and so on to what Sub-divisions there may be among us; so that it cannot be expected that I should give you in this short Dialogue his Picture at length; no, I only pretend to present you with him in Miniature, in Twenty Fours, and not in Folio.[2]

2. From *The History of Mademoiselle de Beleau; or, The New Roxana, The Fortunate Mistress: Afterwards Countess of Wintselsheim. Published by Mr. Daniel Defoe. And from Papers found, Since his decease, It appears was greatly altered by Himself; And From the said Papers, The Present Work is produced* (1775)

When I first published the life of this beautiful Lady, which was in the year 1724, I sent one of the books, as a present, to my old friend and acquaintance Mr. Thomas Southern, author of the *Tragedy of Oroonoko*.[3]

When he had read my book, he paid me a visit at my house in Islington; and agreeable to his usual facetiousness, for he was an excellent companion, rallied me severely in my making the Lady, the Heroine of the work, so unnatural to her children in her dis-

---

1 Those who refused to take an oath of allegiance to the Anglican church.
2 A sheet folded into twenty-four pages rather than the two pages that make up a folio.
3 Thomas Southerne (1660-1746) was an Irish playwright whose adaptation of Aphra Behn's novel *Oroonoko* (1684) in 1696 was wildly successful.

owning them; and added, that what I had related concerning her circumstances, as to her poverty, in the latter part of her life, he knew to be false; for, on the contrary, he knew her not only to be rich, but very rich; and he was so free with me, as to tell me that I knew it also; and that, he imagined, I afflicted her, in that particular, for the sake of the moral only, that her wickedness, he said, as I was pleased to call it, might not go unpunished. He further added, her deportment, elegance of manners, and graceful behaviour, were equal, if not superior, to the beauty of her features, and that he ever attributed her successes to the former, as much as to the latter; yet, said he, her complexion and features were so happily, and so agreeably united, that when she was at the age of forty, no person whatever in her company could have believed she exceeded four-and-twenty; nay, he added, when he say her in the fiftieth year of her age, had she not told him herself to the contrary, he should not have taken her to be much above thirty.

He still further added, she was in the possession of two inestimable jewels; that is to say, a good head, and a good heart; the fruits of whom, her friends were sure always to be plentifully provided at her table; the one from her generosity and liberality; as were likewise the poor, who had their share of the latter, and who were seldom or ever sent empty away. And though she frequently in her reflections calls herself a prostitute; a strumpet; yet, said he in the true sense of the words, she was as chaste, with respect to the person whom she lived with, as the most virtuous wife could be to a husband.

In my excuse, for Mr. Southern is an excellent judge of what is proper in history, as well as in poetry; I told him, as to that part concerning her children, I not only had it from her original papers, but also from the lady herself, in the several conversations that had passed between us, and those so lately as the year 1723, in which year she died; and the reasons she gave me were; she was, she said, terrified, in her thinking of her two eldest daughters, who survived her, and who are both married, to whom she gave ample fortunes; I say she was terrified, for fear they should ever come to the knowledge of the wicked course of life she had formerly led, both in England and in France.

But upon my Friend's saying so much to me, and he giving me some few hints, has occasioned me to restore the children, and alter the catastrophe, by rescuing her from that pretended poverty, though not from her remorse, which at the conclusion, I before had plunged her in.

3. John Howlett, *The Insufficiency of the Causes to which the Increase of the Poor's Rates Have Been Commonly Ascribed* (1788)

In 1704 corn again rose to almost six shillings a bushel, and out steps Mr. Daniel Defoe, and addresses the Knights, Citizens, and Burgesses, in Parliament assembled, and displays much brilliancy of genius, and some plausibility of argument, upon the idleness in advices of the Poor, and makes his Proposals for their better regulation and employment.

4. George Chalmers, *The Life of Daniel Defoe* (1790)

In 1724, appeared the *Life of Roxana*. Scenes of crimes can scarcely be represented in such a manner, says De Foe, but some make a criminal use of them; but when vice is painted in its low-prized colours, it is not to make people love what from the frightfulness of the figures they ought necessarily to hate. Yet, I am not convinced, that the world has been made much wiser, or better, by the perusal of these lives: they may have diverted the lower orders, but I doubt if they have much improved them; if however they have not made them better, they have not left them worse. But they do not exhibit many scenes which are welcome to cultivated minds.

5. Thomas Ruggles, *The History of the Poor* (1797)

In the third section, the wickedness and profligacy of the poor are considered: the increment of their expenses or actual distress; although he acknowledges that there are some considerations which incline him to think, that there is really a greater frequency of vice among our poor than there were formerly; but this increase he, with great humanity, argues to have been the *consequence* of their poverty, not the *cause* of it. In the pursuit of this investigation he takes notice of, and treats with no great respect, the opinions of Mr. Firmin, Mr. Locke, Lord-Chief-Justice Hale, Sir Josiah Child, Mr. Defoe, Mr. Godschall,[1] and others, who, respectively, at different times, from 1678 to the present period, have declared themselves of opinion, that the relaxation of discipline and corruption of manners have occasioned a general aversion to honest employment.

---

1 "Mr. Firmin, Mr. Locke ...," were prominent social reformers and theorists of the late seventeenth century.

6. *The Penny Magazine of the Society for the Diffusion of Useful Knowledge* (1833)

In the ensuing week occurs the anniversary of the death of this great writer, whose name is doubtless known to most of our readers as that of the author of Robinson Crusoe; but who, although more than a century has now elapsed since he ceased to live, has not yet obtained in the general estimation that share of fame and that rank in English literature to which he is justly entitled. Defoe's was a life of extraordinary activity; an account of which, therefore, if given in detail, might occupy volumes. Here we must confine ourselves to a very rapid and general sketch. He was born in 1661, in London, where his father was a butcher, of the parish of St. Giles's, Cripplegate. The family name was *Foe*, to which he appears to have himself prefixed the *De*. His father, who was a dissenter, sent him to be educated at an academy at Newington Green, kept by a clergyman of his own persuasion. Here he distinguished himself by his fondness for reading every thing that came his way, and his industry in storing his mind with useful knowledge. On leaving the academy he is supposed to been bound apprentice to a hosier; and he afterwards set up for himself in that line in Freeman's Yard Cornhill. It is probable, however, that he had scarcely finished his apprenticeship when he made his first appearance as an author; for in one of his later writings he mentions a political pamphlet which he published in 1683, and in terms which almost seem to imply that even that was not the first production of his pen; he was then, he says, "but a young man and a younger writer."

Literature was destined to become Defoe's chief profession. His speculations in trade among which was a brick and tile work near Tilbury Fort in Essex, were not fortunate; and about the year 1692 he became bankrupt. His conduct in relation to this event was highly to his honour; for, although he had obtained an acquittal from his creditors on giving up every thing he had, he appears to have persevered to the end of his life in the endeavour to pay off the full amount of his debts, and to have succeeded to a great extent in effecting that object. About a dozen years after his bankruptcy, he states in one of his publications, that "with a numerous family, and no helps but his own industry, he had forced his way with undiscouraged diligency through a sea of misfortunes, and reduced his debts, exclusive of composition, from seventeen thousand to less than five thousand pounds." He had married in 1687.

Although Defoe had come forth so early as a political writer, his next appearance from the press was in a different character. In 1697 he published a work bearing the title of "An Essay on Projects." It is full of new and ingenious schemes, connected not only with trade and commerce, but with education, literature, and the general interests of social improvement. This same year, however, we find him re-entered upon his old field of politics, where he continued to distinguish himself as the most active, the most able, and the most conspicuous, among a crowd of fellow-combatants, throughout a stormy period of about eighteen years. Our space will not permit us to follow him through the various incidents of this part of his history, or even to enumerate the productions of his fertile and unwearied pen. Subordinate and comparatively humble as was the sphere in which he moved, and exposed as he was from his circumstances to all sorts of temptations, Defoe's political career was distinguished by a consistency, a disinterestedness, and an independence, which have never been surpassed, and but rarely exemplified to the same degree by those occupying the highest stations in the direction of national affaires. His principles repeatedly drew upon him obloquy, danger, persecution, and punishment, both in the shape of personal and pecuniary suffering, and in that of stigma and degradation; but nothing ever scared him from their courageous avowal and maintenance. The injustice he met with on more than one occasion was not more shocking from its cruelty than from its absurdity.

It was on the 19th of February 1704, during his imprisonment on a conviction for publishing a satirical pamphlet, entitled "The Shortest Way with Dissenters," that he commenced his political paper, entitled, first a "Review of the Affairs of France," and afterwards, (namely from 1st January 1706,) a "Review of the State of the English Nation." It was originally published only once a week, but at last appeared every Tuesday, Thursday, and Saturday, printed on a half sheet, or four quarto pages. To the political news and disquisitions, was regularly appended a short chronicle of domestic incidents; and the whole was written by Defoe himself. The work was continued till the completion of the ninth volume in May, 1713; when a tax which had recently been imposed, the same which probably occasioned the dropping of the Spectator ... induced the author to bring it to a termination. He was then in Newgate for the second time. Defoe's Review, which, at its commencement at least, had very great success, has been usually regarded as the parent, and in some respects the model of the Spectator. But it has not enjoyed the good fortune of that celebrated work; for while the Spectator has been reprinted many times, a perfect copy of the Review, we believe, is not now known to exist. There are only the first six of the nine volumes in the Museum. But many other works proceeded from Defoe's pen while he was engaged with this publication. Among books, entitled "Jure Divino," an able attack on the notion of the divine right of kings,—and his History of the Union with Scotland, an event in the negotiation of which he had a considerable share, having been sent down by the government to Edinburgh for that purpose. Defoe appears to have accounted his services on this occasion among the most important he had been able to render to his country; and probably few individuals of that day saw so clearly the advantages of the arrangement which thus converted the two nations into one people.

Conformable to the fate which had pursued him through life, the accession of the house of Hanover, although the end and consummation, it may be said, of all his political labours, instead bringing him only to neglect and poverty. The treatment he met with seems to have affected his health, though it could not break his spirit. In 1715 he was struck with apoplexy, and for some time it was apprehended that he would not recover from the attack. The strength of his constitution, however, which had been sustained by a life of unsullied correctness and temperance, carried him through. But he was now resolved to abandon politics, and to employ his pen for the future on less ungrateful themes. The extraordinary effect of this determination was to enable him, by a series of works which he began to produce after he had reached nearly the age of sixty, to eclipse all that he had formerly done, and to secure himself a fame which has extended as far and will last as long as the language in which he wrote. Robinson Crusoe, the first of his admirable fictions, appeared in 1719. The reception of it, says Mr. Chalmers, was immediate and universal; and Taylor, who purchased the manuscript after every bookseller had refused it, is said to have gained a thousand pounds. It has ever since been continued, as every reader knows, to be one of the most popular books in the English tongue, the delight alike of all ages, and enchaining the attention by a charm hardly possessed in the same degree by any similar work. Other productions in the same vein, and more or less ably executed, followed in rapid succession from the pen of the industrious and inexhaustible author. Among them are especially to be mentioned his Journal of the Plague, a fictitious narrative, published in 1722, which is said to have deceived Dr. Mead, and to have been taken by him for a true history; his Memoirs of a Cavalier, which appeared the same year; and his Life of Colonel Jack, published the year following. All these narratives, the mere fabrications of the writer's invention, is almost impossible during the perusal not to take for genuine. Defoe died in his native parish on the 24th (not as has been often stated the 26th) of April, 1731, and consequently in his 70th or 71st year. He was buried in Bunhill Fields, then called Tindall's Burying-ground. He left several children, the descendants of whom still survive.

Select Bibliography

Bibliographies

Furbank, P.N., and W.R. Owens. *Critical Bibliography of Daniel Defoe*. London: Pickering and Chatto, 1998.

Biographies

Backscheider, Paula R. *Daniel Defoe: His Life*. Baltimore: Johns Hopkins UP, 1989.
Novak, Maximillian E. *Daniel Defoe: Master of Fictions*. Oxford: Oxford UP, 2001.

General Studies

Backscheider, Paula R. *Daniel Defoe: Ambition and Innovation*. Lexington: UP of Kentucky, 1986.
Blewett, David. *Defoe's Art of Fiction:* Robinson Crusoe, Moll Flanders, Colonel Jack *and* Roxana. Toronto: U of Toronto P, 1979.
Bowers, Toni. *The Politics of Motherhood: British Writing and Culture, 1680-1760*. Cambridge: Cambridge UP, 1996.
Dijkstra, Bram. *Defoe and Economics: The Fortunes of* Roxana *in the History of Interpretation*. New York: St. Martin's Press, 1987.
Furbank, P.N., and W.R. Owens. *The Canonisation of Daniel Defoe*. New Haven: Yale UP, 1988.
Hunter, J. Paul. *Before Novels: The Cultural Contexts of Eighteenth-Century English Fiction*. New York: Norton, 1990.
Kahn, Madeleine. *Narrative Transvestism: Rhetoric and Gender in the Eighteenth-Century English Novel*. Ithaca: Cornell UP, 1991.
McKeon, Michael. *The Origins of the English Novel, 1600-1740*. Baltimore: Johns Hopkins UP, 1987.
Novak, Maximillian E. *Defoe and the Nature of Man*. London: Oxford UP, 1963.
Richetti, John J. *Daniel Defoe*. Boston: G.K. Hall, 1987.
Rogers, Pat, ed. *Defoe: The Critical Heritage*. Boston: Routledge & Kegan Paul, 1972.
Rosenthal, Laura, *Infamous Commerce: Prostitution in Eighteenth-Century Literature and Culture*. Ithaca: Cornell UP, 2006.

Sherman, Sandra. *Finance and Fictionality in the Early Eighteenth Century.* Cambridge: Cambridge UP, 1996.

Shinagel, Michael. *Daniel Defoe and Middle-Class Gentility.* Cambridge: Harvard UP, 1968.

Sill, Geoffrey M. *Defoe and the Idea of Fiction, 1713-1719.* Newark: U of Delaware P, 1983.

Starr, G.A. *Defoe and Casuistry.* Princeton: Princeton UP, 1971.

———. *Defoe and Spiritual Autobiography.* Princeton: Princeton UP, 1965.

Sutherland, James. *Daniel Defoe: A Critical Study.* Cambridge: Harvard UP, 1971.

Uphaus, Robert W., ed. *The Idea of the Novel in the Eighteenth Century.* East Lansing, MI: Colleagues Press, 1988.

Watt, Ian. "Defoe as Novelist." *The Pelican Guide to English Literature.* Ed. Boris Ford. Vol. 4. Baltimore: Penguin, 1965. 203-16.

———. *The Rise of the Novel: Studies in Defoe, Richardson and Fielding.* Berkeley: U of California P, 1967.

Zimmerman, Everett. *Defoe and the Novel.* Berkeley: U of California P, 1975.

Articles

Aikins, Janet E. "Roxana: The Unfortunate Mistress of Conversation." *SEL: Studies in English Literature, 1500-1900* 25.3 (1985): 529-56.

Backscheider, Paula R. "The Genesis of *Roxana.*" *The Eighteenth Century: Theory and Interpretation* 27.3 (1986): 211-29.

Baine, Rodney M. "*Roxana's* Georgian Setting." *SEL: Studies in English Literature, 1500-1900* 15.3 (1975): 459-71.

Blewett, David. "*Roxana* and the Masquerades." *Modern Language Review* 65 (1970): 499-502.

———. "The Double Time-Scheme of *Roxana*: Further Evidence." *Studies in Eighteenth-Century Culture* 13 (1984): 19-28.

Bowers, Toni. "'I Wou'd Not Murder My Child': Maternity and the Necessity of Infanticide in Two Novels by Daniel Defoe." In *Writing British Infanticide: Child-Murder, Gender, and Print, 1722-1859*, ed. Jennifer Thorn. Newark: U of Delaware P, 2003. 172-95.

Castle, Terry J. "'Amy, Who Knew My Disease': A Psychosexual Pattern in Defoe's *Roxana.*" *ELH* 46.1 (1979): 81-96.

Cohan, Steven. "Other Bodies: Roxana's Confession of Guilt." *Studies in the Novel* 8 (1976): 406-18.

Conway, Alison. "Defoe's Protestant Whore." *Eighteenth-Century Studies* 35.2 (2002): 215-33.

Durant, David. "Roxana's Fictions." *Studies in the Novel* 13.3 (1981): 225-36.

Flynn, Carol Houlihan. "Defoe's Idea of Conduct: Ideological Fictions and Fictional Reality." In *The Ideology of Conduct: Essays on Literature and the History of Sexuality,* eds. Nancy Armstrong and Leonard Tennenhouse. New York: Methuen, 1987. 73-95.

Furbank, P.N., and W.R. Owens. "The 'Lost' Continuation of Defoe's *Roxana.*" *Eighteenth-Century Fiction* 9.3 (1997): 299-308.

Gabbard, D. Christopher. "The Dutch Wives' Good Husbandry: Defoe's Roxana and Financial Literacy." *Eighteenth-Century Studies* 37.2 (2004): 237-51.

Griffin, Robert J. "*Roxana*: The 1740 Version." *Center & Clark Newsletter* 38 (2001): 5-6.

———. "The Text in Motion: Eighteenth-Century *Roxanas.*" *ELH* 72.2 (2005): 387-406.

Hentzi, Gary. "Holes in the Heart: *Moll Flanders, Roxana,* and 'Agreeable Crime.'" *Boundary 2: An International Journal of Literature and Culture* 18.1 (1991): 174-200.

Hinnant, Haskell. "*Moll Flanders, Roxana,* and First-Person Female Narratives: Models and Prototypes." *Eighteenth-Century Novel* 4 (2004): 39-72.

Hume, Robert D. "The Conclusion of Defoe's *Roxana*: Fiasco or Tour de Force?" *Eighteenth-Century Studies* 3 (1970): 475-90.

Hummel, William E. "'The Gift of My Father's Bounty': Patriarchal Patronization in *Moll Flanders* and *Roxanna.*" *Rocky Mountain Review of Language and Literature* 48.2 (1994): 119-41.

Jacobsen, Susan L. "A Dialogue of Commerce: Defoe's Roxana as Mistress and Entrepreneur." In *Compendious Conversations: The Method of Dialogue in the Early Enlightenment,* ed. Kevin L. Cope,. Frankfurt: Peter Lang, 1992. 218-233.

Kibbie, Ann Louise. "Monstrous Generation: The Birth of Capital in Defoe's *Moll Flanders* and *Roxana.*" *PMLA: Publications of the Modern Language Association of America* 110.5

(1995): 1023-34. *MLA International Bibliography*, EBSCO-*host* (accessed 14 Feb. 2007).

Maddox, James H. "On Defoe's *Roxana*." *ELH* 51.4 (1984): 669-91.

Maurer, Shawn Lisa. "'I Wou'd Be a Man-Woman': Roxana's Amazonian Threat to the Ideology of Marriage." *Texas Studies in Literature and Language* 46.3 (2004): 363-86.

Richetti, John. "The Family, Sex, and Marriage in Defoe's *Moll Flanders* and *Roxana*." *Studies in the Literary Imagination* 15.2 (1982): 19-35.

Rivero, Albert J. "The Restored Garden and the Devil as Christ: Defoe's Inversion of Biblical Images of Salvation in *Roxana*." *Essays in Literature* 11.2 (1984): 285-91.

Scheuermann, Mona. "An Income of One's Own: Women and Money in *Moll Flanders* and *Roxana*." *Durham University Journal* 80.2 (1988): 225-39.

———. "Women and Money in Eighteenth-Century Fiction." *Studies in the Novel* 19.3 (1987): 311-2.

Sill, Geoffrey. "Roxana's Susan: Whose Daughter Is She Anyway?" *Studies in Eighteenth-Century Culture* 29 (2000): 261-72.

Sloman, Judith. "The Time Scheme of Defoe's *Roxana*." *English Studies in Canada* 5 (1979): 406-19.

Snow, Malinda. "Arguments to the Self in Defoe's *Roxana*." *SEL: Studies in English Literature, 1500-1900* 34.3 (1994): 523-36.

Sorensen, Janet. "'I Talk to Everybody in Their Own Way': Defoe's Economies of Identity." In *The New Economic Criticism: Studies at the Intersection of Literature and Economics*, eds. Martha Woodmansee and Mark Osteen. London: Routledge, 1999. 75-94.

Stephanson, Raymond. "Defoe's 'Malade Imaginaire': The Historical Foundation of Mental Illness in *Roxana*." *Huntington Library Quarterly: A Journal for the History and Interpretation of English and American Civilization* 45.2 (1982): 99-118.

———. "Defoe's *Roxana*: The Unresolved Experiment in Characterization." *Studies in the Novel* 12.4 (1980): 279-88.

Wall, Cynthia. "Gendering Rooms: Domestic Architecture and Literary Acts." *Eighteenth-Century Fiction* 5.4 (1993): 349-72.

Westfall, Marilyn. "A Sermon by the 'Queen of Whores.'" *SEL: Studies in English Literature, 1500-1900* 41.3 (2001): 483-97.

Wiegman, Robyn. "Economies of the Body: Gendered Sites in *Robinson Crusoe* and *Roxana*." *Criticism: A Quarterly for Literature and the Arts* 31.1 (1989): 33-51.

Zomchick, John P. "'A Penetration Which Nothing Can Deceive': Gender and Juridical Discourse in Some Eighteenth-Century Narratives." *SEL: Studies in English Literature, 1500-1900* 29 (1989): 535-61.